Dark Angels

Also by Karleen Koen

Through a Glass Darkly

Now Face to Face

Dark Angels

A Novel

Karleen Koen

THREE RIVERS PRESS
NEW YORK

This is a work of fiction. Names, characters, places, and incidents either are the product of the author's imagination or are used fictitiously.

Published in the United States by Three Rivers Press, an imprint of the Crown Publishing Group, a division of Random House, Inc., New York.
www.crownpublishing.com

THREE RIVERS PRESS and the Tugboat design are registered trademarks of Random House, Inc.

Originally published in hardcover in the United States by Crown Publishers, an imprint of the Crown Publishing Group, a division of Random House, Inc., New York, in 2006.

Library of Congress Cataloging-in-Publication Data

Koen, Karleen
Dark angels : a novel / Karleen Koen.
p. cm.
1. Charles II, King of England, 1630–1685—Fiction. 2. Catherine, of Braganza, Queen, consort of Charles II, King of England, 1638–1705—Fiction. 3. Courts and courtiers—Fiction. 4. Great Britain—History—Charles II, 1660–1685—Fiction. 5. Great Britain—Kings and rulers—Fiction. I. Title.

PS3561.O334D37 2006

813'.54—dc22 2005030734

ISBN 978-0-307-33992-8

Printed in the United States of America

Design by Lauren Dong

10 9

First Paperback Edition

For X and, one more time, for Carmen

ACKNOWLEDGMENTS

FOR ANGELS ALONG THE WAY: my agent, Jean Naggar; my writing pod, Joyce Boatright and Sandi Stromberg; my friend Ann Bradford; my editor, Allison McCabe; and Crown Publishing.

When I was a child, I spake as a child. I understood as a child, I thought as a child: but when I became a man, I put away childish things.

For now we see through a glass darkly, but then face to face: now I know in part; but then shall I know even as also I am known.

And now abideth faith, hope, charity, these three; but the greatest of these is charity.

—I Corinthians 13: 11–13

Author's Note

The history of kings and queens is seldom a happy one. But in 1642 there was a happy royal family. It was the family of Charles I of England, married to a princess of France, whom he loved and who loved him back. Theirs was a true romance. They had six healthy children. The queen was Catholic, however, a bit too Catholic for public tastes. Once upon a time, all kingdoms of the Western world had been so, but a prior king—one Henry VIII—had broken from the Church of Rome and established the Church of England. Charles I and his Parliament parted company over the rights of a king to rule absolutely and over questions of religion. A civil war ensued. The family of Charles I shattered to pieces. His last child, named Henriette, was born while her father was in battle, and she never saw him. Charles I was captured and sentenced to be beheaded. His son, the Prince of Wales, sent a blank sheet of paper to Parliament, with a signature. They had only to dictate the terms to spare his father's life; it was to no avail—Charles I was beheaded in 1649. His wife wore the last letter he had sent her inside her gown, against her breast, until the day she died. The Prince of Wales became Charles II, a monarch without a kingdom. England became a protectorate, dour and narrow, ruled by General Oliver Cromwell. Charles wandered from France to Spain to the Dutch Republic for ten years, looking for aid, for enough soldiers to invade England and win. (He had invaded before and lost.) At last, in 1659 Oliver Cromwell died, and no one was strong enough to keep the kingdom together. Certain generals, particularly one, decided a monarchy would be best again. Charles was invited to return. Return he did in 1660, and he ruled until he died, holding together a kingdom that still threatened to split to pieces over religious freedoms and the authority of the king. This novel opens ten years after Charles II was crowned king. History named him the merry monarch.

Part I

Chapter I

May 1670

Facing white cliffs in a strait of ocean separating two kingdoms, a fleet of ships lay at anchor. It was the fleet of the kingdom of England, sent to escort precious cargo: a princess of England and France, the most famous princess in Christendom, in fact. A yacht with a rakish bow slashed through the water toward the best and greatest of these anchored ships; the king on board liked fast yachts, fast horses, fast women. The princess was his sister, and he and those with him could not wait to see her.

"Monmouth's on the yacht!" said a young woman leaning over the side of the princess's ship. She had stepped atop a huge coil of rope for this view, and a sailor, eyeing her satins and the single strand of fat pearls at her neck, had warned her to be careful, but she'd sent him off with a withering comment to mind his own business. She wasn't one to suffer fools—or even those who weren't fools—telling her what to do. The sight of King Charles's yacht racing toward them was thrilling. She could see the crowd waiting on shore. The queen and her father and her best friend were among them. She was so glad to see England again, she wasn't certain she'd be able to keep herself from kneeling on the beach and kissing the sand of it when she landed.

"And who else is there?" asked the friend with her, like her a maid of honor to the princess, and like her, excited to be witnesses to this,

King Charles and his sister meeting again after so many years—ten if it was a day. Flags were flying from all the topmasts, whipping smartly in the breeze. The day was bright and clear. Everyone was dressed in their finest, felt high-spirited, mettlesome as horses, stirred and thrilled by this reunion.

"Climb up here and see for yourself!" Alice said.

"Don't tease, Alice, and don't fall—" Her friend, Louise Renée, grabbed Alice's gown, for by now Alice was leaning over the edge at a dangerous angle, the feet in her dainty satin shoes on tiptoe.

"The Duke of York is with His Majesty and Prince Rupert—oh, they're close enough to hear me—Rupert! Prince Rupert! Monmouth!" Shrieking the names, Alice waved a gauzy scarf back and forth with wild abandon and was rewarded with a hearty wave from the king's cousin, a smile from the king's son, and a startled glance and then a grin from King Charles himself. Loud cheers had come up from hundreds of throats, the throats of the sailors manning the ships, the throats of the crowd on shore. They, too, were waving and clapping, cheering the king. Gulls, who'd idly settled among the rigging, rose like winged blessings into the sky.

"He hasn't changed a whit," Alice said.

"Who?"

"The king. I wonder who he'll be flirting with by midnight—"

"Mademoiselle Verney, get down from there at once! Mademoiselle de Keroualle! You will join the other maids immediately! The king is boarding—"

It was the keeper of the maids, Madame Dragon, Alice called her.

Alice and Renée ran across the deck to join the elite circle of young women around the princess, all in satin gowns, in dainty shoes with stiff gauze bows, their hair coaxed by servants into curling orderly disorder, fat strands of pearls around their slender necks, drops at their delectable ears. As young women, unmarried, their very youth was beautiful. As part of the household of the foremost princess in France, they were everything that was fashionable. There wasn't a woman on shore who wouldn't be biting her lip with vexation and determining to buy new gowns once theirs were seen. They couldn't wait.

Princesse Henriette—her formal title at the French court was Madame—glanced toward Alice and Renée as they slipped in among the other women, a slight arch in her brow, both questioning and condemning.

"Pretty behavior," sneered a lithe young man to Alice, one of a group of restless and handsome noblemen, but then the orchestra that had been sent to accompany the princess struck up a lively tune, and all about them another cheer began from sailors in the rigging, from those standing in order on the deck as the sardonic face of the king of England, Charles, the second of that name, appeared just above the brass of the ship's railing. In another moment he had leaped to the deck.

"Minette." He held out his arms, his face made handsome by joy, and his sister ran to him, and he hugged her close and then swung her around, her skirt swelling out like a bell. Men had followed him over the side, appearing one after the other, dressed almost as sumptuously as any woman, laces, blue ribbons, diamond pins, long, curling hair, false, a wig but magnificent nonetheless. The princess was immediately surrounded by them. Her other brother, the Duke of York, hugged and kissed her, and their cousin Prince Rupert elbowed York out of the way unceremoniously and said, "Little beauty. I thought we'd never pry you from the Frenchies' grasp." Unfortunately, he spoke in French and loudly, so everyone near heard him.

The Duke of Monmouth, King Charles's son, insisted on his hug, and the princess danced from one male relative to another, kissing their faces and wiping at tears running down her face.

"She's ruining her rouge." It was the same young man who spoke before, with the same sneering, spiteful tone.

"We're in England now, d'Effiat. You'd best watch your tongue," Alice told him.

"Oh, I am afraid," he mocked her, and the others with him laughed maliciously, even Beuvron, who was her friend.

Alice turned her back on them. The day was too happy to spoil with quarreling. There had been enough of that in France. This was adventure, huge adventure, and she was home at long last, about to see her best friend in the world, and the queen she so loved, and her father, and there was nothing d'Effiat or Beuvron or any of them could say to ruin a single moment.

Her eyes met Prince Rupert's, and he winked, then made her a bow.

Renée pointed to the king's son Monmouth. "He's handsome." She wasn't the only woman who'd noticed Monmouth.

"Yes, and he knows it, so beware."

Protocol, dear to French hearts, was being ignored. Everything was becoming very confused. The maids of honor had broken rank in spite of the Dragon's frowns, lured by Monmouth's smiles, by Rupert's twinkling boisterousness, by King Charles's laughter, by the sense of froth and frivolity that seemed to have climbed right on board with him.

Those who accompanied the princess from France, a *duc* here, a *vicomte* there, a priest or two, the captain of her household guard, tried to push past the clustered maids of honor, past the princess's tall brother and cousin, to introduce themselves over the noise of the orchestra and the bellows of that cousin, who seemed to be ordering something from above in the rigging.

He was. A great willow basket was being lowered from a pulley. Squeals from the maids of honor added to the growing melee as they rushed here and there to be out of its way. Once the basket was on deck, Prince Rupert patted it fondly, fell on one knee before his princess cousin, and made a motion for her to climb in, using his knee as step.

"I'm not to go overboard in this?" Princesse Henriette cried, delighted and horrified. She spoke in French because she'd lived in France all her life, and her English was small. "I haven't introduced—"

King Charles swept her up in his arms. "Introductions aren't necessary. We'll do what's proper on shore. But for now, I claim my sister as a prize of the sea. She's in English waters, and she's mine." With that, he placed her into the basket, giving one and all a glimpse of her stockings—vivid green—the princess laughing so hard, she couldn't speak.

"This is highly irregular—" began the French ambassador.

"Pay me a formal call to complain," said King Charles. His eyes, a rogue's eyes, swept over the maids of honor. "One beautiful woman isn't enough. My sister must have escort."

Young women everywhere held their breath, dropped into giggling, graceful curtsies as his eyes touched, considered, and admired each of them. The captain of the household guard cleared his throat. The Dragon hovered, fluttering, not certain what to do. No one knew at this point.

King Charles's eyes found Louise Renée de Keroualle, the most beautiful among them.

"Why am I not surprised?" Rupert said to his cousin York.

In a heartbeat, Renée stepped up on Rupert's knee and over into the basket. For a moment, her stockings showed, and they were the same green as the princess's. It was shocking and exciting.

King Charles's eyes found Alice. She had dropped as gracefully as a flower drooping. A gliding, natural grace of movement was one of her beauties. He walked over and stood before her, looking down at her bent head, the riot of curls there.

"My dear Verney."

"Sir."

"Her Majesty has missed you dreadfully."

"And I her." Her heart was beating very fast. He was her liege, her lord, her king. She'd known him since she was a child and he a penniless, beggar sovereign without a kingdom. This was a great and powerful moment.

"Did you behave yourself in France?"

"No, sir. And I am happy to say I have acquired the most beautiful gowns in the world."

"The better to finally find a husband with?"

A child of court, her skills polished to high gloss by going to France, she met his eyes. "That was my plan, sir."

"Lord Colefax was a fool. I do believe we've missed you." He held out his hand to help her rise, a signal honor. Enormously proud, Alice walked to the basket, cutting her eyes in a deliberate, provocative challenge to the group of sneering, fashionable young Frenchmen, impressed in spite of themselves. She stepped up onto Rupert's knee.

"Are your stockings green, also?" asked Prince Rupert.

It was all she could do not to kiss him on the cheek and add to the complete breakdown of decorum. She could see how shocked the French around her were. She bunched her skirts to climb into the basket, and the answer was evident. Sailors began to cheer, but whether it was for the glimpse of stocking or the jerking rise of the basket was unclear. There was an immediate bustle as the king, his brother, his cousin, and his son climbed over the side of the ship and down the rope ladder to the yacht, as nimble, as quick as any man in the rigging.

People from the French court ran to the ship's side. Everything was happening so fast! No one had been properly introduced! Nothing was going as planned! Other boats, yachts, wherries, rowboats, bobbed like corks some distance away—clearly those boats would bring them to shore, but they'd thought to have a reception on board, a long dinner. Speeches were planned!

Suspended over the water, Alice felt her heart rise like a lark. The sun was high and bright, the wind strong. The crowd on shore waved hats and large handkerchiefs, calling, hurrahing. The sea near the shore sent in wave after wave of little white frills, as if hundreds of serving maids had dropped caps in the water to celebrate this day. At the top of the sheer cliffs, the huge fortress of Dover Castle awaited them. She could see people standing on the parapets. Flags flapped at the corner turrets. The basket lurched toward one side. Princesse Henriette and Renée screamed. Alice took her scarf, held it over the side, where the wind clutched at it. The scarf was long, gauzy, made of spiderweb and forbidden Dutch lace by nimble nuns' fingers. Good-bye to quarreling, good-bye to meanness, and here's to my good fortune in England, she thought, and she let it go and screamed herself as the basket lurched straight downward, to the sound of a high, shrill trill of laughter from the princess.

On board the yacht, the king's Life Guards settled the basket, and one of them stepped forward to help the women out. Alice had the sensation of falling as she met his eyes.

"I know you," she said in English. "You're Robin Saylor, aren't you?"

"Richard, Lieutenant Richard Saylor, at your service."

He signaled for the basket to rise, led Princesse Henriette to a bench covered with cushions as the rest of royal family stepped one by one from the ladder. Another Life Guard quickly pulled up the anchor, the Duke of York took the tiller, Monmouth unfurled the sails, and the yacht was moving away from the ship.

"Mission performed admirably," said King Charles. "I didn't have to listen to a single speech. Rupert, you owe me twenty guineas." He smiled upon his sister. "As you can see, we are not as formal as King Louis."

Princesse Henriette leaned back against cushions, raised her face to the sun. "I don't know when I've laughed so much." She still spoke in French, but half the English court knew the language. So many had lived abroad during England's civil war.

"Are all your ladies wearing green stockings?"

"Only the pretty ones." Roses and lilies, mint and balm, lay on the floor of the deck like a carpet. She picked up a rose. "Is all this for me?"

"Everything is for you. By the by, Buckingham has tried to fast himself into the shape you last saw him wearing, but in truth, he resembles nothing so much as a pregnant sheep these days, doesn't he, Lieutenant Saylor? Tell her."

The Life Guard King Charles addressed smiled but was silent.

"Lieutenant Saylor has the gift of diplomacy."

The yacht had come in very fast to the shore, but it was large enough that it had to stop yards out. There was a harbor built, but it was dangerously silted with sand and shingle from the cliffs.

"I see my father. I'm certain of it," Alice said to Renée. She pointed to the group standing under a canopy with the queen. Alice felt as if her heart were going to fly out of her chest. "And there's Barbara." She stood to wave her arms. "Barbara!"

Efficiently, expertly, the Life Guards dropped the sails and the anchor, and the yacht stopped as obediently as a docile mare. The water was choppy and deep. Other young officers from the king's

Life Guards standing on the shore walked into the water, then swam to the yacht. A rowboat was clumsily maneuvered close to its side.

"Your carriage awaits," said King Charles to his sister. "The harbor is silted up. This is the only way I can land you without wetting you." He was over the side and into the rowboat, followed by his brother and his cousin and his son. Those who'd rowed it forward slipped into the water like seals to make room for the king and his family. From the rowboat, Monmouth, smiling, held out his arms to the princess.

"I'll catch you," he told her.

The princess stepped up on the railing of the yacht, and even though a Life Guard held her arm to help her balance, when she dropped into Monmouth's arms he staggered back, and they would have fallen overboard if it hadn't been for Prince Rupert, who blocked the fall but in the doing so, fell overboard himself. The rowboat rocked furiously, dangerously, and the king's brother, the Duke of York, fell forward onto his hands and knees and cursed. King Charles went down on one knee, but the Life Guards in the water steadied the boat so that Monmouth remained upright, the princess safe and dry in his arms. Rupert spat out sea, then floated on his back like a whale. His fashionable hat and great wig went floating by.

King Charles began to laugh, one hand slapping the wooden seat near which he knelt. That made his brother laugh, and then everyone was laughing except the princess. Monmouth set her to her feet, and she wiped at her eyes.

The smile on King Charles's face faded. "Why are you weeping, dear one?"

"He would have been so furious at all of this. It is so wonderful to laugh instead." The princess leaned on the side of the rowboat and held out her hand to Prince Rupert. "Come, sweet cousin. The least I can do is help you aboard again."

"You can't pull me in, gal. I'm as fat as Buckingham."

She leaned even farther out, coaxing, and Monmouth moved swiftly to grab the back of her skirts, which made King Charles laugh again.

Prince Rupert swam forward. She kissed him on the mouth, and with Monmouth's hand still fastened to the back of her skirt because the rowboat was tipping back and forth again, she went to King Charles and kissed him on the mouth and then raised her brother, the Duke of York, from his knees and kissed him, too. Then she turned to face the shore, and putting her hands to her mouth—the jewels in her bracelets gleaming a moment in the sun—she threw a kiss to the shore, where people erupted in applause, and courtiers, certain wild men of King Charles's court, dropped their great fashionable hats and their great fashionable wigs and began to walk into the water, one after another like lemmings, to meet her.

"We're not formal, but we do have our own style," drawled the king, highly amused and therefore pleased at the way his landing was unfolding.

Laughing, feeling outrageous, and not to be outdone, Alice took off her beautiful shoes, stood on the railing of the yacht with bunched skirts, her green-stockinged feet sure and certain, and balanced there a long moment like an acrobat at some common fair.

"Don't touch me," she snapped to Lieutenant Saylor, who did not know she was the best dancer at court.

"Well done. Now jump," called Rupert, who did, from the water.

"Your Grace, if you please," she said.

The Life Guards, primed now, held the rowboat steady as Monmouth stepped forward, gave his hand, and she leaped into the rowboat in a neat, clean movement. Only Renée was left, and it was clear that she was afraid and that she was ashamed because she felt her fear was spoiling the fun.

Lieutenant Saylor stepped forward and said in flawless French, "Mademoiselle, take my hand. I promise that I will die before I let you fall in the water."

"Push the rowboat against the yacht and keep it there. Jemmy, you and Jamie man the oars." King Charles touched the side of the yacht, held a hand up to Renée. "Just sit on the railing, mademoiselle, and trust the lieutenant and me."

By now courtiers had waded to the rowboat, were introducing themselves to Princesse Henriette. It was as if it were the most natural thing in the world for them to be wigless, bobbing in water wearing satin coats. In another moment, Renée was on board, and York and Monmouth began to row the party ashore.

On shore, officers of the Life Guards walked forward to help beach the rowboat. The king's orchestra, greatly excited, began to play. The musicians played violins, of course, for that was the fashion from France, and whatever France created, in art, in dress, in music, in war, in policies, others mirrored. King Charles and his brother and son stepped out onto the wet sand, but that would not do for their precious cargo. Princesse Henriette was carried by the king himself to dry beach, the waiting queen hurrying out from under her canopy into the sun to embrace her sister-in-law, still in the king's arms. York followed with Renée. Wet and bedraggled, Prince Rupert walked out of the waves. "You grab Alice," he told Monmouth. "I'd do it, but I'm wet through."

Monmouth held out his arms to Alice. Just before she let him lift her up, she looked back, to the ships, at rest like great swans, their sails, instead of wings, folded in, to the people climbing down ladders, the rowboats and wherries filled with the French court. In her ears was the sound of wave and hurrah and violin. It was May, England's happy, Druid festival of a month when hawthorn bloomed and roses opened wide and fish leapt out of green reeds in the river and folk danced around the Maypole to begin the month and pinned oak leaves to their hats to end it. It was her birthday month. She felt drunk with excitement, felt aware of time and place in some keen, sharp way. I'll never forget this, she thought, never.

"Out of my way."

She turned. It was her father. He'd left the crowd of courtiers under the canopy to come for her. And with him was Barbara, her dearest friend. "You made quite a spectacle of yourself on that yacht, missy. Green stockings indeed. What's next? Rouge?"

"Well, I had to do something to remind you I was home."

"My dear, dear girl," her father said. They embraced, she in the rowboat, he out of it. He held her tightly. "I've missed you so, poppet."

She began to cry. So did he.

It was mayhem. There was no point even to fight it. The French were arriving, some of them so determined that they waded ashore in the splashing waves, others bleating like sheep, refusing to wet gowns or shoes, waiting for soldiers to carry them to dry sand. The princess had brought a large retinue with her, ladies, gentlemen, servants, priests, officials. People milled about the beach as the king's household guards tried to bring order and direct people to the carriages and wagons that would take them up the cliff to Dover Castle.

The princess remained under the canopy surrounded by the important ladies of court, Monmouth's and York's wives and the Duchess of Cleveland, who was the king's mistress. Members of the high council crowded around, too, as did various children, some belonging to the king, some to York, some to important noblemen. The king's spaniels were there, growling and barking and generally getting underfoot. Beyond the canopy were carriages, wagons, horses, servants, the royal pages chasing and shoving one another like the boys they were.

Her father ahead of her, Alice walked arm in arm with Barbara toward the canopy.

"Is he here?" she whispered, not wanting her father to hear.

"Yes."

"Is she?"

"No." Barbara stopped. "I may as well tell you this now. Their son died last month."

Before Alice could respond, young women came running toward her from under the silk canopy, her friends, maids of honor to Queen Catherine of England. They hugged and kissed her, walking her forward to the canopy, their conversation and questions as clamorous as magpies' chatter.

"Those green stockings. Everyone is talking of them. I want some!"

"Oh, Alice, I can't believe you're home. You have to tell us everything, everything. We hear that the beautiful La Vallière is in disgrace. Is it true?"

"Colefax is here. He's been pacing up and down—I think he's still in love with you!"

"What did you bring us? Did you bring us anything?"

A very slender man no taller than Alice planted himself in front of her. "I saw your exhibition on the railing of that yacht. Excellent balance, and the leap was perfect. I want to know everything you've learned at Madame's, and I want to know it now. Never mind these rattlepates. None of them practice as they should, and they're all clumsy as cows."

She stepped into his arms for a hug. It was Fletcher, the queen's dancing master.

"It's about time you were home," he said softly, then in another tone entirely: "Move along, cows, there's talk of leaving for the castle now. Alice, we are packed like straight pins into the smallest space found in this fortress. I am in a barn sharing space with horses—horses, I tell you—and glad for it."

"It's only thirteen days," said one of Queen Catherine's maids of honor, a willowy beauty named Gracen. "Do stop complaining."

Thirteen days, thought Alice. Not enough time, and yet it must do. She walked in under the canopy. Princesse Henriette was hidden by the bulk of men surrounding her, men in long coats that came to their knees and the great curling wigs King Louis of France had just taken to wearing. Their shoes had high heels, lacquered red, so that they towered even taller than they were. The king and his brother, York, were like giants.

There was Colefax, the black armband for his dead child around his sleeve. Alice turned so that she wouldn't meet him. Gracen grabbed her hand.

"Queen Catherine is asking for you."

The queen of England was tiny and dark haired and birdlike. Alice swept into a low curtsy for her, but Queen Catherine took her hands and raised her up to kiss both her cheeks. She was flushed with excitement, looking almost pretty, as she could sometimes.

"The princess is leaving. Hurry!" It was her father.

"Majesty, with your permission?" Alice said to Queen Catherine.

"Of course. Go at once."

"We'll meet later!" Alice called to Barbara and Gracen and her other friends among the maids of honor.

King Charles's gentlemen of the household were directing people to carriages. Grooms brought forward horses for those who'd come down to the beach on horseback, but King Charles's yapping spaniels made the beasts nervous, and they were pulling at the reins, attempting to rear. Children cried, musicians wandered about searching for some transport back to the castle, people speaking French demanded carriages, but no one was listening. Alice saw the princess climb into a carriage with the king, then someone called her name. It was one of the royal pages, her favorite.

"Where have you been? What carriage am I to ride in?" she asked him.

But he ran off without answering, and she saw that Queen Catherine and her ladies were leaving. She felt a hand on her arm.

"This way. You're to ride in this carriage." It was Lieutenant Saylor. "I told you I wouldn't let you drop," he said to Renée as he helped her inside, smiling. It was a dazzling smile. Alice caught her breath and then took Saylor's hand to be helped inside herself. The carriage was crammed with other maids of honor from the Duchess of York's household. They nodded coolly to Alice, aware that she served the French princess, that she had served the queen, that she was, so to speak, above them.

"You great clumsy oaf, you've stepped on my gown and torn it."

The voice was unmistakable. Alice poked her head out the window of the carriage. It was the Duchess of Cleveland, the king's mistress, and she was glaring at Prince Rupert, wigless still and drenched.

"Bloody cow," he said to her.

"Stupid ox."

Beyond them was Colefax, frowning, looking around as if he were searching for someone. He saw Alice. She pulled her head back inside the carriage, bumping it on the edge of the opening in her haste.

The carriage jerked forward. Nothing changes, she thought, thinking of the Duchess of Cleveland and Prince Rupert, of other quarrels that kept this court unsettled. But then it was no different in the household of Madame, as Princesse Henriette must be called in France, and Monsieur, her husband.

And then there was Colefax, with the band of black around his arm and sadness in his eyes. Nothing changes and everything does.

Chapter 2

In a huge, echoing chamber of the keep of Dover Castle, the arrival banquet for Princesse Henriette was in full force, had moved its massive way through speeches and merry toasts, interspersed with soup, carp, pig, tongue, eel, crayfish, goose, venison, lamb, mackerel, pigeon, artichoke, green peas—something new, something French, of course—and salads. King Louis of France had sent French wine and brandy as part of his largesse, and any number of those bottles had been uncorked in the last hours. Servants were bringing in trays piled high with jellies, tarts, chocolates, creams. People began to push back chairs, to move up and down the long banquet table. The maids of honor from the various English royal households—Queen Catherine's, the Duchess of York's—sat in a cluster at one end of the table.

Alice sipped slowly at a goblet of wine and watched as two fresh fifteens, maids of honor, full of wine, threw bread at each other. Everyone was talking to someone. She was barely acquainted with half the young women and girls sitting here tonight. Before she'd left, she'd known every one of them, and what's more, they'd known her. If there could be such a thing as chief maid of honor, she'd been so.

"We've been talking about your hairpins, Alice." It was Kit, younger, a maid of honor to the queen and known to Alice. Alice's hair was thickly riotous and had to always be held back with pins.

The ones she wore this night were roses of beaten gold with pearl centers, quite old. She'd won them in a game of cards in France, from one of Princesse Henriette's ladies-in-waiting who swore they'd been her grandmother's, that the great Henri IV of France himself had pulled them out of her grandmother's hair when he made love to her.

"And those stockings," continued Kit. "I want a pair just that shade."

"I'll give you mine tomorrow."

"Aren't you the kind one, Alice."

It was Gracen, another maid of honor to Queen Catherine, cool Gracen, mocking Gracen, grown up in the time since Alice had left. Now there was an edge to her that made her formidable. Alice didn't remember Gracen being formidable.

Alice could be mocking, too. "I thought you'd be married, a babe on each hip."

"Oh, I but follow your example."

Touché, thought Alice.

"We were spiteful to Caro, Alice," said Kit, sopping her sleeve in food as she reached for her wine goblet. "We repaid her for you."

Dear Caro, bumbling Caro, loyal Caro, who had married Alice's affianced. It had been the scandal and jest of the court. Had Alice thought it wouldn't hurt to hear of her again? Yes. I hate hearts, she thought. They're unpredictable and capricious.

"Their little boy just died."

The little boy whose beginning made the marriage imperative.

"Another on the way. Colefax is clearly an attentive husband." Gracen watched Alice to see what her face would show.

"Hush, Gracen," said Kit. "You're unkind."

"Do drink another goblet of wine, Kit," said Gracen. "It becomes you so."

"You're nasty."

"And you're ugly."

"I'm not." Kit began to weep the easy tears of someone who has had too much to drink. "Am I, Alice? Tell me."

"Of course you're not. Excuse yourself and go and dry your eyes. Hurry, before Brownie sees you." Alice sat back in her chair, met Gracen's eyes, big and innocent. "That was cruel."

"Only if she were really ugly." Gracen pointed to where Barbara and Renée sat, men standing two and three deep behind their chairs, courting them. It was one of the sports of court, to seduce a maid of honor. A young woman had to be very beautiful or very clever to survive. Barbara was the reigning beauty—languid and fair, and when she blushed, it was as if cream were suddenly mixed with new strawberries. Though now Gracen could give her a run for her money. But Renée was simply dazzling—a pale oval of a face, crowned with crisp, dark, curling hair, eyes the color of beryls, dropped like jewels in the midst. "And her name would be?" Gracen asked, nodding toward Renée.

"Louise Renée de Kerouালle."

"Now the fashion will be for sheep." Gracen made a bleating sound, and the young women around her, who heard, laughed.

Well, thought Alice. What sharp eyes and what a sharp tongue our Gracen had grown. There was a wide space between Renée's eyes, so that it might be said she resembled a sheep, albeit a very beautiful one. Did Gracen set the tone these days? It hadn't been so when Alice had left. It had been Alice—well, Alice and Barbara, with Caro as their faithful third. "Who is that directly behind Barbara's chair?" Alice asked.

"John Sidney. Do you remember him?"

"Slightly."

Frowning, Alice watched an earnest young man hover over Barbara, something possessive in his stance. Alice pointed to the tall Life Guard with eyes like blue ice who had been aboard the yacht, and who had stationed himself behind Renée's chair early on and had not moved. "Tell me about him."

"Richard, Baron Saylor," Gracen said. "Our handsome soldier, as handsome as Monmouth, I think. He came to court as you were leaving. His sisters are at court, too."

Yes, that was what one did at court, clawed a position and then brought in family and scattered them hither and yon, to pick up honors and positions as they might. The old order had been destroyed with the long civil war and the protectorate afterward. The new order King Charles brought in ten years ago was still coalescing. If

Alice had had any family to speak of, she'd have done the same. As it was, she treated her friends as family.

"Point them out to me, Gracen." Alice followed the line of Gracen's elegant finger. The Saylors were a handsome family. Something proud, bright, tawny about all three.

Kit sat down among them again, her tears dried, her eyes on Gracen. "Louisa Saylor is a dreadful flirt and after your father, Alice. Her sister took Lord Cranbourne right out from under Gracen's nose and married him. It was too funny— Ouch! Gracen! Don't pinch!"

"Who are you tearing to pieces?"

Barbara had left her admirers and sat beside Alice in her chair, scooting Alice over with a swift motion of her hip. She leaned her head against Alice's shoulder and smiled happily. "Not me, I hope."

"We were talking about the Saylors," said Alice.

"Richard is an archangel dropped among us. He looks an archangel, don't you think, that straight nose, those eyes?" Barbara had had too much wine. Her normal demeanor was reserved and quiet, but wine made her talkative and funny. Everyone loved it when Barbara drank.

"Not an angel. A Viking. He looks as if a Viking warrior ravished a woman of the family long ago, and he's the living proof." Gracen shivered suggestively, then turned charmingly wheedling. "Alice, I want to meet your friends. They seem so witty and worldly."

Friends? thought Alice. She had none in Princesse Henriette's household, save for Renée and Beuvron. Gracen was looking at the Marquis d'Effiat and the other handsome, glitteringly fashionable young men who held a kind of court of their own in another part of the chamber. They weren't supposed to have made this visit; they'd been forced on the princess by her husband. There had been a huge quarrel over it.

"The Marquis d'Effiat is not my friend. He is rude beyond measure to Madame—"

"Madame who?" interrupted Kit.

"Madame nobody. 'Madame' is what Princesse Henriette must be called in France, and her husband is called 'Monsieur,' " Alice said impatiently, thinking she'd never end if she began to explain the intricacies of the etiquette of the French court. "The French are very particular about titles. You'll be burned at the stake if you make a mistake. D'Effiat belongs to the household of Monsieur and makes no bones about despising the princess. He slanders her every chance he may. And he really is dangerous."

"Then I really must meet him." Gracen made the others listening laugh.

"You're stupid to say something like that."

Gracen sat back, color in her cheeks. She flicked her head in an angry gesture, looking lovely and a little dangerous herself.

Alice stopped. She was making it worse. Of course they wouldn't understand. They hadn't lived for two years in a war between two households, a prince's and his princess's, everyone from master to servant involved, where bitter accusations began in the morning and hadn't ended by night, where revenge, no matter its hurt, was never finished. King Charles could be cruel, but his court was lazy and easy, the way he was himself, and he despised quarreling, would do anything to avoid it, was angered, in fact, by being made to summon the energy to argue. One of the things she wanted to do during this visit was talk to someone about the unhappiness in the princess's life. But she wouldn't do so with these friends. She moved to another topic. "Where is His Grace the Duke of Balmoral?"

Balmoral was not among the great men sitting to either side of the royal family, where he should have been. He was her savior. A true gentleman. The only one of them with any dignity in the stupid little drama she and Cole and Caro had played.

"I haven't seen him," said Barbara.

"Why don't you ask Lord Colefax?" Gracen paid her back. Colefax—Cole—was Balmoral's nephew and heir.

"What an excellent idea." Alice dropped a great damask napkin in a bowl and rose from her chair. "My compliments, Gracen. I may just do that. And by the way, if a Viking had his way with the Saylors once upon a time, I do believe a spider performed the same deed among the Sidney women. I'm sorry, but John Sidney has spider shanks."

Everyone, even Barbara, burst into laughter. If it was the fashion for a woman to hide her legs under long skirts and petticoats so that a glimpse of ankle was erotic, it was also the fashion for men to show their legs in tight breeches that came to the knee, in stockings that clung to every muscle of the calf. Handsome, muscular legs were as much admired as a woman's shoulders. Campaign begun, thought Alice. Score one against this John Sidney.

Her friends watched her sail away, her shoulders rising pale and bare and taut from the bodice of her gown, the beautiful little golden roses shining dully here and there among her curls.

"She wouldn't talk to Colefax, would she?" asked Gracen, wide-eyed, admiringly.

"She might," said Barbara.

Gracen stared after Alice with narrowed eyes. "She's not going to stop me from flirting with whomever I please. I'd be a perfect comtesse."

"You don't speak French," said Kit.

"I have other charms. What's the matter with you, darling?" Gracen noticed that Barbara was slumped in the chair she'd been sharing so happily with Alice.

"Mister Sidney doesn't have spider shanks, does he?"

Kit exploded into laughter.

"As long as another shank is made well, never mind, I always say," said Gracen, making even Barbara, never as rowdy as the rest of them, smile.

"ALICE."

A royal page gave her a hug, his arms clasping hard around the waist of her gown, the smile on his face and in his voice genuine. She stroked his shoulder a moment. The pages, boys anywhere from eight to thirteen, served the royal households as messengers and aides. To Alice they were like the young brothers she didn't have. "Where's Edward?" she said, asking of her particular favorite.

"Somewhere near the queen."

"Well, you find him and tell him I have need of him. It's very important."

She heard loud laughter and glanced toward its cause. There stood the intruding men of Monsieur's household, d'Effiat foremost among them, speaking rapidly in French, their hands gesturing and animated, and whatever they were saying clearly amused the crowd they'd gathered. And why not? They were richly dressed, of noble birth, proud as wild falcons, and all that was fashionable at the moment in Paris, belonging as they did to the second most important household in the kingdom of France, that of Monsieur, the only brother of the king of France. Already they'd attracted the wits of court. Beuvron saw her and quietly detached himself from his friends.

"Are you having a good time?" she asked after they'd touched cheeks. He was the only one of them she liked, and even he she only half trusted.

"Surprisingly so."

"Why surprising?"

"We expected chickens to be wandering among the chambers and hay in everyone's hair."

"We English can be civilized upon occasion."

"Alice, my sweet—"

She knew him. "How much?"

"A guinea?"

"I don't have that, but I'll give you what I can." She turned and fiddled with her skirt, pulling out a small bag from a secret pocket, shaking coins from it into her hand. She always kept coins about her. It was a legacy from her precarious past, a precaution drilled into her by her father.

"You are an angel, Alice."

She didn't answer, watched him return, just as discreetly as he'd left, to the group. He didn't want the others to see that he'd approached her. There was some new edge to these men. She'd been noticing it, feeling it, for weeks. It couldn't be a good sign. Where in this crowd was her father? Dancing had begun, the intricate, stately steps the French court had made the rage, and everyone was watching the royal family, who danced the first dance by themselves. King

Charles partnered his sister. The Duke of York was with the queen. Monmouth danced with the Duchess of York; and Prince Rupert, in dry clothing, bowed to Monmouth's wife. There would have been a fit in Paris if an illegitimate son like Monmouth had joined the royals proper, but here it was different. He's grown up, Alice thought, her eyes measuring him, her first friend. They'd known each other in the wild, uneasy days when King Charles was in exile and no one in the ragtag court around the king knew where the next meal would come from. She and Monmouth had been children of the exile and children of the return. Her feet began to move into the positions of the dance even though she hadn't a partner. There was nothing she loved better than dancing.

Young Edward appeared before her, and she circled the court page in measured, graceful, gliding steps, saying as she did so, "You've grown two inches, Edward. How dare you be so unmannerly?" She sank into the curtsy reserved for the end of the dance, even though the music continued.

"I'm told you had need of me."

"I do. First, you have given me no kiss of greeting. I am heartbroken. Who has replaced me in your esteem? And if you tell me Gracen Howard, I shall wring your neck. Second, is the Duke of Balmoral here?"

"I haven't seen him."

"Well then, my sweet boy, it is terribly important that I know where he is. Can you burrow that out for me? There's a coin in it for you, as always."

His eyes twinkled; he had a merchant's heart combined with a boyish beauty that made people trust him. He had often been invaluable to her.

"Beware them—" She nodded her head back toward d'Effiat and the men with him. "Tell the other pages. And help me to play spy upon them, will you, but safely, always from a distance? There will be more coins for you."

He nodded, excited by her request. She watched him disappear among the courtiers. She ought to have asked him where her father was. The first dance was ending. She smiled at her friend Monmouth, and he walked forward, an answering smile on his face. She dropped into a curtsy, talking all the while, falling back into their old friendship, trusting it, as if she hadn't been gone for two years. "Jamie, I need a favor. It's important."

"Wonderful to see you again, also, Alice."

"Don't tease. I want you to think of a way to keep the Marquis d'Effiat and his friends as far away from Madame as possible during this visit."

"And why would I do that, other than that he seems an arrogant toad?"

"He's here to spy on her."

"What do you mean, Alice?"

"I mean that Monsieur did not want her to make this visit, sent some of his household along for the sole purpose of watching her. They'll report every smile as flirtation or disloyalty. Trust me in this, will you, Jamie? I'll be in your debt for it."

What he did next took her completely by surprise. He seized her hand and pulled her forward to him, so that his face was too close, his smile too seductive. "A kiss will pay," he said.

She was so shocked—and hurt—that she was silenced. What was this? Who was this? They'd weathered the exile and the heady triumph of the return together. This man was as much a brother to her as anyone could be. How could he gloss over what she'd just said, treat her as some easy flirt? She took in his loose smile, the easy, proud set of his face. No one says no to him anymore, she thought. It was one of the curses of royalty. Even illegitimate royalty. He'd been too much spoiled. He was England's Restoration darling, dark eyed, dark haired, high-spirited, as handsome as the day was long, cherished by his father. She pecked his lips chastely, her face stern, her mind racing. She needed an ally in what she must do, not a flirt. She'd thought to pour out her frets to him. Now, suddenly, jarringly, she was no longer certain. Nothing changes and everything does. "There's your kiss, Jamie."

Chastened, he stepped back, reading the hurt in her face.

"Will you do it?"

"Perhaps."

His answer simply wasn't good enough. She walked back toward where the maids of honor sat, thinking rapidly. It had to be her father, then. To trust her father was never a certain thing. Spider-shanked John Sidney and Barbara had their heads together, and from the expression on their faces, he was saying something she clearly liked hearing. In another moment, Alice was beside them, sitting down abruptly in Barbara's lap, circling her friend's neck with one arm, ignoring John completely. "How like him," she said, making her face sad. "He's abandoned me."

"Your father would never do that," said Barbara, knowing at once of whom she spoke.

"He always does that."

"I'm certain he's near."

"Come help me to find him, please, Ra." Coaxing, Alice used the pet name all of Queen Catherine's maids of honor called Barbara.

But Barbara didn't have to be coaxed. Alice was her dearest friend. "Of course I will."

As they walked away, Alice looked backward over her shoulder to John Sidney, who was staring after her in a perplexed manner. Slow-witted, thought Alice. You're going to have to rise early in the morning to best me, sir.

"What on earth have you done to offend Mistress Verney?" asked Richard Saylor, who was sitting near and had seen it all.

"Nothing that I know of," John said. "I have scarcely made her acquaintance."

"Well, if I'm not mistaken, you've been considered, found wanting, and ambushed, old man."

"Ambushed? What do you mean?"

"Remind me never to soldier with you. Come with me while I make another attempt to flirt with Mademoiselle de Keroualle. I'm dancing with her tonight, as many times as she'll allow. Four. Bet me, cousin, that I persuade her to dance with me four times."

"You admire her that much?"

"I love her."

GRACEN STOOD A moment just outside the alcove where d'Effiat and the others were gathered. She could see they were seated round a table, Englishmen and the French, playing cards for coins, a language all understood.

Gracen unfurled her exquisitely painted hand fan, walked in as if she knew everyone there, stopped, and gasped theatrically. "I beg your pardon," she said, fluttering the fan in agitation.

The men stopped what they were doing, stood.

"I was searching for someone. I didn't mean to interrupt."

"And who is this lovely?" asked d'Effiat in French.

"It's Mademoiselle Howard, one of the maids of honor to Queen Catherine," answered an Englishman.

D'Effiat took in her large eyes, the wide cheekbones. "Introduce me."

"Mistress Howard, may I introduce the Marquis d'Effiat," and the man went round the table introducing the other Frenchmen who were there. One after another, they nodded to her, their faces admiring.

"I've interrupted your game," said Gracen. "Do say you forgive me."

"Won't you join us?" asked d'Effiat.

Beuvron, who spoke English—he practiced daily with Alice—translated.

"Alas, no. I was just going to walk along the parapets, admire the moon. I was looking for a friend to escort me." She batted her eyes at d'Effiat as Beuvron told him what she'd said.

"So you shall," said d'Effiat, knowing he was being flirted with. Handsomely sullen, he expected admiration. "The game may wait; a lovely woman, never." He left his hand of cards, the coins stacked before him, and walked to Gracen, offering his arm. She ran her eyes over his face, disdainful, attractive, and smiled, quite pleased with herself.

"Beuvron, come with us, play go-between for me with this delicious little straying lamb," ordered d'Effiat.

Chapter 3

Alice and Barbara talked in a corner tower adjoining the great hall. Windows were open, and they stood at one of them. Night hid the sprawl of the castle enclosure, its outer walls that overlooked the sea, but lights glimmered here and there, from another tower, from the guardhouse, and one could hear the ocean, a muted roar. Alice closed her eyes and sighed. There was so much to tell Barbara, much to ask. Two years was a long time. Letters between them could never hold the whole of it. Another sound outside made her tilt her head.

"What's that?"

"King Charles had silver bells hung in the parapets so the princess could fall asleep listening to them."

The bells pealed lightly, sweetly in the breeze, something in their sound catching the heart. Behind them, through a door, revelry continued, musicians playing, people dancing, talking, laughing, flirting.

"How many of you came over with the princess?" asked Barbara.

"Too many." Alice thought of d'Effiat and his friends. "Two hundred or so."

"My word."

"King Louis does nothing sparingly. He wanted you—us—to be impressed with his splendor."

"We are."

"When did you and this Mister Sidney become such friends?" She asked the question offhandedly, as if she didn't care.

"It's just . . ." Barbara groped for a word. "Grown."

"And how does Her Majesty the queen?"

"It's been a difficult spring, Alice. She lost another babe. The king's taken an actress to bed. She's just had his child—a boy. It hurts me to speak of this. Let's go and find your father."

They walked back into the great hall, moving through the crowd, peering into corners and alcoves, finally to find him sitting with a striking, fair-haired young woman on the long, wide steps that led up to the hall itself. The Viking angel's sister, thought Alice. Well and well again. Kit's warning echoed in her mind. Did she think to capture Alice's father and pillage his fortune? It was the fashion for men as old as her father, the age of King Charles, forty or more if they were a day, to moon over women just barely women. Her father was not one to be behind fashion. But I, thought Alice, am too old for a new mama. She swept forward. Barbara, reading her mood from the set of her shoulders, stayed back a step or two.

Sir Thomas Verney rose. "Poppet, I want to introduce you to Mistress Louisa Saylor."

Alice was silent, not even glancing at Louisa.

"Well," said Louisa into the silence, "I must be going. The music calls. Now, Sir Thomas, don't forget you've promised to dance with me, and I'll be pining, just pining away, until you do."

Alice watched her father swell.

"A lie, miss. I'll have to fight my way through your admirers."

"Nonsense. You have only to walk forward for me to send them on their way like that." Louisa snapped her fingers, and her earrings danced. She was tiny and blond, flirting and forthright. "I am so pleased to make your acquaintance at last, Mistress Verney," she said to Alice's haughty profile. "Your father speaks of you with such love." Her gown hissed against the stones of the steps as she moved upward toward the music, toward the crowd.

Sir Thomas Verney drew dark brows together in a frown; Barbara made a noise. She didn't thrive where there were quarrels, and when

Alice and her father were together, there were often quarrels. One hung over them now. "Do excuse me," she said. "I know you have so much to speak of." She fled.

"Was there any talk of an arrangement, a . . . well, let's just say a treaty? You're a clever girl, Alice. It would be secret, of course, not bandied about, but you hear things, notice things," said Sir Thomas.

"If it were secret, I would be out of bounds to speak of it—"

"Don't play games, Alice." Her father was harsh. "One hears gossip. Monsieur, for instance, was said to be furious that he was not included on this journey."

"Monsieur, Father, is furious if his coat doesn't fit him in the way he thinks it ought. He has only two moods, sulks or fury. What are you on the hunt for?"

He tapped his nose. "I smell a rat covered in French perfume. I cannot help but wonder if this familial visit doesn't cover some state business between King Charles and King Louis. It doesn't, does it?"

Alice shrugged indifferently. Her father swelled again, and this time it was not because he was pleased. "You were rude to Mistress Saylor."

"Accept my apologies for interrupting your ridiculous flirting, which is of course far more important than anything I might have to say—"

There was a soft, interrupting cough from above. Alice turned, saw Edward on an upper step. She hurried to him.

"Balmoral is ill," Edward whispered.

"What do you mean, ill?" Alice whispered back, very fierce. "How ill?"

"I don't know. He remained in London, at Whitehall. And Mistress Howard is walking on the roof with that Frenchman you don't like."

"Edward, you surpass my expectations. Find me in the morning, and I'll give you three coins instead of one." She turned back to her father. Light from flambeaux that were anchored to the stone walls of the great open stairwell flickered over his face. Its play of shadow seemed to show his vanity, his ambition, his twisting and turning from one great man to the next to further himself. Nothing changes.

She must tread skillfully, now. She walked downward to him. "Did you know His Grace Balmoral was ill?"

"I don't think it serious."

"Do you know that for certain?"

"No."

"Can you find out?"

"If I wished. Something's afoot." Sir Thomas looked about discontentedly. "I tell you I smell it. Are you certain there's nothing you've seen, nothing you've heard, about an agreement, a contract, between the kings?"

"I know nothing, but I am concerned." She paused, careful now, uncertain how much to say. Since King Charles had been crowned ten years ago, her father had remained just on the edge of the great men who advised him, one of their minions. He wanted in on the circle of influence. The wanting made him dangerous. "Are you or are you not still allied with Buckingham?"

A shadow passing over his face told her much. "I'm his man. Who questions my loyalty?"

"No one, Father." She had only thirteen days in England and was uncertain whom to trust. How did she begin to explain the atmosphere of Princesse Henriette's unhappy household, the hostility, the war that was being waged between the princess and her husband and his absent lover? She'd thought Monmouth would aid her in this. To be forced to trust her father made her wary, more anxious than she already was. "Will you tell the Duke of Buckingham for me that I have some frets for Her Highness? Perhaps he might allow me to speak with him before I return?"

"Tell me your frets."

"I'm too tired this night, Father, but I will, I promise, first thing in the morning. We'll breakfast together. That will be delightful, won't it. Now you tell me why you have allowed this John Sidney to court Barbara."

"What are you talking about? She's a ward of the court, Alice, not my responsibility."

"I expect you to look after her. You promised me you would."

"Sweet Jesus, I do! She receives a handsome little sum of pin money from me once a quarter. Why? Not because I owe it, but because you asked it. What have you against John Sidney? He seems a good man, comes from a good family."

"He's a nobody. She can do better than him. I intend to see she does."

"You do, do you?"

"I have a plan."

"You have not been home six hours, and you have a plan? I've had too much wine, and I can't listen to plots tonight."

"No plots, Father. This is a serious matter. I have thought everything over carefully, and I—"

He interrupted. "I'm well aware it's past time we married you. I haven't been sitting here picking lint from my navel while you've been in France, my girl. I've got my eye on the young Earl of Mulgrave for you. Quiet, I know, but you more than make up for that. The family is willing—"

"Father, I have every intention of marrying His Grace the Duke of Balmoral."

Sir Thomas, never at a loss for words, went silent, staring at this only child of his.

"I've been writing to him."

"Writing— God's eyes, poppet! When did this begin?"

"He wrote not long after I left to see if I was settled in, if I was sick for home, asking if there was anything further he could do, and I answered, and he replied, and we've been corresponding—"

"He is as old as the hills, Alice. Older. You'd be a widow before the wedding oaths were done."

"Be that as it may, I've made up my mind."

"It can't be done, pet. He's been a widower for over twenty years, and you're not the first to have set her cap at him. You're too young to know—"

"It has Princesse Henriette's blessing."

"Madame? You've managed to obtain Madame's interest?" Sweet Jesus, thought Sir Thomas, almost in a panic. There were things

Alice didn't know, plots begun in her absence, cabals broken and reformed, Balmoral and he not the cautious allies they'd been when Alice was engaged to his nephew and heir.

"She said she'd speak to King Charles—"

"Alice Margaret Constance Verney, I insist— No. I demand that you not go rushing into this. I am your father, and I—"

"Should be very pleased and do everything in your power to help me."

He stopped himself from saying what he really thought, smiled heartily, falsely, at her, his charm heavy and practiced but charming nonetheless. "We won't quarrel on our first evening. We'll talk again tomorrow before I've had my first glass."

She knew when to quit. Her courtier's instincts were every bit as good as his. "I leave you to your flirting, Father."

He caught her arm as she turned from him to walk up the stairs. "Tell me true, poppet, does King Louis of France really keep both the old and new mistress by his side?"

"True as rain."

"Is the new one as beautiful as they say?"

"She glitters like gold, Father." Golden hair, golden laugh, golden charm, but, unlike her predecessor, no golden heart.

"Like gold," repeated Sir Thomas, pleased with this gossip. He kept his arm on hers, his eyes still on her face. For a moment, two pairs of dark eyes under dark brows reflected back the image of the other, and there was affection and wariness in each set. They loved each other, had been together through lack and disgrace and exile to reach the pinnacle of this day, but neither trusted the other, he because he could do no differently, and Alice because at the age of six she'd stopped being stupid about him.

ATOP THE ROOF of the keep, Gracen prattled away, certain of her charm, certain she had d'Effiat's interest—being a maid of honor was no small thing—asking him question after question about King Louis of France, about his new mistress, the gossip of the moment in most courts.

"I've heard she was friends first with La Vallière? Is that true?" she said, her eyes shining with curiosity. This betrayal between friends had been much discussed among the maids of honor. The old mistress had unwittingly introduced her successor. Wasn't that always the way? Every one of them knew the story of the shy, gentle little maid of honor named Louise de la Vallière who had stolen the tender young heart of the king of France when he was only three and twenty. It had been the scandal of Europe, and he'd loved her purely for a long time. But now that was ended. Someone more glittering, higher born, had taken her place, and that, too, was the scandal of Europe.

Beuvron translated. D'Effiat looked Gracen up one side and down the other. The wind whipped her hair out of its pins and pulled at the skirts of her gown, so that her shape was there to be seen. She was a beauty. "Insipid," he said to Beuvron. "I'm bored. Make my excuses." He walked away, not bothering to bow a good-bye.

Amazed, Gracen stared after him. "I don't understand."

"He remembered something he must do. He makes his apologies and says he will talk with you tomorrow or the next day."

"You're lying."

"No, I assure you it's true. Let me escort you back inside. The wind is becoming fierce."

They walked in silence to a corner tower. Inside it, Gracen went to a window where there was enough light from the flambeaux that she could see her reflection in it. She began to fool with her hair, working it back into its pins. "He thought me dull. I'm not dull, you know, far from it."

Beuvron sighed. What was it about d'Effiat that attracted women? Did they think they could warm his heart? He hadn't one, not for women. "He does you a kindness," he said. "I'd leave him be." And then, because her face was becoming mutinous, because she looked ready to argue, he, too, left her on her own, alone in the tower, thinking that perhaps rudeness was kindness, after all, with this one.

"DID YOU QUARREL?" Barbara asked as Alice sat beside her at the table, reached for a goblet of wine, and drained it.

"Not really." Her mind looped over and around her conversation with her father. Why was he not pleased that she'd set her mind on Balmoral? He'd been so pleased before, when she was to marry Balmoral's heir. She'd expected excitement and a full falling-in with her plan. With their two heads plotting, Balmoral had no chance of escape. She was both surprised by and suspicious of his lack of enthusiasm.

A familiar voice caught her attention. She glanced toward the bend in the banquet table, to the king's mistress, the notorious, the brazen, the brash Duchess of Cleveland. Alice hated her, hated her rudeness, her temper, her vanity, but most particularly her behavior to the queen. She called her "the great cow." The only thing cowlike about her were her big eyes. She wasn't placid, didn't chew her cud, wouldn't be put out to pasture. The great cow had thrown back her head to laugh, and like her life, the laugh was big and bold, not to be missed. Her jewels were large, as glittering as Princesse Henriette's and certainly Queen Catherine's. She hung over one side of King Charles's shoulders, an intimate and revealing gesture telling anyone who wished to see of her significance. King Charles stroked one of her creamy white arms absently as he talked with his sister.

"The great cow still reigns, I see," Alice commented.

"Perhaps not."

Alice pounced on Barbara's words. This was news indeed. "What? Tell me everything."

"King Charles didn't accept her last child as his, and"—Barbara drew closer, looked around to make certain no one was listening—"word is she is moving out of Whitehall."

"Well, well, well." There just might be justice in the world after all.

"Caro wrote you a letter," said Barbara. "I have it—"

"No, Ra. I'm sorry her child is dead, but I can't forgive her."

"Can't or won't?"

She wouldn't quarrel with Barbara, not on this first night. She couldn't face the muddle that was her feelings for Caro. She'd rather celebrate the news the king's favorite mistress might be ending her rule. "Listen," she said. They could just hear the voice of someone singing. It came from an adjoining chamber.

Can you make me a cambric shirt,
Parsley, sage, rosemary and thyme.
Without any seam or needlework?
And you shall be a true lover of mine.

"Does the great cow still have the habit of kicking off her shoes?" Alice asked.

"Why?" Both dread and excitement were in Barbara's voice. "What are you going to do?"

"Avenge. I know she's been mean to the queen while I've been gone."

"You're going to steal her shoes? Alice, you've had too much wine!"

"I've had only just enough. . . . What shall we wager that they are kicked off and under the table? I desire a good old-fashioned fit of rage from her. Let the French see her at her finest."

"She'll suspect!" They were standing up now, whispering furiously.

"Why?"

"After all this time, for the pranks to begin again—"

"She won't make the connection. I swear it! Go and engage her in conversation."

"She likes me not. She won't— Alice!" Barbara's whispers were like a goose hissing. "You're not to do this!" But she was smiling, and there was a light in her eyes that egged Alice on. They walked together, arm in arm, innocent and charming, toward where the royal family was sitting. Barbara began to giggle. She always did before the crime.

"Do it," Alice hissed.

Barbara moved gracefully, humbly, drawing eyes with her beauty, toward the woman who had been mistress to King Charles for over ten years.

"My earring," Alice said to no one in particular, touching her ear.

At those words, Richard, who was pouring wine for the king, turned. Alice bent down. No one was paying any attention. All were intent on their talk, on watching the dancing. She was under the skirted tables in a flash, trying not to laugh as she snatched exquisite shoes—soft white kid with embroidery—then out again in nothing flat and walking away. She left the chamber, holding the shoes into her skirts, ran down the wide stone stairs of the entrance, out into the night, toward a fountain near the kitchen. She dropped the shoes in. If the great cow danced again tonight, it would be in stocking feet. Alice would return later, fill the shoes with dung, and leave them before the lady's doorstep.

Inside the keep, biting her lip, Barbara waited breathless at the top of the stairs.

"In the fountain," Alice said. "They needed a wetting."

Barbara's trill of laughter attracted the attention of Fletcher, the queen's dancing master, as he whirled by. He was in his element, had stopped at every plate to visit or flirt, was like a bee moving gossip from one guest to the next.

"What are you two up to?" he asked. "You look as if you've swallowed candles, your eyes are shining so. Tell me at once."

"Nothing," replied Alice. "Let's go hear the singing."

Without another word, she and Barbara and Fletcher walked through the crowd into the chamber, where a soldier, a trooper, stood at one of the room's long ends, singing. Sitting on chairs and cushions and footstools in the light of dozens of candles, people were clustered close to listen. Most of the maids of honor were here, and therefore so were many of the men they attracted. It was that witching time of evening, the wolves and jackals among the court out, circling, manners dulled by drink, no statesmanship and certainly no wives to keep them from the magic maidens, they whom everyone adored, the maids of honor. We thrive on their notice, don't we? thought Alice, aware of the pride she felt to be one. We bridle if we obtain it. We're ready to dance with disgrace for a glance, sighs, love letters, promises, all ours for who we are. It was heady stuff to be the maid of the moment, to be the subject of ballad, song, poem, play—not to mention someone's passion—few could withstand all the glory it brought. Some survived, flew like swallows to greater heights. Others fell, crushed by seduction and disgrace and a court as fickle as it was fun.

Monmouth was here, as was his wife, both surrounded by admirers, sycophants, and the ambitious. People were as respectful to him as if he were a crown prince. Maids of honor sent glances and little smiles his way. Alice wondered how much beyond their friendship was changed. Queen Catherine sat with a few of her household. Barbara went to the queen, settled in beside her, nesting like a sweet mourning dove.

"And where are you going?" Fletcher asked Alice when she didn't follow Barbara.

"There."

"I'm coming with you, then."

Alice and Fletcher walked straight over to Colefax.

Leaning with a shoulder against a wall, he straightened at the sight of them, his face changing, his eyes lighting with welcome and more.

"I've heard your uncle is ill," she said. No greeting. No polite talk. It was emotional to speak with him, more emotional than she had imagined; her heart was pounding in her ears.

"It's nothing serious, just a recurring vexation."

"I'm pleased to hear it. You'll give him my regards, tell him I asked of him, please?"

"I will."

"I'm sorry for the death of your son." It might have been our son, Cole, she thought, and her heart ached, and she clutched Fletcher's arm, glad he was there because she didn't know what she might have done otherwise.

"My uncle said I treated you abominably. I have no excuse for what I did, but many regrets."

Yes, Balmoral was the sensible one among them, mending scandal, demanding honor, sending Alice away. Best, he said. "How is your wife?"

It was as if she'd dashed cold water on him. His face closed. Poor Caro, thought Alice. She turned on her heel and went to sit at the feet of Queen Catherine. The maids of honor were whispering among themselves, her little scene with Colefax witnessed, her old scandal in mind and, if not known or forgotten, retold now, revived.

Left almost at the altar. Poor Alice Verney. Am I glad your son died? thought Alice, meeting Cole's eyes a moment across the space that separated them. No. Am I glad now not to be your wife?

"You be careful," Fletcher whispered. "It's in his eyes. He still wants you."

Yes, he wanted what he couldn't have but had been careless when it was his for the taking. She turned away from all that was in her, listening to the words of the song and, since everyone was watching her anyway, making certain the shocking green stockings showed just a bit.

Can you dry it on yonder thorn,
Parsley, sage, rosemary, and thyme,
Which never bore blossom since Adam was born?
And you shall be a true lover of mine.

Queen Catherine's small hands were clasped tightly in her lap, her face unsmiling. The emotion of the trooper's tender voice, the words, were stirring. Queen Catherine looked wound so tight that the slightest touch might shatter her. Alice had been the queen's maid of honor since she was twelve, beginning the day Queen Catherine had arrived as a new bride on these shores. She touched the toe of one of Her Majesty's pretty satin shoes where it peeped out from under her gown. Poor queen. Good queen. Kind queen. Barren queen. Living among the wolves, living with a husband half wolf himself.

GRACEN STOOD AGAIN in the opening of the alcove. Her fan, open, whipped back and forth before her face as she contemplated d'Effiat, his small hands, his concise gestures. When finally he raised his eyes to meet hers, he did not smile but returned to the game as if she were not there. She remained where she was. D'Effiat might be ignoring her, but the other men with him were finding it harder to do so. Their glances touched on her again and again and then away. She made them all uncomfortable standing there, haughty, righteous, vengeful. Their fun, the easy jests in English and in French, dried up. D'Effiat laid down a card. Beuvron did, also, and laughed a little as he raked coins toward himself.

"Remain where you stand, O vengeful goddess," he said softly. "You bring me good fortune."

At those words, d'Effiat stood, walked to Gracen, looked her up and down once more. He wasn't that much taller than she was, but he might have been a giant. He made a jerking gesture with his head to Beuvron, who cursed under his breath but obeyed, joining them at the alcove's opening.

"Do we quarrel here, before everyone? Or in private? Ask her," d'Effiat ordered.

"She says here, before everyone," Beuvron translated.

The expression on d'Effiat's face shifted. He almost smiled. He bowed to Gracen as if to say, Ladies first.

"Your kingdom's reputation for courtesy has been greatly exaggerated. I'm angry with you." She spat the words, furious, quite willing to make a scene. "How dare you treat me so rudely. I am many things, sir, and none of them are dull." She turned on Beuvron. "Tell him every word. Don't change one. And don't change his for me."

"Tell her virgins are always dull. It can't be helped," d'Effiat replied when Beuvron had done as Gracen asked.

"It's you who is dull, dull and stupid and rude."

"This is a childish exchange. Tell her I offer my apologies for speaking my mind. Tell her I invite her to join us at cards."

Beuvron looked at d'Effiat. "Don't do this. Send her on her way."

"Tell her."

Beuvron did so. D'Effiat held out his hand, waited for Gracen to put hers atop it, which she did. He escorted her to the table, put her in his place, waited, again impatient, his foot tapping, while a footman found another chair for him, and sat down in it.

"We're playing a guinea a game," Beuvron told Gracen.

"I haven't a guinea, but I will tell you backstairs gossip, as malicious as I know, until I begin to win. Then I'll wager coins."

"This is ridiculous," Beuvron said as he translated. "I'm not going to play." He sat with his arms folded.

"Let me hear your gossip," d'Effiat said.

Gracen smiled. "The Duke of Monmouth's mother died from drink and from the pox. She was so awful that King Charles had his son kidnapped. Before he was made a duke by the king, his name was James Croft. You can enrage him by mentioning his mother." She arched her back, preened like a peacock as Beuvron translated. One of the Englishmen at the table folded up his cards, stood, and left the alcove. Gracen stared after him, her face changing, some of the preen leaving her.

"Was his mother a common whore?" asked d'Effiat.

"No. She was a maid of honor gone bad."

D'Effiat smiled, moved the coins he had piled before him in front of her. "A loan. I'll tell you my terms later," he said. "I warn you now they'll be high."

Chapter 4

The next day, certain high personages of court met in the chapel of the keep. Early morning sun streamed through the colored glass of the windows, made the gold of the crucifix gleam. King Charles's Life Guards stood at the closed chapel doors, in each of the corner towers, and along the stairs. The French ambassador unfurled papers while a Jesuit priest, fluent in English, French, and Spanish, stood ready. King Charles was there, and his brother, York, and Princesse Henriette. A few, not all, of the king's closest advisers were there. Buckingham was not. Balmoral was not. The exclusion was deliberate.

The Jesuit quickly pointed out different sections of the treaty, and King Charles listened, nothing lazy, nothing easy, in his face now. He and these carefully chosen men had been working on this treaty for months, as had his sister in France. He dipped the quill he held into a bottle of ink and signed his name. The Jesuit dripped wax, and King Charles pressed the great seal of England into it.

"There, it's done," he said.

Princesse Henriette rushed forward, hugged her brother. He pulled her into his lap, kissed the top of her head. There were fourteen years between these siblings and so much more, but they might have been born under the same star. She was small and fair, with chestnut hair, like her brother, York, while Charles was large and dark as a gypsy. It was their wit that met and sparked. It had always been so, since she was a child of four and he a great gawk of eighteen, on their very first meeting ever, when he'd knelt before her and taken her hand and said, "I'm your eldest brother. I pledge you my heart." She'd given him her heart in return, and the affection had never varied. This treaty—a secret treaty, a dangerous treaty—was the result of that loyalty.

"Well, Jemmy," King Charles said to his brother, "you'll have your ships now." York was admiral of the navy.

"And you your war," said York. They planned a war with the Dutch Republic, subsidized by the French, who would be their allies in it.

"And I my heart's desire," said Princesse Henriette. She took King Charles by the hand and led him to the altar rail, and they knelt, York joining them.

The French ambassador rolled up the treaty, and the Jesuit took it, put it inside his robes, then went to the royals to hear confessions and prayers. The others, the ambassador, the advisers, slipped out side doors, through back corridors, Life Guards before and after them, to make certain that no one else saw them or came near. For all anyone at court knew, the royal family attended chapel together this morning. It could only be thought affectionate and appropriate, after all their time apart.

"You won't regret this," Princesse Henriette said to King Charles when her confession and prayer were done.

His dark eyes glinted. He hadn't taken confession, in spite of certain promises in the treaty. His sister and brother were the devout ones. He'd been warned as a boy by the great duke who was his mentor, his teacher, his governor, not to be too devout. One can be a good man and a bad king, that duke had said, and had added another piece of advice: above all, my prince, be civil to women. He'd taken both pieces of advice to heart. Mischief was in his expression now, a mischief that made him beguiling to women. "Our business is done. We do nothing serious from this moment on, other than poke fun at Jemmy here. Is that clear, Minette? As your sovereign brother, I command the diversions to commence and your plate to be filled with nothing but jewels and laughter."

She kissed him.

That afternoon, they went sailing; that night, they danced on the roof of the keep, after they'd sent kites flying high into the evening dusk above them, Life Guards holding the lines steady, while the kites' tails fluttered whitely, like angels there among the stars.

A WEEK INTO the visit, Alice woke out of a sound sleep. Someone was shaking her arm. It was her servant, Poll, a lighted candle making odd shadows play across her face, and behind her Edward, Alice's favorite court page.

"You have to come with me," he whispered. "It's Mistress Howard. I think she's in trouble."

He stood with his back turned as Poll helped Alice pull on a gown, find slippers and a mask to wear. When a lady didn't wish to be recognized, she wore a small cloth mask over her eyes. They all held their breath as Renée, sleeping in the bed with Alice, tossed fitfully but didn't wake.

"I've called Poppy," Poll whispered. Poppy was Alice's groom. "He's waiting."

Once outside in the hall, Edward spilled over with talk, like a cup too full, while Alice's groom listened, frowning. "They're in the chapel, Alice, and I don't know what they're doing, but Mistress Howard is crying. She snuck out of the queen's chambers an hour ago. It was luck that I saw her. Leo and Geoffrey and I were playing dice in a corner, and we looked up, and there she was, sneaking by, with a mask on her face. She gave us a coin to be silent, but I followed her. She went into the chapel where the marquis and the others were. I didn't like it, Alice. They'd been in there for hours, drinking. So I went up a stair and into the balcony to see what I could. Some of them are half-dressed, and they've taken a crucifix down and leaned it upside down on a table, and the altar has a black cloth over it, and candles are lit everywhere on the floor. And Mistress Howard wanted to leave, but the marquis said no."

A black mass? thought Alice. It was the latest rage among a certain set of noblemen and women in Paris, spoiled, too privileged, wild animals in their search for farthest pleasures. If Gracen was in the middle of that . . . She didn't want to take her thoughts further. She raced down the corridor with Edward leading and Poppy, the groom, following.

Can you wash it in yonder well,
Parsley, sage, rosemary, and thyme,
Where never spring water nor rain ever fell?
And you shall be a true lover of mine?

Voices, accompanied by a guitar, mingled and fell out into the hall as they passed by. Alice peeped into the chamber. It was Lieutenant Saylor and John Sidney and that trooper with the massive shoulders and tender voice singing, several wine bottles on the floor between them. They looked like choir boys, and the harmony of their voices was beautiful. Something in their faces, something clean and strong, still innocent, boyish, made Alice risk stepping into the chamber.

John stopped singing at the sight of her. "Isn't that—"

"A lady who doesn't wish to be known," Alice said quickly, cutting him off. Richard stood a little too carefully, put down the guitar a little too carefully, and walked over to her.

"Someone's in trouble," Alice said softly. "I might need your help and your discretion."

Richard bowed, his head almost touching the floor. "At your service."

She nodded toward John and the trooper. "Can they hold their tongues?"

"Of course," Richard said. He turned to face the others. "We have to help Mistress V—" Alice pinched him. "This lady, I mean, and we have to be discreet." He hiccuped.

"Whatever you need," said John, stepping forward to bow, like Richard, a bit haphazardly, and Alice smiled, suddenly liking him, seeing what Barbara liked.

"Lead the way," said Richard.

A boy, a groom, two slightly drunken soldiers, and a clerk, thought Alice, running behind Edward as he led them to the floor where the chapel was. It will have to do.

At the closed chapel doors, Alice put her hand carefully on the handles. The doors were locked. She put her ear to the door. She could hear what might be crying, what might be talking, but nothing clearly.

"This way," whispered Edward, and he led the way up a steep, narrow stair that opened to the balcony. Richard followed Alice. In the balcony, as dark as night, the three crept forward.

Below, in the chapel, they could see Gracen, masked, her cloak off, her gown in disarray, twisting and crying to free herself from men who held each of her arms. D'Effiat, his shirt off, his chest bare, and Beuvron, fully dressed, argued. Lighted candles were everywhere on the floor of the chapel, making odd, frightening, flickering shadows play about the room, and the altar table had been pulled forward. The men holding Gracen were trying to put her upon the table, but she fought them too hard, and Beuvron and d'Effiat were telling them conflicting orders, to let her go, to hold her and tie her down. Other men stood in monks' dress, cowls pulled up so that their faces were in shadow.

"Hands of Jesus Christ," Richard swore very softly, recognizing Gracen. He motioned for Alice and Edward to follow him back to the stairs. He ran down them, taking them three at a time. If he been mildly drunk before, he seemed completely sober now.

"Are there other doors to the chapel?" he asked Edward.

"Yes." Edward's eyes were small saucers.

"Take—" He stopped, looking at Alice's waiting groom.

"Poppy," she told him.

"Take Poppy and see that every door out of that chapel is locked. If you can't lock it, barricade it. Then find every priest you can and send them here, find the French ambassador, find His Majesty's lord chamberlain."

"I want to stay, to help you fight them," Edward said.

"No fighting!" interrupted Alice. "The scandal will ruin her, and someone may be hurt!"

"Run on, Edward," Richard said. "There won't be any fighting. You," he said to Alice, "drag her off to safety, to privacy, the moment the door opens."

"Is it going to open? What are you going to do?"

He didn't answer. "John, once the woman in there is out, get the key and relock these doors. Trooper"—this to the man who only moments ago had been raising his voice in a tender rondel—"you help him. The pair of you keep that door shut, and if you can't . . ." Richard pulled the sword he wore from its sheath, threw it handle foremost to John, who caught it and stared down at it. "Stop them any way you have to."

"No—" began Alice, but Richard had sprinted back up the stairs to the balcony, his mind moving far swifter now than his legs.

He moved again to the edge, looked down. Not a pretty scene, the upside-down crucifix, the drunken, quarreling men, their faces slack, some vicious, some simply vacant. He recognized a few, the rogues of court, Rochester, Sedley, Killigrew, who would try anything once, particularly if drunk. Gracen's pleading hurt to hear. Thank God for the one called Beuvron, who was arguing fast and hard, or there was no telling the state they might have discovered her in. If he had to jump over the balcony, onto d'Effiat, could he do it? He measured the distance, tense and ready for whatever must be done.

Then he stepped forward, speaking in hard, deliberate French. "Let go of her at once!" The command fell like a thunderclap on the disarray below; the men holding Gracen dropped her arms, looking around to see who had spoken. "Unlock the doors! Now! I command you in the name of King Charles and King Louis!" He then said in English, "Run, mademoiselle! Leave this place!"

Gracen needed no second urging. She ran from the line of Richard's sight, and d'Effiat and Beuvron raised pale, startled faces to him.

"Who is that?" asked d'Effiat. His speech was slurring, he'd drunk so much.

"We're caught," said Beuvron, his tone disgusted. "Well done, Marquis. You've brought disgrace to the gentlemen of Monsieur's household. The king will be furious."

He ran toward a door to open it and save himself, but it was locked. Others were doing the same, running to doors, but all were locked. Beuvron looked upward to the set face of the English soldier, who was leaning both arms on the balcony, staring down at them as if they were animals. He went to the crucifix, crossed himself, gently turned it right-side up, hung it on its nail again, and sat down in a pew.

JUST OUTSIDE THE doors, Alice caught a fleeing, sobbing Gracen in her arms.

"Follow me at once," she said.

And they ran down the corridor, down stairs and more stairs, out into the night, across the gravel of the keep to the constable's gate, a collection of massive towers that framed the entrance to the castle and where Queen Catherine and her household were staying. Alice could hear Gracen crying behind her, but she didn't stop, not until they'd run past a startled Life Guard at the entrance and up stairs. There in the stairwell, Alice stopped, untied her mask. Gracen sat on a step, sobbing into her hands.

"I was so afraid," she said over and over. When finally she'd quieted, she untied her mask, wet with tears, used it to dry her face, and looked up at Alice. "Thank you, Alice. I'll never forget this, never. I'll always be in your debt."

"Did you think I lied? How could you be so foolish?" Gracen flinched, but Alice was past caring. "What if Edward hadn't seen you? Do you realize you might now be—"

Gracen put her hands to her ears. "Don't say it!"

"What did you call them? My friends? Only one is that, and even he isn't completely trustworthy. Being a maid of honor isn't a talisman against harm, Gracen."

"I shouldn't have gone. It was my vanity. I'm sorry, Alice."

"We have to go to Brownie."

That was their pet name for the mother of the maids, the woman responsible for the safety and reputation of Queen Catherine's maids of honor.

"No! No, Alice. Let's just see if everyone is still asleep. If everyone is still asleep, no one has to know. Please, Alice. What will I tell her? I can't think. You have to help me."

Gracen had begun to cry again, and Alice could see she was on the edge of hysteria. She turned and began to walk up the stairs. After a moment, Gracen followed.

The door to Brownie's chamber was ajar. Was an alarm already raised? Please not. Please let there be time to tell a suitable lie and get this over with. Alice put her head into the chamber. Brownie sat with one of the queen's household, he who was master of the queen's horse, an important position. Their heads were together, their expressions serious. Alice knocked at the door, stepped inside, wadding her mask, a telltale sign she had been up to no good, in her hand.

"Lord Knollys," she said to the queen's master of the horse. She walked forward, her eyes on Brownie. "Oh, Brownie, the most terrible thing has happened, and it is all my fault. Gracen and I were playing cards and sneaking wine, and we fell asleep. We just woke, and we've walked across the bailey with my groom, and Gracen is sobbing like a child, she is so afraid." Alice looked behind her, pulled Gracen forward. She was indeed sobbing. "It's all my fault, but Poll was with us the whole time, I swear it, and Poppy is waiting for me below, and I'm in trouble myself. I have to go, Brownie. Please don't be too angry—" And then she was out the door, on its other side, shutting it, leaving Gracen to get through on her wits. She retied her mask, ran down the stairs to the Life Guard.

"Will you escort me back?" she asked. At the keep, she gave him a coin. "For your silence," she said. "My friend and I have been foolish." He winked. Alice walked up the great entrance stairs. There was a crowd milling, and the Dragon, her French keeper of the maids, shawl over a nightgown, was among them. Her groom, Poppy, appeared out of nowhere, and she and he exchanged a look. He nodded, as if to say, All right, then.

"Where have you been?" The Dragon breathed fire on her, furious to have been waked, even more furious not to have found her in her bed. She didn't like Alice to begin with.

"With my father," Alice said coldly. "My groom escorted me. Surely I have a right to visit my father." She saw John Sidney standing against the wall and walked over to him. "Tell me."

"Seven priests, the French ambassador, King Charles's lord chamberlain, and the Duke of York are on the other side of that door," he said. "Is she—"

"Fine." Alice put out her hand to shake his. "Thank you, Mister Sidney. Where's Lieutenant Saylor?"

"Inside with them."

"And Edward?"

"There, too."

The Dragon was bearing down on her. She followed the woman to where Princesse Henriette's maids of honor were sleeping, listening to a lecture on how she must always let the Dragon know if she left the sleeping room, that if this was the way all young Englishwomen behaved, well, it was a pity and a sin, young women who misbehaved in France found themselves behind convent walls, yes, they did. Alice pulled off her clothes, dropped into bed beside Renée, who didn't move, and closed her eyes. It seemed they hadn't been closed a moment when her servant, Poll, shook her awake again.

"Your father says come at once."

Groaning, Alice sat up. All around her in the dark chamber, young women were still sleeping. "Is it dawn?"

"I've no idea, miss. I just know he roused me from my bed and said fetch you." Poll placed the candle and its holder on the floor. "Put this cloak around you, and here are shoes."

"I'm so sleepy."

"That'll be two of us, miss." Poll was sharp.

A single lantern sat on the floor of the stone hallway where a dark shadow detached itself from among the other shadows. It was Sir Thomas Verney.

"Here she is, sir," said Poll.

Copper caught just a glimmer of lantern's light as a coin went whirling in the air, and Poll caught it.

"Come along, poppet."

Alice stumbled behind as her father took her down winding corner stairs.

"That mix from France are a bad lot," he said, talking over his shoulder. "There was some sort of ugly mix-up in the chapel this night, some girl involved, a serving wench, we think. Nasty business. They are locked in their bedchambers now, but must leave first thing in the morning, banished to the ships, king's order." He stopped before a stout door set into a stone wall and knocked on it.

A servant in full livery—as if it were daylight and he waited upon His Majesty himself—opened it, and Alice walked into a chamber twice the size that she and half the maids of honor were packed into. Candles blazed on a table. In a far corner through an archway was a heavy dark bedstead, and Alice could see someone lying there, a white arm flung out from under the covers. His Grace the Duke of Buckingham, one of King Charles's foremost friends and foremost councillors, sat in a chair. Sir Thomas pushed Alice forward, and blinking, she almost stumbled as she made a small curtsy. She found she couldn't tear her eyes from the loose robe he wore, lapis-and-citron-shaded dragons twisted and curled into one another, breathing fire, the fire embroidered with shining gold-flecked threads.

"Well?" Buckingham drummed fingers impatiently on the table.

Not understanding, feeling stupid, Alice raised eyes to his face, well fed, showing its high living in certain lines and sags, in pouches under eyes that weren't smiling. The servant came forward to offer wine on a silver tray, knelt on one knee, just as if Buckingham were royalty. Buckingham waved him away. His face rearranged itself into an expression of hauteur. "Have I waited up for nothing?"

Behind Alice, her father put his hands on her shoulders. "Tell him, pet."

"What, Papa?" Surely he didn't know about Gracen or her own part in everything?

"What you told me this morning of the princess."

Alice bit her tongue on the word "now?" It was almost dawn. She'd slept only an hour or two. The two men with her hadn't slept at all. She felt halting, exhausted, tongue-tied. "Relations between them are very bad, Your Grace."

Buckingham made a dismissive sound. "I dislike abusing the ideals of one so young, but that's the state of many marriages after a time, my dear."

"Is it? Do you dismiss most of your wife's servants, her ladies-in-waiting and maids of honor, her majordomo, her priest, the governess for her children? Do you then put in their place creatures who spy and gossip and make trouble, who are loyal to your creature?"

She had his attention. "Creature?"

"The Chevalier de Lorraine." Monsieur's lover.

"Banished last year, I thought. To . . . where was it, Tom?"

"Spain."

"Italy," Alice corrected. "Banished in body, not in thought and not in spirit. His letters arrive weekly by courier. Monsieur droops until he receives one, then storms about like a tyrant for days."

Buckingham had placed his elbows on the arms of the chair, had brought his fingers together, was regarding her over the steeple he made of them. "What else?"

"Tantrums, furies, not allowing her to go to Versailles when all the court is there, when he himself is there. He tried to prevent this visit."

"A husband's prerogative."

"He told her a soothsayer had read his fortune and prophesied that he was to have two wives. He wondered, as if he were musing on a horse race, when she might die. Her little daughter now tells anyone who asks that her mother loves her not. How would a child of those young years say such a thing, unless someone fed it to her with her broth at night?"

"The governess?"

"Who else? And there's someone new in the household who arrived a few weeks before we left. I'm told by one I trust that he comes from Italy, from the chevalier." There it is, thought Alice, that's when the mood in the household changed, became frightening, with the arrival of this man.

"Is he handsome?"

"Of course."

"A pretty boy sent to solace Monsieur."

"Or torment Madame."

"Torment is a strong word, Mistress Verney."

Alice hugged herself inside her cloak, lifted her chin, met his eyes. She was not going to take the word back. Why didn't he offer a chair? She was trembling with fatigue.

"Go and wait by the door, girl."

Her father and Buckingham kept their voices low so that she couldn't hear them. She felt as foolish, as bothersome, as one of the princess's little spaniels, while Buckingham and her father seemed great, powerful, hunting mastiffs. One bite, and the neck of anything they wished to kill was broken. Her father left Buckingham, took her hands.

"Poppy will see you back."

He opened the door for her, and there was Poppy again, in the hallway, his face never showing that this wasn't the first time he'd been up with her this night.

"This way, miss, you're about to drop. Take my arm," Poppy said to her.

I sounded the fool, she thought. Had she sounded hysterical? Was she hysterical? Husbands were the law over their wives. Not all husbands were kind. Did she imagine too much? Make things worse than they already were for the princess?

"Here you are, miss."

Exhausted, ready to faint, Alice opened the door of the bedchamber. Dawn was just swimming upward over the horizon so that light began to break the darkness outside the high windows cut into the stone like an afterthought. She dropped her cloak, kicked off her shoes, dropped into the bed beside Renée.

So that was the great and noble George Villars, Duke of Buckingham, he whose father had been best friend to the king's father, he who was reared in the nursery of the royals, he whose brother had died a boy on the battlefields for the king's cause, old to her eyes, blurry eyed from his night of drinking, wearing ridiculous blue velvet slippers with silver fringe on their upper edge, the requisite red heels at their back, his mistress, a notorious countess, sleeping in his bed. He had killed her husband in a duel three years ago. Rumor said she'd held the horses and laughed when her husband fell. Rogues of court, wild animals like d'Effiat and his friends. Even being a princess did not protect, just as being a queen did not protect Queen Catherine. Marry well and wisely. It was the vow she and Caro and Ra had taken. A man who would not beat you. A man whose position would sustain you, even though he wandered. Caro had done it, even if it was over Alice's own bones, and she was going to do it, by heaven, climb so high that she'd be at no one's mercy, ever, and break Cole's heart in the bargain.

She crashed head over heels into sleep.

Chapter 5

The next day, news of the black mass and exile to the ships was the talk of court: Who was the woman, had she been ravished, what was a black mass? But those involved shook their heads, gave no gossip to feed the curiosity. Richard was summoned to Princesse Henriette's chamber in the afternoon. He smiled down at Renée, who'd been sent to keep him company in the hall while he waited to be allowed inside. "Too soon you'll be gone from me. I'm going to write to you. Tell me I may write to you."

There was a smile from her, but no answer.

"I'm going to write to your father, tell him my intentions. I'm going to come over to France to present myself to him." He was on yet another day of determined, persistent wooing.

"What will you say when you present yourself to him?"

"I will say I love your daughter with all my heart and wish to make her my wife."

Taking advantage of the empty hallway, he leaned forward slowly, giving her time to pull away, which she did not do. He put his mouth on hers, their first kiss, what he'd been working toward since the moment of seeing her. He let his mouth stay gentle, but he reeled with the feel of her lips, their taste, the scent of her hair, the desire he felt for her. "I will lay down my life for you," he said, lifting his head, looking her straight in the eye. "I will make you proud of me." There was strength, certainty, in his face, in his voice.

"I have no fortune."

"Neither have I. We'll make our fortune together."

The door to Princesse Henriette's chamber opened. Reluctantly, he released Renée's hand, walked inside.

It was a large chamber, windows cut high in the stone walls so that sunlight gathered and fell in pools. Ladies-in-waiting sat in chairs in the sunlight, talking, embroidering, and their needles stilled as they watched Richard walk forward. In one of the pools sat Princesse Henriette, small spaniels in her lap and at her feet. In a corner of the chamber was a huge bed. Gold embroidered silk swirled down from a gilded crown, swirled around bedposts to land in a spill of silver fringe. Seed pearls picked out a pattern of crisscrosses which quilted the silk into a thicker material for the bed curtains. Lace, the most costly, so fine that it was called "stitches in the air," hung down in festoons from the top of the bed frame. The coverlet was quilted out of the same gold silk, shiny and wondrous, as if all the precious metal in France had been melted down and poured to make it. A crown was embroidered in its center, and the same lace finished the edges. It was costly, delicate, as fragile as if fairies had crept in at night and woven it from moonlight. The bed coverings had been brought from France with the princess, as if there were nothing fine enough the English could manage.

Richard blinked his eyes at the finery on the bed. The cost of the coverings could dower his remaining unmarried sister. The princess smiled at Richard. Masses of chestnut curls were held with pearl pins over each ear. Her eyes were large, very round, very blue. She was twenty and five, had lived all her life in France, at the French court, having been sent to it as a babe as war tore apart her family and kingdom. She had married the brother of the king of France and so was the grandest princess in that kingdom, after the queen. "Leave us," she said to her ladies. "Except for Verney and Keroualle."

There was a murmur of talk, the sound of skirts swishing against the stone floor, heels tapping. All eyes were on Richard, not all of the glances friendly. Richard bent and put out his hand to a spaniel. The dog, pretty and cautious, blue bows tied over her ears, smelled it, put out a hesitant pink tongue, and licked his fingers.

"She likes you," said Princesse Henriette. "You're the hero of the hour."

"Am I?" He answered her French with his own, and she smiled. His accent was perfect.

"You know you are. I wanted to thank you myself for what you did."

"Any man would have done the same."

"On the contrary, Lieutenant Saylor. Verney, if you please."

Alice walked forward, put something into Princesse Henriette's hand. She, in turn, held it out in her palm to Richard. It was a ring, a twisted gold band with an emerald held by tiny golden dragons. "It was my mother's."

"You honor me hugely. I must tell you there were others who did good deeds last night."

"I've thanked them. Mister John Sidney, Edward Capelet, Trooper Thorton."

Richard glanced at Alice, who frowned at him, which didn't bother him in the slightest. "One more."

"Who?"

"If it hadn't been for Mistress Verney, we'd have known nothing. She's the one who summoned me."

"She did?"

"Yes. If anyone deserves this ring, it is she."

Alice was silent, red coloring her cheeks.

"I will give her another reward. Thank you, Lieutenant."

Dismissed, Richard bowed and backed out of the chamber. The gift was excessive, but he felt honored and touched to be noticed by this princess, who was famous in many kingdoms beyond her own. There was something charming but vulnerable about her.

Princesse Henriette held out her hands to Alice, who took them and knelt at the princess's feet.

"Why did you say nothing?"

"I didn't wish my presence known."

"Yes, you're wise. They'd blame you, make you pay for it, wouldn't they."

"The Dragon found I wasn't in my bed. I've told her I went to see my father."

"And the woman?"

"Safe. Not hurt, except for pride."

"How did you know what they did?"

"I paid Edward to spy on them."

Princesse Henriette laughed. After a moment, Alice joined in.

"So, thanks to your spying, I am free for the remainder of the visit."

"Might we not stay yet a while longer, at least until your birthday?" King Charles had already requested a few more days be added, and they had been granted. But Alice was greedy for more.

"Monsieur is furious with what we've already received. He calls me ungrateful."

Alice was silent. Monsieur reached across the Channel to command them, to corral them, even now, to make the bars of the golden cage visible.

"What may I give you, Verney, to thank you?"

"Champion my suit with His Grace the Duke of Balmoral."

"You know I do, but he's ill. He's not even here."

"Talk to my father. Tell him you think it a suitable match."

"You will be a splendid duchess. I will talk to your father. Is there nothing more?" When Alice shook her head, the princess reached up into the ringlets around her ear, slowly unscrewed huge pearl drops, set them in Alice's hands.

"These are too fine, Highness—"

"Take them anyway. I'm so happy. Six days without his men spying on me. You're a treasure, Verney. Is your friend Mistress Bragge as good as you?"

It had been arranged for months now that Barbara was going to return to France with Alice. "Better."

"How wonderful for me. That's all, Verney."

Alice joined Renée, who sat on cushions in a corner, dreamily picking at embroidery.

"What are you thinking of? Or should I say whom?" Alice asked her. Lieutenant Saylor's pursuit of Renée had been noticed by all, just as Renée had been noticed by all. She was the belle of the visit. That would be a good match, thought Alice. In France, Renée had not enough fortune or name to be appealing, no matter how lovely she was. In England, loveliness often overcame those obstacles. "We're going to have such fun in the next few days." Picnics, dancing on the village green, a treasure hunt, a horse race, sailing were planned.

"I'm glad they're gone, glad they're punished," said Renée.

Yes, thought Alice, we all are. But will we end up paying for it in the end?

MUCH LATER THAT evening, when the night's dancing on the green of Dover's village was done, and the carriages rolled back up the hill to the castle, and yawning courtiers found their beds, certain men strolled in the late night, went down the cliffs to the water to swim—or stood talking on a parapet that overlooked the sea in the late hours of the night. King Charles and the Duke of Buckingham spoke for a long time.

And then still later, King Charles watched the bobbing of lanterns that showed the path his brother, his cousin, and his son walked as they came back up to the castle from the sea, where they'd been swimming. He sent a Life Guard to fetch them, and after a time there was a little cabal of family, Life Guards stationed along the parapet to keep everyone else away, though sleep likely did that.

"Send me back with her," said Monmouth after his father explained what Buckingham had told him. "I'll kill Monsieur, run a sword right through his heart."

King Charles smiled in the dark. "While I can't fault your sentiment, I'm afraid that's no solution, Jamie."

"You're too young to ruin your life. I'll do it," said the king's cousin Prince Rupert. "Send me."

"No one is killing anyone." The king's brother, the Duke of York, was perturbed, but then, of them all, he had the least humor.

"However, the notion of sending someone back with her is an excellent idea." King Charles leaned an elbow on the thick ledge of the stone wall. "Someone who could report daily, so that if I must demand a separation for her, I can tell our cousin Louis that I do it on the basis of clear evidence. She won't do it; her pride's too great."

"You forget her faith," said York.

All of them were silent a moment. For a princess of France to separate from a prince of France would be a huge thing, a terrible scandal that would involve the pope and the Church of Rome. And there were reasons now, known only to King Charles and York, not to wish an upset to King Louis of France.

"Whom might we send?" said King Charles, making, as only his brother knew, a decision that might change the destiny of the war they were plotting.

They were silent again, the sound of the sea in their ears and now and again silver bells.

Monmouth broke the silence. "Send Saylor. He showed wit and courage in Tangier and certainly in the situation with the black mass."

No one spoke. Lieutenant Saylor was rumored to be lovers with Monmouth's wife. Saylor was discreet in it; the Duchess of Monmouth was not. Sauce for the gander was sauce for the goose in Charles's court, but Monmouth was young and much indulged.

"He speaks French," said Prince Rupert. "You could send him back as a tutor for her. She's told everyone she is going to improve her English. Monsieur would accept it. It might not be liked, but it would be accepted."

"That Monsieur dares dismiss her favorites," said York, finally catching up in anger over what the king told them. "At the very least, we'd have someone in the household, a spy that Monsieur cannot dismiss without displeasing you, which will displease King Louis. Send me. I'll run Monsieur through and eat his heart."

Prince Rupert and Monmouth laughed, and Prince Rupert slapped York on the back as if in congratulation. They talked more of whom else they might send but kept coming back to Richard Saylor.

"His discretion is excellent," said Prince Rupert. Not only did he not play the part of swaggering lover to a high-ranking duchess before the court, he would not name the woman involved in the black mass, claiming she had worn a mask, that she'd run away before anyone could question her. The page swore the same thing. "To have called in the French priests was brilliant. We might have had a nasty incident on our hands."

"True," said King Charles.

"Monsieur's gentlemen won't be pleased. It was Saylor who arrested them," said York.

"Perhaps his presence may remind them to act as gentlemen," said King Charles.

"Perhaps not," answered York.

"It seems to be decided. If you'll excuse me, then, Father."

The other three were silent as Monmouth left them.

"Young hound," said Prince Rupert when Monmouth was far enough down the parapet not to hear. "His wife is a spirited gal. Did he think she'd take all his indiscretions without some of her own?"

King Charles and York made no answer. Queen Catherine was too religious and too kind to be indiscreet, and while kindness was not her strong point, the Duchess of York had found solace in food. Prince Rupert wasn't married. He could be as indiscreet as he wished.

"I like that boy. I'd send him to France before Monmouth's duchess ruins his reputation and makes your son hate him. Now, with your permission . . ." Rupert bowed, then walked down the parapet as Monmouth had done to a tower that held stairs.

King Charles and his brother listened to the sound of his steps and then to the sea and its endless roar.

"We ought to just keep her here." It was York.

"You above all people know we can't do that and why."

"My little Anne is to go back with her. Ought I to refuse to send her now?" The Lady Anne was York's young daughter, near the age of Princesse Henriette's daughter. It had been thought it would do the little cousins good to know each other.

"To do so would cause great offense and raise suspicion. It isn't to our interest to do that, as yet. There is always the possibility that Monsieur will behave himself."

The brothers stared out into the night as the surf below them clawed the cliffs. They knew King Louis's brother, their cousin, from their exile. Both of them had been at the French court, had seen the French royal prince both at his finest and at his worst. His best could be very fine indeed; his worst, a tyrannical, vengeance-seeking fury that might last weeks.

"Just the three of us, Charles," said York. The rest of what had once been their large family was dead from imprisonment, from smallpox, from beheading, from bitterness.

"A holy trinity," said King Charles, only half jesting.

It was true there were only three of them left, but the holy piece of it had shifted. He and York weren't close now, as once they'd been. The Duke of Buckingham saw to that.

TWO DAYS LATER, Richard turned his horse down the avenue that led to Tamworth. Burned-out oaks, a remnant of the war, lay charred and ruined and rotting on each side of him. The avenue had been replanted with straight lines of limes, but the limes were young yet. Near some of the fallen oaks had sprung new trees—dug up and planted elsewhere, twenty years old now were these children of the old oaks, and while it would be another thirty before they were even a shadow of the spreading grace of their forebears, it was a sign, Richard's mother said, that left alone, most things heal.

The war had been over for twenty years, but the house whose gables he could see in the distance still bore its scars. There were wings and buildings that, once burned, had never been replaced. Ivy and lichen covered their stone foundations, crawled up charred timbers. Until ten years ago, his mother had served as housekeeper in her own home, serving the Roundhead, which is what those who'd taken the side of Parliament in the civil war were called, for the soldiers of the Parliament had cropped their hair short, a great contrast to the king's men, who wore long flowing locks called lovelocks. The

Roundhead had taken Tamworth as booty during the war. It was he who had replanted the woods and orchards, bought new livestock, rebuilt barns and stables, but he'd left the house itself alone. He was a London man, part of the city Puritans who were the mainstay of Cromwell's rule, and the house and estate were his reward, but he could never stay long. He missed the squalor and fuss of London, said Richard's mother, and she'd smile a certain smile, and Richard would wonder just what her part was in the Londoner's longing to leave.

Followed by his groom, Richard trotted his horse into the curve of the courtyard. Vases of flowers sat in the opened windows of the first-floor parlor. His mother and Susannah must be at the end of one of their housecleanings. Four times a year, his mother and her servant scoured the house from its attics to its ground floor—fresh sand, beeswax, and oil of roses part of their arsenal to repel moths, fleas, dust. The house rose three stories, and there were bays rising the same three stories on its front ends. It had been built to honor Queen Bess by a courtier who had pleased that queen.

She'd given him this land, much favor, and an earring, a large pear-shaped pearl that Sir Francis Drake had brought back from his sojourn around the world. The pearl was long gone, sold to support King Charles I in his war against the Roundheads, but Tamworth was theirs again, the Londoner simply a tenant for a time who restocked the barns and fishponds and kept the house from going to the rats and owls, said his mother, and for that, we'll bless him. The parlors had dark paneling, the staircase deep, steep stairs; there was an overgrown labyrinth in the gardens.

"Master Richard," said his mother's servant, Susannah, in surprise when he walked into the kitchen. She was at a long table, rolling out dough. Before her, lying in flour, were the flattened circles she'd finished. The kitchen was cool and dim, the doors at each end open to the beauty and breezes of summer. A skinny child sat at the end of the table, making animals out of leftover dough.

"I didn't see you in the fire's ashes last night."

Susannah read leftover ashes, the sunset, and animals' entrails. She read palms, people's expressions, and the snuffing out of a candle by wind. She prophesied the sweetness of a summer's honey by the way the bees swarmed and warned about early frosts if the swallows and wrens nested in a certain tree. Richard took her prophesies for granted.

"What's this, Annie?" he said to the child. "No smile for me?"

The girl frowned at him, stuck out her tongue. Swiftly, Richard moved around the table, grabbed her before she could dart away, and swung her into the air. She never made a sound, just stared at him in scorn. He kissed her soundly on both cheeks before setting her back on her stool.

"Frown at me again, and there will be another kiss," he warned, and Annie looked down at the table, a flush under her sallow skin, but out of the corners of her eyes she followed Richard's every move.

"Where's my mother?" Richard rummaged among the earthen bowls to see what Susannah was putting into her pies.

"On the hillock. There's cheese over there under a cloth, and I've bread from yesterday. Annie, find the quince jam for Master Richard. We roasted a chicken yesterday. I was for putting some of it into my pies, but I'll give it to you instead."

Richard was out the door, bending a little so the center timber didn't strike his head. "Bring it to me, Annie, if you would be so kind."

"There now, I told you not to pine for him," Susannah said to her granddaughter when he was outside. "You thought the Lord didn't hear your prayers, didn't you? Find the pint of ale and take that to him, too. From the looks of him, he rode straight here."

The hillock was to the northwest of the house. Richard stepped down the terrace that had been his father's project for the last years of his life. Cromwell's soldiers had torn the stones from their places, for nothing more than meanness, said Richard's mother, and it had been his father's work to order them set into place, from his bed at the window, to select new stones to replace those broken, so that it was woven all together into a gracious whole. Stone balustrades had been carved by a marblesmith in Maidstone and shipped piece by piece lying in straw in a wagon. There was lawn beyond the terrace, another of his father's projects, lawn that lay level and flat for a time before rising in green coolness into the hillock, where spreading, ancient oaks the Roundheads had left alone grew, and in summer bluebells bloomed, and at its top the stream could be seen meandering through fields before it wound its way back into the woods, and the Tamworth village church tower rose above the trees, and the chimneys of their neighbor's farm showed.

Near the crest of the hillock, Richard saw his mother asleep under the oaks in what his sisters described as the fairy circle. He moved softly, not wanting to wake her just yet; but his mother's eyes opened when he was within a few feet of her, and she smiled. Richard knew, without putting thought to it, her love for him. In memories that had no words to them, she'd held him close, rocked him, cradled him, murmured his name, sung to him, and walked through fields with him. She'd fed him pasties and sweetmeats from her own fingers, porridge and French ragout with a spoon. Sometimes he thought she read his mind. He knelt now on one knee, and they hugged, and she pulled him down beside her, and they looked up through the oaks at the sky, their profiles identical, the same straight nose, the same slant to the eyebrow.

"The wheat is planted, and barley and oat. Sir Winston"—he was their neighbor—"brought some Dutch seed from London, which Squire Dunwitty and I are trying in some of our fields. Old Mistress Marrow is selling the family farm and the flour mill. I think you should purchase them. We could borrow from Lizzie's husband." Elizabeth was one of his sisters, the married one, who'd captivated a lord, an earl, and brightened all their prospects.

"I'm going to go away for a time. I don't know how long I'll be gone. I've met a woman I want to make my wife. I'll be asking her father's permission to court her. She's French, Mother."

His mother turned on her side to regard him. Annie appeared, lugging a basket that weighed almost more than she did. Richard sat up, fished in the basket for the first thing he could grab, and ate it ravenously as Annie and his mother laid out a starched cloth and placed food neatly on it. Between bites of cheese and chicken, he described Renée to his mother, told her how he'd known he loved her from the moment of seeing her, told how he was going to France to guard Princesse Henriette, except that it was a secret, and that Renée was her maid of honor, so he would be able to continue his courting.

He smiled that smile of his, and Annie, restless as a titmouse, was pinned to a moment of stillness by its beauty. She had to run behind a tree to recover. She lingered in the background, blending herself into the oaks so that no one might notice her and so that she could listen as much as she wanted.

"Louise Renée de Keroualle . . ." His mother repeated the name softly. "What do you know of her family?"

"They live in Brittany."

"So her father hasn't a place at court?"

"No, I believe not. I think her marriage would be blessed by the princess, and there might be a favor given. I know King Charles thinks her very beautiful and pleasing, so there might be a place for her at this court after we're married." He swallowed down the ale as if it were water, wiped his mouth with the back of his hand, not the least doubt in him that everything would go his way. "I thought to walk over to the Ashfords and see if Sir Winston will loan me his horse. I've ridden Pharaoh too hard. He has the heart to take me back, but I don't wish to lame him."

"You leave today?"

"Yes, the French court departs soon."

Jerusalem Saylor was silent. Her son had ridden the miles from Dover simply to tell her he was in love, and that he left for France, with no more mind to it than if he were walking across the fields to Ladybeth Farm. She patted her lap, and Richard, who'd eaten enough to be sated for the moment, laid his head there, and she smoothed his forehead with her fingers, grateful to have him to herself for even these few moments. You're to leave him be to be a man, Dicken had told her before he died. You're not to cling on him. He has his way to make.

"Annie," Jerusalem said, "run and tell Susannah that Master Richard leaves in a few hours. He'll need food and drink to take with him. You'll ride Mandy back to Dover—" She put her fingers over Richard's mouth. "I can do without her for a few days. Effriam is going with you?" Effriam was Richard's groom. "Well then, he'll fetch her back. Now, close your eyes and rest a while."

She lifted her eyes from his face a moment and stared out at Tamworth, allowing herself the luxury of the feel of Richard's forehead cupped in one of her palms. She guarded Tamworth for him, had loved it from the first moment of viewing it as a bride, not yet knowing how its seasons, its roof over her head, would at times be her only constant. To everything there is a season, she had learned in this place, learned in anguish and in joy, and surely the anguish had carved out the preciousness of the joy, seasoned and prepared it, for joy was what she felt at this moment, little as it was, that her son should be lying in solid sleep before her, a man now overlying the boy, taking him farther away from her each time she viewed him, and yet the boy in him had ridden many hard miles to tell her his news.

RICHARD OPENED THE door of Tamworth church, dipping his fingers in the holy water and kneeling a moment toward the direction of the altar. He moved aside the panels of the side chapel and stepped in. His father was here and his grandfather and his grandfather's grandfather. Their coffins were beneath his feet, beneath the broad stones on which he stepped. Tablets in memory of them were among the stones and fastened to the walls. Sunlight was dimmed, cooled, changed to something else as its light was filtered and stained through the colored glass of a window, a window his father had had made by artisans in Italy to celebrate the restoration of King Charles II. They'd mortgaged a farm, and it had been quite a day the day the window arrived. It had sat in state at the front of church for three Sundays in a row, so that all of Tamworth, all of the district, could view it. The vicar had blessed it with holy water. The village blacksmith had soldered it into place, and his father watched from his bed the burning of the boards that had covered the hole of the window for some twenty years, for the Puritans didn't trust joy in their worship, no joy or beauty, either. Everything must be as stark as their souls.

Richard closed his eyes and prayed, asking God's blessings on his mission, asking that God watch over his mother and Tamworth, over his sisters. He asked that God make his eyes and mind sharp, so that he might help the princess, asked that the Duchess of Monmouth might forgive him, and his mouth be filled with the words that would make Renée and her father trust him. That he should be returning to France with her was a blessing he had not expected. He was besotted, a weak word that—he was bewitched, enchanted, bowled over. He was in love, the fire of it scorching, leaving nothing else standing. And in France, it was his hope to make the acquaintance of the two greatest generals in King Louis's army, the Prince de Condé and Maréchal de Turenne, who led soldiers in an army that was the wonder and envy of Europe.

Later, after Richard had been fed again and changed his shirt, and his mother and Susannah had packed his saddlebag with food, and he and Annie had walked around Tamworth so that Richard could see fields, sheep, apple trees, he knelt for his mother's blessing, then swung himself up onto his mother's horse, with Effriam, the groom, clambering up behind him in the saddle, and they rode away.

Jerusalem and Susannah went at once to the kitchen fire, and Susannah looked into the flames for a long time. She threw in some holy water that Annie had gotten for her when Master Richard was in chapel and listened to the resulting sizzle and hiss. Finally she shook her head.

"I can't see a thing about the sweetheart. Annie, go and fetch Nana her shawl."

Annie, sitting on the stool, blinked, did as she was told, but only after she lingered near the doorway long enough to hear her grandmother's next words.

"Bad times in France, though, I see that. Come here and look for yourself."

Dear God, thought Jerusalem when she'd done so. She went outside to walk restlessly along the stream, among the marshmallows and summer lilies blooming there, sending Richard blessings with every breath of her body. Someone would die in France, that's what the embers said. She knelt among the marshmallows. Let it not be Richard, she prayed. Please.

Chapter 6

In Dover, one merry day led into another. There seemed to be no end to laughter, dancing, flirting, amusement. But on the morning of the day before they were to leave, all the English maids of honor were summoned to the chapel. Barbara came rushing to find Alice, still dressing, and pulled her to one side so they wouldn't be overheard.

"She knows—"

"Nothing," Alice said. "Whatever happens, you are to admit to nothing."

"How can you be so calm?"

"Well, for one thing, I'm not summoned, am I? It means they haven't a clue as to who is doing what. Think, Ra."

But still, she and Fletcher crept into the back of the chapel at the appointed hour, sitting in the farthest corner, where the dark of the balcony hid them. Maids of honor from Queen Catherine and from the Duchess of York sat in the front benches used as pews, their chatter flying up high to the vaulted ceiling. Fletcher poked her in the side, pointed. From where they sat, they could see King Charles hidden behind a wooden screen. He sat twisting a ring around and around his finger.

"You're going to end hanged," Fletcher whispered.

The king's lord chamberlain stood in front of the altar. It took the man a long moment before he finally had the attention of all the young women.

"Someone," he began, "has been playing a game with the Duchess of Cleveland, which has ceased to be amusing. We all understand high spirits, particularly on this festive occasion." The lord chamberlain's eyes swept over the sets of maids of honor. Alice shrank farther back in the corner, and Fletcher, beside her, couldn't help but smile. "The high spirits of youth. But it is time to rein in such spirits. The duchess feels that certain attacks—"

At that word, a low murmur rippled through all the maids of honor, and they turned to one another, exclaiming, protesting, questioning what was meant; but the lord chamberlain spoke over the noise, subdued it. "Attacks against her person have come from among these quarters." The murmuring grew again. "I feel certain she is wrong," he continued, "but I have promised that I would bring her suspicions before you. I have assured the duchess that she may rest easy for what little bit is left of our happy time. I should hate to see the last evening of Princesse Henriette's visit ruined by antics that make everyone look foolish."

Barbara stood up. Alice took a breath. What was she going to do? Confess?

"Of what do we stand accused?" Barbara asked.

"Dung in dancing shoes, frogs in bed, salt in a sugar bowl . . ." The lord chamberlain paused.

"False mastic," King Charles called out from behind the screen. Alice could see that he was amused.

"False mastic," repeated the lord chamberlain. Alice had remixed the mastic with which patches were glued to one's face. The fashion was a few years old. Still, women were mad for the little dark spots of silk shaped like half-moons or stars or other things that could be put on their faces, at their mouths, upon their cheeks, or near their eyes. Only married women might wear them. Men patched, too. One of King Charles's councillors wore a patch, like a thin lightning bolt, across his nose to disguise an old dueling scar. Queen Catherine swore it was why half her maids of honor married—to be able to patch and wear rouge. The Duchess of Cleveland's patches had fallen, one after another, into the first course of the supper served last night. Alice considered it one of her finest moments.

"Is there any one of us who is suspected?" Barbara asked. She looked very regal and very pretty, color the shade of strawberries high on her cheeks, as if she had been accused.

King Charles walked out from behind the screen. Young women stood, dropped into curtsies as best they could standing in the narrow spaces confined by backless benches. His eyes swept over them. The sight of them, woman after woman, head bowed, earrings dangling, the bolder of them peeping through their eyelashes at him, was charming. "You've done your duty," he said to the lord chamberlain, who let out a huge sigh. King Charles looked from one woman to another. Alice could see he was holding his mouth not to laugh.

"It would be a great service to me," he said, "if the pranks might stop. In other words, behave yourselves, I command you as your sovereign. I beg you as a gentleman. It would be an even greater service if there were no gossip about this. Be gone, now. Shoo."

Women obeyed him, talking nonstop, leaving the chapel in groups. Alice and Fletcher caught up with Barbara, dragged her away from the others.

"We need to outdo ourselves this evening," Alice said excitedly.

"Alice Verney, are you mad?" interrupted Fletcher. "As your dancing master, I forbid it. Bragge, I forbid you to have anything more to do with her if she so much as glances at the great cow."

"You were magnificent. I had no idea you could lie like that," Alice said, and she and Barbara both laughed.

"It's our last day, pets," said Fletcher, taking them by the arm so that they were on each side of him.

Barbara's face changed. Alice saw it, looked away in irritation. Gracen would have been beside herself to go to France. Caro would have given diamond earrings. But Barbara drooped. The cause was doubtless one John Sidney. Too bad. The deed was done.

IT WAS AFTERNOON of the last day.

"We're so jealous," murmured Gracen. She'd survived her escapade, the mother of the maids never suspecting anything near the truth. The only evidence it had happened was that she was as sweet as island sugar to Alice.

Touching the ribbon tied tight around her neck, Alice said nothing, but then she had no need to. Every day of this visit, the princess and her ladies had worn something unique—starting with the vibrant green stockings—something that set them apart, and every day the English ladies of court had grown more excited to see what would be next. Today, the last day of their visit, Princesse Henriette's ladies wore ribbons of black tied tight around their necks. It was charming and symbolic—the princess mourned leaving her brothers and England, but in a way none of her household could prove or protest.

"Blast!"

It was Prince Rupert. Ladies immediately began to fan themselves with their elaborate, spreading hand fans and to giggle at his language.

"Beg pardon," he called to them.

They were watching the men play at bowls. The gentlemen's long jackets were off, the loose sleeves of their shirts pushed up, held with women's garters Monmouth had collected like medieval tournament trophies from among the more daring of the women. The day was sweet, a breeze teasing skirts and wigs, the sun shining and warm. The men's admiring audience, Princesse Henriette, Queen Catherine, the other great ladies, sat in chairs or on footstools, and everyone else thronged around them, sitting on rugs, lying against cushions piled everywhere, fat cushions with tassels at their corners. The orchestra performed from atop a castle parapet.

The men played in a specially designed area of the garden of the warden of the castle, where grass was thick, green as an emerald, cut to precise and even height. They rolled heavy lead balls at a jack, an earthenware ball of white. The object was to come as close to the jack as possible and to keep anyone else from coming near. The king rolled a ball close to the jack, and at Monmouth's turn, he edged a ball away from King Charles's. Princesse Henriette rose to her feet to clap. Alice saw two of the princess's ladies-in-waiting put their heads together and whisper, clearly about the princess. Were they gathering evidence to present to Monsieur? And what would the accusation be? Your wife had too much fun, smiled, and laughed, and actually enjoyed herself? It was easy to forget what awaited them in France sitting here, where formality was dismissed for frivolity, where the princess had put down her guard, so loving, so affectionate were King Charles and the Duke of York, and the court followed suit. Every day had been one of diversion arranged to the princess's taste. She must be amused, must be delighted. No wonder she glowed, her face softened, and she seemed as young as one of the maids of honor. But tomorrow they left this paradise, went back to the cage Monsieur and his lover had constructed bar by bar. Trust no one, thought Alice. That must be her litany beginning tomorrow.

Scoring a point, Prince Rupert whooped like a boy. The Englishmen were playing the French. Alice turned her head idly and saw Monmouth's duchess slip from the queen's side to walk toward an ancient oak, one of the few to survive the war. Lieutenant Saylor stood under it. When had he returned? thought Alice. And where had he gone? The duchess began to speak to him quite earnestly. Fletcher said they were lovers. Alice looked around. Did anyone else notice? She saw Monmouth, on the bowling green, look up, see them, and his face became unreadable. Spoiled as he'd become, he was still her friend. Alice stood, picked her way through pillows and cushions and lolling bodies, walked over to the spreading oak.

"Do look at that." Richard's sister Louisa nudged his other sister, nodded her head toward Alice.

It was colder under the shade of the oak. The bells in it jingled. The smell of ocean was strong. Neither of them saw Alice. They were quarreling, or at least the duchess was.

"—abandon me the way you intend—"

"Do excuse me," said Alice. "Everyone is watching."

The Duchess of Monmouth turned in a whirl of skirts to face Alice, furious as a cat. "Who do you imagine you are?" she exclaimed, and before Alice could answer, she shoved past her, strode off. But she walked right into Richard's sisters, who were strolling together toward the tree. They surrounded the young duchess at once with chatter and laughter and themselves, bearing her back to the seated ladies as if nothing in the world were the matter and life was just grand. Richard, on the other hand, was dismayed and embarrassed.

"You're as red as a rose petal. Oh, dear, I do believe I've dropped my earring. Will you help me find it, Lieutenant?"

She said it to give him time to recover—and because it amused her—leisurely fanning herself, while Richard crawled on the ground at her feet, searching. She glanced back at the crowd of courtiers. Yes. Alice Verney and Lieutenant Richard Saylor under the old oak tree wasn't nearly as interesting as the Duchess of Monmouth and the lieutenant had been. Richard knelt on one knee, staring up at her.

"I regret to say I can't find it."

There was a moment of heart-stopping silence as she looked down at him, as she thought, over the sensation of falling that was making her heart beat fast—as it had done the first time she saw him on the yacht—His eyes are the clearest shade of blue I've ever seen. Richard tilted his head to one side, wondering why she stared at him so. "You look exactly like one of my father's hounds," she said. "Do get up."

She turned. Cole was walking toward the oak, and with him was his uncle, the Duke of Balmoral. Alice's hands flew to her heart. She sank into a curtsy deep enough for a king, watching the elderly duke as he advanced, one arm on Cole's for support. Cole was pleased with himself, Alice could see. He thought to worm himself back into her affections with this gesture, little knowing he brought the noose with which she would hang all his ambitions. Her eyes went to the duke. He has aged even more in these two years, she thought. He was slight and thin, and the hand he gave her to help her rise was bony, its skin dry, leathery; yet there was some strength to it. His face seemed to be made of a hundred seams coming together at the mouth and nose and eyes. She had forgotten how old he was—his youth the time of cavaliers and court masques, his middle age the war, his old age the Restoration. It frightened her a little, all that lined and marked and bent him.

"How long has it been, my dear?" he asked her.

"Two years, Your Grace."

"France becomes you."

Alice found herself blushing.

"It does me good to see you," he said. "I wished to do my duty and say Godspeed to the princess. Her father, the king, was a man of great integrity. Colefax tells me you have decided to renew your acquaintance as friends. . . ."

Alice found Cole's eyes. They had decided no such thing. You avoid me as if I carried the plague, he had complained to her. Yes, a plague of lovesickness that might make her ill still. I practice pretty speeches but never have the chance to say them. What might pretty speeches win you? she'd asked. Restoration of your regard. And she'd run away from him since, from the confusion in her.

"And I am glad for it, Mistress Verney, for I always thought him a fool to lose you."

Now it was Colefax's turn to become red.

"Will you do me the honor to escort me to the princess, so that I may make my apologies for missing so many days of her visit?"

Proudly Alice stepped forward, and he leaned on her as they walked toward where Princesse Henriette sat. Alice had to walk very slowly, and he breathed unevenly, laboriously, as if the walking took all his strength. Can I do this? Marry a man so old? she thought. Fear pushed up in her.

Leaving him with the princess, she moved around people until she was between Barbara and John Sidney. She plopped herself down, whispered in Barbara's ear, "I could not leave without a final gesture. Keep your eye on the great cow's left cheek."

Barbara put her hands to her mouth to smother laughter.

"What is so amusing?" asked John. After two weeks, he was having to make an effort to be gracious to Alice.

"Secrets. Silliness." Alice leaned back on her elbows and regarded him through slitted eyes.

"Yes . . . well . . . if you will excuse me, Mistress Bragge, Mistress Verney."

Barbara leaned back on her elbows, too. "You've chased him off."

"I don't think it possible."

"Why don't you care for him?"

"I can't abide the idea of your marrying someone with those legs. Only think of your children."

Fletcher, sitting to the other side of Barbara, laughed. "I'm going to cut my hair," he announced.

"No," said both Barbara and Alice. There was something dapper and crisp about Fletcher, a small man with large eyes and luxurious, long, curling hair as beautiful as a woman's.

"It's the fashion to wear a wig. There isn't a Frenchman here with his own hair on his shoulders. I cannot be behind fashion, Alice. Not a man in Monsieur's household was without a wig. I wonder what they plot out there, on the ship."

"They were so handsome," said Barbara, as if handsomeness erased evil.

"They resemble angels, but one evening in their company finished me," said Fletcher.

Angels, thought Alice. The new man in Monsieur's household, the one from Italy, was named Henri Ange, or in English Henry Angel. Queen Catherine made a gesture, and Barbara rose to go to her, leaving Alice and Fletcher behind.

"I don't like the idea of your going back to them," said Fletcher to Alice.

"Barbara will be with me."

"Well, I don't like the idea of that, either. She's much more . . ." He paused.

Alice tapped him on the head with her fan. "Delicate? Sensitive? Kind?"

"Almost too tender for this world."

"It will do her good to see the French court, to learn French ways."

"Planning her marriage, are we?"

"She can do better than John Sidney."

"The question, my dear Alice, is does she wish to. What's happening?"

The men on the bowling green had abandoned it. Women were rising from their rugs and cushions, from their chairs, greatly excited.

"We're to play," Gracen called to Alice.

Women crowded around Princesse Henriette and Queen Catherine, begging to be allowed to be the first to play, and Alice left Fletcher, took her place among them. Last afternoon, she thought. Roses in the garden sent thin celadon-colored arms fat with blossoms upward to the sun. Their heady smell was as strong as perfume. Amid the music of violins in the orchestra, silver bells rang, high, clear, thin as the air that carried their single note. Chosen women took their places, their gowns melon and moonlight, apricot and old gold, apple and amber, Princesse Henriette like a beacon among them in white, the deep green of the grass, the azure of the sky, making every color, every hue, vibrant and alive. It was as if the bowling green had become a stage, and nymphs and sprites and fairies played to an enchanted audience.

His wig off, King Charles leaned back among the cushions and pillows on a rug and picked up his favorite spaniel, his eyes lingering on the French beauty Renée de Keroualle. Between glances, he examined the spaniel in his lap. "Will you look at this. Mimi has a sore patch on her back again. I wonder which of the other little devils is biting her?"

"Storm to the south." His cousin Prince Rupert nodded to the edge of the green. King Charles saw that his mistress had not been included among the queen's players. She was marching toward where they sat.

"I want to play." Plump and sloe-eyed, the Duchess of Cleveland was sullen, and there was nothing subtle about her when she was sullen.

"And so you shall, in a little while when this game is over. Come now and sit beside me, and I'll whisper the finer points of the game to you," said King Charles.

"You just want to fondle me."

"What else do I pay you for, sweet?"

She laughed and sat beside him. Queen Catherine bowled her turn, and a heavy lead bowl traveled solidly to settle near the king's rug.

"You've got to try to hit the jack, my dear," called King Charles, "not me."

"She was aiming for the duchess," said Prince Rupert.

"Ass," Cleveland said to him.

"It wouldn't have hurt you if it had hit you. It would take a cannonball, fired at close range."

"Charles, make him stop."

"Don't quarrel, children. It makes the king fretful. Where are the rest of the dogs, Rupert? They all want to see the lovely ladies play, don't they, Mimi?" King Charles stroked his spaniel's head, while she, eyes on him, cocked her head to one side, alert and adoring. "Go and fetch my dogs, Rupert."

"Why do you indulge him?" Cleveland asked once Prince Rupert walked away.

"Because he's my cousin, because he fought like a Roman for my father and pirated the high seas for me when I was in exile. Because. Because. Because."

Silenced, the Duchess of Cleveland looked around her. There was a great deal of laughter and much teasing and flirtation this afternoon, just as there had been all the visit. In his best of moods, Charles encouraged such frivolity. Servants had begun to walk among those watching, offering wine and roasted chicken and fresh oysters lying in their translucent shells. The air was soft, languid, as silky as a fine shawl. The smell of the sea was mixed with that of roses. It was a lazy, slow, pointless, delightful day, a perfect end to a perfect visit. The silver bells jangled gently, in tune with the laughter and squeals of the women. Birds chirped, bees droned, butterflies made dashing, quick feints at flowers and then sped away. She felt the softness of the afternoon in her bones, felt the distance between herself and this man whom she had enchanted for so long.

"We did love each other once upon a time, didn't we?" She'd risen with impudence, reigned with impudence, and would go down with impudence.

Bright canine eyes regarded her. Cynical human eyes did the same. "That we did, pet. Do fetch me a chicken leg, won't you."

Cleveland gestured to a servant. As she did so, one of the patches she wore on her face, a dark half-moon thought pasted securely on one cheek, peeled off and fell on her bosom.

"Blast and damnation," she cursed.

King Charles bit his lip not to laugh.

THE FAREWELL HAD none of the celebration of the arrival. The morning began with fog; the day itself was overcast, clouds low and gray, and there was rain, not hard, but a continuing drizzle that wet through clothing and sent people who had waited on the beach back into carriages. The French were dry-eyed, ready, already gossiping of this court compared with their own.

But nearly everyone in the English court wept when Princesse Henriette was carried by her brother to the waiting rowboat. Now she was in the royal yacht with her brothers and a priest, and the yacht remained at anchor midway between beach and ship, as if the king and York were loath to allow her from their sight, while rowboats and wherries, crammed with French, waddled through a choppy sea to board the waiting ships.

"You'll be back within six months, sooner if I have my way," Sir Thomas said to Alice, who was hanging on his arm, unwilling to let go, never mind the rain, which was beginning to soak through her cloak. "And in the Duchess of Monmouth's household, as a lady-in-waiting."

"The queen's." They had been quarreling about this since last night, whose household she would return to serve in, and quarreling in general, each upset that she was leaving again. She was suspicious of her father's pushing so hard toward the Monmouths. Fletcher told her a cabal was forming around Monmouth, to proclaim him the next heir, which was insulting to York, the heir as long as King Charles did not have children from the queen. Not only was it insulting, but it was dangerous. Monmouth was illegitimate. There could be a war over something like that. Buckingham's fine hand was stirring the pot, said Fletcher. If Buckingham was behind it, it meant her father was, also. "Her Grace likes me not."

"And you make certain you buy as close to the castle of Versailles as possible. I want to be fastened like a snail to a side garden."

One of her tasks from him was to buy property in France. His peddler, as innate to him as his easy smile, had been summoned up after listening to the French brag of Paris, of the neighborhood called Marais, of their king's rebuilding of a hunting château called Versailles. His greed, his insatiable lust for property, stirred.

"I'd like to return affianced, Father. Remember you're to speak to Balmoral on my behalf." A good night's sleep had quieted her fear, waked her to fresh resolve to have him.

"But not too high. Find out what others have paid. Don't be afraid to bargain. I will consider anything in the Marais, if the price is right—" He broke off and turned to see who made Alice's face light up as if a candle were inside her, and here was Lord Colefax, with his uncle the Duke of Balmoral. Alice dropped into the lowest of curtsies on the sand and shell of the beach, and Balmoral reached out a hand to help her up. His face was almost hidden under the felt hat he wore.

"You should not have come out in this rain, not after just leaving your sickbed," she told him.

"I could not have you leave without wishing you well, Mistress Verney." Rain dripped from the brim of the hat he wore.

He could care for me, thought Alice, I know it. "Will my letters still be welcome?"

"Uncle, we must get you out of this rain," Colefax interrupted.

"I will continue to look forward to them. Good-bye, my dear. Godspeed. Walk me to that useless quay, Cole. I had no idea such silt had built up in this harbor." Balmoral bowed and allowed himself to be walked away by his nephew, talking all the while about the silted harbor and the state of England's defenses. He was captain general of His Majesty's army, as well as being on the privy council.

"Mistress Verney, we must leave." It was a Life Guard, Richard, in fact.

Alice clutched her father's sleeve.

"You're not the beauty your mother was—" Her father reached out a hand to touch her hair, her cheeks, the corner of her lips, saying words Alice had heard too many times to have much feeling for. "But I've been reminded this entire visit of my own mother, Alice. She had a style, a character to her, which I very much have seen in you."

Touched, Alice took his hand and kissed it. Sir Thomas lifted her up and into the rowboat among maids of honor and ladies in waiting. In her ear, he whispered, "Keep your eye out for any sign there's been a treaty signed."

"Father," Alice said in irritation.

"There are Jesuits along on this visit. Where there are Jesuits, there is intrigue."

"Princesse Henriette is Catholic. Of course there are Jesuits."

A grunt was her answer. Like many, her father believed the religious order of the Society of Jesus capable of greatest machinations. Waves splashed at the boat's stern as Life Guards and sailors put their shoulders against its wood and began to push it backward. Sir Thomas walked into the waves alongside the boat. "Give me a kiss, Alice. . . . Another. Mistress Bragge, you keep an eye on this daughter of mine."

Alice held fiercely on to his hand until a swell tore their grip apart. A kiss for you, Father, and a blessing, she thought. Her eyes were on shore, on those under the canopy who waited in the drizzle, Queen Catherine, Fletcher, Edward, Gracen, Kit, and others, like John Sidney, who walked out into the wet and all the way to the edge of the water, waving. Barbara waved back.

The rowboat worked its way past the royal yacht, still at anchor, as Alice took Barbara's hand. "Tell me you're excited to be returning with me."

"I'm excited and sad to be leaving those I love."

Yes, thought Alice, me too.

"I see you found your earring," said Richard. As satisfied as a young lion after feeding, he sat in the rowboat by Renée. To Alice's surprise, he was returning to France with them. She felt respect for him to have maneuvered such a thing, then she felt a chill and shivered with it. An old folk saying came to mind, that someone had just walked over her grave. Her eyes sought and found the Duke of Balmoral back on the shore, walking with his nephew. God bless and keep you, sir, she thought. And bless and keep us in France.

She looked back to her father.

"Jesuits," he mouthed silently.

Chapter 7

Princesse Henriette looked as if she were finally asleep. Alice paused in her reading aloud, stood, and then the ship groaned, and the princess opened her eyes, staring at something beyond Alice. They were already near Calais, on the French coast, would anchor soon and wait for the morning light to disembark. "How old are you, Verney?" she said.

"Twenty."

"I remember twenty. Pull the curtains, so I may see the stars, then leave me. I'll sleep soon."

It was a lie; she hadn't slept either night of this voyage, but Alice was tired. She went to one end of the cabin and pulled back the long draperies that hid the windows across the ship's broad stern. She opened a casement to the breeze, and draperies fluttered out like white ghosts—the ghosts awaiting us in France, thought Alice—and on the bed, the princess stared out at the night somberly, unblinkingly, as if she thought the same, and Alice left her to her thoughts, slipping out the door, thinking to go out on deck, feel the air on her face.

Richard leaned against the wall in the galleyway outside Princesse Henriette's cabin. He was taking his role of guardian seriously. "How is she?"

How did he think? She'd come on board sobbing, both her brothers weeping. King Charles had walked back to hug her three times before he could bring himself to leave the ship. It was wrenching for all the English who saw it. Alice shrugged, climbed up the stairs and onto the deck, went at once to the railing, leaned into the wind and spray. The droplets refreshed her, gave her hope. Perhaps there would be little quarreling tomorrow, a reconciliation, kindness. She stared up at stars, the same stars the princess was likely watching from her bed. Star bright, star light, first star I see tonight. Wish I may, wish I might, have the wish I wish tonight. What did the princess wish for? The contrast between what they left and that toward which they sailed was staggering.

THE NEXT MORNING, they woke to the fact that the ship was anchored beside the quay at Calais, on the other side of the narrow channel of water that separated the two kingdoms. As Alice watched the princess's ladies prepare her breakfast, select the gown and jewels she'd wear this day to be received by the king of France and his brother, her husband, she listened to complaints about England. "We waited for hours on board," ladies around her whined. They were practicing what they'd say to the waiting court, thought Alice.

"We got wet landing on the beach."

"The harbor was filled with silt and shingle."

"Don't the English repair their harbors? No wonder the Dutch trounced them in the last war."

Those words were for Alice, but she ignored them. Alice saw the princess's captain of the guard approach the chief lady-in-waiting. There was a long conversation between them, and then the pair left. Renée, who'd been on deck, hanging over the railing to see who of the French court might already be on the quay, found Alice, dragged her to a corner under stairs.

"The king isn't here," she whispered.

King Louis not in Calais? "Impossible."

"Shhh. Don't speak too loudly. He isn't here, nor is Monsieur. There's no one from court at Calais."

The Dragon saw them. "Get dressed immediately." In their cabin, the other maids of honor were buzzing with talk. No one knew precisely what had happened, but everyone knew something had. As soon as she was dressed, Alice went on deck, went to the railing herself to see. There was a carriage there, an expensive lacquered vehicle with six black horses at its front.

"Colbert's," said Richard, coming up behind her. "He's waiting for the princess to be ready to receive him."

Colbert was King Louis's most important minister.

"Has there been a death in the royal family?" asked Alice.

"No."

"Then what's happening?"

"I don't know yet."

And Richard left her, walking down the gangplank of the ship over to the carriage, engaging the grooms in conversation. Alice saw that d'Effiat and his little group were clustered near the foresail, talking among themselves. She also saw that Henri Ange, the mysterious messenger from Monsieur's lover, stood in the midst of them. Well, she said to herself, here was at least one person who'd traveled from Paris to greet the princess. She didn't like it.

"Who is that?" Henri Ange asked, his eyes on Richard. It was hard not to notice the straight-backed, icy-eyed Englishman.

"An interfering fool they've sent back with Madame," answered d'Effiat.

"Fools seldom are."

"Alice, come at once. We're to go to our cabin, stay there." It was Renée, sent to fetch her.

Alice waited impatiently with Renée and Barbara and the others. It seemed an hour or more; she put her head out the door any number of times to see what might be happening or to grab a passerby and question him or her, so she knew Monsieur Colbert was on board speaking with the princess. Finally, the Dragon came to tell them to assemble themselves on the main deck. Chattering and curious, they climbed the stairs to find everyone on the ship was on the deck, going down the gangplank, assembling on the quay.

"What's that smell?" d'Effiat said when Alice passed near him. "I do believe it's the stench of England." He made a face and waved the hand fan he carried, but in another moment he was stumbling forward as if he'd been pushed from behind.

"I beg your pardon," Richard said. "I didn't see you."

D'Effiat's nostrils pinched in. "You, you—"

"Peasant, fool, lout?"

The tension between the two was dangerous. It had been so since Richard stepped on board and d'Effiat saw him.

"He means no harm," Alice said to d'Effiat.

"He can speak for himself," said Richard. "Amusing, is it not, that a man who mocks his Christ with behavior that is reprehensible might have any comment on my character, or any man's, for that matter?"

D'Effiat turned white. "I will kill you."

Richard bowed. "We understand each other, then." His tone was pleasant.

Henri Ange interposed himself between the two, said to d'Effiat, "This is ill timed."

D'Effiat bowed stiffly to Richard and walked away. Alice was surprised that d'Effiat would obey anyone, much less Henri Ange.

Henri, his face open and friendly, bowed to Richard. "Allow me to make apologies for him. He is not himself."

"I disagree."

The other man smiled, didn't answer, moved away.

"I thought you returned with us to tutor the princess in English, not to fight duels." Alice looked up into his cold eyes, chunks of ice dipped in paint, she thought. "D'Effiat will make trouble for you now."

"Well, that will keep me awake at night."

"It should. He has the ear of the prince, Lieutenant Saylor. Monsieur could forbid you the household."

"I am here by King Charles's order. How may Monsieur stop it?"

"We're not in England anymore, Lieutenant. You must be more discreet, for Madame's sake." She found Barbara, made her way down the gangplank. Richard followed, staying near Renée.

"I wish I knew what was happening," Alice said once they were on the quay.

"We are to travel to Paris on our own," Richard answered. "We will be received at the palace of Saint Germain en Laye, where the king and his brother are. The word is Monsieur is unable to travel. Apparently, Colbert was sent by the king to give Madame the news."

Alice felt stunned. It was a staggering insult, as if Monsieur had publicly slapped his wife. The princess's progress toward Calais had been a daily pageant, everyone in court along, as King Louis both escorted the princess toward her destination and showed off to his court the territories his army had conquered in a recent war. Another war—a small one, between husband and wife—continues, thought Alice. The princess was right to be unable to sleep as they sailed back.

Carriages waited, and beyond them, in the shade of trees, a buffet, so that they might eat before they journeyed. Colbert was nothing if not efficient.

"I'm already tired," Barbara said after they pushed their way through courtiers to get something from the buffet. Richard, Alice saw, made certain Renée received a full plate of food, found her a chair, and then draped himself at her feet to smile up at her as she fed him with her fingers.

"We're leaving." It was d'Effiat, snapping at Alice and Barbara as if they were disobedient dogs. With him was Henri Ange, who lifted an eyebrow ironically to Alice.

"Now?" Alice said. She and Barbara had not eaten more than a few mouthfuls.

"We depart for Saint Germain immediately. It is Monsieur's wish. Find your carriage and place your bony English ass into it."

Ignoring his insult, Alice put down her plate, walked over to Renée. "Renée," she said, "we're ordered to leave. See if you can get into the princess's carriage, and save a place for Barbara and me. Hurry, or we'll have to ride with the Dragon, and you know what she's going to say to you."

Richard stood, dusted himself off as Renée rushed away. "What will the Dragon say to Mademoiselle de Keroualle?"

"She'll lecture her about allowing you to take so much of her time on the journey over, not to mention kissing her fingers as we all just witnessed."

"I intend to marry her."

"Excellent. The sooner you let the Dragon know, the better. And I'd call upon Madame, if it were me."

"You would, would you? Do you always know what everyone else should do?"

"Yes." She grabbed Barbara's hand and ran to the princess's carriage. In the carriage, Princesse Henriette sat silently, her face stony. Beside her, sitting gravely and quietly, as if she felt the upset, was her little niece the Lady Anne, York's daughter.

"No chatter, please," said Princesse Henriette. "I have the headache." She looked down at the Lady Anne. "Do you think you can be very quiet for me? Just for a while."

At a knock upon the carriage door, a lady-in-waiting leaned out the window and took a small glass bottle from Henri Ange. His eyes met Alice's, and each considered the other for a long moment.

"For your headache, ma'am," said the lady-in-waiting, and Princesse Henriette uncorked the bottle, drank the liquid in a gulp, and closed her eyes.

THE JOURNEY TO the royal palace of Saint Germain was a tooth-rattling five days by carriage. On the first day, when they stopped to rest at a château, Richard found Alice, who'd hidden herself away in a window seat to read, and he asked her about Monsieur and the household, watching her face closely as she marked her place in the book with a finger and bit her lip, thinking, he could see clearly, about what to say, considering every word. Her caution amused him, but it also alerted him. There were undercurrents in this household that even he, a stranger to it, could feel.

"There is no love between them anymore, though she tries to do her duty. It is a most unhappy household. There was a lover, his—"

"The Chavalier de Lorraine?"

"Yes, and Monsieur was besotted with him, and the chevalier hated her, took command of the household, began dismissing her servants, Monsieur doing anything he asked, and she fought him, going to King Louis, who has a high regard for her. At any rate, the chevalier encouraged Monsieur to disobedience and arrogance against his brother, which was a mistake, and he was exiled. Monsieur blamed Madame, and even now he stays in contact with his loved one."

"Tell me about Monsieur." The information in the official file on Monsieur was thus—loved by his brother, the king, yet allowed no responsibility, no real service. He did not sit upon the council. He did not even have the governorship of a city or a province. Spoiled by the court, his brother, their mother. Petty and cruel as well as brilliant and sometimes kind. A man of discernment and distinctive taste. Still distraught over the exile of his lover, the Chevalier de Lorraine, a troublemaker to the highest degree.

Alice wrinkled her nose. "A man who may weep for days over nothing and shed not a tear for that which matters. He worships his brother and yet is not always loyal. Fickle. Vindictive. I have a few questions for you, Lieutenant. Why are you here? I find it hard to believe that your task is the simple one of teaching English."

"You do, do you?"

"Yes."

"You know the old saying?"

"Apparently not."

"Curiosity killed the cat."

She frowned and went back to her book.

ON THE SECOND DAY, Richard managed to obtain an interview with Princesse Henriette. He was brought to her bedchamber in the château at which they were resting by one of her ladies-in-waiting. The princess sat in a chair in afternoon light made by long, opened windows that overlooked the château's park; Alice, sitting on a footstool, read to her. It was the duty of the maids of honor to accompany, to amuse, to assist. At a gesture from the princess, Alice glanced at Richard and then moved away obediently.

He's going to ask for Renée's hand, she thought, and something in her didn't like it, but she walked over to Barbara and Renée, who played cards in a corner of the bedchamber. Women were in and out, bustling everywhere, taking the gown the princess would wear that night to be pressed, choosing the jewels she'd wear at supper, brewing the special chicory water she liked to drink in the afternoons, doing all the necessary small chores that made her life comfortable.

"I think he's going to ask for your hand," Alice whispered, her eyes sharp to see what would show on Renée's face. Happiness. Alice went to a window, pleating the long drapery there, staring out at the stretch of lawn, the trees that made a shady walking path, gardeners moving to and fro. Barbara came up behind her.

"Whatever is the matter?"

"It's a good match. She hasn't the dowry or name to attract a soul here, so it's a good match. You know how I want all of us married well. I'm happy for her."

"Alice, you don't . . ."

"I don't what?" The question was sharp.

"Mind, do you? Because you seem out of sorts."

"Nonsense. I'm not out of sorts. Leave me alone."

Richard knelt on one knee before the princess.

"Now, my dear tutor," she said, "shall we speak in English or French?"

"French might be easier for what I wish to ask."

"And that would be?"

"Your permission to court Mademoiselle de Keroualle."

"I thought so. You've been very open in your regard." There was reproof in her tone. Before marriage, a woman's reputation was as important as her inheritance. "What can you offer her?"

"My heart. My most steadfast regard, the promise that I would treasure her all the days of my life."

"Very prettily said, but life, as you know, requires more."

"My estate is not all that it could be, I will not lie. We have not recovered yet from the war. But I can offer her a good home, with farms and orchards and sheep, which keep us from lack and provide some income, and I mean to make it better, to add to it, to build it back to what it was and more. I mean to make her a countess one day, if she will have me."

"What need do you have of my permission? I am not her father."

"I would not want you to think me forward, to think that I have improper intentions toward her, when what I feel is respect and what I wish to do is take care of her in all ways. I would teach her, as I have been taught, of love, that it bears all things, believes all things, hopes all things, endures all things, that it never fails."

"What do you quote to me?"

"From the Bible, Madame."

"The Bible. You are a man of God, then?"

"I would hope so." He leaned toward her. "And I would say to you, while I have this opportunity to speak so privately, that I am commanded by your brother His Majesty to watch over you, and I take that command to my heart. I am your praetorian guard, Madame, your defender, your protector, your champion. Whatever you need of me, you have only to ask."

He knew she was aware of the fiction of his being a tutor, but he'd been wishing to say something to her since the return voyage began. In Dover, they'd called her fairy princess because she was so enchanting and charming. Now, it was as if he witnessed invisible gossamer wings fold back into themselves.

After Richard was seen from the bedchamber, Princesse Henriette motioned for Renée to join her at the window, examining the maid of honor's face in light that hid nothing. Words came into the princess's mind, words the English trooper had sung in his tender voice: There's garden in her face, where roses and white lilies grow. Dangerous to be so beautiful. There were already those who desired her for it. "You know what he wished to speak of?"

"Yes, Madame, I do."

"It pleases you?"

The cheeks were suddenly, vividly roses. "I would like to be a wife."

"His wife?"

"Yes, if it please you."

Princesse Henriette was stern. "Please me? I've nothing to do with it. A husband and wife must please each other. I want you to remember your reputation. Don't allow your regard for him to make you less than all your mother would expect. And he must ask permission from your father to court you."

"Of course."

Relenting a little, remembering her own happiness at what now seemed long ago, the princess said, "I imagine I can find a little something extra to put in your dower." She reached out and touched one soft cheek. "He seems a good man. You are fortunate in that. Tell Alice to come and read to me again."

LATER THEY ALL walked in the park of the château, down a lane of chestnut trees toward a landscape canal, the latest fashion, a long rectangular pool of water set in a garden. Richard walked among the maids of honor and ladies-in-waiting, as if he were one of them. In high spirits, he teased one and all; his sisters had taught him much about teasing females. He insisted on beginning English lessons, making them laugh as he called out words in English, then explained them in French: "Tree, leaf, sunlight, stones, bad dogs, beautiful women."

At a bench, Princesse Henriette sat down abruptly, waving the others onward with their walk.

"I'll stay with her," Alice said, and she sat on the bench, watching the spaniels, who were running back and forth, torn between their loyalty to their mistress and the delight of a longer walk. Alice had something she must ask the princess; this thing with Richard and Renée brought it to the forefront, and here was her moment, but the princess did not seem well. Her face was pale, even with the rouge on it, and there was perspiration above her lip. Dark circles were under her eyes.

"Are you well, Madame?"

"I feel strange."

"Madame, had you time to speak with His Grace the Duke of Balmoral about me?"

"I did not."

Hugely disappointed, Alice turned her face away, but the princess was no fool. She put her hand on Alice's chin and made her look into her eyes. "I've disappointed you."

"No."

"You lie, but you do love me, don't you?"

"Of course."

"That's what Queen Catherine said, that you serve firmly and steadfastly, that I was fortunate to have you in my household. I know you don't tattle on me, even though you've been offered a pretty coin to do it. I will write your duke a letter broaching the subject as soon as I'm settled. I promise."

They could hear laughter from the direction of the landscape canal. Princesse Henriette stood up, smiling. "Whatever is he saying to make them laugh? Monsieur would disapprove." She smiled more genuinely at the thought of that. "Come, no sulks from you. They are not becoming to a future duchess. We mustn't miss the fun. I must learn my English, too. It will upset Monsieur. I think I approve of this Lieutenant Saylor. What do you think?"

"There's something fine in his eyes." Something strong and solid, thought Alice, that a woman could warm her hands and heart upon in a cold, cold world.

WHEN THEY ARRIVED in Paris, Princesse Henriette ordered her ladies to dress in their finest, and she returned to her chambers in the Palais Royal, her palace in that city, to do the same. Everyone was on alert. Only the handsomest, fastest horses would do, only the most decorated of carriages, of harnesses. Everyone was to sparkle with jewels. They would go to Saint Germain in grand style, as befitting a princess of England and of France. Alice was excited that Barbara was finally to see the grandest, most sophisticated court in the world. They journeyed toward Saint Germain en Laye, King Louis's favorite château, the palace of his ancestors where he himself had been born. It nestled on a high hill overlooking the Seine River. When the palace was in sight, word passed through the entourage that His Majesty himself waited outside the forecourt, all the court with him.

The carriage Alice and Barbara and the maids of honor were in stopped. The Dragon was at the door, breathing fire. They were to assemble behind Madame, and quickly. Princesse Henriette had stepped from her carriage, was going to walk on foot to the king. It was the kind of gesture the French adored. Alice and the others hurried to take their places behind her ladies-in-waiting. It was a perfect day, the sun shining down on grand spectacle. Troops were lined all along the road, to honor the princess. They stretched for a mile or more. Ahead could be seen the king, behind him his court, and behind them, behind an enormous opened gate, the beautiful towers of the huge palace of Saint Germain en Laye.

"My soul," breathed Barbara, taking in the gowns, the jewels, the feathers and laces, the silver and gold trappings on horses, the ribbons tied in manes and tails, the troops of soldiers, both household and army, standing at attention, the full spectacle of the court gathered in a semicircle behind King Louis. Princesse Henriette, hand in hand with little Lady Anne, walked to King Louis. He was the altar she must approach before she could properly return to court.

"There he is," Alice said to Barbara, though any fool could have told which man was king. "Isn't he handsome?"

"Yes."

The word was a gulp. King Louis was dark eyed from his Italian forebears, with a sensual mouth from his French ones; he was muscled and lean from acrobatics and dancing, from riding and walking, from hunting and fencing. A man of all parts, he was a graceful dancer in court ballets, an accomplished musician, a patron to artists and craftsmen, a firm ruler over his kingdom, and a warrior. He'd spent the last year conquering the Spanish Netherlands to the shock and dismay of the rest of the world. The only man wearing his hat, its thick white feathers nesting about the brim like birds at rest, he raised Princesse Henriette up out of her curtsy and kissed her cheeks before taking off the hat—an enormous compliment—to bow to the Lady Anne.

"Which one is Monsieur?"

Alice scanned faces, not believing what she saw—or didn't see. "He isn't here." If the insult at Calais had been huge, this one was even larger. There would be fireworks, and not the ones King Louis had likely ordered, over this.

"Which one is Madame de Montespan?" asked Barbara. The new mistress had been the talk of the visit to Dover, with the French bragging on her as if she were a goddess.

"That one, see? In the blue."

Barbara took in the sight of a lovely, lively, smiling, smooth face with big eyes and a painted red mouth and the thickest head of blond hair possible, hair woven through with sapphires and pearls, which also were in ropes around her neck.

"And La Vallière?"

"There. In ivory."

A very slender woman stood beside the sparkling Montespan.

"I thought she would be more beautiful."

"She is."

"She looks sad."

"Yes. He has not treated her well."

"The queen?" asked Barbara, when she could tear her eyes away from the slender woman who did not smile and the lively one who did nothing else.

"There."

Barbara took in the sight of a woman so short, she was barely taller than the dwarf standing on each side of her. Stout and short armed, the queen had a large nose, and her hair, never mind the many diamonds sparkling there, was frizzy. Barbara was silent with amazement, and Alice was pleased, so pleased, to show her friend this new glamorous world where the handsomest king in Christendom, the young lion of Europe, did as he pleased with a practiced politeness and grace that put other men to shame. He ruled his court with a courteous iron will. A morning frown from him could distract everyone for hours. This was the center of the world, and one ought to see it, at least once.

King Louis led his sister-in-law toward the palace. Official decorum was breaking as courtiers rushed to surround them and watch, never minding now who should be where.

"What's happening?" asked Barbara.

"Oh, there will be some endless banquet or another. Just stay by me. Renée, there's the Prince de Condé. Introduce Lieutenant Saylor to him." Alice shook her head at Renée's lack of imagination. She'd overheard Richard talking of the French general, and here the great man was, only a few feet away. Princesse Henriette was a favorite of his. For that, he'd be polite to her maid of honor, and Renée's beauty usually assured politeness anyway. If she was going to be wife to this young man, who had his way to make in the world, she was going to have to do her part.

RENÉE AND BARBARA cowered together, their hands over their ears at the sound of the quarreling, which came from Madame's bedchamber in this, the part of Saint Germain en Laye that Monsieur used; but Alice had her ear to the door to hear whatever she could. It was night. The quarrel that had been brewing since the return, the quarrel that never ended, was in progress on the other side of this door. Her eyes moved over the other women in this outer room. Let them tattle on her all they wished.

"—dare you treat me so!" said the princess.

"I treat you any way I wish!" answered her husband.

"You'd best beware, Philippe! My business in England was important, as you well know! Your brother is not pleased with your behavior!"

"And I am not pleased with yours!"

"I'll make you pay for this!"

"You make me pay with every breath you take!"

On those words, Monsieur opened the door. Alice stepped back, but it didn't matter; he didn't notice her. He was furious, striding through the withdrawing chamber ready to destroy anyone who might stand in his way. Once he was gone, ladies rushed into the bedchamber, draped and festooned with everything that was beautiful—

the finest of fabrics, embroideries in gold and silver, furniture with lovely curving legs, walls of finest walnut polished to a soft patina. But none of it mattered because of the unhappiness that was the other occupant. Madame was standing in the center of the enormous ornate rug, beginning to weep.

"Get out!" she screamed as they rushed toward her. "You don't serve me! You serve him! I won't give you the satisfaction of my tears! Get out of my sight!" Her voice, steadily rising, ended in a shriek. Her dogs, already distressed, barked, growled, began biting at skirts, and the princess rushed to the bed like a madwoman, picked up a pillow, and threw it straight at a lady-in-waiting. Anything she could put her hands on, she began to throw, blankets, books, a hairbrush, a crystal jar of rouge. Women retreated as rapidly as they'd rushed in.

"Verney, Keroualle, Bragge, stay!"

Alice shut the door. Barbara was already near the princess and, with her instinctive kindness, held out her arms, and Princesse Henriette moved to her. The pair sank to the floor, Barbara holding the princess close. Renée sat beside them. She stroked the princess's arm, not quite daring to hold her the way Barbara did, and dogs pawed and whined among the bunched skirts of gowns, squirming to get to their princess, to lick her face and make soft sounds of sorrow for her.

After a time, crying eased, and as if it were the most natural thing in the world, the princess moved to lie with her head in Barbara's lap, and Barbara stroked her forehead. Renée sat snuggled into Barbara, several of the dogs in her lap. The three of them might have been sisters or best friends.

Alice knelt down. "Can I get you anything? Wine? Your chicory water? A cordial for your head?"

"My head. Yes, something for that. I didn't have my headaches when I was in England. Did you notice, Verney?"

Alice walked into the withdrawing chamber. Women waited, their eyes on her, their faces proud, curious, disdainful, but Alice didn't care. "Madame desires a headache cordial. Immediately."

One of them stepped forward with a sealed letter. "This came from His Majesty."

"From His Majesty, and you didn't bring it at once. Pretty behavior."

"I had no wish to disturb."

"On the contrary, that is all you care to do. Sweet Jesus, you should all be ashamed of yourselves." She was reminded too closely of Queen Catherine's periods of disfavor, when courtiers—including her father—had deserted as if a plague sign had been painted on the doors. Alice despised moral cowardice. The only fixed point she'd known in her life was service to the queen. When she gave her loyalty, she meant it.

She brought the letter to Princesse Henriette, who tore it open at once when she saw King Louis's seal. A smile came to her face. "I am commanded to see him tomorrow afternoon. Ha. Monsieur will be furious. How I shall laugh. I shall smile so sweetly when I walk past him. I'm so sorry, I'll say. You're not included in this discussion, my dear— I've said too much. You three did not hear me say I am to meet the king alone tomorrow, is that clear?"

They nodded their heads obediently. Princesse Henriette sat up straighter, as if the king's message were a tonic that cured her. "Mademoiselle Bragge, I regret that you should see me thus reduced." She patted at her face with a handkerchief, began to touch and smooth her curls. "I don't forget myself often, but he . . . well, I won't say more on it. You're very kind. I felt it when you held me in your arms. Verney told me you were so. We must have her, she told me, and already I see she's right. You three are my musketeers. King Louis has his, and I have mine. Help me to the bed, dear ones, so I can sleep away this headache. Verney, stay until I sleep, then guard the door. I don't wish to see anyone."

"Yes."

At a knock on the door, Alice opened it to Henri Ange, who handed her the small dark bottle that held the headache mixture. Again, they considered each other. "How is the beautiful and kind princess?" he said, his English as plain, as distinctive, as broad, as any merchant's on a London street. The exactness of it shocked Alice.

"What concern is it of yours?"

"The concern of a well-wisher."

"You wish her well?"

"You doubt me?"

"Yes."

He laughed. He had small, even teeth. "The princess has a fierce watchdog. G-r-r-r-r. Don't bite. I'd be an ally if you wished it."

She didn't answer.

"Or not."

The way he said that, the way the light in his eyes vanished like a candle snuffed out, disconcerted her. Everything about him disconcerted her. She shut the door in his face and sat in the darkened chamber as the princess went to sleep, thinking. Why would King Louis summon the princess to meet with him alone? Why was it important no one know? Was there, as her father suspected, a treaty?

King Louis made up for his brother's rudeness. He took the princess for a walk in the enormous terraced gardens, the whole court flocking behind them at a respectful distance. There was a dinner that evening held in her honor, afterward fireworks in the vast gardens. Alice watched as courtiers fell over themselves to press forward to have a word with the princess. King Louis's regard for her was clear. If there was a contest with her husband for the king's affection, at the moment she had the lead.

But Monsieur had the last laugh. The court was leaving the next day for Versailles, the old château the king was redoing. There were further fetes, further pleasures awaiting there, and Princesse Henriette, rouged, jeweled, gowned to perfection, petted, admired, sought after, left the fireworks in her honor still fading in the sky to walk to her chambers and find her household packing, but not for Versailles. The only taste of celebration she'd enjoy had passed.

"We go to Saint Cloud, Highness," said her lady-in-waiting, not daring to raise her eyes to the princess's face. Saint Cloud was a summer palace just outside of Paris. The entire court, the world, might go to Versailles, but they weren't joining them.

"It's an insult, a way to thwart her. You see the honor she was given. There was to be more. We'd have been days celebrating at Versailles. I hear there was a ballet planned and a mock battle on the long canal. She's one of the lights of this court." Alice tried to explain to Richard when they stopped on their journey to allow the dogs to run in the grass. "She sets the fashion; the king has always depended on her to add style and verve to his court. It's been that way since she married. Monsieur used to be proud of her. Now he hates any notice she receives. This is cruel to her, not to be allowed a place by the king's side. We spent all the winter away from court; she hated it." Alice shuddered, thinking about marriage and all it could entail. "To be at the beck and call of a fool or a madman or someone cruel . . . I'd leap out a window first."

"Or he would."

Alice laughed, saw Beuvron standing alone near one of the carriages. They'd scarcely spoken a word since he'd been sent to the ships in Dover. That disgrace had not yet been dropped into this latest quarrel, but Alice knew the princess well enough to know she'd bring it up at the proper moment, when she needed something to goad her husband with, and then woe to everyone. "Hello, old friend," she said to him. To her surprise, he stepped away as if there were something offensive about her. "Beuvron?"

"I am aware I owe you money. You'll be repaid."

"I don't care about that."

"Keep away from me, Alice." To her hurt and amazement, he walked away, but took only a few steps before returning, seizing her hand, kissing it, saying quickly, as if he said them fast enough the words would disappear and absolve him, "You've always been a good friend to me. There's a line in the sand now, Alice, and you're on one side, and I'm on the other."

She watched him join d'Effiat and those crowded around Monsieur, talking, laughing, jesting, all their attention on him, on keeping him amused—the litany of the household was "Monsieur must be amused." Like slender, slightly tamed tigers, they all vied for his attention, particularly now, when he was in a bad mood. In among them, aloof and watching, Henri Ange saw her. He tilted his head and stared, but Alice lifted her chin and returned to the carriage.

When they arrived at Saint Cloud, the mood changed like clouds moving to show sun. Monsieur and his gentlemen melted in one direction and Madame and her ladies in the other, and there were enough calming, charming, gracious places to hold both. Paris was within easy distance. Monsieur loved Paris, and Princesse Henriette loved this house. Splendid and multiwinged, the house was on the highest point of land at a bend of the Seine River, and its gardens ran downward to the water. To make the setting perfect was one of Monsieur's amusements, and there were vast acres of trees, planted in precise rows called alleys, which led to a vista of the river or a shady arbor in which to rest or dine or talk, and parterres, which were flower beds outlined with rigidly pruned shrubs, everywhere. Inside the parterres grew pinks, hyacinths, citron, myrtle, jasmine, the fragrance as strong as perfume. Water was part of the beauty, not only the ribbon of the river, but water displayed in fountains, in reflecting pools, in jets, which, when turned on, created fantastic sprays leaping into the air.

Alice and Barbara walked the gardens. "Have you ever seen anything more beautiful? I do love it here," said Alice.

They were at the cascade, a staircase of water spilling down a hill in froth and spray to end in the sudden quiet of a long reflection pool. It could be heard before it was seen, the sound of the rushing water beckoning and inviting. To stand anywhere near it was to be cooled, as if a breeze had come in directly off the river. When Barbara could move her eyes from the beauty of the cascade, she saw that simple marble benches were placed around the reflection pool, and a swan, its long neck arching, swam in solitary splendor at one end, away from the spray and sound. The household had already scattered, leaving the majordomo and servants to unpack and settle, and two ladies-in-waiting sat on one of the benches, their fans fluttering as they talked, almost as if the women were posed to grace the scene: the sweep of soft feathers in their hair, the sheen of fashionable, fat pearls at their throat and ears, the glimpse of soft shoes that matched some shade in their gowns, the gowns embroidered and tiny-buttoned and gleaming with a combination of fabrics that were lustrous even from a distance. Several of the princess's spaniels lay at their feet, their paws crossed, as if barking at swans were something they never thought to do. Coming to Saint Cloud was like walking into the pages of a fabulously painted book, where nothing was not perfect.

The quarreling seemed to melt away under the charm of the house, of the month of June, when days were warm, nights cool, and roses fragrant. Monsieur spent much of his time in Paris. Princesse Henriette and the children and her ladies spent their time in the gardens, picnicking, playing cards—gambling was the vice of court—and receiving visitors. The world of Paris came to call, as did the English ambassador.

Richard announced he would conduct English lessons in the gardens, and anyone might come. All the women were his pupils. He explored the house, he visited with the captain of the household guard, he watched the group of young men who were devoted to Monsieur, their preening, their purring, their disturbing tension. Through Renée, he learned of the odd comment made to Alice by the one called Beuvron. It stayed on his mind. They left him alone, except for Henri Ange.

Richard was on the quay, fishing. He cast back his line, and it caught. He turned, and there was Henri Ange. "My God, I didn't hook you, did I?"

Henri walked forward, held out his arm. The hook was fastened into the sleeve of his jacket. Richard stepped forward, began to undo it, apologizing.

"Someone else was a fisher of men," said Ange.

"I'm hardly that. Merely clumsy. I didn't know anyone was behind me. There, I've done no harm to your jacket."

"You like to fish?"

"I do. I grew up fishing a creek near my home."

"You speak beautiful French."

Richard bowed.

"May I sit here awhile?"

Richard cast his line out into the river. "You're from Italy, I'm told."

"Who told you that?"

Richard was silent, his mind moving quickly. The undercurrents in this household were treacherous. He didn't wish to make trouble for Alice or Beuvron. He shrugged.

"Does my accent betray me?" Ange prodded.

"On the contrary. You sound a Frenchman."

"Tell me of England. I've been thinking of visiting it."

And so Richard talked, noticing that every question he asked was not answered, or it was deflected away. Alice did not like this man, but to Richard he seemed harmless enough. After a time, Ange stood, bowed, and left. But he joined Richard the next day as he walked along the river, and the day after that.

"You've made a friend," Alice said when she saw them talking on the third day. "I can't say I approve your choice."

"I can't say I asked you to do so."

Richard was thinking of that as he put his hands to the ropes of the swing and pushed Renée out and up. She laughed, and the swing returned, and he put his hands to her waist, to the place where the gown swelled out, thinking how someday she would be in their marriage bed and he would painstakingly untie and unbutton all the pieces of material that covered her and taste every inch of flesh he saw. Alice and Barbara and the little girls were picking flowers in the distance. Princesse Henriette sat in a chair on the lawn, talking with a favorite friend in from Paris. There was a breeze off the river. The day was perfect, and I, thought Richard, could be quickly bored with this idyll. There had been much to write to the king about the household, the quarreling, the odd atmosphere, but now, in a space of days—it had been a week since they'd left Saint Germain—there was nothing.

In the house, in one of the many chambers, d'Effiat panted and groaned and cried out, putting his hands in the thick dark hair of the man who knelt in front of him. Then it was here, the mountain to which all men journeyed, the peak high, wide, hot, and he moaned and staggered back and sat in a chair, shivering, watching as Henri Ange, who never allowed embrace, rose to his feet, went to a mirror, and shook his head so that his hair fell in handsome darkness all around his face. Ange went to stand outside on a narrow balcony. Before him was the view of the gardens, the princess, and her guest; farther on, he saw Lieutenant Saylor pushing Renée de Keroualle in a swing that hung from a magnificent and ancient tree. D'Effiat joined him, put his hand to the man's shoulder, but Ange shook it off.

"He's made himself quite the pet," said d'Effiat.

"It's an intelligent move, to make himself comfortable among the ladies. Women talk too much, and if he were of a mind to seduce, he could have his choice already. Women tell everything once you've bedded them."

"He's a spy."

"Yes."

"I think it should be ended now."

"Are you certain?"

"Finish it."

Chapter 8

The next day, hidden from view behind a table used for dining, Richard flipped playing cards into a porcelain foo dog's open mouth. Monsieur collected porcelain. Monsieur collected everything. As far as the eye could see there were paintings, gold and silver plate, candlesticks, ewers, statues, objets d'art made by the artisans housed in the Louvre Palace in Paris. It was late afternoon, and the royal couple were entertaining, except that Princesse Henriette had fallen asleep among cushions on the floor.

"I don't think she looks at all well," Richard heard their guest say.

He stood and watched Monsieur—elegant in a satin coat, calm in manner, charming for the guests' sake—walk over to his sleeping wife and stare down at her. She woke, and for a moment their eyes met.

"You're quite right." Monsieur smiled, the smile as handsome as that of a Greek statue and as cold. "She looks terrible."

Princesse Henriette sat up, touched her face with her hands, a sleepy, bewildered expression still on her face.

"Some rouge might help," Monsieur told her.

Does the war between them begin again? thought Richard, because if ever a salvo between man and wife had been fired, he'd just heard it. Then a footman announced another guest, and there was the bustle of greetings and ordering of refreshments, coffee and flavored waters. Renée brought coffee to him, and he took the opportunity to hold her hand a long moment. He saw Princesse Henriette abruptly put down the drink she'd just finished, clutch at her side, and lean over. "What pain!" she said. There was an odd, long moment in which her eyes locked with Richard's. "I'm poisoned," she said. And then she began to fall as Richard, not even knowing what he did, leaped over chairs and past floor cushions to catch her in his arms.

"Take her upstairs! Put her to bed! Fetch a physician!"

Monsieur shouted orders as Richard carried her up the stairs, taking them two at a time, feeling her body convulse in his arms, seeing perspiration stand out in beads on her face, her dogs nipping and yapping at his heels.

"ALICE! ALICE!"

Startled, Alice put down the book she was reading. Renée was fairly screaming.

"She's ill. They've taken her to her bedchamber. Oh, do come quickly! Richard carried her in his arms," Renée chattered hysterically as they ran to the princess's bedchamber. "She was shaking in his arms, groaning with every step!"

It was pandemonium in the bedchamber: servants, maids of honor, her ladies, Monsieur's gentlemen. Monsieur was at the bedside. At the sound of a groan so agonizing that it made the hair on the back of her neck rise, Alice pushed aside enough people to be near the bed.

Sweet Jesus, she thought. The princess's face was gray, her lips spread against her teeth in a grimace. She saw Alice.

"Poison."

She whimpered the word and began to convulse. Women nearby screamed as Alice and a few others grabbed her arms and legs so that she would not hurt herself. Then there was a physician there. He held open the princess's eyes as her teeth clattered against themselves in a ghastly sound, poked at her abdomen, and the cry she gave made Alice loose the arm she held.

"Colic," the physician said.

"I'm dying!" Princesse Henriette shrieked.

Her husband fell back in a faint, and now people rushed to care for him, but Alice looked for Richard, who stood with Barbara and Renée near long windows.

"What happened?" she demanded.

"Princesse Mickelberg came to call," Renée choked out.

"We were in the summer room, she was lying on cushions, sleeping," said Barbara, her face white with shock at all that was happening around them.

"Madame de Lafayette said she looked ill." It was Renée.

She has looked ill, thought Alice, since the moment she returned. A terrible suspicion formed in her mind, too monstrous to be borne.

"A servant came with coffee, with flavored waters," continued Renée, her words punctuated by small, half-hysterical gasps because the princess was screaming again, as Monsieur was carried from the chamber, the physician ordering much of the crowd from the bedchamber with him.

"She drank some of her chicory water," said Renée.

"Then leaned over," said Richard.

"She said she was poisoned," said Barbara.

"She said that?"

Richard, hearing the word *poison* again, ran from the chamber, down the stairs, taking them two and three at a time.

"Where's the Englishman going?" d'Effiat asked as Richard ran by him. "I was in the pantry today."

"Were you?" Ange was calm. "You were thirsty, I would imagine."

"Yes," said d'Effiat.

Richard burst into the dining salon. It took him only a moment to see that all the cups had been cleared away. He found a cluster of footmen in an antechamber, talking in furious, upset whispers.

"Show me what was served for refreshment just now."

One took him to the end of the chamber to a small pantry. There were silver and pewter cups and rare Venetian glass bottles on the shelves, a brewing pot for coffee, the brazier upon which to heat it, on a table.

"Madame didn't drink coffee," Richard said.

"No, she always has chicory water in the afternoon," said the footman nervously. He pointed to a bottle, which Richard grabbed, taking a clean goblet from those arranged on the shelf.

"What are you doing?" Alice had followed him. "Where are the cups, the glasses?"

"They're cleared away," began the footman.

"Who cleared them?" Alice demanded.

He shrugged, looking from Alice to Richard with a sudden, frightened, stubborn expression that said, Whatever may have happened, it is no fault of mine, never was, never will be.

"Leave us." Alice pointed to the goblet Richard had in his hand. "What are you going to do with that?"

"Actually, I have no idea. I just felt compelled to make certain that it doesn't disappear. Does it seem odd to you that the cups are already cleared away?"

She nodded, her face as pale as the beautiful lace at her sleeves.

"I'm going to Paris to the residence of the English ambassador to tell him what has occurred."

Alice clasped her hands together. "Yes. Tell him to come at once."

"Do you think she's been poisoned?"

"I don't know. It's too awful to contemplate. Where's her cup?"

"Her cup?" Richard repeated.

"She has a favorite cup, always drinks from it."

"I have no idea." Richard handed her the goblet of chicory water. "Hide that."

"Hurry, Lieutenant Saylor!"

At best, it was going to be several hours before he returned.

WHEN RICHARD RETURNED, he came without the ambassador, who had not been home. He'd waited until he could stand it no longer, then left a note. He found all of the servants, grooms, cooks from the kitchen, footmen, maids, weederwomen, gardeners, in the hall that led to the withdrawing chamber that led to the princess's bedchamber. In the withdrawing chamber, Renée was huddled with Alice and

Barbara. Everyone was on his or her knees, praying. She's no better, Richard thought. He knelt beside Renée, who put her arms around his neck and cried. It was improper to embrace him, but no one cared. Many were weeping, holding on to one another. Richard stroked her back, met the gaze of Alice, who closed her eyes again and continued her own prayers.

"She hates the priest attending her," said Renée, sobbing into the front of his shirt and waistcoat. "She wants her confessor, the one Monsieur dismissed, but he's so far away. Oh, I don't want her to die. What shall I do if she dies? Where shall I go?"

Richard brought her hands to his heart, held them there. "You'll go to your father's and wait for me." He made his way over to where Alice knelt.

"Is there any further talk of poison?" he whispered.

"That priest won't let her speak of it." Alice jerked out the words, her eyes angry, her face streaked with tears. "Whenever she does, he tells her to mind her soul, to make peace with God, to accuse no one. He tells her she is a sinner! I hate him. But she did say to Monsieur that he hadn't loved her for a long time, but that this was unjust, that she'd never abandoned him. He wept like a child."

"What was unjust?"

"I don't know, Lieutenant."

A servant came out carrying a bowl of blood. They'd bled her, a remedy for sickness. A footman brought soup, but word soon passed around the withdrawing chamber that she couldn't eat it.

"She says she's cold." Alice brought news she'd gathered after a discussion with those near the doorway of the bedchamber. "She says her hands and feet are numb. She said a moment ago that if she weren't a Christian, she would kill herself. They've sent for the king."

She sat on the floor beside Barbara like a doll whose stuffing was gone; Barbara leaned back against the wall, her lovely face swollen from crying.

"It's my dream," Barbara whispered. She had bitten her lip so hard that blood was beading. "I always thought it was me, and all the time it must have been her."

"Hush, Ra, hush, darling."

They hugged each other, and after a time Barbara dozed, not waking when a stir swept through the chamber as someone tall and magnificently dressed strode by without a glance or word to anyone.

"That's Condé," Alice said to Richard, "your great general."

NIGHT HAD FALLEN.

The long hours of shock and despair had exhausted everyone, and some were dozing, sleeping on the floor like dogs. Richard stepped past bodies, positioned himself in the doorway. The Prince de Condé sat in a chair, his hands holding Princesse Henriette's. Richard would not now have recognized her, her hair matted with sweat, her eyes sunken, agony etching her face.

Her friends, people he didn't know who'd arrived while he was gone, as well as ladies-in-waiting, knelt at small, individual wooden prayer stands, beads of their rosaries working through their fingers. Windows were open to the night. Monsieur wept into his hands. I wasn't able to protect her, thought Richard. He'd not even suspected she needed protection of her life. There was a dull ache in his chest.

"Move aside," someone ordered, and Richard stepped to one side to allow another physician to enter the bedchamber, his long gown making whispering sounds against his legs.

"Sent by King Louis himself," he heard d'Effiat whisper. "His own doctor."

A sudden impulse rose in him to cross the space between them and choke the life out of d'Effiat. As if he read his thought, d'Effiat met Richard's eyes. Henri Ange rose, led d'Effiat to a dark corner.

"He knows," said d'Effiat.

"No," said Ange. "He doesn't know he knows." His eyes glinted. "It's more amusing that way."

Richard glanced over to where the young women were. Renée lay with her head in Barbara's lap. Barbara sat against the wall, her eyes closed. Alice was on her knees, praying again. The sight surprised Richard and, for some reason, moved him.

Servants went by, carrying towels, bowls of water. The princess's moans, as yet another physician put his hands on her, were unceasing.

Why do they not give her an antidote? thought Alice, her prayers straying. Unless there was no antidote. . . . She moved to sit back against the wall like Barbara. She watched Richard, who was pacing up and down. The waiting was interminable. She had forgotten how many chimes the clock had last rung, or the church bell, had no idea what time it was, except that it was dark. This afternoon she had been in the garden, talking to Barbara about Paris, about the seamstress they would visit, about Notre Dame, the medieval cathedral that Barbara would love, about the Luxembourg, a grand palace belonging to a grand French princess, where they would call with Princesse Henriette to drink chocolate and Barbara would see, yet again, the luxury and sophistication that this royal family took as its due, and with time, enough of that would make someone like John Sidney seem a rustic. It all seemed days away, another time, another life.

She fixed on d'Effiat and Henri Ange, huddled into one corner of the withdrawing chamber. Earlier Beuvron had been sobbing, weeping hysterically, and now he was shaped into a ball on the floor, his face to the wall, his back to everyone. Ange's face was remote, sad, and Alice had seen him praying when Princesse Henriette's screams had driven her to hold her own hands over her ears. Could they have helped Monsieur to poison her? Was such an evil thing possible?

Musketeers entered the room, their swords and uniforms intimidating; Alice stood. People began to drop into curtsies or bow. Richard made his way to her. "What is it?"

"The king," said Alice, and she dropped into a low curtsy as King Louis and a group of women drenched in perfume and jewels swept through the chamber. With Richard at her side, she fought her way to the door; everyone was crowding into it, moving themselves into position along the walls to see this, the king of France come to say good-bye to the foremost princess in his kingdom. King Louis knelt by Princesse Henriette, who had been moved to a cot by the window, spoke softly to her.

"Who are they all?" whispered Richard.

Another time she would tell him the women were the king's cousin, his queen, his mistresses, current and past. Another time she would cluck her tongue, but now she just felt a sadness so deep, it was impossible to speak.

The entourage gathered around Princesse Henriette, talking in low voices with her, and she, racked with pain, held out her hand and had something to say to each of them. Everyone wept. Though only those near could hear what was being said, no one along the wall moved. Everyone knew they were witnessing history.

King Louis spoke with his brother, with the physicians, asking them what remedies they'd tried. He leaned over and held Princesse Henriette's hand, bringing it to his mouth to kiss. Once they'd been lovers; that's what the scandal sheets said. They spoke. Those nearest whispered the words into the ears of those who couldn't hear. You are losing a good friend, she told the king. Don't leave me, he said to her.

Then, after a time, without warning, the king strode from the cot, out of the bedchamber, tears standing on his face, followed at once by all who'd come with him. In a moment the court was gone from the bedchamber, Monsieur hurrying away with them. Even with death lying in bed with his wife, he must see his brother, the king, off properly. The bedchamber seemed strangely empty, as if some essence of vitality and life, some possibility of hope, had also departed.

"Why did he leave?" whispered Richard.

"The king of France may not witness death."

The captain of the household guard motioned for Alice to come forward, and she found herself standing at the cot.

"Thank you for your care of me," Princesse Henriette whispered. "I'm glad to leave, I am."

Others were being brought forward to say farewell; she was calling out last bequests, taking rings from her fingers to give to dearest friends. Alice walked into the withdrawing chamber, sat numbly in a chair. This couldn't be happening, and yet it was. Renée and Barbara were nowhere to be seen. Perhaps they'd stumbled on to bed. She would stay until the end. She moved so that she was kneeling before the chair, put her elbows on the cushion, making her own prayer stand. When she lifted her head, she saw the English ambassador, Lord Montagu. Oh, thank God, she thought. Face grim, he acknowledged no one but went directly into the bedchamber and did not reemerge.

Richard, a cat that couldn't be still, came to tell her details every now and again. She prayed and slept and woke to pray, not knowing what was real, this time in the antechamber or the fragments of her dreams.

"Lord Montagu asked her if she'd been poisoned, but I could not hear what she said. That priest interrupted, told her to accuse no one, to offer her death up as a sacrifice."

Black crow, thought Alice, and she dreamed of crows.

"They've bled her again," she heard Richard say.

"Where are her children?" he asked her another time.

Sequestered far away . . . Monsieur wouldn't allow them to see the manner of their mother's dying, even for a good-bye. The little Lady Anne, thought Alice. Well, she had her governess, and Alice would find the woman later and see how the child was faring. . . .

"Monsieur has left. Why wouldn't he stay?" Richard said in the dream or perhaps in real life. Royalty may not witness death. She thought she'd told him that. She dreamed she saw a priest, his gown purple and flowing, a large cross dangling from his belt, sweep by. This must be a dream. She heard a clock chime twice and fell into a dreamless sleep in which a church bell rang three times. She felt arms on her shoulders. She lifted her head from the cushion of the chair.

"It's over," said Richard.

He sat on the floor by Alice, then lay on his back, gazing up at the ceiling painted with cherubs and clouds. Alice looked around her. Servants were scurrying forward from the hall; Lord Montagu walked out of the bedchamber. The door closed behind him. The public viewing of a royal dying was over; death had her to himself. The full impact of this night crashed over Alice like waves. She fell back on the floor beside Richard, keening sounds coming out of her mouth.

Lord Montagu sat in the chair she'd been using as a pillow and prayer stand, said tiredly, "A bad business, a very bad business." And to Richard, "No sleep for you, my boy. You're to take my letter to the king. I need paper and ink."

"Go to the circular chamber," said Alice, "just off the gardens." And then, when she saw Richard didn't know which chamber she spoke of, she wiped her eyes, sat up. "It would be my pleasure to accompany you both. Come."

She led them downstairs to a chamber shaped like a circle, one of the most beautiful rooms in the palace, the princess's favorite, small panes of mirrors set into faux windows one after another until they joined actual windows and handsome glass doors to the garden.

All around them the house was silent. Nothing and no one stirred, as if every man, every beast, were exhausted. Richard brought candles, and Lord Montagu sat down to write, openly crying at times, as he filled sheets of paper, demanding Richard's or Alice's memory when his own failed him, his frowning reflection doubling back on itself in mirror after mirror. Done, he sprinkled sand over the ink to dry its blots. Richard melted wax onto the paper once it was folded, and Montagu pressed his ring, in which his seal was carved, onto the wax.

"You are to take this at once to His Majesty, tell him I will make a further report when I am not so disordered from grief. You are to take my carriage to my house, have my aide give you coins, and fly to England, Lieutenant, for His Majesty must know, as soon as possible, what has just occurred. Tell him I follow you by a day or two at the most. I beg you your discretion should he ask you questions. She told me that if she had indeed been poisoned, King Charles must not know, he must be spared that grief, that she did not wish revenge upon King Louis, for he is not guilty. Those were her very words. Do you understand what I'm saying to you, Lieutenant? There may be talk of poison, but I am to be the one to choose when and how it will be discussed—if it is at all—with His Majesty."

"I will not lie if I am asked a question by His Majesty."

"Nor am I asking that." Lord Montagu was cold. "I am asking that you make certain you report only what you saw or heard, not what you conjecture or imagine."

"I took some of the chicory water."

Lord Montagu's eyes widened slightly, then he gave Richard a hard glance.

"She drank it, clutched at herself, and said she was poisoned. I took some of the water."

"Where is it?"

"I have it in safekeeping," said Alice.

"Lord above us all, what a mess this may be. I depend on you, Lieutenant, not to make it worse." His glance moved to Alice. "And you."

"Sir," said Richard, "may I have just a moment to write a letter?"

"A moment, no more."

Richard's hand moved swiftly over the paper. He gave the note to Alice. "You'll see she gets this?"

"Of course."

Richard stepped out into the night and into the carriage, which jolted and swayed down the drive toward the road to Paris. The ferocity of the night was reverberating in him. He wished he'd choked d'Effiat. The carriage went through the elaborate iron gates, which opened to Saint Cloud, Saint Cloud sitting on its hill, stars shining down on its perfect gardens and its grand rooms and its glittering occupants. That death had touched it with one bone wing seemed impossible. He couldn't believe he was bringing the news he was. Could he have done more? Was there something he'd missed?

ALICE SAW THE reflection of herself sitting near a candle, opening the note. He vowed his love and devotion, told her, no matter what, to wait for him, that he'd be back to France, back to her. He wrote very firmly, very evenly. She touched one of the letters, the R in his name, before refolding it and walking slowly, wearily, like an old woman, up the stairs to the bedchambers.

Chapter 9

Paris exploded with rumors. The Chevalier de Lorraine held Madame and poured arsenic down her throat. Monsieur commanded the poisoning. No, Monsieur knew nothing of it. The poison was in the chicory water. It wasn't in the chicory. It was on the cup. Where was the cup?

Louis, king of France, walked a long gallery in his palace in Paris, the Louvre. He passed statues brought up from the dirt of ancient Rome, molded and shaped by other empire builders who understood the passion for empire. He passed heavy tapestries whose bright threads depicted tales of the Bible, tales of mythology, tales of his reign, which he was turning into mythology, woven by the finest artisans in the world, right here in his own kingdom, part of the industry he and his minister Colbert were creating. He passed paintings by Titian and Rubens and Correggio, a collection his forebears had begun, to which he added—some of the paintings, ironically, purchased from the Roundhead Oliver Cromwell, when England had been in its protectorate and sold off the treasures of its beheaded king, who was Louis's uncle. The chamber was long, high ceilinged, made of marble, and cold—so that the fireplaces, big enough to roast oxen whole, never warmed it in wintertime.

Was it true? Had his brother killed Henriette? His brother

embodied—in a way that even he did not—that wild Italian streak in their heritage, that of the grand gesture, prodigious art, immense intrigue. It was why he kept him hobbled, encouraging vice, encouraging greed, encouraging pettiness—keeping his brother like an overgrown child. A child was easily diverted. A man was not.

But this?

Lord Montagu, the English ambassador, had been as cold as this marble chamber, accepting an autopsy by France's most eminent physicians, but only in his presence and the presence of English surgeons. Word had just been sent: The autopsy was done. Their findings: Her stomach was flooded with bile, the organs of her abdominal cavity in an advanced state of gangrene; a natural death from cholera morbus. It would be published in the *Gazette de France*.

But Louis knew—as he knew the ambassador knew—there were poisons capable of producing any symptom. The English physician insisted there were traces of poison in the body. The French disputed. A dog had been given the chicory water. It had not died. He knew that the Marquis d'Effiat had been in the pantry where cups and glasses were kept the afternoon of her death. When questioned, as were all of his brother's household, the marquis said he'd been thirsty after playing tennis and gone into the pantry for a sip of water. Where was the cup out of which she'd drunk? Did his brother know she was to die? Had Philippe ordered her poisoned?

No, Philippe swore. No, he wept. I regret all my sad dealings with her, he cried. If I could do it over again, I would be a saint to her. He sniveled, he sobbed, he shouted. He crawled on his hands and knees, begging Louis to believe him. I was jealous, Philippe wept. You favored her over me. I could not bear it. But I would never hurt her. You are my brother. Protect me from this vileness they whisper.

She had brought back a treaty with Charles's signature and the signature of two of his ministers. A secret treaty to wage war on the Dutch, for which Charles would be handsomely paid; his English cousin always needed money. But the treaty was more than a contract of war, so much more than that. It was something that would assure his name lived hundreds of years beyond his span of years.

Charles of England swore to convert to Catholicism.

Not only a personal conversion, but to bring the kingdom of England back within the Mother Church's fold. England, that rogue nation, that Protestant bastion, would once more kneel, as did all civilized nations, before His Holiness the pope. And it would be he, Louis, the fourteenth of that name, who would be revered as the warrior saint king who brought it all about.

Now Charles was distraught, unapproachable, seeing no one. And yet Louis knew a wise king recovered from disloyalty, disobedience, treason. Had he not done so himself? Had he not feelings himself? She was one of his first loves. She died a sister, a friend, an aide to grander schemes. All of thirty and two, handsome, revered, and increasingly feared, the king of France continued to walk the long gallery of his immense palace, his heart the growing stone it must be for the sake of the greater glory he pursued.

PHYSICIANS AT SAINT CLOUD, the princess's body being opened and explored, sent Barbara into a state of near hysteria. Unlike Barbara, Alice lingered near the chamber in which the autopsy was being performed, then bribed the footmen to tell her when the physicians were finished with their grim work.

A footman found her sitting by herself in the circular chamber that had been Princesse Henriette's favorite. "They're cleaning themselves now." The princess's body would be touched this evening by yet another set of men—the embalmers.

Alice ran down side steps to catch the carriage of the English physician. She was wearing a mask on her face. A footman was holding a torch to light the man's way into his carriage. Like a slim, black-gowned ghost, Alice opened the door on the other side and slipped inside. The physician stepped up and sat down with a groan, then saw her.

"Who are you?" he asked, and put his hand to the pull to stop the carriage.

"Please, I must ask some questions. I mean no harm, and I will pay you well." She put a small leather bag of coins on the seat beside him.

He lifted the sack of coins, testing its weight, and set it down again. The carriage lurched forward, began its slow rattle down the driveway of Saint Cloud.

"The princess?" She didn't finish, left the sentence open. In the dark, she couldn't see his face, but she could feel his heaviness, his tiredness.

"Dead and gone, that's for certain."

"I have to know. Did she die of poisoning? Please. There's more where that came from." Alice pointed to the sack of coins.

"Why should I tell you?"

"Because I loved her. Because someone must know the truth."

He sighed. "There were traces of poison, I'm certain of it. But my distinguished French colleagues disagreed. And I must tell you, they performed the autopsy like butchers, as if to hide truth rather than reveal it. If I had to swear in a court of law, I'm not certain what I'd say. There's nothing left I could point to."

Alice opened the door of the carriage.

He put out his hand. "Young lady, wait. I don't want these coins—"

But Alice had already leaped to the ground, catching herself as certainly as an acrobat, and was running back through the gardens, to the palace.

PRINCESSE HENRIETTE LAY in state at Saint Cloud. King Louis and Queen Maria Theresa, accompanied by courtiers, sprinkled holy water over the body and prayed at solid silver prayer stands. Alice, Renée, Barbara, and the other maids of honor huddled in a corner like lost kittens. No one paid them any mind. Candles burned everywhere, casting odd shadows. A small silver casket lay at the foot of the corpse. It was Princesse Henriette's heart and would be taken to Val-de-Grace, a convent that had comforted both her and her mother when they had been hangers-on to the French court, despised, pitied because they had nothing, their men dead or in exile, their kingdom lost. Alice held hard to Barbara's hand, and Renée held hard to Alice's. They felt abandoned and frightened. No one had any time for them. Everyone was impatient, wept easily, rushed here and there, accomplishing nothing.

Alice glanced over to where Monsieur's men were gathered. Their clothes were darkest black, the lace at their throats and sleeves white as first snow, like their faces, handsome faces, young faces, cheekbones angular, making shadows in the candlelight. Despite their beauty, their appearance brought to mind unholy things, creatures of the night who tapped on closed windows and brought bad dreams. Her eyes met those of Henri Ange. His face was as smooth as a marble saint's, no puffy lids, furrowed brow, or twisted mouth to mar it. He looked kind, approachable, almost simple, like a handsome boy in a village somewhere, heart still pure. Did you poison her? thought Alice.

As if he read her mind, he winked at her. Dropping her eyes, she squeezed Barbara's hand hard enough to make Barbara wince. He frightened her.

The praying, the viewing of the body, ended. The majordomo of the household made a gesture, and people of the household began to file by, taking a last look before the lid of the casket closed.

Barbara shrank back. "I can't," she whispered.

Alice and Renée walked forward, Renée crying. Alice took a quick glance at the face, but it seemed to belong not to Princesse Henriette, but rather to some badly done wax figure. As she moved away, she had to pass the gathering of Monsieur's men, and one of them caught her by the arm. Then handsome young men in darkest black surrounded her on every side. The circle they made around her was too close. She could feel their breath on her. She pushed forward and was pushed back. As simply as that, she was encircled and cowed.

"Stop it," she whispered, and her voice cracked.

From behind, someone put arms around her like a lover, whispered in her ear, "I'll rescue you."

She swallowed back a sob.

"But first you have to say thank you. Thank you, my dear Henri Ange."

"Thank you, Henri Ange," she whispered. Tears rolled out of the corners of her eyes.

"My dear Henri Ange," he corrected.

"My dear Henri Ange," she repeated.

The circle opened, and ahead, in the half-light made by candles, stood Barbara and Renée, waiting for her. Her dignity broken, Alice managed not to run, managed to swallow back sobs.

"You're someone else when you're with them," she accused Beuvron furiously later.

"I am," he answered. "Beware us all."

THE NEXT EVENING, the body left Saint Cloud by torchlight in a magnificent procession of priests on foot and royalty in carriages. The princesses of the blood, those descended directly from kings, were the handmaidens. Barbara and Alice stood at windows overlooking the courtyard, watching as the train of horses, people, and carriages wound down the long driveway, on to Paris, to the Cathedral of Saint Denis, to the Abbey of Kings. It would be hours before they would arrive. A drum beat out a solemn, eerie rhythm. They could hear it long after they could no longer see anything but the flames from the torches in the distance.

Monsieur was already waiting at the cathedral with his household guard and bosom companions to receive the body of his wife, and then he would stay in his Palais Royal in Paris, receiving condolences, dressed in black from head to toe like a god of the underworld. His two daughters, princesses of the blood, were in the procession bringing their mother's body, even though one of them was a baby. Little Lady Anne was in the procession, though Alice hadn't wanted her to be. It is not your decision to make, Lord Montagu had told her. It is her duty as a princess of England. Lord Montagu was in the courtyard. He'd come to see off the procession. His carriage was in the courtyard. He would join the procession at some point, see the princess into the abbey. Alice left Barbara and went downstairs to speak to him.

He turned at the sound of her footsteps in the gravel. "I want to thank you for your care of the Lady Anne. She tells me you were very kind to her, slept at the foot of her bed every evening."

"I wanted no harm to come to her in this house." There was silence as they both considered the implications of what she'd just said. "And I thought she might be afraid to sleep in a house in which her aunt had died."

"You'll be pleased, then, to know she leaves for England tomorrow."

"Very pleased. How does His Majesty King Charles?"

"Not well. He is holed up like a fox to the den, will see no one, speak to no one. He refused to receive the special messenger sent by Monsieur to announce the death and extend condolences."

She heard satisfaction in the ambassador's voice. Monsieur and Lord Montagu were not on good terms. In the hours after Princesse Henriette's death, when everyone was bereft and emotionally drained, Monsieur had walked into his wife's chambers, demanded her keys from the ladies-in-waiting, and opened cabinet after cabinet, taking jewels, a small casket holding letters—which Alice had learned from Beuvron were from the king of England—as well as another holding coins King Charles had given his sister as a parting gift. Alice had walked in on a scene in which Lord Montagu was shouting that Monsieur was a thief—and worse. She had asked that those coins be given her servants, Montagu was shouting. But Monsieur was not moved by deathbed requests and English ambassadors.

"London is as aflame with rumor as Paris," said Lord Montagu. "The apprentices have set fire to a house in which Catholics live, they burn effigies of the pope, the Duke of York had to order a guard around the house of the French ambassador, and I'm told the poor queen dares not set foot outside of Whitehall for fear a mob will pelt her carriage." Queen Catherine was Catholic, a princess from Portugal.

"You've written the king about the autopsy?"

"I have."

"May I ask what you wrote?"

"That the majority of the physicians believed she died of cholera morbus. Anything more is conjecture."

"Conjecture? She said herself she was poisoned. She said it to you—"

He interrupted her. "She said many things to me, Mistress Verney."

Alice pushed on. "I think Henri Ange did it."

"Who is no longer to be found in the household of Monsieur."

"He was there last night."

"He is not there now."

"They're horrid. They deserve to die." She wiped at a tear that trickled down her face.

"It is an ugly business."

"And King Louis?"

"Distraught, I promise you that. Dismayed and shamed by the rumors sweeping the streets. Comfort yourself by the fact that what princes do is not always punished by man, but all must be judged by God."

God? thought Alice. How can God allow what He does? "I want to go home."

"Yes, of course you do. I have coins from your father, and I've booked passage for you and Mistress Bragge. In a week you'll be in England and away from this place."

"Lord Montagu, I don't wish to stay here in this palace another moment. Might you help me find suitable lodgings in Paris?"

"You'll come and stay with me in Paris until you leave for England. Let me take care of our little princess, see her on the road, back toward the arms of England. By the way, Lieutenant Saylor was sent to escort her back. He wished to come here, but I wouldn't allow it, asked him to join the procession when it reaches Paris, to stay with the Lady Anne from then on. He bade me give this letter to you." Lord Montagu reached into a pocket, fixed her with a stare. "I'm not aiding a romance, am I?"

"No, of course not."

"Good, for I don't believe in them. I'll send a coach for you first thing in the morning. Can you be ready?"

"Yes."

When he was gone, she ran to an empty chamber, shutting the door behind her, and opened the letter. Out dropped two more, one addressed to Renée and one to Barbara. Why would Lieutenant Saylor be writing to Barbara? It made no sense. One eye on the door, the other on the letter, Alice opened the one to Barbara. Inside was yet another letter, and this handwriting was not the lieutenant's. Opening it, Alice read the words. It was from John Sidney. So. Lieutenant Saylor acted as a go-between for his cousin. She wondered if there had been other letters. Likely. She tore it into pieces and put the pieces inside a perfume brazier as something dawned on her, something forgotten in all the drama of the last days.

Princesse Henriette had never written to the Duke of Balmoral.

She went to the bedchamber of the maids of honor, but Barbara was nowhere to be seen. Alice found her on her knees in a small chapel, praying. Alice waited in the hall until her friend was finished, then grabbed Barbara by the hand as soon as she walked into the hall. "We're going home."

"When? How?"

They walked arm in arm toward the bedchambers. "Lord Montagu is sending a carriage for us in the morning. And Beuvron left me a note. He says that I can rest easy; they've all gone to Paris. Not that I will." Alice pulled the cord that summoned servants. "We'll spend the next few days in Paris, too, with Lord Montagu, until we travel to the coast to catch a ship home."

"Home." Barbara rushed to put her things in a pile, her brush, her silver hand mirror, a box of ribbons. She stopped at one point and hugged Alice, who smiled to see happiness back in her friend's face and felt not a shred of guilt about tearing up the letter.

Word of their departure, the fact that Alice had asked for her trunks to be brought from the attics, spread through the household. Hearing it, Renée entered the bedchamber and saw Poll placing clothing in a trunk.

"You're leaving?" Her eyes filled with tears. "What will I do? The Dragon hates me."

"Write to your father and have your family come to fetch you," suggested Barbara.

"They need me here. They won't want me to come home."

"Her stipend," Alice whispered to Barbara. "I have something for you." She waved the letter from Lieutenant Saylor, and Renée took it and read it, but it brought no smile to her face.

"He writes it will be some time before he can return." She refolded the letter.

"At the most, you'll have to wait only a few months, six, perhaps. You can wait a few months," Alice said.

But Barbara sat beside Renée, taking her hand, frowning at Alice. "It's difficult to be separated from those we love, isn't it? Our mind goes tumbling in directions that are frightening, that they'll forget us, that what we desire will never come to pass." She kissed Renée's cheek and stood. "He adores you. You have nothing to fear."

Renée went to a chair, her face somber, watching Alice and Barbara, who were beginning to play cards, to wager silly things, like a footman's mustache, the Dragon's slipper, the cook's big spoon. It was as if they'd forgotten the heartbreak and shock of the last days, as if they'd already left. And they have, they've left me in their heads, Renée thought. She shivered.

Bide your time, Lord Montagu told her, whispering to her the interest of a certain very great man. "Trust me," wrote Richard.

She didn't know how well she could do either.

The next morning, Alice stood a moment in the vestibule of Saint Cloud. But for servants moving trunks and bags, there was no one to say good-bye to her and Barbara, no one from Monsieur's household, no one from the princess's, save Renée. All the mirrors were covered with black cloth, the custom at a death. Draperies were drawn, windows closed. Princesse Henriette's ladies stayed in bedchambers, writing letters to family, to those in high places at court, maneuvering their next move as ladies-in-waiting.

This house, this lovely summer villa, had always been filled with people coming and going. Monsieur and Madame were famous for their dinners, their fetes, their gardens, which were open to anyone who wished to stroll in them. Now all was silent, left to its mourning. A piece of her life was over in no uncertain terms and not in the way she'd imagined at all.

Renée sat on the bottom step of the staircase, sobbing as if her heart were breaking. Alice took a little bag of coins from her pocket, placed it on Renée's lap.

"To tide you over," she said. "My father believes all things can be overcome, waited out, if one has some coins put by."

"I don't want to be left here."

But Alice was already walking away from her, out the door, to the carriage, to her other life.

Chapter 10

In England, the first thing Alice did was weep in her father's arms. The second thing she did was examine the house he brought her and Barbara home to—a new one; he never stayed in one place for more than a year—from top to bottom. It was an old London mansion off the Strand made of flint and stone, many gables and chimneys, and it had its own river landing. Large, grand, and completely out of fashion, it had heavy dark wood everywhere inside, intricately beamed ceilings in a great hall, and a musicians' gallery off in a high corner. "Archaic," she said to Barbara. Then she fell into bed and woke the next morning, lingering awhile, which was not like her. She hadn't expected to have to begin again. She felt dismayed. That was also not like her. The pall of the princess's death hung over her, so unexpected, so horrid. In her dreams, she had rushed down a long hallway, calling for the princess. She had something she had to tell her, must tell her. But the corridor had no end, no beginning. . . . She shivered and sat up.

Time to begin whether she wished it or not.

She would begin with her father.

"Did you speak with Balmoral?"

"I can do nothing there, poppet. But we have a nice offer from Lord Mulgrave."

She closed the cover of her jewel case with a snap and looked at herself in the mirror. She was dressing to go out. She wore her mother's diamonds screwed in her ears and looked well enough—if dark, bright eyes and dark curls meant anything.

"Never you mind ignoring me," her father said. "I've brought a handsome specimen to the table, and you'll do me the respect of considering him. You're twenty. It's indecent. I thought I'd be bouncing boys of yours on my knees a good three years ago! If you're not careful, I'll end up marrying for the both of us and providing my own heir, and then your jointure will be cut down to a quarter of its size, and we'll just see who lines up to have you then."

Alice considered her father. He'd done nothing about Balmoral. He was viewing himself in a pier glass, a long and rare and very expensive mirror that Alice had had shipped to him from Venice. The only things fashionable in this house were what she'd sent him over the last two years. He drew in his stomach, puffed out his chest. Was he still flirting with that Saylor chit? she wondered.

"Where are you off to?" he asked her, suspicious, but then suspicion was his nature.

"I'm going to call on Aunt Brey. There was a note from her last night. She wants to hear about the"—Alice swallowed past a sudden lump in her throat—"the death."

He sat down. "Tell me about the death."

She did, but not quite everything: Her own suspicions about the poisoning and that Monsieur had taken a casket of letters from King Charles she kept to herself. The truth was she couldn't trust him, and so she'd give him no fodder for his ambitions until she was far clearer about their direction.

"Those goddamned benighted Frenchies," he said when she was finished. "They need to be taught a lesson. If His Majesty wants war, we'll give him what is necessary." The "we" was the House of Commons, which by law funded—or not—the king's ventures. Her father ran a faction there for whatever great man he was supporting at the moment. "It was hard to see your princess die. I know that, poppet."

"What am I to do with myself, Father? I feel as if I've lost a . . ." She groped for a word. Her mother had died when she was born, so she didn't know what a mother was. She had no brothers and sisters, so she didn't know that, either. Her father was a weather vane, turning first with that wind, then with this. She had only her duty to anchor her, first to Queen Catherine, then to Princesse Henriette. Now, to whom?

"We're all still head over heels," said her father. "The king just left his bedchamber yesterday. He'd been there since he heard the news. I thought a party of us were going to have to go to the privy council and beg them to break down the door."

"She died so horribly, Father." She put her hand atop his. "What was your position in the Lord Roos bill of divorcement?"

His face went blank. "Lord Roos? That was in the House of Lords. I remember little of it."

She changed direction. "Would you see about a place for me in Queen Catherine's court again?"

"Difficult, poppet."

"Queen Catherine adores me, and King Charles would do whatever you asked in this. He knows my service to his sister."

"What about the Duchess of Monmouth's household? She's young and lively, and her ladies cut quite a swath at court."

"She likes me not."

"Easily gotten around."

"I'd like to be Queen Catherine's maid of honor again." Alice watched her father's face very carefully.

"All that praying and going to mass, girl. Bah."

"I prayed and went to mass at Princesse Henriette's court every day. It didn't seem to bother you."

"That was France. This is England. Stay with me until you marry." He dropped a kiss on her head, blew another at her from the door. "Give your aunt my continued dislike, won't you?"

Alice went into the adjoining chamber, where Poll was just doing the last of the buttons on Barbara's overgown. It was Alice's gown, but she always shared with Barbara. She had much, and Barbara had little.

"I'm off to Aunt Brey's. We'll meet at the queen's later."

"Yes."

"You look markedly happy, Ra."

"I'm glad to be home again. And glad the court is at Whitehall. I thought they'd be at Hampton Court, which would make it harder for us to . . . to see everyone we would wish to see."

John Sidney, thought Alice.

Poll curtsied. "Ready, miss." She and Poppy, Alice's groom, would accompany her since young unmarried women of quality were not supposed to venture out alone, not so much for safety, but to ensure there was no question they came to their marriages virginal.

Barbara went to a window, waited until she saw Alice and her little entourage walking away, before going to the bedchamber, and standing before the pier glass where Sir Thomas had been admiring himself only moments ago. She looked well, very well. Her heart began to sound in her ears, the beat quick like a small bird's. Silly not to tell Alice she was meeting John. Yet what else could she do? Not since the black plague five years ago had she seen death so closely. Eat, drink, and be merry, for tomorrow we die. She understood the motto of the rogues of court in a new way. We did all die. And it was tomorrow. And she was going to live to the fullest this day.

HER AUNT TURNED her cheek, and obediently Alice kissed it.

"Go stand there and turn around slowly."

Alice went to the middle of chamber and slowly turned around. Her time in France stood her well. There was no one, no one, as fashionable as she at this moment. The band of black mourning around her arm for the princess detracted from nothing, and the band of black around her throat was genius, sheer genius. Her hair was curled a new way, the way the mistress Madame de Montespan had just taken to wearing hers. There was a new, sharper V cut in Alice's gown at the waist—de Montespan again—and jeweled clasps holding back her overskirt. It was all new, expensive, and what she needed to give her some edge over her return.

"You've improved. I'd heard you had. It was among the gossip from Dover," said her aunt, Alice-Hester, Lady Brey. "Those brows of yours—you've been plucking them. They're less fearsome; in fact, one might say they give character to your face now. The influence of Princesse Henriette, God rest her soul. And this would be . . . ?" She pointed with her fan to an elaborate silver box that Alice had placed in her lap.

"Open it."

Her aunt did so. Inside the box were tiny black shapes.

"Patches, Aunt Brey. You can no longer afford not to wear them. La Montespan has made them necessary."

"How do they stay on the face?"

"They're gummed." Alice pointed to the various stars, hearts, quarter-moons, even a carriage and four horses.

"It will be the rage, I suppose."

"It is the rage. Every lady in Dover patched, and no Frenchwoman would be caught without at least one on her face. Come, wearing one won't kill you. Only a woman of the streets wears more than four. You must, Aunt, or you'll look dreadfully old-fashioned."

Her aunt's severe face relaxed into a smile. "You imagine I care. You're too thin; that's not fashionable, is it? But you remind me suddenly, I must say to you, of your mother."

Behind her aunt was an enormous portrait of her aunt and Alice's mother; at her aunt's breast was pinned a cameo, a profile of Alice's mother. They'd been beauties. If it hadn't been for the war, her aunt always said, we'd have married dukes at the very least. But there was no court in which to marry dukes. The king was imprisoned, his queen remained in France. And Alice did not resemble her mother. Changeling, her aunt had said on their first meeting, when Alice was ten and far thinner than now. In the portrait, two smooth-faced beauties, their arms wrapped around each other, looked down on the world, very alike, except for their eyes. One had eyes of deep blue, one almost violet. Alice's eyes met the painted ones of violet blue. Hello, Mother, she thought. When she'd first seen the portrait, she'd fallen to the ground and wept. It was the first time she'd ever seen what her mother looked like. Her aunt had promised that after she died, the portrait would be Alice's.

Her aunt motioned for her to sit, and Alice obeyed, looking around herself. The style from France was to have chambers filled with things, vases from China, huge candlesticks the size of boys, small tables, great armchairs, pier glasses on walls. Her aunt's house seemed sparsely furnished after the abundance she was used to seeing.

"They're painting chambers white and cream and green the color of spring grass now," said Alice.

"Are they?"

"And the princess was having a chamber at Saint Cloud painted a butter yellow."

"Was she? A bad business there. The talk at court is horrid, this poisoning. The ballads sung in the streets frighten me. We could go to war. The king is still holed away, I hear, his council becoming quite fretful in his absence."

" 'A penny's worth of bread to feed the pope,' " sang Alice, mimicking right down to the gestures a street balladeer she'd heard on the walk over. " 'A penny's worth of cheese to choke him, a penny's worth of beer to wash it down, and a good old bag of sticks to burn him.' "

"Don't be vulgar."

"King Charles is out in the world again, Aunt. My father told me this morning."

"Well, your uncle will be pleased to hear that. So, my dear, what are you going to do with yourself? I hear the Mulgraves are looking in your direction. Your uncle Brey thinks it a good match."

"A whim of Father's. Aunt, I need you to talk with me about Queen Catherine, about what occurred this spring. I want to go back into service to her."

"You're old for a maid of honor."

Stung—because it was true—Alice said quickly, "It's just until I marry. Otherwise I have to live with Father."

Aunt Brey's nostrils pinched in. She and Alice's father were never on good terms. "I had not thought of that. You could stay with me."

"If I were Barbara, that would be a wonderful thing. You know you love her more than you do me. I fear, Aunt, you and I would quarrel."

"Yes, we would. He's let you off the reins too often, and it's gone to your head. I've always said so."

"He never put reins upon me. It was easier not to, and now I am quite used to none, I'm afraid."

"Things will be different when you marry, Alice. A woman must be obedient unto her husband. Of course, if it's Mulgrave, you'll lead him about by the nose. He is not the brightest candle in that family chandelier."

They laughed like witches, one at midage, one young.

"The queen, now that is quite another matter, Alice. She has, frankly, never been in a more precarious position than she is now. Brey and I were talking of it just the other night, he saying that if I were with her household, he might insist that I leave it. You cannot imagine the rumors that were swirling in the spring."

"Divorce, I'm told."

"There was a case that came to the Lords, Lord Roos wishing to divorce his wife for infidelity. Brey was most upset with it, even more upset by the fact that His Majesty came every day to hear the arguments. The queen had miscarried again, you know. The cruel fact is, Alice, there will likely be no children from her. He can litter boys all over the kingdom, but his queen can't carry to term. Ironic, is it not?"

Alice's hands were clasped tightly in her lap. "I think it sad, Aunt."

"Yes, well, perhaps it's that, too. At any rate, the talk of his divorcing her just consumed the court. You cannot imagine it. I know that both the Archbishop of Canterbury and Bishop Burnet were summoned to counsel with His Majesty, and he was told it was within his legal and moral right, as king, to do it. Not being able to conceive is grounds for divorce within the queen's church, I believe. The Duke of York was adamantly against the Roos divorce bill and spoke most forcefully upon it, but Roos was allowed his petition. The harm done to the queen's position was just awful, Alice. Though nothing has happened, the king and queen are estranged—or estranged as much as anyone can be with Charles Stuart as her husband. Certain of the council, the Duke of Buckingham for one, are dead set against her."

So my father's position is against the queen, thought Alice.

"Brey said there was someone on the privy council—he wouldn't tell me who—who was ready to swear in a court of law that the king had married Monmouth's mother ages ago during the exile—a lie, of course—so that Monmouth could be declared legal heir," continued her aunt. "That rumor was everywhere this spring, too, driving a wedge between Monmouth and York. The Duke of York is outraged at the suggestion a bastard would be put in line to the throne before him."

And Jamie is caught in the web, too, thought Alice.

"My advice, my dear, is go to another household. The Duchess of Monmouth is a favorite with King Charles. Go there, or even to the Duchess of York."

"You're good friends still with Lady Suffolk?" Lady Suffolk was Queen Catherine's mistress of the robes, a powerful position in the queen's household.

"Yes."

"Can you see Barbara placed again with the queen? Please, Aunt."

"Of course. Immediately. Our little Barbara needs her stipend, doesn't she?" Barbara was quite a favorite with her aunt.

"Until she's married properly." A thought occurred to Alice. "You know, Aunt, I might push Mulgrave in Barbara's direction."

"Isn't that what happened with Caro? Your pushing her toward Colefax—he might have a friend or relative for her, I remember you saying—and look what happened. You meddle too much, Alice. Don't cut those eyes at me, young lady. I am your aunt, and it is my duty to tell you the truth."

"Let's not quarrel. I came today to see Barbara placed, for I know she's fretted about it, and as for me, I'm determined to go back to Queen Catherine's service, also. So can you help me?"

"If I say no, you'll simply find someone else to aid you. I know you." She sighed. "I'll do what I can." The last words were reluctant, but they were enough. Aunt Brey's word was as good as gold in the hand. "Now, tell me about the death. We've heard the most outrageous tales. The Chevalier de Lorraine is not in France, is he? They're saying he was summoned to kill her."

And so, one more time, Alice told of it, biting her tongue on the suspicions that filled her, thinking as she spoke how she no longer knew this court. The players had changed positions, and she must maneuver carefully, but it had come to her last night that there was one in this court to trust, whose decency she knew firsthand. She was aware, now, in a way she never had been before, of the treachery that lay beneath the surface of things.

King Charles took a long and furious walk in St. James's Park with his dogs. The lines on his face were marked deeper, his eyes dark wells. He conferred with his council, went to a play, and allowed his lord chamberlain to set up the meetings for formal condolences from various ambassadors and courtiers, everyone warned to keep their condolences as brief as possible. The court packed to leave for summer palaces, Hampton Court and Greenwich, already talking about the horse races that would be held in Newmarket in July. It buzzed that because of the death the tide had swung to the Dutch, that King Charles was going to further alliances in that direction—there was already in place a treaty with them that had stopped King Louis in his land grab for the Spanish Netherlands. Of course, there were also two wars between the Dutch and English in the last ten years, but His Majesty was going to declare war on France, it was all but agreed.

"It's what I think wise," Sir Thomas said to Alice, who'd found a window seat in which to begin composition of the letter to the Duke of Balmoral that told all, or nearly all, of what she knew. "King Louis won't stop with the Spanish Netherlands. He's a threat to us all."

"And you'll lead the way to give King Charles all the coin and men he needs for such a fight?"

"All?" He smiled, truly amused. "There'd have to be some bargaining done between His Majesty and us, wouldn't you think, poppet, tit for tat, so to speak."

"Depend on it, Father, if you think that, so does the king."

Chapter II

July

The body of Princesse Henriette lay in state in Paris at the Cathedral of Saint Denis all the month of July, the vigil around the sarcophagus kept by Monsieur's guards in their handsome uniforms, the light of a hundred candles, and monks chanting masses for the dead. Her funeral was to take place in August, and word was, neither the king of England nor his brother nor his cousin Rupert nor his illegitimate but best beloved son, Monmouth, would attend. As that news ricocheted through royal courts from Sweden to Spain, something else dropped into the mix. England would be represented—not by Lord Arlington or Lord Shaftesbury or the Duke of Lauderdale or the Duke of Balmoral, all august members of his council—but by the Duke of Buckingham, apparently most august of them all.

In England, July was a crimson month, pimpernels, roses, currants, strawberries in the gardens, cherries in the orchards, robins with crimson breasts singing in the green trees. In the fields, laborers began to scythe rye and barley and wheat, and to wash sheep for shearing, herding them into rivers and streams to clean their fleece before it was cut from their bodies and spun into wool cloth. It was the month the king traveled up-country to the village of Newmarket to enjoy a week or more of horse racing under serene blue skies.

On the outskirts of the village of Newmarket, Alice, Gracen, and Barbara, all good horsewomen, kept their restless, prancing horses in order. The queen's carriage followed. The maids of honor—of which Alice was not yet one—wore matching gowns and hats with large brims to protect a lady's complexion, which must be as fashionably pale as possible. King Charles waited in the village, where the races were held and where the actress who was his mistress had a house he'd given her.

"You were groaning," said Gracen. "That same silly nightmare." Gracen and Barbara were talking about their dreams of the last night. Barbara had slipped back not only into her position of maid of honor, but also into her close friendship with Gracen, which was fine, but when had Gracen and Barbara become such friends that Gracen knew about Barbara's nightmare? thought Alice.

"Hello, you two," she said. "You're going to help me with my plan, yes?"

"At your service," said Gracen.

"I hope you don't hurt yourself," said Barbara.

"If she falls on her head, she'll be fine."

Barbara gave a soft laugh.

Alice turned her horse abruptly, galloped to the queen's carriage, and leaned down to the window opening. "Are you comfortable, ma'am? It's a wonderful day."

"It is, my Verney. It's good to leave Whitehall." The queen spoke with a Portuguese accent. "Is" became "ezz," and "yes" became "jess."

They were off to visit the Duke of Balmoral, who had an estate near Newmarket. Alice was along as an invited guest of the queen and at the express request of Balmoral. She kept her horse trotting by the carriage, her glance going now and then not to the fine day, the sun shining, the cloudless sky, the trees around them full and green, but to the two riding ahead, Gracen and Barbara, whose familiarity bothered her. She had not realized in Dover what friends they had become. Barbara could have more than one friend. She had more than one friend. Saying that to herself made her feel she had herself in command, and she flicked her riding crop against her horse's haunch and rode back toward them.

"—one's heart has its own path, and I think I should listen. It's God speaking," Barbara was saying.

"It could be the devil," answered Gracen.

"What could be the devil?" asked Alice.

"Barbara has a softness for John Sidney," Gracen said even as Barbara spoke over her:

"Don't tell—"

"Don't tell me what?"

"Oh, she thinks you'll disapprove and lecture her and tell her what to do," said Gracen.

"I do disapprove. He has no resources but must live on his wits."

"I have no resources," said Barbara.

"Which means you must marry wisely," said Alice.

"Is the heart never wise?"

"Not that I can see."

"She wants to flirt with Mister Sidney," said Gracen. "Whatever can a little flirtation matter? Practice for greater things, I say."

"Flirt with whomever you please, just don't do anything hasty. My aunt says passion is fleeting, unseemly. It flames high, dies cold, and the embers leave heartbreak—"

"You were hot for Colefax," Gracen pointed out.

I could slap her, thought Alice. "I was, and you see where it got me."

"You're a court favorite."

"That has nothing to do with Colefax."

"It has everything. If he hadn't gotten Caro with child, you'd have never gone to France. If you hadn't gone to France, you wouldn't have come back so fashionable and full of fun things to do, everyone wondering who is going to snatch you up in marriage and shaking their heads over Colefax's mistake. So maybe Barbara's little flirt will lead her to great things— Oh look, there are the entrance gates ahead. All right, Alice, let's begin your game. Last one there is the last one married."

With a flick of her riding crop, Gracen was off, Barbara following. Alice deftly turned her horse in a couple of circles before riding after them, thinking, So, Gracen defended Barbara now. That had always been Alice's task.

The Duke of Balmoral stood waiting on the top step of the house. In the courtyard, Alice raced through the gates, then pulled too hard on her horse's reins, and, startled at such treatment, her horse reared. She took a breath and let herself slip off—but her trick didn't go as planned. She hit the ground with a jolt and lay stunned. Gracen screamed, Barbara leaped off her horse and came running as the queen's carriage rumbled into the courtyard.

Queen Catherine stepped out of the carriage; her page Edward ran ahead to Alice.

"Alice, please open your eyes," he said.

"Say something, Mistress Verney, at once."

At the command in that voice, she opened her eyes to look up, dazed, at the Duke of Balmoral. "My horse, someone please see to my horse," she said.

"Spoken like a true horsewoman," said Balmoral, and he smiled.

Alice closed her eyes again, allowed herself to be picked up and carried into the house, upstairs to a bedchamber, people bustling all about, Edward holding her hand, the duke walking behind with the queen.

"What hurts you?" Balmoral questioned once she was laid down in a bed.

"My leg." And badly.

"We'll send for a physician."

"One is with us." Queen Catherine sat on the bed, took Alice's hand, and held it as a housekeeper bustled to put her leg on a pillow. "Edward, fetch him. I pray you have not the leg broken, Verney." The queen's English was lilting and prettily said but fractured.

"Your Majesty," said Balmoral, "let us leave Mistress Verney to rest. I've refreshments prepared for you." He led her away.

Alone, Alice moved herself to the edge of the bed, gingerly, carefully, stood, putting her weight on her good leg. Then she tried to walk to the window. It hurt horribly, but she could do it. Thank goodness the filly hadn't stepped on her. She sat in the window seat made of warm, almost golden oak. It's begun, it's begun, it's begun, she sang silently. He wished to talk with her about the letter she'd sent. She wished to empty her heart of its suspicions to the one person she could trust, and in the doing so, courtship might begin. A shame she would miss the meal and talk and walk in the gardens. But she wouldn't be able to go on to Newmarket with the others, either, would she? She smiled. Nothing ventured, nothing gained.

IN THE LATE afternoon, a butterfly sunned itself on the opened windowsill of the bedchamber. Her leg wrapped tightly with cloth from knee to ankle, Alice lay still as Queen Catherine, Dorothy Brownwell, the mother of the maids, the queen's physician, and Balmoral discussed her.

"It's a bad sprain," said the queen's physician.

"She must stay here. I insist," Balmoral said.

"It was an awful fall," said Dorothy, her mouth trembling at the very memory of it. She looked ready to weep. Everyone loved Brownie, as the girls called her; she was kind and disorganized and incapable of running a firm household, which made all the maids of honor quite happy. Before Alice had left for France, she'd been running the maids as much as Brownie. "I thought my heart would stop," she said to Alice.

"She cannot ride a horse. You haven't room in your coach, Your Majesty. Mine has a broken wheel but will be up tomorrow. She's to stay here, and I will send her to you tomorrow. Nothing could be simpler." Balmoral spoke with such authority that everyone was silenced.

Queen Catherine leaned over. Warm brown eyes met snappish dark ones. "You rest, Verney. I send the maidservant to you attend, and I tell your papa."

"I am so dismayed to be of such trouble," Alice said happily.

Queen Catherine smiled. At first glance, she failed in beauty in any number of ways. She wasn't fashionably pale; her nose wasn't small; her mouth wasn't well shaped. At best, her stature was childish, slight, whip thin; she could be as darting and nervous as a bird. But her smile was fresh, pure, kind, like her heart.

Dorothy leaned over and kissed Alice; then the maids of honor came in to say good-bye. "Might Mistress Bragge stay with me?" Alice asked the queen.

"Mistress Bragge and I are to sing for the king tonight," Gracen said quickly.

"You and Mistress Wells sing," said Queen Catherine. "Bragge stays to see for Verney."

Alice had Barbara help her to the window to see the good-byes. In the forecourt, the duke helped the queen into the carriage. I've done it, she thought. She turned to Barbara. "Let's leave this bedchamber. If I lean on you and you walk slowly, I can hop."

A hall led to a grand sweep of stairway. They began a halting descent. Balmoral, walking into his great vestibule, looked up. "Whatever are you doing out of bed, Mistress Verney?"

"I will die of boredom in that bedchamber, Your Grace. Mistress Bragge is helping me to the gardens. I know you must have charming gardens."

"I do." Balmoral walked up the stairs. "There's a rolling chair somewhere about for when I have the gout. We'll find it." He offered his arm to Barbara. "Mistress . . . ?"

"Bragge."

"Come with me to command it found. Mistress Verney, you sit here on the stairs while I send for a footman to carry you. I want that leg healed so I may have the pleasure of watching you dance again."

The rolling chair was found, and Alice was rolled into the gardens, a footman pushing her, Balmoral and Barbara walking ahead, as he gave them a tour. There was something she'd never seen before, a maze, a labyrinth of concentric circles, made by turf grown thick as carpet and cut short to form circles within circles within circles. Dirt paths intersected every so often to bring he who walked the maze ever closer to the center.

"I'm told it was created by monks." Balmoral gestured back toward the house. "This was an abbey before Great Harry had them destroyed. Look at the end wall there, and you see where once a great stained-glass window was. It's said you must walk this maze on your knees, praying, and the guidance you need will come to you by the time you reach the center."

"Have you done it?" asked Alice.

"I have."

"And did you get your answer?"

"I did." He smiled, wrinkles seaming his face into a hundred furrows. "That's why King Charles sits upon the throne."

They walked on. There was a long, smooth lawn cut into squares, gravel paths making their borders. There was a walled orchard, trees espaliered onto the wall as well as standing in neat rows, apples visible among the leaves, baby apples, not yet ripe. It would take the hotter month of August to perfect them. There was an herb garden and a kitchen garden, heads of lettuce unfurled in the sun, beans wrapping tendrils around reed support poles. At the wall that separated his woods from the house, small, quaint garden houses, a single high-ceilinged chamber in them, had been built into the wall's corner ends, so that one might spend the day there, reading, or supping, or dreaming.

"This is delightful," said Alice, who made the footman carry her inside. There were arched openings on every side of the garden house, and the interior had been painted with trees and birds and flowers.

"I never come here," Balmoral said.

Back at the house, on a square of lawn, servants brought out chairs and a rug, and there was a footstool for Alice to prop her foot upon. Barbara sat on the rug, tucking in her skirts, leaning against Alice's chair. The sun was soft on them, the sky blue. Birds sang as if summoned to choir.

"What you must see, Your Grace," said Alice, "is Versailles, and all King Louis is doing there. Acres of land are becoming his park and walking gardens. His orangery is finished, a huge hothouse for hundreds of trees, and its roof is the terrace for the first floor of the palace. Great steps connect them on the outside. There are fountains and statues to be found everywhere. There is to be one of

Apollo rising in his chariot, the heads and shoulders of his horses just out of the water. It will go in a huge circular fountain. The sketches for it are quite magnificent. I saw them at Madame's." She looked around. "You might, if you desired, put in such a fountain, if you took down your garden wall." She pointed, and Balmoral rose and walked to the edge of a garden wall to see.

"So I might," he said. "The trick would be living to see it finished."

The sun moved into twilight, and a servant appeared to tell them a supper was ready.

"Your Grace, might we have supper here?" His gardens were lovely in this long July twilight. The beautiful thing about summer was that the sun hung in the sky for hours at this time of evening, so there was this long, pleasant lingering time.

Balmoral smiled. "I will go inside and arrange it at once."

Alone with Barbara, Alice leaned forward. "It hurts me that you will talk of John Sidney to Gracen and not to me."

"Let's not talk of it now."

Servants were carrying out tables, and on the tables they were placing heavy silver candelabra. One of the servants, a tall man with a saber scar along the side of his face, kept glancing at Alice as he lit candles, but she didn't notice. Barbara rose.

"Where are you going?" Alice asked her.

"My head aches. I thought I'd lie down."

"Oh, Ra. Stay here, please. I don't want you to go. Supper will be no fun without your presence." Never before had she had to beg for Barbara's company, and the newness of it was sharply painful, but then Balmoral was with them, and there was wine to drink if they wished it, though Balmoral refused any, and it seemed he had a musician under his roof, and the man came to softly play a guitar, and the duke's majordomo was brought forward to be introduced to them, one Will Riggs, a tall man with an old saber scar that ran along one side of his face into his hair, dressed not in livery, as was the fashion, but in plain clothes, as were the rest of the servants. Livery on servants was the newest, smartest fashion from France. The duke didn't follow fashion, it seemed.

"The Prince de Condé has a fine orchestra. He takes a portion of them even to the battlefield to entertain him in his tent. He says it soothes him and makes his mind clearer," Alice happened to say.

Balmoral leaned forward, his eyes sharp with interest. "He does, does he?"

And Alice thought, Of course, he's a soldier. Where is my mind? He is the captain general of His Majesty's army. It was he who negotiated with our exiled king to bring him back. Balmoral was a kingmaker.

"Have you met this Louvois?" he asked. Louvois was King Louis's minister of war.

"I can tell you only gossip."

"Tell it to me, then."

"Well, there is rivalry between him and Monsieur Colbert. Each wishes to be of the most use to the king. Louvois does not forget that it is his father who gave Colbert the opportunity to rise, and Colbert has risen high enough that he does not wish to be reminded of such. Louvois, who is the king's age, mocks Colbert." She almost said "who is older" but managed to swallow the words.

Balmoral laughed. His teeth were long and yellow in the candlelight. "The two ministers don't get along, do they? Well, I'm gratified to see His Majesty of France's council is no better than His Majesty of England's."

The sun had lowered and set itself, and candles flickered in the dark while music played. Barbara remained silent, and Alice glanced down and saw that her friend was dozing, lying on the rug with her arm as a pillow.

"Your friend sleeps," said Balmoral. "Your fall is a most happy accident. I was wondering how I would detach you from the queen to talk with you, for I've thought again and again of the letter you wrote me."

"You have no idea how much I've been longing to speak of it."

"Speak, then. Begin by telling me, even if you wrote it in the letter, everything you remember of the death."

And so she plunged in, telling it all, the writhing, the sweating, the screams, the horrid priest hushing the princess, the visit from King Louis, his tears, Condé and Lord Montagu staying until the end, Monsieur's odd dignity at times, his hysteria at others, the way the princess's dogs huddled under her bed, the way no one brought her daughters, the way she seemed to shrink into her bones before their eyes, the weeping, the confusion, the fact that the princess spoke many times of poison, Lieutenant Saylor's search for the cup, its disappearance, the autopsy, her words with the English surgeon. Finally she stopped, emptied at last.

"Lord Montagu. I was most interested in his instructions to you."

"He said he must be the one to speak of poison to the king, he and no other. Lieutenant Saylor and I were not to conjecture, he said."

"But, of course, you did. Do you think Monsieur killed her?"

"I think the poisoning began on her return."

"Ah, yes. The mysterious Henri Ange. Tell me about King Louis's regard for Madame."

"It was high, very high. The fact that she was sister to King Charles meant much to him. And would not her closeness to King Charles make friendship between the two kingdoms more likely? Things might be said by her to King Charles, I would think, that no one would know of."

"How true."

"Lord Montagu told Lieutenant Saylor and me that her dying wish was that the manner of her dying not hurt the friendship between the kings. That is why he asked for our discretion."

"Oh, that was the reason, was it?"

Something in his voice caught her ear. "Do you think my conjectures too wild? I swear I've told no one else of them."

"I think only that Lord Montagu has been a very busy man," he said dryly. "Monsieur did not come to Dover, did he?"

"No, and he forbade her to go without him, but King Louis somehow arranged it."

"And so you've told no one else these thoughts you share with me. I'm flattered."

Alice could feel her face growing warm. He referred to her father. Did he think her an undutiful daughter? Which, of course, she was. Her father wasn't trustworthy, but those weren't words she wished to say to the duke, no matter their truth.

"M-my father's concern was more with whether there was a treaty—"

"A treaty?"

"Something secret, perhaps, between the kings that Princesse Henriette aided. I know the princess spoke in private with King Louis. And Monsieur took a casket of letters from her cabinet."

"A casket of . . . whose letters were they?"

"I'm told they were letters from King Charles to Princesse Henriette."

There was a long silence. She couldn't read the expression on his face in the candlelight. "What does Lord Montagu say about this casket?" he asked at last.

"I am not aware he knows of it. I did not tell him. I am telling you."

Balmoral leaned forward. He spoke softly and clearly, kindly but deliberately, so that each word was like a blow, but through velvet. "What you have shared is extraordinarily dangerous. I want to ask you, for your sake, to say nothing to anyone else, as yet. You have done me a great honor to trust me with it. May I ask for further trust about this?"

"I am yours to command."

Balmoral shivered, and Riggs, the majordomo, stepped forward with a shawl and wrapped it around the duke's shoulders.

"You should go inside, Your Grace," Riggs said.

"The night is so very beautiful," Alice said. "Could we not stay outside a while longer?" She felt so relieved, as if a huge burden had been taken off her soul, as if she'd perhaps done something for Princesse Henriette. She couldn't bear to go inside just yet.

"Another song for the lady," Balmoral commanded, and the musician strummed the guitar and sang a sweet love song:

Have you seen but a bright lily grow
Before rude hands have touched it?
Have you marked but the fall of the snow
Before the soil hath smudged it?
Have you felt the wool of beaver,
Or swan's down ever?
Or have smelt of the bud of the briar,

Or the nard in the fire?
Or have tasted the bag of the bee?
O so white! O so soft! O so sweet is she!

It was an old song. I wonder what he is remembering, thought Alice, thinking how the men of her father's time and before, for all their loss and tribulation, seemed to find more meaning in life from those desperate years. She glanced down at Barbara and saw that she leaned on an elbow, awake. "Will you play for us, Ra? She has a lovely voice," Alice said to Balmoral.

"Oh, no," Barbara protested.

"Please. She plays beautifully, like an angel."

"Yes, I remember you were to sing for the king tonight. Let me add my pleas to Mistress Verney's."

The musician brought her the guitar. Barbara strummed the chords a bit and then began to sing. Her voice rose clear and true into the summer night, mingling with the smell of roses, myrtle, lavender growing in distant beds.

Shall I wasting in despair
Die because a woman's fair?
Or make pale my cheeks with care
'Cause another's rosy are:
Be she fairer than the day
Or the flow'ry meads in May,
If she be not so to me,
What care I how fair she be?

Alice sat still in her chair, listening to some beauty in Barbara's voice that made her seem far away and grown up in a way Alice wasn't. John Sidney put this lilt in her voice. I won't have it, thought Alice, and her jaw became strong and hard in the darkness.

BALMORAL REMAINED SITTING in the gardens after the young women went to their bedchamber.

"It was good to see you smile tonight, Your Grace," said Riggs, as he placed a branch of candelabra closer and then stepped into the shadows to wait until he was summoned again.

Balmoral smiled no longer.

Confound it and deuce take it. The letter Lieutenant Saylor had near killed two horses to deliver had not been shared with the council. Or, let me be more precise, Balmoral thought, it had not been shared with me. As captain general of His Majesty's army, he stood ready to declare war, to sound the drum for soldiers. Buckingham had been his ally in demanding war with the French but was now hot to go to France and negotiate a secret treaty on behalf of King Charles. The others of the privy council felt this was a good time to gain concessions from France for a war with the Dutch.

Would that make two treaties, one for His Majesty and one for his council?

If a wily, ambitious rogue like Sir Thomas Verney had been on the scent of a treaty in Dover, it meant something. Depend on it. Jesuits were involved, had wangled some leniency toward Catholics. And money was probably already in King Charles's private pockets. It was part of Louis's policy to bribe first and attack later. Guileful of King Charles to keep secrets, to play his council against one another, the mark of a statesman. Confound it! Charles would need to be one to keep Louis at bay. He'd need to be one to keep the confounded crown on his confounded head!

There were tremors, splits waiting to crack open wider. Whatever truce kept them together for the purpose of governing the country was fragile now, frayed after ten years' wear. He'd like to die knowing that selfish, unsettled roués couldn't tear it apart for the sheer whim of it—roués like George, the Duke of Buckingham, Georgie Porgie, pudding and pie, kissed the girls and made them cry. He kissed his old friend Balmoral, didn't he, played games on his own when they'd sworn to play together. Confound his confounded, deuce take it and the devil, too, scheming!

Floating somewhere was a report that young Lieutenant Saylor had written of his time in France. Where was it? Why had it not circulated to the confounded captain general of His Majesty's confounded army? Little Alice Verney was a born courtier, had told him more in one letter and a conversation than he'd gotten all this summer from spies at court and in France. I am yours to command. Her words touched him as much as he could be touched with a heart that had turned to husk long ago. A casket of letters from King Charles. Now that would be worth putting one's hands on, wouldn't it? Not to go to war when a beloved sister was murdered. The mark of a statesman. And a scoundrel. And a king.

God save the king.

Chapter 12

When Alice returned to Newmarket the next afternoon, Poll brought her a letter from Renée, who missed her dreadfully, who rattled, she said, like a tiny, ignored seed in the household of Saint Cloud. The English ambassador had promised to aid her, but she'd not seen him in weeks. The notes she sent him went unanswered. Renée was so lonely, so at loose ends. Was there nothing Alice could do to help? Was there anyone Alice might recommend her to? Alice had been such a good friend to her. She would never forget such a favor at this time of her life, would be so grateful. She remained her friend, her lonely, sad, forgotten friend.

Alice refolded the letter into its square, tapped it against her chin, thinking.

Why not bring Renée over and find a position for her? Her presence would make it easier to foster a marriage to Lieutenant Saylor. . . . Besides, she needed something to keep her occupied while she plotted for Balmoral. And she needed another good friend.

That evening at the king's house, there was a full moon in the night sky, musicians in the great hall, dancing, and gambling. Alice was sitting among her friends when Gracen touched her arm. "Look who's making her way toward you."

Alice looked over to see Caro walking toward her.

"She ought not to wear that color," Gracen said.

Her child must be due soon, thought Alice.

"Be kind," Barbara said anxiously.

"Don't either of you dare leave me," said Alice. Caro's face was pink cheeked. Too pink. Full of wine, thought Alice, and felt her heart beating very fast.

"I want to talk to Alice," Caro said.

Gracen stood up gracefully, grabbed Barbara by the hand, and before Alice could stop her was walking away. She turned her head to give Alice a cool smile. How Gracen, thought Alice, surveying Caro's perspiring face.

"I w-want your forgiveness."

Well, Caro had always been forthright, stammering, blunt, but even so, this caught Alice completely off guard.

"He took me by surprise. I'm n-neither clever nor handsome like you. And for him to even n-notice me was so amazing, I was—"

"Foolish. Deceitful. Lying."

"Yes, all those things. I never m-meant to hurt you. I—he—when he kissed me—"

"Stop."

Rustling in layers of silks and laces, Caro sat down clumsily. Everything she did was clumsy, but the pregnancy made it more so. She dressed badly, too, always had. Clothes wore her rather than the other way around. "Please forgive me, Alice. I'm not asking that we be f-friends again—"

"We can never be friends."

"I know that." Caro began to cry. "He isn't k-kind to me, you know. He didn't care for me. Not in the least. He hated me for getting with child. He—"

"How long were we friends?"

Caro wiped a wet cheek and said through a sob, "Years, five years, six."

"The whole court laughed at me."

"No, Alice, they l-laughed at me. I was the court fool, not you. You left me behind to be eaten by w-wolves. I needed you, Alice. I needed your forgiveness. They've been cruel to me, my friends, c-crueler than you can ever imagine."

"You forget yourself." And then because Caro was so red faced and bumbling and sincere and had been, once upon a time, her dear friend, she said, "You've had too much to drink, Caro. Go to your bed."

Alice stood, one hand on the handsome cane she'd borrowed from Dorothy Brownwell, and limped toward Cole, who was flirting with the Duchess of Monmouth. He broke off what he was saying at the sight of Alice, and his hawk's face began its sweet smile.

"Your w-wife is w-weeping there in that corner, sir." Alice's tone and mimicry broke his smile to nothing. "Command her to bed before she embarrasses herself further."

"By God, you've still got the sharpest tongue at court, Alice."

"I whet it daily on married men who stray. As you may imagine, it's never difficult to find a subject." She turned, didn't look back to see what might happen. Her heart felt like a cold stone, Caro's words beating in her pulse. Friend. Friend. Friend. I needed you. Forgive me. Gracen was in among the dancing couples, as was Barbara. Was there any warmth to Gracen? Anything other than cool self-interest? Had her help in Dover meant nothing? Should she have told Dorothy Brownwell the truth? Dorothy stood smiling at Lord Knollys, and the way she smiled at him made a tidbit of gossip come to Alice's mind. Gracen swore they were lovers, had been for ages. Did I love Cole? she wondered. She'd been excited by his regard, adored being paid court to, been proud of his title, his being heir to the Duke of Balmoral. She had been enraged and humiliated by his conduct, but love? What was that? This emotion Barbara seemed to feel, willing to become a nobody's wife . . . and Lieutenant Saylor, when he spoke of Renée, there was a light in his eyes that hurt the heart. He, who had his way to make, had abandoned the regard of a duke's wife for it. . . . The balladeers sang of true love. What was that?

Her father appeared out of nowhere and grabbed her arm. "The king would see you, poppet."

"His Majesty?"

"Take my arm, and I'll lead you to him. What's this nonsense of you falling off a horse? There isn't a horse alive you can't ride."

"Do you think I hobble like this for sympathy?"

"I think you're up to tricks, missy, and I won't have it. Falling off a horse at Balmoral's. Interesting, I thought to myself when I heard it. I've half a mind to send a note of warning to His Grace."

"You wouldn't have to send a note if you'd do your duty as a father and see if he'd consider marriage with me." Neither looked at the other in this game of emotional chess, played since Alice was old enough to reason. "I've something of importance to discuss with you, Father."

"Later, after you've seen His Majesty."

Her father opened a door and more or less pushed her through it. She found herself inside a small chamber in this rambling great house the king used as his palace when he was in the village for the races. Some of his ministers sat around a table with him, the Duke of Buckingham, Lord Arlington, and Thomas Clifford, as well as others of the court, Bab May, Thomas Killigrew, the Earl of St. Albans. A slim sprite of a woman perched on the arm of the king's chair. It had to be Nellie Gwynn, the actress the king was keeping, thought Alice. Fair haired, sharply pretty, she wore a magnificent gown and good jewels and far too many patches. She patches the way a whore would, thought Alice. King Charles laid down a card, and Nellie pinched his ear.

"You'll never win if you play like that, sir. It should have been this one," she said.

A servant stepped forward and whispered in her ear, and the actress looked up and saw Alice, who had remained in the shadow of the door, a bit overwhelmed by the scene before her, like a tavern, with men and smoke and intimate laughter. Nell came forward and curtsied. "Nellie Gywnn, Mistress Verney."

Her accent was as common as a fishmonger's or weederwoman's. She can mimic anyone, said Fletcher, and sings like an angel, dances as well as you. Alice didn't acknowledge her.

"Nell, take my place," called King Charles.

"Thank God for that." Nell settled in his chair, small in it, and smiled at the men, completely at her ease. "Call me a highwayman, for you may as well give me your coins now." Everyone laughed.

King Charles led Alice to a chair at a far corner of the chamber, motioned for her to sit, then sat beside her, his face shadowed by the brim of his hat, the charming, caressing, easy manner that got him his way, except with his House of Commons, in play. "I want you to go to France."

She was so surprised, she didn't answer.

"Be part of Buckingham's party. He's goes as my emissary for Madame's funeral, a few others also, Lord Sandwich, Lord St. Albans. It's fitting that you be included, as her former maid of honor, and there's something very special that is coming back from France, something that needs a woman's kindness. I'm going to want you to cosset it carefully. Your father will explain."

What was he talking about? A dog? Was she to escort Madame's dogs back? She opened her mouth to question, and he put a finger to his lips.

"No questions from you, Verney. You'll know all when you need to, and trust me, you'll be rewarded. That position you want in Her Majesty's household is yours, once you've done this."

She smiled.

King Charles's eyes swept over her. He liked to say he could tell everything about a man from his face. People said he was lazy. He was, and he wasn't. Whatever he saw in Alice's face seemed to satisfy him. He stood. Alice saw she was dismissed. He walked back to the game. "Nellie, have you lost my fortune?"

"On the contrary, I've won fifty pounds from these here cheats you call councillors and friends."

Alice slipped out the door a servant opened for her. Her father waited. "Well, gal?"

"I'm off to France, part of Buckingham's entourage." She saw even as she spoke that her father already knew. "What am I to take care of, Father? Her dogs? He didn't say." She rushed on, not giving him a chance to answer, seeing instead an opening for what she wanted. "I thought to bring this up later, but now is perfect. I want to bring Mademoiselle de Keroualle back with me. She is my friend, you know, and she's written that she's unhappy in France, and I thought we might find her a place in someone's household here. I've had such a sad letter from her, and I know it's sudden, but I didn't expect to be going to France like this, and it would be so easy to bring her back with me when I return. Please, say yes. Please."

Her father stepped back, staring at her for a long moment with narrowed eyes. "What a kindhearted girl you are, Alice," he finally said. "Yes, you write to your friend and tell her to pack her bags. We'll take care of her." Only later would she suspect his quick agreement. "Now, you'll need a chaperone."

"I thought of Aunt Brey."

Her father laughed as if she'd said something witty. "Aunt Brey."

"What am I to take care of, Father? You haven't told me."

"It's as you say, the little dogs, some jewels of state belonging to the king's mother, and now, little Mistress Keroualle." And then he was gone, disappearing down the corridor, and she followed him slowly, limping to the main chamber, but he was across the room near the musicians, beaming down at Louisa Saylor, who gave him a saucy smile.

Alice watched the dancing, her eyes darting over different ladies present. The Duchess of York, the Duchess of Monmouth, the Duchess of Richmond, Lady Suffolk . . . what household might Renée be placed in? She might have to settle for being companion to someone. Until she married Lieutenant Saylor, of course. Fletcher appeared before her, bowed smartly, everything about him crisp, as always, and perfectly done. He wore a huge, curling wig that cascaded past his shoulders.

"I've seen the actress at last," she told him.

He sat down at once beside her. "A tidbit, don't you think? Not the main course."

"Who has the king's regard, then?"

"La belle Stewart."

Alice wrinkled her nose. The woman he spoke of had married a duke. There was a long, involved story between her and the king. "He isn't courting her."

"We don't know that, do we? She was always more discreet than people gave her credit for— Cow!" Someone among the dancing couples caught his eye. "It doesn't matter how many lessons I give

Luce Wells, she dances like a country clod. Look how her elbows stick out. Now, Gracen is perfection."

"Too leggy," said Alice.

"He dances well. Look at the way he holds those shoulders, that head. Like a young god. And his legs. Divine, simply divine. I love it when he and Monmouth stand together, the light and the dark angels of court." He spoke of Richard, dancing with zest and grace in the middle of the floor. "They do say Her Grace of Monmouth is on a tear, determined to have him dismissed from the king's service, but Monmouth won't do it. He's racing tomorrow—Saylor, I mean. I hear he has a magnificent horse."

Alice watched. Her time in France had made her more demanding of the art. There was nothing the French royal family loved more than dance; everyone had a dancing master. She sniffed. His partner did not do him justice. I could, she thought. They'd adored her dancing in France, calling her fairy, feather light. "I'm going to France with the funeral entourage," she told Fletcher.

"Are you? You have all the good fortune. I want to go. Pack me in your truck. Hire me as a groom."

"And I'm to be maid of honor again."

"But that's wonderful. When?"

"When I return."

He brought her hand to his mouth and kissed it. "Thank God for that. I will tell Her Majesty tonight. That will make her smile."

"She is smiling, Fletcher. Look at her."

"My dear girl, that is for the jackals of court. None of us who serve her have smiled in months. Ugly rumors about. . . ." He shuddered, flicked at his coat sleeve as if an ugly rumor had landed there. "Disheartening, hurtful. I talked of it in Dover."

"When I'm back, we'll put our heads together and hatch a plot to put her in the king's good graces again."

"Only one thing will do that, Alice, and I fear it's impossible. It's been eight years."

"She is still queen. She deserves the respect of that."

"Yes, we've just turned up on our bellies like whipped dogs, is all. We need your backbone, Alice. Barbara is too good, and Gracen . . . well, if it doesn't serve our Gracen, it doesn't happen, does it? Caro's gone and preoccupied with family. And I doubt Kit and Luce have a full brain between them. The ladies-in-waiting, they were always Cleveland's creatures, never the queen's. It's been terrifying. Your Fletcher has thought of leaving her household like the coward he truly is. But I take fresh heart, I do. Oh, there's Lord Rochester! He wishes me to create the dances in the intervals of a play he's penning. They say Buckingham is writing something new, too, something that pokes fun at our august poet laureate. I cannot wait. A duel between the Duke of Buckingham and John Dryden. Inkblots at forty paces! He's taken on an actress, you know, Dryden. I may have to support one myself, it is becoming so the fashion. I leave you, my pet, to your crippled self. What was this humor of falling off a horse? Really, Alice. I was most upset. If I haven't you to teach, I might as well herd cows. You must allow your leg to heal properly."

He was gone in a snap of fingers, stopping here and there, visiting, collecting, exchanging gossip, a bee with court's pollen.

Alice limped outside to stand on the terrace, to look up at the silver moon, thinking of the queen in disfavor, of Dryden's wife, who now had an actress as a rival. Was constancy simply a poet's dream? We must marry you off to a grand man; you're made for it, Princesse Henriette had said. And in that moment, she'd hatched revenge on Cole and safety for herself. She sighed. It was all harder than she'd thought it would be. She turned at a sound. Richard had stepped out to catch his breath. He pulled his long hair up and off his neck, shaking his head the way a horse would, and she was struck dumb at some spark that crackled out of him. Monday's child is fair of face. Tuesday's child is full of grace. So it was said about Monmouth, but to her, so it might be said of Richard.

"They're saying you fell off a horse," Richard said to her, at his ease, coming to stand beside her, looking up at the full moon. " 'Methinks it were an easy leap to pluck bright honor from the pale-faced moon.' I heard that in a play the other afternoon, and it caught my fancy."

"I'm going to France, to Madame's funeral."

"A signal of honor, Verney."

"Have you any messages you wish me to take to Mademoiselle de Kerouaille?"

"God's eyes, yes! You'll be seeing her, then?"

"Of course I'll see her." For some reason, she didn't tell him Renée was returning.

"When do you leave?"

"Soon, I think."

He smiled at her. "Thank you. Thank you from the bottom of my heart." And then he left her. At the wide doors that opened into the night, he leaped up and touched the ornate carved stone above the doors in triumph.

My second good deed for the day, thought Alice. She frowned up at the pale-faced moon.

Chapter 13

August

"All noble and devout persons pray for the soul of the most high, powerful, virtuous, and excellent Princesse Henriette-Anne of England, daughter of Charles the First, king of Great Britain, and of Henriette-Marie, daughter of France, and wife of Philippe of France, only brother of the king." So chanted a high official of the king's as he marched in a procession through the streets of Paris, preparing the world for her funeral.

It was the spectacle of state expected, flambeaux and wax candles burning, incense rising, the coffin covered in cloth of gold edged with ermine, everyone in satiny, shimmering yards of midnight black, pearls in ropes around women's necks and hanging in drops from ears. Monsieur with a cloak that trailed twenty feet behind him if it trailed an inch, the greatest, longest black feathers encircling the crown of his hat, the king's mistresses ethereal angels in mourning, the funeral sermon given by the most popular bishop in Paris, the ring Madame had willed him glittering on one thumb. "Madame is dead. Oh, help us, Madame is dead," he began, and sobs broke out under the soaring arches of the cathedral.

"My word," said Aunt Brey afterward as she and Alice stood in the milling crowd of people, waiting for their carriage.

"Yes," said Alice. The funeral was grand, the manner of her dying swept under a table. It was taken for granted she was poisoned. It was taken for granted all was forgiven. Life, as they say, had moved on.

A FEW DAYS later, still in Paris, at the house of the English ambassador, Alice waited by a window that overlooked his courtyard, and when she saw a carriage pull in, she ran down the stairs and out onto the cobblestones. Renée was barely able to step from the carriage before Alice pounced on her.

"Tell me everything!"

"In my day, we didn't talk in the street for all the world to hear us," said Aunt Brey in the carriage, acting as Renée's chaperone. "Let us go into the salon, if you please, Alice." And then, as she walked arm in arm with Alice, Aunt Brey whispered, "It was very odd."

In the salon, Renée began to tell Alice of her visit to the Louvre Palace while Aunt Brey stood before a pier glass, examining herself. "The king, I was commanded to see the king, if you can believe it, Alice. I thought my appointment was with Monsieur Colbert only, but His Majesty was there. His Majesty knew that I was returning to England with you, and he said that I was very fortunate and that it was my duty to do as I was told and be agreeable." She smiled a lovely smile. "As if I would do anything else."

"A very odd thing to say, I thought," Aunt Brey said into the silvered glass that reflected her face. "I really must have some gowns made while we're here. I looked the dowd today. Yes, it was very odd, Alice. Why on earth would King Louis himself bother with any of it, I want to know? And there's more. Go on, tell her, Renée."

"I am going to be maid of honor to Queen Catherine."

Alice met Aunt Brey's eyes as Renée impulsively hugged Alice.

"I owe your father a debt I cannot repay. I never expected this, never. I'm going to write him a letter of thanks. Oh, I must go and change my gown, Alice. Madame Colbert has asked me to call on her this afternoon." At the door, she turned to face the two women. "This is like a fairy tale." Then she was gone in a rushing sound of skirts.

"There's still more." Aunt Brey pulled a letter from her sleeve. "I received this from your father yesterday."

Alice took the letter. Renée was to buy whatever she needed to make her appearance in England. Her father would pay. Alice walked out into the garden. Bright summer sun shimmered off the high whitewashed walls, but there was a bench in the shade. Sounds from the street rumbled over the garden wall, carriage wheels creaking as they lurched into muddy pits, coachmen's curses, the snap of a whip, a horse's whinny. The streets of Paris were a torment to walk along, messy, narrow, muddy, but this garden was an oasis, ivies growing thick against the stone of the house and walls, trees grown high and sheltering, flowers blooming, birds singing. Her aunt followed her out and sat on the bench beside her.

"My father is paying for her gowns?" Alice said. "Maid of honor to the queen?"

"Yes. It's most unusual. Alice, I think you'd best prepare yourself."

"For what?"

"Forgive me for speaking against your father, but I'm not at all certain that his intentions toward Mademoiselle de Keroualle are honorable."

Alice opened her mouth to argue, then closed it again as her aunt continued. "He's of an age where men lose their heads over something younger, and she is, if I do say so myself, startlingly lovely. My mother used to say young women of a certain age have a bewitching time, their maiden time when no man can resist them, when youth and high spirits carry the day. And to her credit, I think she has no notion of it whatsoever, is, quite frankly, simply bowled over by her good fortune, as so she should be," Aunt Brey finished dryly.

Alice could feel her mind spinning, going back over details, clues she might have missed. Could it be that her father had designs on Renée? The thought made her physically ill and completely furious, and yet it might be true. Only look at his determined flirting with Louisa Saylor. He was susceptible. This kind of generosity—let her buy what she needed in Paris—was not his style. Did he think he was going to seduce Renée? That Alice would sit by and allow it to happen?

She thought back to Dover, to her father and his cronies clucking over Renée's dramatic beauty like uncles. Renée was without powerful family to protect her. Uncles be damned. She twisted the letter furiously.

"It may be worse than you imagine," said Aunt Brey with a sniff. "What if he marries her? It's the kind of thing men do at his age, marry someone half their years and imagine themselves young again. One may sup with the devil as long as there's a long spoon."

Coldness replaced incredulity and fury. There would be no marriage except the one Renée and Lieutenant Saylor contracted. Alice had every intention of championing it with all her heart. "I'll handle it."

"I've gossip for you. The French court was buzzing with it. Arabella Churchill is in Paris, has been delivered of a son." Arabella was mistress to the Duke of York. The son was his. Aunt Brey swelled with the pleasure of having more scandal to repeat. "And the little actress Nellie Gywnn suddenly has a town house in Pall Mall. His Majesty strolls across St. James's Park and visits with her over her garden wall. If he thinks to set her up among us, he is sadly mistaken. I will not make a curtsy to an actress. And guess who is no longer in Whitehall. You'll never believe it. The Duchess of Cleveland has moved out of the palace into another lodging."

"The great cow falls at last," breathed Alice.

"What did you say? There are no cows in Whitehall. They're in St. James's Park, as you well know. What are you talking about?"

Renée walked out into the garden, bright sunlight making her shade her eyes. Alice considered her. You'll return with me, Alice had said to her. I'll see you placed properly, thinking she'd find something for her as companion to one of the ladies-in-waiting. Ha. We'll have fun, you and I, she'd said. You'll be my little cousin. Little cousin seemed to be doing very well on her own.

"I wanted to say good-bye before I left." She leaned down and touched her cheek to Alice's. "Are you cross?"

"No," Alice lied.

Her aunt sniffed.

THAT EVENING, ALICE tracked down the English ambassador before he left for his evening engagement. Dressed in satin and laces, a full dark periwig hanging down over his shoulders, Lord Montagu looked grand and unapproachable, his pen scratching importantly over the paper in front of him. Alice didn't leave him in peace like a good girl but waited coldly before the table at which he sat, willing him to look up.

"I'll be finished presently."

"Oh, it's nothing. Just a few questions I have, such as when might His Grace be leaving for England again?"

"His exact departure is not yet fixed."

Buckingham was at this moment the toast of Paris, had attended Princesse Henriette's funeral like a potentate, cutting a swath through court, was being entertained by one and all as if he were the king of England.

"Mademoiselle de Keroualle is confused about what is to happen when we reach England. I fear I am, too." She watched Lord Montagu purse his lips, put down his pen carefully so that the ink would not make a blot on the letter.

"Your father has graciously offered his protection, as you know, as you so kindly came across to offer. She will reside with him under his full guardianship, until assuming her position in the royal household." His voice was bland.

"Yes, that's where I'm unclear. No one told me of such a thing. That position would be?"

"Maid of honor to Queen Catherine, as you are." Montagu did not betray by so much as a flicker of the eyelid what a surprise these arrangements were, but perhaps, thought Alice icily, they are no surprise to him. "King Charles feels a responsibility to her," continued Montagu.

"The Queen of France cannot shelter her?"

"Forgive me for my frankness, but you know how the French are about bloodlines. Those who serve their queen must be of the highest families. It would be quite impossible."

"La Grande Mademoiselle?" La Grande Mademoiselle was a princess of the court, cousin to King Louis.

"Has the same high standards as the queen of France. I cannot tell you how glad Mademoiselle de Keroaulle's parents are that she goes to a family such as yours, who will care for her. They've sent a letter to your father thanking him." Lord Montagu smiled at Alice. "I am beholden beyond words that you are with her. It makes her crossing over to a foreign land so much less frightening. You are consideration itself, Mistress Verney."

Consideration itself? thought Alice. I'm a fool.

HIS GRACE THE Duke of Buckingham was taking his own sweet time about returning to England.

Let us make the most of our time in Paris, Alice told her aunt.

She led Renée and her aunt from shop to shop, to exclaim over the selection of fabrics, colored feathers, soft leather for gloves and shoes, fans, ribbons, buttons. She introduced them to her seamstress. She arranged to have the dancing master to the court call and give her aunt lessons. She bit her tongue when, without being asked, he gave Renée lessons, too. She took her aunt to meet Madame de Lafayette, who had been great friends with the princess; they walked in the large gardens of Luxembourg Palace, which belonged to La Grande Mademoiselle, and admired the elaborate fountain built by Catherine de Medici; they went to look at the huge stone triumphal arches King Louis was having built as part of widening the streets in Paris. They drank coffee and hot chocolate at small cafés; the Spanish queen of France had brought with her the habit of drinking chocolate, and the Turkish ambassador had introduced coffee sweetened with sugar. They went to the Palais Royal, Monsieur's residence in Paris, and called upon the two little motherless princesses, and there, Alice had a note delivered to Beuvron. "Call upon me," she wrote. "I miss you. Come and gossip. I must look at properties in the Marais. Come and be my guide." But the days in August glided by, and he did not call. She persisted, sending him a second note, and then, a third. And in the midst of it all, she wrote Balmoral a very long letter describing the funeral.

Alice threw down her embroidery needle in disgust. She sat before a wooden stand, a large circle of embroidery held in its frame. She was doing beadwork. It was all the fashion to work hundreds of tiny beads into elaborate embroideries. "I'm going blind. Oh, when are we returning to England? Let's pack our trunks and go, Aunt Brey."

"There's no need for that." Aunt Brey looked up from a letter that had been delivered. "His Grace the Duke of Buckingham has his secretary write that we leave in four days."

A footman walked into the salon. "Comte Armand Beuvron asks if you are receiving?"

Alice clapped her hands, ran to meet him at the door. He looked his old self, lively, fresh faced, ready to be diverting or diverted.

"I had given up on you, Beuvron! We're just leaving for the Marais. Nothing could be better. Do say you'll come with us. Aunt, I want to introduce you to the man who took me under his wing when I first came to Princesse Henriette's household. I don't know what I would have done without his good advice and kindness."

"You're her Beuvron, are you?"

"But you're too young to be Mademoiselle Verney's aunt," Beuvron said. "There must be some mistake, or your niece lies to me. Surely I speak to no more than an older sister."

"You're too kind." Aunt Brey was frosty, but Alice could see that she was flattered. After an afternoon with Beuvron in his spirits of old, he would have her eating out of his hand.

Outside, she and Beuvron walked a pace or two ahead of her aunt. "Why haven't you called on me?"

"Shame. I don't forget how I've treated you, even if you are kind enough to do so."

So what's driven you now? thought Alice. They strolled around the elegant square called Place Royal, a statue of King Louis's father at its center, stately town houses offering an even expanse of windows that overlooked the square, talking of Princesse Henriette's funeral. He had been among the mourners representing Monsieur's household, and now he shared long-ago gossip about the princess with her.

"King Louis and Princesse Henriette were lovers. It was a terrible scandal. The Queen Mother had a fit, demanded they behave more decorously. That's how La Vallière happened, you know. She was to be a decoy—flirt with my maids of honor, Madame told him—only King Louis fell madly in love. La Vallière was the only one he had eyes for, and believe you me, others tried to entangle him, including the highborn witch who has now succeeded."

"That must be ten years ago. How can you know this? You were but a child."

"How old do you think I am?"

"Twenty if you're a day." His face was pleasant and smooth, but his eyes, as Alice stared into them, said something else. "No," she amended. "You're as much as twenty and five."

"Add seven more years to that and you'll be close to truth."

"Do you take some potion to make you ageless?"

"As a matter of fact, my sweet, I do. There's a witch called La Voison who sells them and many another thing. Everyone goes to her."

"Was Monsieur jealous?"

"Well, his taste does not truly run in that direction, but Princesse Henriette was his new wife, and they were young and so beautiful together. You cannot imagine it, the couple they made then. They both liked dance and music and people around them; and their taste was exquisite, their coffers bottomless, and at once their chambers were filled with such fun, and our queen, you know"—Beuvron lifted his shoulders, shrugged good-naturedly—"half nun, half dwarf, worse then than now. Not really a companion to the dashing young man our king was. Madame was so engaging—it was as if no one saw her until she was to be married, and there under our noses was this sparkling, vibrant sprite. And fun, what fun she was to be with! We all flocked to her chambers, and the king enjoyed himself there, too, and began to realize that he was, after all, king. He took her from Monsieur, just scooped her up, and where it had been the three of them together, it was suddenly the two. Shocking. His mother nearly had a fit. Monsieur was numb with surprise and hurt, and then La Vallière ensnared His Majesty, with innocence no less."

"And lost him, too."

"Oh, that was foretold. She simply wasn't able to keep pace. And she had no flair, no head for court politics. Wouldn't ask a thing of him, let her looks go. She looked like a hag only three years ago, I do assure you, thin as a rail, starting like a rabbit if anyone said boo to her. Everyone was ashamed for him. And who was she, after all? A soldier's daughter, a nobody. I'll say this for the new one, she may have a tongue like an adder, but she comes from among the highest families in France, and it shows. She dresses superbly, keeps a fine table, knows everything that is going on, and is the wittiest woman in France to boot. She had us crying with laughter at supper the other night. If you could see her do her imitation of La Grande Mademoiselle, you would die with laughter. We nearly did. The king was choking with it. He can't be bored. That's where La Vallière made her mistake. She began to bore him. And children?" He shuddered as if they were talking of street rats. "Children ruin a woman, or at least they ruined her. La Montespan spits hers out like a cat, doesn't look back, and no one is the wiser."

"So there is a child between them?" asked Alice, greatly pleased with this gossip she would take back.

"Secreted away. The husband, you know, is a wild man who would claim it as his if he could find it. He is not taking the loss of his wife with sangfroid. Wore black all last year, and when anyone asked him why, he said he was mourning his wife. His Majesty is not used to anyone saying no to him. And make note, if you please. Gossip says both are his mistresses, but only one of them continues to conceive. Interesting, don't you think?"

They stopped before the huge carriage opening of the town house that had once belonged to the great Cardinal Richelieu. It was on the market for an enormous sum, and Alice was considering it for her father. She squeezed Beuvron's arm. "I'm so glad I screwed up my courage and wrote to you, though I'd given up that you were going to call. That which put a wedge between us is past."

"Dead and buried. This is a very grand town house. Is your father so rich?"

"No, but he has many friends among the gold merchants in London. I was thinking he might put together a group to buy this." Gold merchants were the ones who made loans. She glanced at Beuvron's face and then away, said lightly, "Have you need of money?"

"Is the sea filled with water? I owe you far too much already. Come, let us look through this great pile of stone the grand cardinal built and see if we find any ghosts. There ought to be a few. If these stones could speak, what a tale they'd whisper. He and the Queen Mother were great enemies. We were at war with Spain, and she was Spanish, and her loyalty was not to France, at least not then."

And so, charming, full of gossip, he led Alice and her aunt from chamber to chamber as if it were his and it would be his honor to sell it to them. The clerk who'd opened the doors for them scarcely had the opportunity to open his mouth.

BACK AT LORD Montagu's, Alice left Beuvron in the gardens, went to her bedchamber, picked up a small box, and came back down the stairs with it. Her aunt sat in the chamber overlooking the gardens, her view Beuvron, as she played solitaire. "What have you there, Alice?"

"Some letters I wish to share with Beuvron."

"Ah. Stay where I can see you, please. He is a charming but completely frivolous man, I must say."

In the garden Alice sat so that her back was to her aunt, opened the box with a key she kept in a secret pocket sewn in her gown.

"Fortunate you," said Beuvron, his eyes on the coins piled within the box.

"My father insists I take it in case there should be some misfortune. Be without anything, friends or family, but never coins, is his motto." She quietly stacked some between the two of them. "Yours."

"Alice, I cannot—I owe you far too much as it is."

"You possess knowledge of something I wish to know. Answer my questions, and we're even and more. I want to know about the day Madame died."

"I cannot speak of it."

Alice replaced the coins inside the box, shut the lid, but something in Beuvron's face, a flicker of desperation, caught her eye. He had huge debts, as she knew. She decided to gamble. She took a stack of coins back out, placed them beside him, and shut the box, saying, "I must go inside now. Enjoy the sun a moment before you leave. If you go through the door on that wall, you'll find yourself on the street. Now, I expect you to come with me tomorrow. There's a different house, one that belonged to some high constable of the kingdom and looks like a fortress."

He put his hand over the coins. The pleasant convivial mask of perennial boy slipped, and he looked older, sharper. "Ask me what you will."

"Was the poison in the water? The same water was given to a dog, and it didn't die. And the prince drank some of the water. So it couldn't be. Did the Chevalier de Lorraine send some special poison?" And when Beuvron made no answer: "So he sent the poison through Henri Ange, yes? Did Monsieur know?"

"Every time someone dies in Paris, the world screams poison." Beuvron spoke wearily, looking past her as her servant, Poll, brought dogs to the door leading to the garden. The small spaniels scampered across the terrace to paw at Beuvron, whom they recognized.

"Her dogs? You take them back with you? I'm glad."

"King Charles wants them."

He stood, bowed to her. "At what time do you desire my company tomorrow?"

Annoyed, she knew better than to push. "Ten of the morning."

THEY STOOD TOGETHER in the courtyard of a house built in the fifteenth century, looking up at intricate iron balconies while her aunt examined the stonework under the windows, magnificent boars' heads set on medallions. Beuvron dropped something into her hand. It was a tiny fobbed watch with a blue enamel cover, a diamond at the center of its face. It was the current fashion for men to pay their bets with little watches like these. "My luck's changed. I won last night. It might be that something was rubbed on the rim of the cup."

Alice became still, afraid any move would silence him.

"And your own little queen had best beware. His grace the noble

Duke of Buckingham plays a double game. He spent an hour with the Marquis d'Effiat, and they did not speak of fashion. And he had the witch Voison brought to the house at which he stays."

"I don't understand."

"She sells potions, Alice, love potions, powders. Poisons."

Just then a man paused in the huge opened gates, wide and high enough for carriages to pass through. "Mademoiselle Verney, is that you?" he called.

Beuvron's face went pale, and he took a step back as Alice watched Henri Ange enter the courtyard, walk up to her, smiling his even smile, his eyes intent on her face. Her heart began to beat loudly in her ears.

"Imagine meeting up with you again. A small world, is it not?"

"How do you do?" said Alice, remembering his arms around her, the ominous whisper in her ear, Thank you, my dear Henri Ange. "Where are you now? Not with Monsieur's household anymore, I understand?"

"No," he answered, not answering. "Beuvron"—Ange's eyes flicked over the other man—"it's been some time since we've seen each other. How are you?"

"Well."

"He's escorting my aunt and me as we look at property," said Alice, linking her arm into Beuvron's. "No one knows Paris better. In truth, he's not well. I dragged him from his sickbed." That's why he's acting the odd way he is, she almost babbled; but she was able to bite it back.

"You're moving here?"

"Oh, no. My father dabbles in property. I play his chamberlain."

"Fortunate father to have such a devoted daughter. Might I borrow Beuvron from you if you've finished your business? I'm thinking of buying some property myself."

Alice could literally feel Beuvron shudder against her. "Not today," she said firmly. "We have more to see, and I must have his opinion, even if I put him on his deathbed." Dismayed by her unfortunate choice of that word, she turned abruptly toward her aunt, blurting, "Let me introduce you to my aunt."

"You were in Monsieur's household, too, were you?" Aunt Brey said in her bad French after Alice made introductions.

"I was."

"Were you at Madame's funeral?" asked her aunt.

"Alas, no. The cathedral was packed, and there was no room for underlings such as myself, no room, so to speak, at the inn."

"That Bossuet's sermon was magnificent. You must buy a copy of the broadsheet and read it. What a pity her death was," said Aunt Brey. "You know people in London believe her poisoned."

"Is that what they're saying?"

"Indeed they are. They say the young men of Monsieur's household did it, that that lover of his was behind it all."

Ange smiled, as boyish as a cherub. "People will gossip, won't they? The truth is too prosaic." He looked directly at Alice. "They want someone to blame."

She shuddered the way Beuvron had done earlier. Ange saw it, and his smile broadened. "I must take my leave of you, but it's a pleasure to have come upon you so unexpectedly, Mademoiselle Verney. Are you and your aunt in Paris long?"

"No," said Alice.

"Well then. Mademoiselle, Lady Brey, I'll take my leave. Beuvron, old friend, we'll meet up again soon, I promise."

He bowed and walked through the stone arch of the courtyard gates. Alice and Beuvron followed him to the street and watched him cross the square.

"I'm going to faint," said Beuvron. "Did you hear him threaten me?"

"Come with me to Lord Montagu's. Tell him what you've told me. Come back with me to England."

"I won't say a word to Lord Montagu." Beuvron was on the verge of hysteria, his voice shrill. "And I'm begging you to say nothing! If you value me as a friend, you'll keep what was said between us, because if I'm asked by anyone, I will deny everything! Everything. Sacred heaven, I feel ill. I must have a glass of wine at once. I'll have to test every bite I put in my mouth for months. What ill luck that he should be passing. I leave you, Alice, and I beg you, for your sake and mine, to keep silent."

And he, too, crossed the cobbled street, choosing the opposite direction Henri Ange had.

"Where is your little friend?" asked Aunt Brey when Alice joined her in the vestibule of the house.

"He isn't feeling well."

AT THE PALAIS Royal, Beuvron ran upstairs to the attics, which overlooked all of Paris, to a bedchamber he was allotted when his coins were low and he could afford no rented lodgings. He slammed the door behind him and stood gulping in air, as if it hadn't been safe to breathe before.

"Lovely afternoon."

He jumped, turned, said, his voice shrill, out of his control, "You frightened me out of my wits. What do you think you're doing in my chamber?"

Richard lounged back in the chair in which he sat. "It seemed the perfect place to wait."

"How did you get in?"

"No one pays any attention if you know how to dress."

And Beuvron realized the English lieutenant was dressed in livery, like all the footmen in the house, his hair tied back in a neat horse's tail, black ribbon to hold it.

"Do I owe you money? Is that it?" He was undone by seeing Ange, by Richard showing up in his chamber like a ghost. "You've come at the proper time, if so." He pulled coins from a pocket, tossed them on the bed. "If you want more, you'll have to wait in line."

"I desire information."

"Doesn't everyone?" Beuvron was sharp.

"Who else is talking to you?"

"Alice Verney."

Richard smiled. The smile was wide, startling. Sacred heaven, Richard was beautiful. Beuvron felt himself half seduced. "What does she ask for?"

"Why should I tell you?"

Richard pointed to the coins on the bed. "For more of those than you can imagine."

"Who would pay?"

"A great man."

"What does he want?"

"He wants to know about a certain casket of letters, would like the letters."

"I can't do that." Beuvron was shrill again. "I won't do that."

"Copies of the letters, then. Come, my friend, think. That could be arranged, couldn't it? Is Monsieur really so interested anymore?"

It was true. With the funeral over, it was as if the princess were a bad dream they'd all dreamed. The little translator hired for the letters was already bored, already playing truant to his task. Monsieur had been involved for a brief moment, become impatient, and moved on.

"I'd like to see the casket. Can you take me to see it?"

"Now?"

Richard was caressing. "I won't do anything to put you in danger. Let me but see the casket, know it really exists, and I'll make it worth your while."

The next thing he knew, Beuvron was leading Richard down a back stairway, down a hall, all the while thinking, What am I doing? Why am I doing this? The Palais Royal was filled with chambers and halls. He opened a door, put his head inside. Sure enough, the translator was not there. He and d'Effiat were having a fling. Beuvron stayed at the door while Richard examined the chamber. He allowed himself to admire the crisp, efficient way the Englishman moved. There on a table, for all the world to see, was the small casket. At least the translator had the sense to lock it, thought Beuvron, ashamed suddenly of how like spoiled children they all were, tired of toys too soon, treasuring nothing. He watched Richard pick up the casket and look at it from all sides before putting it back to pick up a sheaf of papers held with a red ribbon.

"What have we here?" Richard said softly. He untied the ribbon, looked through the papers, smiled again.

Beuvron watched in horror as Richard rummaged through loose paper and books on the table, watched as he tied the red ribbon around blank paper, not the ones it had originally held. "What are you doing? Stop that!"

Richard put a finger to his lips, walked to the door, and led the way back to Beuvron's chambers.

How does he find his way back? thought Beuvron. Is he a bloodhound? In the bedchamber, he exploded. "You put my life in jeopardy with what you've done! I demand you hand over those papers—"

"Or what? You'll strike me?" Richard laughed. "I'm going to take these with me, and then tomorrow, I'm going to return them. No one will be the wiser, and our great man will be pleased."

"I cannot allow this! I'm going to tell Monsieur."

"Who is at Versailles, is he not? By the time you ride there and back, I'll be gone."

Beuvron felt desperate. "How pleased?"

"Six louis d'or worth."

It was an enormous sum.

"Ten." But Beuvron sensed the Englishman knew he'd be satisfied with less. He cursed himself for a fool. Let him offer five, he thought. I'd be satisfied with five.

"Eight."

Beuvron smiled. Richard was a gentleman. For eight he'd live with fear and much more.

"I'll be back in the morning with the papers and with your coins." Richard stood, held out his hand. "Have we an agreement?"

"We have."

"What was Mistress Verney asking about?"

"The day the princess died."

"How many louis will that cost?"

"It can't be bought." Beuvron had only to think of Henri Ange to feel fear snake up his spine. Once the door was closed again and Richard was gone, he went to the window that overlooked the rooftops of Paris. The shadow of Henri Ange shrank. If he didn't talk of him, he wouldn't conjure him. Eight louis d'or. He could pay off his debts and start fresh. He breathed in soft summer air. Or he could continue to gamble.

In a servants' hall, Richard shrugged on his own jacket, untied the ribbon and let his hair fall to his shoulders, picked up the livery jacket, folded to a neat square, and walked out of the palace. In the gardens, he was just another Parisian citizen enjoying Monsieur's generosity. Another few blocks and he was at the clerk's, who had his inkstand filled and his pen poised, ready to copy the letters.

"I'll be back by nightfall," he told the man.

Then he walked to a monastery nearby; they'd given him an empty monk's cell, used by pilgrims, accepting that he was an English Catholic—not to mention the coins he gave them. The urge to call on Renée, to send her a note asking her to meet him in secret, was insistent, powerful as a heartbeat, but to do so would jeopardize what he'd been asked to do. Balmoral was not one to suffer fools; one misstep would finish him with the duke, who did him a great honor by trusting him. He changed clothes, putting on the satin coat and breeches of a Parisian dandy, powdering his face pale, affixing a patch to his right cheek the way they did here. A heavy wig, and he would no longer know who he was if he caught a glimpse of himself in a pier glass. There were gambling dens to frequent, losing a few coins, finding men Balmoral had asked him to contact, setting into motion the gathering of certain information Balmoral wished to know. So Alice had asked questions, too. Richard smiled. Why was he not surprised?

HIS GRACE THE Duke of Buckingham cut into another slice of beef.

"The first time she came to England was when she was seven and ten. The world knows the story of her being left by her mother only weeks after she was born, never seeing her father before he was beheaded." The duke swallowed back emotion, but to Alice's eye the gesture was practiced; he'd said it too many times before, and real emotion had died. "Of course, I saw her when she was a little girl hanging on her mother, hanging on the edges of the French court. We were all on the edge in those days." He shook his head. "Hard days."

"You landed on your feet, if memory serves me." Aunt Brey was acidic, out of patience with this great duke. The truth was Buckingham had left the life of an exile, returned to England before the Restoration to marry a Roundhead heiress and make love, it was rumored, to Cromwell's daughter besides.

"Won't you ladies have some more wine? Fill their cups again." He waved his arms grandly, ready to launch into another memory of Princesse Henriette. "God, I loved her once upon a time—"

"I believe we heard that tale on the trip over," said Aunt Brey.

They were in Buckingham's cabin in the forecastle, his windows open to the sound of sails. There was a good wind blowing them to England. The ship's keel sang a quiet lament as it strained against the water through which they clipped. Through the windows one could see the night, filled with stars, like diamonds scattered on a black court gown. The table was set as if they were in London, with linens and silver. There was lantern light, the sound of sails whipping out hard, the ship groaning and creaking. What were you doing so long in Paris? wondered Alice, staring at Buckingham's florid face. What mischief do you brew? Do you threaten my queen, who harms no one, and perhaps for the likes of you, that is her crime? And where was her father's place in all this? And Renée's? Her courtier's instincts told her intrigue was brewing.

"It's quite late, Your Grace." Aunt Brey, her duenna up, was determined that his drinking companions would have to be the sailors on board. "I fear these two young ladies need their beds." I had to listen to his boasts all the way over, she'd told Alice as they walked on board ship to return. I refuse to listen all the way back.

Buckingham grimaced, then smiled—charm there, clear evidence of a man who had always been the beau of court and knew no other role. "Well then, a final toast. To the memory of our precious princess, our pale pearl, the favorite of two kingdoms, two kings, may she rest in peace."

Everyone raised their goblets and drank. Renée crossed herself.

"Beware of doing that in England." Buckingham's charm disappeared. "There's great feeling against your kind just now."

"My kind?"

"Indeed."

Renée stood, put down her napkin, and, swaying against the motion of the ship, left the cabin.

"A little touchy for my tastes," said Buckingham. "She'd best swallow that. But lovely, very, very lovely, I will agree."

With whom? thought Alice. She excused herself and went to Renée, knocking on the door of the cabin they were sharing. She had half hoped Renée was being brought over by her father for Buckingham, but that didn't seem to be the case. Putting her ear to the door, she could hear sounds of weeping. Alice smiled, thinking of her father. He hated women's tears, fled from them at the first drop. And then her smile faded. Her father, the potential poisoner. Opening the door, she entered, then sat on the edge of the bed, willing herself to be kind. "Why do you weep?"

"Oh, for her, and for his memories of her, and for myself, leaving everything I know. I was a fool to come, a fool to listen to cajoles."

Cajoles? thought Alice. Did I cajole? "Perhaps not."

"I am not to worship my God in your country?"

"It's just that you must be discreet with it, that's all. Our good queen is Catholic, the Duchesses of York and of Cleveland, even some great men high in His Majesty's regard. Barbara is. You'll find yourself among friends in this. As a maid of honor, you may accompany the queen to prayer several times a day. She'd be glad of it."

"I wish I had not consented. I am alone."

"You're not. And everyone admired you so in Dover. They will be ready to do so again."

"Madame was there. I belonged to Madame, and for her sake they were kind to me."

"Not just for her sake. You know you captured more than one heart, and if I'm not mistaken, you possess one true one, someone who will be filled with joy at your return."

"My dear lieutenant. Yes, he'll take care of me, won't he?" She sat up, wiped at her face. "I forget that. You were so kind to bring me his letters. Your aunt would disapprove to know how bad we were. There—in that little bag—they are. Please be so kind as to fetch one and read it to me, and perhaps I can quiet my fears."

Alice selected a letter, thinking to herself she wanted to read it almost as much as Renée wanted to hear it.

Mademoiselle de Keroualle, I am afraid you will think by my wandering writings that a midsummer moon has taken possession of me. It's true. I am possessed. There is a saying in England that it is unwise to wear one's heart upon one's sleeve, but I can do nothing else when you are in my thoughts.

Alice took a breath and continued.

You told me you'd entrusted your own dear heart to mine. Such knowledge fills me with elation, and I vow my devotion, my loyalty, my being, to you again and again, a hundred times over, a thousand. When I have the privilege to claim you in marriage, you will never lack for affection or passion, and whatever is mine will be yours also. I will take you to the place of my boyhood, called Tamworth. It is my legacy and my treasure, as you are my treasure. There are woods and a stream and a village. The house is old. There is a hillock from which one can watch fine sunsets. One day you will watch a sunset with me. When I was a boy, I fished in the stream and dreamed dreams, which are my guide to this day. I think I dreamed of you. I must close as my paper ends. I remain, yours to command in anything, Richard Saylor, Lieutenant in His Majesty's Life Guards and lieutenant to you.

Alice refolded the letter carefully. "I would be very proud to receive such a letter."

"He knows what he wants. I adore that in him. I am so often confused."

Wait until we land, thought Alice.

Chapter 14

September

"But look," said the dressmaker, holding the shimmering dress against herself. "The shade will be perfect with your dark hair and those great eyes and that complexion. I call it seashell. Come, my lady, let me put it on you, and we'll have it pinned to fit in a twinkling."

Alice frowned. "And my dress would be which one?"

"Your dress?"

"I am Sir Thomas's daughter."

"You—of course. Of course. You must forgive me. I was carried away by the beauty of—of you both. For the daughter of Sir Thomas, I think this white—"

"I like it not."

"Why, then I have the pale gold. Do look at the embroideries—"

"No."

"Take this one." Renée offered the gown whose soft color was so lovely, it mocked a woman's blushes. "You have dark hair and eyes, it will become you most handsomely."

The truth was it would become Renée best. The truth was the dressmaker had been sent to please Renée; there hadn't been a thought of her. The truth was her father was an old fool, a potential poisoner, and it broke her heart and muddied all her plans.

"I'll try the gold," Alice said.

Once it was upon her, she had to admit it was handsome. The dressmaker, knowing she'd displeased, fussed and fretted, pulling the belled skirt this way and that. Cut through billowing sleeves were openings, the same down the very tight front. The dressmaker pulled through touches of a gauzy gold-threaded undergown. Between each opening was a square button of opal encased in a tiny gold frame. The undergown spilled from the bodice and showed off Alice's handsome shoulders.

"We'll thread a gold ribbon through your hair; we'll make your maid curl it in a hundred ringlets, the way Madame de Montespan wears hers, and it will be perfect," said Renée.

But it was Renée who was perfect.

Her gown was striped, blush and palest gray. It, too, had the long tight waist, and there was tied a narrow ribbon belt with a small silver buckle. The only bit of undergown showing was lace at the bodice, framing her creamy shoulders and equally creamy face. She looked as luscious as a young plum.

"I've fans and gloves and hair ribbons," exclaimed the dressmaker, walking around Renée as if she'd created her herself. There would be business off this, if the young lady could be brought to buy the gown. Other women would see her in it and wish the same for themselves, not knowing how little Renée's beauty had to do with the beauty of what she wore.

"No," said Renée reluctantly. She already owed Sir Thomas too much.

"Yes," said Sir Thomas, walking into the bedchamber. "Anything she desires," he said to the dressmaker, running his eyes critically up and down Renée.

"No, please, I couldn't," said Renée.

"Yes, please, you could. I stand as your guardian while you are on these shores, and I am responsible for your upkeep, and I won't be shamed by your appearance. Pearls," he said. "Mademoiselle's gown would be best set off with pearls. Did you bring your jewels, mademoiselle?"

"Yes, sir."

"Well, go and fetch them."

He then considered Alice, who was watching him with one eyebrow lifted. "A handsome color for you, poppet. I like it. We'll have this gown, too," he said to the dressmaker. "The king of England comes to call tomorrow, and I wish them both to look their best."

Renée had returned with her jewel box, held out her pearls.

"Why, I can barely see these," exclaimed Sir Thomas.

"They were given to me by my father."

"Alice has pearls you can wear, a necklace and bracelet and earrings and a pin, too."

"No pin," said the dressmaker, "and I think no necklace. But drops at her ears, that would be lovely, youthful, angel-like, if you will, sir."

"Very well, we'll get Alice's drops, and you'll wear those."

"And what will I wear?" Alice inquired in a steady voice.

"Oh, something gold, I think. You've any number of earrings."

"Something with the brown of the buttons would be pleasing," said the dressmaker.

"I like my pearl drops. They were given me by the princess."

"Get the ones I gave you. You're to share them, like a good sister. She's never had to share," he said, winking at Renée.

"I've some earrings that match the gold gown," the dressmaker said. "My brother is a jeweler," she explained, as if anyone cared.

"It's settled, then," said Sir Thomas.

"May I see them?" Alice inquired coldly. "I may not like them," she said to her father and the dressmaker and anyone else who cared to challenge her. But, unfortunately, no one—not even she—could deny that the dressmaker's earrings were wonderful with her gown.

"Distinctive, perfect for the young lady," said the dressmaker, adding up in her mind all that she would be putting in her account box from this day and already giddy with the sum. "If I may say so, mademoiselle," she said to Alice, "it is my opinion that you must favor a distinctive style. You wear it well—"

"You may not say so."

"Our little guest will need fans and gloves and other things. Go through Mrs. Tuck's trunk of pretties while she's here, pick what you like, Mademoiselle de Keroualle." Sir Thomas was expansive, full of himself. "We've a special visitor tomorrow, and you must look your best. He is coming to see how your voyage across the sea was and how you are. And my daughter, too," he added hastily, seeing the look that had settled on Alice's face. "Whatever either of them desires."

Renée went to Sir Thomas and knelt before him, took his hand to kiss it. There was dignity in her gesture. "No one has ever been so kind to me. I don't know how I can repay it." She looked up at him. "But I thank you from the bottom of my heart and promise you one day I will."

"Get up, young lady. Those sweet words and the sight of you in that gown is payment enough."

Alice could see her father was touched. Oh, she was going to need her wits about her to make this tangle unravel the way she wished it. And if he were part of a plot to poison the queen? Well, she didn't know what she was going to do with that.

AFTER FANS AND gloves and ribbons were picked—Alice going through the dressmaker's items with an ice cold intent, determined to cost her father a pretty penny—and the dresses were taken away to be sewn to fit perfectly—the dressmaker and the young women who worked for her would sew through the night by candlelight for this—Renée knocked on the door of Alice's bedchamber.

Alice sat at a table, shuffling cards. The court was back at Whitehall Palace settling in for winter. August had ended while they were in Paris. Fall danced forward in small steps. Outside, in the garden of this barn of a house, leaves were beginning to turn, crimsons, ambers, golds, the shades Lady Nature wore for autumn. Buckingham had lingered long in Paris, over a month. He and his wretched plots, thought Alice.

"I cannot believe it is already September, Renée. Can you?" she said, to say anything other than what was in her mind. "Marry in September's shine, your living will be rich and fine. My mother was born in September, but her living was neither rich nor fine. She died bearing me."

"I don't need to wear your pearls, Alice—"

"Suit yourself."

"Am I wrong to accept your father's generosity? Does it upset you?"

I must remember she is no fool, thought Alice. I must remember none of this is her doing. "He may do as he pleases, but I do think you might be wise to be a bit wary of him. He can be an old dog. But come, we're going to pay a call upon the Duchess of Monmouth, and guess who will very likely be there?"

"Richard?"

Yes. The sight of Richard would dampen whatever might have been sparked by her father's generosity today. Let her father, whose bloody ambition and bloody greed were never to be trusted—and might have drawn him into a plot to hurt the queen—buy as many dresses and fans and gewgaws as he pleased. It would be for Renée's trousseau to someone else.

Which was amusing, when one thought of it. Ha.

THEY WENT BY water, with Poll and Poppy to accompany them. The tide was high, and they could step from the house stairs directly into the wherry. It was a short journey to Whitehall Stairs, and Alice wanted Renée's first sight of the palace to be by river. Ahead of them, on the other bank, were the spires and turrets of Lambeth Palace, home to England's highest prelate, the Archbishop of Canterbury. And there was the long sprawl that was Whitehall Palace, her world, her milieu. Ten years ago, she'd arrived there with her father as part of the king's threadbare, ragged, beggared court. Growing up in rented chambers, moving often because there were never coins for the rent; this was the only home she knew.

Whitehall Palace was a hodgepodge of buildings dating over five reigns, a sprawling complex of courtyards and linking galleries, a cobbled-together warren of chambers, halls, stairways, balconies, gardens. There were as many as two thousand rooms within its boundaries, and any number of courtiers, not to mention servants, as well as the royal family. Its north faced St. James's Park, its south flanked the river; it began near Charing Cross and ended near Westminster

Abbey. A royal rabbit warren, her father called it, but he was dismissive only because he had never lived within its walls, a grief to him.

It had its own wharf and brewery and timber yard. It had been taken as booty from a bishop who displeased Henry VIII and been a royal palace since. King Charles I had died on a scaffold set outside one of its great buildings.

"I'll show you the spot where the king's father died," Alice said to Renée. "Some say his ghost walks at night."

Renée shivered and crossed herself.

"Catholic," said the waterman, eyeing Renée, and then spat into the river.

Ahead of them lay a long, low stone pier.

"Whitehall Stairs," cried the waterman.

These stairs were between the kitchen buildings and the queen's suite of apartments. Farther on was an elaborate, covered river entrance, but that was the privy stairs, for the use of the royal family. The waterman helped them onto the pier, and Alice darted forward, pulling Renée by the hand. They walked between buildings, the chapel, the butteries, and pantries, to Whitehall Street.

It was a melee of carriages—both those stopped and those attempting to turn around—and noise. Sedan chair bearers waited for passengers, grooms sauntered about or gathered in groups to talk to one another, coachmen shouted warnings and curses from carriages as they maneuvered horses this way and that.

Added to the mix were porters, young court pages, servants, Londoners on business or pleasure, and barking dogs, some tied to stiles, some running free.

"There," said Alice, turning in a slow circle, "was the scaffold built for our dear Majesty King Charles the First. They built a scaffold before one of the banqueting house windows, and he stepped out to die."

At this juncture, the palace was built across the street in the form of Holbein Gate, and the only way a Londoner could continue by foot or carriage to Westminster—other than by river—was to pass through Holbein Gate, the palace rising on both sides, and rattle on through to King Street.

Holbein Gate's octagonal turrets and slate roof gave it an old-fashioned look. Its opening was wide enough only for a single carriage to pass through, so there was always a jam of carriages and impatient coachmen waiting their turn. Alice pointed to the gatehouse's second story, where there were sets of narrow, high mullioned windows.

"A wicked one lived there."

"Who?"

"The Duchess of Cleveland."

"Ah . . . ," said Renée, for if her king's mistresses were famous, so was this one, whose reputation for wildness, beauty, and ruthlessness had followed her even when a girl.

"I used to see her at the windows or on the roof of the banqueting house. She loved it when the coachmen brawled among themselves."

Behind the gatehouse, one side of the palace was devoted to the king's privy garden; the other was a warren of royal buildings in which various dukes lived.

Alice knocked on a door, and it opened, and they stepped into the handsome ground floor of the Duke of Monmouth's apartments. Poll and Poppy stayed below as Alice and Renée gave over their cloaks, looked at themselves quickly in pier glasses to shake their curls, and walked upstairs toward the sound of music and conversation.

The chamber was long and large, everything in it of the latest fashion, from the beautiful oval plasterwork on the ceiling to the sets of matched chairs to huge silver firedogs at the fireplace. Twilight had come, and footmen were at the candles, lighting them. Musicians played a viola and a violin at one end of the chamber. The Duchess of Monmouth sat on cushions on the floor, surrounded by her maids of honor and various friends. In a window seat farther down the wall sat Barbara and Gracen, talking with their heads close together. John Sidney sat beside Barbara, Alice saw at once.

She made her way to the duchess, curtsied, said, "Ma'am, I do bring my guest, Mademoiselle de Kéroualle, to meet you."

"Back from France, are you? Monmouth will want to know all of the funeral. He's somewhere about." And then the duchess said in French, quite coldly, to Renée, "Mademoiselle." She turned back to the others even as Renée was curtsying, and Alice led Renée from one friend and acquaintance to another, introducing her.

Richard, who was watching one of the card games being played, saw them. In two strides, he was beside them. "You're back," he said to Alice, but his eyes were on Renée.

"Yes, I've brought you a surprise."

"God's word, you have." In French, he said, "Mademoiselle de Keroualle, I am overcome to see you. I had not expected this."

"She's to join our court," said Alice.

"What good fortune is this?" exclaimed Richard, smiling down at Renée in a way that was dazzling.

"Indeed, she's to be a maid of honor for the queen. Where's His Grace?"

"In his closet playing dice." Closets were the most private of chambers, where only those invited might enter.

"Will you tell him I've arrived—and stop staring at her in that way. You'll make her noticed."

Richard saluted and sauntered off. Barbara and Gracen came running, John Sidney following them. "Alice!"

Barbara kissed her cheeks, and Gracen followed suit.

"When did you arrive back? And you've brought Mademoiselle de Keroualle with you. How delightful." Barbara spoke in French to Renée, "Welcome, mademoiselle."

"Now why have you brought the beauty to outshine us?" said Gracen in English. "I was the most beautiful after Barbara, and now you ruin my chances with this chit."

John Sidney stepped forward to greet Alice, but she ignored his presence, saying to Barbara, "Why are you not with the queen?"

At once, Barbara looked guilty.

"Boring," said Gracen. "We play truant."

"We have stayed rather long. We ought to go back," Barbara said.

"Pooh," said Gracen. "Kit and Luce are on duty, not us. We don't have to be at her side every second."

"But the evenings," said Alice, all the while thinking, How bold Gracen is becoming. Evenings were difficult for Queen Catherine, when shadows she held at bay during the day gathered and pounced.

"You're quite right, Alice. I forget my obligations. We'll go at once," said Barbara.

"Go where?" It was the Duke of Monmouth, who took Alice's hand and kissed it.

"To the queen," said Alice, dropping into a quick curtsy.

"You may not leave. You've only just arrived. And we must talk."

"Let me go to the queen and pay my respects—"

"And introduce Mademoiselle de Keroualle. She's to be a maid of honor," said Richard.

Monmouth stared at Renée for such a long time that she flushed. Not understanding what anyone was saying, she stepped closer to Alice.

"All is well," Richard said to her in French. "We argue about where next we go."

"We're not arguing," said Alice.

"Because you're not leaving," said Monmouth.

"If it please Your Grace, just for a little while, to pay my respects to Queen Catherine. And then I'll speak with you, tell you everything about the funeral. There's so much to tell."

"We could all go," said Richard.

"A capital idea," agreed John Sidney.

"Bring the musicians," said Richard. "They can fiddle us to her chambers. We can dance in the gardens."

"That would be amusing," said Barbara, and her soft excitement seemed to settle it for Monmouth.

"But what is happening?" cried the Duchess of Monmouth as Richard spoke a word to the musicians, and they ended their tune in its middle.

"We go to pay a call on Her Majesty," said her husband. "Come along, madam wife, you and all your ladies. It's my wish."

And in another moment, most in the chamber were trooping down the stairs, out into the dusk, across Whitehall Street, and into the privy garden, where night bloom and roses, bay and rosemary, perfumed the air. The violinist led the way.

Alice tossed her head to the rhythm of the music, loving the evening and the music and the scents and the silliness of what they did, thinking, I could dance out here all night. Thoughts about queens and poison, fathers and treachery, lessened. The spell of the dark and garden and music seemed to enchant others as well. Men and women danced here and there; some of the duchess's ladies began to dance together.

Renée said to Richard, dancing toward him, "Why did they stare at me so?"

"Because you're beautiful."

She laughed. "This is madness. Is everyone mad?"

"We've gone mad because you're here."

"You mustn't speak so."

"Because I haven't your parents' permission yet or because you wish it?"

"Because you haven't my parents' permission."

He took her and twirled her, and they smiled at each other in the dark. "I love you," he said, but he spoke in English.

"I love you," John Sidney said to Barbara, who was holding out her skirts on each side, sashaying toward him. There was no mistaking the look that passed between them, and it was a good thing that the garden was dark, except for torches burning from the buildings that formed part of its boundaries, and Alice couldn't see it.

The noisy, babbling group entered Queen Catherine's withdrawing chamber, led by the fiddler. Alice glanced around. The maids of honor who must be on duty this evening were there, and the lady-in-waiting, and then the loyal ones: Dorothy Brownwell; Fletcher; Queen Catherine's master of the horse, Lord Knollys; and the queen's old nurse. A dreary little group. The canary cages were not covered yet, and the birds sang and flitted about the cages. The queen's pet fox leaped from her lap to hide under a cabinet. The draperies were the same apple green they'd been when Alice left. Edward and the other pages smiled, happy to see her. Here was home, the only permanent home she'd ever known.

"Verney!" cried Queen Catherine. "You return. No one tells me."

"Ma'am," said Monmouth, bowing handsomely. "We came to pay a call."

Queen Catherine's cheeks colored. It was clear she was touched. "I am happiness that you do."

"We brought our musicians and vagabonds we found along the way."

"I adore it." Queen Catherine clapped her hands. "To the privy garden. Monmouth, lead the way."

And back through halls and corridors they went, Edward carrying a chair for the queen. In another ten minutes they were within the privy garden, and couples were dancing, and Edward brought more torches and pushed them into the soft dirt of the gardens, so that there was more light, and Queen Catherine danced and talked with everyone, as happy as a girl. On the two sides of the garden that were bounded by buildings, courtiers came to their windows or out on their balconies to stare.

Alice brought Renée to meet the queen. "I bring you Mademoiselle de Keroualle. She's to be your new maid of honor and will be presented formally in a day or so, but I wanted you to meet her. She has been a dear friend to me in France."

Queen Catherine's face changed. Alice glanced down at Renée to see if she noticed, but Renée was too busy with her curtsy.

Then Monmouth found Alice and led her away from the crowd, toward a bench against the privy garden wall. "Everything," he said. "I want to know every last thing."

"It would be to your advantage, you know," said Alice, settling herself, "to be kinder to the queen."

"And how would that be to my advantage?"

"Beyond the courtesy of a gentleman, do you mean? Most despise her because she cannot bring a child to term, Jamie. Yet if she did, even once, where would you be? Perhaps not His Majesty's dearest darling then." She patted the bench, wondering, Was he, in this new arrogance she wasn't familiar with, part of the faction of courtiers who were set against the queen, who schemed of dreadful things like divorce? Would she and Jamie, who had always schemed together, now scheme against each other?

"Haven't you heard? I take lectures from no one these days, Alice," he replied. "Not even old friends."

She dropped her eyes, felt the burn that must be showing on her cheeks. Without missing a beat, she began to talk of the funeral. "The funeral was magnificent. The coffin lay in the center of the choir, covered by cloth of gold edged in ermine and embroidered with the arms of both France and England. There were hundreds, hundreds of flambeaux and wax candles. Monsignor Bossuet gave the sermon, and it was magnificent. I have a broadsheet for you, but I've memorized some of it. Listen: 'O, disastrous night, O, dreadful night, in which resounded like a clap of thunder the unbelievable words: Madame is dying! Madame is dead! Like the flower of the field in the morning she was gone from us by night. What haste! In nine hours His work was done.'"

MUCH LATER, NEAR to dawn, Alice walked the paths of the garden.

Poll lay on a bench, huddled in her cloak, sleeping. Her groom was asleep on the floor of a hall in Holbein Gate. Renée had left with Barbara and Gracen a few hours ago to sleep in their bed with them. The party had broken up by bits and pieces, yet even the last of the most hardy had drifted away some time ago. It seemed that only she was unable to sleep.

She became like this sometimes, so keyed up that restlessness wouldn't abate.

She walked through a silent courtyard until she found herself near the kitchens. She thought she might take off her shoes and sit on the quay and put her feet in the water. But a man and a woman stood on the quay of Whitehall Stairs, embracing. Alice waited back in the shadows, not wishing to disturb them. The woman had a cloak over her nightgown and embroidered slippers on her feet. The man stepped back into a boat, which a riverman rowed out into the current. The woman remained for a time on the quay, watching. At last she turned and walked back into the palace, and the hood of her cloak slipped. In the light of a torch that was still blazing, Alice saw it was Dorothy Brownwell, the mother of the maids of honor.

She tried to find some place to hide herself, but it was impossible, so she stayed where she was. Dorothy, after a moment in which she saw Alice, hurried on by. Alice walked out onto the quay, watching the river. She would wait for the sun to rise. Surely it was near sunrise.

In her mind were scenes from this night. Jamie snubbed her. She could no longer go to him with anything on her mind and have his help unconditionally. She must now bow and scrape first. Her old friend grew away from her, too important, too almost a prince, to heed her anymore. His reprimand stung like venom in her heart. John and Barbara danced together, Richard and Renée, Brownie and Lord Knollys—for it must have been Lord Knollys who embraced Brownie a moment ago on the quay. Queen Catherine, the expression on her face when Renée was introduced, sadness, a sudden sharp etching of it. Why? Barbara continued her foolish flirtation. Everything changes and nothing does. King Charles came to call on her father today, and she'd been up all the night and kept Renée up with her. Her father would be unhappy. Good.

The sun rose quietly in the distance, coloring the sky ocher and peach and old gold. The tide was out. The mud of the river stank. Time to go home.

Chapter 15

"Turn around," commanded Sir Thomas.

Renée did as she was told, while Alice watched with narrowed eyes and mounting temper. Never, not even when Colefax had come to make a formal request for her hand in marriage—an alliance at which her father had been overjoyed—had he demanded to see what she would wear or offered an opinion on such. Yet here he was in her bedchamber, scrutinizing her—but it was really Renée, she saw that clearly—as if they were fillies he was about to put up for auction. Did he wish to show off before the king? My pretty little mistress-to-be?

"She's perfection, Father."

"That she is," said her father, rubbing his hands. He was dressed richly, in one of his best satin coats with longer skirts on the jacket, the newest style. She'd had it and other things made for him in France, but now she wished she'd thrown them overboard or, better yet, given them to the sailors.

"It's about time you stopped frowning, Alice," he said to her. "You'd no right to keep your friend out until all hours, not when you knew the king was coming to call. Not that she shows a wink of it."

"And I do?"

"That damned temper of yours shows it."

"If you say one more word to me, one more, I won't come downstairs."

"Stay up here and sulk, missy."

"Bah!"

"Bah, back!"

Renée twisted a handkerchief in her hands. "Please . . ."

Both turned to look at her. Renée swallowed, and tears began to glisten at the corners of her eyes. Why am I not surprised? thought Alice.

Sir Thomas took hasty steps forward. "Now, mademoiselle, don't you cry. I won't have it. Alice has a nasty, snarling temper, and I'll lock her in a room if you say the words."

"Oh no. If Alice isn't with me, I can't meet His Majesty. Oh, please don't be angry. Either of you. Please."

Sir Thomas ran his hand over his face, and a huge smile emerged. "I'm not quarreling. I won't quarrel, little girl."

"I will," said Alice.

Sir Thomas turned to his daughter. "You look like a jewel in that dress, a dark, exotic jewel. You're the prettiest I've seen you, poppet. Now, I need you to go down these stairs and charm the king of England and whomever he deigns to bring with him today. I need smiles and that quick wit of yours. It isn't every day—it isn't any day—that His Majesty calls on Sir Thomas Verney. And I need Mistress de Keroualle to feel at her ease. His Majesty won't be happy with me if he sees she's upset. Now, can you do that for me, Alice, my dear? Help your poor old papa who simply wishes to win the king's regard?"

He'd disarmed her. Oh, how I always want to believe you will do nothing despicable, she thought.

He took her face in his hands and kissed her on the lips. "I thought about beating you when you finally showed up this morning, our little French guest drooping like a drowned cat, but you both look magnificent at this moment, and I couldn't be prouder." At the bedchamber door, he said over his shoulder, "I'll send someone up directly we see the king's barge." And then he was gone.

"I'm afraid," said Renée.

Alice led her to the window seat, sat beside her, took her hands, and said as patiently as she could, "What nonsense. All you have to do is smile. It's as if we were at Madame's and King Louis had come to call, that's all. No more, no less."

"Please, Alice."

"Of what are you afraid?"

"I can't name it."

"Well, perhaps it's only sensible to be afraid. You've left your family behind. You're in a new court. You don't know anyone yet. But think—this afternoon we're going to walk in St. James's Park with Lieutenant Saylor. Then we're going to eat supper in New Spring Garden with Brownie and whatever maids of honor can join us, so that you can begin to make friends. And tomorrow, my father will take us to court and formally present you to Her Majesty, and then you and I will live at Whitehall, and it will be easier there to see Lieutenant Saylor. And in a year or so, if you wish it, I'll sponsor your marriage to him. Would you like to marry him? I think you would. He's mad for you, any fool can see. And I'll be godmother to your first babe." Crossing her fingers for luck, she thought, May I be Balmoral's duchess then, and I'll see that your lieutenant rises as high as the stars.

Poll came running into the chamber, practically shouting, "The king! His barge is in sight! Your father says come!"

"Tell him we'll be right there," said Alice. Her father had the entire household in an uproar. She led Renée down the hallway to a window that overlooked the river. There in the distance was the king's pleasure barge, its flags and pennants waving in the breeze. "There's His Majesty," Alice said. "He does us a great honor to call to see how you do. He's a kind man, but I need to warn you he loves to flirt with pretty women, and so likely he will flirt with you. He has wonderful wit and easy ways, not stiff like King Louis. The story of his life is amazing."

"Tell me."

"There isn't time for everything—"

A footman bounded up stairs. "Your father asks for you to join him on the terrace."

"Yes, tell him we're on our way."

The footman bounded back down the stairs.

"He was on campaign with his father by the age of nine," Alice said as she and Renée descended the stairs. "At ten he went before the House of Lords to plead for the life of an adviser of his father. By ten and four, he was fighting in the West Country, separated from his father. The royal family was scattered to the winds. His mother was in France with the child who was Princesse Henriette; his other sisters and brothers were all imprisoned. By six and ten, he was sent away so that he would not be captured as his brothers and sisters had been."

Ahead was the river garden with its terrace. Through sets of opened doors, Alice could see the barge, landed at the river steps. Her father was descending them to welcome His Majesty.

"We'll wait here," said Alice, stepping just outside the doors and onto the stone of the terrace. Poppy stood there with the princess's dogs on leashes. Alice patted a spaniel before assuming her place beside Renée. "When I say so, drop into a curtsy. . . . By the time the king was twenty, his father had been beheaded. It's said he sent Cromwell a blank sheet of paper with his signature affixed and told him to list whatever conditions he wished that would spare the life of his father. But for naught. He fought a last battle against the Roundheads at one and twenty and was very nearly captured, but he escaped. His kingdom was in the hands of the Roundheads, and he was in exile again, poor as a church mouse, going from one court to another to marshal funds and an army with which to take back his crown. By thirty, when all hope was extinguished, he was proclaimed king. It all shows in his eyes, Renée. If he weren't such a roué, I swear I could be in love with him myself. I thought I was when I was twelve. Poppy, release the dogs."

Chapter 16

The Duke of Balmoral was among those the king had brought with him. Alice's heart began to pound at her good fortune.

Dogs went yapping and scampering toward the men. King Charles laughed and bent down. "Little absurdities, come to your uncle. Come here, Puff Puff, Melon, Lulu. Bad. You are all very bad dogs, just what His Majesty likes." He straightened, a wide, amused smile on his face, and saw Alice and Renée.

"Now," Alice said, and she and Renée dropped into curtsies, which they both held as King Charles sauntered toward them.

"He's very tall," whispered Renée. "I forgot that."

"Hush."

"My legs are hurting." Another whisper from Renée.

King Charles held out a hand to each, and taking it, they rose. "Charming, upon my word. Mistress Verney, greetings to you."

"And to you, sir."

"And Mademoiselle de Keroualle, welcome to England." His French was accented but impeccable. Living on his wits, begging for aid in France and Spain and the United Netherlands, had sharpened it.

"Thank you, sir."

He settled Alice to the arm on his right and Renée to the arm on his left and turned the three of them around to the others.

"You know, of course, His Royal Highness the Duke of York, His Royal Highness Prince Rupert, His Grace the Duke of Buckingham, but, Mademoiselle de Kerouaille, I think you've not made the acquaintance of His Grace the Duke of Balmoral."

Balmoral bowed, and to Alice's delight, a smile seamed his face at the sight of her.

"I have a gift for you, Sir Thomas." King Charles snapped his fingers, and a page ran to the barge and returned with two small trees, their roots bound in sacking.

"From my plantations in the New World, arrived only yesterday on a ship. One is a magnolia, and the other is an oak. From . . . where are they from now, brother?"

"New York, I believe, sir, named after me." The colony was booty from the Dutch wars. It had been New Amsterdam. The Duke of York smiled. He was tall and loose limbed like his brother, but ruddy rather than dark.

"No," said Prince Rupert, "it was from farther to the south. South Carolina, named after our dear, blessed, departed Majesty."

"And where in your garden shall we plant these trees from New York or South Carolina? I say here and here." The king pointed with his long cane, an affectation from France because he certainly didn't need it to walk. It had a golden dragon's head, bright ribbons tied under the chin.

Buckingham looked at the house with distaste. "You need to tear this old wreck down and build anew." They started toward the opened doors, Sir Thomas calling for the dogs to be leashed, to be put in the barge.

"Oh dear, something in my shoe." Letting go of the king's arm, Alice turned to Balmoral, who led her to a bench and gently took off her shoe and just as gently shook it.

"Might we sit a moment?" Alice asked. The others were inside the great chamber, surveying it.

"Thank you for your letter about the funeral. How is your leg? Healed, I trust?" Balmoral said.

"Yes, Your Grace. I have something of import I need to say."

He waited. The brim of his hat, where it wasn't pinned back to the crown, threw a shadow on his face.

"You know my belief Madame was poisoned."

"Yes."

"I—I do believe that perhaps Their Majesties might be in danger. Her Majesty, I mean. I know there is talk the king should remarry, though that be against all laws and the conduct of a gentleman."

"And you think someone might poison her to allow him to do so? A serious statement, Mistress Verney."

"His Grace . . ." She cut her eyes to the Duke of Buckingham, standing in the open doors, pointing out broken floor marble to Sir Thomas. "He stayed overlong in France. He talked with those who killed Madame and with others whose specialty is poisons. Someone I trust told me."

Balmoral's eyes narrowed, and he, too, regarded the Duke of Buckingham. "What an interesting fact you share with me, Mistress Verney," he said finally. "Doubtless our duke does some digging for truth on his own. It's likely as harmless as that. But we don't know, do we? And I assume you haven't told your father because he is Buckingham's man. Discreet. Discretion is an art. Why do you tell me?"

"I am only a woman, and a young one at that, and I do not think others will listen to me, and I thought if I shared what I'd been told with someone such as yourself, someone who has His Majesty's full respect and has proved his allegiance to this kingdom in so many ways, someone who knows me a bit, has some regard for me, that my concern might at least be looked into, not dismissed as the hysterics of a female."

"Will you do something for me?"

"Anything."

"Will you write it all out, everything, every word your friend told you, who this friend was. They're looking our way; they've marked how long we've been speaking to each other. I can see His Majesty is amused, will jest with me later of flirting with you."

"If only you would, Your Grace." She watched his face. She was too bold. But what choice did she have?

He stood, stared sternly down at her. "You mock an old man. I'm not certain I care for it."

"It isn't mockery. I hold you in highest regard. One of the reasons I bring my concerns to you is that I want you to see my regard." She held his glance, even though she could hardly breathe. This was a most foolhardy gamble. He could think her a jade, a wild piece, so many unflattering things that might make him turn from her in contempt.

"You do not know me," he said.

"I want to."

He began to cough and had to sit back down on the bench, the cough so racked him. He waved her away, and she went into the great chamber, not at all certain about what she'd just done.

"You'll need to spend a pretty penny on this, Sir Thomas," said King Charles.

"Or I can sell it, turn it into a square of houses like Covent Garden."

"The property is too small for that," said Buckingham.

"How did you come to purchase it?" asked Prince Rupert.

"I won it from His Grace here at cards."

"If he'd asked nicely, I'd have given him the old wreck," said Buckingham, wiping his hands with a large handkerchief edged in lace, as if the dust of the old-fashioned place were too much to bear.

"I hear you're often fortunate in cards," said King Charles.

"I am," said Sir Thomas.

"I should finance my treasury from gambling," said King Charles.

"You'd have to tax the winners, trust them to 'fess up to winning. I, for one, would lie," said Prince Rupert.

"The flaw in the plan. I shall have to continue to depend upon my obstreperous House of Commons for my coins."

Sir Thomas was often one of the more obstreperous members, but he ignored the barb.

"Lead me up the stairs, Sir Thomas. Let me see what Buckingham has lost," the king said.

They toured the floors above, peering into bedchambers that were scattered down the long, wide landing, and then went down into the cellars, Renée remaining on the king's arm. Finally, back in the big chamber that looked upon the river, King Charles said, "Do you play, mademoiselle?"

"Play?" asked Renée.

"Cards," said Alice.

"Yes, sir, I do."

"Excellent. You and Mistress Verney shall play me a round or two of what? Basset, I think. I'll leave the others to themselves. That way I won't lose Hampton Court to Sir Thomas."

"It's how I kept my daughter fed in the old days," Sir Thomas said, holding out a chair for the king. "Have you no memory of needing a new suit to call on La Grande Mademoiselle, and none of us, including yourself, had a pence between us, and it seems we'd used up our goodwill with the tailor because he demanded coins before he'd thread a needle? I went to Paris and gambled all night, and won three gold louis d'or to buy a new suit so you could go-a'courting."

King Charles threw back his head to laugh, a booming, surprising laugh as big as he was. "Was that you?"

"It was indeed. And I don't believe you ever repaid me."

"Doubtless I didn't. Take it up with my lord treasurer."

"Which means you'll never be paid," said Prince Rupert. "We haven't an extra feather to fly with."

"Ships of the line," said York. "We place all our funds into building ships of the line."

"There are other ways I can be repaid," said Sir Thomas.

But talk of the royal navy and treasury funds and repayment was left for the other table of players. King Charles kept up the lightest of banter with Renée, asking her questions about her family, about the journey, about what songs she liked to sing, about what instruments she played. Alice could see her friend slowly regaining her poise. And one thing about Renée, she played cards well. A strain of common sense and ruthlessness showed itself.

"Shall we make it interesting?" King Charles's eyes glinted. He put coins upon the table, dividing them among Alice, Renée, and himself. And then he proceeded to lose every hand, except when Alice might win. Slowly her coins, as well as the king's, piled up before Renée, who laughed and raked the coins toward herself with an open, charming greed.

"Worth every pence," said King Charles at the sound of her laughter, and Renée smiled, at her ease at last and very lovely.

Alice moved restlessly. It was near the time they'd promised to meet Richard. She'd had no idea the king would stay this long.

"Do I bore you?"

She looked up to see King Charles's dark and wickedly alive eyes upon her.

"No. I just hate losing, sir."

"We had some plans to walk in the park," Renée said.

" I can easily send round a note—" began Alice, but King Charles cut her short.

"No." He gathered the cards in his large hands. "I would never think of interfering in your plans. And a walk would be a good thing. Put the roses back into the cheeks of Mademoiselle de Keroualle. Her cheeks are paler than I remember. Where do you go?"

"St. James's. Then to New Spring Garden."

"Delightful." The king rose from his chair. "You must tell me what you think of my gardens, mademoiselle. They can't match what your king is creating at Versailles, but they are handsome enough for us."

"It's Alice's fault if she's pale," said Sir Thomas from his table. "She kept her up all the night."

Again, Alice found dark eyes regarding her. "We were dancing in the garden," she said hastily.

"Was that you? I heard the music."

"It was Her Majesty's idea," said Alice.

"Was it? Perhaps she'll be persuaded to do it again, and I'll come and watch. Do you like to dance, Mademoiselle de Keroualle?"

"Very much, sir." She looked at Alice, and it was clear she was ready to depart.

"If you'll excuse us, sir," said Alice. She glanced at Balmoral and then away. She had no idea what he was thinking, no idea if she had offended or not.

"Of course. You two run along and have your walk. Tell the cook at New Spring Garden that I'll pay for your supper."

King Charles followed the pair with his eyes, strolling out into the entrance hall to watch them run up the stairs. Back in the great chamber, he walked around the foursome playing cards, stood a moment behind his brother's chair before tapping him on the shoulder. York surrendered his chair. The others stared at King Charles.

He smiled. "Jemmy has the best hand."

"Dash it, that's cheating," said Rupert. "I'm too old to duel with you and too strapped for coin to lose."

"Oh, very well. She'll be at court tomorrow?"

"Before noon," answered Sir Thomas.

"Excellent. Who is winning?"

"I am," he answered again.

"He's unbeatable when fortune smiles on him," said Buckingham. "She doesn't always smile, though, does she? Remember that run you had last year?"

"Sweet Jesus, yes. I very nearly went bankrupt, sold properties to recoup that I regret to this day. Sold them to you, if I remember correctly. I've been buying in the hell the fire left, from people too discouraged to rebuild, glad to rid themselves of the bit of land." Four years ago, a huge fire in the city of London destroyed much of it. Sir Thomas glanced at the king, proud to share that he knew court gossip, too. "They do say Christopher Wren has given you a grand plan for the rebuilding."

"But I haven't the funds in the treasury to buy the land," said His Majesty. "Already shacks and hovels breed like rabbits. Why don't you donate your London land to the crown, Sir Thomas. It would be much appreciated." The king was sardonic, and Sir Thomas stared at him, uncomfortable, not certain how in jest he was.

"Your daughter was buying up properties in Paris," said Buckingham.

"Looking only."

"The talk at Madame Rouge's in Paris was that you were moving to France."

"Not likely."

"Were the whores pretty?" King Charles asked Buckingham.

"All the whores, male and female. And clean. I don't know where Madame Rouge finds them."

"They say if you want someone dead, begin at Madame Rouge's," said Balmoral.

"If the whores are pretty, when we declare war, we'll have to make certain we leave it standing and divide the whores among us. Spoils of war," said Sir Thomas jovially.

None of the others responded to his jest. He looked from one face to another and felt suddenly, coldly, how much he was the odd man out, no matter the old days. In the silence he felt knowledge here that he wasn't privy to, and that in spite of his latest favor to Buckingham, he would never be privy to it, unless Buckingham needed him to know. I'm his dog, he thought, no more, no less. And to the others, I'm less than that.

"Does Your Majesty ever fret?" asked Balmoral, as if Sir Thomas had not spoken.

"Over?"

"The fact that some factions do indeed want you dead."

"Religious fanatics, you mean? No. It's been ten years. I think the worst of them have tired or fear the tyrant my brother would be."

For a moment all eyes went to York, whose ruddy face flushed. The king spoke what people feared, but with a humorous tone in his voice.

"They do say it's become quite the thing in Paris to poison one's wife or husband or mother or father, whoever is in the way," said Balmoral.

"Like my sister?" The words were so unexpected, King Charles's voice so quiet, his expression suddenly so forbidding, that every man except Balmoral cleared his throat in discomfort.

"Precisely like the princess," Balmoral said in clipped tones. "I think you should have a taster. You and Her Majesty and Their Graces the Duke and Duchess of York."

"Oh hell and damnation, Balmoral, I won't believe there's a plot to poison me."

"Did you probe into the poisoning rumor while you were in Paris?" Balmoral asked Buckingham.

"Why would I?" he answered indifferently.

"What if she was afraid?" said Prince Rupert. "It's something I can't forgive, that I never asked her that."

King Charles slammed his hand on the table, and the cards jumped. "I don't want her mentioned. I don't want her name said." He looked around into each pair of eyes. "Am I clear?"

"Very clear," answered Balmoral, calmly. "May one ask why?"

"If I think too long on all that's happened, all who've been lost, particularly this last, if I think on the betrayals upon which this kingdom rests, I'll gladly take poison, and if it doesn't kill me fast enough, I'll hang myself. When the black mood comes to visit in her long ebony gown and her hollow fiery eyes, I'll hang myself and thank God this bloody business is over. And you'll all have to deal with Jemmy here as your liege lord. Lord, Buck, look at your face."

No one spoke. No one moved. Anger of this sort was so unlike the king that all of them were shocked. And some of them, the one or two who loved him, were saddened.

York put his hand on his brother's shoulder. "Listen to Balmoral. Hire a taster for a time."

"How long a time, Jemmy? A day? A year? Two years? If I start fearing some madman will kill me, I'll go mad myself."

"Just for a while," said Prince Rupert, gruffly.

"A precaution, nothing more," said Balmoral.

"It might be a blessing if she were poisoned."

Aghast, every man there turned to look at Buckingham.

"She's useless."

"She is the queen of England, married under the eyes of God! What God has joined together!" York thundered. "Are you an assassin now, George? Is that your latest fancy?"

Buckingham shrugged.

"I'm fatigued," said Balmoral. "Might we return, Majesty, if you can forgive an old man's weakness?"

The way he said the words, the quietness in them, as if an older age looked down on this one and shook its head at its contemptuous folly, affected every one of them. King Charles stood so abruptly that the chair behind him fell over. "Hire a taster," he said to Balmoral. And to Buckingham, "Make your presence scarce for a time, my dear George."

When the king was on the barge again, everyone with him but Buckingham, Sir Thomas came back inside. Buckingham still sat at the table, playing solitaire. Sir Thomas sat down near him. The king was furious, and he would remember that he'd been made furious in the house of Sir Thomas Verney. This afternoon he had so looked forward to was smashed to pieces like a dish.

"Are you mad? I don't understand you," he said to Buckingham.

"I only say what he's thought himself. There's much you don't know."

As if he didn't know that! As if he hadn't worn himself to the bone trying to break into the inner circle. As if he hadn't whored and gambled and served one man or another to get there. He'd been there in the old days; and he'd stuck it out, unlike pretty-faced Buck here, who had turned tail to England and married a Roundhead's spawn. King Charles had forgiven it; he forgave too damn much, that was his problem. "Tell me, then. But I tell you now, I won't be a part of harm to the queen," he said.

"No one is going to hurt her. We're not barbarians."

"I thought you were hot for war with France?"

"That was last month, my dear."

Anger filled Sir Thomas and, under that, the gall of humiliation. He had obeyed this man and stirred up as many as possible for a war with the French. And now, like that, like a snap of the fingers, it was not to be. And he wasn't going to be told why. One didn't talk to the dog, did one. "Did your dealings in Paris prosper?"

"Dealings?"

"You went over for more than the funeral."

"Did I?"

"I say you did. I say you ought to tell me the whole of it."

"Do you now? Well, maybe there will be a war, after all."

But with whom? Buckingham threw the dog a bone. Sweet Jesus, he'd lied to his only daughter for this man, used her like a minion, like the minion he was! And for what? For hope of notice from the king. Smashed to nothing today. Smashed right here at this table before his very eyes. Enough. Time to find another master. But of course, no need to announce it. Let the great duke think he still had a loyal servant; the dog had at least learned that trick, hadn't he? Woof.

KING CHARLES, NAKED and very drunk, held up his son, who squirmed and gurgled at him.

Just as naked, Nellie Gwynn the actress stood close, keeping an eye on both the king and their son. "He has three new teeth."

The boy laughed and flailed out his legs, staring down at the king.

"I see them," said King Charles.

He kissed the child hard on each cheek, and Nellie took the baby and nodded to her mother, who stepped forward to return the babe to his bed, her face expressionless to the nudity of a king. God only knew she had seen worse than naked men. She and Nellie were both from the streets, but Nellie had the wit and youth, saucy beauty and voice like a lark, to bring her up to these high places, and she didn't forget her mother—ancient by the standards of this age, when it was said a woman was prime at twenty, decaying at four and twenty, old and insufferable at thirty. The streets were hard. One had to be quick-witted, ruthless, and lucky to survive. Nellie was.

Nellie poured another goblet of wine and gave it to the king. He drank it down like water. She sat on his lap. He had long legs with lean thigh muscles, and the sight of them excited her. She wanted to make love again. After a year, she might, just might, love this man, and love was a fragile seed in her world. But she didn't know him. Her mother before her was a whore. Nellie knew men. But not this one.

"I dreamed the queen had a son the other night. And today, I had an evil thought," King Charles said. In his mind was the reaction to Buck's words—that it would be a blessing if the queen was poisoned, God forgive him, never mind the dower she'd brought, the kindness she'd shown, and the loyalty.

"I ain't a clergyman, sir, but you can confess to me, if you like."

"The church of Nellie Gwynn. Confession to a naked whore. Appealing, Nellie. You'll take the bread from priests' mouths." He smiled at her, and she was comfortable with and comforted by the lasciviousness in that smile. She'd known such smiles most of her life. Her mother had shown her how to use them to her advantage.

Nell kissed his hand, held it to her breast.

He was unable to make his wine-soaked mind command the hand to caress her. He loved women's pleasure, loved, always had, always would, their shape, their smell, their softness, the way their minds worked, their loyalty, and then, if crossed, their treachery. Ruthless, colder than any man's. Life plays the traitor to us all, takes our best hopes and fairest promises and turns them against us, he thought. The only thing to do was make a jest before you became the jest. But he couldn't jest at his sister dead, his wife barren. A bargain with France, and Minette died. Freedom from his House of Commons' parsimony and high-handedness thanks to Louis's coins, but for his sister's life? No one had told him the true bargain. The coins filled his privy purse, and he felt like Judas. But he'd spend them, wouldn't he? And bugger Louis in the bargain. Everywhere he fathered sons, except on the queen. Old Rowley, his subjects called him, for his virility. Life demanded its pound of flesh, played out two right real jests before his very eyes, and he, who loved to laugh, could not summon the strength to do so. His eyes closed. His head lolled back. "Two jests, Nellie, on me. The boy is very fair. I can beget sons."

He laughed, and the actress in her picked up nuance. She put both her arms around him and hugged him, her lust lessening now, a bit of fear in her. Without this man, she was nothing again, plaything to men without the kindness he had. Dust to dust, ashes to ashes, vanity, all is vanity—one of her mother's best customers had been a Fifth Monarchy man, and he would thunder out those words as he finished his pleasure with her mother, before he turned to her.

"Is there a God, Nellie?"

"Oh yes. Come to bed now. Come and play with me." She touched her cheek to his, then drew back, shocked. There was wet against her cheek from where it had lain against his. A king's tear. From this man who always smiled. Worth what? A king's ransom?

"A fine boy. I'll make him a duke someday, and he can play with my other children."

In another moment he was snoring. Nellie moved off his lap,

called for her mother and the footman, and together, heaving, they managed to get him to the bed. She summoned his Life Guards, who waited downstairs, and they came up and dressed him. They eyed Nellie, naked still, as they dressed him, and she saw the lust in their eyes, enjoyed it with a wicked zest that was part of her spark. They'd never get a piece of her, not while the king desired her, but they could have a look at what pleased a king. They carried him off as tenderly as a babe in their arms, out into the night, back to Whitehall. Nellie went to look in at their son, sleeping in innocence. A future duke, was he? Nellie Gwynn, tart of the stage, mother to a duke.

He talked about two jests. She couldn't read, and she couldn't write, but she could count. That made three.

Chapter 17

Under the trees, sitting at charming tables built round their trunks, lanterns flickering from branches, Charles's young court flirted with one another, drinking wine in the dark. Most of them had been children when he was restored to the throne. They remembered the poverty, the want, the shifting—but barely.

Alice had shown Renée the king's garden house, which his father had built, and the bowling green where Monmouth and his cronies did play many an afternoon. They'd walked the pall-mall court the king had had built. He liked all things of the outside, walking, tennis, fishing, boating, riding horseback, archery, bowls, pall-mall, a game of sticks hitting balls, which he'd made the fashion. They'd strolled along the long canal of water in St. James's Park nearby, a landscape pool that would do pride to any French palace. Richard was sitting with them, along with Barbara and John Sidney, and Dorothy Brownwell and her Lord Knollys. Gracen was here, and Kit, and Charlie Sedley, and some of his friends.

Alice allowed the wine's expansive mood. She had decided to be hopeful about her conversation with Balmoral. Barbara and John stood up. "Where are you off to?" Alice asked.

"A walk, nothing more," said John.

"Without chaperone?"

Dorothy stood, but Lord Knollys put his hand on her arm in a proprietary way. "Will you trust me instead?" he asked Alice as if she were the queen.

"And me?" said Gracen, going to stand with Barbara.

"I grant you your walk." Alice laughed, amused with her grandness, with the fact that her disapproval carried weight. Maybe she'd gain back the old days. To her right, Renée and her lieutenant were talking about this Tamworth of his.

"You don't like John Sidney?" Dorothy asked Alice when he was in the distance.

"It isn't the match she should have."

Dorothy played with a ribbon on one of her full sleeves. A widow, she loved the maids of honor she was given charge of, each and all, no matter how they might tease her and trick her. Girls will be girls, she would say when some mischief happened. And then she loaned the coins or upheld the lie that would keep the girl from dismissal, telling her in her soft lisp, You must beware, you must behave. She had large, protruding eyes and golden hair—falsely golden, Gracen swore—and a heart as soft as goose's down.

"You saw me last night." She looked Alice full in the face, her great round eyes begging.

Alice sipped at her wine. "I saw nothing."

Dorothy leaned forward and kissed her. "I knew you'd say that. I fretted all the day, but the heart of me knew you'd say that. I'm glad you're back."

The truth was Dorothy Brownwell had been too lax, especially with Barbara, but Alice would begin to deal with that tomorrow, when she took her place again among the maids of the queen.

Behind them, at another table, revelers had begun to sing, pounding their hands on the table as they sang. It was a soldier's song.

Who comes here?
A Grenadier.
What do you want?
A Pot of Beer.

Where is your money?
I've forgot.
Get you gone home
You drunken sot.

"See what you'll have to put up with," Richard said to Renée, and winked. He was off to France again in a day or two for Balmoral.

Chapter 18

October

Clear moon, frost soon. If the moon shows a silver shield, be not afraid to reap your field.

Alice jerked off gloves, said to the new footman, "Fetch my father at once." She strode to the fire in his great chamber, putting her hands to it. It was cold out. September's feast day of Michaelmas, with its roasted goose, its paying of rents, was over. So, almost, was October. All Hallows' Eve, time of spirits and magic, the ending of the month, was only days away.

Reading his daughter's mood from her face and the way she stood, Sir Thomas paused in the doorway of the house's great chamber. So, the moment he'd been dreading was here. But to his surprise, she ran to him, kissed his cheek.

"There's something you have to know. It's awful. The king is paying too much attention to Renée. He has spent an hour with her every day of this last week. I'm there, but I might as well not be. You must tell him to stop it, Father. You're her guardian. You must go to the king and tell him to stop it before there are duels and scandal."

"What duels?"

"Well, Lieutenant Saylor, of course," Alice said sharply. "He's a man of honor."

"Why the devil would he duel?"

"You're not listening, Father. Tell the king to find another flirt. Tell him Renée is a respectable girl. Tell him he can't do this to us again—"

"Us?"

"The queen. He did it with Frances Stewart when he was in love with her. He would come in and talk with her and then take her off to a corner and be kissing her and touching her. Poor Queen Catherine was afraid to enter her own chambers for what she might see. She used to make me do it for her. It was awful. Unendurable. He's going to make the queen dislike Renée." And she had plans that Queen Catherine would dower Renée; she'd done it before for other maids of honor. "Tell him to stop."

"Frances Stewart married a duke. Perhaps Renée will, too."

"There are no dukes to marry, except Balmoral, and I have him."

"An earl, then."

"Father, you must stop this. I thought you of all people would want it stopped." Isn't she your sweetheart? Don't you care? she wanted to say but didn't.

"It doesn't hurt a young woman to be admired by the king, Alice. On the contrary, it makes all the bucks of court sit up and take notice."

That was true. Alice calmed a bit. And King Charles wasn't one to force his attentions. Renée would simply have to tell him to quit. Only Renée was afraid to do so. I can't, she'd said. He's the king. "You must tell the king that his attentions aren't returned, that Renée doesn't want them."

"I must?"

"You're her guardian. You brought her over. It's your place."

Sir Thomas skirted the issue. "Are his attentions unwelcome?"

"Of course they are."

"Are you certain, Alice?"

"Yes."

"Has she told you this? Did Mademoiselle de Keroualle tell you with her own words that the king's attentions were unwelcome?"

"Well, of course she did."

"Alice . . ."

"I know they are."

"Then she didn't tell you?"

"Not precisely, but anyone can see she's uncomfortable and doesn't know what to do. It's horrible, Father. You have to stop it."

"I'll certainly speak with the king."

"Will you? Oh, thank you, Father."

"Where are you off to? Aren't you going to stay?"

"Oh, no. Barbara is waiting for me in the hall. We have to get back to court. We're going to the theater this afternoon with the queen."

"What's playing?"

"The Conquest of Granada."

"That's right, Nellie dances again. I completely forgot. I may join you, poppet."

"Come and play basset with us later if you do."

"Play's too timid at the queen's. I like my cards fast and dangerous. There's a letter for you. Ask Perryman on the way out."

"Who's Perryman?"

"My new footman. A treasure."

She left in her usual whirl, and Sir Thomas stood looking at the fire. A coward I am, he thought. Sooner or later, Alice will have to know. He'd take later. He always did. And he had promised nothing, really—simply to speak with the king. He hadn't said about what. He smiled, pleased to put off reckoning for a time, comfortable with his treachery.

In the hall, Alice said to Barbara, "It's done."

"As easily as that?"

Alice linked her arm in Barbara's. "I almost think he doesn't care for her as I thought he did. A coach for us—what's your name?"

"Perryman."

"Perryman, if you please."

"Aye, ma'am, and while you wait, I'm heating some bricks for your feet, and I gave a letter for you to your maidservant."

Poll held it out.

It was from Beuvron, Alice saw. Wanting money, most likely. She'd read it later.

AT THE THEATER, courtiers and Londoners filled the main chamber. Word of Nell Gwynn's return to the stage was the topic of court and London, and everyone was excited to see a new play by John Dryden, the poet laureate.

"There you are," said Gracen to them. "I've saved a place by me."

Alice and Barbara curtsied to Queen Catherine and then sat down. They were in a special section reserved for the queen—only those she invited might sit there. In the pit, directly in front of the stage, were scores of young men from both court and the city, who openly ogled the maids of honor. The young women were used to it; it came with being a maid of honor, and those of maids who were older, like Barbara and Alice, paid no attention anymore. The men in the pit—from merchants to courtiers—stared at Renée today; she was new to them. The bolder of them pointed at her openly as they talked. It was the gauntlet every lovely woman of court ran. Some thrived. Some wilted.

Alice leaned over to whisper to Renée, "I've spoken to Father about the king's attentions."

"He'll hate me," Renée whispered back. "He'll dismiss me from court."

"He seldom dismisses anyone for anything. Don't fret so."

"I don't want to make His Majesty angry."

"He won't be angry. Look, there's Lieutenant Saylor."

From the pit, Richard bowed.

"Why is everyone staring at me?" asked Renée.

"Because you're lovely. Never mind it."

Kit grabbed Alice's arm hard. "It's the Duchess of Cleveland. She's coming over to us."

"She's not."

But there she was, larger than life in all things, advancing toward the queen's stall like a languid lioness. The men in the pit watched her, elbowed one another so that none should miss her. She drew eyes. She always had.

Barbara Palmer, Duchess of Cleveland, was still magnificent in a court that liked its beauties barely grown. At an age when women at court retired to their country estates to rear children and left their husbands back in Whitehall to drink themselves to death, there was no retiring for this woman. She no longer held King Charles in the palm of her hand—or, as the wits would say, in another place—but she did hold his regard as mother of four of his children. In her heyday, she'd blatantly made Queen Catherine's life miserable. In the firmament of court, she remained one of the stars. Tall, full figured, she held her head the way a queen of wild savages might.

"A word with you, Verney." She made a slight, cold curtsy to Queen Catherine. "Majesty, might I steal your little Verney for a moment?"

"Only a moment."

"Of course," said Cleveland, as if she'd ever obeyed this little Portuguese, a waif to her Amazon.

Alice meekly followed the duchess to the stall that was hers. Cleveland could have sent a footman or page to fetch her; this drama boded no good. Dread began to fill her. This woman had helped to bring down the cleverest of the king's councillors simply because her cousin Buckingham asked her to. She was so openly jubilant at his downfall that the councillor had said to her, "Pray remember, madam, if you live, you will grow old."

"Alone at last," Cleveland said, shutting the gate behind them and sitting down, but not inviting Alice to, only turning large, dark, contemptuous eyes on her. She let a silence build. When at last she did speak, every word was a lash.

"You know, for quite a while, I just couldn't fathom it. Who would play such tricks on me? Who would dare? For years, I've wondered. I didn't really note that they stopped while you were in France and began again with Madame's visit. But my confusion has lifted."

"I don't understand."

"You're clever, Verney, I give you that. Not many could fool me for as long as you have. But, come, no more insincerity between us. The game is up. I have you, fair and square. And there must be justice, there must be retribution. A little bird tells me you've picked the Duke of Balmoral to conquer. You do aim high."

"That's not true."

"Good, because I'm going to make certain that it doesn't happen. I'll see you married to an idiot first, but Lord Mulgrave's an idiot, isn't he? Better yet, not married at all. You'll die on the vine, Verney, wither like an old gourd. And I shall laugh and laugh as I watch it."

"You can't do that."

"Can and will. Who am I not related to in this court? Who doesn't owe me a favor in one form or another?"

Alice opened the door of the stall. The play was beginning, the actress Nellie Gwynn taking her place on the stage for the prologue. Alice turned back to the duchess. "Once you might have done so. Not anymore, I think. When I'm a duchess, I'll see you banished from court." She didn't know why she said the words. She'd gone stark, raving mad, most likely, saying anything to push past the feeling of having been crushed. King Charles had arrived, and in the noise and confusion around that, she slipped into the queen's stall and sat down, breathing hard. It was an effort even to find breath. Dread filled her.

"What did she say?" hissed Barbara.

"She's on to us over the trick we pulled last week."

Barbara gasped and fell back as if shot in her chair.

"It's me she suspects. Don't fret. I won't admit a thing, and I won't give you away. You know you can trust that."

"I knew we shouldn't have done this last one. I knew it!"

"Hush."

A tear rolled out of Alice's eye. In the dark, she found Barbara's hand and held tight. The prologue had begun, but her pulse was beating so, she couldn't hear it. The laughter in the pit told her the play was starting well. Nellie, dressed as a French courtier—it was a trick of clever managers to have the actress wear breeches so that their legs might be shown—gave Dryden's apologies for the play, as well as the great moral ideas the play would touch on. In addition to tight breeches and the laces and ribbons of a court fop, she wore a huge hat; it was so big that if she leaned to one side, she could touch the ground with it. She leaned to one side and touched the ground. Men in the pit began to applaud.

Not only did she mock the dress of the Frenchmen who'd come in the summer with Princesse Henriette, she mocked the style of the other company of actors, who used outlandish costumes to draw laughter. King Charles could be seen pointing a finger at his brother, who sponsored the other playing company. Nellie, actress to her core, began to play the part even more broadly, hilariously burlesquing a courtier full of himself. She threw the hat on the stage and danced around it. The audience clapped. King Charles stood and tossed her his hat, which she put on her head and wore to finish the prologue before tossing it back to him and bowing like the most graceful of courtiers. Cheers and whistles followed her exit. This was to be a tragedy, but Dryden was not above beginning with a broad laugh.

Alice could barely take in the tragic plot set in Spain, with star-crossed lovers, Queen Almahide played by Nell, popular, handsome Charles Hart as the warrior Almanzor, who loved her. There was a temptress and a jealous husband. There was a conversion to Christianity, wonderful scenery that transported the audience into another world, songs that were faintly erotic or political. A little actress was emoting. Fletcher, sitting behind Alice, pinched her on the shoulder.

"That's the actress who has Dryden," he whispered, "breaking up another happy home." Boos and applause erupted at certain lines:

See what the many-headed beast demands—
Cursed is that king, whose honour's in their hands.
In senates, either they too slowly grant,
Or saucily refuse to aid my want:
And, when their thrift has ruin'd me in war,
They call their insolence my want of care.

Prince Rupert, who was sitting on the stage, as was the fashion, stood and called out just as if he were one of the actors, "Andrew Marvell, Thomas Verney, Rob Howard, do you hear?" He wasn't bothered in the least that he was interrupting the play, nor were the actors, used to this and more from their audience. The day would be a good one if there wasn't a fistfight in the pit.

Alice saw her father sink down where he was sitting, put his hat over his face. She turned around to Fletcher. "I don't understand."

"The loss of the last Dutch war," Fletcher whispered. "It's felt it was because the Commons wouldn't grant enough funds for a proper fight, but when it was lost, they went on a hunt to blame the council."

So, she thought, putting together other pieces of gossip she'd heard this last month, that the king and his Parliament were more and more at loggerheads. My father is in it, thought Alice, and behind him is Buckingham. He was behind much, it seemed: Monmouth's pride, York's retreat, the divorce. A dangerous man. The play continued, treason, revolt, near suicide, death of an evil king, and finally, with that, it was over. Applause swept the chamber. The audience began to depart or leap up on the stage to join the actors as they undressed behind the scenery.

Alice glanced toward the Duchess of Cleveland, who blew her a kiss. She was no longer so frightened—she'd come up with a plan while watching the play.

Stagehands came out to douse the candles at the foot of the stage. Since the king was still in the theater, they left those in the chandeliers burning and sat on the edge of the stage to wait. King Charles opened the gate of Queen Catherine's stall. A smile lit her face as he sat beside her in his lazy, easy way. "Did you enjoy the play?" he asked.

"Most thrilling."

"And you," he said, turning to the maids of honor, waiting for him to notice them.

"Oh, yes!"

King Charles switched to French. "And you, Mademoiselle de Keroualle, it wasn't too savage for you, the prologue? She did make most cruel fun of your countrymen. Perhaps it is a good thing that your English is, for the moment, weak."

"It was very well done. And no, I did not understand, but everyone seemed most amused, and she who played the queen was most graceful." Renée spoke slowly, some of her words in French, some in English; she was improving each day, thanks to Richard.

"Everyone in the pit was admiring you tonight. You grace our court."

Renée didn't answer.

Queen Catherine stepped into the uncomfortable little silence with her own hazardous English. "Come you will to my apartments tonight, sir. I would have most honor. My brother he sends a new lute and the Madeira to drink."

King Charles stood, bowed to her. "You always have the most honor, my dear." He took her hand to lead her out of the stall and was pleased enough with her invitation for the evening to walk her out of the theater. The maids spread out behind them like ducklings.

"Wait," Alice whispered to Renée. "Lieutenant Saylor's just there. Talk with him about your fears. I'll tell the queen we've lost your earring and we're looking for it. Go on. Hurry."

The stagehands hoisted the heavy ropes that held the chandeliers high. They were eased to the stage, and the men began to blow out the candles in them. Richard stepped easily over the railing of the stall. They were almost in the dark.

"What's the trouble, my heart?" he asked. "Did Nellie's song offend you? I won't sleep tonight if you don't tell me what troubles you."

"Nothing. Everything. The king flirts."

"So would I if I were king. He likes pretty women. There's no harm in that."

"Are you certain?"

"Of course."

There was no one in the theater now except Alice. "Hurry," she hissed, and waited while they kissed, no longer shy with each other now, their bodies melding the way lovers did, the sweetness between them more and more unfolding.

Queen Catherine's apartments were filled to the bursting because King Charles was there. Near midnight, Sir Thomas walked in, did not see his daughter in the main apartments but found her sneaking a pipe of tobacco with Prince Rupert in what was called the Shield Gallery. Its walls displayed huge shields from the yearly birthday tournaments of the great queen Elizabeth. The memory of Queen Bess was revered by all; the Roundheads had not destroyed her legacies in this palace.

At the sight of him, Alice inhaled too strongly, choked, and the pipe with its very long and slender stem dropped from her mouth. Prince Rupert caught it deftly.

"And where did you learn this nasty habit?"

In between coughing, Alice answered. "Everyone smoked at Madame's court."

"You are not at Madame's court."

"I'll take my leave of you, Verney." Prince Rupert tapped out the burning tobacco against a tile of the fireplace, opened the top of a glazed box, and put the pipe inside. He nodded to her father and walked away down the long length of the chamber.

"I've just left the Duchess of Cleveland's apartments. What a harridan she's turned into. She had some ugly things to say of you, Alice, tricks being played on her, this one last week especially ugly. I told her her suspicions were lies, and damned lies at that. Now precisely what have I perjured myself about, missy?"

"You'll have to help me."

"Cleveland wants your head served on a platter. Fortunate for you it isn't three years ago, or that's precisely what would happen. She's furious."

"You have to help me play a trick on her, only we must do it in such a way that no one can possibly think I could be involved. That will throw her off."

"I am not playing schoolboy tricks on the most dangerous woman at this court!"

"She isn't the most dangerous anymore. You have to, Father, or I'm ruined."

"You'll go to her, and you'll apologize."

"I will do no such thing. Besides, it wouldn't be enough. You know how she is."

"I am not— Where are you going?"

"The queen is playing the lute. Can't you hear it? I want to see. Come along, Father."

"We aren't finished speaking of the Duchess of Cleveland."

"We certainly aren't. Barbara agrees with me—"

"Barbara? Barbara isn't—she wouldn't—"

Alice spoke over him. "A trick of which I cannot be accused is the only way. We just have to think of something."

Protesting, he was led into the main apartment. The queen was indeed playing the lute her brother, the king of Portugal, had sent her. Her master of the horse, Lord Knollys, was there, playing cards with Dorothy Brownwell, Gracen, and the queen's ancient, half-blind Portuguese nurse. Courtiers were there, Lord and Lady Arlington, the Earl of St. Albans, Thomas Clifford, Thomas Killigrew, others. But no Duke of Balmoral. He never came, in spite of the invitations Queen Catherine sent him on Alice's behalf. He'd sent Alice flowers, the loveliest bouquet she'd ever seen, but when she'd gone to thank him, his majordomo said he wasn't receiving visitors.

Fires in the fireplaces were roaring. Unlike the Louvre, with its vast rooms and stone floors, so cold in winter that one had to almost sit in the fire, Whitehall had chambers that were smaller, less unpretentious. When filled with a crowd, they were almost cozy. The queen sang a song composed during the first Dutch war. It had been enormously popular for a time:

To all you ladies now at land,
We men at sea do write,
But first I hope you'll understand
How hard 'tis to indite:
The muses now and Neptune, too
We must implore to write to you.

Fletcher, his voice lilting and soft, joined her on the next line. "With a fa, la, la, la, la."

"Just one last little trick, Father," said Alice, under cover of the singing, squeezing her father's arm. "That's all I ask."

Chapter 19

That same night, a few hours before dawn. Alice threw down her cards. "You best me."

Smiling, King Charles folded his cards into a neat stack without showing what they were. Alice began to unscrew an earring. The third player, Buckingham, back in favor with the king again, yawned, stood just as a servant entered and added more wood to the fire. Sparks flew up the chimney and bounced against the fire screen.

"I won't take your jewelry, Verney. Keep the earring in your pretty ear." The king looked around him. "Ye gods, are we the only ones awake?"

"It's a dull lot here. I'll be glad when your courting is done," said Buckingham. His shirt was undone at the neck, the laces and ribbons there bedraggled. He'd been drinking steadily, but it didn't show except in the boredom now expressed, the disdain behind it. Nothing would please him in the next hours except something outrageous, unexpected, different. Restlessly he paced around the table at which they'd been playing cards.

It was, as Buckingham said, a dull scene. The queen had retired several hours ago. Barbara and Renée sat slumped and sleeping over the great cushioned stools Alice had brought from France as gifts for Queen Catherine. Gracen was awake, tucked into a window seat, talking with Lord Knollys, whose lap cradled the head of a sleeping

Dorothy Brownwell. Kit and Luce were drunk and sat in the shadows on the knees of one of the king's favorites, a young courtier, the Earl of Rochester, who was kissing first one, then the other.

And that was the reason Alice was careful in whose company she drank.

She'd waked one morning before dawn when she was fifteen in this very chamber, a snoring courtier beside her—a man she didn't even like—with her gown undone to her waist. She was weeping by the time she found Barbara, fast asleep in her bed, and the two of them had gone over every detail, Alice having to remember that at a certain point she'd liked the kissing, the fondling, but she remembered nothing else. For the next month, she'd waited to see if she might be with child. She wasn't. But the fear around that had kept her sleepless for weeks. She'd been twelve the evening a newborn babe appeared, mewing like a kitten, during the midst of a dance the king gave. She'd seen the baby in its birth blood on the floor amidst the dancing, and then she'd seen it scooped up, she knew not by whom. It had happened so fast she believed she'd dreamed it. Except that one of her favorite friends, another maid of honor, stayed the next day in her bed sick to death, and whispers about her filled every hall and corner of the queen's apartments. And then her friend left court, so ill with fever that she had to be put upon a litter and carried out. Who was its father? Some said the king. Some said the king's brother.

"Wake the mother of the maids." King Charles stood. "See that our little sleeping French flower is escorted safely to her bed." Then he was striding out the door, Buckingham with him.

"Where do we go?" Buckingham said.

"I can't speak for you," said King Charles, "but I go to see Nellie."

"I'll wait in her hall."

"Don't."

"Why not? You won't be long, will you?" Their laughter followed them out.

Renée, her head in her arms on the cushioned stool, opened her eyes and stared into the fire. Its light flickered over her face; it was clear she'd heard his words.

Rochester stood to follow the king, and the young women on his lap fell to the floor. He stepped around them. Kit began crying. Luce began to retch. Rochester never looked back. Gracen left Lord Knollys, went to Barbara, and shook her awake. She and Barbara helped Kit and Luce to stand up.

"I'm going to be sick," wailed Luce.

"Not here," said Gracen. "You wait until I find a bucket."

Alice touched Dorothy's arm. She sat up, blinking rapidly, looking like a confused, plump child. "I drank too much wine. I fell asleep," she said to no one in particular. Her hair was falling out of its pins on one side.

"So you did," said Alice. "You need to see to Kit and Luce. They're sick and, like you, have had too much wine."

Dorothy looked around herself, bewildered. Kit was still crying, and Renée had taken off her heeled shoes and was walking in her stockings toward the door that led downstairs to the maids of honor's chambers. Barbara and Gracen held Luce between them, urging her not to be sick, to wait just a few moments more.

"The king asked most particularly that you see Mademoiselle de Keroualle to bed," Alice told Dorothy, who immediately got up and followed her maids down the stairs.

Alice sat in the place on the window seat where Dorothy had been, her eyes narrowed on Lord Knollys. Who was this man Brownie favored? Was he good enough for Brownie? He was certainly one of Queen Catherine's favorites. He did not mingle with the king's men, join in their gambling and whoring and writing of wicked verses, but served the queen quietly and well. There was little respect given to that by the young courtiers who had the king's ear. They called him the queen's gelding, but King Charles didn't join in the mockery. It seemed to Alice as if the king appreciated the loyalty and courtesy shown, as if Lord Knollys acted toward the queen in a way King Charles might wish to do but did not.

"How is your lady wife?" asked Alice. The question was not innocent.

"Not well. Never well."

"So Mrs. Brownwell tells me. Mrs. Brownwell has been my friend since she came to court. I have such a deep regard for her."

"She has my deep regard, also. If I may be so bold, what age are you, Mistress Verney?"

Alice lifted her chin and lied. "Nineteen."

"Mrs. Brownwell told me you'd seen us. And it's evident you have your judgments, of me in particular. When you are forty and one, as I am, or thirty as Mrs. Brownwell is, we three will talk of life and its vagaries, of loneliness and duty, of sickness and health, easy to vow but hard to keep when it stretches on and on and on." Lord Knollys spoke patiently, but only just.

"I know something of heartache."

"You know nothing, and you presume much. Good night, Mistress Verney." He stood.

"I don't want her hurt."

"I trust I have brought no hurt to Mrs. Brownwell, but rather kindness, more than kindness. Mrs. Brownwell has been a source of great comfort to me, and I, I pray, to her. Do you always meddle in what is not yours? It's a bad habit, if you'll forgive my saying so. Good night."

Alice leaned back against the corner of the window seat, thinking about what he had said. What concern of hers was it if Brownie bedded the Earl of Knollys and seven other men besides? She was a widow and could do as she pleased. Alice went to the fire to stretch out her hands to it. It was going to be one of those nights when she fretted about everything and couldn't sleep—and then she remembered the letter.

Slipping it out of her pocket, she sat before the fireplace screen and opened it. Beuvron wrote only a few lines. Henri Ange was coming to England. He wrote to tell her because she had always been a friend to him, because he knew her love for Queen Catherine. She was to burn this letter.

Alice's eyes darted back to the date. Sent over a week ago! Ange might already be in London, likely was. He'd come to kill the queen; she knew it. Balmoral said he'd put a taster at the royal tables. A taster ate of every dish, drank of every wine served. But Ange could get round that. It would be child's play. Well, the Duke of Balmoral could expect another visit tomorrow. She'd put it on his shoulders. She stared into the fire. Beuvron's note just added to the thoughts circling one another in her mind. She stood and walked down a hallway to the stairs to the maids of honor's chambers.

In the maids' chamber, they readied themselves for bed.

"Who's Nell?" asked Renée, pulling her head away from the brush. Behind her, brush in hand, Barbara frowned.

Gracen, sitting in bed in her night smock, smiled a cat's smile.

"The actress you saw tonight," said Barbara.

"She is the king's mistress?"

Gracen made a sound like a giggle and fell back in the bed.

"You mock me?" Renée asked her.

"I mock you?" Gracen repeated the question, tone for tone. "Yes, you silly French girl, she's the king's mistress. Would I were."

"She's the one who danced tonight?"

"Danced and sang," said Gracen.

"Who else is the king's mistress?"

"At the moment, only Nellie that I know of, but he loves where he wills. One time, we were watching a play, all of us, do you remember, Ra, and he—"

"You shouldn't tell this story," said Barbara. "It isn't kind."

"King Charles seems so kind," said Renée.

"The play was performed here at court, for us, and there was an interval, and Moll Davis—"

"An actress," explained Barbara.

"—came out to sing, and she sang so suggestively—" Gracen jumped from the bed and pulled down the front of her nightgown so that most of her breasts were showing. She leaned forward, began to sing, swaying her hips provocatively as she walked around Renée and Barbara, singing:

> *Then since we mortal lovers are*
> *Ask now how long our love will last;*

But, while it does, let us take care
Each minute be with pleasure pass'd.
Were it not madness to deny
To love, because we're sure to die.

She jumped back on the bed, pulled the blanket around her shoulders. "The king stood up right then and there, grabbed her by the arm, and left with her. It was clear to an idiot what they were going to do. And Queen Catherine, her face turned such a color, and she sat as if stunned, and no one spoke, not the actors, no one. The musicians almost stopped playing in their surprise. Oh, I'll never forget it. It was Christmas, I think." Gracen laughed, the sound joyous. "Compliments of the season."

"Don't listen to her," said Barbara.

"Isn't it true?" said Gracen.

"It is true. But not everyone is like that."

"Who isn't?" asked Gracen.

"Lord Knollys, for one."

Gracen nodded. "That's true enough. Who else?"

"Richard Saylor, John Sidney—"

"Puritans, secret Puritans—"

"What are Puritans?" interrupted Renée.

"Not of the faith," said Barbara, who was.

"They don't believe that the sacrament is God's body," said Gracen, making devil horns with her fingers.

Renée crossed herself and put her hands over her ears.

"She's going to cry," Gracen said to Barbara.

Barbara sighed, put down the brush, knelt before this new maid of honor who came from a more decorous court.

"Richard is this Puritan?"

Barbara pulled the shawl tighter around Renée's shoulders and hugged her. "He is not a Puritan. Gracen makes fun."

"But he isn't of the true faith. I know that, but can't help loving him."

Barbara pulled her up, pushed her toward the bed, where Gracen lay now. Under the covers and quilts, and in the half-dark of the candles,

Barbara could see the gleam of her smile. Barbara snuffed out candles, climbed into bed. Under the covers, Renée reached for her hand.

"It doesn't matter here," Barbara said to her.

"Perhaps your love might save him," said Gracen, laughter again in her voice.

Barbara felt Renée shiver beside her. It was simpler where Renée came from. There was one faith, and those who worshipped differently were few and far between. "Those in the Church of England believe they have the true faith, and the Presbyterians believe they have the true faith—"

"Don't forget the Quakers. Here's why they're called Quakers." Gracen began to move her arms and legs and head erratically. The bed holding them shook.

"Gracen, you're not amusing."

"But I am."

"Only to yourself. There was a great and long war here about true faith. What we learned from it is that we have to live together in our differences, that perhaps there is more than one way to God."

Renée didn't say anything, just held Barbara's hand hard. When she and Gracen were both asleep, Barbara slipped out of the bed, dressed hurriedly in the dark, crept out of the bedchamber, praying she wouldn't meet Alice, who must still be up and wandering about somewhere.

BUT ALICE HADN'T gone to the maids of honor's bedchamber. Instead, she had tapped on Dorothy's door, then carefully opened it.

"My lord?" Dorothy walked forward, her long fair hair brushed and hanging thickly on her shoulders, her nightgown sheer and clinging, a Portuguese shawl vivid, bright against the nightdress. The fire in her fireplace crackled and spat. On a table between two chairs sat a tray with wine opened, a goblet waiting. The other goblet was in Dorothy's hand. At the sight of Alice, she stopped short, disappointment so clear on her face that Alice began an apology.

"Forgive me for disturbing. I only wanted to . . . Of course, it's so late."

"Shut the door behind you and come in. He isn't calling on me tonight, is he." Without waiting for an answer, Dorothy poured wine in the other goblet, held it out to Alice while refilling hers. She sat in one of the chairs and showed her feet to the fire. All of Dorothy was sweetly plump these days, and her legs were moon pale and shapely in their roundness. Of course Lord Knollys would desire her, thought Alice, seeing her, as she had since the night she'd discovered the affair, in a new light. On her feet dangled high-heeled, fashionable, backless, embroidered slippers, their toes ending in steep points, the latest style at the French court.

"Fetch my other slippers just there, will you, Alice? My feet are cold. And in the cabinet there is cake. Bring it out, will you? Are you hungry? You're thin as a stick. Eat some cake, put some meat on those bones. Men like women with flesh on their bones."

"So I'm told." Alice pulled off the beautiful slippers and placed wool booties on Dorothy's feet.

Dorothy took a chunk from the crumbling cake Alice had found and ate it, licking her fingers and reaching for more. "Once I was tiny . . . well, not tiny, but smaller."

"You were small when I left for France."

"When was that, Alice?"

"I left just as the court was abuzz with Caro's marriage."

"I thought she'd be dead by now." Dorothy gestured for more wine. Alice poured it.

"Caro?"

"The Countess of Knollys. She hangs on and on. Sometimes I think she'll never die. She's not left her bed in over a year. Here's to the Countess of Knollys, God forgive me, whose death I wish. I can't believe I wish it, but I do. The awful thing is, she was always kind to me." She shook her head, drank, then raised her glass to the fire. "Here's to me, countess next, someday." She drank again.

"He'll wed you?"

"Oh, yes. We've often talked of it."

"How long—" Alice stopped, not quite knowing how to ask. But Dorothy knew precisely what she meant.

"Have we been lovers? Six years."

"No."

Dorothy smiled tenderly, the tenderness edged with pride. "I cannot tell you how kind he's been, how much he's done for me. There's debt, you know. I was left in debt when Mr. Brownwell died. I still owe. Of course, some of it is my own fault. I like the cards, just as I like cake. He urges me not to gamble, but when he's not at Whitehall, and everyone is playing cards and laughing, I don't want to come here to my chambers, where my thoughts go round and round in circles like rats within the walls." She looked over to Alice, her big eyes very wide, very like a child's. "The thoughts frighten me."

"What do you think of, Brownie?"

"That I will be here forever, nursemaiding ungrateful wenches who half of them despise me—"

"We love you! I thought you loved us."

"You love me. Barbara loves me. Caro loved me, and Frances and Margaret and Simona before her. But this new lot. They're little more than baggages, all of them. I'll be fortunate if one of them gets from here without carrying a growing babe beneath her skirts, and who'll be blamed? Dorothy Brownwell, mother of the maids, for not guarding well enough. As if I could."

"Like Winifred." Alice whispered the name; she'd dreamed of the baby on the floor for years.

"Winifred." Dorothy shook her head. "Married now, settled in, her sins forgotten. I'll say this for the king and Her Majesty the queen: They bear no grudges. Thank God for it, or half this court could never show their faces in public again. Oh, sweet God in His heaven, I want to be safely wed, settled in, to fret no more when I gamble too much, to buy any gown I wish, to eat cake until my stays pop, to let go the thoughts that say he'll abandon me for another. Those are thoughts that torture me."

"You're young and handsome. There are many fish in the sea."

"The fish want to swim among the young maids or with the actresses and whores."

"I'll find a husband for you."

"You'd best find one first for yourself."

"I've found one."

"Oh?"

"Balmoral."

"The duke? You don't mean it!"

"Well, it's not settled yet."

"What does that mean, it isn't settled yet?" Dorothy mimicked her, then smiled at her mimicry. "I did that as well as Gracen. There's one who's grown up. I turn around, and she turns into a beauty. Balmoral. Tell me about Balmoral. He has one foot in the grave."

"Well, I'm determined to have him, and my father—"

Dorothy snorted.

"My father is going to help me do it."

"Your father hasn't anything on his mind but being king of the House of Commons."

"Brownie, when did the talk of divorcing the queen start?"

"Oh, don't bring up that dreadful subject. I've never seen her weep the way she did this last year—"

"This last year? Is that when it started?"

"Well, let's see. You were gone . . . Caro had married your Lord Colefax . . . Frances had the smallpox, and all the talk was that she'd lose her looks, and the king went to see her in spite of the sickness—I always thought he truly loved her. The war with the Dutch was over, disastrously. The House of Commons was howling to investigate the council and officials right and left . . . the queen had miscarried again . . . yes, there it was, not long after that there just grew these whispers. There was something in the House of Lords—some divorce case—and I really thought for a time he'd leave her, and then nothing happened. Everything became Madame's visit, what were we going to do to entertain Madame. Who is dead now. Oh, I want more wine. I don't want to think about these things. There's another bottle in the cabinet. Fetch it, Alice, that's a good girl."

"I will find you a husband, Brownie."

"I have a husband. He calls me wife, I call him husband." Dorothy began to weep.

Dorothy was in her weeping stage of drunkenness. Best to get her into bed, thought Alice. "There, there, yes, yes, you do. Lord Knollys is a fine man."

"He is, oh, he is. I love him so."

"So you do, I know that. Come along here, let's go to bed now."

"The sheets will be cold. If I had a proper husband, I wouldn't have to lie in a cold bed."

"Unless there was a quarrel."

Alice took fire tongs, tossed some coals in the warming pan, walked to the bed, at which Dorothy stood sniffling like a lost child, and carefully—the handle was long, it was easy to tip open the pan and then hot coals would fall out onto the sheet and start a fire—rubbed the bottom of pan against the sheets, up and down, up and down, all around.

"There, jump in, quickly now."

Alice emptied the coals into the fire, hung the pan by the mantel.

"I'm sick. The room is spinning," said Dorothy from the bed.

"Here, sit up."

Dorothy did as commanded. Alice fluffed pillows behind her, took the ones on the other side, placed them behind Dorothy's back. "Now, lie back carefully—carefully; you want to be sitting up as much as possible. There. Close your eyes . . . Better?"

"My head will hurt in the morning."

"So it will."

"Stay."

"I will, Brownie. I'll be right here. In fact, when you wake in the morning, I'll be on the other side of the bed."

"You'll sleep here? Good. Oh, I wish I hadn't eaten the cake. Lately, he complains that I eat too much. I know I do, but I can't seem to stop."

"Never mind it. I'm going to find you a husband who will spoon-feed you himself."

"He'd be jealous."

"Indeed he would. He thinks he has you all to himself. Well, we'll show him a thing or two."

"I want no other."

"Hush now, just hush, my dear, dear Brownie. What would we do without our dear, dear, Brownie. . . ."

It was a kind of lullaby she sang, the way she imagined her mother might have sung to her. Dorothy closed her eyes. There was a hiccup, and she began to snore. Alice sighed. She'd forgotten that Dorothy snored.

She went back to the fire, moved the fire screen, poked at the burning wood there, added another piece, moved the chair closer, and considered whether she'd open the bottle of wine for herself. There was an ache between her eyes, and her mouth felt dry, and if she drank more, she would be sick. So she'd just sit awhile with her thoughts, which were sad. What was that verse, when she'd been a child, she'd thought as a child, spoke as a child, understood as a child, but now she saw more clearly? She could bear that, seeing more clearly.

Outside the window, a pale sun was rising. It was sad, what men and women did to themselves, to one another, but, yes, she could bear that.

Chapter 20

While Alice dozed in a chair in Dorothy's chamber, most of the palace slept.

But not everyone. At just past dawn, Richard stepped out from the Life Guard house and looked around. No one on the street in either direction. It was too early in the morning for any servants to be up yet, but soon this part of the palace would be bustling. "All clear," he called.

Barbara stepped from an alcove and ran across Whitehall Street and through a door in Holbein Gate that would take her into the royal quarters of Whitehall Palace again. Richard grinned at his cousin, who was watching Barbara run. Then he shivered; the morning was cold, more than cold. Winter was so close, you could feel her frosty breath. "So you're her morning prayers now, are you?"

"She's mine, Richard. I think I will die if she doesn't marry me."

"She'll marry you."

"Not with Verney back."

"You forget the good book, John. 'There be three things which are too wonderful for me, yea, four which I know not: the way of an eagle in the air; the way of a serpent upon a rock; the way of a ship in the midst of the sea; and the way of a man with a maid.' Come, I'll buy you a cup of milk. The milkmaids should be done with their milking."

They walked through the alley by the tilt yard, out into St. James's Park. Milkmaids herded their cows in from the little hamlets of Chelsea and Marylebone. Ducks still hid their heads under one wing in the long landscape canal. None of the pelicans or peacocks were around. Doubtless they were nestled in some shrubbery from the chill. Richard handed a milkmaid a coin, and she quickly dipped two metal cups into her full milk pail. John was in among the young trees that shaded Pall Mall Alley. King Charles had planted these ten years ago when he was restored to the throne. Richard clinked his cup against John's. "To true love."

John sipped the milk, glanced at his cousin as if he wanted to say something. Richard saw it but said nothing.

"Barbara says the king is eyeing Mademoiselle de Keroualle," said John at last.

"He can eye all he wishes. I won't begrudge her the pleasure of the king's admiration."

"You trust him?"

"I trust her. She's beautiful. Why shouldn't the world notice?"

"How stalwart you are. I, on the other hand, cannot sleep for fear Barbara should suddenly know how unworthy I am of her. I think my heart will break."

"She's of age to marry as she wills. You have only to convince her of it. Have you a letter for me?" Richard delivered John's daily letters to Barbara and hers back to him. "Ah, but you've been telling her in person what you'd write in a letter, haven't you?"

"We'll meet for dinner at the Swan, and I'll give it to you then."

"You'll write a love letter when you should do accounts? For shame. No wonder the Commons investigates the doing of the war."

"Dinner at the Swan, Richard. I'm off."

Richard tossed the cups back to the milkmaid and went to the royal mews to check upon his horse. There was to be a drill upon the parade ground today, thank God. He could feel restlessness within himself. Things were moving too slowly. Maybe his brother-in-law, Lord Cranbourne, was right; maybe he should give up his commission with the army and ask for a place in the navy. Since the Dutch wars, it seemed every penny went to victual or to build ships. King

Louis had commissioned thirty-seven cavalry regiments five years ago. His army was huge. It had been Richard's intention to join the French army and court Renée from there, but then Renée had surprised him and ended up on this side of the Channel. It couldn't be that the rest of wars would be fought on the sea, could it? Patience, boy, Balmoral said, his watery eyes narrowing. There's war coming, but that's between you and me and the fence post. He'd say no more than that. War. Richard had two Dutch wars under his belt and Tangier. A man was never more alive than in the midst of a battle, where death picked and chose with a randomness that changed you forever, that made every sense in your body sharpen to crisp awareness of all that was life, all you would never do again if you died in the next moment. His horse whinnied at the sight of him, and he gave the handsome beast pieces of Indian corn and park grass out of his pocket. He'd brush him down and braid his mane and tail with ribbon. And after drill today, he'd call upon the Duke of Balmoral, see if there were any further errands in France that needed doing.

THE SUN OF this day rose higher, warming some of the chill. It was going to be a beautiful October day, but not everywhere, not in the queen's quarters.

"Don't weep, ma'am, please don't weep," begged Alice.

But Queen Catherine kept the note clutched to her breast and paid no mind. The Duchess of Richmond, the lady of the bedchamber on duty, knelt on the other side of Alice, adding her own pleading to Alice's. Barbara and Dorothy stood guard at the bedchamber door to make certain no one entered and saw the queen in this kind of distress. The queen put her face in her hands and, in doing so, dropped the note. Alice picked it up.

"Three sights to be seen," were the words written on the paper, "Dunkirk, Tangier, and a barren queen." The sneer was an old one, part of a street ballad that pilloried the king's most faithful councillor, a man who was one of the architects of the king's return but was now in exile. It touched on what were considered the man's failures, the sale of Dunkirk to the French; Tangier, which had come as Queen

Catherine's dower but had to be defended continually from the infidel Moors; and, of course, Her Majesty's failure to carry a child to term.

"Bring me that bowl of water," said Frances, the Duchess of Richmond. Frances dipped the queen's hands in the water. The shock made the queen catch her breath. Frances dipped her own hands in, put them to the queen's face again and again, until the queen stopped her and slumped back in her chair. The sobs had hushed, but in her face was a wild sorrow. "Send for Father Huddleston," she whispered.

Nerves jangling, Alice stepped into the withdrawing room, where the rest of the maids of honor were waiting, as well as Her Majesty's pages and the other ladies who attended Queen Catherine. They were past time to go to morning mass. It wasn't like the queen to be late. Whom to trust here? she thought. Few. That knowledge was clear and stark, as real as the awful note. Any one of the older women in the chamber could have consented to sneak it into the queen's bedchamber, put it in a place where it could not be overlooked. And there was another note, the letter in her pocket. Could they be connected? "Edward"—she kept her voice calm—"will you go for Father Huddleston?"

"Whatever is the matter?" It was the Countess of Suffolk, the highest ranking of the ladies of the bedchamber, in charge of the queen's wardrobe and privy purse. "Is she ill? Let me in at once."

"She's asked that no one else attend her. There's a fever."

Lady Suffolk's imperious impatience changed. Fevers were dreaded. They might be harbingers of plague or smallpox. It was only four years since plague had decimated London. It had killed Barbara's father. Only two years or so since smallpox had embraced the court beauty.

"Could it be her flux? Has she her flux?" asked another untrustworthy hag of the bedchamber, Lady Falmouth.

"It wouldn't matter," said Lady Suffolk. "The king has not been fishing in this pond."

At that moment, Alice hated these women with all her heart. They had no mercy.

"May I come in?" It was Renée. She asked quietly, humbly, with dignity.

"I said there's a fever."

"I mind it not."

"No."

Lady Suffolk eyed Alice disdainfully. If it hadn't been that there was fever, she'd have marched right past her and seen precisely for herself. The bright spot in it was that this cheeky young woman might be stricken with it herself, might even die. Lady Suffolk smiled. High-backed, difficult Alice Verney dead in her prime before she was even married. And the other piece in this was that the queen might sicken enough to die—one never knew. Then they could all of them wash their hands of a bad bargain and begin again. She shook out her skirts with satisfaction and left the antechamber to carry the gossip that Queen Catherine was sick with a fever.

In the bedchamber, Barbara and the queen knelt together at her prayer stand, murmuring, their fingers touching beautiful silver and gold—and, for the queen, diamond—rosaries.

"Where's the note?" Alice whispered to Frances, the Duchess of Richmond.

Frances took it from a pocket. "She's asked that no one see it."

"Keep it safe," said Alice.

"Who would be so cruel?" whispered Dorothy.

"Anyone outside this chamber," answered Alice. "I don't think we should speak of this to anyone just yet. Falmouth and Suffolk are like cats out there waiting for birds with broken wings."

She pulled Frances to a corner by the fire, where they might talk and not be heard. "Is it true the king isn't visiting Her Majesty in the bedchamber anymore?"

Frances nodded.

"How long?"

"Months. Since the spring." Frances looked away. Smallpox had lightly kissed her profile, not killing her, as it did many, or disfiguring her so that she must wear a mask for the rest of her life, as it did others, but leaving its telltale marks in a broadening of her features, so that her once sharp beauty was blunted.

Father Huddleston interrupted them. The door to the withdrawing chamber behind him closed, but not before Alice saw curious faces clustered at the door, peeking in to see what was to be seen. The priest went at once to Queen Catherine. Her face, which looked up from its prayers, was streaked with tears, ravaged by them, actually. He led Queen Catherine up the stairs to her closet, to her most private space, a small chamber filled with handsome, gilded furniture, paintings, relics, crosses, things she loved, where no one might enter, where her life was finally and most completely private.

Barbara sighed; something in Alice exploded. "We must talk."

Leading her by the hand, Alice slipped out a door so intricately made, so joined to the wall, that at first glance, or even second, no one would know there was a door there. They hurried down a back passage. Doors were open here and there, and one of them opened to the queen's oratory, her little chapel where she might worship privately. A woman was kneeling in prayer there, and she raised a startled white face as Alice and Barbara ran by. It was Renée.

"Alice!" Renée rushed into the passage, caught up with Alice and Barbara. "The queen. How is the queen?"

"Well enough."

But Barbara took pity. "She's a little better. I think her fever will pass."

"If there is anything I can do—"

"You can leave us alone. We have important business." The words were sharper than Alice meant, but there they were, out of her mouth, too late to call them back, and anyway, it was none of Renée's concern.

Renée took a step back. "Yes, of course. If there is anything I can do—"

But they were rushing on, leaving her alone.

"Your prayers," Barbara said, tossing the words over her shoulder.

There were few people in the Matted Gallery. On the top floor of the palace, it was the longest of the galleries, full of statues and paintings that King Charles had meticulously acquired, attempting to restore at least a portion of what had been his father's collection. Prince Rupert and the Duke of York had lodgings at its farthest end. Alice stood a moment at the roaring fire, as if to gather her wits.

Barbara put her hands to her chest. "My heart is beating so, I think it will fall from my chest. Oh, Alice, who would do such a thing to the queen—" She stopped, her words dying in her throat, seeing the expression on Alice's face.

"You knew of the bill in the Lords about divorce, of all the gossip and talk before Madame came, and yet you wrote me nothing? Nothing! Where was your mind? Where was your care for her? You promised me you'd write everything of importance! Do you not remember? We swore it to each other. I trusted you, and you failed me!"

"I didn't know—"

"The whole court was singing it, that the king should put her aside. You didn't know"—Alice stepped forward so that her face was inches from Barbara's—"because you were caught in your silly romance, thinking of nothing but John Sidney! I could slap you witless, Barbara. This note is no game! Someone is trying to hurt the queen, truly hurt her, have her cast off and sent away, have her divorced and abandoned, perhaps have her killed!"

"Killed? What are you talking about?" Tears were rolling down Barbara's face. "Please, Alice. You're too close. Don't stand so close."

Alice stepped back. "Tell me everything. Everything you remember."

"I don't remember anything!"

"You don't remember the queen crying? You don't remember gossip, rumors, talk of divorce?"

Barbara wiped at her face, but her tears continued. "Yes, of course I do."

"When did they begin?"

"I'm not certain. Perhaps after the miscarriage—"

"Tell me of that."

"Her little fox jumped on the bed, startling her, and she cried out, and we started to laugh, only she clutched at herself and began to say, 'Oh, no,' over and over. She was so happy, so sure this one would . . . Her face, Alice, I've never seen such sorrow. And no one but those who truly loved her came to comfort. Even the king was cold this time—"

"He was cold? Tell me precisely what those words imply."

"He didn't call to see how she did. She lay in bed for three days, and there was not a note from him. Nothing. Prince Rupert came, the Duke of York, the Duke of Monmouth, all called on her, but he didn't. She was beside herself with fret and worry. There was nothing we could say to calm her."

"So I would imagine. Were you with her when she called upon His Majesty?"

"How do you know she called upon him?"

"She would, wouldn't she? Go to him if he did not come to her, even if she had to crawl?"

"No, I wasn't."

"But what did you hear?"

"It was so long ago, Alice, two years now—"

"Damn it, Ra, think! There used to be plenty of wit in you. Has John Sidney taken it all?"

"Don't curse at me."

"Don't be foolish, then."

There was silence. Barbara sat in a chair by the fire and leaned her head back, eyes closed, tears steadily seeping down. Alice didn't move, didn't change the steadiness of her gaze.

Finally Barbara spoke. "We were at peace—"

"Of course we were. Otherwise I could not have gone to Madame's court."

"Please don't interrupt me. We were at peace with France. It seems that he received her graciously—"

"Who said so?"

"I don't remember now, Alice. I'm told he said something to the effect that his heart was too moved by the loss to visit her. At any rate, I remember she was fretted for his sake, for his sorrow. That was her concern. Oh, yes—"

"What?"

"The Duchess of Richmond was ill then, too, and the court had just learned she had smallpox, and so the king was busy with that, with his worry for her, and everyone was talking of his bravery and his regard there. And there was the Duke of York's conversion—"

Barbara stopped, clapped her hands over her mouth, but it was too late to call back the words.

"Conversion?"

"I shouldn't have told you. You must keep this a secret!"

"You wrote me nothing of this?"

"Alice, if you weren't so angry at this moment, and I so desperate to please you, I wouldn't even be speaking of it. It is a secret. You must promise me, you must swear not to speak of it. You know how certain members of the privy council are, how your father is, not allowing even the slightest indulgence to us."

"How do you know of it?"

"We know one another." It was a simple statement.

"You of the true faith?" The question was sardonic.

Barbara lifted her chin. For the first time, there was an answering hardness in her face. "I would die for my faith, Alice. Do not mock it."

"Tell me everything."

"Well, there was that bill in the Lords, and there began to be talk of divorce. The queen told us not to worry, that they could not undo the hand of God, and so we didn't. The Duke of York himself defended her in the Lords. He wouldn't do so without the king's permission. That's what we all felt. That's what she felt. And then there was his infatuation with Moll Davis, and then shortly after, Nell Gwynn had his eye."

"You should have written it all to me."

"I wrote you of Nell Gwynn. They can't put the queen aside. It's the law of the land and the law of God."

"You are a ninny, Barbara. They can do anything they please. They tore this country apart for God, your God, their God. They destroyed lands, drew and quartered men and women for God—your God, their God. They made rules that no one might dance or play cards. Then they made rules we might. Which was God's will? Does He really care whether we dance or not? Do you think they cannot make a rule to rid themselves of a queen if they so desire?"

Barbara was crying again. "It seemed as if it had gone away. I didn't think—"

"No, you didn't." And then Alice was walking away, down the long gallery. There was only the sound of her heels clicking against the polished inlaid wood of the floor for a long time, and then there was nothing but the sound of the fire's crackle.

Barbara put her face in her hands and wept.

After a time, someone touched her arm. Gracen knelt down so that her face was near her friend's. Barbara's eyes were red, her face swollen.

"Ra, my precious Ra, what is it?"

"I thought you might be Alice. Foolish me."

"Is it the queen?"

Barbara didn't answer.

"Is she terribly ill? Whitehall is buzzing with rumor. Some say she's with child. Some say she has the plague."

"She isn't—she's not very ill. And there is no child."

"Why do you cry, dear friend?"

"Alice is angry with me."

"Why?"

"I failed her."

"I don't like her when she's angry."

"She's right to be angry. I'm not as clever as she. I don't see things the way she does."

"Ra, I can imagine little that you would do to make someone angry. Are you certain it isn't just Alice being the way she can be?"

"I don't know. Let's not speak of it."

Gracen sat on the edge of the chair in which Barbara sat, took her friend's hand in hers, began to rub it. "Shall I be mean to her for you?" The question was light. The steady gray gaze was not.

Barbara shuddered. "I couldn't bear it if there was more quarreling. She'd be even angrier."

"She isn't right about everything, Ra, she just thinks she is. I think she's worse since she came back from France. More imperious. Pooh, is what I say." Gracen snapped her fingers in dismissal of Alice.

"She says it's because of John."

"What?"

"She says I was too busy flirting, making a fool of myself, she implied."

"She hates it that you love him as you do. She'll never love anyone that way. She hasn't enough heart."

"Don't say that."

"Why? Isn't it true?"

Barbara was silent. After a time, she said, "She wants what is best for us, for her friends, that is all. John hasn't an estate, nor have I. I can see the wisdom in her fret for that."

"Is it best that you abandon John?"

"I couldn't, not now."

"Then marry and be damned to Alice."

"I'm afraid to marry."

"Why? Because of what happens between a man and a woman? I'm told it's very pleasing." Gracen smiled to herself. Any man passing at that moment would have been intrigued.

"It's silly."

"Tell me."

Barbara was silent.

"Does Alice know?"

Barbara didn't answer.

"She does. You and she and Caro were always like sisters. Sisters who had no secrets from one another. I used to hate you for it and yet want to be your sister, too." She leaned her face against Barbara's shoulder, wrapped slim, long arms around her. "Her going to France gave me a chance to grow in your regard. I love you, Ra. You are my sister. Don't allow Alice so much. Is she more than your God?"

"Of course not."

"Then ask Him what He thinks of John Sidney."

Barbara laughed. "He loves him."

"Then so may you." Gracen reached up to kiss her lingeringly on the cheek. "You are the loveliest person I ever knew." She leaned her head back against Barbara's shoulder, and they sat for a long time in silence, arms wrapped around each other, Barbara shivering and sighing once in a while, until the logs in the fire broke apart and sent great sparks up the chimney.

Chapter 21

That very afternoon, they played cards in the queen's withdrawing chamber. Queen Catherine remained in her closet, asking for no attendants. She'd sent her regrets to the king, her assurances that she had only a slight headache, that he was to come to her chambers whenever he wished, enjoy himself, which meant he could enter her chambers and flirt with Renée. He took her at her word.

He was in a high-spirited, jaunty mood this afternoon, laughing when his spaniels chased the queen's little fox and overset a canary cage, amusing the maids of honor by telling their fortunes. At Alice's and Renée's turns, King Charles scooped up cards and reshuffled them. They moved like magic between his hands.

"I kept myself from going mad once by playing cards with the subjects of my kingdom. A tavern keeper had the best skill. Cromwell's soldiers were about, searching for me, and playing cards passed many a long hour while I waited until it was safe to move on." He talked to them as if he were a page at court, as artlessly as a boy. It was quite flattering.

"When was this?" asked Alice.

"After the battle of Worchester. I was twenty, as tall as I am now but gawky, awkward, running into things." He spoke directly to Renée, as if he wanted her to envision the awkward lad he'd been.

But he hadn't been awkward ever, only large. "I traveled for days in disguise as a servant, wore shoes that were too small, had my cavalier's lovelocks shorn most roughly, I do tell you, slept in priests' hiding holes. Many people risked their lives for me, many of them Catholics, which my archbishops don't like me to remember." He smiled. "Once I hid in a tree while Cromwell's soldiers searched for me. An acorn had only to drop for them to look up and see me. I was to sail to France, you see, to raise armies with which to return and help my father. But first I had to cross the countryside. We reached the coast, but it was the very devil to hire a boat—once we had it hired, the captain's wife persuaded him not to endanger himself—and so I was some days at a tavern, hiding in the attic, soldiers all about the town, looking for me, while those with me worked to convince the captain otherwise. The tavern keeper recognized me. My height, I would imagine, my dark hair, not to mention this." He passed a hand over his long face. "Even though there was a price on my head, my weight in gold, he said not a word, only quietly kissed my hand when it was time to depart and asked God to watch over me. It was the last true loyalty I was to see for many a year. But I digress. I was to tell fortunes, wasn't I?" Swiftly, he dealt cards before Renée and Alice, then turned them over.

"You shall be mistress of the robes someday," he said to Alice, tapping a finger on an ace and a queen nearby. He turned over a card in front of Renée. It was the king of spades. He said nothing, turned over another card quickly. It was the queen of hearts. He laughed, his whole face lighting up. "Your palm, mademoiselle," he commanded.

Renée held out a hand. He stared into her palm, then ran his finger lightly down a line. "You'll be mistress, too. It's in the cards and in your hand."

He leaned forward and quickly, boyishly, with just a hint of a beguiling and unkingly shyness, kissed Renée's palm. "Not of the robes, however. Unless you wish it. Then I'll snatch it from Verney in a moment."

Various courtiers in the chamber looked at one another, having noted every gesture he made.

Renée pulled her hand away. "With your permission, sir." She stood, curtsied, walked out of the chamber.

King Charles gathered up the cards, shuffled them slowly, his face rueful. "I can read cards. It's like touching for the king's evil, a second sight that Jemmy calls devilish. You will be mistress of the robes someday." He pulled the king of spades from the deck with a deft movement of his fingers. "That is me. When my father was alive, it was my father, and I was the jack. But now I am king. So, Verney, does she hate me? My portraits show an ugly fellow, but I am told I have some charm."

"I—That is . . ."

"You dismay me. You are never at a loss for words. And yet you sit before me like a cow poleaxed before butchering."

"Lovely comparison, sire."

"That's more like it. I'll ask again. Does she dislike me?" Cards tripped from one hand to the other, lightning fast. Alice tried to forestall him.

"What did the cards tell you, Your Majesty?"

"You're playing for time, Verney. Answer me."

"I have no answer."

"Does she talk of me?"

"No."

He made a sound, gathered up the cards, and then spread out a few before him. He tapped a jack. "That's Buckingham." He tapped the queen of spades. "That's Her Majesty. Interesting they should show up together. Have I brought her all this way for naught?" It was as if he were talking to himself. He turned over another card, then another. Then he looked directly at Alice. She felt pinned by the acute intelligence of his stare. "What's a king to do, Verney?"

"Play the game slow, sir." It was all she could think to say.

"I thought I was. Slower still? I thought there was an understanding of my interest, that her journey here was an acquiescence to hear my suit. Have I been misled?"

"I don't know. I knew little or nothing—perhaps she, too—" The words came jerking out, making no sense, as it occurred to her how much she'd been duped, and by whom.

"Ah well, so little in life is straightforward, I've found, and people do prefer to lie to kings. It makes their life easier, truth being a disordered bitch. Speaking of which—" He whistled. "Come along, girls."

Two ladies-in-waiting stopped their talk and glanced in his direction.

He smiled at them. "I refer to my dogs, of course." He stood, as did the spaniels lying at his feet and around his chair. Alice hurried to stand, too, then dropped into a curtsy. Courtiers and spaniels followed him from the chamber.

Alice sat down the moment his back was turned. The little fox pawed and whined from behind the door that hid her, and Edward let her in. She ran to Alice and curled herself on her feet. My father, thought Alice. Up to his neck in this and telling me nothing. I will flay him alive. And then something else occurred to her. If Richard and Renée were not to marry . . . She shivered, and the queen's little fox jumped up from her feet and ran to Edward, who was playing dice in a corner with another of the pages. She went to stare at herself in a pier glass. Her curls were thick and glossy, dark, just like her eyes. But she was no beauty. Richard could never prefer her in place of Renée. . . .

And it didn't matter anyway.

She would have Balmoral, no one else.

Her father always took the easier route, even if it meant betraying her. Why should her eyes fill with tears for that old truth? Because she was tired. Because she was running now on court air. Because Cleveland stalked her, and the queen had been treated treacherously, and she'd quarreled with Barbara.

This day was not done. There was a letter in her pocket that must be dealt with. And the queen's note spoken of—but only to he whom she trusted. She thought again of Richard. Her mouth trembled. Tired, that's all. Tiredness made things seem more important than they were. She couldn't appear before Balmoral in hysterics, and they were there, crouched all low and tensed in her chest, in her throat. Made a fool of by her own father. It wasn't the first time, was it? She'd find a napping place, a hidden corner in this labyrinth of a palace she called home, and nap. Then she'd go to Balmoral.

"HE'S IN HIS closet with someone," Edward whispered. "But I gave your coins to his majordomo, and he says he'll make certain you have an interview."

Alice wore a mask and a short cloak that came only to her shoulders; the hood framed her face and hid her hair. Rested now, her hysteria quieted, she looked mysterious and fashionable. She put a coin in Edward's hand, and true to form, he took it.

"Shall I wait for you?" he asked. He had good instincts and knew something was brewing. She shook her head. He pointed to a man adding wood to the fire in this antechamber, where several others besides Alice were waiting. It was Riggs, the servant from His Grace's country estate. "I gave him the coin. He's the one who will inform the duke that you are waiting."

"Thank you, Edward."

Balmoral was standing at long windows that looked out onto St. James's Park when Riggs ushered Alice inside. Every inch of the wall in this chamber was filled with paintings by Verrio or Holbein or Titian. Interspersed among them were ceremonial swords in ornate scabbards. Jade figurines stood atop cabinets. There was an elaborate and huge chimneypiece that took an entire wall, a suit of armor in a corner, such as a warrior of another century might have worn, but strange to Alice's eyes, its helmet oddly formed, with horns coming out of it like a devil, the color of the armor a dull red, and the armor itself rounded, skirted, floating out at the shoulders. Balmoral gestured toward one high-backed stiff armchair, then sat in the other. She pushed back the hood, untied the mask.

He smiled at her. "Do you fear for your reputation?"

"I'd be honored to have my name linked with yours." He pursed his lips, and Alice hurried on. "I wanted no one to know that I was visiting you. I come on a matter of great importance." She handed him the letter.

Once it was read, he carefully refolded it, leaned back, closing his eyes, his hands together before his face.

"Henri Ange. Henry Angel. Skilled in the use of poison. Father French, mother Italian. Known to have apprenticed in Rome under Michaelanglo Exili, a poisoner of first rank. Went with Exili to the court of the queen of Sweden for a time." He opened his eyes. "Left the household of the Chevalier de Lorraine to join the household of Prince Philippe of France. Left that household at the death of Princesse Henriette, went to stay with our same Exili, who it seems now lives in Paris. Seen out and about in Paris, but not exclusively in the company of Monsieur's men. If he paid a call upon the Duke of Buckingham, or was summoned, there is no one who has spoken of it other than your Beuvron, who will not speak of it again, no matter the coins offered him. As you can see, I have taken your confidences to me much to heart. Why do you think this Ange has come to England?"

"To kill the queen. It's the easiest way, isn't it? It makes it unnecessary for you or the council to instigate a divorce and wrestle with the consciences of Parliament and the nation, perhaps provoke another war."

"There would not be a war over her death." Balmoral spoke without emotion.

His certainty was disturbing. "Yesterday the queen received a note. It said, 'Three sights to be seen—' "

" 'Dunkirk, Tangier, and a barren queen,' " finished Balmoral.

"She was—" Alice stopped. What word described touching a wound that did not heal, tearing it open afresh?

"I can imagine."

"No, Your Grace, you cannot. It is not a face she shows anyone. There is to be a gathering tomorrow, Father Huddleston and Lord Knollys, others, who take her hurt to heart. I beg that you meet with them and listen to their concerns, perhaps advise them. I am very afraid for her."

"I've put tasters in place in the royal households."

"He doesn't have to poison the food to kill her. The water Princesse Henriette drank wasn't poisoned. Will you be able to follow the path of every fork, every plate? There was a tale in France of someone poisoning gloves. Can you guard the queen's gloves, her combs, her shawls? I saw the princess die of his poisoning, and it was neither pretty nor short."

"Has His Majesty been informed?"

"No. We've sworn ourselves to silence, fearing to stir up talk of divorce again, but I bring it directly to you." She looked at his suddenly inscrutable face, tried to read it. "Unless you, like others, wish the queen gone. I've never asked it of you." She felt tired suddenly. If Balmoral were against the queen, what would she do?

"I think this kingdom needs an heir from the king's loins. I think that which God has joined together should not be sundered. A conundrum, is it not? Perhaps it isn't the queen who is to be the victim. Have you thought of that, Mistress Verney?"

"Who else would it be?"

"His Majesty."

"But why?"

"Oh, some men must always dabble in intrigue. If he died, in the chaos others might rise as regents or advisers or favorites. I must ask if you've shown this note from Beuvron to anyone else."

She looked down at her hands, didn't answer.

He took the gesture to mean no. "You do me great honor in your trust of me; you have from the beginning. I saw you looking at that armor in the corner. It is my proudest possession, from a samurai, which is what they call a warrior from the land of Nippon, on the other side of the world. Their honor is their most sacred attribute. They kill themselves if it is soiled. I find the thought of such a place comforting. If I weren't so old, I'd go there, learn to be a samurai. I'd like to see with my own eyes a place where a man kills himself because his honor is soiled. We must see you married so that we may advance you to a place of honor in the royal household. You are a loyal servant to Her Majesty. Such is price above pearls. There is a suitor for your hand, I'm told."

"He won't consider me."

"Nonsense. He is eager to have you as his bride."

"No, Your Grace, he isn't."

There was a long moment in which neither spoke. A clock in the chamber—King Charles was enamored of clocks, gave them as presents—began to strike the hour of nine of the night. At the ninth stroke, Alice said, "There is one more thing."

Balmoral waited.

"The Duchess of Cleveland likes me not. She's told me she is going to say evil things of me to you because she knows my—that your respect for me is something I hold close to my heart. I beg you won't listen to her, or if you do, you allow me to defend myself against what she might say. I could not bear it if you came to dislike me."

"That would be quite impossible, my dear."

Alice retied the mask about her face, pulled up the hood of her short cloak, took the letter and refolded it, waited at the door for Balmoral to open it for her. He stood beside her; his hand was on the crystal knob, but he did not turn it. "I'm very old." It was quietly said.

"So am I."

He took her hand, gazed down at it before raising it to his lips for the lightest of kisses.

Door shut, Balmoral remained standing where he was for a time. Foolish to be stirred even in the slightest. He shivered. He was always cold, yet another reminder of his age. Opening the door again, he made a signal that told Riggs he would see no one else this night, drew a huge, fur-lined cloak about his shoulders, stirred the fire, added a log, sat down to watch it burn.

When winter began to breathe its icy arrival, every old battle scar he had ached. And there were a number of them, from the Roundheads, from the Irish, from the Scots, from the cavaliers. He'd fought on all sides in his lifetime, no shame to it. The times had been too treacherous for shame. And it had ended with him here, a duke and captain general of His Majesty's army, such as it was.

Such as it was. He grimaced at the fire. The words were those of Lieutenant Saylor, his adroit young spy. One of the letters copied from France hinted at an agreement of some kind. And King Charles wrote about a cipher. Why give his sister a cipher unless she handled secrets? What had the king promised Louis? Whatever it was, he did not share it with his ministers. Was there some colony he gave? Some concession of trade? Something about the succession? He was pleased with Saylor's work. He'd put him to finding this Henri Ange. And once found, what then? He ran his hand along the fur of his cloak as he ran his mind over the king's closest ministers. Was there a decent man among them? Was one of them trustworthy?

Not to his mind. The last trustworthy adviser to the king had been the Earl of Clarendon, as much an architect of the Restoration as he himself was. And where was Clarendon now? Banished. Living in the Dutch Republic, writing his memoirs. Oh, this flirtation with poison had the smell of Buckingham, old Georgie Porgie, that confounded, treacherous, lecherous, lightning wit of court. He'd like to see Buckingham fall. What pleasure there would be in that. A last service he could do this kingdom. Did the fall include Buckingham's minion Sir Thomas Verney? He had regard for Alice, always had. She had a quick mind and the wiliness of a born courtier. And lovely, lovely dark eyes. Ambitious little climber, said the Duchess of Cleveland. After you. Is it not too amusing, Your Grace? Thinking she can gather you in her coils, said Cleveland. Exactly what she seemed to be doing.

ALICE CROSSED WHITEHALL Street, stepped into the Life Guard building, and walked down a hall until she stood before a door. She could hear music from inside the chamber. Richard must be playing his guitar. She put her ear to the door. He was singing. She leaned against the door, her eyes closed so that she might hear better. After a time, she straightened her shoulders, knocked decisively. He stood framed in the doorway, holding up a sealed letter, which she took from him.

"Are you not engaged to go to His Grace's?" she asked.

"Later. For Monmouth, it's early yet."

"You don't enjoy it?"

He shrugged. "What adventure are you upon, masked like that?"

"No adventure." Words were in her throat. She wanted to tell him about the letter, the note to the queen, her fears about Renée. But she was silent.

He cocked his head to one side, his expression quizzical. She took a step backward, turned with a light step, the letter for Renée clasped to her breast.

"Verney."

She faced him again.

"I think we ought to call each other by our Christian names. Have I your permission to call you Alice?"

"Yes."

Richard watched her walk away. She moved with an instinctive grace. Her mouth was lovely. The mask accentuated it. Had she a secret sweetheart? Who knew with Alice? He shook his head and closed the door.

In the maids of honor's apartments, Renée sat on the floor, skirts bunched around her, staring into the fire. A note had come to her that the French ambassador would be calling. He would ask how she did, if she had need of anything, and then he would come to what he really called upon her for. What news have you for me? Anything, no matter how small, he wished to hear. She was spy to this court. He was impatient with her, not understanding why she dallied when the king's interest was so pointed. And there was a note from Lady Arlington, a lady-in-waiting to the queen, wife of one of the king's privy council members. She wished to call upon her. The story of the king's kiss on her palm was all over the court, doubtless in a letter on its way to King Louis at this very moment. What would Richard say when he heard of it? But perhaps no one would be foolish enough to tell him. The great ladies came to flatter, to be on her good side now that they saw for certain which way the grass grew. Renée smiled with the pleasure of knowing that a little nobody, one Renée de Keroualle, had caught the attention of a someone so important. She looked down at her hand, turned the palm over, starting at the place the king's lips had brushed.

She was not unmoved by his kiss or his clear desire. What to do with that? What to do with anything?

In the queen's bedchamber there was a low, ornately gilded railing that separated the bed from the rest of the chamber, the way a railing separated the altar from the rest of the church. One had to have express permission from the queen to step inside. This night, the queen's old nurse dozed on a cot just inside it. The queen had needed her presence—the vicious note had struck hard, struck well. The curtains around the bed were pulled shut.

Alice tiptoed inside the bedchamber to Barbara, who was sleeping as best she could, huddled in a chair some distance from the queen's bed. Barbara started awake at the touch of her hand. Alice knelt down, thinking about Richard. Had she indeed stood before a man who was not run by pleasure? An amazing thing. "I lost my temper today, Ra. Say you forgive me."

Barbara was silent. Alice couldn't read her expression, but from another armchair, legs extended themselves out, and the face of Gracen appeared over the back of the top of the chair.

"I'm so, so sorry," Alice repeated. "I don't know what got into me."

"Never mind it," Barbara said.

Chapter 22

All Hallows' Eve

A day later, Alice swept into her father's drawing room before his new footman could announce her. She drew up short at the sight of Louisa Saylor and her sister, Lady Cranbourne, sitting, very much at their ease, with her father. The sight of the sisters took her cold anger and heated it to fury.

"Mademoiselle Verney," said Lady Cranbourne, "what a pleasure to see you. I was just remarking to your father that we don't see enough of you."

"Try calling upon Queen Catherine once in a blue moon. You'll find me there, on duty."

The smile on the two sisters' faces stopped looking quite so genuine.

"You haven't taken off your cloak, poppet," said Sir Thomas. "Whatever is the matter with that footman of mine? Perryman!" He bellowed the name, and Alice was pleased to see Louisa repress a wince.

"Perryman!"

"I did not wish to give him my cloak. Do we speak alone, Father, or do I enlighten your guests as to precisely the kinds of plots you make?"

Lady Cranbourne stood. "It's time Louisa and I took our leave."

Alice waited coldly while the Saylor sisters said good-bye to her father. She noted how he lingered over both the shapely hands held out to him, how he fussed over the gathering of their cloaks, how he had to help Louisa Saylor tie hers under the neck, how Louisa smiled up at him. Strumpet. She said not a word to the sweeter-than-island-sugar good-byes the sisters gave to her.

Once they were out the door, ushered away by her father's treasure, young Perryman, the pleasantness on her father's face dissolved. Brows drawn together, he advanced on her. She knew this trick. Pumping himself full of hot air so that he could blast away whatever was blown—rightly or wrongly—in his direction. She wasn't having a bit of it.

"When did I become a procuress?"

The question stopped him. Alice watched him gather his wits together.

"How dare you do this to me? Were you ever going to tell me?"

"Of course I was."

"You made a fool of me!"

"Never. You're chilled through, that's what it is. I'm sending for spiced ale, and you're to drink it, my girl, whether you have a mind to or not. Perryman! Perryman, some ale for the pair of us. Now then, give me your cloak, sit down a moment, and let's discuss this reasonably. That's my poppet."

"I'm not your poppet, Father. I'm someone you use the way you'd use the least servant in the house."

"I'm a worthless devil, Alice, who ought to be horsewhipped for the way I've handled things. How is Mademoiselle de Keroualle?"

"Distraught."

He considered this, and Alice watched him do it. Had he a single decent moral? Was he nothing but shifting sand? Richard was in her mind. And Balmoral. Honorable men.

"She should have said something before all my expense and bother."

"Let me understand this, Father. Did Renée know that she was being brought over to bed the king?"

"You put it so baldly—"

"Answer me!"

"Well, who's to say on that? I wasn't there when she was first approached, now, was I? And I myself said nothing to her, depending on those in France to have handled the matter."

"Father, she isn't a woman of the streets, a whore to be bought and sold at whim!"

"Of course she isn't. She's a good, decent young woman, a far cry from those actresses he's been after of late."

"And if she doesn't bed the king, there will be no harm done. We'll find her a decent husband, and King Charles may go on his merry way."

"Who says so? Why wouldn't she? I've not spent my coins to dower her for some other man, Alice."

"But you'll spend them on gowns and jewels to catch the king's eye, like a pimp?"

"Where do you learn the language you do? You shock me, Alice, indeed you do!"

"From court! From Rochester and Sedley and Buckhurst! From Sheffield and Killigrew! From you!" Ferocious anger rose in her as she named the rogues who amused the king. If her father had had any part in the queen's despair, she would poison him herself. "You should have enlightened me!"

"It's no dishonor to be mistress of the king."

"Father, there have to be some proprieties. She is unmarried, has no family here to protect her. The wolves are already gathering, wanting to be in at the kill."

"Who?"

"Lady Arlington. The Duchess of Lauderdale. The Countess of Suffolk."

"Those conniving—excuse me, Alice—but I'm the one who has spent all the coin—"

"And used his own daughter as procuress! How could you allow this? You know my loyalty to the queen!"

"Yes, well, if you love the Portuguese, you'd best keep her husband distracted." The words were harsh, but no more so than the expression on his face.

"She is good and loyal and does her duty. She brought millions to the treasury in her dower."

"That was then, and this is now. She's barren. It's her duty to give us princes. There are none. Some of us believe there never will be. It's what, ten years?"

"King Louis was born after twenty years of barrenness."

"His father fancied men. Our king is a proper man. His wife isn't a proper woman."

"The marriage cannot be undone. Marriage is a sacrament. Those who say otherwise are unholy."

"And she's a Papist. I was against it at the time. Let us have a proper Protestant, a German or Austrian or Dane, as our queen, I said. No one listened." He stared hard at Alice. "You've not become a Papist, have you?"

"Would you hate me if I had?"

There was a strained silence between them. A pulse beat up high in her temple. He would hate her. And she loved him in spite of everything, all his flaws, his betrayals.

"I won't help Renée become the king's mistress." Her voice was trembling.

"Not even if the king would be grateful, do anything he could for you in return? He might, for instance, have a word on your behalf to Balmoral, and his word counts for something, wouldn't you say? Ah, your face, Alice, not quite so high and righteous now, are we? Truth is, Balmoral isn't keen to ally himself with me at the moment. We've some differences between us, and that's all I'll say on that. And word is the Duchess of Cleveland has put a bug in his ear about you— That reminds me. I've thought of a trick we might play, just this once so, as you say, suspicion will fall elsewhere."

"I'm leaving now."

"Life isn't filled with easy choices," he called to her retreating figure. "We all of us get our hands dirty after a time. How do you think I kept you fed when we were abroad?"

Outside, Alice huddled in her cloak as the sedan chair borne by bearers lurched from side to side in its journey back to Whitehall, her groom walking alongside the chair. She was chilled, especially in her heart. How much was her father a part of the plot against the queen? Today was the day of All Hallows'. Evil spirits abroad. She leaned back against the straight, uncomfortable seat. King Charles to help with Balmoral. Her father knew precisely what to say to her. Weren't all her schemes for this, to be his duchess, to be above the fray, to set her friends in fine marriages like so many pieces on the chessboard, to know she was at the whim of no one, to aid the queen, to repay Colefax for scandal and distress? That's what being a duchess meant. And to be the duchess of a man of honor, well, there was nothing higher. Her mind moved here and there, around the situation, thoughts glinting like silver fish surfacing in the river of her mind . . . Richard loved Renée, and she loved him in turn. Was there a way she could seem to aid the king's suit but actually aid theirs? King Charles had forgiven Frances Stewart. He would forgive Renée. For him, there was always another woman. In her mind, she saw a series of keepers, saw a long finger wagging up and down at her, the child Alice, naughty, willful, running wild because her mother was dead and her father was absent. Would you both have your cake and eat it too? The question was ridiculous. Yes, was the answer. Always.

She looked out the glass window in the door; they were passing Charing Cross, where once there'd been a statue of Charles I, pulled down by the Parliament. Years later, those who'd had him executed were hanged, drawn, and quartered on the very spot, their gamble failed. The statue was found, placed again at this crossroads where London ended and Whitehall began.

Everything was a gamble, wasn't it?

She'd have to think hard on this, very, very hard.

WHITEHALL HAD BEEN preparing itself for All Hallows' Eve for days. Torches dipped in tar were placed in the privy garden to be lighted once darkness fell. Wood for the big bonfire on the hill in Hyde Park was piled high. The Duke of Monmouth was giving a masquerade to begin on the hour of midnight, when spirits were known to walk about. The astrologer Elias Ashmole was to be there, as well as a magician. Ashmole was going to tell fortunes. The maids of honor had been talking of nothing else for weeks. The cooks in the kitchen were even now blending flour and sugar and butter into the light and tiny soul cakes Queen Catherine would distribute after an All Hallows' mass. Apples had been kept in the darkest and coolest of cellars so there should be some not withered and pie-bound for the bobbing that would take place in the public courtyards. And nuts, everyone had hoarded autumn nuts like squirrels, for all the divining they'd be doing later, crowded around their fireplaces. Alice walked into the bedchamber, flung off her cloak, and Poll took it from her.

"You've mixed the gum and wine?" she asked her servant.

"Don't I always?"

She'd put herself behind by going to see her father. She had to place the queen's patches and help with the curling of her hair, she had to put the tincture of gum and wine on all their cheeks so they'd be blooming—none of them were allowed rouge yet; only married women or harlots rouged—and she had to find Renée and speak with her. That was first and foremost.

"Where are you going?" cried Poll, Alice's costume in her hand. There was a final bit of fitting and sewing yet to be done, but Alice was gone, running down the corridors of Whitehall.

Renée was in the queen's withdrawing chamber. Everyone was sewing colored beads to their masks. The floor was a welter of colored ribbon, mulberry and grape, citron and beryl, canary and cadmium, primrose and peach. Edward sat in the corner, playing the lute and singing for them. They must look handsomer than the Duchess of York's maids of honor, better than the Duchess of Monmouth's. It was, as the French said, de rigueur, necessary. They had their reputation to uphold, now more than ever—or so Alice had convinced them. Alice whispered to Renée, who put down her mask.

"Oh, Luce, do finish mine for me," Alice begged. "I'm . . . what flower am I?"

"Primrose," said Barbara. "I'll do it, Luce."

Alice led Renée away. Gracen raised an eyebrow. "Do finish mine," she mocked.

Alice led Renée through a back chamber where the king's seamstresses worked. They barely glanced up from their sewing. Yards of glittering fabric lay in pieces on the floor. A great artificial papier-mâché head made to resemble a sultan stood perched on a table. The chamber led to a waterside gallery with large, old-fashioned mullioned windows overlooking the Thames. It was for the king's private pleasure, but the guards posted at the king's door knew Alice and nodded to her as she hurried to one end of its long length, pulled two chairs together where they might whisper and not be heard. Just beyond, through another door, were the many chambers that made the apartments of His Highness the Duke of York, but he and his wife and her maids of honor were across the park at St. James's Palace. They'd not yet moved into Whitehall for the winter.

"We haven't seen you all of today. I asked Gracen where you were, and she said you were out 'scheming.'" Renée said the last word in English, as Gracen must have done. "What does it mean, this 'scheming'?" The way Renée pronounced it, it sounded like "sky-ming."

"Plotting and planning, like you. You've not been honest with me."

Renée's smile faded.

"Am I your friend?"

Renée nodded.

"Do you trust me?"

"The only one," said Renée. "Others, they want—" She stopped.

"They want you to be the king's mistress," Alice finished for her, and waited.

Renée didn't say anything.

How could I have ever thought her a fool? thought Alice. "Is that what you want?"

"No. Yes—I don't know!"

"How can you not know? Explain that to me."

"They tell me I must do this, for the sake of my family, for the sake of my country. They tell me I will have so much—jewels, and homes, and honors. They tell me I am so fortunate to have attracted his attention. I'm alone in Paris. Perhaps they're right, I think. And the king, the king is very kind, Alice. He makes me smile. . . . I know

I have promised Richard my heart, my hand in marriage. I can't bring myself to tell them that, yet. You mustn't tell them. They will be so angry with me."

"But if you told them, it would put a stop to everything!"

And when Renée didn't answer, Alice said, "You don't want it stopped, do you."

"It is pleasant to be admired, more than I imagined. I like His Majesty. Am I bad?"

"Do you love Lieutenant Saylor?"

Renée nodded, and Alice saw it was so.

"Do you still wish to marry him?"

"When I am with him, I am certain, my head and heart are clear, but then, when the king compliments me and shows me with his eyes all he is feeling, I am not longer so certain."

"I feel the fool in this."

Renée took her hands, looking up at her with the dignity that was always under the beauty. "Oh, no. You have been the dearest of friends. I could not have made the journey over without you, without knowing that Richard was on the other side, and that you, the pair of you, would watch over me. I thought I would simply tell them I had changed my mind. But now I don't know my mind. I am not strong like you, Alice. My mind goes every which way, and I feel lost and confused. I want everybody to be happy, to be happy with me. I don't like anger. I don't like displeasing. They frighten me, and I cannot think."

Alice's mind, resilient, scheming, restless, went every which way, too. "It's been done," she said slowly. "The king was mad for Frances Stewart, crazy for her, and yet she married another right under his nose, and he forgave her, and they became best of friends."

"Who is Frances Stewart?"

"The Duchess of Richmond."

Surprise showed on Renée's face. "The queen's lady-in-waiting, the one who is not quite lovely anymore, yet is. He admires many, doesn't he?"

"He does indeed. That's something you need to think on—if you want to be one of many."

"He might be faithful."

"If he promises that, he lies, Renée. Look at me. I do not think he can be faithful. So you must consider this carefully. And I think you must tell Lieutenant Saylor."

"No, he will hate me, think me weak and wretched, think me lying and deceitful. I love Richard. I don't want him to think such awful things of me."

"It is his right to know where things stand."

"Please, oh, please. Promise me you'll say nothing! Promise! There's nothing to tell him. I've done nothing!"

It was hard to withstand her. "I promise for now."

"Not for now, forever. It is my place to tell him this, Alice, not yours."

Alice was silent. Renée was correct, but what a mess they were weaving.

"Alice!"

"All right, I'll say nothing. I hope I dance at your wedding."

What a tightrope Renée walked. It would be so easy to fall. And the truth was, whichever side she fell upon, Alice intended to stay in the king's graces, to reap the reward of Balmoral. Dislike it though she might, it was the ugly truth.

"Just be my friend, Alice. Don't abandon me."

"I won't."

"Forever and ever."

"Forever and ever."

Renée smiled. Alice leaned forward and they touched lips once, lightly, sweetly, chastely, in its own way a new seal on friendship.

Off Wych Street, which was near the square of Covent Garden, Richard finally found the alley called Wych Court. There it was, the house with the red door. A burly man opened it at his knock, looked him up and down, and, at the coin offered, allowed him entrance. Richard walked down a long hall, small chambers to each side, sheer curtains drawn shut if there was a customer, open if not, so that the passerby might view the wares: boys, young men—some dressed as women, made up with paint and patches and curling hair, some not. And the closed curtains were sheer enough to allow a view of various acts of coupling. Sounds of groans and panting, of cursing and crying, followed him into the main chamber, a handsome room with ornate furniture, every piece French and gilded silver. Men—merchants and goldsmiths, ship's captains and noblemen—stood in groups, sipping wine, talking. Boys and young men Richard's age mingled with them. A footman, his cheeks and lips highly rouged, patches on his face like a woman, approached.

"A word with Mrs. Neddie," said Richard. He handed the footman the note Balmoral had given him, then stood awkwardly. The hair on the back of his neck prickled. He was aware of the gaze of men falling on him in a way he wasn't used to. A boy, twelve or so, walked over. Richard shook his head. "I'm not here to buy anything."

"Not even a glass of wine?"

"No."

"One glass of wine. I'll be beaten otherwise. We have to make money for her in whatever way we can. One glass of wine and you're rid of me for the evening, I swear it."

Richard considered the boy, measuring the truth in his eyes. They were clear, his face smooth, open. He was lying. He said to a servant, "A glass of wine for . . ."

"Etienne."

"Etienne and myself."

"I've not seen you before," Etienne said.

"Nor are you likely to again. Etienne?" He mocked the French name.

The boy grinned. "It's fashionable to be French these days. Sometimes I pretend I don't speak English, and they pay more."

"Go away, Etienne."

"Yes, sir. Thank you, sir."

The footman had appeared, was beckoning Richard. He followed him up a flight of stairs and into a handsome chamber done in the best style, French furniture, large, elaborately framed Italian landscape paintings on the wall, shimmering draperies of fine silk.

Lounging on a sumptuous daybed was a beautiful woman dressed in a gown the color of midnight, ebony shot through with threads of blue. Diamonds glittered around her neck and at her ears. She smiled at Richard, who blinked. She might be the most beautiful woman he'd ever seen.

"Do sit down, Lieutenant Saylor. How is my very dear Duke of Balmoral?" Her voice was low, with a provocative rasp to it.

"Well, thank you."

"How is it that I may aid you? I know it isn't a boy for the duke. Have you come on his behalf for someone? I can give you tough boys, ruffians, or soft, sweet ones. I am the soul of discretion, I assure you." She smiled. "Or perhaps it is you? Do you desire a boy? A young man? Handsome like you?"

Richard flushed, feeling color stain his neck, his face, like fire.

Neddie snapped open a fan, flowers painted on its panels, and began moving it back and forth near her face. "No. I didn't think so, but it's always so amusing to ask."

"I've come for information. We're looking for a Frenchman, whose . . . taste . . . er . . ."

"Runs to the wares I carry?"

"Yes, thank you. His name is Henri Ange, though he may be using another. He speaks English well, so he might pose as an Englishman."

"And this Frenchman who might pose as an Englishman, what does he look like?"

"Medium height, very slender, light eyes."

"Any one of the men downstairs answers to that."

Richard pulled a small bag from his pocket, held it out. She took it from him, weighed it in one hand. "He understands me so well, always," she murmured. "What do you want with this gentleman, should I see or hear of him?"

"Simply to talk to him, to ask a few questions."

"All these coins for that? The questions must be very interesting."

"They are." Richard bowed. "We wouldn't want him to know we were looking for him. We'd just like to know if you see him and where we might find him. Thank you for receiving me, Mrs. Neddie."

"The pleasure was all mine, I do assure you, Lieutenant. Give His Grace my sincere regards and tell him I am, as always, his humble servant, that I love him like a daughter."

The moment the door closed behind Richard, she rose and opened one of several concealed doors in the chamber. Her bedchamber was as ornate as her receiving chamber. The bed was huge, framed by twisting columns that ended in wooden putti—fat cupids carved in Italy and given her once upon a time by an admirer. The bed hangings were expensive, crushed velvet, trimmed in silver braid. A man lay on the bed, medium height, slender. He turned his head to watch her. She sat on the bed in a graceful movement. "I was just thinking of you."

He made no answer. His shirt was open. She placed some of the coins Richard had given her on his nipples, down the line of dark hair that inched to his navel. She placed the last coin on the button of his breeches. "A little present for you because I find you so attractive."

She traced the line of one of his brows; they arched naturally, giving him a look of amused cynicism. If the soldier sent to see her had been more acute, he would have described those brows. They were quite distinctive. "I have a love of other languages. Do you speak other languages, my sweet prince?" She leaned forward, moved a coin with her tongue, and kissed his nipple.

"Yes," he said in French.

"What is that?" she asked.

"French, as I'm certain you know. And this is Italian. It's dangerous to play games with me. Do you want me to embrace you, beautiful whoremonger, or kill you?" he said in Italian.

"What are you saying? It quite thrills me! When we play, you must speak to me in it. You're so clever. Are you very bad as well?" she murmured against his chest.

He made no answer, closed his eyes, accepting her caresses like a cat, as his due.

She moved her hand to touch him more intimately. "You are, I just know it. Neddie loves bad boys. Let me show you how much."

Downstairs, Richard tried to pay for the wine, but the footman told him there was no charge. He walked down the corridor, the sounds from the little openings following him to the door. Outside, he stood in the middle of the street. Night had fallen, and already here and there in the distance were the soft lights of All Hallows' Eve bonfires. He pulled in air like a bellows, wanting to clear his mind, his lungs, his being. It won't be pretty, Balmoral had warned. Jesus God.

He looked back to the red door, unsatisfied.

Back he went.

"Etienne," he said to the burly man, who smiled in a way that made Richard consider hitting him but decide against it.

"If you want Etienne, sir, you've got to come inside, sir."

Richard held out another coin. "No one has to know but you and me."

"I can't. I wish I could."

She ran a tight ship; so Balmoral had warned. Flirt with her, if you can, he'd advised, but Richard couldn't do it. He'd been too shocked at all he saw. He'd felt as thick and stupid as a country bumpkin. "All right, then, lead me to him."

Etienne sat on the cot in his tiny chamber. He looked up as Richard entered, drew the sheer curtains shut, and his face remained as clear as a young angel's. "Coins there," he said, pointing to a bowl. "Then tell me what you'd like."

Richard dropped them in, placed three more on the blanket. "For you, if you help me." In a flash, Etienne moved the coins under a pillow. Figures walked by outside the sheer curtains, glancing in. It was as if they were ghosts, figures from a netherworld.

"I want you to watch for someone." There was the sound of weeping and of a violin being played, and somewhere near a man was groaning. Richard described Henri Ange. "I'll come again to ask if you've seen him," he said, then held out his hand. Etienne shook it.

Outside, Richard walked briskly and carefully down a narrow street, little more than an alley, which brought him to the Strand, one of the broader streets of the city. From here, it was easy to cross over to the walls of the houses built along the river, find a side street to river stairs, hire a boat to take him to Whitehall. Here and there on the opposite shore were more bonfires, beacons in the dark night. Richard breathed deep of the night air and the river, pulling cold deliberately into his lungs again and again.

AT WHITEHALL PALACE, Alice tied a last scarlet ribbon into Queen Catherine's hair, curled to twisting ringlets everywhere. They both contemplated the queen's image in the mirror. She wore a stiff, scarlet high stomacher out of which her chemise framed her shoulders with handmade lace. Her shirt was black velvet with satin stripes of red overlaid. It was very short, so that her ankles and shoes showed. And in her ears and around her neck hung Portuguese emeralds, mined in the Americas, part of her dowry, set in heavy gold. Her mouth was rouged vivid red, and Alice had taken great care with the rouging of her cheeks.

"Four," said Queen Catherine.

"I think three."

"Tyrant."

Alice placed three gummed dark patches on her face, a coach and horses on her forehead, a star by her left eye, a heart by her bottom lip. With her mask on, only the heart would show. The mask was red. Queen Catherine was an apple vendor. She would carry a basket filled with the best of autumn's last apple crop. On her black stockings, clearly and shockingly showing, were embroidered red apples. Her cloak was red velvet, lined with emerald green.

They were all going as street vendors, vendors of flowers and herbs. All of the maids of honor wore provocative short skirts high enough to show off their ankles, stockings, and shoes. On their stockings, the queen's embroiderers had embroidered the flower or herb they were selling. For days beforehand, they'd debated among themselves as to the propriety of showing their ankles, the queen and Barbara holding out, feeling they were going too far. But somehow it had been resolved that they'd do it, and then Queen Catherine had fallen into the fun of it as if she had been its advocate all along. But that had been before the note arrived. It had been Alice's idea that they perform as a surprise to the king. So they had called upon Fletcher to organize them, and they were going to enter singing and dancing—really it would be as if they were stage actresses, at least that is what they had secretly convinced themselves—and it was all going to be slightly shocking and therefore quite wonderful. The king would like the naughtiness of it. Each of them had a line to sing all by herself. It would end with the crowd of them dancing through costumed courtiers, offering flowers, herbs, apples, as favors to whomever they chose—another source of great excitement—and they would end by encircling the king and pouring whatever remained in their baskets into his hands. This last was the result of Alice's having seen his sultan's costume today.

None of the other ladies' households, that of the Duchess of York or the Duchess of Monmouth, was doing anything other than dressing up—Edward and other court pages were their spies and told them so. It was all great fun, or would have been if the queen were not so dispirited.

"I want not to do this." Queen Catherine dug her fingers into the fur of the little fox sleeping in her lap, and it yelped and stood up.

Alice knelt beside her. "You look wonderful, Your Majesty."

"In here"—she touched her breast—"I am have such sad."

"Shall we put it out that you are ill?"

The canaries in their cages and lovely little birds dabbed with different colors, from one of Portugal's colonies, were singing in their cages. It was a last aria before dark. "And give more for talk to my enemies to do? No. Dress yourself. Mass, she is in half an hour."

THE MAIDS OF honors' adjoining bedchambers were a welter of black velvet shirts, embroidered stockings, high-heeled shoes, giggling young women, servants running here and there, curling tongs heating in the fireplace, secrets being whispered, earrings being screwed in, laughter everywhere. Big ewers as well as a few silver tubs of water and the damp rags showed that bathing had preceded the dressing.

"Our faces!" Luce squealed as Alice rushed past.

Poll poured boiling water into a tepid tub, and, fingers flying, Alice untied, unpinned, rolled down, stepped out of clothing to bathe. That done, she began to reassemble herself as fast as she could. In no time she sat on her bed, tying the garter that held up her beautifully embroidered stocking. Poll was at the fireplace, heating the tongs for her hair. Everyone else's hair was curled and beribboned.

"Our cheeks . . ." Luce stood beside her bed.

There was a knock at the door. Gracen opened it enough to see who it was, talked in a low voice with Edward, then turned to tell them all, "The queen is ready to go to mass."

"Tell her we need but a few moments more," Barbara said.

Alice stood up in her one stocking. "Is the splash ready?" she asked Poll.

"Yes, but your hair—"

"Never mind it, Poll. We'll pin it up one way or another. Bring the splash."

At once they sorted themselves into line, Luce sitting first in a chair before the fire. Gracen brought candles and set them all along the mantel so the light would be better. Wishing to miss nothing, several of the servant girls gathered around Alice. Carefully, Poll began to measure out the gum benzoin, which had been mixed in spirits of wine and very lightly boiled.

"Fifteen drops apiece," Alice reminded her.

"As if I didn't know that like I know my own name." Poll dropped the amount into a very small pewter bowl of water and stirred it once with a thin stirring stick made of bone. Alice dipped a paintbrush into the mix and dabbed at Luce's cheeks. Gum benzoin drew blood to the surface and gave a girl blooming cheeks. It wasn't rouge, so Alice—discovering the recipe in a household book of her aunt's that had belonged to her grandmother—had convinced Barbara it was fine. If Alice and Barbara agreed, all obeyed.

Giggling and whispering had stopped now. This was serious business; a girl could look as though she had scarlet fever if it wasn't done properly, and no one had the art of it like Alice, who needed silence for her work. It had been two years since she'd done this. Every one of them was different, some needing more, some needing less. Alice put on a glove dirtied with coal dust. Poll handed her the shaved piece of coal. Deftly, she touched under the lashes of Luce's eyes. Again the effect had to be subtle. Kit, Barbara, Renée. Gracen. Alice touched lightly at a last cheekbone, under a last eye, and it was done.

"Go on to mass," she told the others. "I'll slip in once Poll has pinned up my hair."

"I'll stay and do your hair," said Barbara.

"Everyone has her mask?"

"Don't let your cloaks open."

Like mothers, Barbara and Alice called out instructions.

In the silence left behind, Alice tied her other garter in its place at the top of her stocking, while Poll checked the temperature of the tongs with a wet finger. Alice sat, her mind calming as Barbara began to curl her ringlets.

"Her earrings, Poll." Barbara screwed in the pearl drops they all wore—badges of their position. "The brush, Poll."

A paint stroke here, there, and Alice's cheeks bloomed.

"We're done. Go and look at yourself in the mirror. The color becomes you."

Alice stared at herself in the glass. She wasn't pretty exactly, but she was—she tilted her head—very interesting. Cloaked and ready, Barbara came up behind her and draped Alice's own cloak over her shoulders, smoothing out the material the way a mother would. Alice turned, and Barbara fastened the ties, pulled up Alice's hood, then her own. They stared at each other and smiled.

"We'll break hearts tonight," Alice said. "Let's find Edward and be on our way."

They took each other's hands, just as they'd done since they were twelve and learned they were best of friends, and began winding their way through halls and sets of chambers until they were walking through the gallery whose end was Holbein Gate.

They walked down the stairs that led to the park, pulling their cloaks close to them. Winter was in the chill. In the sky a sliver of moon was surrounded by haze. Edward took a torch dipped in pitch from its place. In another moment it was lighted, and he walked out into the night before them. He was their linkboy—young boys who carried lanterns or torches to light the night—for the walk across the park and to St. James's Palace. Other courtiers and Londoners, too, strolled in the park, the lanterns of their linkboys bobbing like small stars fallen from the sky.

The queen's chapel was across the park, in St. James's Palace, built by old Henry VIII, he of the many wives. The chapel was beautiful, its grace and intimate elegance the legacy of a man named Inigo Jones, who had been fascinated with the great Renaissance architect Palladio. Its ceiling had set the fashion for honeycombs—deep frames of gilded wood set one after another in the ceiling, resembling the outside of a bee's hive. Inside each shallow honeycomb was a painting. The king's mother, French, Catholic, had worshipped here with her ladies and gentlemen.

They crept in, tiptoeing around statues of saints and memorials to the dead, to the queen's pew. Candles shone from huge candle stands and from gilded chandeliers, saints held out marble hands to bless, carvings of angels smiled in forever faith, bunches of flowers scented the air like perfume. It was ornate and, in the evening, dark, mysterious, beautiful.

In a moment, Barbara was kneeling and saying the prayer, and although Alice knew it by heart, she didn't say it. Her father's words were ringing in her ears: Are you a Papist? Perhaps. She had been Papist while with Madame's court, chanting the prayers. What if she had been? What did it all mean? Across the aisle was the Duchess of Cleveland, near her the Duke and Duchess of York. There were Lord and Lady Arlington, Sir Thomas Clifford, Lord Knollys, other ladies and gentlemen of the household. How many were here out of courtesy to the queen? How many were here out of a faith that was unfashionable, out of favor? It was said Papists caused the terrible plague of 1665, set the great fire that had burned London within a year. She glanced up into the gallery. There were John Sidney, the Earl of Rochester, and Lord Mulgrave. Mulgrave nodded shyly to her. Why were they here? To hear the prayers and chanting? To ogle the maids? To celebrate that which they did not admit openly?

Alice wanted to believe, yet it seemed to her God was capricious, cruel, a trickster who delighted in the trick. Was this how one fooled the trickster, by agreeing with Him that, yes, it was indeed a very good trick? How could one do that? She didn't understand. Her history lesson taught her that King Henry IV had converted to Catholicism to rule France. My kingdom is worth a mass, he'd said. That she understood. Could her father not love her if she converted? Would he hate the Duke of York now if he knew of his conversion? Barbara said the bonfires were lighted tonight to aid souls out of purgatory; Rochester said Druids lit them in ancient ceremonies acknowledging life and death, and Christians took the ritual and made it theirs. Was not life purgatory enough?

Everyone was rising. Mass was over. She followed the others into the vestry, where plates of soul cakes rose in fragrant, bite-size piles. A soul cake, a soul cake, have mercy on all Christian souls for a soul cake. The Duke of York was murmuring names as he piled his plate high: "Mother, Father, Elizabeth, Mary, Henry, Minette . . ." His family gone. There were two cakes on the queen's plate, no more, no less, for the babes conceived and ended. Alice turned her face away, went to stand with Luce and Kit, who were wild and giggling and eating cakes simply because they were there and dusted with sugar.

Chapter 23

In the upstairs viewing gallery in the banqueting hall of Whitehall Palace, Luce ran to Alice and Barbara. "There are four sultans, not one!"

"It's true," said Dorothy, waving a hand in the direction of the great banqueting hall below. At one end was a throne. Paintings by Rubens sat settled in dozens of ornately gilded ceiling frames. Massive cherubs lifted their arms in blessing in the corners. Their blessings didn't always work—the king's father had stepped out one of the evenly spaced windows to his scaffold and beheading. But tonight, no one was thinking of that. Laughter and conversation echoed up to the gallery.

Alice maneuvered through the musicians playing for the crowd below, leaned one hand on the balustrade, and looked over. Milling among the costumed courtiers were indeed four sultans, not one. It was impossible to miss the papier-mâché heads with their ornate cloth of gold turbans. And because the head was so big, the king's height couldn't be used to mark him, at least not looking down from this level.

Fletcher clapped his hands to capture the maids' attention. "It's a bother, but I've thought it all out. We do everything just as we've practiced, but at the end, stand before the audience in a row, like flowers in a garden, and sing the last verse. The queen will be your anchor. Wherever she is, fan out on each side of her—Wells, are you listening?" Of course, Luce wasn't. "Where's Verney? Someone go and fetch her at once. She hasn't heard a word I've said." Fletcher fanned himself impatiently. "I'm as warm as if it were summer. It's nerves. Let me live through this moment. It's like herding cats. We'd never get a play done if the actresses behaved so. Who'll be blamed if it doesn't go well, James Fletcher, that's who, not Verney or Wells, who is, I note, still talking. Grant me patience! May we begin, Your Majesty?"

At her nod, he signaled the musicians, and they ended their music at a stanza, while Queen Catherine and the maids walked down a staircase. After a time, many fell silent, looking up at the gallery, where Fletcher stood, silently counting to let drama build and the queen's party assemble themselves in their places near the throne.

He raised a hand, and a single flute began to play.

The great hollow center of the hall took the notes and flung them toward the matching sets of windows at the gallery level, where they echoed back to the courtiers standing below.

"Pippins, fine pippins to sell . . ." Queen Catherine sauntered forward from behind the throne, her beaded scarlet mask covering her eyes, her skirt swinging out with every step. People moved back, leaving her that actor's delight, a natural entrance.

"The apple has no seeds," said the Duchess of Cleveland, arrogant in her five children. People around her tittered. An audible hiss rose up to mingle with the flute. Queen Catherine froze. Suddenly a sultan was before her, holding out his hand for an apple, his eyes behind his mask encouraging, well-known to her. She took a deep breath and recovered her poise. He bowed and moved back, handed the apple to Cleveland with an ironic bow.

"Whatever am I to do with this?" she asked, recognizing the king.

"Reflect upon your bad deeds."

"But, darling, they were done with you."

"Here's lady of the autumn, here's mistress of fall," Queen Catherine began to sing, her voice trembling, but then taking hold, strengthening, as she advanced to the center of the hall. "I live not alone, but sisters have many, come, my dear sweets, to sell all your wares, one and two and three, three for a penny, one, two and three, three for a penny." At that moment, violins swelled out to join the flute, and from every corner of the room, the maids danced out, calling:

"Flower, buy a flower, sir."

"Primrose, bundle a penny."

"Daffodils."

"Rosemary, remember rosemary."

"Buy my fine myrtle and roses, my myrtles and stocks, my sweet-smelling balsams."

They held out roses and sweet williams, daffodils and stock, made of silk by the seamstresses, tied to fresh herbs cut that afternoon from the kitchen gardens. Once in a semicircle around the queen, they waited until applause had died back, then began to sing an old poem Fletcher had set to music.

Go and catch a falling star,
Get with child a mandrake root,
Tell me where all past years are,
Or who cleft the Devil's foot,
Teach me to hear mermaids singing,
Or to keep off envy's stinging,
And find what wind
Serves to advance an honest mind.

Alice stepped out in front of them, began to dance. She danced lightly, gracefully, to each of the four sultans and then to the queen. Alice and the queen leaped into the fast-moving steps of a Morris dance, centuries old, something mysterious and reminiscent of ancient times in it. The maids around them sang.

If thou beest born to strange sight,
Things invisible to see,
Ride ten thousand days and nights,
Till age snow white hairs on thee.
Thou, when thou return'st, wilt tell me,

All strange wonders that befell thee,
And swear nowhere
Lives a woman true and fair.

Breathless, as applause rose, the queen and Alice stepped back into the semicircle of maids, and, music still playing, they all wove in and among costumed courtiers, handing out flowers, herbs, apples, as favors to end as they began, back in a semicircle. On the last long note, all of them dropped into the deepest of curtsies.

Applause rained on them.

All the sultans were clapping. Above in the gallery, Fletcher was clapping. Alice and her friends met one another's eyes, their mouths smiling below their beaded masks. They'd done it, surpassed all the other maids, brought novelty—always a treasure at this court—and in the surpassing, gathered notoriety to themselves, to the queen. They were, for the moment, the most fashionable, the most envied. They'd be the most sought after tonight, and for a few days, the court would talk of them. It would pass, of course; but it did for now.

A wizard, carrying a staff crowned with laurel and crow's feathers, stepped forward. It was the Duke of Monmouth.

"As Merlin of this fete, I implore all evil spirits of this night to depart and leave us in peace."

"Now that will be confoundedly boring," said Buckingham in a low tone, dressed as a playing card. The man beside him, also dressed as a card, smiled.

"Never mind it. They're within us," the man said.

"I call upon all sprites and spirits everywhere to bless our gracious monarch, His Majesty, my father, and I command the dancing to begin."

The four sultans stepped forward, selecting Queen Catherine, Renée, and the Duchesses of York and Monmouth as partners. Monmouth selected Alice and led her among the dancing couples. "Beautifully done, my fair primrose."

"Jamie, I want you to do something for me."

"If the dancing hadn't betrayed you, the first words out of your mouth would."

"I want you to flirt outrageously with Louisa Saylor."

"With utmost pleasure. May one ask why?"

"One may not. Jamie, last year when Lord Roos brought his bill on divorce, were you a piece of that?"

"I thought it despicable," he said quickly, and Alice thought, He lies. "The men who surround my father haven't always his best interests at heart."

"Yes, they'll betray anyone, won't they."

"My uncle—"

"Isn't, perhaps, the wisest of men, but he has a noble heart, and he is heir to the throne, and if ever he should wear the crown, he will need wise and loving councillors who have the best interests of us all at heart, men like yourself, Jamie."

"You continue to confuse me with a schoolboy. What boredom. I thought to enjoy my dance with the most graceful woman at court, and I find myself lectured once more."

The music ended. He bowed to her, and she sank into a curtsy, feeling flat, saddened.

She grabbed his hand, still in the curtsy. "I was your first friend. Remember that."

"Remembering is what keeps me from cutting you out of my circle, Alice."

"And flirt with Louisa."

In spite of himself, he laughed, reached out to flick her under the chin before turning away. She stared after him. Her first true friendship was walking away.

"There you are, poppet," said her father. "I thought I'd gather a dance while I may. You won't be free this night, I don't need that mountebank Ashmole to predict that. Sweet Jesus, you should see the crowd lined up to have their palms read by him! Come dance with your father."

"How did you know which one I was?"

"The moment you began to dance, I knew you. And Monmouth always danced with you first, didn't he, before France? Tell me you forgive me. It frets me to have quarreled."

Just like that, he touched her heart, and yet he'd say anything to stop quarreling, as she well knew. "I want you to do something for me."

"And if the dancing hadn't betrayed you, those words certainly would. Up we go, turn, and bow." He liked to talk aloud the dance steps.

"Patch whatever quarrel you have with Balmoral, Father. For my sake."

"Right, then left, skip, and turn. I don't think it can be done. If you want him, you'll have to help the king win Kerouallle. You'll be invited to sup with the Duchess of Cleveland in a day or so. Don't refuse."

"She'll never invite me to dine."

The Duke of York danced by. Sir Thomas glowered at him.

"She'll invite you, and that's all I'll say. Skip left. Back right. York—I'm told the Jesuits are corrupting him, including the one who is the queen's own priest. They're everywhere, Alice. All in the court, behind closed doors, quietly doing their worst because King Charles won't listen to reason and ban Papists from court. So men like me, faithful, loyal, wait in line behind those whose first duty is not this kingdom, but the Church of Rome, that old whore of Babylon."

She was so startled to hear him say that—the old Roundhead description for Charles I's queen as well as for the Church of Rome—that she stumbled.

The dance was ending anyway. He left her without a parting kiss.

Breathless, disturbed, she sat down beside Dorothy. Across the chamber, a woman raised a goblet to her. Jesuits—were these the phantoms her father feared? Was this how they blamed the queen now? Who did the blaming? Was her father in league to poison the queen or not? If Buckingham was, he was . . . She stood, unsmiling and grave, as someone approached her to dance.

ANOTHER SULTAN WAS enjoying his third dance with Renée.

"I've seldom been happier," King Charles said. "How well you dance. Your gracefulness enchants me. We must have all our dancing masters come from France." The papier-mâché face couldn't smile, but a smile was in his voice. "My cleverness tonight also pleases me. I'd forgotten how love gladdens the heart, makes the mind nimble."

"Love is a strong word, Your Majesty, one I hold most seriously."

"I'm smitten. All four sultans danced with you tonight, but I am every one of them."

"One of them should dance with Her Majesty."

"One of them is."

"But he isn't you."

"No one knows that. I commanded them not to speak."

"Do you think she doesn't know her own husband? She planned our entertainment this night for your sole pleasure, and this is how you repay her? She has all about her those who would hurt her. Will you hurt her, too?"

"Am I understanding you, mademoiselle? Are you demanding I dance with my wife?"

The caress in his voice was quite gone.

"One can be kind. Kindness makes up for much."

The dance had ended. A sultan came forward and, after a conversation with the king, took Renée's hand. Richard stepped forward to claim a dance. He hadn't bothered with a costume, wore his guard's uniform—a blue coat—and a black mask upon his face.

"In one more dance," Renée said to him.

Something in her voice caught his ear. "Is everything well with you?"

"Yes, oh yes. Just wait for me, Richard."

Annoyed, wary now from the tone he'd caught in her voice, he walked about the perimeter of the chamber, declining to join any of the groups talking and laughing. He passed by the line waiting to see the astrologer Ashmole. Sitting before the man was Barbara Bragge, John standing behind. It must be Barbara for John's smile to be so broad. His sister loomed in front of him, masked, pert, pretty, and, he could see from the set of her shoulders, determined. She took him by the arm. "Walk me around the chamber, Richard. I scarcely ever see you."

"That's because you keep yourself busy collecting admirers, Lou."

Delighted, she laughed. "Sweet brother, you're the only one who calls me Lou." They were passing Alice, who was not dancing. "She'd be a good catch for you."

"I've asked her to marry me." His mind was somewhere else.

"Alice Verney?"

"Mistress de Keroualle. What are you talking about, Lou?"

"I am talking about Sir Thomas's only heir. I hear he owns half of the Thames's left bank."

"And here I thought from all your outrageous flirting that you were set on marrying him yourself and providing a new heir. What then would be left for me?"

"A handsome dower, my dear brother, enough to repair our precious Tamworth."

"I believe I can find my own wife. I have."

"Someone else is interested in her, Richard. Your passion may be dangerous. Do you find her ugly?"

"Who?"

"The heiress."

"No."

"But not pretty, either."

He saw dark brows, taut shoulders, a full underlip. "Not exactly."

"She likes you."

"Why do you say that?"

"The way she looks at you."

"Go away, Lou. Find someone else to order about." He saw Alice, whispering now to one of the pages. He walked forward. She seemed to order most of them about as if they belonged to her, and they seemed happy to serve. When we were small, she was my first true friend, Monmouth had told him. I did whatever she asked; it never occurred to me that I might disobey her. Alice and Edward saw him, stopped whispering.

"Conspiracies," Richard said. "May I join them?"

But Edward was off, as if he had orders. He did, to find Balmoral for Alice.

"Will you dance with me?" Richard asked.

"Would you mind terribly if I didn't? My leg is aching."

Richard shrugged and sat down, leaning his chin on the back of the chair in front of him, his eyes on the dancing, on one couple in particular.

Alice followed the direction of his gaze. "Court is treacherous. You'll have to be clever to keep her."

She stopped; he'd turned his full gaze on her. The black mask made the ice blue of his eyes startling. "Am I being warned?" The second time tonight, he was thinking.

"Yes."

"Did she ask you to tell me that?"

"No."

"All right, then."

Was that it? thought Alice, studying his profile. If the words did not come from Renée, did he believe no threat existed? "You think it so simple?"

"What?"

"Relations between a man and a woman?"

Again, eyes framed by a black mask regarded her. "We've pledged our love."

"An ideal, like the stories troubadours once told of the knights of old."

"Is love an ideal?"

"Look around you." She gestured toward the groups of courtiers, less decorous now, with the night passing, with the wine flowing.

"Is this where you've always lived, Alice, at court?"

"Yes, except when there was no court. And this is where you must live, Richard, if you are to prosper. And this is where she lives—"

He stood. Without a parting word to Alice, he threaded among the dancers until he stood between Renée and the sultan with whom she danced, taking her in his arms, leaving the sultan standing alone, something so direct and clear in his action that Alice pressed her hands to her heart. If it was the king, Richard had just deliberately insulted him. Foolish, and daring . . . and something to be admired.

She stood and walked swiftly around talking groups to where the Duke of York stood. He had his mask and wig off and stood amid various maids of honor, some from the queen, some from his wife, some from the Duchess of Monmouth. Alice slipped in among them, put her arm around Barbara's waist, and hugged her. "Did you have your fortune told?" she whispered.

"I did indeed."

"Now who among you beauties will I dance with next?" York was saying. The handsomer of the brothers, he hadn't the hooded eyes of the king or the craggy face, but he hadn't the charm, either. Alice moved gracefully in front of him and dropped into her deepest curtsy.

"The fair primrose, is it?" Pleased, York tossed his wig to a page nearby. "It is you, Verney, isn't it?" he asked a few moments later as they stood in front of each other, waiting for the first notes of the next song from the violins.

"It is indeed."

"I thought so. I can scarcely tell who is who. When is everyone to unmask?"

"On the stroke of two, I believe, sir. Sir, I come as a messenger."

"A messenger? Fair Hermes, are you, in female form? And yet you look like a primrose."

"There's a beautiful maiden among us, someone who wishes to dance with you, who has long admired you from afar."

His interest was caught; he had a weakness for pretty girls. Alice felt a faint prick of guilt to do this to Richard's sister, but then she thought of her father, of his treachery, and her resolve stiffened.

"I'll give you a riddle, sir."

"I'm no good at riddles."

"Who's blond and fair, tender and kind, sister to a sailor who never sails the sea?"

She watched him mulling over her words, watched his pale eyes go to where Monmouth and Louisa Saylor were dancing—tiny and graceful, Louisa was laughing, and her laughter was like silver bells ringing out—watched his eyes widen.

"You don't mean . . . ?"

"But I do. Yet have a care. Her brother is jealous of her reputation. Discretion is the order of the day. I've said not a word."

Exhausted suddenly, Alice thought, I want to sit down, my leg is hurting, I'm tired of myself, I'm ashamed of my scheming. Where was Barbara? She'd find Barbara, and they'd find a place to hide away from suitors and wine-filled gallants, as they used to do when they were younger and the court, with its many cruelties, hurt them. But Barbara was sitting with John Sidney, who, like Richard, couldn't be bothered with a costume and was talking to her earnestly, and Barbara was listening just as earnestly. Bah. Where was Dorothy? thought Alice, looking around to find the mother of the maids, she who was to guard them, protect their chastity and reputations. Dorothy was sitting holding hands with one of the sultans. Lord Knollys, judging by the silly smile under the bottom edge of Dorothy's mask.

ON THE DANCE floor, a sultan walked forward to Renée, who still held Richard's hand in hers, though the music of the last song had ended. "My dance," the sultan said.

It was the king. Richard recognized his voice.

"Begone, soldier," His Majesty drawled.

Richard bowed. "You command me in all things but this. Only she may ask me to leave."

"Do it, then, mademoiselle." The voice was not the least angry, but not to be argued with, either.

"Go, Richard, please," Renée whispered. "I will walk with you later in the gardens."

"Well, I've done what you asked," King Charles said, his tone clipped, crisp, as they began to dance. "What is my reward?"

"You're angry with me," said Renée.

"Are you—" The king stopped, so that York and Louisa Saylor, dancing near, almost fell into them. He took Renée by the arm, led her to some chairs, motioned for a footman, spoke a moment to him, then sat beside her, fishing in a pocket for a handkerchief, but there was none. He unwrapped the gauze belt around his waist and handed it to her as two sultans appeared, along with a few of his Life Guards. "Sit in front of me, and you others move to each side. I don't wish anyone approaching. Knollys, are you there?"

No one answered. "Buckhurst, help me take this damn head off . . . There. Eyes front. You're all deaf and dumb tonight, is that clear? Killigrew, do you hear?"

"Yes, sir."

He turned back to Renée, his hair clipped very short, so that his face looked every bit its age and hard besides. "Don't weep. I never meant to hurt your feelings. Please, don't weep. I'm a cad when I don't mean to be, not to you. Do you love him? Say the word, and I'll let you be."

"I do love him."

Shocked, he was silent for a time. He leaned back in the chair, staring at her as she wiped at her tears with the gauze belt he'd given her. "You're the first woman I've ever admired who has ever asked me to be kind to my wife." Madness, he was thinking, to be touched by that. But he was.

"Handkerchief."

One of his guardsmen turned around long enough to hand him one. The king gave it to Renée, who sniffed, untied her mask, and then blew her nose. He smiled at the gesture, so common, so ordinary, so everyday. And coming from her, so moving. "I lie. I would woo you anyway." He took her hand and held it. He felt like a boy, with a boy's eagerness and fear. "Say I may have my chance."

She was silent.

"Send me away, then. Tell me to leave you. I must hear it directly from your lips." He was harsh now. "I'm no different from your lieutenant."

"I would not hurt Her Majesty."

He knew banter, particularly flirtatious banter. He did not hear that in her voice, but he also did not hear that she sent him away. She sidetracked, wasn't certain. Her soldier hadn't all of her heart, then. He smiled to himself. Very well. Very good. He would sidetrack right with her until they ended where he wished or until he was defeated. It added zest to the chase, which pleased him. She wasn't a whore, to drop into his lap at a glance. About time.

"If you should ever consent to love me, you will hurt her. If you do not, you will hurt me. There's no escaping hurt, my sweet, not in affairs of the heart. She is a good woman, and I do care for her after a fashion, but she is my wife for reasons of state, not for reasons of love. I must love someone. It is my nature, and a man can't go against his nature. I would that someone were you. I'd see you dressed in silver and gold, hang diamonds upon you simply to see if they could possibly match the sparkle in your eyes."

"Do you think to buy me?"

"Can I?"

She laughed, and he raised her hand to his mouth, turning it over and kissing the center with all the passion he felt for her. "I'm an ugly fellow, not handsome like your soldier. Could you care for me?" he said to her when he was done. She didn't say no, which was enough, as was the fact he was still holding her hand. He did love this game. He felt vital, alive to the possibility between them. He loosed her hand, stood, leaned over, and dropped a kiss on her mouth. Before she could speak, he was striding off, sultans and guardsmen with him, and she was alone.

She sat where she was, her hand to her mouth, which felt seared. Her heart was stirred. What had she just done? But another, deeper part of her knew. Richard walked toward her, mask off, face angry. "That was charming," he said, standing before her.

"I told him I loved you."

The grimness dissolved into a sudden smile. He sat beside her and took the same hand King Charles had just held. "It's done, then."

"Let's dance, Richard. I don't want to talk anymore. I don't want to quarrel. I have cried before the king of England at my first court fete. If you make me cry again, I will not forgive you. I just want to dance and dance and dance until I drop from exhaustion."

"THAT'S THE SECOND time this night he's danced with her," Buckingham said fretfully. He was referring to King Charles, who had not put his sultan's head back on and danced undisguised with Queen Catherine.

The fete was reaching a frantic pace. In another dance or two, masks were to be taken off. The wearing of them relieved a man and a woman of the need to be discreet—not that this was a discreet court—but the costumes added extra fillip. Couples were in dark corners, behind columns, in the gardens, touching and kissing, the bolder of them doing far more, the fact that anyone might see adding spice.

"Ahhh . . . ," breathed Gracen, wrapping her arms around the man who kissed and licked her breasts, pushed out of her tight vest. She bit his earlobe.

"You make me wild," he said.

They kissed, tongues entangling, mouths ravenous. She kissed until she wanted to scream, then pushed him away, and he staggered back, almost falling into the large sultan's head he'd taken off.

"Go away now." She was cold, turning and pushing her breasts back into the vest, leaning over as if she were alone. He wiped a hand over his face, picked up the head of his costume.

"Wait," she commanded. There was a pier glass on the wall. She stood before it. "Come stand here behind me."

He did so, dared to drop a kiss on her shoulder, but she tossed her head. "Now go away."

He left the chamber. She found her mask on the floor, retied it, went to the alcove's opening, and looked out, feeling powerful, unsettled, ripe for danger. She loved this feeling, knowing a man desired her, knowing she could make him beg, could issue a command and he would obey. She loved that she'd made him forsake his vows to his wife and to his lover. She felt ruthless, like the tigers in the king's menagerie. She could claw open hearts, lick the blood, not blink an eye.

"AREN'T YOU GOING to dance with me?"

Frances, the Duchess of Richmond, looked lovely as Artemis, sister to the Greek sun god Apollo. The costume allowed her several simple drapes of fabric that showed off her willowy figure.

King Charles bowed. "Of course I am. Later tonight."

"You're flirting with the French chit."

"She isn't a chit. She's your age."

Frances was two and twenty, had been at this court since she was fifteen. "Ah, ancient, then. She's very pretty."

"Indeed she is. How does your husband?"

"Very well. Have I thanked you for sending him to Denmark?"

The king laughed, took her hand, kissed it before walking away.

"FOLLOW ME."

Lord Knollys took Dorothy by the hand and led her through a hall and then to the stairs that led to the upper gallery. He pushed open a door, and they were in a chamber with chairs and tables, a retiring room for the king. "Begone," he said to a dozing page. "Wait." He found a coin, gave it to the boy. "Stand outside the door and give warning."

Dorothy helped him take off the sultan's head, turned around so that he could untie her mask. They leaned into each other, and she twisted her head back to kiss him, his hands on her breasts, touching them, stroking the tips. She'd meant to be colder tonight, to behave, but she'd had too much wine, and wine made her think too much, and this, his hands, his kisses, was what she wished.

There was a table; she sat upon it, facing him, pulling up her skirts to bunch around her—she shuddered at the feel of the wood against her bare skin, at the feel of his hands, already on her legs, bare above her garters, bare to her waist. He knew exactly how to touch her. She moaned into his mouth, touched him. He was ready. A part of her watched as she undid the buttons and guided him, both of them breathless with the haste, the suddenness, the feel of her hand on him.

"Ahhh," breathed Dorothy. I'm liquid fire, she thought. She bit her lip and felt the cold wood of the table upon which she sat, the cold only adding to the heat of what they were doing. She must remind him to pull out in time, but for now she clawed at the table and leaned forward to bite his neck. He raised his head, and they looked at each other, their faces slack, their mouths longing to touch. There would be no later for them this night, when she might lie in his arms and pretend that such was hers forever, only this snatched moment, which in its very desperation made the pleasure unbearable. She tried not to moan. Music was playing outside the door, couples dancing far off in the center of the hall. And then here it was, everything she'd ever wanted, and she clawed his back and whispered his name.

"MIGHT, ER . . . I call, er . . . upon, er . . . you tomorrow?"

To tease her father, Alice danced with poor Lord Mulgrave. It had taken all his bumbling courage to blurt the sentence he just had. She knew it, and she didn't care.

"Perhaps."

The Duke of Balmoral had not graced the fete with his presence.

And Richard was in the garden with Renée, no doubt kissing her passionately. And Barbara and John Sidney were nowhere to be seen. And the woman who raised her goblet in a toast earlier was Caro. She hadn't tried to approach Alice, and for some reason that bothered Alice more than an approach might have. And Colefax had danced with her twice, making compliments that should have pleased her vanity but made her feel guilty and ruthless. And not knowing, she'd danced once with wild Lord Rochester, who was very drunk, who waited until the very end to tell her he wanted to touch her breasts and something else much more intimate, only the word he'd used was obscene.

She let go of Mulgrave's hand, wondering when the queen would call the maids to leave.

"A dance, mademoiselle?" someone asked.

She waved good-bye to Lord Mulgrave, examined the man who'd just spoken. He was dressed as a playing card, the jack of spades, and she didn't know who he was, and it didn't matter if he danced well. They danced in silence, which suited Alice, who gave herself over completely to the turns and circles and promenades, her hand resting lightly atop his. It was divine to move in silence, to give herself to the music and steps, to close herself off from the world of choices and betrayals and guilt. The dance ended, she knelt in a curtsy, her head bowed, her chest rising and falling as she caught back her breath. Her leg was aching. Really, it was painful.

"Magnificent, as always. I bid you good-bye, but not adieu."

This time he spoke in French.

Her head jerked up, and she stood clumsily. He was walking away, the face of the big playing card on his back mocking her. Henri. It was Henri Ange! She ran after him, ignoring the pain in her leg, calling his name, managing to grasp the edge of the card. He stopped, throwing her off balance. He pulled her to him, kissed her hard on the mouth, and at the same time caught her leg with his foot, so that when he let her go, she fell backward, her treacherous high heels slipping out from under her. She landed hard on her backside, her breath leaving her in a surprised sound.

"You've had too much to drink, Alice Verney. For shame."

His English was the accent of the streets outside this palace. Even as people were rushing forward to help her, laughing—this was a court that lived off gossip, and arrogant Alice Verney's drunkenness would be chewed over tonight and tomorrow—he slipped away. When she was standing, rubbing her elbows, he was nowhere to be seen. All around her, people were pulling off masks, and some of the men, their heavy, long French periwigs, too.

"Disgraceful. I'm going to speak to your father. Really, you know better." An austere and frowning shepherdess glowered at her.

"I'm not drunk, Aunt Brey."

"Dorothy Brownwell does not oversee you maids the way she ought. In my day, the maids would have been in their chambers hours ago."

Someone was tugging on her gown. Gracen. "The queen's retiring. And Luce is quite drunk. You're going to have to help me walk her out."

Alice looked in every direction. There were bare faces everywhere now. He was gone. What could she do? Nothing. It was deliberate. The dance. The kiss. The push. A kind of dare. She walked away from her aunt's sour face, walked by the Duke of Buckingham, sitting sprawled in a chair, looking weary and drunken.

He was a playing card too, the king of spades, but she didn't think about it.

CHAPTER 24

Queen Catherine placed the last patch pulled from her face into its silver box, accepted the damp cloth her tirewoman gave her, and rubbed her face. A somber, birdlike woman looked back at her from the mirror propped upon her dressing table, no red bows and rouge to give her charm anymore. All around her was the litter of her position, India embroidered cloth sheathing this table, the table itself a welter of silver or jade boxes, crystal and gold candlesticks, silver brushes, silver hand mirrors, ivory combs, French powders, Spanish rouges, silver or wood ormolu trays, the jewels she'd worn tonight tossed aside like nothing.

So, she thought—her thoughts, as always clear, unlike the mangled mess of her English—he has fallen in love again, this time with Renée de Keroualle. I hate her. It isn't her fault. Dunkirk, Tangier, and a barren queen . . . Enemies striking out, wishing to frighten, to crush her. The months of it were weighing on her. His pleasures. He must have them. . . . They were stronger than any tie of loyalty or affection. A taster . . . The Duke of Balmoral set a taster in her household. All the royal households, he soothed. Poison . . . Her old nurse whispered it was the fashion in France to poison those who'd become a bother, useless, as she was, the queen who seldom conceived, could not carry to term. They hissed at her. They tittered at her. Thank the Mother of Jesus for the king's kindness tonight. They would like for her to die. She was nothing to them. Worse than useless. The one thing a princess, a queen, must do, she could not. Would they lock her away? Would he divorce her? Commit a crime against all that was holy for the kingdom's sake? What would she do if she were divorced? Insist, like another queen of long ago, that it wasn't legal and beat sad wings against the bars of disgrace, banishment from court, while the king went, as this long-ago king had done, on his merry way, to another wife?

Barbara Bragge had entered the bedchamber, was waiting permission to approach. Barbara was one of her favorites, and she turned in her chair to nod her head, watching as she walked forward. Something about her has grown older, thought Queen Catherine. Is she in love? She ran her eyes over Barbara's lovely face. Sweet, steadfast, slow to anger. Will I lose you soon to that young man you seem to adore? Barbara knelt before her. Yes, I think so.

Barbara raised her eyes. They were glowing with a light that seemed to come from far, far within. The queen saw it and reached out to touch Barbara's cheek fondly.

"This night I have been given two of my dearest wishes—" Barbara's voice broke, but she continued on. "My friend John Sidney wishes to study the true faith. May I ask Father Huddleston to appoint someone to him?"

"But that makes delightful! I have overjoy! Father Huddleston studies with Mister Sidney, I command. And I am godmother when he is baptized. It is honor."

Barbara seized the queen's hand and kissed it. "You're so kind."

Queen Catherine had been happy, too, this particular way, once upon a time. The memory of it was treasure to her; she was as tender of it as she would have been a living child. "So? And when are there marriage?"

Barbara blushed and didn't answer.

"A dower I give."

"No, Your Majesty."

"Nonsense. Go, now. They burn hazelnuts. You put your John Sidney in the fire."

She turned back to her mirror. Ten years ago she'd been one and twenty, like Barbara. Princesses weren't promised happiness, were they? How good to know it did exist. She would dower Barbara Bragge £2,000.

The fire in their antechamber was roaring. It was tradition; no fire might go out this night, or evil things might enter through the chimney. Alice washed her face with a cloth. The other maids were in their nightgowns, sitting before the fire, waiting for her, huddled in their warmest cloaks, ones lined with wool or velvet or, if you were Alice Verney, softest, warmest beaver's pelt brought over in a ship from the Colonies across the sea. Alice dried her face on another cloth, stepped back into the cloak Poll held, pulled it around her. Last All Hallows' she'd been in France, Princesse Henriette alive. Now she was home, and they would do the old ways tonight, just as they always used to do, and tonight she'd danced with an evil spirit who threatened the queen.

Alice looked about her, thinking about the spirits said to be roaming outside the windows. Did Princesse Henriette's spirit rest, or did she walk the corridors of Saint Cloud demanding revenge? Was she in a place of purgatory, or had she ascended to heaven? Luce was retching in a chamber pot over in a corner, her servant holding back her hair. The baby of them, Kit, was already in bed, asleep. They'd only just managed to unfasten and unpin her gown and take the ribbons from her hair before she closed her eyes and went to sleep. Alice had been that way at fifteen, too, awake one moment, romping like a wild thing, asleep on her feet the next. Barbara wasn't here. Where was she?

"By earth, by air, by water, by fire, this circle is cast," she said. The words were Poll's, from her mother's mother. So was the ritual they would do this night. All Hallows' was one of the best nights for divining sweethearts.

"You sound like the magician tonight," said Gracen.

"He was good, wasn't he," said Dorothy. "He took two coins from behind my ear."

"Are we ready?" Alice took the basket of hazelnuts from Poll, held it before each young woman, and they took hazelnuts into their hands.

"One for you, and one—or two or three—for a sweetheart," Alice reminded.

"Tell me again," said Renée.

Alice repeated the instructions in French. "You hold it against your heart, think of your beloved—or admirers—then put it on the grate with your own. If it cracks open, he's untrue. If it pops out, he won't marry you. If it burns beside yours, you'll wed and live in peace. If it begins to blaze and burn, he adores you."

All became laughter and talk and teasing, as one after another they attempted to place hazelnuts on the hot grate without burning their fingers. Then came the anxious watching and waiting as the fire crackled and whispered, and then screams and questions as hazelnuts began to crack open, or blaze, or pop completely out of the fire, or burn quietly. A hazelnut flew off the grate and into the fire.

"That's yours, Brownie!"

"I didn't do one!"

"Yes, you did. I saw you!"

"Renée, one is blazing, and one popped out. Which one is Lieutenant Saylor? And who is the other?"

"Alice, both of yours are blazing! Who are they? Colefax and Mulgrave?"

"Gracen, Gracen, look! Yours just popped!"

Gracen grabbed the offending hazelnut and threw it into the fire, where it blazed up and then exploded. "Pooh."

Gracen sat down by Barbara, who'd just joined them, still in her costume. "Come with me tomorrow to see Ashmole," Barbara said very quickly, very quietly, so that Alice might not hear.

There was more laughing and teasing, and then the basket was passed again for another turn. Nothing ventured, nothing gained, Alice always told them. Barbara let the basket pass her by. Beside her, Gracen dug through the remaining hazelnuts.

"He's going to be faithful this time."

"Are our games too silly for you these days?" Alice asked Barbara. How mocking my voice sounds, she thought. What did Barbara and

Gracen whisper about? I'm a jealous witch, thought Alice, but she couldn't stop herself.

"I saw Caro toast you tonight," Barbara answered.

Everyone became silent.

"Ah, but you didn't see me acknowledge it, did you?"

"Alice, why don't you forgive her?"

Dorothy stood up, clapped her hands together. "Time for bed, everyone." She shooed the young women off right and left, then picked up the basket of hazelnuts. But Alice and Barbara didn't move.

"She betrayed me. I don't forget betrayals."

"She was with child. He had his part, yet you danced with him tonight. Why is hers so wrong and his forgiven?"

"It isn't forgiven. I do it—" Alice stopped. She did it to hurt Caro, to show her she could take Colefax back if she wished, and to show the court the same. Not a pretty mix. "Friends don't betray friends," she finished.

Later, in bed, Alice lay on her back, unable to sleep, a knot in her heart. Barbara lay with her back to her. And Alice couldn't bring herself to say words that would mend over their quarrel.

Over in another bed, Gracen snuggled against a sleepy Kit. "I saw my beloved's face in the mirror," Gracen whispered.

It was an old custom, to go alone to a looking glass, eat an apple before it, and comb your hair. The face of your future husband might be seen, looking over your shoulder. "Let's play, Kit. Put your hand there, and I'll put my hand here."

"I don't want to. They'll hear us."

Gracen put her lips on Kit's neck. "No, they won't. We won't make a sound." But later she had to cover Kit's mouth with her own to stop her moaning.

Chapter 25

All Saints' Day
November 1

Balmoral stood with his back to Richard, staring out at St. James's Park. "You've been to every alehouse and tavern?"

"Every one between London Bridge and Whitehall. I thought I would go to those around the palace today, and across the river tomorrow."

"Good. Someone will inform. It's the way of the world."

Richard cleared his throat. "If I may, Your Grace, why do we not raise a hue and cry, have it known from every pulpit that the queen's life is in danger, describe Ange to the public?"

"This is a matter of great sensitivity. It is not to be bandied about on every corner of London or, indeed, every corner of Whitehall. There are larger fish to catch than Ange. I am placing you directly into the queen's household. You will be captain of her bodyguard."

Richard was silent. The promotion was a double-edged sword. On the one hand, he became a captain, with greater pay and rank, with an officer's place in the cavalry. On the other, the queen's bodyguard hadn't the respect of the Life Guards. And the queen herself was not in favor at the moment.

"You have my permission to order her personal guard howsoever you see fit, to protect Her Majesty to the fullest. There is a council of her household in which you will participate, but it is imperative that you report directly to me, and it is imperative that you speak with no one, I repeat, no one, about what is discussed in that council. It is a secret council at the moment, whose concern is her welfare. Willbert in the treasury has your orders. You will be lodging near the queen's quarters, just off the guardroom. Dismissed, Lieutenant—forgive me, Captain Saylor."

Richard walked through the antechamber. Curious glances followed from those waiting to attend the duke as he dressed for the day—it was the custom, taken from France, to attend the dressing of great noblemen. A man on the way up allied himself with a nobleman by attending him, by listening to what was discussed, and by trying to be of use. It was a custom that Richard was impatient of, so he'd more or less ignored it, attending the Duke of Monmouth only occasionally. The talk there was of taverns and whores and escapades from the night before, or complaints as to how this or that councillor of the king had slighted him, of how his uncle, York, was cold to him. And lately talk of Jesuits in secret places, of the city filling with Catholics sent from France to spy and make trouble.

Alice told him he must attend several men's dressings—Buckingham's, York's, Balmoral's, Arlington's. You must hear what is said in each and begin to know those who attend regularly, make friendships with them, for they will be carrying out the will of those they attend. That way, you will begin to see the blowing of the winds at court. They're always blowing, Richard, and a wise man pays attention, so that he may survive the storms that arise.

Odd. He'd thought he'd be reporting to Lord Arlington, who was in charge of the secret service; he'd thought other councillors would be involved in this affair of the secret letters, now the poison. . . . Likely they were, he was simply at too low a level. Captain of the queen's bodyguard. He didn't wish to leave the Life Guards, but he was honored that Balmoral trusted him. He crossed Whitehall Street, walked through Holbein Gate, through a passage near the banqueting hall to the great public courtyard, to the buildings where the clerks for the army had a chamber. "Orders for Lieutenant Saylor."

An officious clerk didn't look up from his pen and paper but continued to scribble as if Richard weren't standing there.

"Direct me to Mr. Willbert, please. I've orders from His Grace the Duke of Balmoral."

That got the clerk's attention.

Richard followed the clerk in and out of tables over which other men sat hunched, the sound of quill pens scratching over parchment, to stand before Willbert, one of the assistants to His Majesty's secretaries of state, who rose and bowed to Richard, handed him a folded and sealed letter.

"You'll present this to the lord steward. Lodging, firewood, and three meals at the queen's open table are part of your pay. Good luck to you."

"Have you supped, Mr. Willbert?"

"I never eat until two."

"The beef at the Swan is very good. Will you let me buy you a tankard of ale to celebrate my promotion?"

"That I will."

"I'll be standing at King's Gate."

"Good enough, Lieutenant Saylor."

Richard grinned. "Captain, it's Captain Saylor."

Whistling, he walked back through the tables of clerks. Might as well begin now, with this Willbert, a clerk to the secretaries of state. We supped at the Swan, he'd tell Alice later, and he told me all the secrets of the affairs of state. He'd call on Monmouth, tell him the news, go to the stables and check on Pharaoh, his horse. Then he'd walk across Whitehall Street and through the banqueting hall, into the privy courtyard and through the Stone Gallery, find Renée, kiss her, and tell her. Captain of the queen's bodyguard. Order the household guard as you see fit. He smiled. He'd take his cue from Balmoral's old regiment, the Coldstreams, the best regiment in Cromwell's army, which had been the best army the country had seen. They weren't ready for him in the queen's bodyguard, but he was ready for them.

Several hours later, Richard walked into the queen's guardroom and looked over the men lounging there. Some were sleeping, some were playing cards, some were drinking ale. An older man looked up.

"Captain Richard Saylor, appointed captain of this guard," Richard said to him. They had the discipline to leap up from their places, be it bed or chair, and salute him.

"Sergeant, present yourself."

It was the older man. "Thomas Miller, at your command, sir."

"Where are my lieutenants?"

"Not on duty at the moment."

Richard didn't like that, but he'd deal with it later. One lieutenant should always be on duty here in the guardroom. It's what ruined us, his father had told him, arranging tiny lead horses, tiny lead soldiers, across the quilted coverlet of his sickbed, our laxness and overweening pride. Courage is part of victory, but so is chance, and when chance is allied to discipline, a man conquers. Study Cromwell, my boy, study Monck, study Balmoral; they know how to lead armies.

"Present the men. I'll want your name and how long you've been in service."

The guardsmen lined up, making a square around the chamber, whose walls held muskets, swords, and pikes, their weapons. As Richard stood before each, the man told him his name and history. Only of few of them were old veterans, having served in Cromwell's armies. One of them had been in Spain in the 1650s when King Charles had pulled together a regiment to fight for the king of Spain. The rest had begun their life as soldiers with Queen Catherine's arrival. They'd seen service fighting the great fire of London and protecting the palace and city gates during the Dutch wars. And a few, a very few, had served on ships as part of a landing force when the last real war with the Dutch had been fought.

"Send word to my lieutenants to call on me by this evening. Send me the duty roster. Muster yourselves on the parade ground tomorrow at dawn, and we'll see how you drill. That's all."

"Cocky bastard," said one once Richard was out of hearing.

"He did well in Tangier, distinguished himself," said the sergeant. "And if I'm not mistaken, he was on board the *Revenge* with the Duke of York in the first Dutch war. I remember a lad that very well may have been him. Held his own there, too, running messages in a longboat for

His Royal Highness even though cannonballs were exploding in the water all around him. We may have us a real soldier here." The sergeant sighed. He'd been with Cromwell. He knew what real soldiering meant. It meant the easy life was done.

IN THE CHAMBER the king used for his privy council meetings, Balmoral finished the last of his report to that council, the smallest, most powerful of the king's. There was nothing in the report about a Henri Ange. "And last, I've appointed Richard Saylor captain of Her Majesty's bodyguard," he said.

"Saylor?" Buckingham, who had been slumped in his chair, eyes closed, dozing—a habit of his during the reports of other council members—sat up. "Sent by His Majesty back to France with our dear princess?" There was a note of incredulity in his voice. "The young man who bungled the business in France?"

"I think highly of him," Balmoral replied.

King Charles, who had been examining the spaniel in his lap for fleas, stopped, raised his eyes to his councillors.

"He acted with greatest caution, almost killed two horses bringing us the news, made an excellent and most thorough report afterward." Balmoral was calm. A report, he did not say, that the captain general of His Majesty's army had had to pull strings to find and read for himself.

"Which I found full of rumor and unsubstantiated statements," Buckingham replied. "Why such a change at this time?"

"We have just spent the past quarter hour listening to His Grace explain to council that he foresees Guy Fawkes as well as Ascension Day will be unusually dangerous this year," said Lord Arlington, these days the king's favorite councillor. It was over Arlington that Buckingham and Balmoral had allied. Arlington referred to the coming date of November 5, when London remembered a plot to destroy both houses of Parliament by blowing them up with gunpowder. Although the event had happened in the time of the king's grandfather, the plotters had been Catholic, and that was not forgotten.

Balmoral would be stationing guards throughout Whitehall and up to the Strand on each of the celebration days.

"We have word there is some stirring among the Anabaptists and Presbyterians." Balmoral stared hard at Buckingham, who used both groups to his own ends.

"No Quakers?" It was King Charles, who spoke for the first time. "But, of course, all of them are still imprisoned, are they not?" The question wasn't meant to be answered. It was the king's way to point out one more time how displeased he was by the various acts passed against his will by Parliament and the machinations of different men seated at this table to suppress all religion save that of the Church of England.

There was a silence.

"I don't think this is the time to change the queen's bodyguard," Buckingham said.

"It is precisely the time. The bodyguard had been without a captain for some time. The appointment of one is necessary. The recent death of a beloved member of the royal family, the talk surrounding it, has stirred feelings, and we lie perched between two celebrations most apt to set off those feelings. I would not have Her Majesty—or anyone—harmed." Balmoral spoke dispassionately. He might have been describing an experiment in a laboratory.

"Saylor has my blessing," said King Charles.

Buckingham shrugged indifferently but exchanged a look with another man around the table, which Balmoral caught. Confound him, Balmoral thought, he's plotting with someone else against me now. "I have no more to report."

King Charles went back to scratching the belly of his spaniel.

"Our next item is His Grace's journey to France in the next month," said Arlington.

"I remind everyone that this treaty Buckingham goes over to sign commits us to war with the Hollanders, and our most pressing need is new ships," said one of the councillors.

"And soldiers, unless you intend to fight every battle at sea," said Balmoral.

"Am I to delay the signing while you quibble over funds?" Buckingham looked around the table. "I'll fund the building of a ship myself. I'll fund a regiment myself."

"Enough drama, George. My ministers are within their rights to bring up the matter of funds, since we are inevitably short of them." King Charles didn't look up from his spaniel. "Our cousin King Louis will give us funds."

As I wager he's already begun to do, thought Balmoral, watching the king.

"And I'll go to the House of Commons at the proper time and ask for money, as I always do." At a snap of King Charles's fingers, the little spaniel jumped from his lap, sat on her haunches, and raised her front legs beguilingly. "Mimi teaches me how, don't you, girl?" The men around this table had tired of his dogs long ago. Not a one of them smiled.

"You shouldn't have to beg," said a council member.

"No indeed," agreed the king in an affable way. "I will be highly displeased if the purpose of Buck's journey is bandied about. We don't need the mob screaming popish plot—or plot of any kind—at this particular moment. And if I am to beg for funds from the obstreperous gentlemen who make up my Commons, I want to do it on my own terms."

"Your Majesty will have no trouble coming up with reasons to fight the Hollanders again," said Balmoral.

"Particularly since last time we did, they sailed down the Thames and were allowed to burn half our fleet," said Buckingham.

"Allowed?" Balmoral rose, his chair clattering noisily backward behind him. "Implying what, sir? If we weren't before the presence of His Majesty, I'd draw my sword and fight you in this very chamber! You are an impediment to this kingdom and this council. I don't forget that it was your jackals who called for an investigation and very nearly toppled this council. I challenge you, you confounded, whoring son of a bitch dog—"

"Do sit down, Edmund. At once. I won't have any dog maligned in such a way," said King Charles. And when the jest failed to turn the moment: "Gadzooks, man, sit down. How are we to conduct the business of this kingdom if my council murder one another at the council table? If I thought you'd been at fault, I would have removed you as captain general of my armies. George, your words are amazingly ill judged."

"A poor jest. My wit falls flat. I do beg your pardon."

Balmoral sat, but it was evident he was furious. His hands shook as he gathered his papers.

"I will now make a report upon the state of the treasury," said the council member in charge of the treasury. Buckingham closed his eyes and leaned his head back to doze, while King Charles gazed out a window. The report from the treasury never changed. The crown was in arrears, back pay was owed to servants from musicians to hawk keepers, from sailors to soldiers. There was always some fresh plea from someone to be paid. There was always some new plan to borrow, but this was always atop old loans, which were never repaid. No one enjoyed the reports from the treasury because no one knew how to remedy the situation. The House of Commons granted money, but it was not enough for His Majesty's pleasures, all their ambitions, and certainly not enough to fight wars. A large and grateful sigh emerged from Buckingham when the report ended.

"Are we finished? Is there more?" asked King Charles, but it really wasn't a question. He stood, effectively ending the meeting, his spaniel held in the crook of his arm. Balmoral remained at the table, so when the others had left, the king nodded to him. "Don't take all day, Edmund. I want to walk in the park while there's still a bit of sun outside."

"You are aware I have placed a taster in your household, the queen's, and York's."

The king's eyes moved over Balmoral's face, considering each blink of the other man's eye, each change in the fold of a wrinkle. "I am, but I repeat I am seriously doubtful someone will poison me to make Jemmy king."

"There's word, not yet verified, that an expert in poison is now in London. This person"—Balmoral cleared his throat—"was most recently in the household of Monsieur."

The king stilled.

"I would, at the moment, sir, prefer to keep this information between you and me."

"Who is behind this?"

"That, sir, is what I would wish to ascertain, and why I wish for secrecy."

"Fifth Monarchy? Jesuits? Those Scotch Presbyterians of yours?"

"The queen's life may be in real danger." Balmoral was calm. "A reflection, perhaps, of certain rumors afloat, certain actions of the last year. I've not spoken of this with the others," he continued in the way he fought his battles, steadily, sending in pikeman after pikeman until sheer numbers tired the enemy.

"The others?"

"This council. Nor do I intend to, yet."

"I trust you have your reasons?"

"I do."

"And you will share them with me at the proper moment?"

"I will."

"I want this person found."

"The poisoner and he who is behind it all? I have your permission to seek both? For that is what I do."

The king didn't answer, and after a moment, Balmoral stood, bowed, took his portfolio, and left the chamber. To his annoyance, Buckingham was in an adjoining chamber, drinking a goblet of wine. Balmoral could smell its red grape from the doorway. How much I desire a drink, he thought.

"I wanted to ascertain there were no hard feelings between us."

Balmoral was silent, and Buckingham added offhandedly, "You seem hasty in your appointment of the queen's captain. I can think of a dozen men who would have liked the position and deserved it more."

"If all goes smoothly, I will be congratulated. If something should—God forbid it—happen, Captain Saylor bears the brunt of it."

Buckingham smiled. "I hadn't thought of that. It was a game in there, Bally, old man, to make others think you and I are enemies, to throw them off the scent of our friendship and mutual intention, nothing more. Mustn't let them think we're plotting."

Your confounded plotting, thought Balmoral, not mine. Yes, we should have a queen who can birth an heir. Yes, he should divorce, and we've made the way clear with the Roos bill. Yes, he knows it and will act upon it or not in his own time. But to kill the queen? If you are behind such, and I suspect you are, you go beyond the bounds of decency. You always have. God save me, but I despise you. Rumor has it Monmouth will assume my place as captain general the moment I breathe my last. I see your touch in that. Rumor has it the king, in exchange for your favoring war, has promised you will lead the army against the Dutch. Over my dead body. I am going to serve your fair, fat head to His Majesty upon a platter. A service to this kingdom before I die, as I am surely doing. Confounded Salome herself will have nothing on me.

Balmoral bowed. The two dukes smiled falsely and ruthlessly at each other.

In his most private of chambers, stirred to anger and more by his encounter with Buckingham, Balmoral stared at a beautiful crystal decanter. He kept it inside a handsome cabinet, so that he might ignore it. But it was a siren. Singing to him through closed doors at any time it chose. To have some of what was inside it or not, was the question, whether he could risk a small taste of the ambrosia it held? What else had he to do this day, in case the drinking should not cease, as it was wont to do . . . this day and the morrow, for it was always a morrow when he woke, ill unto death and with little or no memory of the hours before and with guilt screeching in his ear, as his wife had done before she joined him in drink and died a drunken fool.

Riggs knocked, poked in his head. "A lady awaits."

Balmoral frowned, his temper up, as always it was when this siren witch devil tempted, and he held her at bay. "I am not receiving visitors."

"Not even Mistress Verney?"

A few moments later, Riggs ushered Alice into Balmoral's closet. She wore her mask and short, hooded cloak, which told him at once that something had occurred.

"A moment only, Your Grace. It is of great importance."

She sat in a chair whose arms and legs were twisting serpents of wood carved by Grinling Gibbons. At the ends of the arms, each serpent's mouth held a small, darkly grained apple. If one looked closely, one could see that at the ends of the tails were tiny women, long hair flowing into more serpents. Alice untied her mask, let back the hood of her cloak. Her face was pale. "I've seen Henri Ange."

"Our dark angel? Where?"

"Here. Last night, at the fete. He danced with me, but I did not know it was he. We'd not taken off our masks yet. Why did you not come to the fete, Your Grace? I was vain enough to think I might tempt you to one dance."

He ignored the irrelevant. "What did he say to you?"

"Nothing of any importance. A hello, a good-bye."

"My word, he has his gall."

"He frightens me."

"Let me summon the captain of the queen's bodyguard. Will you have some refreshment, Mistress Verney? Some wine or a cordial? There's a sherry from Portugal of which I am particularly fond." He gestured toward the open doors of the cabinet, toward the beautiful decanter, its own kind of sweetest poison within.

She refused, and they waited in silence, she too upset and he too irritable for words, until there was a knock upon the door.

"Enter."

Richard walked in, and Alice's eyes widened. He bowed to her as she clapped her hands. "But this is delightful! Oh, you've made a wise choice, Your Grace. Lieutenant—I mean, Captain Saylor—showed such care in France. He—"

"He gave service before France and after. I believe myself quite capable of judging a soldier's mettle, Mistress Verney." He turned to Richard. "Mistress Verney saw an angel last night, Captain."

"Henri Ange. He danced with me. I had no idea it was he. Then he spoke to me in French, and I knew. He wanted me to know."

"He's daring us to catch him. It's a game," said Richard.

"Captain, you will put the queen's bodyguard on high alert. A taster is in place for both Their Majesties. They'll take nothing, absolutely nothing, from anyone's hand but his."

"I will speak with the captains of Prince Rupert's guard, His Majesty's, York's, Monmouth's. Ask them to be alert to any strangers, any Frenchmen," said Richard.

"He won't be a Frenchman," said Alice. "Last night he spoke as if he'd been found in a cradle in the rushes of the Thames."

"Then an alert to any strangers—"

"And a description of him," cut in Alice.

Balmoral watched them, their youth, something in them sparking off each other. Saylor had been tested in Tangier, hadn't he? And done very well on his little missions in France. If the queen died, the young soldier would be ruined. A pity—but so be it. "I wish him captured alive, Captain. I will be satisfied with nothing else. You will report to me on a daily basis."

"Yes, sir."

Balmoral closed his eyes at a sudden dizziness and took a step backward, a half stagger. Richard caught him by the arm. "Your Grace!"

"It's nothing. Call my man. And leave me."

"Let me stay," said Alice.

"Leave me."

Richard waited with Alice in the bedchamber as she retied her mask, fingers fumbling, and pulled up the hood of her cloak. "I don't want to leave him," she said.

"Do you—have you feelings for His Grace?"

"Yes. Richard, please, let us work together on this. I will tell you anything I gather. Will you do the same for me? You may have all the glory of it. I just want to make certain Her Majesty survives."

"As do I." He held out his hand to her, and she shook it before hurrying away.

Alice and Balmoral, thought Richard. Well and well and well again.

Chapter 26

A court page walked across the open courtyard of Whitehall's wood yard. Henri Ange, leaning against a wooden pillar, straightened.

"You there," he called.

The page turned. "Sir?"

"I've lost my way. I've come to see the queen dine in state." Henri held up a coin. "That's for any clever boy who can show me my way out of this place." He nodded his head to the piles of stacked firewood and dark piles of charcoal under the porches on each side of him.

"She doesn't dine in state today. On Sundays at three of the clock, sir. And you'll need to go past the guards at the banqueting hall."

"Do I need a ticket?"

"No. Just a clean coat."

Henri nodded his head toward the colored sash around the boy's waist. "Are you a queen's page?"

"No, I belong to the Duke of Monmouth's household. The queen's pages wear green hose and ribbons."

"Green. Very good. Thank you, boy."

The page held up the coin. "Thank you."

Henri smiled. "Where do you think I see a bear baiting?"

"On the south bank, sir. That's where you'll find them."

"I've heard they're fearful."

"That's what I hear, too."

"Never seen one?"

"No, sir."

"Well, seeing as I've never seen one and you've never seen one, and I'm new to this great city, what about you showing me my way about and the pair of us going?"

"You'd take me to a bear baiting?"

"Unless that's wrong. I hadn't thought of that. Am I wrong to offer it?"

"No." The boy put out his hand. "John Howard."

"Henry Jones."

"Pleased to make your acquaintance, Mister Jones."

That made two of them.

Chapter 27

November

Please to remember the fifth of November, the gunpowder treason and plot. I see no reason why gunpowder treason should ever be forgot.

Queen Catherine sat at her embroidery stand, colored threads and boxes of beads jumbled in a cloth bag nearby. Maids of honor chatted and played cards. A fire roared in the fireplace. A page played a guitar. It was the month of rain, of fog, of branches bare, naked to leaden skies. It was the month of Guy Fawkes Day, Queen Elizabeth's Ascension Day, St. Catherine's Day. Needle poised, as it had been for some time, the queen stared down at the pattern, Adam and Eve in the Garden of Eden. In her mind, she wrestled with what to do.

"Ma'am," said Frances, her lady-in-waiting, "Lady Brey is here to speak privately with you and Mrs. Brownwell."

"Send for Brownwell."

Frances shooed the others from the chamber, ushered in Lady Brey. Queen Catherine put down the needle she couldn't seem to pull through fabric and waited as Alice's aunt marched toward her purposely, began speaking even as she curtsied.

"You will forgive me, ma'am, if I speak frankly, but I know no other way. I'm not pleased with the way my niece, Alice Verney, is being overseen. At Monmouth's fete, I found her sprawled on the floor and, if I am not mistaken, drunk."

Queen Catherine was silent.

"It is the duty of the mother of the maids to protect the reputation of the girls she oversees. Alice must make a proper marriage, and if her reputation is spoiled, that will not be possible. I am most upset, most displeased. I've half a mind to withdraw her from court."

"We protect the maidens."

Lady Brey made a dismissive sound. The king set the tone of the court, and everyone knew it, the king and a queen who had power. This one had none.

Dorothy Brownwell, out of breath, entered the privy chamber, hurrying to curtsy before the queen. "A thousand pardons, Your Majesty. Lady Brey, how do you do? I apologize for my tardiness."

"Lady Brey has no happy with care of the maids." Queen Catherine was cold, tiny and frowning and cold.

"My concern is with one maid only, and that is my niece, Alice Verney. My sister died giving birth to her, so I feel a special responsibility, and of course she had to grow up like a gypsy before her father returned with her to England, and I quite fret for her. I encountered her drunk at Monmouth's fete, and I am here to make certain that such does not happen again."

"There must be some mistake," said Dorothy. "Mistress Verney is decorous, I do assure you. Not that she doesn't get into—what I mean to say is that she is quite lively, to be certain, but drunkenness is not one of her—"

"I know what I saw."

"We protect the maidens," Queen Catherine repeated stubbornly. "Good day, Lady Brey."

Dismissed, Lady Brey curtsied abruptly and left the chamber. It was clear she was not pleased.

"Oh dear," said Dorothy once the door was closed behind her.

"Perhaps you watch a little closer."

Dorothy blinked with surprise.

"Not so much time with Lord Knollys, heh?"

Dorothy caught her breath.

"Someone, they tell me, not one, but more times. Whisperers of court, they look for bad. The reputation of a woman, she is all she has. Go."

Dorothy left the chamber, eyes blinking with tears, a fury working itself up into something fierce. How dare Her Majesty fuss at her! She could do nothing! The king moved among the maids as if they were his personal harem. A proper queen would stop it. For her to criticize—she did the best she could in impossible circumstances!—well, it was too much, really it was. What were they saying about her and Knollys? That she ran after him, that she made a fool of herself over him? A woman became lonely. A woman became afraid. A woman became older. Oh, why didn't his wife just die so she could leave this position where she was clearly unappreciated? Watch a little closer. Was she just to sashay up to the king and say, No, go away, sir? It's a maid of honor, sir, mustn't touch, sir? Respect, sir, you do remember what that means? Oh, that would be pretty. Before Renée it had been Frances, and before Frances it had been Winifred, and before Winifred it had been . . . she couldn't even remember the name. Running after Knollys!

She slammed the door to her chambers shut with a bang, sat down in a chair, and cried until she could cry no more, then found the last bit of cake in her cupboard and ate every crumb.

BARBARA SLIPPED AWAY with Gracen and a maidservant to visit the famed astrologer Ashmole. They walked down streets where boys and apprentices piled lumber and hay into high mounds that would be burned this night, the night of Guy Fawkes, along with effigies of the pope. When they found Ashmole's lodging, his servant said to Gracen, "If the young lady would be so kind as to wait here."

"I'll join mademoiselle." Gracen was as imperious as a queen.

"No, I'll be fine, indeed I will," said Barbara.

Elias Ashmole bowed to her and opened a door to a more private, smaller chamber, and Barbara went inside. Gracen made a face at the maidservant who'd accompanied them and began to prowl the place she was left in, several chairs, a table covered with a Turkey carpet, a bed with fine hangings, stars and moons embroidered upon them. She went to a cabinet, made of wood stained ebony, and tried to open one of its doors, but it was locked. She sighed, went back to the table. There was a pack of cards. She sat down and began to play solitaire.

In the other chamber, Barbara shivered inside her cloak and drew it closer. Ashmole's eyes didn't miss the movement. She gave him nothing else to draw upon. Her cloak covered her clothing, and a mask covered her face from forehead to chin. Her voice, however, was young. He continued to shuffle the cards, biding his time. They sat in a chamber that had been tinted a blue just verging on black. Planets and stars were painted upon the walls. Even the windows were painted over. The only light was the branch of candles on the table between them. The air was close. Bathing seemed to have no part in Ashmole's telling of fortunes.

"You told my fortune at All Hallows'," Barbara said. Don't tell too much, advised Gracen. Make him work for his coins.

"I told many fortunes that night," Ashmole answered smoothly, watching her.

"I'd hear mine again."

He was silent, shuffling the cards. At last he began to place them upon the cloth of the table. He put seven down, turned one over. "Fortunate in love."

She made no movement, but he could feel her smile. He turned over two more, said nothing, turned over the rest. Quickly he picked up the cards, reshuffled them, and dealt out seven again. He turned three of them over. Now he knew exactly who she was—the laughing lovely who would die soon.

"Mademoiselle has a wonderful life ahead," he said, pulling the cards back into the deck. "She will live a long life, surrounded by children and then grandchildren, and her husband will prosper. It's in the cards."

"They say I'll die, don't they?"

He never answered questions like that, no matter what the cards said. "No such thing. They promise—"

"How much for truth? I've brought guineas, gold guineas. How many of them will it take for you to tell me the truth?"

"What is truth, mademoiselle? An imp, a wisp, changing from moment to moment, ephemeral, hard to grasp."

She put a guinea on the table. Even her hands were gloved. But he knew who she was. It was rare to see a woman who had so marked a fate. She and the young man were deep in love. Time would never mar that. There would be no opportunity. So her beloved would always remember her with blazing love. She was fortunate in that, at least. He took the guinea and smiled, showing missing teeth, reshuffled cards, laid them out. "I see long life, happiness, oh, perhaps a quarrel or two, but a—"

Barbara touched the Death card with the tip of a gloved finger. "It shows every time. It did the same before. I saw your surprise. You shuffled the deck three times before you would talk with me. You did that with no one else."

"Because your future is so handsome, I had to do it over to believe it. Travels, your husband will travel in his life, but you—"

"Tell me this, at least. Will my child live?"

"Oh, you'll have many children. And that husband, he'll travel to faraway places, the empire of China, the mountains of India . . ." On and on he went, describing the full life she would have, telling her how many boys, how many girls she would birth, telling her whatever came into his head, telling her everything but what she came to hear. Her silence was a presence, rebuking him, but he ignored it. At last she stood, dignity in her movements. At the door, words came from him that he would later ponder. Perhaps the dignity forced them. "She will live."

She opened the door and closed it silently behind her.

He sat where he was. What had made him speak? There was so much that was unseen by most. The child wouldn't live, nor would her beautiful mother, who had always known this. He'd seen it the other night in her eyes, staring at him through her pretty mask, felt it from the spirits, which hovered over her and showed themselves to him. There was much sorrow in this life, his fate to see it, but not necessarily to tell.

"You've not spoken a single word since you came out of his chamber. What did he say?"

Barbara didn't answer, just kept walking, head down, as Gracen and the servant hurried to keep up with her. When they finally entered the maids of honor's apartments, she took off her cloak, untied her mask, found her rosary beads, and said sharply to Gracen, "When Alice comes, send her to me, please."

"Where will you be?"

"In the queen's oratory."

Gracen stretched out a hand. "Let me—"

"Do as I say."

Gracen pulled back her hand, her face mutinous, but also sad.

Richard walked down Whitehall until he was at the mews, the vast royal stables that were just on the other side of Charing Cross, the intersection where Whitehall, Strand, and Cockspur streets met. Grooms and stable boys, street vendors and sedan men, liked to loiter about the base of the statue of the king's father at the center of the intersection. He walked into the stable yard, into a barn of horse stalls, down the alley between the stalls, opened one, and his horse snorted at him, nudged his shoulder as he walked closer. "Hey, old man, I got here as soon as I could. I'm busy these days." He found a brush, began to curry the horse's coat, even though it was gleaming, began to whistle.

"Is that your horse?"

Richard saw the boy from Madame Neddie's standing on the other side of the stall door. He seemed thinner than Richard remembered, more awkward and young. "How'd you find me?"

"Soldiers like yourself have horses. Horses have to be stabled. I waited at the statue until I saw you."

Richard slapped Pharaoh's rump. "Do you hear that? He tracked us down. You have the makings of a spy, Etienne, isn't it?"

"It's really Walter."

Richard brushed Pharaoh's neck a stroke or two. "Outside the door, down a bit, is a barrel of dried apples. Get one," Richard told him, and when Walter was back, "Walk slowly toward the horse, holding out the apple so he can smell it . . . Let him have it . . . Now pet his nose. Pharaoh, meet really Walter. Really Walter, this is Pharaoh, the strongest horse in His Majesty's stables, won the King's Cup at Newmarket this summer. Here, make yourself useful. Brush his mane. Have you ever brushed a horse? Steady and firm. Pharaoh likes it if you pat him once in a while and talk to him. I tell him my troubles."

"What does he answer?"

"To stop whining and brush him properly and then take him for a gallop. You have to mind not stepping behind him because he'll kick you. Have you eaten?"

"No."

"What time must you return?"

"Before dark."

"Good enough. We'll get you back before dark. Get on with it. I'm hungry. Have you seen that man about?"

"No Frenchmen."

"It's said now that he may not speak in French, may speak like you and me."

ALICE ENTERED THE oratory quietly. Barbara was still kneeling at the altar rail of solid silver, her fingers flying over her beads. Alice sat on a bench. Barbara finished her last prayer, crossed herself, and sat by Alice, leaned her head on Alice's shoulder.

"What is it, Ra? I'm to sup with the Duchess of Cleveland this evening, if you can believe it. At my father's command. Some kind of silly Guy Fawkes supper."

"There will likely be gunpowder under your chair."

"I don't doubt it."

"Alice, how long have we been friends?"

"Since you came to court."

"And you love me."

"With all my heart."

Barbara raised her head from Alice's shoulder, shifted so that she could see Alice's face. "I'm going to marry John Sidney."

A storm was there in Alice's suddenly drawn brows, but Barbara felt strangely at peace. "I want your blessing."

"And if I don't give it?"

"I'll marry him anyway."

"Sweet Jesus, I could get you anyone if you'd let me! With your beauty and my father's interest, you could have your pick. Don't do this, Ra!"

"It's too late."

"What do you mean?"

"I'm with child."

"Ra!"

"I want your blessing."

Alice stood, stepped back. "I can't give it. We promised each other better than this. You said you were never marrying, and then I come back from France and you're hanging all over him! There are a dozen better matches you might make if you must. You deserve better than him! I want to kill him and slap you!"

"It wasn't his doing, Alice. I wanted it as much as he."

Alice put her hands over her ears. "I don't want to hear."

"It isn't so simple when you truly love someone. It's so sweet, the flesh is honey, like fire— Oh, Alice, you felt something like it for Cole. You talked to me of it, how hard it was to stay chaste, how close you came to yielding. I understand now. I didn't then, but I do now. I love him so. I want this, more than anything. I want to be his, completely, to be one in the eyes of God. And he wants it, also."

"You don't have to marry. Father will send us to France. We can live there while you grow the baby, and then—"

"I'm to abandon it? Is that what you'd have me do?"

"No, no, of course not, but—"

"I'm marrying John Sidney. I want your presence at—"

"No."

Alice took another step back. Barbara reached to take her hand, but Alice snatched it away. "I have to tell you something, Alice—"

"I don't want to hear another thing from you. You're a fool, Barbara Bragge. Stupider even than Winifred. Acting like a whore! Throwing yourself away! A fool, a fool, a fool!" Alice picked up her skirts and ran from the oratory, not knowing where she was going. She had to be alone.

She felt murderous. All her plans, all her hopes, knocked to pieces. She knew how it should be. Not Barbara. She was the clever one. Not Barbara. Never Barbara.

Somehow she was on the first floor in Dorothy Brownwell's chamber, moving swiftly past a surprised servant, moving to the little chamber that was Dorothy's closet. She tried to open a window there. She must have air. She banged on it, then somehow had the sense to push, and it hinged open. She drew in drafts of the cold air, breathing in and out. Such stupidity on Barbara's part! There wasn't a happy marriage. She'd never seen one. There was lust to begin with, perhaps, but it cooled, particularly for the men. It always cooled. It was the fashion, and no one could be behind fashion. A woman had to choose with care, think of the time when she'd be bearing his children, think of the life she must build for herself. There had to be a handsome allowance, perhaps something only of hers. There had to be a title, or the promise of a title, else why do it? Why endure a man's boredom and cruelty, indifference and selfishness? Ra was one of the loveliest young women at court. She could have married on her beauty alone. She beat her fist on the stone ledge. Stupid! Stupid! Stupid! In three years there would be three babies and not enough coin, and John Sidney would be pinching and ogling any woman who took his eye, just to add some spice to their humdrum life. It wasn't what she'd planned at all. She didn't want Barbara to leave her—

The shock of that thought stopped her.

She leaned her face against the metal of the window. There was such a hard knot in her heart. She didn't want Barbara to love anyone better than her. That was the truth of it.

Her friend, her sister, her keeper of secrets, moving on, leaving her behind. She'd desired Cole, but she'd never truly loved him. What was love? Blindness, nothing but momentary stupidity. She couldn't see what Barbara saw.

And she hated her for that, for seeing what she couldn't and for leaving her behind.

AT DUSK, HER father was waiting outside the Duchess of Cleveland's house in the neighborhood of Westminster, to the east of Whitehall. On the meadows and hills in the distance, bonfires were burning. They burned in Hyde Park, in the hamlets of Marylebone and Chelsea. For Guy Fawkes. In London itself, bonfires burned in the streets, and people danced around effigies of the pope. The great fire that had burned nearly four hundred acres of London had started with far less, and London wasn't rebuilt from it yet.

"You're late, Alice. His Majesty has already arrived." Sir Thomas waved Poppy toward the back where the servants would be, took her by the arm as if he would shake her. She pulled away from him.

"Don't trifle with me, Father."

He looked her up and down. "What's brought on this pretty little mood?"

"Nothing. What am I doing here?"

"You are accompanying your father, who is creating a truce with the Duchess of Cleveland so that you are not ruined. You will behave yourself."

Alice made a sound.

"You are not to show that dreadful temper of yours tonight, or I swear I'll do as your aunt asks and send you to live with her."

"What do you mean?"

"She was most perturbed by some behavior of yours on All Hallows' and has made a formal call on me to say that you are not being supervised properly as a maid of honor, and that if you wish to make a respectable marriage and not disgrace the family, you need to live with her."

"Ha."

"My sentiments exactly, but she called upon the queen to say the same thing."

"She didn't. How stupid. Everyone is so stupid."

"Alice—"

"Leave me alone."

They walked silently up the stairs to the duchess's presence chamber. She thought she saw her father's new footman, Perryman, lurking down a hallway, a bad wig upon his head and a false mustache under his nose, like some actor in the king's troupe of players.

"Is that Perryman?"

"Where?"

She pointed.

"No."

And then they were in the presence chamber, and because she was late, she went and made a deep curtsy to His Majesty, who was jovial, his attention upon Renée, who was also there. Then she had to go to the Duchess of Cleveland, who didn't reply to any of her apologies, and then she had to greet the other guests, the actor Charles Hart, and the actress Peg Hughes, and the Earl of Rochester, and Lord Mulgrave, who smiled shyly as he bowed over the hand she held out—what her father had been saying to him, sweet Jesus only knew—and finally, thank goodness, there was Frances, the Duchess of Richmond, and Prince Rupert. And everything was drinking wine and silly, light banter. King Charles had done the same thing with Frances, courted her under Cleveland's nose, with Cleveland's permission. Now it was happening with Renée. What perversity underlay that?

"—Buckingham is writing another play."

"—Sedley has the pox."

"Will the Commons be friend or foe this spring—"

"The Hollanders are grown overbearing. There will have to be another war—"

"—she's his latest mistress."

It took Alice a moment to gather they were talking of the actress Peg Hughes and that her protector was Prince Rupert. It will be an actress next for my father, she thought. It's become the fashion. And part of her was glad, because that would stop Louisa Saylor, and part of her was tired of lust's latest fashion. At one point, a fly was somehow in the chamber and buzzing around, and then its presence began a rowdy, wine-driven game—people were tossing pillows and swatting at it, Renée laughing at the antics, and Alice watched it all dully, smiling mechanically and thinking what great fools everyone was.

After supper, Prince Rupert tapped her on the shoulder, and she slipped away with him even though it was cold, too cold, on the balcony upon which they stood. Bonfires were bright on the horizon. She and Rupert shared puffs of the long-stemmed pipe while he philosophized to her, of which she listened only to snatches.

"—it's a jumble, it is. There was never enough coin to begin with—"

"—the king and Parliament can't subsist together. Too at loggerheads—"

"—Buckingham has put a wedge between His Majesty and York. It breaks my heart—"

"—reduce expenditures of the household, but how, I ask you—"

Alice puffed the pipe, exhaled smoke slowly, until Prince Rupert urged her to come back inside before they were missed. Their sweet, an apple pie the size of a small table, was sitting in a place of honor, the duchess's majordomo beginning to cut into it. Alice sat near her father, who was arguing with Rochester over whether to go to war against Holland or France, which of the pair was the most natural enemy of the kingdom, when a shriek cut through festivity. Mice were crawling out of the pie!

The shriek had been made by the majordomo, who began to slap at them with his knife, but this made the pie fall over onto the floor, and in the falling more mice were released, and they were darting everywhere. Renée screamed as a mouse tried to scamper up her gown. King Charles picked her up in his arms. Rochester and Mulgrave and Sir Thomas were stamping their feet as mice skittered everywhere, and then Alice was scrambling to climb up a chair, screaming, shrill and hysterical, adding to the pandemonium.

"They're gone, they're gone!" Prince Rupert was trying to coax her down, but she couldn't stop screaming.

Her father reached up and slapped her, and she collapsed sobbing into his arms.

"Deathly afraid of them. Bitten when she was a child," she dimly heard him say.

And then a solitary mouse crept out from the overturned dish and stood on hind legs, sniffing the air. Alice screamed again; her father turned her head away and hugged her tight.

The Duchess of Cleveland, who was standing on a chair, looked across the chamber over the mound of broken pie and dish and crumbs and met King Charles's eyes. Biting his lip not to laugh, he held a whimpering Renée in his arms, looking like a bridegroom about to cross a threshold.

"Never let it be said," Cleveland called to him, "that I provide you a dull evening." And then she let out a laugh, earthy and full, part of her inherent allure, and then everyone was laughing, as the lone mouse stayed where it was, frozen with fear; but Alice still sobbed into her father's shoulder, and he patted her head and said between gasps of laughter himself, "There, poppet, there . . ."

"Do you remember the mice at the Louvre during Louis's Fronde?" Prince Rupert said to the king. The Fronde was civil war the French king had endured as a child.

"I could have played tennis with the largest every morning," said King Charles.

"I made them serve on ship with me," said Prince Rupert. "They became pirates, and no one has seen them since." Prince Rupert had served as a privateer during the exile, going out to sea to capture prize ships for the king.

"Were you very poor, sire?" Renée asked King Charles.

"Poor as . . . well, you have to forgive me the obvious, a church mouse, dear."

AN HOUR LATER, back at Whitehall, King Charles ordered Alice away. She walked to the door.

"Please stay," Renée called, and so Alice sat in a chair in a corner of the antechamber. I don't want to do this, she thought. I don't want to see him make love to her. King Charles led Renée to the fireplace, pulled forward a footstool that she might sit on it, sat down on the floor before her.

"I liked holding you in my arms tonight," he said in French. "I liked being able to sup with you. When you're mine, I'll expect a handsome supper every night, but no mice."

"Where will I serve you this handsome supper? Here?"

"In your handsome apartments in Whitehall. They shall be built to your desires. Say the word, and I'll order them begun."

She was silent, staring past him into the fire. King Charles reached into his pocket, pulled out pearl eardrops, huge, magnificent, and put them in her hand and folded her fingers about them. "From Surinam, made especially for beautiful maidens a king loves. May I?" He began to unscrew the earring in her ear very carefully. His hands did not fumble, were certain, warm where he touched her. When the second earring was in, he turned her to face him. "Perfect. You need only a necklace and bracelet to match."

He reached into another pocket and pulled out a long strand of huge pearls and a bracelet with a diamond clasp. Alice could see the glitter of the diamonds from where she sat. Kneeling, he dropped the necklace over Renée's head and pulled back her curls behind it. He took her wrist and fastened the bracelet. All his movements were deliberate and easy. He sat back on his heels, pummeled a nearby pillow to fatness, dropped it, and stretched out on the floor with the pillow under his head. He pulled off his thick, dark periwig and bunched it up under his head to join the pillow.

"I cannot accept these," said Renée.

"Of course not. I just wanted to see how they'd look on a beautiful woman. Wear them simply to please me. Do you know what this Guy Fawkes of ours is about?" He began to talk about the time of his grandfather and the plot to blow up the Parliament and all in it. "I can understand their impulse," he said, smiling, shadows playing over his face.

Alice pulled her legs up into the chair, settled herself like a cat, and closed her eyes wearily. She dozed, dreamed she was back at Madame's, and it was evening and snowing, and they were all around the fireplace. Do eat this poison for me, Madame said to her, holding out a baby, and Alice opened her eyes. King Charles and Renée kissed. He knelt before her, his hands on her bare shoulders, her face turned up to his, her throat long and white, her hands at her sides passive, their mouths locked together. He raised his head, and the fire outlined her profile and his. Renée didn't move, and it seemed to Alice she was in a kind of swoon. He gave a laugh, sharp with joy, and Renée started. He stood, held out his hand to her to raise her up.

"You made me immortal with a kiss. Little witch, you have my heart." He picked up his wig and hat with feathers curling the brim. "I'm happy," he said to the hat. "We could be happy, witch," he said to Renée. "Don't you desire happiness? Ah, our duenna wakes." His long face was alive and laughing, his mood vibrant. Alice loved him best when he was like this. "You make a poor duenna, and I thank you from the bottom of my heart. Sleep well, sweet maidens."

"You let him kiss you," Alice accused once he was gone.

"I couldn't stop it. And it was only one kiss."

"You were kissing back."

"He's very good at it." Renée touched the great fat pearls hanging from her neck. "Where shall I put these?"

"I have a jewel box. We can lock them there." In the silence of the maids' bedchamber, they unlocked Alice's jewel box, placed everything there. "You have a decent dowry just with these," Alice said.

"But I must give them back."

"I doubt it. He's very generous to the women he fancies. Oh, I'm so tired. Good night."

"Good night. And thank you for staying with me."

"Next time I won't fall asleep."

Barbara wasn't in their bed. Alice put her feet to the hot brick Poll had covered in flannel and placed in the bed and bunched quilts about her neck as Poll pulled the bed hangings shut. Where was she? With him. Alice knew it. How could she? She was ruining herself. She tossed and turned and pounded her pillow as if it were Barbara's face. Sleep touched her, surprising her with its swift arrival. In her mind she saw the king and Renée kissing again, their mouths melded, his hands gripping her white shoulders, Renée's eager stillness. She remembered Cole's kisses, feverish, hot, drugging her with pleasure. Give me a kiss, and to that kiss a score; then to that twenty, add a hundred more. . . .

She would never have that with Balmoral.

PRINCE RUPERT MET King Charles as he walked up the stairs to his bedchamber. Life Guards with the king saluted Prince Rupert.

"There's a fire in London," said Prince Rupert.

The king stopped smiling.

"I sent a troop out to reconnoiter, Saylor's in charge of them. Might as well make the lad earn his captain's pay. And keep him from discovering your poaching."

"Balmoral agreed?"

"He was not in a condition to make a decision."

"Ah."

"The poaching went well, I trust?"

"Ask me no questions, I'll tell you no lies. Tennis in the morrow?"

"It's nearly dawn."

"Good, you'll be all the more easily beaten."

Chapter 28

Walter was on the rooftop with the others, watching the fire. It was cold, but they didn't care. They would do anything to leave the warren of rooms that bound their lives. "Do you remember when all of London was burning?" asked Hugh, a reed-slim young man much in demand.

"Yes," answered Walter. He'd lost his family in that fire, when London as he knew it turned into an inferno. And since then his life had been here.

"Look at her. The empress is happy tonight," said Hugh.

"Who is he?" asked Walter.

"Her new love."

"Feel here." Nan put Walter's hand on her middle, where there was a slight hardening. Nan was his best friend; she and her sisters washed the sheets and emptied chamber pots and cleaned the chimney of ashes and built the fire again. She wasn't a whore, but one of Madame Neddie's customers had done this to her, held her down and taken her, and now there was a child growing. "You know what this is?"

Walter nodded.

"I might as well throw myself off this roof."

"It will be all right. I'll take care of you."

"Walter!" Madame Neddie called to him. When Walter came forward, she caressed his face. "You're going to be a handsome lad. All the better. Go and fetch us another bottle, sweetling."

Walter returned with the champagne. The cook and door porter were on the rooftop now, the last of the customers gone, except those too drunk to move. They lay snoring in beds Madame Neddie kept for just such occasions, clean sheets, pillows stuffed with feathers and lavender, the best.

"What's that you was talking to her?" Walter asked the man with Madame Neddie.

"Italian," Madame Neddie said. She leaned into the man's shoulder and sighed.

"You Italian?" Walter asked.

"No," the man said. "As English as you. It's just a game I play. I speak in gibberish, and she thinks it's Italian."

Neddie slapped at his arm. "It is Italian."

The man winked at Walter. "Sure it is, love."

Walter went back to stand with Nan, put his hand on her arm. "Let's go look at the fire."

They ran down the stairs and out into the night, braving bully boys who prowled in gangs. The fire was down Fleet Street, close to the ditch that ran to the river, close to the prisons. Walter made out a line of guards around a burning building that had collapsed in on itself, saw Captain Saylor, without his coat, smears of soot on his face and shirt, shouting orders. Guards had formed a line, were passing buckets of water from the ditch to the fire.

"I know him," Walter said to Nan. "He's my friend. A soldier. Stay here."

He ran to Richard. The fire was loud, cracking and roaring, like a demon eating bones. "Sir," he said to Richard.

"Not now. Go away, Walter."

"Yes, sir."

RICHARD TROTTED HIS horse back to Whitehall, half the queen's bodyguard marching behind him. So much for the first unexpected event. They hadn't done badly, had obeyed orders, two of the three lieutenants even showing initiative. In front of the Horse Guards building, he said to them, "Assemble in one hour." He handed his horse to his groom.

At the door of his chamber, he paused rather than throwing open the door, hit it hard a time or two with his fist. John opened it. Barbara sat on his narrow bed, fully dressed, feet tucked up under her. There on the table was a freshly baked loaf of bread and some cheese. John went to the fire, began to pour out some warmed ale from a pail in the ashes. Richard's mouth watered at the smell of the bread. Barbara began to slice it, steam rising with each cut. "How did you manage this?" he asked her.

"One of the queen's cooks has a fondness for Barbara," answered John.

"Why am I not surprised?"

"And she fetched it herself moments ago."

Richard stuffed his mouth with the bread and cheese. John brought the warmed ale, and they shared the tankard.

"Was there hurt?" asked Barbara.

"A house burned to the ground because they were French Catholic. There are perhaps four dead. Someone told me the apprentices were dancing around their fire earlier, shouting that Queen Catherine was a daughter of the pope. They threw pitched torches at the house. Those who died were French, but they'd been here twenty years."

"I'm to be baptized in a week," John said.

Richard drained the tankard, gave himself a moment. "Not the best of times."

"Will you dance at our wedding?" asked Barbara.

He looked from one to the other. "What's this?"

"It's to be a private baptism and then a wedding."

"You waste no time. Throw in a christening, and you can be done with it."

Barbara blushed a fiery color.

"Wait about seven months," said John.

Barbara put up her hands to cover her cheeks. "He'll think me wanton, John."

"I think you dear. You could do nothing to mar my admiration of you. And I thank God something pushed you to put this man out of his misery, even if it had to be seduction."

"You're glad, then, Richard?" Barbara asked him.

"With all my heart."

"I'll tell your servant to fetch you water, and then I'll walk my lady home," said John. Barbara kissed Richard's cheek, and they were out his door.

Richard sighed. He could wish his cousin something other than Catholic. . . . That thought brought him to Renée, who was Catholic, too, but Richard would never ask her to change her faith. He thought of various things they would do their marriage night. . . . It was a good thing the water his servant brought was ice cold. Richard whistled as he washed his face, pulled off his shirt, and found a clean one.

King Charles and Prince Rupert had finished their game of tennis and walked into St. James's Park so the king's dogs might relieve themselves. King Charles made his way to the long landscape canal he'd had built the first years of his reign, began feeding his ducks. Prince Rupert had gone to inspect the lime trees but quickly reappeared by the king's side. "There's a drill going on in the tilt yard!"

"You've dreamed it. Or it's Cromwell's ghost," answered King Charles.

"No such thing. It's young Saylor. He is actually drilling the queen's bodyguards."

"Mind the dogs," King Charles told a page, and walked with Prince Rupert to the outside stairs that led them up and then across top floors of Holbein Gate. They climbed stairs until they could peer down into the tilt yard and watched as the queen's bodyguard ran at wooden dummies with their pikes—long wooden weapons with a pointed steel head. The men formed small defensive squares, the sharp tips of their pikes pointed toward the imaginary cavalry charging. The tilt yard had once been the scene of many a Tudor tournament, when tournaments were the fashion.

"Stand still, my beating heart," said Prince Rupert.

"You ought to join them," said King Charles. "I might obtain a better game of tennis out of you."

"At ease," called a sergeant.

"Let them sleep until noon," they heard Richard tell the lieutenant. "Then march them into London to relieve those guarding the house. And everyone is to be here tomorrow an hour after dawn."

King Charles walked back down the stairs to a gate in the wall surrounding the yard. Once inside, he sauntered forward, and surprised soldiers at once formed a line to salute him.

"They told me in Tangier you ran the regiment for half a year," he said.

"Colonel Dillion was quite ill," answered Richard.

"Mad enough for Bedlam, you mean," said Prince Rupert.

Richard was silent. He didn't speak of those days ever.

"I don't think I was told the half," said King Charles, who had been watching Richard's face.

"The Moors are fierce fighters," said Richard.

"Was much burned in London?"

"One lodging, and some who lived there died in the fire. I thought we would stand guard until this evening, make certain nothing else catches."

"It's the damned embers," said Prince Rupert. "Spread them thin and damp them with water. I thought the fire of '66 would never die out."

"I'm sorry for the deaths. You'll make a full report to Balmoral, and we'll see what we can do. How does your mother?" asked King Charles.

"Very well, sire."

"When next you write her, pray send my regards."

Richard bowed.

Prince Rupert and the king walked out of the tilt yard, crossing the wide expanse of street before the banqueting house. Servants and pages were scurrying with firewood or coals, with trays of food from various kitchens, as the palace awoke. This was the king's favorite time of day, fresh, clean, the possibility that anything might happen still real, and the workers, the drones, as he liked to think of those up with him, about and buzzing.

"I like that lad," said Prince Rupert.

"That's a man, not a lad."

"I heard there was a mutiny, hushed up."

"His father had both legs broken at the battle of Worchester, made Wilmot prop him against a wall and gather up pistols so that he might pick off Roundheads while I escaped. I'll never forget the sight of him singing a ballad as his manservant handed him primed pistols, Roundhead pikemen in front of him as far as the eye could see. He wouldn't let us take him with us. They didn't cut off his head because they hadn't time; they were so close to capturing me. I'm told Jerusalem Saylor walked through the battlefield, turning over every body until she found his. She put him in a cart and carried him home to die, cursing any Roundhead patrol that tried to stop her. And he lived, God bless him."

Prince Rupert crossed himself. "Did you ever see him again?"

"No. And then his three children showed up one day, every one of them with some version of that red gold hair of their mother's—Norsemen's blood somewhere there." They were silent awhile, their footsteps echoing in the courtyard they now crossed.

"I hear the Vikings liked to cut their enemy's heart from his chest and eat it raw."

"Do you, now? Is that a warning?"

"Do you need warning?"

King Charles smiled and didn't answer.

Alice took the nosegay she'd requested from one of the king's gardeners, marched across the privy garden, across Whitehall Street, down the alley that led to the part of the palace where the Duke of Balmoral had his apartments, Poll following.

"He is not receiving visitors," a footman told her.

"I wish to see his majordomo."

And when Will Riggs appeared: "I wish to give these to His Grace the Duke of Balmoral."

"He isn't receiving visitors." The scar on Riggs's face drew it up on one side.

"I am not a visitor. Take me at once to His Grace."

"That isn't possible, ma'am."

Whom did he think he was talking to? A tradesman? "Don't tell me what is possible. He may be more ill than anyone can imagine. I want to see him."

"I have very strict orders—"

Alice moved around him and walked up the stairs.

"Please, Mistress Verney, he has asked that no one be allowed in. He has these fits often and never desires company."

Alice turned around midstair, so that Riggs all but bumped right into her. As it was, they were nose to nose on the stairway. "Are you telling me that he has fits often and sees no one? He might die. He might be dead even as we speak." She continued her march up the stairs.

Riggs moved around and ahead of her. "I cannot possibly allow this, ma'am. Do forgive me. Please. I will take him the nosegay myself, I vow it."

Alice walked by him, through the presence chamber, the bedchamber, Riggs before and around her, hovering like an anxious, oversize hornet. At the door of the duke's closet, she slapped her open palm against the door twice. "It's Alice Verney, Your Grace. I've come to—"

The door opened.

With a triumphant glance at the majordomo, she stepped inside. Balmoral remained at the door, swaying as if there were a great wind. "Who is it?" he asked, his words slurred.

"Alice, Alice Verney. Are you all right? Shall we send for a physician?"

"Physician, heal thyself." He stepped back and caught himself on the intricate marbled mantelpiece jutting out two feet from the wall. "Now I am a great boy. I'm fit to serve the king," he sang a folk song, "I can handle a musket, and I can smoke a pipe, and I can kiss a pretty girl at twelve o'clock at night."

Her sense of triumph withered. Alice met the eyes of Riggs, who had remained just inside the door. His Grace Edmund Colefax, the first Duke of Balmoral, was drunk to the point of not knowing what he did.

"I brought you flowers." Alice put them down quietly upon a table. Papers were scattered on it and pots of ink. He'd been writing or trying to write. There was ink over the cambric shirt he wore. "I interrupted your writing."

"Writing memories—no—that's not right, memoirs, battle instructions, such-like, war, you know, fighting, war, blood everywhere, is this blood on my shirt, is that you, little Alice, sweet Alice, who is bleeding, you or me?"

Alice picked up one of the sheets of paper. It was indeed some kind of warrior's memoir, but the ink was blotted and the handwriting wild and difficult to read. She placed the paper back on a random pile. "I will come and visit again, Your Grace," she said softly.

He crumpled, half falling, half sliding down the side of the mantelpiece. Riggs knelt at once to see to him. Alice left the closet, and Riggs followed her into the bedchamber.

She turned on him, dark eyed, heartsick. "Are these his fits?"

"I am not at liberty to say, ma'am."

"What if he falls and hits his head?"

"I stay with him, ma'am."

"Until?"

"He goes to sleep, as he's just done."

"And when he wakes?"

Riggs shook his head, sighed.

"How often does he have these . . . fits?"

"Not often, now, ma'am."

Now? "How often?"

"Once a month or so."

"I will call upon him tomorrow."

"He won't receive you tomorrow."

"I will call upon him tomorrow. You will tell him that I called upon him today and appreciated his kindness in receiving me."

Riggs opened his mouth to protest, but Alice cut him off. "Not a word from you. Good day."

Halfway down the stairs, she stopped, turned around, walked

back up, found Riggs in the closet, lifting Balmoral in his arms. She stood to one side as he laid the duke on his canopied bed, propped pillows behind him so he was almost sitting. Balmoral was as limp as if he were dead. "How long have you served him?"

Riggs sighed, as if wondering why this particular plague were being visited upon his house at this particular time. "Years now. I was his body servant when he was a lieutenant colonel. But that was long ago."

"Very good. Good day to you, Riggs. Don't forget my message."

He opened his mouth, shut it again. It was just as well. Alice was already out the door.

Downstairs, she walked past a formal chamber where there was a huge painting of His Grace on one wall. It drew her in. It was taller than her and half the width of the room. It had been painted years earlier; he stood in his battle armor, a sword in one hand, a helmet with plumes in the other, against bloodred draperies that floated behind him and partially obscured a distant scene of London, with its many church spires, its bridge across the Thames River. At his feet was a curling map of England, Scotland, Ireland, Wales, architect's tools strewn near balanced scales of Justice. Her heart hurt. She put her hand against it and stared up at the painting's face—he was a legend in the court, one of the architects of the Restoration, important enough to ride directly behind His Majesty during the entrance to London ten years ago, crowds cheering, women weeping, her father among the riders, and she in new clothes of silver lace and pearl buttons watching from a window. He was captain general of the army during the last Dutch war, and there'd been an inquiry into his conduct and decisions, because the Dutch had sailed down the Thames and set fire to any number of warships. He and York had been questioned. Had he been drunk on the morning of the attack, this captain general, this great duke, the last of the old soldiers who'd once ruled this kingdom?

She'd sail in tomorrow in spite of his anger and the way his body would be feeling. She'd sail in as if she were expected, welcomed. She'd be kind, and sprightly, and not say a word of what she'd witnessed. If he could trust that she wouldn't lecture or moralize, that she didn't care, he would see she would keep his secrets, the way he kept hers. He would marry her.

What would she do when he touched her?

Bear it. Remember what once he'd been, something honorable and brave. Was still, except broken. She, too, was brave. She could bear anything to be a duchess, to be his duchess, to have the honor of bearing his name. Startled by wet upon her cheeks, she put a hand to her face. Who was this in her who wept? How strange. But no stranger than that a hero of the Restoration—His Majesty's greatest general—should have come to this.

Chapter 29

Queen Elizabeth's Ascension Day, St. Catherine's Day, November's end

In a small chamber off the queen's chapel at St. James's Palace, Father Huddleston dipped his fingers in the holy water of the chancel, touched them to John Sidney's forehead. "In the name of the Father and the Son and the Holy Ghost, I do baptize you."

Nearby, Barbara sobbed into a handkerchief, Gracen on one side, Renée standing on the other, Richard beside her. Queen Catherine was there, and the Duke and Duchess of York, Lord and Lady Arlington, and the king.

"Another drops like a fly," King Charles leaned over to whisper to his brother. "You're not apostatizing are you?"

York was stiff. "It's the true faith and has its own lure. As you know so well."

When did you and I stop laughing together? King Charles thought, watching his brother keep his eyes upon the baptism. He knew the answer—when Buckingham began to meddle. King Charles observed his brother blow his nose loudly into a huge kerchief and wipe surreptitiously at his eyes. Altar boys began to arrange Communion. Father Huddleston moved to the altar railing, and King Charles watched as his wife hushed Barbara, wiped her cheeks, kissed them, and presented her with a wedding bouquet of winter's hothouse roses and rosemary. Then John and Barbara, with Gracen and Richard, Queen Catherine and York, moved to stand before Father Huddleston.

As the long litany that was the marriage ceremony began, King Charles motioned to Lady Arlington, who came and sat beside him. "What's this I hear about Cleveland falling in the theater yesterday," he half whispered.

"It was too amusing. She made her usual entrance. And when she sat down in her chair, it fell with her. She clattered over like a tipsy doll, and my own lord hurt his neck straining to have a really clear view of her legs. She came up sputtering like a cat, while the pit applauded. And though Tom Killigrew himself came out to see to her, she was seething. Nothing could mollify her. She left the play in a rage."

"How was the play?"

"Not nearly as amusing as Her Grace's tumble."

"I'll see it on the morrow. Gadzooks, how long does it take to marry?"

"Marry in haste, repent in leisure."

King Charles drummed his fingers on the back of the pew and leaned his head back to view the paintings done in this smaller chapel, then closed his eyes. He dozed, as he was able to do, anywhere, anytime, an attribute he'd learned running from capture. And so he missed the litany, the prayers, and the benediction. He missed seeing Richard mouth a silent "I love you" to Renée, missed seeing her return a grave smile. He opened his eyes to see Father Huddleston offering Communion to those there who wished it. The marriage was done.

Richard stepped forward to the couple. "Mrs. Sidney, I salute you."

Barbara kissed his cheek. "Now you are my cousin, too."

Leaving his seat, King Charles walked to Barbara, took her hand in his, kissed it. As everyone clustered around the bride, King Charles looked down at Renée with dancing, amused eyes and kissed her swiftly on the mouth. It was not the first time he had kissed her publicly in the last weeks, but it was the first time Richard had seen it. "Let the wedding feast begin," he commanded, and led the way to an adjoining chamber, where servants began to serve goblets of wine.

A tower of round cheeses and winter nuts sat upon a table. A servant began to carve roast beef just taken off a spit. Richard glanced at the tasters, who nodded to him solemnly. The king and queen would touch nothing they themselves had not tasted first. A guard had been in the kitchen for the cooking of this. I ought to set one permanently, thought Richard. And I ought to talk with the cooks, warn them against the hiring of new servants. Meet any new servants hired since All Hallows' . . . He kissed her as if she were his. I could kill him.

Toasts to the bride began.

"To a beautiful maid of honor who has graced this court."

"To a cherished servant who has been faithful and loyal."

"To John Sidney," interrupted York, raising his goblet, as John, who was in the midst of a swallow, choked to be singled out, "who has bravely followed the call of his conscience."

Can he never stop preaching? thought King Charles to himself. He walked over to his brother. "Your heedlessness will plunge him into trouble if you're not careful."

"How?"

"Look around this chamber. There are servants everywhere. Pray remember it is against the law of the land to be Catholic and hold public office. I ignore it, but I won't if it causes me trouble."

"I'm a fool."

"Precisely. Drink the wine and flirt with the ladies and leave off all talk of God, Jemmy, for the bridegroom's sake and my own." King Charles raised his goblet. Everyone fell silent. He felt in a wicked mood. " 'O rare Harry Parry, when will you marry? When apples and pears are ripe. I'll come to your wedding, without any bidding, and lie with your bride all night.' " He drank deeply, not seeming to care that the old rhyme fell flat in this more austere company, where the bride stood blushing and the groom stared at his king bemusedly.

That was for me, thought Richard. The kiss was a first shot across my bow. This is the second.

King Charles held his goblet to be refilled and called out to

Richard, standing on the other side of the chamber, "Captain Saylor, pull me from the abyss."

Third shot, thought Richard. He raised his goblet. " 'Drink to me only with thine eyes,' " he began to sing, his voice tender, true, no sign in it of the anger pulsing in his temples. " 'And I will pledge with mine. Or leave a kiss but in the cup, And I'll not look for wine. The thirst that from the soul doth rise Doth ask a drink divine; But might I of Jove's nectar sup, I would not change for thine.' "

King Charles looked around the chamber, at the sentimental smiles on the faces of the women. Richard had changed the mood entirely.

"To Mrs. Sidney's eyes." Richard held his goblet high.

King Charles made his way to where Renée stood. "Are you enjoying the wedding?"

"Yes, sir."

"Every woman's desire?"

"Indeed."

" 'Come live with me and be my love and we will some new pleasures prove,' the poet says. There are other ways men and women may ally most joyfully, as I intend to show you. I see the bride and bridegroom are retiring. There is to be no flinging of the stockings. No wedding bacchanal, it seems. A pity. I always enjoy those."

It was the custom to see the bride and groom to bed, for her to take off her stockings and fling them out to be caught by any man of the company, for everyone to make bawdy suggestions and ribald comments about this first night the bridal couple would spend together. This age, as had most—except for Cromwell's—celebrated the pleasures that came with coupling. But whatever celebration there had been in the chamber departed with the bride and groom. If there was one thing King Charles would not endure unless forced, it was dull company. In a moment, he had commanded cloaks fetched, was tying them about Gracen's and then Renée's necks. Queen Catherine stood back, watching, and he brought a cloak to her and tied it about her neck, too. "Are you pleased for your little maid?" he asked his wife.

"Very. Thank you. You honor with the presence of yourself."

Something in the high-strung nervousness with which she spoke touched him. He stared down at her, seeing the taut lines around her mouth. "I won't abandon you."

"Divorce is no abandonment? I am stupid for I not understand."

"I never discuss policy at a wedding, ma'am. You'd be wise to do the same." Turning, he held out his arms, first to Renée, then to Gracen, snubbing the queen. She made a sound, and Richard stepped forward, offered his arm.

They all walked across St. James's Park, the night cold, pages running before them with torches, a few of the Life Guards with them. The sky above was clear of cloud, stars sparkling. November moved toward winter solstice, the turning of the year, the longest night, the shortest day, moved toward Advent, preparation for the arrival, the birth, of the Christ. King Charles stopped, pointed. "There is Orion, his dog stars at his heels. Artemis loved him, you know, and her brother Apollo sent a scorpion to kill him, and she set him in the sky, where Scorpio forever pursues him. See, it's just rising there."

"I'm cold," Gracen complained.

"Step lively, then, girl."

King Charles began to run, forcing those with him to do so also. Across the park they ran, the pages, the guards, the queen, Richard. By the time they reached the stairs that took them out of the park and up into Holbein Gate's top floor, they were breathless, laughing. King Charles sent the women up the stairs, calling up to them, "Beauty before majesty. Majesty before the military," he told his guards. At the top of the stairs, he stamped his feet, rubbed his gloved hands together. "A race. Whichever of you two reaches the maids' apartment first shall have a good-night kiss from the king."

Gracen raised her skirts and was off. Renée ran after her, as much to escape Richard's frowns as anything else. King Charles winked to his guards, tipped his hat to the queen, met Richard's eyes coolly, and set off down the hall.

Richard and the queen stood a moment in silent discomfort. Richard's heart was raging. "I know a way," he said, "that might get us there first. Shall we do it?"

His was not the only heart raging. "Why ever not?"

"We'd have to run."

"Then run, captain of my guard."

"Give me your hand, Your Majesty."

They ran toward the back stairs that would take them to the first floor sooner, where the maids of honor's apartments were. Henri Ange stepped out of the deep shadow made by a corner and followed them, until he saw guards standing in a first-floor hallway. Then he faded back into a shadow, like one himself.

"BUT WHERE HAVE you been?" Alice asked Gracen and Renée when they entered the bedchamber to sleep.

"To a boring supper." Yawning, Gracen untied her cloak, stepped out of her shoes, sat down, and untied her garters, rolling her stockings down a white leg. "They do say the way Arabella Churchill caught York's eye was by falling off a horse and lying there with her legs showing. It must be true, because her face is nothing to brag of."

She tossed her stockings at her servant, held her bare leg out at an angle like a dancer, and considered it. "I, on the other hand, have handsome legs and a handsome face, if I do say so myself."

"Still up? It's very late." Renée kissed Alice, sat down, pulled up her skirts, and allowed a servant—she had been given a servant by the king—to take off her shoes, untie garters, roll down stockings.

She likes being waited upon, thought Alice, watching her. He's winning her. "Who was at the supper?"

"The Duke and Duchess of York, Lord and Lady Arlington, Their Majesties." Gracen stood close to the fire, shivering, as her servant unhooked the back of a tight vest. She stepped out of her skirts to stand only in her chemise, a soft gown of finest lawn, with intricate lace at its sleeves and neck. The chemises were sewn by nuns in Portugal, one of the gifts Queen Catherine gave her maids of honor. The nuns made them for no one but the queen.

"Why weren't all of us included?"

"I have no idea. I'm sleepwalking right now. Watch me sleepwalk to bed."

"Renée, why weren't the rest of us included?"

"I'm very sleepy. Come to bed."

"Where's Barbara? Gracen, was Barbara there?"

"She was not."

Alice caught Renée by the hand. "Tell me the truth. Was Barbara there?"

"Yes."

From one of the beds, Gracen gave a sigh. Alice went to the fire and stared into it, her mind busy. The queen wouldn't exclude her from a supper, invite Gracen and Renée and leave her behind . . . unless she'd been asked to by the one person whose every command she obeyed. But why would His Majesty exclude her? And where was Barbara? This could not be allowed—a maid of honor gone all through the night yet again. It was permitted only when it was His Majesty. Tomorrow, she would inform the queen. It was clear Brownie was going to say nothing. It was, therefore, her duty to speak, for Barbara's sake, for her reputation. She shrugged off her fur-lined cloak and slipped into bed beside Renée, who was already sleeping.

Barbara no longer slept in the same bed with her. She slept with Gracen and Luce. Not a young woman said a word at the change of sleeping arrangements—Barbara had just climbed into the other bed, and Renée had moved into Alice's. No one spoke, and Alice had felt how they were all waiting for her to say something, yet she'd been silent, too. Just rolled over onto her side as if it were all perfect. But her anger was huge. And under it was even larger hurt, even though she was at fault. And now she and Barbara weren't speaking to each other at all. Everything was strained and awful, and Alice didn't explode but acted as cold as winter ice from the river outside this palace whenever Barbara was near, all the while with a growing ache in her chest and throat. Sadness, anger, regret, vengeance, all churned around in her. It was almost unendurable.

THE NEXT MORNING, Alice curtsied to the queen.

"Your Majesty wished to see me."

Queen Catherine took a deep breath. In the chamber beyond, Edward was feeding the canaries, who flew about their cages in excitement, shrilling at him. The sound was comforting. Familiar. All the queen's life there had been chambers with cages of birds in them. Training for me, she thought, startling herself. Standing beside the queen, Dorothy twisted the end of the handkerchief she held. "Come and sit at the feet, Verney. There." Queen Catherine took one of Alice's hands in hers and began to pat it. "How long is it that we have know another?"

"Since you came from Portugal."

"You are a small sister to me than a servant. When I first come, hardness, difficulty there is, and you make to smile. You say I have learn English. You and Barbara talk with me. I have shy, have afraid to make the mistake, and you say I talk with you and Barbara without afraidness, you are nothings, maids of honor, you say. You play the tricks upon his whore that have me to laugh so hard."

"No one knows who plays—played—those tricks, Majesty."

Queen Catherine continued on around her objection. "I have watch this the small sister become young woman, clever, lovely, and so determine."

"Too determined," muttered Dorothy.

Queen Catherine and Alice glanced over at her.

"Pray forgive me. My mind was wandering."

"You have care for me, for Mrs. Brownwell, for Barbara, for Caro—" Alice jerked, but Queen Catherine went on. "For Caro. Yes, Caro, who do what she do, but is love by you for long time before. You love very hard, my dear. Maybe too hard, yes? Those we love do not do as we wish, and if we truly love, we must have allow it. Love is the bird she fly or land as she please. One cannot will it. You listen in this, yes? I have some experience of it."

"Charity suffereth long, and is kind," Dorothy interrupted, spouting like a plump parson. "Charity envieth not. Charity vaunteth not itself, is not puffed up, doth not behave unseemly. Beareth all things, believeth all things, hopeth all things, endureth all things." Dorothy paused, at memory's end, while Alice stared at her in amazement.

Queen Catherine took Alice by the chin and gently swung her face back to her own. "I have news to tell with you, delightful news. It make us happy. The friend marries, oldest, most true, last night."

"No—"

"Yes. And I want that you have happy for her. It is will of God that women leave parents—and friends—to cling unto husbands."

"She wouldn't do that without telling me, she wouldn't—"

"She would if you behaved—"

Queen Catherine silenced Dorothy with a flick of her eyes. "I want that you to hear from me." She leaned forward and kissed Alice on the cheek. "That is from Mrs. Sidney."

Alice put a hand to her cheek as if a hornet had stung it. She stood. Out in the withdrawing chamber, the canaries were singing with all their hearts, an aria, an opera of birdsong. "Thank you, Your Majesty," she said. She turned and fled the chamber.

"What she do?"

"The Lord above only knows," Dorothy answered.

"See to her."

"Of course."

Queen Catherine watched Dorothy as she curtsied. Dorothy needed seeing after herself. The queen sighed and walked to a window to look outside. Winter was here. Dark by afternoon. Sleet, snow, ice, cold corridors, cold beds. Queen Elizabeth's Ascension Day had seen rioting of apprentices against lacemakers in Pudding Lane, saying they were all French, all Catholic. It was a slur at her, the Catholic queen—St. Catherine was the patron saint of lacemakers. St. Catherine's Day was tomorrow, her saint's day . . . Kit be nimble, Kit be quick, Kit jump over the candlestick. Everything changes. He laughed last night when Gracen told him his queen was first come, laughed and kissed her. But he also kissed Gracen and Renée, Renée lingeringly, daring Captain Saylor to say a word. If he did not divorce her, she still had to endure his public wooing. The birds in their cages sang and sang. She tilted her head to listen to them. Sweet friends. How did they warble so with a cage around them? Didn't their wings feel the urge to fly unfettered in vast sweeps of sky? Why did they not hold back their song instead of trilling with a keenness that pierced the heart? Some deep wisdom there, but she didn't feel wise. She felt old and tired and useless and abandoned. She put her forehead against a cold pane of glass. Everything changes and nothing does.

ALICE RAN TO the queen's guardroom. "Captain Saylor!"

One of the lieutenants said to her, "Is there trouble?"

"No. I have a message for him from the queen."

"Try the stables," said the sergeant.

RICHARD WAS BRUSHING one side of Pharaoh, Walter the other. In the cold, their breath made little puffs of steam. Richard's groom, Effriam, raked fresh hay into place on the floor. "Is it your child?" Richard asked.

Walter stood on tiptoe to look at him, but Richard was bent down, brushing a leg. "It ain't, but Nan is my friend."

"How do you know her?"

"She and her sisters clean the chambers, wash the sheets and covers."

"How are you going to explain your absence today?"

"I told Madame Neddie you'd sent for me."

"That does my reputation no end of good."

"I told her there ain't nothing like that between us. That I remind you of a brother who died."

"And she believed that?"

"As long as there's coin, she don't care."

"We're paying for every stroke of that brush on Pharaoh," Effriam said.

"And if I don't give you coin?"

"They'll beat me." Walter said it with no pity for himself, nothing but fact, as if he were perfectly willing to be beaten if Richard didn't wish to give him a coin. Richard had not slept well last night, that lingering kiss King Charles had given Renée playing over and over in his mind.

"I could be a groom, couldn't I? If you was to teach me, I could be one."

Richard slapped his horse on the shoulder. "What do you say, boy? Could Walter be a groom?"

The horse nudged Richard with his nose, snorted loudly, and shook his head. Richard laughed. "Go get some apples and bribe him for a better answer."

Richard watched as Walter fed the horse bits of dried apple. He was very thin, at that leggy stage that was the cusp of leaving boyhood, yet still a boy, not near a man.

"What about Italian?" Walter said.

"I beg your pardon?"

"Could that man speak Italian?"

Something in Richard stilled. "He might. Tell me more."

"Madame Neddie has a friend. She says he speaks Italian to her. He says it's Gibberish. I don't know Gibberish from Italian. Where is Gibberish? In the Indies?"

"In China," answered Effriam.

"He's thin, like you said. Dark hair."

"Interesting. Let's saddle Pharaoh and ride him back to Madame Neddie's."

"I could eat first."

There wasn't pleading in his voice, but something quiet, beyond begging.

"The boy's hungry," said Effriam.

"Richard, I have to speak with you." It was Alice, her dark furred hood making a halo around her face.

"Not now. I have business to attend to. Walter, put a blanket on his back, else the saddle will give him sores." But then Richard had second thoughts. "Is it Mistress de Keroualle?"

"No. When may we speak together?"

"This afternoon."

"I'll wait for you in the Stone Gallery."

"Who is she?" Walter asked when Alice had gone.

"A friend."

"A maid of honor," said Effriam. "Too high for you to be gawking at."

"She's pretty."

"Is she?" Richard said absently.

❧

At the Swan, Richard saw the clerk for the secretaries of state, went over to talk with him. As he did so, he watched Walter put the last pieces of a meat pie into his pocket. Caught, he thought, some of his anger from last night sparking. Is he playing me for the fool? He went back to his table. "What are you doing?" He waited for the lie, waited to give him a blistering lecture on stealing.

"For Nan. She's always hungry these days, and sometimes there ain't enough to eat for her. I didn't take none of yours, I swear."

Richard walked to the counter, purchased a tin pail for a few pennies and two more meat pies, set the pail on the table before Walter with a thud, dropped in the fresh pie and added the remainder of his, gave Walter another whole one. "You eat your fill. Here's one and more for Nan. Don't think I'm going to be buying meat pies for nine months."

"No sir. We wouldn't expect it, sir."

Out on the street, atop Pharaoh, Walter felt like a burr against his back. The cold was good on his face. How did those clerks in the treasury and navy do it, live all day in closed chambers lit by candles? He felt he wasn't alive unless he was outside, cold or rain or sun. It was a bright enough day, sun feeble, but no fog. Richard trotted the horse skillfully through carts, some carrying barrels of water, some carrying piles of refuse, through carriages and sedan men carrying sedan chairs. When I'm through with Madame Neddie, Pharaoh and I are going for a gallop, aren't we, boy? he thought.

At Wych Court, Walter slid off the back of the horse and ran toward a corner turn the narrow alley made, calling to Richard, "I'll just take this to Nan."

Richard dismounted, knocked on the red door. The burly giant opened it. "I want to speak with Madame Neddie," Richard told him.

"She ain't receiving visitors just now."

Richard held up a coin. "Tell her Captain Saylor wishes only a moment."

Chapter 30

In her festooned bedchamber, Neddie had her skirts pulled up. Henri Ange sat on a small embroidered stool before her, her feet in his lap. He was painting her toenails. At the knock on the bedchamber door, she called out, "Go away."

"Someone to see you."

"There's no one I want to see."

"That soldier."

Neddie motioned for Ange to stop. "Enter," she called, and the giant opened the door gingerly. "The handsome one with the gold hair?"

When the giant nodded, she lifted her feet from Ange's lap, stood up, and shook out her skirts. "Send him up, Tiny. I haven't a stroke of rouge on, damn it."

"What soldier is this? Why would he come to call on you?"

Neddie winked at Ange's image in the pier glass as she pinched her cheeks and fluffed out her hair. "He's formed an infatuation for one of the boys. So sweet. I think he wishes to make it official. Oh, Madame Neddie sends another beloved out into the wicked world with a new family, but not for nothing. It costs. Wait here, my love. I won't be long." She shut the door firmly behind her, but Ange moved forward silently and opened it just a crack.

"A captain are you now? Bravo, sir. What brings about this visit?"

Neddie stood before a window, and she was still beautiful, but not quite so startlingly so. Richard was trying to determine what, exactly, was different about her as he bowed over her hand. Perhaps the candlelight last time? Perhaps the rouge? "Do you remember the man I asked you about?"

"Not really."

"He was a Frenchman, dark and thin, who spoke English. Well, it's come to us that he may be posing as an Italian. He may speak Italian. Has a man of that description visited your establishment?"

Neddie played with her hair. "My curiosity is up. Why is it so important that you capture this man?"

"Capture? I don't think anyone has said that word. We want to speak with him, that's all."

"It must be a very important question you want to ask him."

"It is."

She bit the tip of a curl and batted her eyes at Richard, flirting.

"There would be some sign of gratitude," said Richard, reading her flirting properly.

"How much of a sign?"

"Ten guineas." Am I mad? thought Richard. Would Balmoral pay that? It was a huge sum.

"My, my, I am impressed."

Richard had an odd feeling. He glanced around the chamber, but he couldn't put his finger on precisely what bothered him. She isn't going to play, he thought, or she is going to lie. He'd set a watch on this house, back and front, to see if anyone who looked like Ange entered or left. That was better than paying ten guineas for what might not be the right man at all. He bowed again, turned to leave.

She followed him to the door, walked out into the hall with him, shutting the door of her antechamber. She said quietly, "For twenty-five guineas I might have seen him. Thirty and a promise from Bamoral himself that this place will never be closed, and I have seen him. There was an alderman up my ass the other day because his son is a regular."

Her crudity shocked Richard. His senses began to tingle. Something was off. "That can be done."

"Bring me a letter from Balmoral and the coins."

"The man first."

"What man?"

Richard started down the stairs. Neddie followed him.

"A letter and half the amount I ask. The other half on sight of him."

Richard held out his hand to shake hers.

"A kiss, my sweet, let's seal it with a kiss."

He put his mouth on hers, and her tongue stroked his lips, darted in between. She bit his bottom lip, held the playful bite a moment before stepping back, her eyes shining. "Sweet as honey," she said. "I knew you would be."

"This man, he's very dangerous." He was telling her too much, but the kiss had thrown him off guard.

"How dangerous?"

"He's killed."

"I'm invincible."

Richard stared after her as she ran back up the stairs, her skirts lifted so she wouldn't trip. Her feet were bare, her ankles shapely.

ANGE WAS SITTING on the sumptuous daybed Neddie liked to drape herself upon to receive visitors. She shut the door behind her and pouted. "Now don't be mad. I kissed the soldier. I couldn't help it. He is so gorgeous."

"Why did he call on you?"

"Don't you know?"

"Are you going to do what he asks?"

"Of course not."

"Why? Wasn't the price high enough? I'd give away any one of the brats you pimp, dead or alive, for ten guineas."

Neddie's laugh was low and throaty. "You heard that, did you?" She sat in Ange's lap, lifted her skirts high. It wasn't the fashion to wear drawers of any kind. She flicked his ear with her tongue. "We need to finish my toes." She bit his ear.

"Do you have a razor?"

She breathed in his ear, "Touch me? We can share the soldier. I know he'd do it. . . ."

"I want to shave my hair off."

She sat up. "Why? I adore your hair." She ran her hands through it. "It's as thick as a sheep's. Don't cut it. It's winter. Wait until summer when it's hot."

"I want to shave it off and wear a periwig. It would be warm, as warm as a hat."

"That might be handsome. Yes, I can see you in a periwig. Yes, I like that vision."

"Shave my head."

"Now?"

"You'll shave my head, and we'll finish the garnishing of your toes and see what else occurs. Something interesting, I promise."

WALTER WAS WAITING outside beside Richard's horse. "Come and meet them. They want to say thank you."

"Who does?"

"Nan and her mother."

"No, I need to be off."

"It won't take a minute. They're just around the corner here."

Richard followed him around the corner of Madame Neddie's, down the narrow space made by buildings that were only a few yards across from one another. The mud separating the buildings was slimy, smelled. It was the habit of Londoners to throw the contents of their chamber pots out a window or a door.

Richard had to stoop to enter the dwelling. He stood in a low-ceilinged chamber that seemed to be filled with people, children from babies to Walter's age or more and, as his eyes adjusted to the dark, an old man in the corner, someone feeding him some pie from the pail. The furniture was sets of beds and stools. There was hay on the floor, fresh hay, a way to keep out the chill of the dirt under it. Sweat broke out on Richard's upper lip. It was the combination of the dark, the dank, and the smell of too many people in one chamber. A thin woman came forward, a baby on her hip.

"This is Captain Saylor," Walter said. "Captain, this is Mrs. Daniell."

"We be thanking you for the food you gave Nan. Come here, Nan, and make your curtsy to the soldier."

At the word *soldier,* the old man stood and saluted.

"Dad be in the war, fought under Fairfax."

Richard nodded to the thin girl, who obeyed her mother and came forward to meet him. Was she twelve? Perhaps thirteen? "Very good. And a good day to you, Mrs. Daniell. Nan."

"My man would thank you, too, but he works in Wapping."

Wapping was past the Tower of London, where the ships docked. Likely he worked on one of the wharves unloading cargo. Her husband had a long walk to and from work, thought Richard. Outside again, he put his hand on the horse's neck. Pharaoh's stall had more light than these people lived in. They looked thin and pale, like plants without enough sun. He would be buying meat pies for nine months. Longer.

He headed up Wych Street to make his way to Drury Lane. Fields lay at its end, and he put just the touch of his spurs on Pharaoh, who knew what to do with open fields and country lanes, the horse running in his bold, nothing-held-back, gallant style and Richard leaning against his neck, leaning into the wind and cold until the pair of them were less restive. Clearheaded again, he trotted a tired Pharaoh back to Whitehall. Now there was the matter of Alice, but more important, there was the matter of Renée.

Chapter 31

Alice was in the Stone Gallery, a long gallery on a lower floor in the palace, just as she'd said. Dozing, she was huddled up into a chair, her skirts bunched around her. Richard stared down at her, at the sweep of cheek and neck, the dark hair curling out of its clips and ribbons. He didn't want to do this, to talk about the wedding last night. That had to be why she had demanded to see him. He pulled a stool close and sat. "Alice."

Her eyes opened at once. There were shadows under them. She's suffering, thought Richard, that's good. He could see a pulse throbbing in her neck, right near her jaw. The blue vein of it was pretty. For a fleeting second, he had the urge to put his finger there and trace it.

"Barbara married John Sidney last night," she said. It wasn't a question.

"Yes."

"Were you there?"

"Of course."

"She didn't invite me."

There was nothing to say to that.

"Tell her I'm never going to forgive her."

"I'm not going to tell her that."

"Where is she?"

"I'm not going to tell you that."

Alice gripped the sides of the armchair in which she sat until her fingers were white. "Why not?"

"So that you can find her and quarrel with her in the first days of her marriage? Tell me why I'd want to do that, Alice, but then answer me one better—why would you want to do it?"

"She's made a mistake."

"If she has, it's over and done with. And I take umbrage at that. John Sidney is a fine man."

"He's a nobody, a nothing."

"You mean he isn't an earl or even a lowly baron like me. One day he may be. Lord Rochester's father was a knight of the squire. It was his faithful care of the king that won his earldom. Do you think there are no more earldoms to be won? Barbara will be a great man's lady one day."

"She should have told me."

"It's your own fault that she didn't. You're as stubborn and arrogant as—" He stopped himself.

"As who said?"

"I am not going to quarrel with you."

"Who said I was stubborn and arrogant?"

"I formed the opinion myself."

"You hate me, don't you."

He pushed back the stool. This discussion was going in directions he refused to follow. It was always so when he quarreled with his sisters. They turned on him and stung him in places he hadn't thought possible, like tiny, determined, completely ruthless blond bees.

"Answer me, Richard Saylor."

He clenched his jaw. "Sometimes I don't like you, it's true."

"Why not?"

"You order people around, people who care for you, as if they were minions, and you think you know what is best, always."

"I do know what is best. Always."

He walked away from her. If she thought he was going to put up with this, she had another thought coming.

"Richard—"

Something small, unlike her, in her voice stopped him, made him turn. Her eyes—eyes so dark that one couldn't see the center—were moist, but no tears were falling. At the sight of a tear, he would walk away without a backward look. She held out her hand beseechingly. "Please don't leave me. Please."

"Don't weep," he said.

She met his gaze head-on, her eyes wet, but not a tear falling, he'd give her that. He pulled out a handkerchief and gave it to her. She blew her nose in it loudly. He grimaced. "The handkerchief is yours to keep."

"I love Barbara like my own sister."

"Then love her like a sister in this."

Alice swallowed. He watched the taut line of her jaw.

"If I can't?"

"Have the courtesy not to tell her so. You forget a piece in this, Alice. You forget that she loves you, too, and that your anger and disapproval hurt her greatly. And there's a third little being in this, to be born in a few months. Barbara mustn't be upset."

She made a growling sound and shook her head the way a wild dog might. For some reason, that made Richard laugh. If Alice sank her teeth in you, you'd never get loose. She was worse than the pit bulls that fought the bears and bulls in Southwark across the river. "Now I have a question for you," he said. "Is Renée in love with the king?" He watched her carefully.

"I don't think so."

She lied well.

He kicked a nearby stool. It flew in the air and landed with a clatter near another chair. "Then what the blazes is she doing allowing his kisses?"

"He likes to kiss the maids of honor, flirt with them."

"Does he kiss you?"

"He has, upon occasion. He thinks her pretty. Her being French charms him."

"Damn him."

"Why don't you just take her?"

"What do you mean?"

"The next time you two are alone, do more than kiss and cuddle, take it all the way."

She shocked him. "Ravish her? You mix me with Sedley or Buckhurst."

"I doubt very seriously it would be ravishment, now, would it?"

He didn't answer.

"May I speak frankly?" Of course, she didn't wait for his answer. "She's not very bright."

"How dare you—"

"I mean that she's an idiot to choose him over you."

"Does she truly choose him over me?" He wanted to throttle someone, beginning with the woman who sat before him.

"You know she loves you. I know she loves you, but it's flattering to be admired by the king. It's turning her head. He can be—" Alice stopped. No use to describe to Richard how King Charles could be. It would only make matters worse. "If you love her and want her for a bride, take her the very next time the kissing leads to . . . well, to where it leads."

"I have this dream, she and I side by side in life, turning front to front in lovemaking, back to back in threat, protecting each other."

"Renée isn't a fighter, Richard."

"She is soft and gentle, isn't she?" His anger surprised him by changing into something almost like understanding. "I won't stop her time of triumph with the king and court. I just don't want to lose her to it."

"What you described is an ideal. It's false. You'll break your heart on it."

He smiled, and Alice was dazzled, as always.

"Tell Mademoiselle de Keroualle that I will call upon her this evening, and that she'd better receive me," he told her.

"Wait. I had a thought I wanted to share with you."

"And that would be?"

"The pages are everywhere in Whitehall. Why not let them in on the hunt for Henri Ange?"

"How could we trust that it would be kept a secret?"

"We could swear them to secrecy, make them take a vow, tell them they're knights performing a task."

"I think it's too many to tell."

"Some of them, then. I'd trust Edward with my life."

"I'll think on it."

"It's a good idea. We want a web around the queen, layers that Ange can't penetrate."

"He's about to be taken."

"You have him? Richard, that's wonderful!"

"I nearly have him."

"Oh."

"I'll present him to you with a noose around his neck."

"He's very clever."

"So am I."

No, she thought, looking at him. You're brave and clever in your own way, but not clever in his way. I am.

CAREFULLY, NEDDIE SCRAPED the razor along the back of Ange's skull to finish. Tufts of dark hair lay at her feet. Setting down the razor, she took a towel and dipped it in warmed water, wrung it, and gently rubbed it over his bare scalp.

He turned to her. His face startled without hair surrounding it, the dark, arching brows punctuating something in his eyes that made her afraid, and there was very little that frightened her. She stepped back, but he grabbed her arm and pulled her into his lap.

"Am I so ugly now?"

"No. Yes. I don't know."

Ange went to the pier glass and looked at his face. Everything he was showed. "It's these eyebrows. Let's shave those, too."

"No!"

He advanced on her, and she retreated. He began to laugh. "Do I frighten you?"

He did. He really, really did. "It's just . . . I feel I don't know you now. . . ."

She never had. He spoke charmingly in Italian. "Come to me, my pet, my sweet. No one knows anyone, you stupid little fool."

He pulled her into his arms. A kiss or two later, and she was quiet. The kissing deepened. Her fear rushed to desire, because that was easier than feeling fear and obeying it, which was stupid of her, but there it was. Ange pulled and unlaced her gown between kisses and touches that weren't tender, but rough, provocative, the way she liked it. Soon she was panting, willing to do whatever he wished because the lust between them was so compelling, stopping thought, hers, not his. He turned her, bent her over, and entered her, and she moaned and arched back against him. He caressed her, making her frenzied, his hand up and down on her, until she was begging, her hands all over his thighs and hers. Then he stopped moving himself but kept the hand he had on her steady.

"So if I pay you thirty guineas, will you say you've never seen me?"

He brought the razor up to her throat with his other hand, and he sliced in just under her ear, making it sweep deep and steady across her throat. She made a sound, and her hands jerked out to clutch his arm. Ange pushed her away, and she fell like a rag doll at his feet, blood spurting, hands and legs spasming. He washed the razor in the bowl, lathered soap, and sat at her dressing table, and shaved off his brows. The body on the floor lifted a hand, farewell, adieu, and became still.

ALICE REMAINED IN the Stone Gallery, staring up at a center portion of the ceiling that was one long mural of the coronation of Great Harry. Balmoral entered one end of the gallery, saw Alice, walked up to her slowly, very stiffly, and bowed. She rose from her chair and took his arm. They began to walk.

"And how are you feeling today?"

"Terrible."

"But less terrible than yesterday?"

"I will give you that. Less terrible than yesterday."

When they reached the end of the gallery, they turned and began to walk the other way. Every now and then, they'd stop to look at a portrait or marble statue, but neither of them spoke. The first time they'd done this, he'd been cranky and protesting, telling her that she must be bored, that she owed him nothing. She knew he was there only out of shame, that she had blackmailed him into courtesy, but now, slowly, it was changing. He seemed to accept her regard, seemed to perhaps like meeting her for this late afternoon walk as outside winter sun gleamed palely. They reached the other end of the gallery.

"Do you think we might venture into the privy garden?"

He frowned at her, ready to be annoyed. "Why?"

"I like the sun. We can see if the holly has made berries yet."

Down a stair and they were in a hall leading to private chambers, anyone meeting them bowing. Outside, Alice turned her face upward like a flower and closed her eyes. Balmoral stared at her profile before they walked over to King Charles's sundial. They admired its intricacy without saying a word of its dials and arrows, its blown glass balls, showing time, date, phase of the moon, and sun sign, Alice touching tiny metal nymphs that played along the perimeter. She did it every time. She loved the dancing nymphs.

"Have you been weeping?" he asked.

"I have."

"Why, if I may be so bold?"

"A friend betrayed me." The words were out before she could stop them, and with them fresh anger.

"What will you do?"

"Hurt her."

"Only after you've reconnoitered so that there is no surprise hurt for you."

"Is that in your memoir?"

"What do you know of my memoir?"

"It was out when I came to visit. Look, there are the hollies. If the king's newest mistress is Catholic, what will people say?" Alice examined a holly tree innocently as she asked the question.

"It won't be liked. It will make certain members of the Commons more difficult than they already are and feed the fringe sects that see the end of the world coming. That particular bias endangers the throne."

Here was a moment. Easy to betray John Sidney's conversion, to hurt Barbara. The words were in her throat. "Ought someone to tell His Majesty so?"

Balmoral smiled sourly. "If someone cared enough to and did not mind being sent to the Tower of London for impudence."

"But you've always cared for this kingdom's stability, haven't you?" She didn't take her eyes from the tree. "Look, there's red there and there. Tomorrow or the next, we'll have our first sprigs of holly." She put her arm back through his, and silently they walked the gravel paths, Alice stopping now and again to examine a plant or break a leaf of some herb so that she might smell it, offering it to him, also, and he watched and inhaled sharp, clean fragrances, saying nothing, but to his surprise enjoying himself.

IN ANOTHER PART of Whitehall, on its top floor, in the king's apartments, chambers he rarely used now that new ones facing the river were finished, Richard and Renée stood in the king's privy gallery, having their first quarrel.

"I don't want him kissing you."

"It was in jest, Richard, too much wine."

"It didn't look like jest to me."

Tears welled in Renée's eyes, dropped down her cheeks, but Richard wasn't moved. "I can offer my love, my passion, my devotion, and little more than that for now. If what I am, what I offer, isn't enough, I want to know once and for all."

"It's enough. It's more than I deserve."

He pulled her to him, kissed her, his mouth tasting her tears, moving to kiss them away wherever they fell, her cheek, her ear, her breast, and then he was back to her mouth, tracing her lips with his tongue, and then another kiss, savoring, demanding, hungry, angry. He felt the moment when her desire caught fire to match his. She kissed him as hard as he was kissing her, and he pulled them both onto a window seat, pulled the draperies shut, all without his mouth leaving hers. In the cold dusk, he pulled down the shoulders of her gown, and her breasts were exposed, and he put his mouth to them, doing what he'd dreamed of doing for too many nights. She wrapped her arms around his neck, saying his name, pulling his head closer. They kissed, and the kiss was a drowning. Richard's hands were in her hair, on her shoulders, under her skirts, while his mouth was everywhere, lips, shoulders, sweet breasts. The draperies opened abruptly. Renée sat back, shielding herself, her hair out of its pins, her legs showing all the way to soft thigh.

"Mademoiselle de Keroualle, you will excuse yourself at once and go to your chamber!"

Renée stepped over Richard's legs.

"At once, I say!"

Richard climbed out behind Renée and frowned at Dorothy Brownwell.

"She has done nothing of which to be ashamed or punished. She is my affianced, and if there is any fault to be handed out, it should go to me."

"It will."

And with that, he was left by himself. He stood before a pier glass in the horn room—called so for all the sets of stags' antlers mounted on the walls—straightening the lace at his throat, pulling down his sleeves, his mind still in the window seat with Renée, still touching her, feeling her, smelling her, tasting her. He felt filled with desire and need, crazed. Crazed or not, he had to meet with the Duke of Balmoral, convince him to part with thirty guineas.

HE WALKED TO Balmoral's in the cold dark of the evening.

"You told her you would give her how much?" asked Balmoral.

Richard repeated the sum, marshaling arguments in his mind, the way one marshaled troops before battle.

"And what if this man isn't Henri Ange?"

"We don't give her the other half."

"No, Captain Saylor, we not only don't give her the other half, we take back, by force, if necessary, the money we've just given her. And if she cries out, we tell her that she may call personally upon His Grace the Duke of Balmoral, and he will explain the situation to her himself. She is a greedy sow, always has been."

"Yes, sir."

Balmoral moved to a chest upon which rested a huge elephant tusk from the East Indies, glancing back to see if Richard was watching. Richard looked away, listened to the sound of keys jingling, the creak of hinges as the chest was opened, the sound of coins being poured, clinking against one another, a dry cough from the duke, the sound of the lid dropping. Balmoral handed him a bag of coins. "Half what Madame Neddie demands. A small fortune in itself. You could take this, disappear, and live like a king in the Colonies or Tangier."

"And the letter she asks for?"

"My mood will have to improve. Bring me back Henri Ange."

"Consider it done."

"I do, Captain."

TINY KNOCKED UPON Madame Neddie's door. "It's that soldier," Tiny called, but the door didn't open.

"I'll wait downstairs," said Richard. The parlors were crowded with people. He saw that Walter sat talking with the Earl of Rochester. Richard found a corner, put himself in it as Walter saw him and walked over.

"Buy a drink," Walter told him, "and I can sit with you."

"You have a customer."

Walter flinched as if he'd been slapped. Richard watched him walk back to Rochester. Anger rose in him; it wasn't precisely at Walter, and it wasn't precisely at himself—but enough was. He signaled to the butler. "A drink for myself and for Etienne."

"Who is visiting with someone," the butler said smoothly.

"Who won't be paying as much as I will," said Richard.

"Very good," answered the butler, and in a few moments, it was arranged, Walter walking to his table and Rochester being escorted toward another slim man, the butler smiling and gesturing, describing with his hands. Richard glanced around at the boys and lads and men in both women's and men's dress, at the flirting and kissing. "Let's go. I'm waiting for Madame Neddie."

"No one has seen her today."

In Walter's tiny chamber, they played cards, ignoring the sounds around them. Every now and then, Tiny would report to Richard that there was still no answer. Finally, Richard lay down on the bed, one hand on the leather pouch tied to his belt that held the bag of coins.

"I've got to sleep for a bit, Walter. Keep a watch. I have to see Madame Neddie tonight. I don't care how late it is. If you see that man who speaks Italian, wake me at once."

"I've only seen him that time on the roof."

But Richard had closed his eyes. Walter sat at the other end of the bed, his eyes on him, on the chest under the blue coat rising and falling. He reached out once and touched Richard's leg lightly, but the rest of the time he dozed himself, his head and back against the wall. Late in the night, they opened their eyes to the sound of screams.

Richard lurched up from the bed. What men were left in the brothel were grabbing clothes and bolting past them out the front door, at which there was no Tiny. Richard ran toward the sound of the screams, up the stairs and into Madame Neddie's antechamber. Those who worked for her were gathered in clusters, some of them hugging one another, some weeping. The butler stood in the doorway to the bedchamber. The face he turned to Richard was slack, the eyes wide. He opened his mouth to speak, but no sounds came.

The screams were from Tiny, who stood over a naked and bloodstained body. Tiny's screams were cracked now, croaks crescendoing up to the ceiling and down again, making the hair on Richard's neck rise. He took the big man's arm, but Tiny didn't stop the croaking sound. Richard slapped him hard, and Tiny stepped backward until his legs hit the bed, where he sat down. In shock himself at the sight of the body, whose beautiful blond hair had absorbed blood almost to the ears, Richard ordered everyone out, then shut the door, leaving the body alone. "Who has the key to this bedchamber?" he demanded.

The butler held up a key.

"I need paper and pen."

The butler pointed to a table, and Richard sat down to write a series of notes, for a squad of the queen's bodyguard to come here, for Balmoral, to ask what he'd have him do. "Walter, do you think you can ride Pharaoh to the mews?"

"Yes."

"Find Effriam, have him escort you to the queen's guardroom, find the sergeant, give him this note, have him give this other one to the Duke of Balmoral. Tell him it's my direct order, even if he must wake the duke. The rest of you wait out on the stairs. I'm going to want to talk to each of you. Tiny, I want to begin with you."

"He can't," said the butler. And indeed, Tiny sat slumped and sobbing.

"Can you?" Richard asked the butler.

"If I have a huge, and I do mean huge, glass of port."

"Make that two, and let's begin."

Richard's mind went to the body, to the surprise there, but he made himself focus on questions that needed to be asked.

BALMORAL ARRIVED BY coach in the early morning. Richard was asleep on the floor in Madame Neddie's antechamber when he heard the sound of footsteps on the stairs. He opened a window and put out his head, hoping the cold air would wake him, take away the sick feeling he couldn't shake. The duke and several colonels of his regiment came into the chamber. Richard saluted and unlocked the bedchamber door.

"Nothing's been touched," he told Balmoral, who stood over the body.

"Ear to ear, by God. Poor Neddie. Search this bedchamber. I'll want letters, bills of account, coin, jewels, anything of value. If you find any men's clothing—"

"There's none," Richard said. "I searched after I'd talked with everyone here."

Back in the antechamber, Balmoral sat down. "What have you found out?"

"She was a man. You didn't tell me she was a man."

"Best confounded actress in this town before the Restoration. No women were allowed onstage back then. Before your time, but for fifteen years Neddie held this town in the palm of her hand, not that there were that many theatricals—stiff-necked Presbyterians and the others, every joy a sin. She made Nell Gwynn and Moll Davis look like the sluts they are. Some important men and, may I add, righteous men, loved her. There were private plays given, if you get my meaning, but she was finished once the king was back on the throne. The theater troupes wanted women to do women's roles. It was novel, exciting to the public. So she began this little specialty. You didn't sleep with her, did you?"

"No."

"Well, you wouldn't have been the first to be surprised at the finish line."

"Henri Ange was here, but few people saw him. He never came downstairs."

"Who tells you this?"

"Majew, the butler, and Simon, the cook. They saw him when they served meals, dinner or supper, but at no other time. There's a back exit in her bedchamber."

"Of course there'd be. So what happened here?"

"I don't know. No one does. No one has seen Ange for days. Majew seldom saw him directly. His back was always turned, or he was in the other chamber. The most any one of them has seen of Ange was the night of Guy Fawkes, when they watched the bonfires from the roof."

"Did Henri Ange kill her? Why?"

"Perhaps he knew how close we were to finding him?"

"But why kill her? Why not just disappear? I think it's just as likely she had a patron who grew jealous of her keeping Ange and killed her in a rage."

"Who would let someone slit his throat? I didn't see bruises on the body."

"It's confounded likely Henri Ange has flown the coop, gone back to France. You tipped him off somehow in your visit yesterday, Captain." Balmoral was not pleased.

"I'd like to post a soldier at the back entrance."

"Why would you like to do that?"

"If he didn't kill her, he won't know she's dead, and he might return."

"If I were Henri Ange and saw a soldier, I'd turn the other way and disappear."

"There's a place a soldier could hide, a lodging that looks out on the back entrance. A man could be posted there, in disguise, on the doorstep like a beggar."

"The word of Neddie's death is already in the streets, Captain. There's a network in the streets. She knew everything that was happening at a certain, shall we say, lower level. I always found her useful, very useful. Deuce take it, I'm going to miss her."

"May I post the soldier?"

"Permission granted, until her funeral. I think Ange is gone, flown away on his angel wings. It's what a wise man would do."

"Thank you, sir."

"You have the coins?"

"Of course."

"Good. Now leave me. We'll finish what needs to be done here."

Richard gone, Balmoral remained where he was. His colonels brought him letters and coins and jewels. He put them all in a saddlebag. When they'd cleaned the bedchamber of the items Balmoral asked, he sent one of them to do the same in the antechamber and the other for the body takers and walked into the bedchamber himself, closing the door. The body held an amazing amount of blood . . . who was it that talked about it, Robert Hooke at a lecture of the Royal Society? But hadn't he seen it over and over on battlefields—heads blown off by cannon, limbs cut away by sword or, worse, hacked by pike. There were times he dreamed in red. He sat down in a handsome velvet armchair some distance from the body and the blood, closed his eyes. Thank God he was old and memories were weak, holding very little power anymore.

Majew, the butler, knocked on the door and entered with the body takers. He stood beside Balmoral as the body was lifted into the winding sheet.

"Her neck will be sewn, and I'll put a lace cravat around it. No one will know. We'll paste and powder and rouge and put a lace cap on her head, and she'll be as beautiful as ever she was."

"How old was she, Majew?"

"Thirty and five."

"Thirty and five."

"Shall you say good-bye? It will be too public later."

Balmoral nodded, and Majew motioned for the body takers to put their charge before Balmoral, sent them from the chamber, and shut the door, waiting to be summoned again. Balmoral bent down, put his hand on the stark white forehead, and closed his eyes to say a prayer. He said aloud the words he had never spoken before, not that Neddie had asked for them; being born on the wrong side of the blanket to a whore shortened a man's ambitions, and Balmoral would have denied any claim as a matter of course. The man who had sired Neddie was so long dead, Balmoral could barely remember him.

"Godspeed, grandson." Beautiful grandson, whom I never wanted to know.

He called out, and they took the body away. He spoke to Majew, who'd served him in the army. "Close for a month, find another location, paint the door red, and open back up. You'll pay me a monthly stipend, as Neddie did, and I'll see you aren't closed."

"Very good, Your Grace."

He'd never made Neddie pay a stipend, but then Neddie was kin.

Chapter 32

Unaware of the drama that had been played out in one of the many brothels of his city, King Charles and his courtiers walked in St. James's Park. Dorothy Brownwell dawdled at the far edge of the group.

"Mrs. Brownwell, His Majesty asks for you," said a page.

Dorothy hurried to catch up with the king, who was walking briskly some distance ahead of her. Spaniels and hunting dogs immediately surrounded her as she approached His Majesty, as if Dorothy were a recalcitrant sheep. "Stop that," King Charles commanded. He came right to the point. "Mademoiselle de Keroualle and Captain Saylor were caught in a compromising position last evening, I hear."

"Not too compromised, sir. No one was lying down."

"One does not have to lie down to accomplish much, Mrs. Brownwell, if you will forgive me for reminding you. Perhaps Mr. Brownwell was not imaginative."

"Her virtue is intact, sir."

"Excellent. I would not like Mademoiselle de Keroualle to be alone with Captain Saylor again. Is that clear?"

"I will do my best."

"No more can be asked."

Richard searched for Alice. She wasn't among the courtiers walking with the king in St. James's Park, and she wasn't in the maids of honor's apartments, but Poll was there, shaking out gowns and letting them air on Alice's bed. "With her dancing master for her lesson, sir," Poll told him.

They were practicing in the old theater space that the king's troupe had used before the company of actors moved out of Whitehall and into a building in the city. A fiddler and a flutist were there, and Fletcher, the dancing master. Alice wore soft shoes that tied around the leg, shoes that actresses and opera dancers wore, and a short skirt that showed her ankles and calves. She was dancing across the stage and back in some kind of complicated step that required her to make a series of small leaps.

"Again," Fletcher demanded.

How beautifully she moves, thought Richard, her legs and her arms as liquid as if they had no bones. An image of Neddie, blood dark, congealed, came into his head. He shook it away, took a deep breath, concentrated on Alice's legs, slim and strong and beautifully shaped. She's mad for dancing, Barbara had said. Fletcher made her do certain movements over and over again. Like a drill, thought Richard, as he watched Alice move backward on her toe tips at a command from Fletcher. The pool of blood was under Neddie's head and halfway down the back of her body. The gash in her throat had looked like another mouth at first glance, a fish's mouth. . . . He sat down abruptly on a bench, put the heels of his hands to his eyes to rub away the vision. Night terrors had come to him in Tangier, bringing him blood-filled dreams, demon's dreams, and there was nothing he could do about them except endure until they passed. Neddie's murder had unchained the dream dragons again. He could feel images waiting on the edge of his mind. He watched as, finished at last, breathless and perspiring, Alice sat on the edge of the stage and rubbed her neck and hair with cloths. Fletcher knelt beside her and felt the calf and bones of one leg. She might have been a horse he was examining.

"You're favoring the left side," Fletcher told her.

"I wasn't."

"You dance like wisps of clouds, ethereal." Richard moved out of the darkness.

Fletcher lifted an eyebrow as Richard pulled himself up to sit by Alice on the stage. "Is this a tête-à-tête?"

"Yes," answered Richard sharply, and Fletcher moved away, pretending to busy himself with gathering music for the musicians.

"Alice, do you think Henri Ange would kill someone with his bare hands?"

"Who has died?"

"A brothel keeper, her—his—throat slit."

"Poison is from a distance. One never has to see one's victim die, never has to touch her." But in her mind, she was remembering the circle of Henri Ange's arms around her, his soft command, Say thank you, my dear Henri Ange, the terror that was suddenly there in her. "Madame suffered terribly."

"Balmoral thinks he may have left England."

"But that would be wonderful!"

"Only if it were true." In Richard's mind, Neddie's sightless eyes stared up at him. His body gave the slightest of shudders.

Alice saw it. "Did you find the body?"

"Yes."

"I've never seen a dead body."

"I pray you never have to, Alice. Good day."

She gazed after him, swinging her legs back and forth from the edge of the stage like a girl. Fletcher sat beside her. "So, the wind blows in that direction, does it?"

"There's no wind, Fletcher, not even a breeze."

"He and Mistress Keroualle were caught in a compromising situation last night. It's all over the court. His Majesty is not pleased."

Alice didn't answer.

"His Majesty has asked for a Christmas revel this year. Purcell, Dryden, and I are to do it. I wonder if this changes things. . . ."

"Why would it?"

"Just whom do you imagine the revel is to highlight?"

"Me."

"Guess again."

"Her Majesty."

"Please. I'll have you both written in, of course, so that it won't look as if we've herded gowned cattle onto the stage, but you are not the main attraction. So, tell me more about this soldier boy, who is obviously willing to risk disgrace for La Keroualle."

"There's nothing to tell."

Her bad temper told Fletcher far more than confession would have.

IT WAS THE first Sunday in Advent. In churches throughout England, priests of the Church of England lit the first candle of the four in the Advent wreath. "Behold, I will send my messenger, and he shall prepare the way before me: and the Lord, whom ye seek, shall suddenly come to his temple," they read from huge Bibles, whose gilt page edges glimmered as the light of candles caught the gold.

HANDS WARM IN a fur muff, Alice walked from Whitehall, Poll and Poppy trailing behind, to have a Sunday supper with her father. A friend of her father's, a Dutchman who visited London, met her in the hall, bowed over Alice's hand.

"One hears you have captured the admiration of His Grace the Duke of Balmoral," he said.

"Reports exaggerate."

"Daily walks in the Stone Gallery. I smell a courtship. If there is any way I may be of service, dear lady, you have only to call upon me. Good evening, Mistress Verney." He placed his hat on his head and walked out the door Perryman held open.

"Well, he was most kind," Alice said to her father.

"Rumors are thick about you and Balmoral. He likes to fancy himself up upon all court news. I hope you know what you're doing. I'm not letting go of Mulgrave yet, in spite of your dallying. Sit down. Perryman will serve us."

"Perryman, was that you I saw the night of the Duchess of Cleveland's disastrous supper, in a bad wig and worse mustache?"

Her father began to laugh as Perryman answered, "No."

"And she fell out of her chair at the theater," said Sir Thomas.

"I thought the agreement was one trick to save me. Father, you'll be caught."

"Not I! It's this blasted servant of mine. I have no power over him, Alice. He is having far too much fun."

"Perryman, I warn you now that if you're caught, my father will deny all knowledge and leave you to swing on the gibbet—and trust me, she will hang you."

"Which just means Perryman can't be caught, if he knows what is good for him."

"Perryman," Alice asked, "is it easy to move about Whitehall?"

"No one pays any attention to servants."

"I hear Barbara made her misalliance aided and abetted by the queen," said Sir Thomas.

Alice was silent.

"Terrible murder in London last week," he went on. "Did you hear of it? A he-madam with his throat slit from ear to ear. Running a he-brothel. That young lieutenant you like—"

"Captain, he's a captain."

"—discovered it. Helping us keep the city decent. He's making a name for himself, he is. His brother-in-law, Cranbourne, and I were talking of it the other day. You ought to buy him a regiment, Lord Cranbourne, I said."

"That would be wonderful."

"You like this Saylor?"

"Very much. He is going to act as secretary to His Grace Balmoral and copy his memoirs."

"Balmoral has written memoirs?"

"All about campaigning, Father. Very interesting."

"You've read them, have you?"

"No."

Her father sipped the ruby-colored wine in one of a set of new Venetian glasses he'd just purchased. He was proud of the glasses and surprised Alice hadn't mentioned them. She had an eye for things of beauty. He watched his daughter for a while. "You've taken this trick of Barbara's hard, haven't you."

"I don't think we can ever be friends again."

"Is this Sidney such a rascal?"

Here was a way to swipe at John, a clerk in the naval office. "He's in Samuel Pepys's pocket, and you know whom Pepys serves," she said, even as another part of her said, Alice, don't, leave it be.

"The Earl of Sandwich, that devil."

Her father and the earl were old enemies.

"Well, I'm sorry for Barbara that she's made such a mistake, but her bed is made, and there's no going back. In time you two may patch up your quarrel."

"Never."

"Never is a long time." Sir Thomas wanted to change the mood. He never liked to encourage Alice in obstinacy, unless it served him. "Winter is upon us. I'm glad I'm not crossing the Channel this time of year like His Grace the Duke of Buckingham. I'm staying close to my fire, I am. He says he's going over to haggle about Madame's estate."

He is hurt not to be going with Buckingham to France this month, thought Alice, not to be a part of the entourage that will wine and dine in the Louvre Palace and meet with King Louis. She watched him in turn, the way he'd watched her. Would she soon be hearing complaints against the duke? And then there would be a break, and then her father would form a new alliance with another great man who had the king's ear, serving as his lackey, directing the votes he could in the Commons, gossiping in the corridors of Whitehall, doing whatever he could with great enthusiasm and even greater hopes for a while. And then the hope would falter. It had happened with Lord Sandwich. It had happened with Lord Arlington. Always her father felt he wasn't repaid enough for his loyalty. Am I like that? She was startled at the thought, and saddened. We're a pair, thought Alice, staring into the ruby liquid in her glass.

THAT EVENING AT Whitehall, the sound of barking, missing in the queen's chambers for several days, made Alice lift her head.

His favorite spaniels preceding him, King Charles walked into the queen's withdrawing chamber. Everyone was playing cards, and all stood at the sight of him, but he waved everyone to be seated, nodded carelessly to the queen, then walked among the tables until he came to the one at which Renée was playing. He stood behind the Earl of Mulgrave's chair, and at once, the young earl stood again and bowed.

"I haven't, er . . . the best of—but, er . . . she, er—I mean Mistress, er—"

"Verney," Alice said impatiently.

"Verney, er . . . is your partner. She'll carry, er . . . you."

"I'm experienced at getting out of scrapes on my own."

"Shall we reshuffle and start again?" Frances smiled up at the king, looking charming and sophisticated with ringlets beribboned and hanging over her ears.

"I wish to go for a walk in the gallery. I'm bored with my gentlemen and crave the company of ladies. Mademoiselle de Keroualle, it would please me if you would accompany me, and Mistress Verney, and Her Grace."

All movement at the other tables ceased as the king left the chamber, Renée on his arm, Alice and Frances following, spaniels prancing ahead. Eyes moved to the queen, who played a card and did not betray by so much as a blink that she'd noticed whom he'd walked out with and that he had not acknowledged her.

"Always lovely to see His Majesty," she said, her eyes on the cards in her hand.

"Was that sarcasm from our little Portuguese?" one lady-in-waiting whispered to another, and they laughed.

In the Stone Gallery, King Charles and Renée sat in one of the deep window seats while Alice and Frances were seated in chairs farther away, near the fire. Alice glanced toward them. King Charles was talking to Renée most seriously. The fact he had not singled out Renée since she and Richard had been reprimanded by Dorothy Brownwell had been missed by no one, least of all Renée. Will she go belly up, like one of his spaniels? wondered Alice.

"She's begun weeping," Frances said.

"He means to have her, doesn't he? Would you be willing to aid in an elopement?" Elopements were scandalous, infuriating families, but Frances had eloped.

"Whose?"

"Captain Saylor would marry her in a heartbeat. We could help them elope."

Frances touched at dolphins carved in the wooden arm of her chair. "I think I'll keep my distance. He's really never forgiven me for mine. And if you value your position at court, you'd best leave her precisely where she is."

"So," said King Charles, watching tears glide down Renée's face but not making a move to stop them, "it does not seem fair I am not at least allowed the privileges of Captain Saylor." There was no softness in his face or his tone. "You were partially unclothed. It would please me very much to see you partially unclothed."

"He earned it."

"What did you just say?"

"He has been my dearest friend since we met; he has never offered me anything but honor. He has asked me to be his wife, offered me the protection of his name and estate. When I am with him, I feel at ease, and what is more, I feel treasured."

She'd surprised him. "I want that ease, that sweetness." He spoke ruefully.

My point, thought Renée.

"Why didn't you become his mistress?" Alice asked Frances. A log in the fire near them made a crumbling sound as it fell apart in a red glow.

"I wanted to be a wife, no more, no less," Frances answered.

"Would you talk with Renée?"

An expression passed over Frances's face that Alice couldn't read. "I'm certain she has enough advisers."

"But they want the king's pleasure, not what is best for her."

"What is best for her, Alice?"

"To be someone's wife. You understand."

"I understand?"

"You married, and for love."

Frances smiled an odd smile. "My passion was not, and is not, for His Grace my husband. I could not marry for love. There's only one man I have ever loved, and he is already married."

Alice looked toward the window seat. King Charles held Renée in his arms, was stroking her hair, his face grave. His dogs were snuggled in her skirts.

"If I'd become what he so desired—what I myself was so very much tempted to—the only difference would be that today I wouldn't be watching him court Mademoiselle de Kerouaille not three feet from me, because he wouldn't want me to know. Because he cannot stand to quarrel. But it would still be happening. I comfort myself on long nights with that. I comfort myself at this very moment, as he courts her using words I very much imagine he used with me. It was a most lovely courtship. Oh, look. Here's our Mrs. Sidney, up from her bridal bed, come to call upon the queen."

Frances rose as Barbara walked into the gallery, and they touched cheeks. It was the first time Alice had seen Barbara since her wedding some two weeks ago. Barbara walked swiftly to Alice to hug her, but Alice sat limply, her heart turned to stone. So, she was thinking, this is what I'm going to do. She hadn't known precisely.

Frances watched them for a moment, then said, "Come. I'll take you to the queen. Mistress Verney has to stay and play duenna."

Frances linked her arm in Barbara's, and after a moment, Barbara walked away with her.

"She acted as if I didn't exist," Barbara said to Frances.

"It will pass."

"She doesn't forgive."

"What a shame. One loses so much when one can't forgive. Let's give her time to enjoy her anger, and then, when she tires of it, as she will, and misses you too much, as she will, she'll come your direction. And it will be your turn to decide if you can forgive. A treacherous game, forgiveness, full of shoals. You look blooming, my dear. I'm going to hazard a guess that Mr. Sidney is showing his affection in every way possible. Alice and I were just talking about this new fashion of marrying for love. Tell me your opinion."

Barbara laughed, and there was such joy in the laugh that Frances stopped her and kissed her cheeks, then allowed herself one last peep at the king and Renée, which was foolish, because it hurt so to see. To see and remember. Once he'd commandeered a skiff, oaring it himself, to visit her at midnight and rail at her for marrying Richmond and breaking his heart. She'd adored his heartbreak and anger. It was all she could do to withstand it. When she'd had the smallpox, she'd thought, If I survive this, I will become his mistress, because as she lay on the brink of death, she knew finally what was most important to her, to show all the love she felt for him. But her moment was past. He would still bed her now and, knowing him, with great zest. But she'd lost his heart, that precious, greedy, inquiring, naughty, lively heart of his. Time and chance stand still for no man, or woman.

My dearest, my beloved one, I kiss this paper a thousand times knowing your hands will touch it. I wait for you, dear one, and remain your faithful Dorothy.

Dorothy sighed, then went about the business of making the letter ready to send. It was for Lord Knollys, who'd left court a week ago to go home to his wife. She was gravely ill. Again. She sprinkled some sand over the page to dry up the blots, blew it off gently, waved the paper about, folded it until it was small, then took her sealing wax stick and held it to the candle.

"Brownie, they haven't sent my trunk here yet."

Dorothy dribbled wax along the last fold, then took a signet ring and pressed it various places in the wax. That done, she turned to face a pouting Gracen.

"Find Edward and have him see to it."

She scratched a name on the other side of the letter.

"Lord Knollys's place is near my father's." Gracen had stepped forward to see exactly what Dorothy was doing. "Give me the letter, and I'll see it delivered. In fact, I'll pay a call and see how his wife does."

"That would be most kind," said Dorothy, not wanting to give her the letter.

Gracen took the letter and kissed Dorothy's cheek.

"Come and help me choose which gowns to take back with me. Why must my mother choose this moment to be ill? I don't want to go. There's the Christmas revel, and everyone is having beautiful costumes made for it, and I want to stay and look beautiful with everyone else. More beautiful. I would. Only Renée is more beautiful than me."

Dorothy kissed her on the brow, wondering if she'd been this selfish when she'd been this young, and they walked to the maids' apartment to help Gracen choose her gowns.

Chapter 33

Second Week of Advent

Near an Advent wreath in which two candles glimmered, Richard sat scowling at the letter from his mother. She asked if he would come home to Tamworth for Christmas. Last night in his dreams he stared down at a bloody, beautiful body, and the face had been Renée's. He had waked with his heart pounding; he didn't dare leave her. She was so weepy and irritable and changeable, one day loving him, the next cold. Words from this week's sermon pounded in his head: "Unto thee, O Lord, do I lift up my soul. O my God, I trust in thee: let me not be ashamed, let not mine enemies triumph over me. . . ." He felt despair. It would be stupid to leave her on her own, and a part of him despised himself for that. A part of him also despised her.

"Captain, meet us later for supper?"

"Do we drill tomorrow?"

"Are you going to the play this afternoon? A group of us will be in the pit."

He shook his head at the three men crowding his door, the lieutenants of his bodyguard. More and more they had become friends, in the loose, companionable style of soldiers who must live and work together in close quarters. They kept few secrets from one another, a man's flaws and gifts were there for all the troop to view. They were proud they had been the ones to put out the fire on Guy Fawkes Day, proud their captain had discovered the murder of a notorious he-madam and thus shut down the brothel. They were proud Richard had been asked by Balmoral himself to copy Balmoral's memoirs. They were even proud he stubbornly courted the king's new love.

He rose, put out the burning candles with his fingers. Two weeks left in Advent, the holy preparation for the celebration of the birth of Christ. What would happen with Renée by their end?

HE WALKED OVER to Prince Rupert's apartments, joining the others who gathered to watch the prince dress, to see and be seen. This was a levee, the rising, from the French court, who made this morning parade fashionable. Prince Rupert, his shirt half on, half off, was laughing with a man who someone whispered to Richard was Sir Robert Holmes, a onetime pirate, an admiral in the last Dutch war, a crack soldier, and an adventurer.

"Do you remember when we were off the coast of Guinea and you got captured by natives?" Prince Rupert was saying to this Robert Holmes.

"Never has my life been so close to ending."

"I saved your life that time. Have you paid me back for that?"

"A hundred times over."

"Then we were caught in a hurricane off the Bermudas." Prince Rupert launched into that story, beginning to talk about his brother, whose ship had been lost in that storm, of the rumors that his brother was in one colonial island prison or another. "He was never there when I'd send a messenger. It was never him."

Holmes saw Richard. "Saylor, isn't it? I had the honor to know your father. You were in Tangier two years ago. I've been wanting to know more of Tangier. Tell me of that." And Holmes pulled Richard off to one side and asked him a soldier's questions, how staffed the garrison was, how the Moors were as fighters. "I can use a good man on the Isle of Wight," said Holmes, who was governor of the island. "If you ever want to leave London, call on me. I'll find a place for you on my staff."

When Richard left to attend Monmouth's levee, Prince Rupert and Holmes walked through the privy garden, through Holbein Gate, to wait on Whitehall Street for Prince Rupert's carriage to be brought round.

"I offered him something in the Isle of Wight," Holmes said.

"Thank you, Robin. I like the lad, don't want him crushed by this."

"The king will forgive all if she yields."

"She's taking her own sweet time."

"She knows her value. Nothing wrong with that. And a man doesn't appreciate something unless he has to work for it."

"You remember my writing to you of those two Frenchmen who put me under their spell with their stories of fur trade in the Colonies, in Canada, the northern Colonies across the Atlantic?"

"Something of the sort."

"They're back from their first expedition for us. I cannot tell you how excited I am about the prospect for trade. The king has granted me land and a charter for a fur trading company. It will be based in Hudson's Bay, a bay a hundred times the size of anything we've seen, I'm told. I'm to be governor and looking for investors. Lord Cranbourne is in for ten thousand."

"Steep."

"Mortgage the family home, man. I tell you this is going to be big. Think of the Hollanders' East India Company."

Holmes laughed and shook his head.

At Monmouth's, the young duke made much of insisting Richard see some new object in his closet, but when they were separated from the other courtiers milling about in the bedchamber, he said, "Richard, I regard you highly. You did what you could to keep me from acting stupidly when I was in drink more times than I can remember. And you behaved discreetly when someone close to me did not. I know your affections for Mademoiselle de Keroualle are true and deep, but I also want you to know that it would be much appreciated by someone to whom I owe everything—as do you—if you dropped your suit. He knows nothing can take her place, but hopes that new duties—and honors—might allay the hurt a bit."

Richard bowed, his face unreadable. "I am commanded in this by no one but her."

Call your dog off, was actually what King Charles had commanded. He doesn't know this dog, Monmouth thought, stubborn in a way Monmouth envied. I think I may be fortunate you did not love my wife, he thought, and he wondered if his growing pursuit of Richard's sister was going to come back to haunt him. He said nothing else but showed Richard a mezzotint he'd been given by Prince Rupert, who dallied with the art the way he dallied with a dozen other things.

When they parted company, Richard went to the royal mews to see his horse. He knew they were hinting him off. Were threats next? Did he love Renée enough to endure disgrace? Yes. One could always make one's way back from disgrace. It was like fashion, changing with time. But the deeper question was, did she love him enough?

"Have you seen Walter?" Effriam asked.

Richard petted Pharaoh's nose. "I have not."

"He's been sleeping here at night, near Pharaoh. I thought I saw him the other morning, and this morning I did see him, but he ran off before I could stop him."

"Another vagabond at Whitehall. Madame Neddie's is closed. I would imagine he's hungry."

"The same thought crossed my mind."

Richard pulled out a coin. "Leave that where he'll find it tonight."

"You could use another groom."

Effriam had known Richard since he was born, had placed him on his first horse, was part and parcel of Tamworth, which was part and parcel of Richard's soul. Richard would have guessed disapproval foremost from Effriam, not kindness.

"I could train him," Effriam said, stern to cover what he suspected Richard would see as softness. "He's quick, and I'm not getting any younger."

"You're sure? Well, when next you catch him—"

"Oh, I'll catch him. He's quick, but I'm cunning."

"Offer him what you please."

"Undergroom, no more than that."

Richard walked to Balmoral's, thinking about what had just occurred. Effriam, full of starch, unbendable as a post, knew Walter's background, knew what he did to earn his living. Was Whitehall going to his head? Was Effriam creating an entourage of sorts? Other servants had them, underservants who were dependent and theirs to command. They flounced around court, self-important as minor kings. Or was he doing his duty as he saw it, bare-bones, harsh, not to his taste, but fair? Richard would bet on the latter. His father had set that example for them all.

THE SPACE IN which he'd been given to work was a small, windowed chamber near the duke's closet. Winter sun shone in. Richard moved so his back was in the sun, shuffled through the papers, stained, ink-spotted papers, the handwriting so wild as to be indecipherable at times. He wrote out what he could understand, leaving great blank spaces that meant he must ask Balmoral directly. He enjoyed the clarity and simplicity of Balmoral's answers. Balmoral had many sets of tiny iron soldiers in wooden boxes; sometimes he'd set them out in a battle formation and talk to Richard about strategies of war, when armies faced each other across the darkling plain, each intent upon victory. Richard absorbed what Balmoral thought of sieges and armies and foreign command through his pores. Do you like war? Balmoral had asked him. I hate the killing, he had answered. Good, Balmoral had replied. You might make a decent commander, then. There'd been a "fit," not long after Madame Neddie's murder.

From what Richard could see of it, Balmoral went on drunks, drinking until he collapsed and his servants could put him to bed. Alice seemed to know this state of affairs and yet continued onward with her determined courtship. He could throw no stones. Did he allow Renée's flirtation with the king to run its course? Or did he make her an ultimatum? There seemed to be no answer in his divided soul.

"I hold it fit that wise and experienced commanders when they meet with a new enemy—that is, of reputation—before they come to join battle should cause their soldiers to make trial of them by some light skirmishes," wrote Balmoral. Richard copied the words, thinking about the practicality of what Balmoral preached, thinking about the tedium of drill that was a soldier's lot. Drill made a soldier sharp and less easy to kill on the battlefield. He lost himself in the writing, in thinking about what he wrote as the pen shaped the words: "A good commander has to be a practical man, gauging the depth of his men's endurance, as well as his enemies."

A sound of bells, sweet and clear, interrupted him. These windows overlooked the park. Richard looked out. Sleighs were pulling up, bells on the horses' bridles. Young women were descending the stairs on the side of Holbein Gate, the maids of honor, hurrying into the shelter of the stair's portico. A last sleigh was filled with branches of holly and oak, enough to decorate chambers with signs of the Christmas season so near.

Richard saw Renée, standing near King Charles.

She was laughing and talking, her face full of life, happy. The cloak she wore was white velvet, embroidered everywhere in silver and green, white fur inside, fur that framed her face like a halo. A gift, no doubt, because he knew she hadn't possessed such before. Huge, fat pearl drops dangled from her ears. I won these in a card game, she'd told him, and he'd been happy for her good fortune. Now, watching, he suddenly knew she had lied. King Charles leaned forward and kissed her, fully, a long kiss, never minding the public eye, and her arms went round him. The gesture of her arms froze Richard. They tried to hint him away. They offered him bribes. He ground his teeth. Help me with my confusion, she begged him. What did she—whom he thought of as his beloved—truly desire?

He knew, and the answer was sharper than a sword blade on flesh.

THAT AFTERNOON, WHEN he went to find her and confront her, she wasn't in the queen's apartments or those of the maids of honor. She had a visitor, he was told, was receiving this visitor in one of the king's chambers, a tiny withdrawing chamber in old rooms His Majesty seldom used anymore to be sure, but nonetheless, Richard didn't like it.

He paced up and down in the hall, drummed his fingers on a window ledge, looking out at the gray day, frowning at any page who had the misfortune to walk by him.

The door to the chamber at last opened, and Richard was surprised to see Colbert de Croissy, the ambassador from His Majesty King Louis of France, walk out. The ambassador saw Richard but didn't acknowledge him. Anger filled him, moved aside grief. He walked in. Renée sat in a chair very close to the fire, her head leaned back, her eyes closed. The great white velvet cloak was lying carelessly on a stool. Before her was a wooden box, its lid off, wood shavings and straw around it. She opened her eyes and turned at the sound of his steps.

"Why does de Croissy call upon you?"

"He wants me to give myself to King Charles for the sake of France, and he wants me to spy on everything King Charles does and make a report to him." She leaned forward to pick up what was in the box. "See what the king of France sends me, to show his pleasure."

"The deuce you say! I'll call de Croissy out and shoot him from twenty paces. And I won't miss! Have you told His Grace Balmoral of this, or Lord Arlington?" What else did she hide? In his anger was an awareness that this was larger than he'd dreamed. When had it grown this large? Was it always more than he knew?

"Sit down by me, Richard. Move that cloak."

"Who gave you that?"

"De Croissy, part of my New Year's, from France."

"Why accept it?"

"Why not? I haven't a beautiful cloak like that. Are you going to buy me one?"

"One day I might. What else have you accepted?"

"You sound accusing." She straightened in the chair. "What are you accusing me of?"

"Of being a simpleton if you think you may accept presents such as these and pay no return."

"Oh, I tell de Croissy gossip I hear, nothing to harm."

"Good God, Renée! Are you telling me you act as a spy?"

"No, of course not. King Charles tells me what to say. He finds this most amusing."

In his anger was growing alarm. The dark shoals and eddies of court, as Alice described it, the intrigue beneath the intrigue. You cannot imagine it, Richard, she said, and you mustn't doubt it. Was it possible Renée was a Trojan horse, a pretense of love by King Charles to throw off the French? That he was jealous of a diplomatic game? He kicked away the offending cloak, pulled the stool close, sat, took the onyx figure of some goddess from her hands, kissed them passionately, wondering in spite of himself if King Charles's lips had been before him. "Come with me to Tamworth for Christmas, away from all this. My mother invites you." Marry me in Tamworth, was on his lips.

"Oh, that would be lovely."

"You'll come, then?"

"Well . . . there's to be a Christmas Eve revel, Richard, and I have the major part. There are special costumes being made, and we've begun to practice our dancing and singing. And the day after, we're going to Windsor Castle, and there's to be a feast and lord of misrule. Such as there hasn't been since the old days, I'm told. Everyone is so excited."

He touched the fat pearl drop at her ear. "You didn't win these at cards, did you." She didn't answer, watched him carefully, something in her withdrawing; he could feel it, a guard against him going up, which brought anger back. "Does King Charles love you?"

"He says he does."

"And do you love him? Answer with an honest heart, Renée. You owe me that."

She threw her arms around him. "Don't abandon me! Don't! So many want me to do their bidding. You can't imagine it . . . I won't be able to be strong if you abandon me! I need you, Richard!" She was crying. "Don't be angry. Don't hate me. I can't bear to be hated. I'm not bad."

He rubbed away tears with his thumbs, in him a mix of tenderness and rage that was killing. You haven't said you loved me, he was thinking as he studied her face, the beauty of it, the broad brow, the full mouth. He kissed that mouth once and twice and three times, but then anger overcame tenderness, and he stopped. There had been excitement when she'd said the king loved her, a tiny spark of pride. Deep inside him, sadness pooled: It was ending, perhaps had ended, that which had been between them. She simply hadn't the courage to tell him. The softness he adored was their downfall, and perhaps greed, but he didn't want to accuse her of that. "I let you free of our engagement."

"What are you saying, Richard?"

"If you don't go to Tamworth with me, I consider our engagement at an end."

"It's winter! The roads will be awful! I will be cold in the coach! It's too far. I am to perform in a masque for His Majesty, for pity's sake—"

He stood.

"You're being unreasonable. Why are you being so mean and unreasonable, Richard?"

He leaned over her in the chair, his mouth close to hers, so that their breaths mingled. "I will not be second after the king."

"But he's the king! What can I do?"

"Choose."

"I warned you, didn't I, months ago? He admires me, I said, and you said, Of course he does. You allowed it!"

"Are you making it my fault that you encourage him onward? No and no again! His anger or mine! It's your choice! I won't be second, not in this!"

She had her soft arms around his neck, and she smelled like lavender and musk, and it would be so easy to lose himself in her touches, her kisses, her tears, her need that he not be angry. He managed to pull away.

"I won't be angry if you choose the king." He surprised himself. Who spoke? Some stupid, noble part of himself. He didn't mean the words, was going to call them back, but her face changed as she took in what he'd said. Dear God, he thought, in shock. I've sealed my fate.

"I'll always love you," she was saying. "You will always be my dear and perfect and most understanding friend."

Blindly, he strode away, not knowing where he was going. It was over.

CHAPTER 34

The Final Week of Advent

Alice frowned. "Tell him," she managed calmly enough, "that I called. Is he anywhere near to . . ." She didn't know how to ask what she wanted to know, but she and Riggs had become allies in their care of Balmoral. At least she had achieved that, the taking of the major rook on the chessboard of his household.

"I would say another day," Riggs said.

"Good enough."

"I'm sorry, Mistress Verney."

She glanced at Riggs's face, at the scar that made him seem sneering, yet he wasn't. He felt pity for her. It was a shock to see that. She walked to the Stone Gallery, found a chair to curl up in. He'd had a fit only two weeks ago, a day or so after that madam died. It was too soon for another. Once a month she could manage, but twice or more? She looked down at her hands. When truth looks you in the face and says boo, pay attention, she told herself; if you marry him, this will be your life. Is a dukedom worth this? With the dignity and honors and pride of bearing his name will come this. Face it, she told herself, so there are no tears of self-pity later; but she guessed there would likely be tears anyway. Richard hadn't given her a letter for Renée in over a week, hadn't called to take Renée for a walk or tried to see her secretly. Was it ending? Had Richard ended it? Had Renée? She didn't want his career hurt in this.

Edward approached her. "Alice."

"Edward, my love. Sit down and tell me all the gossip."

"You look sad."

"Not me."

"There's a new servant."

"Whose household?"

"The queen's."

"What does he look like?"

"Wears a wig, yellow hair, strange looking."

That did not sound like Ange. "Let me slip on a mask, and I'll go down to the open table and see."

"We saw a hanging," Walter told Effriam as they walked over to the kitchen courtyard to eat. Tables were set up in the various kitchens of Whitehall for servants.

"Tyburn Tree?"

"Yes. Mr. and Mrs. Daniell and the whole family went. They wanted Nan to see it, to see this girl hanged for killing her baby."

Effriam thought about that awhile. There were things about the city that shocked him so that he couldn't quite formulate thoughts about them. A girl at Tamworth had to sit shame in church several Sundays in a row for such a birth, but she'd also be taken in and cared for. "Nan doesn't strike me as one who'd kill her child."

"Mrs. Daniell says girls get desperate toward the last. And the parish officers have been by. Who takes responsibility? they asked. Mr. Daniell said he would."

"He sounds like a decent man. Some fathers might throw their daughters to the streets."

They were at the kitchen court now, then down the stairs to the kitchens. Long plank tables sat end to end in the midst of a huge stone basement, and servants crowded at the benches drawn up to seat them. In the middle of the tables were trenchers filled with fresh-baked bread, and kitchen maids brought more right out of the fire on long wooden poles with a broad square on their end. Cauldrons of soup and stews bubbled, in pots big enough to hold Walter, at cavernous fireplaces. Servants were everywhere, eating, waiting to eat, or preparing trays to take to chambers in Whitehall.

"This is a busy place," Walter said.

"It's just one of the kitchens — Where are you heading off to?"

"I forgot something. I'll be back."

"We'll get you a plate —"

It was too late. Walter was out of sight, running up the stairs back to the kitchen courtyard. Effriam sighed. Servants had to bring their own plates and spoons and cups, but used ones were for sale or rent in a back room near the bakehouse, where he headed now. He hoped Walter found his way back. There was more than one kitchen, and rules were strict about who ate where. Some kitchens had open tables, meaning meals were part of pay, and some did not. Walter wouldn't know that.

Walter ran into the stall where Pharaoh was, the horse snorting at the sight at him, felt behind a pile of hay for the pail Richard had given him. Finding it, he dashed back down Whitehall Street in the direction of the kitchen, but there were several gates that opened to courtyards, and when he entered one he wasn't sure it was the same courtyard he'd left. He walked toward arched porches, opened a door, and noise met his ears, mixed into the jumble and rattle of dishes and the smell of food. He ran down a set of stairs, disoriented—for this kitchen didn't look as he remembered it—yet there was the same mix of milling people, the same huge fireplaces in the corners. He walked along the outside of the table, crowded with people, looking for Effriam. Had he eaten already? Gone back to the stables? Walter's stomach growled. Everyone was eating a soup. It smelled so good. He saw where the big soup pot was, walked over, held out his pail.

"I think not," said a kitchen servant, looking him up and down. "Look at this one," she said to servants around her. "He brought a pail. Who do you think you are? The Duke of York?"

"It's all I got. You don't have to fill it all the way." But that's what he was hoping. He was going to take food to the Daniells.

"I won't," she answered.

A dollop of soup slopped in his pail, and he found a place against a stone column, which held up the roof of this basement. He sat on his haunches like a dog to drink it. At the crowded table, someone got up, and Walter quickly sat in his place and reached out for the bread. Across from him was the man, the Frenchman, the Englishman who spoke Italian and Gibberish. It took a moment to register because he looked so very odd, no eyebrows and frizzy false hair, yellow colored. Quick as a flash, Walter was up and away from the table. He found a stone column to hide behind and looked back. The man was standing now, too, looking around. Had he seen Walter? Heart beating, Walter hid behind the column again.

"Whose kitchens are these?" he asked a passing servant.

"The queen's."

"I'm an undergroom—"

"Those that work in the royal mews eat elsewhere, boy."

"Where?"

"Through that door and you're outside. Ask for Scotland Yard kitchen."

Walter fled. He had to find Effriam. And they had to find Captain Saylor.

"ALL RIGHT," SAID Alice, cloaked, masked, half hiding behind the huge stone columns that held up the kitchen ceiling. "Which one is he?"

"There in the middle."

"Which one?"

"I'll go and stand behind him."

Edward did so. Henri Ange turned so suddenly, he startled Edward. "Do I know you?"

"You don't. I was just waiting for a place."

"Well, don't stand so close behind me. I don't like it, boy."

"Edward . . ." A page with Monmouth's colors was sitting across the way. "This is Henry Jones."

"Hello, Henry," said Edward.

"Henry's a friend of mine. His eyebrows got burned off in a fire—"

Ange threw a piece of bread at the page. "No one cares. Be silent, young wretch."

Edward scurried away to Alice. "Well?"

"I'm not certain," Alice said. "He could be him, but he looks so . . . All right, my little bloodhound, I'm off to find Captain Saylor. You keep track of this one."

Alice climbed up a back stairway, her mind running in different directions. She was almost certain it was Ange, but he looked so odd, so dangerous. She didn't remember thinking, on first sight of him, that he was dangerous looking. Where was Richard?

RICHARD WAS IN the small chamber, working on Balmoral's memoirs. Every now and then he heard shouting from inside the duke's closet. Balmoral was roaring drunk. Richard copied words: "Soldiers ought to go into the field to conquer and not to be killed." He wasn't sleeping well. He wasn't eating. One moment he thought he'd go crawling to Renée on bended knee, take whatever crumbs she threw. Another moment he felt he'd call the king out in a duel, never mind that he'd be sent to the Tower immediately. Thoughts of making a scene, humiliating her and His Majesty, even if he was banished, walked in his waking mind like dark crows. If he closed his eyes to sleep, visions embraced him, skulls on a battlefield, Neddie's sightless eyes, Renée dancing naked in a field of corpses. The only thing that steadied him was prayer. In that he could be patient. Wait beside the Christ child, the precious Babe in certain faith that all will be well in the end. It may not end the way you desired, but it will end, and it will be well, so he had been taught. Barbara and John thought his going to Tamworth was a good idea. His mother would have a potion that would allow him to sleep dreamless. He longed for sleep without dreams. His saddlebags were packed; he had permission from Balmoral to take a month's leave. He wanted to be at Tamworth, to burrow in at Tamworth, never mind the woods would be too muddy to walk in, the creek's edge rimed with frost, the trees bare and stark, the great hall too cold to sit in even with fires blazing. It was home. The sound of something crashing in the chamber next to him interrupted his thoughts. He stood, went to the door of the closet, knocked. "Is everything well?"

He put his ear against the door. He could hear voices. Balmoral wasn't alone. Yes, there must be a keeper. Of course.

"Richard." Alice stood in the doorway.

He began to move papers so that she might sit down.

"Richard, I think Henri Ange is here."

Everything in him went still. "Where?"

"At the queen's open table. Oh, Richard, he's shaved off his eyebrows, and he looks odd . . . evil. He has a bad yellow wig. . . . I don't know, it may not even be him—"

"Summon the queen's bodyguard, Alice. At least five men and a lieutenant." He strapped on his sword. "Tell them to meet me there. And alert the Life Guard not to leave Their Majesties unguarded for even a moment. Hurry now!"

He raced down the alley and out into the street, running under Holbein Gate and out into Whitehall Street. He ran through the palace gate and across the courtyard and into the kitchen buildings, into the queen's kitchen, to the basement space where the open table was. Quietly, he moved behind a brick column. He faced a servant talking with several pages, Edward among them. Richard took a long look. Was that Ange? Impossible, and yet . . . He stepped from behind the column and walked forward. The man who might be Henri Ange looked up, and Richard looked into his eyes and knew it was he.

"Henri Ange, I arrest you in the name of His Majesty King Charles."

A page or two gaped up at Richard. Edward at once moved away. Ange stood.

"Who is this Henri?" he said in a flat English accent.

"I arrest you in the name of the king. Come forward, please."

Out of the corner of his eye, he saw that Walter and Effriam were running into the kitchen. In that split second, Ange was on his feet and heading to the stairs that led upward to the courtyard. Walter stepped in front of him, and Ange pushed him hard to the ground and ran past him. In the next second, Richard was running after him.

Outside, Ange ran toward what was called Scotland Yard, the huge courtyard where the practical business of Whitehall was carried out, where the buttery was located and the charcoal house and the wharf for landing supplies, where the fish larder was and the poulterers, surveyors, porters, glaziers, masons, where officials and lesser courtiers had tiny ground- and first-floor chambers and were glad of them.

In the queen's kitchen, there was confusion and shouting. The guards Richard had summoned had arrived, but Richard was not to be seen.

"Which way?" asked a lieutenant.

"I'll show you!" shouted Edward. He set off at a run, followed by the small troop of guards, followed by Walter and Effriam, and now by Alice, too.

Ange ran out onto Whitehall Street, ran among carriages and sedan chairs, back toward King Street on the other side of Holbein Gate. He'll lose me in Devil's Acre, thought Richard. Devil's Acre was a nest of hovels and houses and alleys near the great abbey. There was a ferry that crossed the river farther down.

Richard took a deep breath and redoubled his effort. And as fast as Ange was, Richard was faster. He ran straight into Ange, sent him sprawling into curious bystanders. Ange leaped up, tore himself loose from Richard's grasp, and ran through Holbein Gate, snatching a sword from a bemused watcher who'd unsheathed one to help. By now, the small troop of bodyguards was close behind, and guards from other troops—the Life Guards, Prince Rupert's guard, Monmouth's, York's, off duty and on—had joined in. Two guardsmen had stationed themselves at the end of King Street, pikes crossed. Ange would have to get by them to gain the warren of hovels or the ferry. He stopped, looking back toward Richard and forward to the pikemen. Richard slowed, wary, not trusting him. Ange had lost his wig in the chase, and he looked like something that wasn't quite human; but he smiled, and the old charm was there.

"Give me the sword," Richard said to him.

"We never fought, did we?"

"It was d'Effiat I wanted to kill."

"First blood? Either way"—Ange motioned to the guards around them—"you win."

Why not, thought Richard, a formidable rage in him, compounded by the memory of Madame's death, this man's arrogance, grief and anger at Renée, at King Charles, at the simple treacheries that were as common as clover here. "First blood. Stand back," Richard called to the soldiers. "Open the garden gate. We'll fight there."

"What are you doing?" asked the lieutenant in his bodyguard.

"Settling a score." Richard followed Henri into the privy garden, and men crowded in behind him, Alice among them.

"First blood drawn, and the duel is over," Richard called out. "First blood, and we end it. He goes to the Tower no matter what. Is that clear?"

"They're dueling," said Edward excitedly to the group of pages who had run along with the soldiers and would not have missed this for the world. "The king will be angry." King Charles enforced laws against dueling, trying to keep his young, hot-blooded, pleasure-seeking court alive.

Alice watched Ange take a small vial attached to a leather cord around his neck and sprinkle it along the sword's edge. "What is that?" she called sharply.

"Fair Alice! What a pleasure to see you. It's holy water, my sweet, so that my sword will cut your Richard deeply. Still in love with him? Has he guessed it yet?"

"Ready?" called Richard.

"En garde."

They walked forward, swords raised, then crossed. And then it began, dazzling, frightening swordplay, a dance of death and chance and skill, punctuated by steel meeting steel in light, zinging sounds that made the heart beat fast. They were both skilled, both driven, Ange by survival and Richard by the clearest rage he'd ever felt.

There had been much noise and shouting before; people had gathered at windows that looked down upon the privy garden. Prince Rupert stood out on his balcony in the cold, watching. He knew he should stop this, but he didn't want to. Their swords moved so swiftly that the eye could hardly follow. Both of them were breathing hard. There was a stamina and speed necessary for swordplay that could test the strongest man.

Behind him, Prince Rupert heard his name. King Charles had entered his chamber, Renée on his arm.

"Keep her back!" Prince Rupert said quickly, but they were close enough to see the figures moving in the garden.

"What's this, a duel?" said King Charles.

"Who is dueling?" asked Renée.

"Back!" growled Prince Rupert, giving his king and cousin a desperate look.

"Go into the other room and wait for me," King Charles told Renée as he walked out on the balcony. Renée went to a window and rubbed the moisture settled there from the cold with her sleeve so that she could see into the garden.

"I ought to stop that," King Charles said.

"You'll get Saylor killed if you distract him. Whoever he's fighting is the best I've seen."

"Look, Saylor's drawn blood."

Renée, hearing Richard's name, came out onto the balcony before either man could stop her.

Richard had cut Ange on the shoulder. He stepped back. "First blood," he was saying as he heard his name screamed in a sweetly familiar voice. He looked up toward the windows surrounding the garden on two sides, and Ange, in one graceful, deadly step, stabbed him straight through his side, bringing the sword back out again, bright crimson painting it, staining Richard's shirt, his jacket.

Richard stared at him, stupidly, from the shock of the act and of the sword entering him.

"It's poisoned, my dear." Ange stepped back formally, raised the sword to his forehead, and then let it drop to the ground; but he had not counted on Alice, who heard his words, snatched Ange's sword from the ground, and jabbed it forward blindly, catching his arm.

"If he dies, you die!" she said, and leaned into the sword with all her weight so that it would go deeper, as around them there was beginning pandemonium. Ange had his hand on the sword blade, trying to pull it out of his arm, and she growled in triumph at the sight of blood from the cuts on his hand as guardsmen began the attempt to pry her hands off the sword hilt. That accomplished, she'd have gone after Ange and scratched out his eyes, but someone held her back. She twisted out of that grasp and ran to Richard, who sat in the gravel of one of the walks, holding his side, rocking back and forth. She began to weep. "Richard . . . oh, Richard."

He looked at her, his face very white.

"Oh, God, I love you, I love you," she heard herself saying, but Richard looked past her because Renée was running full-tilt into the garden, and she threw herself at him, making him yelp in pain as she covered his face with kisses.

"A pretty drama there," said Prince Rupert from the balcony.

"Goddamn it," said King Charles.

"That little piece with Alice stabbing that man, better than a play, I tell you!"

"Goddamn it to hell and back again."

Alice was able to stop herself, to draw back. If he dies, she thought—and her thoughts could not go beyond that point. Such feelings of grief came up, she could hardly bear them. It was all she could do not to beat Ange with her fists as guardsmen surrounded him. She wept into her hands.

Ange nodded toward Edward, who approached him carefully, his eyes practically starting from his head. Ange leaned over and whispered into Edward's ear. Then Ange was being marched away, bleeding with every step. Richard was being helped up by his fellow guardsmen, was being led off, Renée at his side. Alice stood where she was, sobbing as if her heart were broken. Edward took her hand.

"Don't cry, Alice, don't."

"He's going to die. He's going to die."

"He said to tell you it really was holy oil. What does that mean? Is that what he put on the sword before? I saw him do it—did you? But I didn't really think at the time; I was so excited to see a duel—"

"Take me somewhere, Edward, where I can be alone."

Of course the sword was poisoned, and of course Ange would say it was holy oil, so that Richard would die. Ange had an antidote somewhere, something to counteract the poison; she'd bet her right hand on it. And Richard didn't. What a devil Henri Ange was, even to the last. Oh, God, she'd made a great fool of herself. Was there any possibility that in his shock Richard hadn't heard her?

"Lean on me."

"Edward, you're so sweet."

So are you, thought Edward. And fierce.

Part II

Chapter 35

March 1671

Pharaoh reached out his long neck and took the corn from Alice's hand. She rubbed his nose, then leaned her face against his neck. Outside, away from the dim of the stall, the spring sunshine was almost fierce.

"I'm so sorry, Richard," she said.

He continued to brush Pharaoh, steady, long sweeps of the brush that made the horse snort in pleasure and whisk his tail.

"Is there anything I can do?"

Effriam said to Walter, "You and me, we'll be getting water."

"You can let the subject drop."

"Yes, of course. . . . I bring a note from her."

Thin, his cheeks hollow, Richard held out his hand, put the note in a pocket.

"Did your mother make it back to Tamworth in one piece?"

"I haven't heard, but I can't imagine muddy roads stopping Mother. Sleet and ice didn't prevent her coming here, now, did they?" His mother, upon receiving word of his wound, hearing the word *poison,* had traveled up to London with her servant, her books of remedies, and dried herbs and flowers from Tamworth's woods and gardens. He should have died. She'd seen to it that he hadn't.

"She's very lovely, Richard."

"Do you think so? Most people consider her odd, even frightening." He laughed.

"What?"

"I was thinking of my sisters, Louisa and Elizabeth. They were appalled to see her. I could have died so long as she remained out of sight."

"That's not true! Your sisters were on their knees in prayer for you. I think King Charles admired her very much—" Alice stopped herself, aghast at her clumsiness in speaking the king's name to Richard.

Richard was silent, his face grim again.

"Well, I only wanted to give you her note. If there's a reply, I can—"

"There won't be."

"Well, then I must go."

"Walking with Balmoral?"

She smiled. "Yes."

Richard stepped back from the horse, hearing something in her voice. "Is that a new gown?"

"It is."

"Very becoming."

"We can only hope His Grace thinks so."

"He will. Answer me this. Do you always get what you want?"

Alice gave Pharaoh a kiss on the nose. "Not always."

"Do you ever give up?"

"Not when I want something and think it possible." I thought you would die, Richard, but I didn't give up on you, and here you are, alive and very well.

"I do—I have. Go away and seduce your duke."

"If there's a reply, you have only to find me—"

"I said there won't be."

"Of course you did. Good-bye, Richard."

"I'm a bear—" He stopped her at the stall's door. "Misfortune in love does it, isn't that what poets preach? Give me a good-bye kiss, Alice."

They kissed chastely on the lips. She had come every day to see him, couldn't stop herself. Their friendship had grown deeper.

"When are you going to see Barbara?" he asked.

"You know the answer to that."

"And still I must ask. John requests me to ask. She's waiting, Alice."

"Our friendship is finished."

"As easy as that you let go someone you love?"

"It wasn't easy, Richard."

He took her by the arm. "She didn't do as you wanted. No one ever does. Will you love no one because of that?"

She shook his arm free. "Is this the pot calling the kettle black?"

He watched her leave. She moved down the alley of stalls gracefully and certainly, nodding here and there to different guardsmen she knew, stopping to exchange a word if she knew them well. Whom didn't she know? Whitehall was her milieu, her world. He could imagine her nowhere else. She was a born courtier, wily, patient, steadfast in her goals. She had taught him much. I love you, she'd said. He pretended for her sake that he hadn't heard it, but he had. It made him consider her in a whole new way, made him observe her and be curious about her. She was jealous and vengeful. He saw it in the way she treated Barbara. Yet he admired her fierceness, even if he thought it wrong. Perhaps it was the contrast to Renée, who had no fierceness.

Alice had been stalwart in this last round with Renée, guiding him, carrying letters, arranging secret meetings, but it was over now. He was in hell, but no worse a hell than that of holding Renée in his arms and hearing her loving words and being allowed to touch and explore her in new soft places, so that his desire was kept a white hot flame, and from that flame he had to watch her with the king and know that he, too, was equally exploring Renée's sweetness. Alice wouldn't tell him this, but everyone else did. Enough. He would bear no more. This second chance hurt more in its betrayal. It was in his mind to take leave of England. Prince Rupert, York, the great French general Condé, they had all made their way as soldiers serving foreign masters.

So might he.

He leaned his head into Pharaoh's broad side, pulled her note out of his pocket. Dear God, he loved her, but dear God, he wanted this over. If he read it, then he let the game continue. It was so tempting to open it, read her sweet excuses, let his heart believe them. In the courtyard was a fire tended by the stable boys. He walked to it, watched the note burn, thinking, The beginning of the end. If he was steadfast, there would be the middle of the end, and then the end of the end. Advice from his father. To see you through the hard patches of life, my son, his father had said, which are always there ahead in the road.

"THERE SHE IS." Balmoral rose from a chair in Stone Gallery, held out his arm in a courtly gesture.

"It's paradise outside," said Alice, taking it.

"Chilly?"

"Yes, but we can fetch your cloak."

Fondly, he watched her signal a page and give the boy instructions for fetching his cloak. She'd get her beautiful day, and he'd be warm, and the truth was it would feel good to sit in the sun, his old bones needed it. They began their walk, up and down the gallery to start. It was their habit—they had been doing this long enough for it to have become a habit.

"What news have you?" She knew so many little tidbits, and when he put them together with what he knew—with the hot-air posturings of Buckingham or Arlington in council, with the bland obtuseness of the king—he'd see the little trails, the little betrayals, before they surprised. Subtleties within the subtleties.

"Captain Saylor says he is ending his attachment."

"Good, if it's true. I'll ask the king to reward him with a promotion, once we're certain it's not just a lovers' quarrel. Prince Rupert's fond of him. Perhaps we'll move him to Rupert's guard."

"Or yours."

"Or mine."

"Her Grace the Duchess of York fell ill yesterday," Alice continued.

"Well, Henri Ange is in the Tower of London. It cannot be blamed upon him."

"Why not? Do you think Henri Ange can't make poisons in the Tower?"

She was like a pit bull on this. "He can't if he receives no visitors, is allowed no letters."

"Does he receive no visitors? How can you ascertain that nothing is sneaked in to him?"

He was testy. "By having the best guards there are. By demanding that no one may see him except with my permission."

"And you have given permission to . . . ?"

"Not that it is any of your affair"—he was winter frost itself—"Arlington, Buckingham—"

"There!"

He ought to box her ears for her impudence, but unfortunately he agreed with her, which only made him more irritable. Yet he could not deny his fellow ministers the privilege of questioning the prisoner—particularly since the imprisonment was creating problems with the kingdom of France, from whom they now had a treaty to join in war against the Dutch signed, sealed, delivered. "Are you implying Buckingham would aid our prisoner in the making of poison?"

"Since I believe it was he who brought Ange over, I am indeed. Henri Ange needs to be hanged, ought to have been hanged months ago. I don't understand it."

Indeed you don't, he thought. All the wrangling, the French ambassador's protests, King Charles receiving a special dispatch from the king of France. Louis wants him, King Charles said, allowing Balmoral to read the letter. "If this is indeed the poisoner of Madame, I demand to question him myself," King Louis wrote in no uncertain terms. And there were questions from certain members of the House of Commons, impudent questions, asking about the imprisonment of the Frenchman, wanting details, following the wild hare of Ange's Catholicism, suspecting a Jesuit plot. They wanted details King Charles was under no obligation to give but that raised further difficulties in a session when the king was working hard to raise money for the coming war, which he had not yet announced to his Commons. Alice's father was stirring trouble, was among those who would not let the arrest fade. Balmoral glanced at her, at those dark eyes behind which ran that feverish and cunning brain, wondering not for the first time her part in the stirring. Did she go straight from him to her father? Those who followed her at his orders said no.

"You should have let him die," said Alice.

My sentiments exactly, thought Balmoral. He had grown quite fond of Alice's ruthlessness. "But then we wouldn't have the chance to question him."

"Have you questioned him? Hard?"

"I've been waiting for him to heal completely."

"Saylor is healed. So is Ange. He's faking if he says otherwise."

"You're quite bloodthirsty."

"I watched my princess die. And he would have done the same to the queen, kill her horribly. He likes to see others suffer. He needs to be killed before he kills anybody else."

"But not before he tells us what he knows."

"I don't think he'll do that. I think he would twist truth for the sheer joy of twisting. I don't think truth can be gotten from him."

"I'm the one with the melancholy humors, not you. You spend too much time with me."

They were out in St. James's Park now. A page walked up just as Balmoral opened his mouth to complain of the cold and delivered his cloak, and as he shrugged himself into its warm folds, he watched Alice, who knew the boy and talked with him. It seemed a letter had just come to the queen from Lord Knollys to inform her that Lady Knollys was dead. Alice had fished this information from the page with just a few short questions.

Balmoral turned to look around him, to take in the smell and feel of spring.

In the distance, a large knot of people made up of the king and various courtiers wound its way toward the menagerie to see the animals. Was there a first treaty with France? One before the one Buckingham had gone to obtain? A secret before the secret, having to do with the princess's visit? It gnawed at him. Certain signs, certain remarks, made him suspect certain fellow privy council members—and there were such tantalizing hints in the letters Richard had had copied in France. The Hollanders were suspicious, their ambassador, their spies, like Thomas Verney's Dutch friend Lowestroft, sniffing the ground, bloodhounds, sensing something. And Ange. What did Ange know? Less than you think I do, he'd said the other day as Balmoral sat in the dank of the cell, staring at the man who was his grandson Neddie's last lover, perhaps his killer. Neddie the catamite, Neddie the sodomite, who came to him in dreams, arms outstretched, hair long and flowing, weeping, Grandfather . . .

He and Alice walked over to the long landscape canal. The page was still with them and ran to bring him a chair. Gratefully, he sat down. Alice was cooing over ducklings following their mama like tiny citron ships of the line. He was content to watch her. He would invite her, in the company of her aunt, to visit him at his estate outside Newmarket this summer. She sat on the broad rim of the canal, leaning elbows against it, raising her face to the sun, which gleamed off her thick, riotous hair. She met his gaze, her expression grave. And he knew, the way one does, that they had come to the crux.

"My father has received another offer from the Earl of Mulgrave."

He chewed on that, leaned his chin on his cane.

"I think this time, I must consider it most seriously."

"Why must you consider Mulgrave seriously?"

"I am not getting any younger. I have been a maid of honor since I was twelve." Caro is gone, she thought. Barbara is gone. Gracen does not return. Renée is increasingly the queen of us. Kit and Luce are fools, Brownie is distracted, melancholy, the queen pale and sad . . . My little family is changed beyond repair. Time to go. "It is past time I had my own household. Mulgrave has waited most patiently. The queen's household is most unhappy these days, and I am at my wits' end."

There is no end to your wit, thought Balmoral.

"You are a dear and trusted friend, and I wanted to discuss it with you before I made a reply. What do you advise me?"

"It's true you've become quite old." He smiled at her sudden smile. "I advise you to wait."

"I have no other offers, Your Grace. Must I go and live as companion to my aunt, or move back to my father's house? I cannot continue as a maid of honor, do not, in matter of fact, wish to. Only my love for the queen has kept me there as long as it has."

She'd thrown down the gauntlet, as he'd known inevitably she would. What he had not known, however, was precisely what he would say. They stared at each other, knowing they'd come to the crossroads of their friendship.

"I am very old, I am very ill. I may not live out the year."

Alice didn't answer, and her eyes didn't leave his face.

"I am far too old for you. But"—he took a breath, and so did Alice—"I ask for your hand in marriage—"

He held out his hand to stop her as she moved toward him.

"With this proviso: that you may at any moment, until the wedding itself, draw back and there will be no imprecations from me."

She knelt before him, flung her arms around him, put her head on his lap. He touched her hair, vibrant with life, and soft, soft for so many curls, as he continued. "We shall marry at the beginning of summer—"

"So long a wait—"

"I want you to have time to consider what you do."

"I won't change my mind. It's you who will."

"I will call upon your father in the next day or so."

She caught the expression on his face. "You believe you ally yourself with a rogue. You do, but a useful one. My father will be your faithful servant. I guarantee it. Within a week, he will be spilling every plot from Buckingham's cabal."

"That will be useful. I will ask that you speak of my proposal to no one until I have spoken with your father and he and I are agreed on terms."

"Yes."

"Well then."

"Well then." She stood, pulled herself up on the wide ledge of the canal, pulled her skirts up enough to show off her stockinged ankles, and began to dance. She leapt and tapped her toes and heels to the stone and sang an old rhyme: "'Little maid, pretty maid, whither goest thou? Down in the forest to milk my cow. Shall I go with thee? No, not now. When I send for thee, then come thou.'" She clapped her hands and turned round and round, keeping her balance when three times he thought she might fall. Finally, she leaped down to dance around his chair, before falling again in a bell of skirts at his feet.

"Pretty behavior for the Duchess of Balmoral."

She saw he was cross. "I am not the Duchess of Balmoral yet. It was a jest, a joy, only for you. May the Duchess of Balmoral not dance before her husband?"

"I'm going to regret this."

She laughed and pulled his age-spotted hand to her mouth to kiss it. "Only every now and again."

"I already regret it."

She let go his hand. "Pretty behavior for the Duke of Balmoral. You've said nothing to my father. I give you leave to change your mind."

"No, no, Alice." He would not draw back now. That would not be honorable, but he didn't say such to her. He'd upset her enough. "It's only that I'm much too old for you." Her zestful dance made him see it too clearly.

She stood up, shook out her skirts. "You hurt me. Until my father comes to talk to me of this, I will not consider you serious in your proposal, nor will I consider us affianced. If I've not heard from my father in three days, I will accept the offer of the Earl of Mulgrave, and you may consider that this conversation between us never took place. Good day, Your Grace."

He watched her walk away in pride and anger.

He watched until she was a small and solitary figure against a horizon colored a soft robin's-egg blue, bare trees showing budding tips, unfurled leaves. Yes, this was the season of life's bounteous unfurling, and he felt old in it, old and withered, with nothing to give, and yet spring offered herself to him, lured him with a long white neck and slender, dancing legs. Did one refuse spring's generosity?

When she returned to the queen's chambers, everyone was busy writing notes of condolence to Lord Knollys. She slipped into a place between Kit and Luce. Dorothy was too happy, and attempting not to show it, to comment on her tardiness. "Be still, Kit, lest you spill ink on your gown," she said. "Alice, help Kit."

Kit could barely spell her name. Spelling and composition were not considered foremost in a young lady's education.

"I want Renée to help me," said Kit. Renée was the bright star among them now. The king's favor did that.

"Of course," said Renée with a resplendent benevolence that frayed Alice's nerves.

"Your English is good enough to write a letter?" Alice asked.

In fact, Renée's English was increasingly better. Mister Dryden, the poet laureate and playwright, tutored her every morning for several hours. It was another source of irritation to the queen, that Renée should learn English faster than she had and already speak it better. Study, Alice had told her. Surprise His Majesty. No, Queen Catherine had replied.

"I write it in French, and then you help on the other, yes?"

"Yes."

For a time, there was the sound of scratching pens, of Kit and Renée whispering. Alice translated Renée's letter to English, and Renée frowned as she copied out the English words:

> *I do not know you well, but I send condolences at your sad news. You have always been kind to me, and we here in the Queen's court await your return eagerly. God and the Holy Mother bless and keep you.*

"May I say that, too?" asked Kit.

"You ought to say something different," said Alice.

"Why?"

"I don't mind it," said Renée, and Alice shrugged.

"Are we done?" Dorothy walked from one to another, blotting ink. Alice brought a candle to warm the sealing wax.

"I haven't a proper seal," said Kit.

"You can use mine." Renée held up a heavy gold signet ring, one of her valentines from her royal cupid. Everyone of consequence had them, their initial or the arms of their house engraved into the flat head of the ring. It gave an official importance to a letter, identified its sender. Dorothy and Alice flicked their eyes at each other. The queen, sitting and writing with her lady-in-waiting Frances, the Duchess of Richmond, said nothing.

"We can count ourselves fortunate he didn't give her the great seal of England," Alice whispered to Dorothy.

"Let's add black ribbon under the wax." Dorothy left to find it.

"Did you give Richard my note?" Renée whispered to Alice in French.

"Of course."

"Was there an answer?"

"No."

"Are you talking about Captain Saylor? He'll answer," Kit whispered to Renée. "He's wild in love with you."

"Everyone has their limit," said Alice.

Kit stared at Alice uncomprehendingly. Alice looked away. It was all too absurd. There was no one left among the maids but giggling, wild children who thought her fussy. Her—Alice Verney!

"Here we are."

Dorothy placed ribbons on the backs of the folded papers, and Alice dropped wax. Seals were pressed, and the letters were placed on the mantel by Dorothy to dry.

"I have a lesson with Fletcher," said Alice, but no one was listening. They didn't listen much to her these days. Not even Renée.

WHEN SHE RETURNED after dinner, King Charles and several of his gentlemen companions were there. Renée was playing upon the lute for them, Kit and Luce at her feet like acolytes.

Dorothy patted a place beside her on the window seat, and Alice sat down.

"I've news I thought you'd want to know. Barbara called upon the queen while you were gone. There is word from Gracen. She wrote to Barbara to say she had been helping with the last days of Lady Knollys and that she sent her love to us. She'll be returning soon, now that it's over. Alice, I'm so happy I can barely contain myself."

"When are new maids going to join us, Dorothy? If I hear Kit and Luce titter on too much longer, I'm going to jump out a window."

"It's up to her," said Dorothy, nodding in Renée's direction. "Queen Catherine asked His Majesty this morning to approve the names of two young ladies, and he said not yet, and when she asked him the reason for the delay, he gave some answer that did not fool her in the least. She returned angry and blamed Renée, calling her the real queen of England. Lady Arlington and Lady Suffolk were in attendance and heard, so of course they'll tell His Majesty, and that will mean he'll be cool and distant for days, until the queen goes to him and begs pardon."

"Her only recourse is to accept this gracefully, allow the king his pleasure, and then he will be kind again."

"It was easier for the queen when his amours were actresses. He didn't bring them to court. This is right in front of her nose."

"You forget the Duchess of Cleveland and our dear Duchess of Richmond when she was plain Frances Stewart. He hasn't changed. Speak with her, Dorothy, remind her of that. If she displeases His Majesty, she does herself a great disservice. The talk about divorce has died back, but doesn't she remember when that was her daily terror? The king gives her respect as a princess."

"As long as she is agreeable."

"As long as she is agreeable."

"It isn't my place to tell her that."

It is your place as a member of her court, thought Alice. Our lieges have to hear the bad as well as the good, else what use are any of us to them? She lifted her chin. She'd talk with Frances and with Father Huddleston. Talk of divorce might have died back since Henri Ange was caught, but the queen's position remained precarious, her only ally His Majesty, because she plotted for no others. She had to be reminded of that again and again, whether she wished it or not.

If only Lord Knollys were here.

"By the by, Barbara is going to be made a woman of the bedchamber as soon as the child is born. King Charles did approve that."

Well, I really must leave Her Majesty's service, thought Alice.

"I wish you'd make up with Barbara." Then, seeing Alice's face: "Well, you can always come and live with me, you know that, don't you?"

"And where are you going, Brownie?" The question was teasing.

"To heaven."

Alice squeezed Dorothy's hand.

"You cannot imagine how I despise being here these days," said Dorothy.

But I can, thought Alice. And so we all abandon the queen. But that wasn't true—Barbara was returning. So would she, when she was a duchess. I already regret it, she heard Balmoral say in her mind. If she was a duchess.

Later, as they sat in the playhouse and the actor Charles Hart was mouthing a tedious prologue, Alice whispered in French with Renée. "I think Richard is hurt beyond words."

"I don't know what to do."

"He is your shield, Renée. As long as you have his love, you have a way out."

"Nothing I do pleases him. The queen is very angry with me, Alice. I'm told she said mean things of me this morning."

So, already they come to tattle, thought Alice. Renée is ascending fast. "She can't help it."

"I try not to hurt her, Alice."

"I know you do, and I admire you for that."

You don't want a way out, thought Alice. Why did her heart hurt the way it did? Why did her head ache a little all the time? Because she very well might have to marry the inarticulate Mulgrave? Because the heady days of being a maid of honor were over for her? Because she missed Barbara so much, perhaps even Caro, in some deep part of her? Knew she was wrong, but knew she would do nothing to change? Was appalled by and yet allowed the size of her pride to grow and grow until it was a prison around her? Because Richard was free? Because she was not? Something was in her, pressing, all the time pressing.

She saw the king's lord chamberlain make his way to His Majesty. Even in the dim light of the playhouse, something about the way the lord chamberlain carried himself caught Alice's attention. He leaned over to whisper to the king, then King Charles said something to those with him and left. Those in the king's box hissed among themselves and leaned over to speak to those around them. People stopped watching the actors as a kind of buzz rose, and then person after person abandoned their seats and left the theater. It was as if a spell fell on the audience, as whatever had been told the king spread throughout the theater. Onstage, the actors continued, but it was to no avail. The strange mood sweeping over the theater touched even them.

Dorothy leaned over to speak with Frances. Alice and Renée and Kit and Luce leaned forward, too. "The Duchess of York is dead," she told them.

EVERYONE AT COURT was stunned. As servants rummaged through trunks and boxes looking for black crepe with which to cover mirrors, as tailors and seamstresses pulled out cards of black thread, found black ribbons, and began to cut black cloth into coats and gowns, as pages and undergrooms scrambled to find cats and lock them away out of sight because there was an old folk custom that cats couldn't be present when there'd been a death, courtiers gathered in small groups, talking of what they knew, conjecturing of what they didn't, mixing rumor and truth to a brew that was neither but from which all drank. They remembered that she was the daughter of the Earl of Clarendon, for years the king's most powerful adviser, an architect of the Restoration, now in exile. Would he return for this? Would the king allow it? Might he sit once more with Arlington and Buckingham and Balmoral to advise the king? Would he take revenge for those among the ministers—chiefly Buckingham—who'd betrayed him?

It was remembered that the marriage had been considered a terrible misalliance, that York should have married a foreign princess, but what they mainly remembered, minced and chopped and turned to one side and then another, was that—because the queen was barren—the Duke of York remained heir to the throne and that now he would remarry, and even though his dead wife had converted to popery, their two surviving daughters were being reared in the Church of England; here was a chance for another beginning.

York could marry a Protestant princess and so perhaps father a Protestant prince, who would take precedence over his sisters. Was York a cat's-paw for the pope? Yes? No? Had he converted, as rumor sometimes said? Yes? No? Oh, they'd be watching this year, to see if he took Communion at Easter. Because it was not a good thing if the heir to the throne was a Papist. And finally, the cruelest scandal broth of all, why had it to be the Duchess of York who died, courtiers commiserated with one another. Why could it not be the queen herself who lay stiff and white on the funeral bier?

Alice made her way among the press of courtiers who were thronging the Duke of York's apartments on the far western end of the palace. King Charles was there, Queen Catherine, Prince Rupert, and Monmouth. Several of King Charles's children by the Duchess of Cleveland were with him. He kept them by him, stroking their hair, as people made their way to his brother, spoke their condolences, and if they were fortunate, King Charles said a word or two to them. Alice looked at the king, whose expressions she knew so well. This day his face was stoic, drawn, tiredness dragging down his mouth.

Alice searched the chamber for Balmoral but didn't see him. Others were there, the Duke of Buckingham, Lord Arlington, other privy council members. Where was Balmoral? He should be here also. Had her scene yesterday sent him on a drunken fit? It was what she feared. Her stomach was in a knot with it. She made a deep curtsy before the Duke of York, whose face was puffy. He wore the slightly startled expression of someone who has sustained a great shock and isn't quite certain of what is happening.

"Your Grace, I am so sorry."

"Verney, you dear thing. No one expected this. It just came out of nowhere, nowhere."

She didn't know what to say, so she simply nodded.

"I'm lost without her."

"So many people mourn with you, Your Grace."

"Do they? Thank you, Verney."

She moved away. King Charles nodded to her, Prince Rupert took her by the arm.

"Come and have a pipe with me," he whispered.

"Gladly."

They left the crowded chamber and walked through an antechamber, almost as full. In a corner were the Duchess of York's maids of honor, some weeping, all huddled together like mewing kittens who had lost their mother. Barbara and Caro were with them, as were Alice's fellow maids of honor. She saw Sir William Coventry and Sir William Penn and Samuel Pepys, all those who worked in the naval office, but then York was admiral of King Charles's navy. Of course they were there. Where is Richard? she thought. He must make his condolences.

In another chamber now, she watched Prince Rupert rummage in a drawer in an ornate Chinese cabinet. This was the Duke of York's set of apartments, yet Prince Rupert knew exactly where the tobacco was kept. In a moment a pipe was filled for her, he was striking flint to tinder, then holding up a slim burning stick to the pipe's bowl, and she puffed to get it burning. Oh, she did love the rich aroma arising, the pale smoke like a benevolent spirit. He was stuffing the bowl of his own pipe, and soon the pair of them contentedly inhaled and exhaled sweet, soothing clouds of tobacco. At some point, they both sighed in unison.

Alice smiled. Prince Rupert sat beside her, patted her hand.

"It's sad times, it is. We're all awhirl. Two days ago she was sitting at my table, eating like the trencherman she was, not a thing wrong with her. Not a sign. Jemmy is beside himself. He sat with the body all night, holding her hand and weeping, remembering back when she was young and slender and had a sweeter temper."

"Poor York."

"He'll be over it in three fortnights. She was a harridan, not like the queen, God bless her. You're looking drawn lately, Verney. What's troubling you?"

"I look troubled?"

"Those bright eyes of yours are dimmed a bit. Is your father giving you fits? He has the Commons in a snarl over the House of Lords changing the amount of tax on imports. We were glad just to be allowed the tax, and the next thing we know, each side is wrangling over whether changes may be made at all, is there precedence, that sort of thing. The Committee on Foreign Affairs has been summoned to find a ruling. I hope they do. We need the tax. The treasury needs coins. His Majesty is impatient. Me, I just tire of the everlasting quarreling. Every single bill in Parliament is a quarrel, and I tell you, I wash my hands of the Commons. If I were His Majesty, I'd hang them all, every man of the Commons, even your father. As for the Lords, Arlington can't agree with Buckingham. Buckingham distrusts Balmoral. I listen to them snipe at one another, and I'm taken back to the war, when our generals couldn't agree which way was south, and so Cromwell cut us to pieces. Sometimes I have half a mind to go privateering again, just commandeer one of the king's ships and sail off and take what prizes I can. I think I'll go to the Colonies, to a place called Hudson's Bay, and live the life of a trader, trapping animals for their pelts. By the by, Alice, you ought to invest in my little trading company, put some pin money in it."

"Have you seen His Grace Balmoral this day?"

"He called upon Jemmy last night, sat with him at the body. They talked for a long time. What's this between you and Balmoral? You walk him around like a pet lion. He's too old for you—and lest you forget, even an old lion has claws. But you'll make a fine duchess if he doesn't die before you wheedle a proposal from him."

"What are you laughing at?"

"Monmouth's duchess won't like it that you'll be her equal. Princess Monmouth, I call her behind her back."

"I'm her equal now."

"Ha!" She made him laugh again. Tobacco smoke was like a fine haze around them, but neither cared. They puffed away on their pipes like two old sailors.

"Your Highness, will you do something for me?"

"Anything."

"Will you have a regard for Captain Saylor?"

"I already do. Too bad he's gotten crossways with His Majesty."

"He should have been rewarded for the capture of Henri Ange."

"Who is this Henri Ange? I have heard the most preposterous rumors, and he isn't discussed openly. Buckingham and Balmoral go behind closed doors with His Majesty to speak of him, and His Majesty won't answer a question of mine. This can go no further than this chamber, and by that I mean your father is not to hear a word of this, but I hear Buckingham and Balmoral are in separate camps over what to do with him."

"Hang him."

"Ha."

Chapter 36

Caro and Barbara sat together in the Duke of York's apartments, among the gathering of courtiers who'd come to pay condolences.

"She didn't even l-look our way," said Caro.

"Perhaps she didn't see us."

"I've given up c-courting her regard. She'll n-never forgive me, and you know, Ra, I don't think I care anymore. One can beg for only so long. If she were to c-crawl to me on bended knee, I don't think I'd blink. I think I'd turn my b-back."

"Please don't say that."

"Don't you think it s-sometime?"

Barbara didn't answer.

"She has Colefax in a twist, I'll g-give her that."

"Because of Balmoral?"

"He's gotten it into his head that she's going to m-marry His Grace."

"What if she does? Colefax is still his heir."

"He's convinced she'll have a b-baby some way, that he'll be knocked f-from the dukedom."

"Oh, Caro, I don't think Alice would be unfaithful, and one can't just conjure up a baby. . . ."

Caro shuddered. "I don't envy her the wedding n-night, or any of her n-nights, for that matter."

Barbara sighed.

Caro reached out and took her hand. "Are you feeling well? You look s-splendid."

"I feel like a small beer barrel."

"M-mothers together. When you're a girl, such s-seems so far away. Do you remember how we'd go to my m-mama on Mothering Sunday? I thought about that this morning, you and m-me and Alice, in our best gowns, eating s-simnel cakes with M-Mother. You always brought her some t-trinket. She loved that."

Barbara had a sudden, clear memory of them at thirteen, at fourteen, and each year after, trooping off to Caro's mother, Alice so excited because she'd never had a mother and Barbara usually sad because she could remember hers too well. "You were lovely to share her with us."

"She adored it. She liked you better as d-d-daughters than m-me. I could never p-please her. How many more months left?"

"Two." A shadow passed over Barbara's face, but Caro didn't notice. Barbara looked around the withdrawing chamber, her eyes lingering over every item, the color of the walls, the sun shining in on dancing dust motes, the expressions on people's faces, the sound of conversation, smiles, frowns, everything in between, the familiar comfort and ease between her and Caro, the way John would glance over at her and smile his love. Every day, now, she thought, this will be the last time I see this, taste this, smell this. The knowledge was a pain so deep, it sharpened every sense. Even ugliness had been transformed. There was nothing ugly. She was aware of the smallest things, of the extraordinary beauty of all, magnificent, not to be wasted, not to be complained of. How she wished to tell John, but she would not mar a moment of their days and nights with sorrow. He'd have his full plate of sorrow soon enough. And how she wished to tell Alice, to lean her face into her shoulder and weep like a child all her fear, all her pain, and hear Alice's protests, Alice's solutions for how to trick death. She'd have them. The truth was life had never been more exquisite. She would have liked to tell Alice that, too.

Alice left Prince Rupert and walked through the privy garden to Balmoral's, Poll a few paces behind her. It was cold, no hint of the long summer dusks ahead, that magic time of talk and dance and laughter with friends in Spring Garden or Mulberry Garden or here in the privy garden, of rowing in the long twilights to Windsor, to Hampton Court, to Richmond or Chelsea. In France, Madame had summoned her musicians for dancing in the gardens, fountains nearby at which to sit, from which to bring handfuls of cool water to faces flushed from dancing, the scent of roses, jasmine, and orange everywhere, the servants gathering to watch, joining in as dusk turned to dark and the night was so alive with possibility, more exciting than the day.

At Balmoral's, no one made any attempt to fob her off. A servant rushed off to find the majordomo. She waited in the antechamber, and then there was Riggs, bowing.

"Is His Grace here?"

"He is not."

She came straight to the point. "Is he here but keeping from company?"

He knew precisely what she meant. "No, I swear it."

She opened her hand, held out the coin for him, which he took. "I must warn you, Riggs, that I have most serious designs on your master."

"Yes." He smiled, one side pulling up by the scar so that it was almost a grimace.

"Is Captain Saylor here?"

"If I may, let me lead the way."

She followed him up the stairs and down the hallway to the chamber allotted Richard. The door was open. Richard sat scribbling, a slight smear of ink on one cheek. Poll sat in a chair just outside the opened door. Alice walked in, went at once to the door leading to Balmoral's closet, put her ear to it.

Richard watched, amused that she would do that even before greeting him—she was nothing if not single-minded. "He isn't in there. I haven't heard a sound all day."

"Everyone is at the Duke of York's. You must go and pay your condolences."

"Must I?"

"Absolutely. Don't hide away. Go and pay your respects and let the world see you undefeated."

"I'm not defeated, Alice, just heartsore. Not in the mood for the eyes of the crowd."

"You must endure it anyway. You must call upon York. Every official from the navy is there. How will the army ever maintain its place if you and Balmoral ignore the courtesies? How does Walter, and the Daniells?"

"Well. My mother wants them to come to Tamworth to serve her after the baby is born. I think they may do it."

"I did not know your mother had met them."

"She was curious about Walter."

"He was most loyal, Richard, slept on the floor at the foot of your bed like a dog." She moved closer, pretending to be reading what he'd written. "You have ink on your face."

He rubbed at the wrong cheek. She put out her hand, touching at the smear with a fingertip, lightly, the way a butterfly might. Surprising himself, surprising her, he took her hand and kissed the palm. She could feel his inner lip, the moisture of his mouth, the hint of his tongue. Her knees went weak. She snatched her hand away, walked to the door, calling out over her shoulder, "Call upon York. Today."

Striding as if thieves were after her, she was back at the privy garden, Poll fussing behind her, before she had any mastery over herself. One of the king's gardeners was tying the long, tender arms of climbing roses to a wall. She walked over to him.

"Mistress Verney. And what can I do for you today?"

"Mothering Sunday is almost here, and I need a nosegay of violets for my aunt."

"Easily done. I'll mix in a bit of juniper and moss. And what about a colonial daffodil for your aunt? There're some just in from a ship from the Americas. His Majesty is quite taken with them."

"That would be wonderful. Thank you."

"Always a pleasure."

Back in York's chambers, she tossed off her cloak, found the queen to curtsy to her, then joined the other maids of honor and ladies-in-waiting, half listening to their talk, her mind playing over and over the suddenness of Richard's movement, the way his mouth felt on her hand, the way her heart was beating still . . . If he'd taken her in his arms, she would not have been able to pull free. If he'd kissed her, she didn't know what she would have done.

He'd heard her.

She'd prayed he hadn't. She'd hoped he hadn't. She'd convinced herself he hadn't. But he had. As evening approached, watching the royal brothers, the queen, Rupert, the Monmouths at their public dinner, she felt still the pressure of Richard's mouth on her hand. Mourning for Her Grace. No dancing. No public performances of plays for weeks. What would they all do with themselves?

THE NEXT DAY dawned. King Charles, a page bringing his spaniels, went for an evening walk, Renée at his side, Alice and the others following, except the queen, who refused to join them. Lord Rochester made stupid, half-bawdy, tasteless comments, as if the maids of honor were actresses, who didn't care what was said to them. Mulgrave, walking beside her, wanted to speak seriously, she could see, so she linked her arm in Renée's. The king and Renée were talking of La Grande Mademoiselle, the most important princess in the French court. King Charles was mocking the French princess's disdainful manner, telling Renée of how he'd tried to court her in his vagabond days and how she would have little to do with him. "And thus she missed wearing the crown of England," he said.

Where was Balmoral? It was day two; her stomach hurt, her head. Barbara looked so big with child. The sight of her yesterday at York's had shocked her. Barbara and Caro huddled in talk. Did they talk about her? Say mean things of her? John Sidney had approached, wanting to speak with her. She must not like him. She wouldn't. He was lucky she did not disclose him to her father as a Papist. Alice had watched Caro, thinking, What if I just went over and began talking; we could repair ourselves. But she didn't. Richard had looked so thin, not quite well, as he entered York's chamber. All the maids watched Renée, who could not keep color from rushing to her face.

But Richard didn't walk over to speak to her.

He made his obediences to King Charles, whose face expressed nothing, whose eyes missed nothing, either. Richard talked for a long time with the queen, as if she were not in disfavor. He seemed to notice none of the mood around him, and he finally settled in between John and Barbara. Not once did he glance at Renée that Alice could see. A muscle showed itself now and then at his jaw. Alice could only guess at what the visit had cost him. He didn't stay to watch royalty dine. And Monmouth and Louisa Saylor. What was going on there? Monmouth had only to look her way for her to smile. Hers was as blazing as her brother's, and Alice felt guilty to see it.

She glanced up. First stars. Wish I may, wish I might, have the wish I wish tonight. She was glad to be walking briskly, His Majesty's only way of walking. She wanted her bed. Wanted to pull covers up over her head and have this day done with. But there was to be no early to bed for her. Back in the queen's antechamber, Rochester amused them for an hour with card tricks. Dryden passed out sheets of his latest play, and they took parts and read them. Strictures of mourning were going to be allowed liberal interpretation, it was clear.

Alice went to sit with Dorothy.

"What further news have you from Lord Knollys?" she asked.

But Dorothy didn't answer, and Alice left the question alone.

She went to stand near the king, who was laughing at Dryden's dialogue as spoken by Rochester and Luce. Dryden recited a poem, then Rochester. King Charles teased Renée to read a poem and show off her English. Alice yawned, found a fat French armchair, pulled up her legs, and, before she knew it, dozed.

She woke to the sound of music. Renée was playing the lute for His Majesty, and the chamber was empty of people. The king's face showed sadness, tiredness, but his eyes gleamed as he watched Renée.

"Another," he said when she'd ended.

"'Had we but world enough, and time, this coyness, Lady, were no crime,'" sang Renée.

The king's heavy-lidded eyes were suddenly upon Alice. "Our duenna wakes."

"Hello, Alice," said Renée, strumming without self-consciousness. The king's attention no longer embarrassed her. "Look how tired she is. I think we can dismiss her."

And when Alice was gone, he said, "What about your reputation?" He spoke in French.

"I weary of duennas. I'm not a child."

"I weary of losing those I love." He sighed, and Renée put down the lute, stood behind his chair, put her arms around him. He pulled off his hat and then his heavy periwig, and she kissed his head, the hair shorn short. He put his hands on her arms and closed his eyes.

"Memory plays its games tonight, Renée, and I am remembering my sister-in-law when Jemmy married her. She was a maid of honor at my sister's court at The Hague. I am remembering how Jemmy would rather be beaten than go and face her when she was angry with him, how we laughed at him. I am remembering her father, who was my savior in those years when I had no place to put my head. He never abandoned me. He was steadfast when I was not. I've a letter from him, asking to return for the funeral, a reasonable request."

Renée, listening, rubbed her chin against his head and said nothing. It was exciting for this man, this majesty, to tell her his thoughts.

"No, is my answer, though I don't say that yet to my council. Let Buck and the others that urged his exile squirm a bit. So many people I loved are gone, one after another. Come here and sit in my lap. My beauty, my little treasure. If I didn't have you . . ." He closed his eyes a moment, and the melancholia that he dreaded descended, a black cloak smothering hope.

Sensing it, Renée kissed his brows, his closed eyes, and, finally, his mouth.

He responded hungrily, a drowning man thrown a rope, his hands caressing her hair, pulling out ribbons, caressing her bare, white shoulders, her covered breasts, her narrow waist. They kissed until they were reeling from it, until they were lying on the floor pressed together. He pulled himself away and stared down at her. "You have the king of England tumbling about the floor like a boy at a country fair."

She traced his full lips with a finger. "I don't like you to be sad."

He put his head in between her breasts, not loverlike, but as a child would, and she wrapped her arms around him. She felt wildly protective. He showed her what no one else saw—he needed her. It was as heady as the finest wine. It went to her head like champagne. No one else saw him so. They stayed quiet for a long time, she hugging him, and he not groping, or jesting, or doing anything but lying against her. After a time, a shudder moved through his body, and he sat up. "You have my heart. When are you going to allow me in your bed?"

There was no reproach, no pleading, in his tone. They might have been discussing the weather. Renée loved this about him, his matter-of-factness. They might have been bargaining for bread. It was very French. She laughed, and he pinched her arm. "I think I ought to have my own chamber," she said.

"Oh?"

Now teasing and more was in his voice. She sat up, too, made him lie down so that she might stroke his forehead, and he sighed again. She kissed that forehead. So much wit there. So much curiosity. So much knowledge. This man who was king. Who loved her above others. "It would be kinder."

"To me, that's for certain."

"To Her Majesty."

There was a silence while he took her words in, a rebuke. "I'm not kind, am I? Not when I want something. Yes, you'll have your chamber and servants to serve you on bended knee. Give me your body, sweetheart, and I'll give you half of Whitehall."

"Do you think you can buy me?"

"God's blood, if we're bargaining, I hope your price is low. My damned House of Commons is like a withered widow courted because coins are under her mattress, and she fears losing a one of them. I bring them my needs, the needs of my navy, of my household. They examine the books, call together committees to question my servants, and still they hesitate to grant what is necessary. Cousin Louis says to his dog Colbert, I'll build this and I'll have that, and Colbert says, Yes, sire, and makes a tax, and that's the end of that. I have to wrangle and lie like a merchant for every pence! And then they complain because the Hollanders are before us in trade, when they won't give money to buy a plank to make the ships that will protect our trading vessels!"

She smiled, pleased that he was stirred, that her words had somehow moved him away from melancholia.

He sat up. "You've managed to chase away the blackness. I'm ready to duel with my Commons." He kissed her with a smack, then bit her shoulder. "Saylor didn't speak to you tonight. What have you done to him?"

Now it was her turn to sigh, to turn her face away so he wouldn't see it.

"Don't tell me he doesn't love you anymore. A fool can see he does."

"I don't please him."

"You won't give me up, and Saylor's angry?"

Still she didn't look at him.

He was touched by that, by her feeling for Richard, which she did not hide. When she gave herself to him, it would mean something. There would be genuine feeling behind it, a heart with the body. He was willing to wait. The foreplay of bedding was so beguilingly delicious. She touched at her eyes. Tears. He didn't feel like staying long to comfort them, if truth be told. Nell had popped into his head, Nell, who wouldn't hold him off, who would meet him kiss for kiss and touch for touch and then some. Pert breasts, trim legs, slender hips. What had Rochester said the other evening, a whore in the hand is worth a virgin in the bush?

"It's your heart I have designs on. Never forget that." The smile she gave him was sparkling. "If you want to keep that maidenhead of yours another moment, you'd best kiss me good night and toddle off to bed."

Outside, his guard following, knowing better than to ask questions, he whistled in the dark. Andrew Marvell was as obstreperous and obstructive in the House of Commons as Thomas Verney, but nonetheless a fair poet. He whistled a Marvell song Renée had been playing earlier, the words singing in his head: " 'Now therefore, while the youthful hue Sits on thy skin like morning dew, And while thy willing soul transpires At every pore with instant fires, Now let us sport while we may.' "

Just what he intended to do.

ALICE HAD GONE not to bed, but rather to Dorothy's chambers.

"There's been no letter." Dorothy poured more wine and added some to Alice's goblet. "At first, I thought nothing of it. But as the days have passed, I've counted back. It's been over three weeks since he's written me."

"The end was likely so difficult that he couldn't bring himself to write of it."

"We have always written each other when distance has separated us. Always. The thoughts I've begun to have weigh so heavy, Alice. Perhaps he no longer loves me. What will I do?"

There was an edge in her voice that made Alice turn the goblet in her hands nervously. "The first thing you will do is be sensible. You don't know anything. It's all your imagination—"

"It's not. I am connected to him here." Dorothy touched her heart. "Something's changed. I feel it."

"We'll write Gracen. We'll write to Gracen and ask her to look around, see if there is some woman sniffing about him. And if there is, we'll command Gracen to hold her off while we put you in a coach, with one of His Majesty's hounds, to chase the wench into the woods!"

Her humor failed. "I can't live without him. He's my life, he's my heart. I need him." Dorothy was collapsing, hysterics close. Alice took away her goblet, and Dorothy grabbed her hands and held on to them, tears spouting.

Appalled, and frightened, too, Alice tried to soothe her. "It's nothing. It's your imagination. Oh, Brownie, don't weep when you don't know what is happening, when it's only your thoughts."

"I can't help it. I want him here now. I want him in my bed. I want to be his wife. I deserve to be his wife. I've waited so long. Why doesn't he write to me? Is he trying to drive me mad?"

She had her arms around Alice, was crying into Alice's waist. Alice pulled herself free. "Brownie, you have to stop. You have to get command of yourself."

"I can't. Oh, don't leave me, Alice, don't go. I can't be alone. Please. I'll be good." And she wiped at her face, took deep, trembling breaths. "Look, I'm stopping. See. I'm going to climb into bed, and you're going to put away the wine and stay with me until I go to sleep, and then blow out my candle."

"I'll sleep beside you, Brownie." Alice almost couldn't bear the cry of gratitude that came from her words. "I'm too tired to go to my own bed. Here, help me unpin."

She blew out the candles, her last sight Brownie's swollen and slack face. In the bed, she stayed carefully on her side, not wanting to touch Brownie and feeling ashamed of that, listening as she tried to cry quietly, tried not to bother Alice. After a long time, Alice said, "There has to be a proper period of mourning, remember that."

Silence answered her. She must have fallen asleep, thought Alice. Thank God.

She threw back the sheets, fumbled with flint and tinder, managed to light a candle. She set the candle in the fireplace, sat in Brownie's rocking chair, and rocked herself back and forth, her nerves feeling frayed, loose, dangerous. Was this true love? This need? This pain. It frightened her to her soul.

Richard. Richard. Richard.

THE THIRD DAY, and no word from Balmoral. Alice looked at herself in the mirror, touched at smudges under her eyes. This evening she would send a note to her father to accept Mulgrave's offer. She stared back at herself, straightened her shoulders, then marched to Queen Catherine's antechambers to begin her day, leaving Dorothy shaking awake Kit and Luce. Renée and Frances were already sorting sheets and blankets, but Lady Arlington sipped slowly at her morning ale and sighed. She was there because it was her duty, little more. She would not lift a finger. Queen Catherine inspected clothing, several of her bedchamber women with her, their needles ready to sew and repair what she indicated was necessary. Alice took a mug of hot tea from a servant.

"How many children?" Queen Catherine asked her. The queen was determined to help the Daniells, of whom Jerusalem Saylor had spoken.

"I believe four boys and eight girls."

"And the babe, we mustn't forget the coming babe."

"Is it really necessary to welcome another fatherless child into the world?" Lady Arlington asked. The question was rhetorical, something said to pass the time, but Queen Catherine rounded on her in fury.

"All God's children we are! You retire, Lady Arlington. I am no need of your services today!"

Everyone was silent. Queen Catherine never spoke harshly to her ladies, and this lady was wife to the king's most trusted councillor.

Injured pride in every movement, Lady Arlington curtsied and, like a great ship, sailed slowly and with regal dignity out of the chamber.

"And you, also!" Queen Catherine spoke directly to Renée. "I am no need of your services, either!"

Renée stood with a blanket in her hand, frozen.

"Say nothing. Leave immediately," whispered Frances, who was nearest to her.

Renée curtsied. When she was gone, all that wasn't said seemed to fill the chamber, but no one dared to speak.

"There." Queen Catherine was false, bright. "Our work we have do in peace."

Dorothy herded in a sleepy, pouting Kit and Luce, while Queen Catherine parceled out clothing that needed mending, and everyone settled down to work, dying to talk about what had happened, not daring to. Frances and Alice sat in a window seat, their needles flying.

Frances spoke quietly, not wanting to draw the queen's attention. "I'm sad, Alice. For five years, I was reason for the queen's grief. It was so alluring to be the king's love, I could think of little else. He must allot Renée her own chambers, as he did with me. It's too difficult for everyone otherwise— Oh, dear God, there's His Majesty. Look at his face. Renée has been crying on his shoulder."

"I'd speak with you, madam wife." King Charles's face was stern.

"Speak," snapped Queen Catherine.

"Before all your women?" He was grim.

"Whyever not? Who in this court does not know—"

"Have your women leave the chamber at once!"

Women jabbed needles into cloth to mark their places and exited in a swishing cascade of skirts. Alice and Frances left a crack in the door they exited and stationed themselves at it.

"You were rude to Mademoiselle de Keroualle!" Alice and Frances heard King Charles say.

"Is that what she tells? Tattle, tattle."

"She told me nothing except that you'd asked her to leave your presence! She was weeping as if her heart would break."

"Her heart? No heart have I?"

"I have never been faithful to you, Catherine! What on earth makes you think I would begin now?"

Alice shivered.

"Here is what I suggest. Accept my amours with good grace, as you have so kindly done in the past, and I welcome your presence in my life! Continue this behavior, and I will put it publicly to the bishops to see whether I have cause for divorce and have you sent back to Portugal, where you may spend your days in prayer in a convent! That won't be amusing, will it, Catherine? You won't be the queen of England there; you'll simply be a woman who has chosen sanctimonious piousness over a very grand and exalted position, a position you have always occupied with grace! I have ordered chambers to be prepared for Mademoiselle de Keroualle! She won't attend you, since that seems to be what you desire, but she remains a maid of honor until I say otherwise! Are we clear in this matter, my dear?"

At the cracked door, both Alice and Frances were crying.

"I don't like discord around me," King Charles was saying, his voice softer. His anger had passed, but not his sternness. "You know that, Catherine. You are my queen. No one can take that from you. I don't desire to." The unspoken implication was that it could, of course, be taken away. "When Mademoiselle de Keroualle gives her first reception, I'm going to expect you to attend it on my arm. Do you think you can do that, my dear?"

They heard no response from the queen.

"I won't demand your presence at public dining for a while or impose myself upon you in the evenings for a time. I am going to allow you to get command of yourself, to remember your position and the courtesy and grace expected of that position, the courtesy I have extended you, my dear, when I assure you I have been urged to do otherwise. Good day, Catherine."

Frances closed the crack of the door very, very quietly, but she remained against it, weeping as if it were her to whom King Charles had spoken. It might have been, thought Alice, pulling out a handkerchief with which to wipe her eyes. If she'd been mistress, it might have been. Will Mulgrave be unfaithful to me? thought Alice. And will I care? On the other side of the door, Queen Catherine must be weeping. Does she weep from pride or from love? What is the difference between the two? It seemed to her, feeling the wildness in her own heart, her aunt was correct: A wise woman didn't allow love to cloud the issue of marriage.

SHE WAS WALKING in the privy garden with Dorothy and Kit and Luce when Edward came to tell her Perryman waited in the Stone Gallery. Alice felt dizzy for a moment, and her stomach twisted tighter into its knot. It was here.

In the Stone Gallery, Perryman bowed. "A boat is waiting at the stairs. Your father asks that you join him."

"I'll be there presently." Edward brought a cloak, and she began a hunt she couldn't stop herself from making. Richard wasn't in the queen's guardroom.

Drilling, a palace page told Edward, who found her and told her. She walked outside, across the cobbles of courtyards, into the melee in the street before the banqueting hall, through the sedan chairs and carriages there to the tilt yard on the other side. But he wasn't there. She walked down the alley between buildings that opened to St. James's Park. There he was. She sighed and leaned on a fence railing to watch him. He didn't see her; he was focused on his men, calling out orders, sending them this way and that, instilling the discipline he so believed in. Walter was walking Pharaoh up and down in the distance. So. There'd be a gallop later. She watched him for a long time, cataloging the different things about him she loved, his seriousness, the way the sun glinted in his hair, the lean, clean strength of his body. She was saying, deep inside herself, good-bye.

Chapter 37

Perryman helped her into a boat. The riverman moved them away from the stairs and into the river's current, his oars slipping in and out of the water expertly. She turned to her father's servant. "So, Perryman, any tricks lately?"

"I have no idea as to what you refer, ma'am."

"Oh, one heard of a fountain in Cleveland's gardens going awry, a metal fish spraying her just at the moment she walked by."

"Poor workmanship, I would say. There are no true craftsmen left these days."

"How does my father?"

"Very well, ma'am. He was saying the other day he doesn't see enough of you."

"I've been scheming, Perryman."

"That's what he said."

"He did, did he? Do you know all our secrets?"

"I would hope not, ma'am."

"Do you always have an answer for every question?"

"Yes, ma'am."

"Has Louisa Saylor been to visit my father again, I mean, since Lady Saylor was here?" Jerusalem Saylor and her daughters had been several times to her father's while Richard's mother was in London nursing him.

"I wouldn't know, ma'am."

Alice fiddled with a frogged toggle on her cloak. It would be too bad if Monmouth ruined Louisa's reputation. Perhaps she'd put her mind to it and find Louisa a good match. She walked through her father's riverside garden and onto his terrace. Smiling, he waited at the opened doors of the house. She walked into his arms, and he hugged her tight, picked her up, and swung her around and around. "You've done it, by Jesus!" he said. "My clever, clever gal, you've done it!"

They walked arm in arm into the great hall of the house. A servant took Alice's cloak as her father's pride and amazement poured over her. "I'm beside myself, don't know up from down—Balmoral, of all people! I'll tell you truly, Alice, I didn't think you could manage it—"

"He's been to call? Tell me, Father."

"Called upon me yesterday afternoon— Perryman, bring us champagne! Very proper, very stiff. I offered him wine, but he'd have none of it. I'm here to ask for your daughter's hand in marriage, he told me, straight off, no beating about the bush. You could have knocked me over with a feather, I swear it, Alice. I never thought you'd bring him to heel. We moved straight to the business of terms, settled without a harsh word between us, as easy as pie. The next thing I know, he is bowing to me—bowing to me, Alice!—and telling me he hoped he and I would not be strangers to each other, that his door was always open to me. You've saved my life, that you have. I haven't told you, but I'm at the end of it with Buckingham. I've been fretting myself to pieces, and now, well, there's just no telling what may happen next. . . ."

"The terms?"

"Most generous. You'll have your own pin money, both from him and from me. One of his properties will become yours entirely and not be entailed to his current heir. Your mother's property of Bentwoodes will be a part of your dowry, but go only to children of your body, not Balmoral's heir, should there be no children between the two of you. The deed to this house and several others will be put in your name, mine for my lifetime, but yours afterward, and again, entailed only to heirs of your body, so that you may remarry and provide something handsome for children even with Balmoral dead."

"It is more than generous, from both of you."

He rubbed his hands together, crowing in triumph. "My daughter is to be a duchess! I can afford generosity! And I'll tell you, we talked of what might happen if he should die before the marriage ceremony. He brought it up, not I. You're to have the property he gives you as his duchess. Handsomely done, I must say. Handsome. He's fond of you, Alice, more than fond."

She sagged suddenly, but he didn't notice. He was accepting the champagne Perryman brought, the liquid glinting in his rare Venetian glasses. "To the Duchess of Balmoral. Long may she reign."

Alice clinked her glass to his. "Long may she reign."

CHAPTER 38

A guard unlocked the chains around Henri Ange's legs and hands. Free, Ange walked straight to a window through which the sun shone. Layers of thick stone made up the towers and prison cells of the Tower of London. Ange held his face up to the light. His hair and eyebrows were growing back. The man awaiting him in this chamber had just arranged that he be shaved again. Balmoral would have had him with a beard to his knees, like an animal. Aren't you an animal? Balmoral had asked.

The Duke of Buckingham, masked, watched Ange carefully, as he did every time he visited.

"I want a cell like this," said Ange. They always began this way.

"It can't be done."

"I want the liberty to walk along the walls several times a day."

"That might be arranged. Once a day."

"Arrange it."

"Your legs will remained chained."

Ange bared teeth. "Arrange it! I'm growing into a madman, some creature of the dark. I don't know how much longer I can hang on. What month is it?"

"It's March. I'm doing everything in my power to get you freed. It is most unfortunate that Alice Verney testified that she suspects you of poisoning Madame."

"Conjecture. I've done nothing more than duel with a queen's guardsman. How long must I remain in the Tower for that? The price for my silence rises with every week I remain here. Can you afford me, Your Grace?"

"I have to, don't I."

"I want out."

"I have done everything I can. The French ambassador requests your release every time he sees King Charles. King Louis demands that you be returned to France."

"Returned to France. Why would I trade this for the dungeons of the Bastille? I think not. Where are my letters?"

Buckingham reached into a pocket, laid down letters. Ange snatched them up, ripped past worthless seals. He knew the letters had been read and then resealed. If Buckingham hadn't done so, he was a fool, which he was not.

"Good news?"

"The money you promised is in Miguel's hands. Excellent. We understand each other, Your Grace." Ange added, almost as an afterthought, except that it wasn't, "If I die in prison, letters will be delivered to Balmoral, Lord Arlington, and His Majesty, detailing the scheme about the queen. Miguel has most specific instructions. They were conceived before I journeyed here. I prefer to plan ahead whenever possible."

"You are offensive, sir. Such a thought has not crossed my mind. Though hanging you has been discussed between His Majesty and Balmoral."

"And you, of course, do all you can to stop it."

"I continue to, yes."

The threat in that lay neatly beside Ange's threat.

"Tell me what's happening outside of this place."

"There's been a death in the royal family."

"Of which I, at least, cannot be accused."

"Our Parliament is quarreling. His Majesty is toying with proroguing it—"

"What is that?"

"It is his prerogative to terminate a session, which must remain terminated until he calls it together again. He courts your countrywoman La Keroualle, but as yet, she has not yielded. She has, however, moved into her own set of apartments."

"Where is His Grace Balmoral? I've missed his growling threats this week."

"Arranging his nuptials."

"You jest."

"He is marrying your dear friend Mistress Alice Verney. It's the news of court, I do vow."

"My little accuser to marry. I'll dance at her wedding. And Saylor? How does he?"

Buckingham lifted his hands in a gesture of not knowing, not caring.

"His mother?"

"Oh, long back to her cave."

"She is a witch."

"So it was believed in her younger days."

"No, I tell you she is one. I would know."

"Is that how she saved her son's life, bewitching the antidote from you?"

Ange didn't answer. Buckingham allowed the silence, while his mind worked in its feverish, leaping frog of a manner. How to kill this man without implicating himself?

"I want a better cell," Ange repeated.

"Yes, we'll see to it."

FROM THE TOWER, Buckingham took himself straight back to Whitehall Palace, to the Duke of Balmoral.

"His Grace is not receiving guests." Balmoral's majordomo was regretful but firm.

Beginning a binge, thought Buckingham. He didn't care. "You are to tell him I'm here."

Riggs didn't dare disobey.

Returning after a short time, he bowed and led Buckingham up to the bedchamber and to the door of Balmoral's closet. Balmoral wasn't one to flaunt his wealth, but this chamber, with the porcelains and figurines, the elaborate cabinet, the suit of foreign armor, the tusks and horns of strange animals, showed hundreds of guineas expended. Balmoral sat at a table, a crystal decanter before him, open, a goblet in one hand. He gestured Buckingham to enter. "Sherry. It's Portuguese, one of the rare ones. I'm quite fond of it."

As we well know, thought Buckingham. "I never refuse."

"To what do I owe the honor of this visit?" Balmoral was still enunciating clearly.

How the gods do look after me, thought Buckingham, who truly believed they did—to catch Balmoral before he was ranting and slopping sherry was proof. "I've just returned from a visit to Henri Ange."

"Who ought to be hanged."

"I begin to be in agreement with you. I could arrange that someone strangle him. The man unnerves me. He is better off dead."

"I quite agree."

"Do you wish to handle it, or shall I?"

"Oh, I'll handle it."

Buckingham smiled. "The Duchess of York's death has quite improved my mood. Leave the queen be, I say. Let bygones be bygones. We'll get our prince through the Duke of York. I've made a list of Protestant princesses, which I shall present at the appropriate time."

"You do that, Georgie. Go away now."

"Bally, old man, we've only just begun our scheming—"

"Riggs," Balmoral called, and when his majordomo appeared, "Riggs, do show His Grace out."

Balmoral waved fingers at Buckingham, thinking all the while, Foolish of Ange to have baited George. One did not threaten His Grace the Duke of Buckingham. It was fatal. Protestant princesses, was it now? He had given it long thought, and he was almost certain he now knew what was in that elusive, was-there-was-there-not treaty. Some concession—some promise about faith—that neither he nor George would agree to, or else they would have been a part of the negotiation. It could be nothing else. Flirting with the Church of Rome! There'd been a war over that once—did His Majesty not remember? What game did King Charles play?

A dangerous game.

One that Balmoral fully intended to join.

This kingdom was Protestant, and it would remain Protestant. Only a confounded, deuce take it, thickheaded fool would try to change it! George might present all the Protestant princesses he wished, but if York was Catholic, it was for naught. Had King Charles allowed York's conversion? Why? The need for cunning sharpened him, enlivened his wait for death. A man with a new bride-to-be ought not to feel so. The marriage was for Alice, not for him. He would give her the honor of his name, all the protection and property that came with that, a last, rare, openhearted gesture from a heart all but dead in him. I ought not drink anymore, he thought. But the sherry had warmed him when little else could, was already offering its familiar harbors. It was too late.

It was Mothering Sunday. Kitchens filled with fragrance: sugar and eggs and butter beaten with dried fruit of orange and its juice and peel, covered with almond paste and baked in ovens to make mothering cakes, simnel cakes. Barbara and John Sidney strolled along the stalls of the New Exchange, a stone building in which shopkeepers set up in stall after stall on a ground floor, while above there was a surrounding gallery with yet more shops. One could find hats, toys, toothbrushes with ebony and silver handles, clothes, books. John tried to buy gloves and fans and combs for her hair, but Barbara wouldn't let him. " 'I'll to them a simnel bring against thou goes a-mothering. So that when she blesseth thee, half that blessing thou will give to me,' " he quoted an old rhyme to her. "Next year, we'll make you accept all those things."

"Who is 'we'?" she teased.

"My son and I."

"What if it's a daughter?"

"My daughter and I." Before the passersby, those strolling, those shopping, he kissed her swollen belly. "May she be half the beloved angel her mother is."

"Buy me a cake now, John."

A bake shop was across the street. They walked in, the smell delicious. John selected a cake in the shape of a heart, and they walked outside, eating it together.

"You have the whole of my heart," he said to her. The sun was shining. Flower sellers had bouquets of violets and fennel, crocuses and gooseberry. "I'm wild for you. If I ever lost you, I'd—"

She put her hand over his mouth. "You'd go on, that's what you'd do. Go and buy some crocuses, my dear. We'll fall asleep tonight with their fragrance in our bedchamber."

" 'Thou are fair, my beloved; our bed is green,' " he quoted to her from the Song of Solomon. " 'Thy love is better than wine.' "

"Hush, John."

"I won't. I can't. I'm besotted."

THAT EVENING, ALICE's groom, Poppy, leaped onto wet stairs and held out his hand to her, and she stepped from the boat onto Whitehall Stairs. She'd spent the day at her aunt's, gifting her with mothering cakes and soft leather gloves, hearing her congratulations, being shown old books, filled with recipes for food, for healing, from mothers and grandmothers and great-grandmothers, that would be hers as a wedding gift, seeing the bed hangings her grandmother's hand had helped embroider, hangings that would be hers, that would grace her marriage bed.

A group of soldiers approached, one of them calling to hail the boat she'd just left, and she stopped when she saw that Richard was among them. He walked forward to her. "I've heard the news. He is to be congratulated, Alice."

"Thank you."

He leaned down to kiss her cheek, but they moved into a hug, and she buried her face in the fabric of his soldier's coat, standing on her tiptoes, longing welling up in her.

"Richard!" His friends, already in the boat, called him. Still he held her.

"I wish you every happiness."

She couldn't force her arms to move from about his neck. But he could and gently did. From the boat, he smiled at her, his expression strained and kind.

I love him with all my heart, she thought, and would have stumbled in her walk to the public courtyard, but Poppy was there and took her elbow and didn't say a word as she brushed quickly at her face, removing tears. Kit ran to her in a hallway as she took off her cloak and gloves.

"Her Majesty is asking for you." Kit was excited, impressed by her again. "We heard the news, Alice! Everyone is talking of it. I'll have to curtsy and call you 'Your Grace,' Brownie says."

"You certainly will."

She washed her face in cool water that Poll poured into a bowl, dried her hands, and stared at her duchess-to-be self in a pier glass, while Poll, standing behind her, fiddled with curls, filled to the brim with talk, Alice could see, and sure enough, it came pouring out.

"Everyone knows . . ." Poll twisted a curl or two of Alice's hair tightly around her fingers, unwound them again in satisfaction. Alice's rise was her rise. "I walked over to His Grace's today, to have a look, you might say."

"I thought you went to see your mother today."

"I did. She came with me. He's got a grand set of apartments, he does."

"Yes, and there's more. There's his property near Newmarket, other places."

"His servants, they're a mixed lot, some good, some bad; old soldiers who served under him, their doxies, is what I hear. You'll need to bring a firm hand there. It's gotten loose in the last years, what with his illness and all. They'll be thinking to take advantage of your youth." Poll frowned at the very idea.

"Are they pleased?"

"I'd say shocked is more like. Curious. Of course, I talked with no one other than an underhousekeeper and His Grace's groom. If I may be so bold, have you and His Grace—oh, ma'am, I'll have to call you 'Your Grace,' won't I?" Poll laughed, a mix of joy and pride. "Is there a date for the wedding?"

"May."

"Oh, my. Well, then, we're to be busy, aren't we?"

"Indeed we are. We may need your mother and your sister to help us."

"That can be arranged, Your Grace."

"You oughtn't to laugh when you say 'Your Grace.' "

"No, to be sure. That's why I'm practicing it now."

QUEEN CATHERINE WAS in her closet, her confessor, Father Huddleston, with her. The sight of him checked Alice for a moment, that and the stillness of the queen's face. She curtsied and stayed down a long moment in the gesture.

"There's been a letter from Lord Knollys," said Father Huddleston. "He sends a letter for Mrs. Brownwell, asks that the queen give it to her, that she not be alone when she reads it."

Foreboding filled Alice. "May I ask why?"

"He's taken a wife."

"Gracen Howard," said Queen Catherine. "Mrs. Brownwell is at the Duke of Monmouth's. Bring her. Say nothing."

ALICE CROSSED the privy garden to Monmouth's. The sound of a guitar being strummed met her as she walked up the stairs behind his majordomo. Courtiers played cards, Prince Rupert the guitar.

"Your Grace," Monmouth greeted her, made an exaggerated bow, kissed her cheek. Over his shoulder, she saw Louisa Saylor. "I'm happy for you, Alice. Everyone is."

There was Dorothy. What am I going to say? Alice thought.

Prince Rupert signaled for her to come to him. "What's this I hear?" He strummed and talked at the same time. "You've captured Balmoral. Well done, girl." A crowd was gathering. Alice was too well-known for the news to go unnoticed, and Balmoral was too important.

"Your Grace," said Louisa Saylor, curtsying to her with a saucy look.

"Kit and I want to be bridesmaids," said Luce.

"It's going to be a small wedding," Alice answered.

"Yes, he's very old, isn't he?"

"Very." King Charles walked forward. "You are going to lead Balmoral a merry chase."

Renée slipped in to kiss her cheek. "My duchess," she said in English, rolling out the word like a flag.

"Where is the duke?" King Charles asked.

"Resting, sir."

"He'd best. He needs to stay in bed until the wedding night. I may command that. I'd hate to have you disappointed, Alice."

Amid the general laughter, Alice said to Dorothy, "Can you come with me back to Her Majesty?"

"Of course."

"Let's leave quietly. She asked that we be as discreet as possible."

"I've taken your advice," Dorothy said as they walked across the privy garden, gravel crunching under their feet. "I'm not allowing myself to imagine the worst. And I've stopped eating cake. And I spent too much on a new gown, but it's his favorite shade."

"I'm glad, Dorothy."

Dorothy breathed in the night air. "I can't wait for the first rose to open. The queen might be in Portugal for all she missed. She must make peace with His Majesty."

"Yes, that's what is wise, isn't it, to make peace with what is."

Dorothy took her arm and began to hum the music Prince Rupert had been playing. She was still humming it when Edward opened the door to the queen's closet. Alice stayed outside, stood by a covered birdcage. After a time, she heard sounds of desperate weeping. Edward, who was hitting dice against the wall, raised eyes to Alice. The door to the closet stayed closed. How brave Queen Catherine is, thought Alice.

When the door finally opened, Father Huddleston walked out with Dorothy leaning on his arm, sobbing. "The queen wishes a word with you," he told Alice.

Queen Catherine stood at her windows, looking out into the night. "Alone she cannot have. You stay with her."

"Of course."

"Cut through the heart. I send sleeping draft."

"I'll see she takes it."

"Coins he send. For her debts, he write. Guilt money. Take it. He ask for it to be his Gracen a lady of my household. Stupid man." Alice picked up the letter, the bag of coins, curtsied to the queen, who had still not turned to face her. "I forget. Blessings on your good fortune, Verney."

Dorothy lay on the bed, her maidservant trying to talk her into putting on her nightgown. Somehow, between the two of them, Alice and the maidservant managed to make Dorothy stand, managed to strip gown and skirt and stockings. All the while, Dorothy wept, a high, keening sound that made Alice's hands shake. How can this many tears be in someone? she thought. Are they in me? Will I sob like this someday over something? She'd wept over Cole's betrayal, but not like this. She could imagine it now because of Richard. It frightened her, the depth and breadth and pain that might be the cost of loving.

Dorothy was still keening when the physician arrived with the sleeping draft.

Silence fell only when she slept.

Alice let out a breath she hadn't realized she'd been holding. The maidservant had pulled out her own little trundle bed for Alice to sleep upon, and here was Poll, and she was fussing, helping Alice out of her gown, and there was a bowl of clean water in which to wash her face, and then Poll was brushing out her hair, familiar and soothing, and Alice felt something inside her let go, loosen. She gave a little hiccup of a sigh, and Poll, folding her gown, put it down to reach over and give her a quick pat on the arm. "You're that tired, Mistress Alice. Into bed with you."

"Leave the candle, Poll."

"Don't you go to sleep with it burning. The last thing we need is for Whitehall to burn down."

"I won't."

With Poll and the maidservant gone, she went to Knollys's letter, unfolded it, but found that she—Alice the curious, Alice the sneak—couldn't bring herself to read it. So she refolded it and blew out the candle. She climbed into her bed and said prayers, for once with feeling, asking God to bless this muddle.

The next morning, when she woke, Dorothy was out of bed, sitting at the table, the letter unfolded before her, the coins spread out neatly on the table. "You didn't have to stay the night, Alice." Her voice was a croak, her face puffy.

"We were worried for you."

"I'll be fine."

Her maidservant entered with a tray.

"Go on, Alice. I need some time to myself today."

Alice kissed her cheek, grabbed a shawl to cover her nightgown, and in another moment was outside, walking to the maids' bedchamber.

"A bath, Poll." She was going to bathe and then go for a long ride, all the way into the little hamlet of Chelsea with Poppy. She was going to listen to birds and walk along the banks of the Thames and let the cold air chill her cheeks, waft away her sad thoughts, celebrate her little triumph, paled in the larger machinations of court.

In another hour, she was dressed warmly, her boots on, in the kitchens coaxing a cook to give her bread and cheese and two bottles of ale. Then she was crossing courtyards, stopping to talk with this one or that as more good wishes came her way, then she was running up the stairs at Balmoral's. He sat in a chair in his closet, his legs covered with a blanket. She paused on the doorstep. He'd never looked so wan, so frail. Some of her happiness faded. This was part of it. Not just honor and safety, but this. She put down her parcel of food and went to him, kneeling as she'd done in her happiness at St. James's Park. "So, having to marry me sent you into a fit, did it?"

He grimaced. "I fool myself, Alice, that I may have one taste, and one taste leads to this. I vow to you that I am not going to drink again."

His hands were trembling in his lap, but whether from this promise or from his last bout, Alice didn't know and didn't want to. She was happy simply to believe him. She laid her cheek on his covered knee. "I would be so glad of that."

"Where are you off to, with your jaunty feathered hat and your riding clothes?"

"I thought to ride to Chelsea. I could wait. We could go together in a carriage."

"No. I cannot stir from this chair today, nor tomorrow. The jolting of a carriage would make my head, which is barely fastened on as it is, fall off."

She told him about Dorothy, about Lord Knollys and Gracen.

"Well, I'm sorry for Mrs. Brownwell. Off with you, then. Be careful."

He leaned forward and kissed her, and a shudder rose in her at the feel of his lips on her cheek, but this, too, was a piece of it. "Shall I come to visit this evening?"

"No. I'll be worse."

Poppy had a horse for her, one from the queen's stables, fresh and sassy and hard to manage. Hoisted into the saddle, she smiled as the horse turned a circle and reared slightly. A hand reached out and yanked her bridle. Alice stared down into the face of Colefax, once her near bridegroom, always Balmoral's heir. So, she thought, here it is at last, what I dreamed. "Let loose my bridle."

"I want to speak with you."

"Later."

"Now."

"Speak, then."

"What are you doing?"

"I'm going for a gallop in the country."

"That's not what I refer to. What do you think you're doing with this business of marrying my uncle?"

"What piece is it you don't understand, Cole?"

"You're doing this for spite, Alice."

She laughed, and the horse tried to rear. Colefax was yanked a few feet in the animal's dancing anxiety, but he still held the reins. "I'm not going to allow it."

"You think you can stop it? How amusing. Do try. It will be fun to see."

She jerked on the reins, and the horse did rear, and Colefax stepped back to be out of the way of the hooves. It danced on hind legs, and Alice allowed it, soothing the animal with little clucking sounds, staying in the saddle. Poppy helped her settle the horse, pulled himself up into the saddle of the horse he was riding.

"Are you finished?" Poppy said. He meant her conversation with Cole.

"Quite finished," she answered and galloped off, her groom following.

She'd thought this moment with Cole would be more satisfying. It had always been in her daydreams. But it wasn't. She didn't marry Balmoral to hurt him anymore, and she didn't know when that had changed.

IT WAS EDWARD who told Richard about Dorothy Brownwell, describing the sobbing. Later in the guardroom, Richard saw her maidservant. "How is your mistress?"

"A watering pot. If you break my heart like that"—she shook a finger at the guardsman who was her sweetheart—"I will stab you with a knife." The guardsman pretended fear, and she slapped at him, and the movements were really rough-and-tumble kisses between them. "She had me dress her up in her finest gown. We curled her hair and rouged her cheeks. She'll be over this in a fortnight."

That afternoon, Richard brought a basket of kittens, born in the stable a few weeks ago, to amuse the queen and her ladies. Cards were abandoned, embroidery circles dropped, as women grouped around the basket.

"I thought I'd show them to Mrs. Brownwell, Your Majesty." With the queen's consent, Richard went down the stairs to the maids of honor's apartments, and there was Alice, her cheeks pink with cold, looking very fetching in a jaunty hat with a feather, at Dorothy's door, knocking.

"Richard," she said, seeing him, "there's no answer. I don't like it."

"Perhaps she has gone for a walk."

"Guard," Alice called to a guardsman whose duty was to stand at attention down the corridor, "has Mrs. Brownwell left her chamber today?"

"Not that I saw, ma'am."

Richard rattled the handle of the door, knocked loudly, then hit the door with his open hand. "Mrs. Brownwell, open the door!" He could hear movement on the other side, a chair being dragged, perhaps.

"I don't like this," said Alice. He didn't, either.

"Mrs. Brownwell, it's Captain Saylor, open the door!" He pounded the door with his fist. "Open at once! Her Majesty needs you!" He stepped back. "We've got to open this," he told the guardsman, who had walked up the corridor to watch. They hit the door with their shoulders, and both fell back.

"I think I've broken my shoulder," said the guardsman.

Alice ran down to the maids of honor's bedchamber, took a key from a door's inner side, returned. "The keys are likely the same."

Richard pushed the key into the keyhole; it turned easily, and the door swung open.

"Sweet Jesus!" cried Alice.

Dorothy hung suspended from a twisted sheet like a slaughtered animal.

Richard heard an odd sound come from himself; behind him, he heard Alice begin to weep and the guardsman shout for help. He bolted across the chamber, clambered up the table, grabbing Dorothy's legs, trying to hold her up, to loosen the grip of the sheeted noose around her neck.

"We've got to cut her down. My God, man, cut her down! Reach into my scabbard and take my sword. Now! Someone hold the table steady; if we fall . . . Grab that chair. Stand on it . . . Saw it, keep sawing! . . . Sweet Mother of God!"

He swore as he fell off the table with Dorothy in his arms as the blade cut through the last of the sheet. He fell so hard that the breath was knocked out of him. Someone screamed, a maid of honor standing in the doorway.

"Get the queen's physician now!" he heard Alice order.

Pushing himself to his knees, he crawled over to Dorothy, pulled at the knot around her throat and managed to loosen it. He turned her over, pulled a knife from his belt, cut through the back of her gown, then through the laces of her corset. It seemed to him he heard her sigh. He slapped her face hard. "Breathe!" he shouted. "Breathe, damn you!"

He grabbed her around the waist as if she were a giant doll, dragged her to standing, pulling in hard at her waist. He prayed the word *breathe,* over and over. She gasped, and then he felt her ribs expand under his arms, heard air drawn in, rasped out. He eased her to the ground.

"Give her that shawl," he ordered the guardsman. Her breasts were exposed. He'd half cut her gown off. "Stop screaming," he said to Luce.

He stepped back, caught himself on a chair, sat down in it. His heart was pounding so hard, he could hardly think over it. Dorothy sat in a chair, her hands at her throat. Luce remained hysterical; the queen was here, kneeling, trying to talk with Dorothy. He watched Alice shake Luce so fiercely the young woman became quiet out of surprise; then Alice walked out of sight into the hall.

Mayhem reigned for a short time, but eventually the physician was there, and Richard carried Dorothy to the bed, laid her down as ordered, was glad someone else was taking over.

"I want to die," Dorothy whispered, the whites of her eyes red and strange from all the small blood vessels in them broken. "You should have let me die."

Richard left the chamber. Out in the hallway, he saw Alice sitting against the wall with Kit, and he was reminded of their death watch for Princesse Henriette. He hadn't known her then. He'd thought her arrogant and rude. He still thought her arrogant. He knelt in front of her, pulled her face to his in a swift movement, and kissed her with everything that was raw and unsettled in him. When he finally took his mouth from hers, she gasped. "I'll beg pardon later," he told her.

Alice watched him stride away.

"Shut up," she hissed to Kit's surprised expression, and Kit quickly looked somewhere else. Alice put her head on her knees. The sight of Brownie hanging there, one shoe dropped to the table, was horrible. And in the horror were Balmoral's trembling hands, his old man's breath when he'd kissed her.

She didn't want to do that which she'd worked so hard to do.

RICHARD WALKED THROUGH the hallways and corridors, not certain where he was going except outside of this rambling, cursed palace. Trees would soothe him. The sight of sky. Prayer brought him back to the same place each time, and now this incident confirmed what he already knew. He was going to resign from the king's service. He was going to cross the sea and join the French army, become a soldier of fortune. His Grace the Duke of Balmoral knew Turenne, the great French general. Alice might wrangle a written introduction for him if he asked. Alice . . .

He walked faster. He didn't know when he'd started loving Alice. He didn't know where Renée stopped and she began. All he did know was that two of the king's personal guards had slit the nose of someone in the House of Commons for insulting His Majesty during a speech. Hired thugs, no different from Buckingham's guard. Is that what they'd come to? A broken promise drove Dorothy Brownwell to hang herself from a rafter in her chamber, and death would likely be preferable to the gossip that would now swirl around her. Courtiers would be amused at her taking a betrayal in love so seriously. She'd end up a scene in someone's next play. He'd nearly died from the poison Ange put on the sword blade. As he'd clawed his way up from death's opaque embrace, he'd wondered what he clawed upward toward. Without Renée, he was bereft. And now there was this confusion with Alice. . . . The season of Lent loomed, of preparing the soul for the holy day of Easter, for death and the promise of resurrection. He felt he had a cross of ashes burned in his heart.

Time to move on, to try his fortune elsewhere.

He could live in this shifting place of betrayals within betrayals, of no loyalties honored, of the strong crushing the weak, no more. He preferred soldiering, where you knew who your enemies were before the battle began.

A FEW DAYS later, Alice sat with Dorothy, trying to coax her to eat a bite of toast.

"What are they saying of me?"

"Nothing," soothed Alice.

Buckingham had staged a mock hanging of a fork last night at Renée's—the dish ran away with the spoon, he'd explained. He courted Renée now, assiduous, flattering, helpful, the way he'd done Frances Stewart when she'd been favorite. Beware, Alice wanted to say, but she held her tongue, no longer certain she knew who Renée was. Dorothy had sewn the coins Knollys had sent her into the hem of the gown she'd worn to hang herself. Courtiers were calling them Knollys's thirty pieces of silver. His stinginess, wits said, saved her life. If there'd been more coins, her neck would have snapped.

A page knocked, opened the door, and announced the queen, who sailed in with Frances, Barbara, Caro, and her little fox in tow. Barbara had an armful of flowers; Caro rushed to give Dorothy a hug; the queen's fox leapt upon the bed, circled, lay down as if he were home. Frances walked to the windows, pulled back the curtains. Dorothy began to cry again.

Alice slipped away, went to the queen's oratory to sit in the darkened, sacred quiet. First, she prayed for Dorothy with all her heart—she was ruined at court, she'd have to leave. Dread kept rising in her. She'd gone to bed with it on her shoulder, woke with it sitting on her chest. It took one misstep for a woman, one, and she fell into the abyss. How did one live life with no missteps? She wanted her mother, the mother she'd never had except in her imagination, to advise her, to tell her what to do. She wanted to crawl into that mother's lap and rest for a while, make everything stop, hang suspended while she got her bearings.

Caro and Barbara were sitting in the great window seat in the gallery. Alice had to pass them to gain the queen's chambers. Taking a deep breath, she walked forward. "Here she c-comes," Caro said. "Are you c-certain you wish to risk this?"

"Yes." Barbara stepped in front of Alice; Caro stayed in the window seat.

"Alice, I want to tell you how happy I am for your news."

"Thank you."

"Caro and I were talking. We thought the three of us ought to put our heads together about Brownie."

"What about Brownie?"

"Well, we were thinking that she'll have to leave court, and that she might stay with one of us."

"She'll stay with me. His Grace will see to it." Alice was haughtier than she meant to be. Barbara reached out to touch her arm, and Alice stepped back. Out of the corner of her eye, she caught Caro's expression. Anger there. Contempt. She hates me now, thought Alice.

"Alice, stop this."

"I have to wait upon Her Majesty."

She tried not to run, though once she was far enough down the corridor, she slipped into an open doorway and sat in a chair in a presence chamber. Did Caro hate her for marrying Balmoral? The look on her face shocked Alice. She pressed hands against her heart. It hurt so much more than she'd thought it would. When Caro had been begging for her forgiveness, it had felt good not to give it. Now that she didn't ask it, she was stunned at what lay between them. Why didn't she put down her pride? Why couldn't she? Would she wait until the day Barbara hated her, too? The thought was so painful, tears came to her eyes. Once there'd been no one closer to her than these two. What happened? Her heart ached, a literal ache in her chest. She wasn't sleeping well. Her temper was shortening. This, when she should be at her happiest. Why was she so stubborn? Why couldn't she bend? Pride goes before destruction. A wisp of a sermon floated up. Pride was heavy, rocks sewn in her skirt, like Dorothy's coins, dragging her down.

Back in the corridor, Caro found a handkerchief and gave it to Barbara. "I told you it was f-foolish. Don't weep, Barbara. It isn't g-good for the child."

Chapter 39

Spring Equinox

Oh come, gentle spring . . .

The door to the cell swung open. Four men carrying lanterns stepped inside.

Startled, Ange rose from his chair, stepped back, but before he could speak, two guards he didn't recognize threw him down and tied his hands together. Then they searched the cell, finding behind a loose stone in the wall the knives Ange had hidden, finding paper and pen and ink and the letters Buckingham had brought. Balmoral dismissed the guards. Only the large, burly man he'd entered with remained.

"Wax candles. Portuguese oranges. Not quite what I had in mind." Balmoral gestured to what was atop the table in the cell. "Kill him." Balmoral sat in the chair Ange had vacated. The other man uncoiled knotted rope.

Ange ran to the door, calling through the small grate, "Help me! Murder!"

"But I've changed the guard, as you ought to have noticed," said Balmoral. "They won't be paying attention. Strangle him, but don't kill him. Finish it with the rope around his head. I want to see his eyes fall out onto the floor." He smiled at Ange, his teeth yellowed.

"It's an old Inquisition trick I'm fond of. Your Miguel is Spanish, isn't he? I do it for him."

Ange fell to his knees in front of him. "What do you want?"

"Some of those coins the Duke of Buckingham has been paying you would do."

"I don't have them."

Balmoral pulled letters out of his sleeve, enjoying the shock on Ange's face. Whatever anyone else pays, His Grace the Duke of Balmoral pays higher—it was the litany of the underworld of the Tower. All guards knew it. Don't send a letter on without making a copy, for Balmoral punished for betrayal, but he punished even harder for stupidity. Copy the letter, then send the original on its way. So many flies caught that way. "Yes. They go straight to Miguel, don't they." He tapped the letters with a finger. "Kill him."

"No—"

Rope dropped around Ange's neck and was tightened ruthlessly. Caught kneeling, Ange twisted, kicking, but the man was strong, and struggling made it worse. Ange gagged and kicked, but it was too late. At the moment he gave up, Balmoral said, "Enough."

Ange dropped like a stone to the floor. At a gesture from Balmoral, the burly man went to a bucket, took a dipper of water, dribbled it onto Ange's face. After a time, Ange opened his eyes, began to gasp air the way a fish would. The man dragged him to sitting by pulling the rope around his neck.

"Was there a secret treaty?"

"Yes."

"Before the one Buckingham negotiated?"

"Yes."

"Can you prove it?"

Ange was silent. Balmoral respected that. Finally Ange answered, "Monsieur talked of it, was angry that he was not allowed any part of the negotiation. I could go to France and gather evidence for you."

"Go to France and gather evidence. I like that. Except I ask myself, Now, why would he come back? If I could detach your confounded head, or take out your heart, keep them alive, you might come back for those."

Ange was silent.

"I have it," said Balmoral. "I'll gather all your coins and your little turtledove and keep the coin in my purse and your love in the Tower, and if you come back, you can have them. If not . . ." He shrugged.

"I need time to think."

"No."

"Yes, then."

Balmoral walked to the door, which opened at his tap upon it. Ange made a small movement, and the rope around his neck tightened fast enough to make him fall over. "Paper and pen," Balmoral told the guard. He came back and sat down, regarding the man at his feet. "No one works a rope like Joshua. You might call him an artist."

When the ink and paper were brought, Balmoral said, "You write your little sweetheart another letter. Tell him to bring all the coins and himself. The day I have him, I allow you France."

Ange scratched out a note.

"Add, 'For God's sake, come to me, my darling.' "

Ange did so, his hand shaking slightly.

"Miguel holds letters accusing Buckingham."

Ange looked at Balmoral with the first real fear he'd felt in his life.

"Tell our Miguel to bring those, too."

Ange wrote the words.

"Give him one more taste," said Balmoral, and Ange fainted when the rope tightened around his neck. Balmoral blew on the note and, when the ink was dry, folded it. He picked up all the copies of letters, stood, and the cell door clanged open. Two guardsmen entered with chains, began to lock them to Ange's legs and arms.

"I want him taken to the White Tower, to a windowless cell like this one, chained to the wall, arms and legs. Food once a day, fed him by Joshua here. If a wax candle or Portuguese orange passes through the door to him, I'll have the man who brings it killed. Make certain that word spreads. He isn't to come out of those chains until I personally unlock them. Good day, my angel. Sleep well. Oh, he's already asleep, isn't he."

Chapter 40

April

Rock-a-bye baby, thy cradle is green.
Thy father's a nobleman, thy mother's a queen. . . .

Arms crossed, Alice sat up in her bed. She slept alone now, no Gracen, no Barbara, and no Renée to share with. She couldn't sleep. It was becoming her habit at night, to sit and fret. This day, All Fools' Day, the first of April, she'd spent with her aunt going through a trunk that held her mother's clothing, gowns crusted with embroideries, lace collars and sleeves, abandoned when her mother ran away to marry her father, kept safe, lavender sprinkled in their folds. We can fashion a gown for your wedding, said her aunt. Then it will be as if your mother were there.

In a month, she would become the Duchess of Balmoral.

No, Balmoral said, I will not have my apartments redone. Yes, he said, you spend any amount on your bedchamber and closet and presence chamber. No, he said, I don't wish to live at Whitehall all the year. Neither shall you. Yes, you may have as many visitors as you wish. No, I don't like too much company. Yes, I feel well today. No, I hurt today. Dance until dawn, he urged. You burn your candle at both ends, he complained.

Someone knocked on the maids' bedchamber. One of the servants lit a candle, and Alice saw in its dim light that Poll opened the door and whispered awhile.

"Captain Saylor is in the antechamber. He says to dress and come at once."

A last April Fools' joke? She, who was queen of the April Fool jest? "I'll do no such thing. Tell him to go away."

The next thing she knew, Richard stood over her. "Get dressed."

"On whose orders?"

"Barbara is having her baby. We're in the second day. She's asking for you."

"I can't."

"If I have to bundle you up and throw you across my saddle in your nightgown, you are coming with me." He was stern and fierce, and he waited in the corridor while she dressed. Outside, her groom was holding the horses. Richard held his hands together for her foot. At the last second she hesitated, pride rearing its heavy head.

"Don't be a fool," Richard said.

"Do what he says, mistress," pleaded Poppy.

Alice settled herself in the saddle. They rode past the royal mews to a row of houses on a quiet lane on the outskirts of the city. Fields and farms and meadows would be visible when the sun rose. The bulk of Leicester House would be visible, almost the only structure to the northeast, sitting by itself among its green fields and to the northwest a windmill that ground flour.

As Alice dismounted, Richard took her by the arm. "It's very serious, Alice."

"What do you mean?"

"I mean, I fear even the queen's physician, who was here this afternoon, can do nothing. I'm riding to Tamworth to fetch my mother." He was back in the saddle and gone before she could respond.

She stood a moment just inside the narrow hall. To her left was a chamber that was used as dining room, parlor, and everything else in between. Directly before her, a narrow stairway marched up to a landing; at the landing a door was visible that must lead to a bedchamber, positioned directly above the chamber to her left. She dropped her cloak near a sleeping servant girl, no more than ten, curled in a ball near the fireplace, in which embers from burned wood glowed. She put her foot on the stair, which creaked with her weight, and above, on the landing, John Sidney appeared, a candle in his hand.

"Alice, is that you? Oh, thank God you've come. Thank God." He met her halfway on the stairs, words falling out almost faster than he could speak them. "I bless you for this. I do. Oh, Alice, it's taking so long. There's nothing I can do. Nothing—" His face contorted, but he took a breath, managed to get command of himself. "I don't want her to hear me." He wiped his face on the sleeve of his shirt. "Why is it taking so long? I fear for the child. I fear for her."

"John." Alice's tone was clear, cold, calm. "Go outside and walk. Go on. You do not help her with your upset."

"No, of course I don't. I'm thinking only of myself, of what I would do if she should— But she's not. We're going to get through this. The physician was telling me this afternoon that sometimes it takes a few days. It's just she is so tired. I don't see how—"

"Go."

There was the single door off the landing. Alice could hear groans and pants. Barbara. Barbara was behind this door having a child, and not easily. All her pride, all her righteousness, dissolved, and she felt shame, piercing and clear. Can I bear what's on the other side? she thought. And then: I can, I will, I must.

She opened the door, took in the sight of Caro on her hands and knees, scrubbing something from the floor, took in the sight of an older woman who she assumed was John's mother, took in the sight of Barbara's faithful servant, with her all the time at Whitehall, on the bed behind Barbara propping her up, took in the sight of Barbara, her face twisted as she knelt, arching, groaning, her hands hanging on to a sheet twisted from the rafter that she could use to pull upon, took in the midwife saying, "That's it, push, breathe out, push, my lady, breathe out."

Caro stood. "Thank G-God you've c-come."

"What can I do?"

"Rub her feet and l-legs if she stops pushing. I've r-rosewater, and it s-seems to soothe her."

But Alice remained rooted a moment, unable to tear her eyes from Barbara heaving, groaning, arching again and again to push life from her. Dust to dust. In sorrow, thou shall bring forth. Weeping and wailing and gnashing of teeth. Purge me with hyssop. Make these bones thou has broken. Suffer the little children. Different verses from endless Lord's Day sermons flew through her head, and none of them captured all that was in this moment. Barbara let go the twisted arms of the sheet, fell back, gasping, into the arms of her servant. "I can't!" It was a wail.

"You can, and you will," said the midwife. "Rest a bit. Time to rest."

"Alice . . ." Barbara saw her. A smile lit her face. What is this inside me? thought Alice, stepping forward to the bed. "Thank you for coming. Thank you. Thank you," whispered Barbara.

Caro leaned across the bed to wipe Barbara's face. She met Alice's eyes, her expression blank.

It's my pride breaking, thought Alice, into a thousand foolish, stupid, wicked pieces. "What can I do?"

"Help me. I must have this baby. He promised she would live, but I have to have her for that to be possible. It's so hard, Alice. Oh, I'm so thirsty."

Caro helped her to sip from a goblet. Spasms began. Barbara groaned, and a ripple of birth took her body. We are nothing, Alice thought, the strength of what was seizing Barbara's body filling her with awe and with fear. Barbara struggled to kneel again. Alice and Caro helped, and her servant leaned once more into her back. "The sheet," Caro said. "Grab the sheet."

"A birthing chair," Alice said to the midwife.

"Over there. We've tried it."

A long groan from Barbara.

"Again," commanded the midwife.

"Johnnnn?" It wasn't quite a scream. And John was there, his eyes reddened, but his voice calm.

"Come, my love, I'm right here." He was climbing into bed beside her servant, his hands on her back. "God be with us. And the Blessed Mother. God be with us, and the Blessed Mother . . ."

TWO HOURS LATER, Alice opened the bedchamber door, stumbled onto the landing, found a corner, and huddled into it, overwhelmed. How could this keep on? How would Barbara survive it? How would the child? In her mind, John was no more an enemy; he was beautiful, calm, and strong, whispering to his wife, kissing her, holding her hands, encouraging her always, not a tear from him. Strong for Barbara, who needed to cling to him, who needed him to be strong when she was so vulnerable. And yet he had to be full to the brim with tears, the way Alice was. Pride goeth before destruction, and a haughty spirit before a fall. All the ways she'd judged Barbara . . . If she survived, she would crawl to her on her knees, begging forgiveness. She would pay whatever penance there was. To see her suffer was so hard. And in that witnessing was the shard, that she loved her friend, always had, always would. Pride had covered it over, but it was unmasked now, its sharp edge glinting. Alice could not escape it: She had made pride more important than love.

She went downstairs, woke the serving girl, took coins from a pocket in her gown. Always have a coin or two about you. She always did. "There'll be a cook shop open in another hour. Go to it and fetch bread, bacon, ale, wine. My groom is outside. Have him escort you." John had to eat, his mother, so did Caro, the midwife, herself.

"She's calling for you." Caro was at the top of the stairs.

"I'll be right up."

Alice opened the front door, stepped out, looked up at the morning stars. Many a night she and Barbara and Caro had been up all night, confessing dreams, hopes, angers, giggling over men. Yesterday. A hundred years ago. All these months she'd wasted. Her groom stepped forward. "Accompany the girl to the cook shop when dawn breaks, Poppy. Spend every pence."

"Mistress Barbara?"

Alice tried to speak and couldn't.

❧

By midmorning, John had set up a prayer stand on the landing, and he and Caro and Alice and his mother took turns at it. People called, Edward for the queen, Fletcher, John's Mister Pepys, His Majesty's lord chamberlain, Richard's sisters, the Duchess of Monmouth, Mulgrave, ladies-in-waiting, grooms of the king's bedchamber, the queen's bodyguards, others, the wits made somber by what was occurring, Sedley, Buckhurst, Rochester, Killigrew, the friends Barbara had made during all her years at court.

"My baby, my little girl, she has to be born, she has to be born. . . ."

Barbara said the same thing over and over, but now she could not kneel in the bed. They had carried her to the birthing chair. The physician arrived. Alice felt sick to watch him examine Barbara, who screamed when he probed. The midwife frowned.

"One must be gentle," she said to Alice.

The physician motioned for John and his mother to follow him out onto the landing. Alice did, too. "I can take the child. It may save her, but will surely kill it."

John leaned into the wall, aghast, staggered at the decision he must make.

"Not yet," he finally said.

Alice ran down the stairs. Dorothy, hollow eyed, her face haggard, already pounds lighter, was sitting in the downstairs chamber; so was one of the king's gardeners. As Dorothy and Alice embraced, the gardener pointed to bunches of flowers standing upright in luminous porcelain vases. "From Their Majesties," said the gardener, "and Prince Rupert, the Dukes of York and Monmouth."

"I think she may die," Alice whispered into Dorothy's ear. Saying the words made her hurt in a way she hadn't since she was a motherless girl. "Pray," she told Dorothy and the gardener, "with all your heart." They sank to their knees.

Outside, Walter walked forward, while Poppy slept in the shade of a tree near the tethered horses.

"It's bad," she told Walter. "Pray."

Alice went back up the stairs. She'd never felt so clear and clean, for once in her life certain. I make myself a prayer, she told God. I make myself a prayer for my beloved friend, my beloved sister whom I have wronged. I make every breath a prayer to You, every moment, every blink of the eye. Bless us. Keep us, O Blessed Lord. I will be good forever if You spare her. I will give to the poor. I will never quarrel. I will be Your most faithful servant.

She walked into the bedchamber. The physician had taken forceps out of his bag. Alice blinked at the sight of them, then knelt at the foot of the bed so that Barbara could see her face.

"You can do this," she said, some power, some assurance, some command, some fierceness from she knew not where, in her voice. "I'll do it with you. Push, my darling, push, and I will push with you." Barbara took a breath, knelt, John standing behind her to hold her up. She grabbed the sheets, let out a groan, and Alice groaned with her, matching her sound for sound, pushing inside herself at an invisible child.

"Ohhhh . . ."

"Ahhh . . ."

Over and over, they moaned together.

"It's coming," cried the midwife.

Barbara smiled. Her face was in that moment as beautiful as Alice had ever seen it.

"Push! Our child is here!" said John. And Barbara gave a primal groan, arched herself upward in a long movement, and at the end of the sound, Alice saw something drop between her legs. Barbara fell forward. The midwife snatched up the child and began to fold a blanket around it.

Why isn't it crying? thought Alice. Shouldn't there be crying?

She and Caro followed the midwife out into the hall. The woman sat on the top stair, the blanket open, her hands moving over the tiny body. Again and again, she put her mouth to the child's mouth, blew; she bent it over her arm and stroked its back; she stroked the small chest, the head, the legs. Then she sighed and began to cover the child with the blanket.

"Let me see," commanded Alice. The midwife pulled back the coverlet. Tiny sweet, thought Alice. Tiny darling, whom my Barbara wanted with all her heart. God bless you and keep you. Her heart felt broken for Barbara.

"I'll clean her and wrap her in swaddling," the midwife said.

"I b-brought a l-little g-gown. . . ." Caro was crying.

Alice went back into the bedchamber. Barbara lay on her back, cradled in John's arms, John's mother smoothing back her hair, murmuring to her, calling her "darling daughter," "precious girl." The physician packed away his forceps and his saw.

"The baby . . ." Barbara hadn't much strength, could only mouth the words.

"Being cleaned as we speak." Alice was bright, clear, decisive. "She looks just like you."

"I don't hear her." Alice had to put her ear on Barbara's mouth and make her repeat the words.

"She's mewing like a very small kitten," Alice answered.

Barbara closed her eyes.

Alice followed the physician out to the landing. "Will she live?"

"She's lost much strength. I'll be back in the morning."

Alice went downstairs to Dorothy, who opened her arms to enfold her, and Alice allowed the indulgence of being held. Her body hurt. Her throat felt stripped from groaning. Warm water, she thought. Barbara must be bathed, and all the bedclothes changed. "Find a fresh nightgown for your mistress," she told the little servant girl. "Are there more sheets for the bed?"

"They all be upstairs in a cupboard, lady."

"Good. Get them. And fetch water. We're going to be doing some cleaning." She wanted Barbara resting in clean sheets, in a clean gown. Let me lose myself in action lest I wither in despair. The quote floated up and back down, as did a glimpse of some despair in her, deep as a river.

BY MIDNIGHT, THERE was a rash on Barbara's legs and abdomen, and she was feverish. She kept asking for her child, as she'd done all night. "I can't tell her," said John. They all agreed they wouldn't tell her yet.

"Nursing," Alice told her. "Latched to a wet nurse."

"Sleeping," Alice said the next time. "I dare not wake her."

When he visited early the next morning, the physician shook his head as he pulled the blanket back up over Barbara's legs. Outside on the landing, he said to John the words every man who has ever loved a woman dreaded: "Childbed fever."

John closed his eyes.

"What does that mean?" Alice demanded, but neither man answered her, so she followed the physician down the stairs. Balmoral was sitting in the parlor, but Alice wouldn't have cared if it were King Charles himself; she was intent on the physician, on finding out what she had to know. "Is she dying?" Alice said to him.

"Yes."

She put her hand on his arm. "How long?"

"It can go as long as a week."

Alice sat on the bottom step, trembling. A week? How could that be possible? A fortnight ago, she had been refusing Barbara's friendship. What had happened between now and then? How had time become so cockeyed? How could she have cared what her pride said? How could she be the great, huge fool that she was and live?

Balmoral walked out of the chamber, stood beside her. "Time for you to go home."

Alice shook her head.

"You need sleep, a fresh gown, some food."

"If you would have Poll come to me . . ."

He was silent.

"If she is going to die," Alice said to no one in particular, her voice breaking, but no tears, "then her last days should be beautiful. Have Poll bring some bedding for me to sleep on. I'll sleep by the fire like the serving girl. In fact, have Poll bring as many fresh sheets and blankets as Queen Catherine's housekeeper will allow. Tell her it's for Barbara. And Queen Catherine must come. She would never forgive herself if she did not say farewell."

A muscle worked in Balmoral's jaw. "I think you should go home for a time."

Alice turned on him, a hissing cat. "For me, at this moment, this is my home! Are you going to aid me in this or not? If not, leave me be! You're of no use to me!"

He said nothing. Alice walked into the downstairs chamber, looking over the flowers, deciding which she might take upstairs. Pillows, she thought, filled with lavender blossoms to lay her head upon. And rose petals, too.

"What else do you require?" It was Balmoral.

"Pillows. Lavender. Roses. Beeswax candles."

"Pillows. Lavender. Roses. I'll bring Riggs. He'll aid you in whatever you need."

With a bow, he left her. Alice heard a carriage pull up. A servant handed down Caro, who had left shortly after midnight. She swept in, the servant following with a large basket. Alice smiled. No telling what was in that basket. Caro was always wonderfully practical. When this was over, she'd make her peace with Caro, beg her forgiveness, too.

"How is s-she?" Caro asked.

"The physician was here. He said childbed fever."

"Dear God." And on those words, no stammer in them, Caro rushed up the stairs.

The day was hard, visitors coming to call, but Barbara would see no one, crying to hold her child, falling into feverish sleep only to wake again and ask for the child. Across the lane, in a field, soldiers were setting up a great, military tent. Balmoral's standard flew from the tip of the tent's top. A base camp, Riggs had explained to her, from which to operate. It will be handy, you'll see.

In the afternoon, Alice and John and Caro and John's mother had a conference on the landing. "Should I tell her the truth?" John asked them.

Caro pointed at the prayer stand. "S-see what He s-says. My heart says n-no."

Alice's father called, and she ran down the stairs and into his arms. He led her into the parlor, held her hands as words tumbled out of her, about the dead child, about how they didn't tell Barbara, about the fever, about how stupid she was to have quarreled with Barbara, about what a prideful, thickheaded fool she was, about how she was going to tell Barbara so, beg her forgiveness; yet she saw as the words were pouring out of her that she wouldn't do it before the others, that she was waiting for a moment alone. So her pride wasn't quite killed yet.

"What can I do?" he asked.

"Make her live."

He pressed her hands. "May I see her? Ask if she will receive me."

Afterward, out on the landing, he cried. "Your mother was that sweet. I wish Barbara's babe had lived. Your mother's face when we placed you in her arms . . ."

When they stood outside the house saying good-bye, he told her, "You need sleep and a change of gown. You're running on air and unshed tears. You'll break, Alice."

"Poll is coming."

"I'll be back this evening. And I'll send Perryman to wait on you."

"I have Riggs."

"Well, you'll have Perryman, too."

Queen Catherine came to call, leaving her attendants downstairs, Luce and Kit silent, tearful, afraid, the ladies-in-waiting quiet, respectful of this dying they all faced to bear children. Queen Catherine sat by the side of the bed.

"Good and faithful servant, none better, not even Verney here."

"My child—" whispered Barbara.

"Beautiful. I make her maid of honor someday."

"I'm so hot."

"God blesses you and keeps you always."

Downstairs, a small, dignified doll, Queen Catherine walked to her carriage. Glancing at her face, those who accompanied her knew better than to speak. Alice went to the tiny back room adjoining the downstairs chamber to wash herself, Poll helping her to dress in a fresh gown. On a table sat the tiny coffin the groom and Walter had made. Caro had collected flowers from the arrangements that had been left for Barbara, and these lay across the coffin's top, covering it. John had sat beside it for a long time this afternoon, one hand touching the wood. And then Alice had an idea. She walked outside. Riggs rose from a chair placed under a tree. Walter, Poppy, and Perryman joined him. "I need a carriage."

He didn't blink an eye. "Anything else?"

"Walter, I'm going to need you to accompany me."

"Yes, ma'am."

"What bee have you got in your bonnet?" Poppy asked.

She put an arm around Walter and walked down the lane a bit with him, explaining her idea. Then she was off to talk to John and Caro about what she wished to do.

"I don't know . . ." John was reluctant. Caro didn't say anything at all.

Downstairs, her father walked in. Alice flew down the stairs, dragged him up to the landing. "Tell John about when my mother died. Tell him what you told me this morning about my being in her arms."

She went into the bedchamber, sat beside the bed. Caro was on the opposite side, holding Barbara's hand.

"There you are." Barbara spoke slowly.

Alice kissed her hand. "I love you. I have been a bad friend."

But it was as if Barbara didn't hear. "Is the baby dead? Please tell me."

The little serving girl entered the bedchamber. "There's a carriage downstairs for you, ma'am," she said to Alice.

"Wait for me, Ra," Alice said. "I'm not going to be long."

Caro followed her outside to the landing. "You're g-going for that baby?"

"Yes. If she must die, let it be with a child in her arms."

"Alice, I-I think s-she's much worse. I don't t-think you should leave."

"I have to give her this if I can." At the bottom of the stairs, she saw John and her father sitting together in the parlor chamber, John's face haggard.

"Have I your permission?" she asked John.

"Alice, I don't know what to say," he said. "I can't think clearly anymore."

"Give me every pence you have," she told her father. He handed her a bag of coins. She was out the door. Walter and Poppy were sitting with the coachman, but what she didn't expect to see was Balmoral inside the carriage. "Your G-Grace," she stammered.

"I thought I'd better keep an eye on you."

She was silent once inside the carriage.

"Where are we off to?" he asked finally as they rolled past the royal mews and into Charing Cross.

BALMORAL FOLLOWED HER into the Daniell house and stood back, not speaking, as she pleaded with Mrs. Daniell and Nan. "It will just be for a while, a few days. I'll pay you handsomely for it."

"How handsome?" asked Mrs. Daniell.

"Twenty-five shillings." It was more than Mr. Daniell would earn in a year.

"I don't want to let go my baby!" said Nan.

"Hush," said her mother.

"Please," said Walter.

"And two golden guineas when it's done," said Balmoral. "Come with the baby. It needs a wet nurse, isn't that true?" He looked at Alice.

"Yes, yes, of course."

"It's done, then," said Mrs. Daniell, taking the handkerchief from Alice's hands, untying the knot, and letting go a big breath at the sight of what was, indeed, twenty-five shillings. "Bundle up what you need and be gone," she said to her daughter.

Nan sat as still as possible in the jolting carriage, overawed to be in one. Only the presence of Walter, who held one of her hands, kept her quiet. Now that it was done, Alice sagged against the leather of the seat. I've gone mad, she thought. This will never work. Barbara will know. What is the matter with me? I'm like some jangling doll made of raw nerves that can't be still a moment or it will fall apart. If it gives her one second of happiness, it will be worth it. Barbara is dying, and I wasted so much time being stupid about so many things that don't matter at all. No matter who is in the chamber, I'm going to ask for forgiveness.

"Your babe is how old?" Balmoral asked Nan Daniell.

"Five days," Nan answered.

"Fortune is on your side, so far," he said to Alice. "She might believe it hers. One looks for such things before a battle, what is working in one's favor. Too much against, and the battle is best left for another day. If your enemy is unwise enough to allow such."

There was another carriage there when they arrived, and Alice saw Richard in the distance, near the campaign tent, standing with his horse, which was unsaddled and grazing placidly. So. Richard's mother was here.

Inside the house there was an intriguing fragrance, sharp to the nostrils, cleansing. Smoke issued from a brazier, sitting at the fireplace, and with the smoke came the smell. John's mother was on her knees there in prayer, not even raising her head to glance at Alice. "Wait here," Alice ordered Nan.

Upstairs, opening the bedchamber door, she saw that Barbara slept. John sat in a chair at the bed, his head buried in his arms atop the blanket. Caro stood looking out the window. Jerusalem Saylor, Richard's mother, held Barbara's hand. There was another brazier on the table, light smoke issuing from it, the same sharp, clean fragrance more intense. And beeswax candles were burning.

"When she wakes, everything is ready," Alice whispered. She was excited, like a child who knows its present will be best.

Caro turned from the window. "Oh, Alice, s-she isn't g-g-going to w-wake. She's gone."

The shock of the words was like being thrown into an icy river. Alice's thoughts went wild, scattered. She hadn't told her over and over how much she loved her. She hadn't begged forgiveness. She hadn't spoken her folly and her shame. She'd thought there was more time. She walked to the bed, looked down. First friend. Her girlhood here, her secrets, her mischiefs, her silliness, her heart. How could it be ended? The pain was intolerable. She fell on her knees, sobs breaking out, jagged and harsh.

John raised his head. "I want to be alone with my wife."

Alice could barely stand, but she groped her way out of the bedchamber. "Caro," she whispered. There on the landing, she put her arms around Caro, clinging. At least I have this, thought Alice. I haven't flung everything away.

But Caro unwrapped Alice's arms, spoke through tears in that slow manner that was her way when she had given a matter much thought. "She a-always f-forgave you. But I d-don't. It was a t-truce for Ra's sake. Now she's g-gone, and so is our friendship."

Alice felt something in herself collapse. I deserve this, she thought. I deserve to be punished. It should be me instead of Barbara. She moved past Caro to run down the stairs, out into the lane, into the dusk. She wanted to scream until the sky cracked, wanted to somehow kill her own shame, kill herself, rather than feel this pain that was splintering in her. She started to run.

"Where's she off to?" said Poppy. He walked into the lane. In the distance, he could see she was still running. Richard walked up beside him. Jerusalem Saylor stepped outside the house. "Go after her, Richard," she called, her voice urgent.

Without a word exchanged, both men began to run.

Alice ran and ran, down Cockspur Street, out into a juncture of Charing Cross and the Strand, down Whitehall Street, into the first open arching gate of the palace, into the courtyard of Scotland Yard, her heels clacking on the cobbles and bricks, her heart hammering in her chest and head. Purge me with hyssop and I shall be clean. Wash me and I shall be whiter than snow. There was the river, the wonderful, deep river. She ran down the wharf where boats and wherries docked, unloading goods for the palace, ran past startled boatmen, ran to the end of the wharf, and leaped into the water. And then she just started walking, water coming up to her breasts, soaking in her skirts, mud pulling off her shoes, now it was at her neck, good, wash this shame, this folly, this pride, from me, and I shall be whiter than snow, she was thinking, under, she just wanted to go under, to get away from thoughts and pains and failures, from ambitions and plots, from wrong decisions, now it was at her chin, and the bottom was falling away under her feet, and the skirts of her gown were heavy, and that was good, she could do this, she wasn't afraid of dying, it would be good to have it over, this business of life. Make me to hear joy and gladness, that the bones which thou has broken may rejoice. Perhaps she'd even see Barbara. She kept her eyes open, took a breath, and let her skirts drag her under.

Running out onto the wharf, Richard saw several rowboats clustered midriver, boatmen diving into the water. In moments, he had his boots, shirt, and jacket off and swam out to meet them. One of them had Alice by the neck. Her eyes were closed. They pulled her into a boat, her wet skirts making her as heavy as two men. Richard heaved himself into the boat. A boatman was pushing on her chest. Dear sweet merciful Lord in heaven, thought Richard. He knelt beside her. She coughed, gagged, spat up water, and began to fight. Richard had to wrestle her to the bottom of the boat to keep her from leaping back overboard. She screamed and clawed at him.

At the dock, he couldn't coax her out of the boat.

The rivermen were terrified to touch her. He pulled her arms behind her, forced her back to the bottom, straddled her. She was still fighting. He tied her hands with his shirt. A boatman handed him rope, and he managed to pin her flailing legs. She writhed and screamed at him. She had to be washed, she said. She had to be cleansed. A crowd had gathered on the quay. She tried to twist her face away from their view.

He took a cloak from some bystander more than willing to give it up, put it around her, pulled up the hood so that her face was hidden by its shadow. Trussed as she was, he picked her up.

"I can't live with this shame," she said into his chest. And she began to cry.

They made quite a sight walking through alleys and courtyards of the palace. They gathered a small entourage of pages, Edward running ahead to open doors, ladies-in-waiting, courtiers joining as they neared the queen's quarters, as Richard carried her to the maids' bedchamber. She was crying now in a way that frightened him. He was astounded at both her will and her anguish. He shut the door on everyone save Poll. He pulled back the hood, looking at her face. She was at some edge he didn't know how to reach toward, and fatigue was hitting him, in body and in heart, so he left her to her servant. In the guardroom, he ignored curious glances at his half-clothed state, went to his chamber, sat on the bed, pulled a blanket around himself, and closed his eyes, shivering at everything this day had brought. Time for prayer. So many needed it, John, the babe, Barbara, and now Alice.

CHAPTER 41

They planned to bury Barbara and the baby in the same casket. Alice dragged herself from bed to attend the service, but heat scourged her body the way regret and recrimination scourged her soul. Fever showed in her flushed cheeks, in her glassy eyes, in an ache that cleft her head apart with the slightest breath. She was at her father's. She'd been taken from Whitehall in a litter a few days ago.

"Your father's waiting." Poll had glanced at her face and then away. "Here," she said when Alice didn't move, "lean on me." She knew better than to say, You oughtn't to go. Outside the bedchamber door, Poll handed her over to her father and Perryman. When Sir Thomas saw how unsteady she still was, saw the trembling, saw that her head seemed too heavy for her neck to bear, he said, "Poppet, you must stay home."

She didn't answer. She couldn't. But when Perryman laid her in the bed, she was crying softly. "Please, let me go."

Her begging weakness upset Sir Thomas more than he already was. "No. The last thing I need is you dying on me. I will throw two handfuls of dirt on the coffin, one for you and one for me." He took her hand to kiss it good-bye and found himself afraid at how hot and dry it was.

❧

The funeral service was crowded, both Their Majesties attending, though King Charles did not even glance toward his queen, who sat in tiny hauteur with her ladies. On the very edge of them was Renée de Keroualle. Like everyone in the chapel, Sir Thomas craned for a view of her. Lovely. Magnificent jewels. Balmoral told him she was not yet the king's mistress but reaped the rewards that she would be. A friend came and sat behind him in the pew, leaned forward to whisper that there had been a Romish service earlier, Their Majesties attending that, also.

"Was York there?" Sir Thomas whispered.

"Yes."

Sir Thomas tapped impatient fingers on the wood beside him. Whether the heir to the throne had gone over to the Church of Rome was Balmoral's chief concern; therefore, it was his chief concern. Eyes would be on the Duke of York at the Easter service to see if he took Communion in the Church of England or not. Do keep yourself on hand for Buckingham, Balmoral had said, smiling thinly. But do let me know whatever he asks of you. Balmoral's sense of clarity was refreshing.

The service was beginning. Sir Thomas looked around to see who else was there. And everyone was, from the king's former beautiful harridan of a mistress, Cleveland, to royal gardeners and musicians, to King Charles's pet wits, Rochester and Sedley, to dukes, royal and otherwise. Balmoral nodded in his direction, and Sir Thomas swelled with pride. Sweet Jesus, to be allied to this man! He'd reached the pinnacle. The history of his climb was in this chapel: Men and women were here who'd been in exile with him, others who had sworn allegiance to Cromwell but bowed to Charles when the fates turned the wheel in that direction. Ten years ago, Roundhead generals had decided that with the death of Cromwell the protectorate would no long support anything but civil war, and the country was too exhausted for that and bowed to the exiled king. Now, of those powerful men, only Balmoral remained. Ten years ago, Sir Thomas had been so poor that he'd had to appeal to Alice's aunt to loan the coins so he could dress himself and Alice for the triumphal entry into London.

Little Barbara Bragge dead. Alice's first friend at court, other than Monmouth. He could not believe he sat at her funeral. He bowed his head as prayers began, noticing out of the corner of his eye Lady Saylor sitting with her beautiful daughters and son-in-law. Her head wasn't bowed, but her eyes were closed. This woman, with her calmness and strange distant eyes, disturbed him. As if she felt him staring, she met his gaze. He felt for a moment as if he were floating in a clear river, then she looked away again. He shook himself at the shock of the simple matter of her dropping her gaze. Beyond her sat his Dutch friend, Wilhelm Lowestroft. Let us begin a mild courtship with the Hollanders, Balmoral had said. Nothing treasonous, a light flirtation merely. It seemed there was a young Protestant prince, one William of Orange, whose mother had been King Charles and York's sister, who hated the French king, Louis. I'd like to know him better, Balmoral had smiled. Do bring our friend Lowestroft to call.

"We brought nothing into this world," the archbishop was saying, "and it is certain we can carry nothing out. The Lord gave, and the Lord hath taken away; blessed be the name of the Lord." Outside in the churchyard, the coffin was lowered into a grave. "Unto almighty God we commend the soul of our sister and of her child, departed," began the archbishop, and when the hymn was sung, Sir Thomas went to stand in a side porch and was gratified to see Balmoral leave the throng, walk forward to join him.

PRAYERS DONE, THERE remained only the throwing of handfuls of dirt upon the grave. People drifted away, walking among the gravestones and table tombs, among greening trees and around clumps of blooming snowdrops, making their way to the porch, to acknowledge Balmoral and ask of Alice.

The new Lady Knollys came up to him. Little Gracen looked the woman with rouge on her cheeks and several black patches scattered here and there. Sir Thomas nodded to her. She was a handsome minx, and she knew it.

"How is Alice?" she asked.

The despair in her eyes shocked him. No bride should look so sad. "Not well."

"Will you tell her I asked of her? Do you know if Barbara had a farewell for me?"

"I don't, Lady Knollys."

He watched her turn toward someone else in the milling crowd as Lady Saylor walked forward. "How does your daughter?" she asked, no coquetry about her.

The jewels she wore were wild and strange, as if from another time, something barbaric and compelling about the stones, the gold work. If her hair had once been the gold of her children's, it was now silver and bound in long braids pinned to her head, flowers and jewels garnishing the knots, like a woman of King Arthur's court. Time touched her face. She did not try to hide it. Sir Thomas found himself a little afraid of her. "Still with a fever."

"I have some claims to healing. Might I visit her?"

"The king's physician has called twice."

"Oh, so she is better?"

"She is not," answered Balmoral. "She's been bled twice and each time fainted. I like it not. I've seen the same on the battlefield to no good effect."

"I have some remedies for fever, old, from my mother and her mother before that. I brought them for Mrs. Sidney. Might I call this afternoon?"

"Please," said Balmoral, and Sir Thomas pursed his lips, noting how Balmoral spoke as if Alice were already his.

"Sir," said Richard to Balmoral, "might I have a word with you?" He whispered the idea that had come to him about the casket of letters.

Balmoral's mouth widened into a smile as he listened. "If you succeed, you do me a service you cannot imagine. Whatever you need is yours for this."

"Thank you, sir." Richard found his mother standing behind a tree with Prince Rupert, who was in the act of kissing her hand. Are they flirting? thought Richard, shocked, but then he was sidetracked, remembering that Prince Rupert, in his checkered past, had been an aide to the French soldier General Turenne.

"Elizabeth is waiting in the carriage," Richard told his mother. He watched her settle upon a time to meet this evening with Prince Rupert, who was like a large dog wagging his tail, all but barking for Jerusalem Saylor. "I wonder if I might have a word with you before you leave?" Richard asked him when his mother was in the carriage.

"Oh, more than a word, my boy. I'm at your service for whatever you need. Now, no need to stare me down. Your mother is going to sup with me and Mrs. Hughes tonight, perfectly respectable, and you cannot fault a man for admiring a lovely woman, can you? That just wouldn't be reasonable."

"I'm leaving His Majesty's service. I'm going to France. If you would be so kind, it would aid me greatly if I might have a letter of introduction to both the Prince de Condé and General Turenne. It would be a greater kindness if you'd speak to no one of this. I'll make my intentions known at the proper time."

"You jest. We need you."

"I must go."

Prince Rupert studied Richard's face for a long moment before replying. "You're a good soldier, well on the way to being a splendid one. Now that I think on it a little, your serving Turenne can only in its turn serve us. If I live long enough, I'll see you a captain general, I do believe. No need turning red, sir. I thought it the moment I saw you attempting to drill some discipline into that lazy excuse for a troop that calls itself the queen's bodyguard. I'll write your letters. Good day." He walked away but came back as if he'd remembered something. "I have a little scheme," he said, "which your brother-in-law has invested heavily in. I'd like to present it to you."

"I have no funds to speak of."

"You have property that can be mortgaged."

"I can't think of such things today."

"Of course you cannot. My manners are abominable. Forgive me. Good day, Captain."

John still stood at the grave. The diggers had begun piling dirt on the coffin now that everyone had scattered to carriages or sedan chairs. The graveyard was suddenly empty. Richard went to stand beside his friend. The sound of dirt on the coffin of a loved one was a lonely sound. The least he could do was bear it with John.

Sir Thomas hovered in the doorway as Lady Saylor bent over Alice, who was mumbling and thrashing about. She touched her hand to Alice's forehead, then to her chest, straightened abruptly. "The fever's too high. We need to put her in a bath to bring it down. At once." Something in her voice made the hair at the back of Sir Thomas's neck prickle, and he found himself shouting for servants. Balmoral, who had been standing behind him, walked into the bedchamber, looked down at the delirious young woman on the bed.

Jerusalem Saylor took off her rings and bracelets, ordered everyone from the room but maidservants, and bathed Alice herself. When Alice was wrapped in wool blankets and her fur cloak, her teeth chattering, Jerusalem took powder from a box she'd brought, dropped it to a touch of wine, added water, and made her swallow it. She ordered a fire built and sat before it, a trunk at her back for support, holding a shivering, bundled Alice, who moaned and trembled as if she were naked in snow. Balmoral returned, pulled a chair nearby, his eyes never leaving Alice, who slept and shook and woke to shake and sleep again.

Afternoon moved into twilight, twilight into night. Perryman came to lead Balmoral to supper and a bed for the night. Sir Thomas, told Lady Saylor had refused to leave Alice to sleep, walked into the bedchamber.

"She needs the touch, the heat, of another body," Jerusalem said to his protests, of someone who has healing in them, she didn't say. "Would you send round a note to Prince Rupert canceling my supper tonight?"

"Of course, dear lady." And Sir Thomas retreated, the sight of his shivering, moaning daughter, eyes half-open, unfocused, too much for him.

Perryman, bringing wine and cheese for Jerusalem, paused in the doorway, his nostrils flaring at the scent from a candle. The fragrance was sharp in the lungs, but calming. "If I might . . . that is, if you would trust me, I will hold Mistress Alice for a time so that you might rest," he said.

Jerusalem's brows rose. "Let me have your hand." She was imperious. She held it in hers, seemed satisfied with what she felt. "Keep her pulled close, your arms wrapped tight as if she were a child."

"Yes, I'll do it just as you have."

"Build the fire again to roaring."

That done, she lay down at the foot of Alice's bed, curling herself up like a cat, and slept for several hours, waking at midnight. She washed her face and hands and went to a window to look out at the night sky. "Perryman, come here."

He laid Alice down, joined her at the window. "Is that someone there, against the tree?" Under a tree in the garden was a shadowed figure.

"Yes, madam."

"Who is it?"

"He, ah, returned with me from Whitehall when I delivered my message to Prince Rupert, asking that I trouble no one with his arrival. He is, ah, a friend, concerned for Mistress Alice's welfare."

"Why not invite him in?"

"I did so, madam. He refused, requested that I, ah, trouble no one with news of his presence. How does she?"

"Continues to toss and fret."

Together, they gave Alice more fever powder. Jerusalem arranged herself to hold Alice as Perryman made the fire spark and roar again. Toward morning, Alice began to perspire. She tried to throw off blankets, but Jerusalem stopped her, wrapped her as if she were a baby in swaddling. When morning light pierced the window and warmed the room with light, Alice fell into a quieter sleep. There was dampness on her forehead and around her mouth, which Jerusalem touched with a finger and smelled, then nodded as if satisfied.

"Is the fever broken?" It was Balmoral.

"Yes. Will you call for the servants to carry her to bed? Perryman, we'll need to warm the bed first, and we'll need a hot brick wrapped in flannel at her feet. When that brick cools, it must be replaced with another hot one."

Sir Thomas appeared in the doorway, plump, vibrant in a robe of blue and yellow, a red silk cap, embroidered slippers. "Is she better? They tell me she's better!"

"A bit," said Jerusalem. "I'm going to leave my fever powders with you. You must give them to her three times this day. There's also another candle in my bag, which has a special scent. I'm going to ask that you light it and allow it to burn to nothing."

Sir Thomas turned on his heel and walked blindly downstairs into his great chamber, gasping now and again at tears he couldn't stop. Alice was never ill. The sight of her high fever combined with Barbara's dying had left him as emotional as a woman. It was only now that he could admit how afraid he had been of Alice dying this night. At the sound of Jerusalem descending the stairs, he wiped his face and walked into the hall. Balmoral was with her, Perryman holding one of his arms to aid him.

"May I give you breakfast, dear lady?" asked Sir Thomas.

"No, thank you."

Balmoral said, "My carriage is outside. I have the honor of escorting her back to Whitehall." To Sir Thomas's eyes, he was the one who now looked ill and feverish, too thin and waxen. "I wish to be called if her condition should worsen; otherwise I will rest this day."

"If this young man"—Jerusalem turned her eyes on Perryman—"cares for her as well as he did last night, she will not worsen. You have a most excellent servant, Sir Thomas."

As the front door closed behind his guests, Sir Thomas turned on his footman. "She didn't offer you a place with her, did she?"

"She did not, sir."

"Well, if she does, you're to tell me at once."

"Yes, sir."

IN THE CARRIAGE, Balmoral leaned back, closed his eyes. He made a sound, something between a grunt of pain and a sigh. "I don't wish that girl to die."

"She won't, not now."

Balmoral opened his eyes. "Was she near death?"

"Yes. The physician attending her was most unskilled."

"I thought so, too."

"She needs to leave London."

Balmoral didn't answer, kept his eyes upon her face.

"I want to take her back with me to Tamworth. Would you allow it?"

"Why should I?"

"I want to guard against the fever returning and let her sleep in the sunlight, under a window where roses and fennel bloom. I think she requires great quiet at the moment, requires being away from this"—a sweep of her hand indicated London and the court—"from memories too cruel yet to bear. She wished to die; you mustn't forget that. She tried to will it."

"Why put yourself out so?" He was truculent, combative.

"My son has always spoken of her with high regard. I believe she has done him some kindnesses, as, indeed, have you." My son stood in the night outside, watching over her, she did not say; for that I would do anything. "And I like to mend things when I see them broken."

"Broken?"

"She's broken here—" She touched near her heart. "I would not like to see that spread to here—" She touched her head.

"It's her father's decision."

Jerusalem didn't bother to reply.

"I want her well by May."

"For your wedding?"

"For our wedding."

They were silent. When the carriage stopped outside Holbein Gate and the door was opened, Jerusalem leaned forward, touched Balmoral on his hand, making him start. No one touched a duke, just as no one touched a king. "You may not have a drop of wine, not a drop. I have second sight. I see things."

"Am I dying?"

"We're all dying." She descended the carriage and walked into the crowd.

IN HIS CLOSET, Balmoral opened the cabinet where his sweet sherry from Portugal lay in its precious Venetian crystal decanter. He liked the first cup to be sherry. After that he cared not. The siren called to him. He closed the cabinet, sat in a chair, thought about being alive to marry this young woman he found he'd grown more than fond of, disobeying him, fetching babies, grieving too hard, walking into rivers, throwing fevers. He thought about secret treaties and Buckingham's betrayals and the fact that if King Charles had agreed to anything with the Church of Rome—if York was indeed Catholic—then Buckingham, king of the dissidents, attracting the odd sects like a candle did moths, would be necessary. He thought about Richard's idea to steal the casket of letters King Charles had written to Madame. With that in his hands, the king would be in his hands, too. He thought about the young prince of the Dutch House of Orange, William, strange, he'd heard, asthmatic, brilliant. He thought about the dark angel Ange. What betrayals was he plotting in that twisted mind of his? He will try to kill me, he thought. No doubt of that. How? If Richard brought the letters, there was no need of Ange. I will kill him first, he thought, and smiled. Odd, here at the end, that life had never been more interesting.

THAT EVENING, RICHARD walked into laughter, faces softened by candlelight, people enjoying themselves with talk and good food. Prince Rupert rose from his chair, a chicken leg in his hand. "Surely it's not time for you to bear her off?"

"I regret that it is, sir."

Prince Rupert, primed with wine, bowed to Jerusalem. "Lovely lady, we're not ended with you. You'll go riding with me tomorrow, yes?" He put his hand on his mistress's shoulder. "We'll go to Peg's for supper, perhaps. She has a cozy little villa in Chelsea. Saylor, I'm trying to convince your mother to move closer to London, lease a little place outside of town, Marylebone or Chelsea. We need to see more of her. I want her to pose for an engraving. She fobs me off."

The thought of his mother anywhere near court made Richard smile. It would be like trying to tether some creature of the forest. He thought of the queen's little fox, the creature's dainty hesitancy, quick, wild ways. Did the fox dream at night of trees and midnight rambles? His mother was not made for court. She would dream of Tamworth and its hillock, its bees, its fields of clover.

He led her to the queen's apartments, deserted of company. Even during the divorce rumors, it had not been this quiet, this empty of people. Everyone who was not on duty to the queen was on the west side of the palace, where the king was, where Renée was.

He knocked upon the queen's bedchamber, and her old nurse opened the door, led his mother inside; he waited for a time, until the door reopened and his mother reappeared. She gave a great sigh when they walked out of the palace, into the dark of the courtyards. She stood a moment, looking up at stars. Richard watched her profile.

"Take me to see Pharaoh."

At the mews, she stood in the dark of the walkway between stalls, listening. She was very sensitive to animals. Richard opened Pharaoh's stall. He could see the dark bulk of the horse lying down, Walter asleep on his belly. Pharaoh lifted his head, snorted, and Jerusalem knelt down, kissed his sleek neck.

"Beautiful boy, prince of horses, how are you?" she asked, paying him his homage. She wrapped arms around his neck to hug him. The horse nuzzled her shoulder, blew softly through his nostrils. As a child, Richard had believed his mother talked to animals. He still did.

"I'll sleep here tonight."

"Mother—"

"Come for me at dawn." She settled down beside Walter like a stable boy herself, flipping off shoes, pulling off her necklace, unscrewing earrings and dropping them in the straw as if they were nothing.

"What do I tell Elizabeth?"

"The truth, if you dare."

Richard smiled at the thought of his sister's response to the news her mother had refused a bedchamber in her elegant new town house in the new St. James's Square near the palace to sleep in the king's mews with Richard's horse.

"I'll be taking Alice to Tamworth," his mother said.

Richard felt something in his heart move. He walked back out under the stars and looked up at them as his mother had done. Thank you, he told them and what was behind them, silently. Alice would heal at Tamworth. Everything did.

Chapter 42

Queen Catherine sat still as her tiring woman combed out her hair. What is it that you want? Lady Saylor had asked. Honor to my position. Children. Love. Affection. Security. Loyalty. Admiration. Everything. Which of those have you any hope of achieving? Affection. Security. Honor to my position. He will give me that; he always does if I let him do as he pleases. "Go to the Keroualle," she told Lord Knollys, "and inform the queen, she calls. This afternoon."

She walked into her withdrawing chamber as, haloed by morning light, Edward took the covers from the canary cages. The birds began to trill and warble. She put a hand against the metal of a cage. Several of them fluttered close, flirted with her. She clucked to them, made cooing sounds. She had come to him trained to love, to obey, and she did both. He liked her, was even fond of her upon occasion. They had laughed together in bed. He had made her trill with passion. She had confused zestful duty with love. But he could not be in love with her. She was not beautiful enough, not English enough, not French enough, not enough enough. She had wanted to bear a child of his, a lusty, long-legged, black-haired boy as he must have been, full of life, naughty. Whitehall was her cage, and there would always be another Renée.

Why do the canaries sing? Lady Saylor had asked. They know no better, she had answered. I believe they do, Lady Saylor had said.

That afternoon, her entourage of ladies surrounding her, she walked down the corridors and through hallways to that part of the palace in which Renée now resided. Heels clicked on the wood of the floors. Gowns made swishing sounds. Her maids—so decimated now, so sad with Alice and Barbara and Gracen gone—laughed and chattered, excited, like children with a special treat promised. Even their demeanor was different, brighter, excited, hopeful. Her isolation had affected them. She darted in like the bird she resembled. Renée was in a curtsy, Lady Arlington with her. Queen Catherine met Lady Arlington's eyes; she had moved to where the power lay. It was the nature of a courtier to follow power, just as it was the nature of a bird to sing.

"I am so honored that you visit me." Renée was sincere, nothing ironic in her voice, her English softly accented, precisely correct. She meant her words. The other mistress, the monster Cleveland, had never been humble, or kind, or excited to receive her. To be accepted by the queen meant something to this one. That would be useful.

"I am have the curiosity to see where you are the live." The sound of workmen hammering, talking, could be heard through closed doors on another wall. "And I am the bring a small gift, a—how do you say it?"

"Housewarming," said Frances.

The queen lifted a kitten out of the basket Frances held, and Renée took it, lifted it high. "I adore cats. Thank you, Your Majesty."

Charles did not. "You are the welcomed."

"May I show you my chambers?"

"Please."

And they walked through several rooms farther on, workmen carefully, with mallets and wooden pegs, joining carvings for oval ceiling surrounds and door moldings. Furniture was covered in sheeting. Queen Catherine lifted a sheet. Lustrous fabric, its embroidery stiff and handsome, graced a chair.

"Yellow is my favorite color," Renée said.

Queen Catherine felt rage surge up. Blue-eyed whore. How dare he give you these chambers! How dare he spare no expense that you might furnish them! How dare he be he! But that was a hole into which it was best not to fall, at least not now.

"How is dear Mrs. Brownwell?" Renée asked. They were seated again in her presence chamber, and a servant was passing around crackers, small cakes, goblets of wine.

"With her brother. Better to be." Queen Catherine looked toward Lord Knollys, who dropped his eyes. Dorothy had left the court the day after the funeral, after the sight of Lord Knollys and his young wife entering the church together.

"It's all been so shocking," said Lady Arlington, placid, the way people are when shocking things have not touched them.

"And Mistress Verney?"

"Better."

Queen Catherine looked around. "Charming. Many windows. Much light. You are having a good view of garden." She'd always liked this side of the palace.

"Will you—would you think of gracing them with your presence tonight?"

She most certainly would. She was not going to sit alone and abandoned in her apartments for one more evening. They could crucify her as they did the Christ; they could whip her with scourges; they could savage her in every street ballad—but she was the queen. "Yes."

Mission executed, Queen Catherine stood, and there were curtsies all around, Luce and Kit kissing Renée's cheeks, laughing and chattering behind the queen as they walked back to their part of the palace, deeper in, darker, its view the Thames River, its windows smaller because it was older, its furnishings not sparkling and new, not the latest fashion from France.

"Crimson and diamonds tonight," Queen Catherine told her tiring woman later.

Frances took up a book she'd been reading to Her Majesty, began. Queen Catherine closed her eyes. After a time, thinking the queen asleep, Frances stopped reading, her expression unhappy. The queen watched her through slitted eyes. She could have taken Frances's hand, patted it, said in the mangled English that never quite expressed what she thought, You would like me to remain prideful. Do you think I can stay the rest of my days here, seeing no one, being visited by no one, under the cover of my cage, never seeing the sun? I cannot.

THAT EVENING, THERE was an air of bubbling excitement in the queen's apartments as women waited for Queen Catherine to be finished dressing. They laughed and talked, whispering among themselves, straightening one another's sleeves or trying on one another's bracelets, so glad to be going to where King Charles would be, where courtiers would be, where the life and pulse of court would be. Pearls for the maids of honor, diamonds and rubies for the queen, diamonds for her ladies-in-waiting. Frances, Duchess of Richmond, looked particularly stunning. Queen Catherine smiled when she saw her. So, she thought, dressed for battle. To remind him of what he never obtained. He will be compelled to flirt. Little Keroualle will be jealous. I will be amused. Edward and the other pages punched one another's arms in impatience to be on their way. Captain Saylor, with six guards, stood ready to escort.

Queen Catherine took a breath. Once she walked through these doors, there was no going back. One more time, she thought. I survived the Duchess of Cleveland; I survived those years of his dallying with our lovely Frances, standing here beside us now, a haunted look in her eyes in spite of her diamonds and gold ringlets brushed to shining. Poor thing. It's her first time. A certain grim amusement welled up. Queen Catherine nodded to Richard, and he opened the great doors that led to the other side of the palace.

They trooped down the corridors, the long hallways. It was dusk. Servants and pages were lighting torches in courtyards and candles in chambers, along the hallways. Whitehall was always beautiful by candlelight, her age softened, her odd rambling turned charming with darkness to drape it. Chambers they passed were in that half-shadow of earliest evening. Gold and silver candlesticks gleamed from tabletops. Courtiers, dressed for supper, for their night ahead, came to their doors to curtsy or bow. Already the word had spread. There was to be a truce between the king and queen and the one who would be the next great mistress.

Music from Renée's chamber spilled out her doors, meeting them in the hall. Edward proudly announced the queen, and silence fell.

There was a full crowd here, His Majesty, a few of his ministers—Balmoral among them—but mostly his favorites, his night companions, his howlers at the moon, Sedley and Rochester, the others who amused him, and ladies, clever wives already attaching themselves to Renée as the next official mistress, one they might receive in their homes, unlike his actresses or whores. Queen Catherine glanced around. The Duchess of Cleveland was not present. Satisfaction in that. What if she, his ugly little queen, outlasted them all?

These chambers were charming. The way candles and flowers were placed, crowded everywhere, among all the splendid objects, gold clocks, enameled vases, porcelain figurines, atop tables, atop the mantels of fireplaces. There was nothing stern in this chamber, nothing austere, from its sunny yellow walls to the cream color of the wood surrounding door and ceilings, to the objects everywhere. Servants were walking among the crowd to offer wine. A long table against a wall held towers of fruit, tarts, tiny pies, amid figures of marzipan and sugar paste. A large sugar-paste swan was in the center, roses in his mouth. This was what her lord craved, sophistication, elegance, style, and, above all, new amusement.

Sapphires at her ears and throat, Renée had dropped into a curtsy at the announcement of the queen. All the women did the same. Men bowed. King Charles walked forward and kissed Queen Catherine on each cheek, pleased that she pleased his heart's desire by coming to her party. "I am so very glad to see you."

"Yes," she answered.

"I've missed you."

"Liar."

He liked her tartness, tucked her arm in his and walked her toward the buffet. "Cousin Louis does this for his evenings in France, I'm told."

Queen Catherine noted royal silver pieces displayed on the table, nodded toward a tapestry hanging large above the long table. "The Gobelins?"

"It was stored away, gathering dust," he said offhandedly. He patted her hand, and she shut her mouth on complaints. There would be spillover from his generosity to Renée; if she was quiet, he would soon feel guilty. She'd have new furnishings, too. She intended to spend a pretty penny.

Seeing the king's approval, courtiers pressed forward to have a word with the queen while she was still on the king's arm. Frances, who had gone to sit beside Balmoral to ask of Alice, sighed at the sight of it.

Balmoral noticed, but all he said was, "Must Captain Saylor scowl so?"

"It hurts him to see Renée."

"He'd best get over it."

"Do we forget true love?"

"Yes, we do."

"How is Mrs. Brownwell?" King Charles asked Queen Catherine. Now that she had acquiesced, accepted what was, he wished to know everything about her household.

Queen Catherine turned dark eyes on him. "Not well."

"Knollys is a dog."

It takes one to know one. "She goes for to live with the brother. I am having the thought, an allowance, yes . . ." She let the sentence drift off.

"Ten guineas?"

She opened her fan. "Seventy-five."

"Twenty."

"Sixty-five."

"Fifty."

"Done."

"Your English is always most excellent around numbers, Catherine."

She kissed him on the mouth, a gesture missed by no one. "My lord and master, so well you have know me."

"I have hoped that we might be friends," Renée said to Richard. She was nervous, twisting her hands together.

Richard bowed, the gesture as stiff as his expresssion. "I am your servant in all things." He looked around the room, its profusion of objects, paintings, rich fabrics, the crowd admiring, envious, ready to serve her. This he could never give her. Frowning, he watched his sister flirting with Monmouth. What was this? Did the royal family think they might bugger all the Saylors? One was enough. King Charles crossed the chamber, stood behind Renée, as Richard made a deep bow.

"The queen is ready to play cards," King Charles said to Renée. His eyes followed her as she went to order servants to set up tables. He cares for her, thought Richard, watching the king with wary, weary anger. Then, in spite of himself, his eyes, too, followed Renée. She was resplendent. The depth of his heartache, which he knew, explored whether he wished it or not each night before sleep, surprised him afresh. Are they lovers yet? he thought. No. It would have been an open secret if they were. Perhaps he would be in France when that gossip made its rounds. That would be a good thing. Turning back to the king, he saw that King Charles, in turn, contemplated him.

"Am I safe in my bed yet, Saylor?" The king's smile did not reach his eyes.

"You are my liege lord. I would protect you with my life."

The way in which Richard spoke, grave, resolute, was not in fashion at this court. King Charles blinked. He could remember being this serious, swearing loyalty to his father before a battle, ready to die for this liege lord who was also father. He'd been pure of heart then, the way Richard was now. It was a treasured memory. "I've never rewarded you for your capture of Henri Ange."

Richard laughed. The sound made King Charles smile. "Alice Verney stabbed him. It's she who should be rewarded—captain of your guard, perhaps?"

"She should be captain of something. Between you and me, I pity Balmoral. She'll put him in his grave for certain."

Alice as widow, thought Richard. There was something interesting in that.

King Charles moved on, and Richard could hear Alice say, Idiot, he gave you an opening to ask for what you wish. But Richard didn't desire King Charles's blessing. He didn't want the royal seal upon his backside for services rendered. He was going to General Turenne in his own way.

Chapter 43

Alice's face was as white as the lace on the pillowcase under her head.

"Mind you don't jolt her too much!" Sir Thomas fluttered and fussed, had been doing so all morning, and all the servants' nerves were stretched to the breaking point, but Perryman and a footman managed to place Alice on the board that had been set across the seats in Balmoral's best and newest carriage. A goose-feather pallet lay across the board, and covers and pillows swaddled it. Poll crawled in and fluffed pillows as Alice closed her eyes.

"Now, mind you drive carefully! There isn't a decent road between here and there." Sir Thomas glanced toward Balmoral. "Have you thought of that? She'll be jolted to death."

"I've given her a draft that will let her sleep the journey," Jerusalem answered.

"Pull down those leather shades," Sir Thomas commanded Poll, "lest the air give her a chill. Has she enough coverlets?" As Sir Thomas circled the carriage, looking for yet another fault or lack, Richard hoisted Jerusalem into her saddle, then mounted his own horse. A caravan was on its way to Tamworth—he was commanding a troop of six men Balmoral was sending for protection, as well as the two carriages, one Balmoral's and the other Jerusalem's. The second carriage contained young Nan Daniell, whom Jerusalem had talked into coming to Tamworth as a serving maid. With her was her child.

Balmoral opened the carriage door, possessed himself of Alice's hand, and kissed it. "Be well. You see you make her well," he commanded Jerusalem.

"But of course I will. You'll be watching her dance at her wedding in a month."

"I'd better be."

"Best to be off," Richard said, "before the sun goes much higher." He saluted Balmoral and rode forward to divide the men into two groups, one riding before the carriages, the other behind.

AS DUSK FELL, they made camp in a meadow just off the road. Troopers built a fire, while Richard rode in a wide circle around their camp, taking the lay of the land, finding a farmhouse. He came back with pullets hanging from his saddle and jars of ale and honey mead in his bags.

That night, he stepped over sleeping men here and there to make his way to Balmoral's carriage. His mother had had Poll open all the shades to the night air. Poll lay sleeping under the carriage, where his mother would sleep when she came to bed. Where was she? And then he saw her, in the meadow, a solitary figure standing quite still under a full April moon, its silvery light as direct as a lantern. He saw Alice through the carriage window. Her eyes were open.

"Do you see the stars?" he asked her.

"Yes." Her voice was a thread.

"Are you warm enough?"

"Yes," she whispered. "I'm fretted for your sister. Monmouth—"

"Never mind Monmouth. I'll care for my sister."

"Don't wait too long," It took all her strength to speak. There was so much more she wished to say. "Where am I, Richard? I don't understand."

"You're going to Tamworth." The thought of it rose in his mind, the house, its brick, its twisted chimney stacks, its gables, its garden with a maze from a pattern of the old queen. The stream, the woods, the lane to the village, the fishpond, his mother's kitchen garden where in summer herbs scented the day and night. Tamworth, where his boyhood mostly was, where his father lay in a family vault in the village church, and his grandfather, also. Rooms with the dark paneling and carving of the fashion of the Tudors, odd hallways, crooked stairs, a great hall. Tamworth, peace of heart, quiet of soul. Tamworth, backwater, old-fashioned, forgotten by time, haven and home. Where he had thought to bring Renée as bride. Funny how standing here with Alice softened all that.

THEY ARRIVED THE next day.

"No," said Richard, "I'll carry her."

He lifted her out of the carriage, shocked at how light she was. Alice leaned her head against his shoulder. He carried her in under the porch, into the great hall, which opened high and wide and echoing.

"I want her here," said his mother, moving to a door that led to a parlor on the ground floor. Great swaths of sunlight cut across the dark of the floor from the mullioned windows across one wall. Jerusalem began to push out the lower windows and open them one by one.

Richard sat in a high-backed chair near the windows with Alice still in his arms. The smell of tansy and thyme wafted in, and he breathed it like balm. Alice trembled, and he pulled her closer to him, wrapped his arms tight around her, willing her his own strength, put his face against her hair, fierceness, protectiveness, young lions in him.

Poll came to drape a cloak over Alice. House servants and some of the troopers were staggering forward through the door, carrying in pieces of a great bed from upstairs, its columns, its frame, its headboard massive.

"In the sun, facing the windows," his mother commanded. The chamber was mostly empty, its furniture burned for firewood during the civil war. A mattress was carried in, and as soon as the bed was put together, servants pulled on sheets that had been dried in the sun, that smelled of green grass and clover. Jerusalem scattered catnip and chamomile among the sheets, atop the pillowcases, so Alice would sleep well.

In another moment, Richard placed Alice in among the sheets, and the moment her head touched the pillow, she closed her eyes, settling into a deep sleep. She opened her eyes once, the next day, to see Poll sitting near and Richard standing by the bed, looking down on her. I love you, she wanted to say, but sleep was calling her back down, and anyway, it was best that she not say that, and any thought made the ache in her head threaten its murder and mayhem; there was something she had to be ashamed of, something she had to feel, but she closed her eyes and went away again into the cool dark.

IN THE FORECOURT, Richard knelt for his mother's blessing. The old-fashioned gesture surprised several of the troopers, and one by one they took off their hats, bowed their heads also, thoughts of home, of mothers far away, in their minds. There was something in his action belonging to that time before the war, and in spite of themselves, the soldiers were touched by it.

"God in His mercy bless you and keep you and hold you to His bosom. May His will be done, may you follow in it, may your journey be safe. God save the king and all who serve him. In Christ's holy name, amen," said Jerusalem.

Richard stood, leaned down, kissed her, was in his saddle and turning his horse to face the journey before she could speak again. The child Annie came out from her hiding place and stood beside Jerusalem. They watched until the horses were over the horizen. Jerusalem went to her stillroom, looked through different books, containing all the recipes and healing wisdom that mothers and grandmothers and great-grandmothers had known and passed down. A small white owl, an embroidered hood over its head, slept on a stand. Poll had screamed at the sight of it leaving to hunt last night, its wings spread in a great arc.

Annie wandered among the drying herbs and crocks of jellies. "What's her name, the sleeping lady?" she asked Jerusalem.

"Alice Verney. She's a friend of Baron Saylor's."

Alice woke at dusk. A thin child she didn't know, all legs and dark eyes, saw and ran from the room. Nan Daniell appeared after a time, carefully carrying a pewter mug on a tray. In the mug was a posset, eggs and sugar mixed in with mulled wine. Poll helped Alice to sit up, and Alice drank it down, saying when she'd finished, "Another, please." After a second one brought in by Susannah, Jerusalem's most trusted servant, Alice felt sleepy again. "Do I hear music?" she asked.

"Lady Saylor is playing her flute," said Susannah.

"What day is it?"

"That I don't know," answered Poll. "But April is here."

" 'This April, with his stormy showers doth make the earth yield pleasant flowers. Purge well therein, for it is good to help thy body and cleanse thy blood,' " quoted Susannah. It was a rhyme from Tusser's *Almanac,* a bible for those in the country. Poll and Alice, who'd always lived in the city, stared at her uncomprehendingly.

April meant Maundy Thursday, thought Alice, the day when the king would wash the feet of beggars in memory of the Last Supper, when the Christ told his disciples, Love ye one another as I have loved you. It meant Palm Sunday, the last Sunday in Lent, the beginning of the Easter week, Good Friday, and Easter itself, death and resurrection. I'd like to die, thought Alice, and she closed her eyes.

A Parisian tailor turned from Walter, stepped back, pleased with his work.

"There you have it, monsieur," he said. "Your brother looks like the young lord he is."

Walter stood in a new satin coat, new stockings, new shirt, new shoes with silver buckles. His hair was trimmed and pulled back into a neat tail, the way Richard wore his. Richard, too, was in everything new, out of his uniform, with satin coat and lace at his sleeves. There was a cameo in the lace at his throat. The coats they wore were robin's-egg blue, and it suited their eyes. Their breeches were fine black wool. They might have belonged to any noble family in France or England, might have indeed been brothers, both thin, both fair, both blue eyed.

"I beg you, monsieur," said the tailor. "One patch on the cheek of my young lord, and it will be perfect."

"What is he saying?" asked Walter.

"He wants to put a patch on your cheek," answered Richard.

"Please have him do it."

Richard gestured for the tailor to do so, and the man rummaged in a small box, came forward with a circle moistened on one side with mastic. He placed it high on Walter's cheekbone, near his eye. "Perfection," cried the tailor. "And you, monsieur, you must have one, only one, near those ice cold eyes. The ladies will be at your mercy."

Outside, bells in the towers of churches in Paris began ringing. It was their custom to ring on the hour, one of the beauties of the city. Walter didn't know himself in this grand suit, but he knew he looked well. Captain Saylor looked magnificent. There was no other word for it. Madame Neddie had liked the word, using it for the boys and men whose faces were strong and chiseled, the way the captain's was. On one cheek was a black patch, not a circle like Walter's, but a star. With the black of the patch, near the blue of Richard's eyes, with the blue satin coat and the black breeches, he looked more beautiful to Walter's eyes than anyone he had ever seen.

"Nothing ventured, nothing gained," said Richard, as they walked across one of the stone bridges that spanned the Seine River. Walter tried not to stare at the clusters of priests, of nuns in their black habits with their black wimples, walking the streets just as anyone else. One never saw a nun in England and very few Romish priests. "Now, remember," said Richard. "You have to do nothing other than keep him occupied. Nothing more. Do you understand me?"

He meant Walter didn't have to kiss or touch or be touched. I need your help only to amuse him for a time, like talking with the customers at Neddie's, nothing more, Captain Saylor had explained carefully. You do not have to do this for me, Walter. You may say no. He didn't understand that Walter would do anything for him. Leap off this bridge, he could have said, and Walter would have done it.

"We'll see if we meet him in the different gaming hells," said Richard. "If not, we'll call at the Palais Royal tomorrow and see if he's still there. I intend to tell him that your name is Stephen Saylor and that you are my cousin."

But Beuvron was in the third gaming house they tried. "That's him, across the room, playing dice," Richard told Walter. "Let him see us. Don't try to attract his attention. You've never heard a word about this man. He is simply some friend of mine you are meeting for the first time. I'll play cards. You stand behind my chair."

"Does he speak English?"

"Yes."

Richard found a table ending a game, sat down, put coins out. Walter stood behind his chair, taking the wine a servant brought and placing it before Richard as if he were his personal servant. They attracted attention, the two strangers, both with pale hair pulled back when every other man in the place, other than servants, wore heavy, curly wigs. Yet their patches and handsome satin coats proclaimed them somebody, and somebody not afraid to be distinctive, something Parisians always noticed.

"Lieutenant Saylor, I thought that you." Beuvron walked across the room. "You're out of uniform. Will you be hanged, or have you quit?"

"Very likely hanged. How are you?"

"Well."

Beuvron glanced at Walter. "My cousin," said Richard. "Stephen Saylor."

"How do you do?" Beuvron said.

"He doesn't speak French."

"A handsome lad, your cousin." Beuvron switched to English. "How do you do."

Walter held out his hand. "Stephen Saylor."

"Are you in Paris long?"

"A few days," answered Richard.

Beuvron glanced again at Walter, said in French, "So you haven't come to see me?"

"Not this time."

"I don't know whether to be relieved or sorrowful. Let me buy your supper tomorrow."

"Perhaps. I've come to gamble."

"I'll join you."

They played cards for several hours, coins going back and forth, others joining and leaving the game. Beuvron gossiped of the court, was in good spirits, talkative and pleasant, so that Richard learned what he needed—Monsieur was not at the Palais Royal at the moment, and neither was Beuvron. Richard put down cards, picked up coins. "It grows late. Let me get this lad to bed. It was good to see you, Beuvron. Good-bye."

"Saylor, wait. I insist. Let me give you supper tomorrow."

"You mean today." Outside, dawn would begin to light the dark in just a few hours.

"I won't take no for an answer."

"If you insist. Where?"

Beuvron gave a street's name, and Richard and Walter walked out into the early morning, to the monastery at which Richard stayed whenever he was in France. He stood in the doorway of the single cell in which Walter would sleep. "I will make my attempt today. I won't need you to distract Beuvron after all. He isn't living at the palace. Instead, you'll help me. First we'll reconnoiter. If all looks well, I'll proceed."

"Reconnoiter. What does that mean?"

"It means to check every gate and door, every watchman and guard. It means to know what you're going into, so nothing takes you too much by surprise."

"He has a kind face."

"Who?"

"Your friend."

"I suppose. Sleep well, Walter. I'll be waking you in a few short hours."

THEY WALKED TO the Palais Royal, Monsieur's palace in Paris. He and Walter no longer wore satin coats, but the sober brown of tradesmen or merchants. They were Frenchmen, out to enjoy the palace gardens. When Richard was satisfied that all was well, he walked into the stables, into an empty stall, and changed into the Palais Royal servant's livery he had stolen months ago, while Walter served as lookout. Outside again, he nodded to Walter, who gave him the package he carried and took the clothes Richard had changed out of. Richard guided him to a bench. "Sit here. Stay here. If night falls and I haven't returned, go to the monastery, take the coins, go back to England."

"No—"

"Yes. Balmoral will need to know, and I need to know you will obey."

"Then I will."

His hair loosed, swinging in his face, Richard walked into the palace through the servants' entrance, the bulky package under one arm, whistling as he walked up the stairs, nodding to other servants he saw, but never doing more than glancing at them. He found Beuvron's old chamber and from there traced his steps to the chamber of the translator who labored over King Charles's letters to his sister. He opened the door, ready with an apology—his being new, not knowing all the chambers of the palace, excuse me for disturbing you, sir—but there was no one inside. He walked to the desk.

Quill pens arranged neatly, their tips, when he touched them, dry.

No letters spread out to be read and translated. No small brown leather casket to hold them anywhere in sight.

He searched the chamber. He searched again. He sat down in a chair to think. It wasn't here. Did he risk looking in nearby rooms? What were the chances he wouldn't be caught? The child of his brain, an identical leather casket crafted to his specifications in England, wrapped like a package, lay at his feet. There were even letters with broken seals inside, blank letters. He had wanted to write, "Greetings from His Grace the Duke of Balmoral" on each page. While I applaud your exuberance, Balmoral had said dryly, I am appalled at your stupidity. He walked into the hall, began opening doors. The rooms were empty, so he searched them. He could feel time passing. Finally, he opened a door and a man in the chamber looked up him, an eyebrow raised.

"A thousand apologies, monsieur." He closed the door. Instinct told him it was time to quit, time to gather up his unused casket and take it home. The mission had failed. Balmoral would not be happy. With the package back under his arm, he walked outside the palace. Walter, pacing in front of the bench, ran to him.

"Captain—"

"Be silent."

Walter followed him mutely to the stable, waited while Richard changed. Richard stood in the dark of the horse's stall, looking down at the package. It was over. He'd failed. He returned with empty hands. No last triumph to present to the grand old man. He picked up the folded livery, which he'd keep. One never knew.

He and Walter walked to the Pont Neuf, the oldest bridge in Paris.

They sat on a bench to watch Paris go by, nobles in their fine carriages, men on horseback, farmers on mules, magistrates from the law courts walking in their long robes, a cow herder driving cows to slaughter, groups of students, ink stains on their fingers. A stall sold rabbits, alive and dead, the dead ones hanging by their legs. A group of actors from the Commedia dell'arte set up shop near a statue in a large side plaza of the bridge. The actors wore elaborate masks and stylized costumes. Walter laughed aloud at their antics, particularly the zanni, whose baggy pants dropped at every important moment. In a moment of finality, Richard gave the packaged casket to the zanni, and the actor began an elaborate improvisation around it, and when, finally, he looked to return it, Richard and Walter had vanished.

THAT EVENING, THEY walked to Beuvron's for supper. So, thought Richard, walking up a stairway to the first floor of a small town house near the great medieval cathedral of Notre Dame, Balmoral's coins brought Beuvron ease.

Since it was the season of Lent, of Easter, Beuvron offered fish, all kinds, smoked, pickled, sautéed in butter, oysters, bread freshly baked, a jar of new butter. He had wine and champagne and port. He chatted happily, but Richard said little, and Walter less than that, even though he felt Beuvron's eyes on him often.

"You must see Versailles," Beuvron said at the end of the evening, when the champagne and wine were drunk and Richard refused another bottle.

"We return tomorrow."

"What a shame. You should stay for Palm Sunday; let your cousin view it. There will be processions, a blessing of the palms, extraordinary to see, flowers everywhere, the singing of the Gospels. You can show him how we wicked Catholics celebrate the resurrection of our Lord."

"Another time." Richard rose, walked to a window, putting his head out to take a breath of air. He'd wanted to end with a triumph. Now he brought failure along with the news he was leaving the army. Balmoral would not be pleased.

Glancing at Richard still at the window, his back to them, Beuvron put his hand out, touched Walter's knee very lightly, nothing disrespectful or forward in the gesture. His face had changed from its pleasant, heedless expression. He looked almost grave. "You're very beautiful, young Stephen. You belong here. Not there. You would be happy here. No bonds against being as you are. Do you even understand me?"

Walter didn't answer, stood, and Richard turned around. The moment passed.

He did understand, more than Beuvron realized, but he'd never leave Richard.

ALICE SAT IN a chair in the sun. Tomorrow, if she was stronger, Lady Saylor would allow her to attend church. People would be waving palm fronds, waiting to have their foreheads touched with ash. Perhaps in the afternoon she would sit on the hillock, a soft rise she could see in the distance, covered with huge oaks. It called to her. She longed to lie under its trees. A bird flew by, landed on the ledge of a window. It was a swallow. All the household talked of not having seen one yet, wondering who would have the good fortune to see the first swallow of spring. Alice began to weep. The weeping became Barbara's. Perhaps you'll be years grieving her, said Lady Saylor, and years more forgiving yourself.

Chapter 44

Balmoral stood with a dozen men at the edge of the river on what was called the Isle of Dogs, nearer the sea than London, but no real isle and no dogs; just a narrow creek eastward separated it from the mainland. Across, on the opposite bank, windmills turned, for the draining of the marshes upon which they stood. Henri Ange was there, too, looking almost bloodless, so pale was he, a streak of gray that had not been in his hair before, legs and one wrist chained to the burliest of the men. A sleek Dutch yacht had just dropped anchor.

Ange moved forward as best he could, the trooper with him. Two men on the deck leaped into the water, climbed through the mud toward him, one slightly behind the other. "Miguel," Ange said, putting his free hand on the shoulder of one of them. He touched his cheek to the man's, said very quickly, very quietly, "Say nothing. Trust me. You'll be rewarded."

Balmoral stepped forward, nodding toward the second man. "And who would this be?"

"The servant, Pedro," Ange answered. The servant cowered and stepped back as troopers surrounded Miguel. Before Miguel could speak, his arms had been pulled behind his back, and he was dragged away.

"Silence him," Balmoral called when he began to shout in Spanish for Ange to help him. There was the sound of hand against flesh, a yelp, and then silence as troopers boarded the yacht and returned with a small strongbox, which they placed before Balmoral. Balmoral opened the lid, and coins glimmered. "Where are the letters accusing Buckingham?"

"I have letters. I know not what they are," whispered the servant in Spanish to Ange, who held out his hand, took them, gave them to Balmoral.

"Search every inch of that vessel," ordered Balmoral, who went to stand in the shade of a tree, reading through the letters. Ange remained where he was, tethered to the trooper. The servant sat at his feet, as still as stone, whimpering every once in a while, but Ange kicked him each time he did so. When the yacht had been searched and nothing else found, Balmoral walked over, gestured, and a trooper unlocked the chains from around Ange's feet, but his wrist was still tethered to the trooper. Balmoral considered Ange. He didn't wish to set him free, but Richard had failed to bring the casket. "A deuce of a way to spend my Palm Sunday," he snapped. "You have one month to bring me proof of the treaty. If I haven't heard from you in precisely thirty days, your sweetheart dies. Slowly."

"You'll have your proof."

"What about this one, Your Grace?" A trooper nudged with his boot at the servant, still sitting at Ange's feet. The servant began to weep.

"For pity's sake, let me have him to help me sail the yacht, or I'll never make shore. And I could use a coin or two while you're at it."

Balmoral tossed two coins at Ange, turned on his heel, walked to his carriage. The coachman flicked the reins; the carriage lumbered away, followed by mounted troopers, the body of Miguel lying across a saddle. The last trooper left unlocked himself from Ange's wrist, eyed Ange and the cowering servant for a long moment as if he might just kill them anyway, then went to his horse, tossed the key toward them, and rode away.

"The key," Ange said.

Wiping his eyes with the tail of his shirt, the servant ran to find it, knelt before Ange, and unlocked the chains around his legs. Ange knelt, too, held out his hands, took the other man's hands in his. "I thought he meant to kill me," Ange said. "You were so brave, my darling."

"Our poor Pedrito. What will happen?"

"He will die in the Tower of London, but you and I won't."

"All your coins. It killed me to bring all your coins."

"So, did you?"

"No."

"And that is why I love you." Once in the yacht, Ange opened the sail and turned the tiller so it caught a gust of wind.

"France is that way," said Miguel.

"I know," said Ange. "I'm not finished."

Chapter 45

It was Maundy Thursday. Everyone was at the banqueting house watching the king and queen and their attendants wash the feet of the poor. Ange, a full curling nobleman's periwig on his head, a respectable coat and breeches on his body, walked into Balmoral's front hall. He was up the stairs before a servant appeared in the hall to answer the bell that opening the door made ring. Balmoral's bedchamber was simple to find. Ange went straight to the closet beyond it, shutting the door behind him quietly. He worked with concentration, opening cabinets and drawers, every sense open to sounds that would warn him of an approach. When he saw the sherry in its crystal decanter, he smiled. It was just as Buckingham had described, once upon a time long ago and far away. Pulling on gloves to take a folded paper from a pocket, he then poured its bit of grainy powder into the decanter, and shook it gently.

"For you, Alice," he said aloud.

Quick as a flash, doors and drawers were closed again and he was crossing the bedchamber, walking down the stairs and out the front door. It took only moments for the coat and wig to be gone, his hair loosed, his sleeves rolled up. He might have been any servant at the palace. He walked into the mews, asked a stable boy where Captain Saylor's horse was kept. The great dark head appeared over its stall door when he whistled.

"I've something for you," Ange said. He opened a gloved palm, and the horse sniffed, then snorted at the smell of sugar. He licked it all, licked even the glove, while Ange whispered to him and told him how handsome he was. He gave him the glove to chew, and the horse did so. For you, Richard, he thought. He heard footsteps, stepped back into shadow. A half-grown boy walked forward, put out his hand, pulled the chewed glove from the horse's mouth.

"What are you eating, Pharaoh?" Walter dropped the glove, kissed the long front of the horse's nose.

Ange recognized him. Madame Neddie's. Staring at him in the Whitehall kitchen. Part of the crowd who'd watched his duel with Richard. This one would be for Henri Ange. He stepped forward, as quiet as nothing. But Pharaoh whinnied, pulling his head from the boy's embrace, and in that moment the boy saw him, and in one lithe turning movement, even as Ange's hands grazed him, he ran from the dark of the stalls toward the light of the street, as if he knew this would be the race of his life.

Alice sat on the hillock. Before her spread a view of daffodils, a field of them, their trumpets belled out and fragrant. In the summer, said Lady Saylor, the hillock is covered with bluebells, a carpet of the sweetest blue you've ever seen. Letters from her father and from Balmoral sat in her lap, unopened. A box had come from London, inside it the gown in which she'd marry Balmoral, the gown she and her aunt had created. The seamstress would come to her from London to finish it. Poll had lifted it reverently from its paper, but Alice wouldn't look at it. She'd gone away, here to the hillock. If she tried to think, her head ached, so she didn't think. But soon she was going to have to.

It was Good Friday. Alice held a kitten—yours if you wish it, said Richard's mother—exhausted from her afternoon of watching flowers arranged in the church for Easter, exhausted from the service and prayers of this evening, exhausted from her thoughts, which circled one another relentlessly. Richard appeared at the far end of the arbor where she sat with his mother.

"My dear boy," exclaimed Jerusalem, who held Nan's baby in her lap.

Richard remained half-in, half-out of sun, shadows made by the arbor's vines playing across his face. He slapped his riding gloves in one hand. Jerusalem's eyes narrowed. She stood up, the baby in her arms. "Is something wrong? Louisa or Elizabeth?"

Alice put down the kitten. Like Jerusalem, she suddenly knew he bore bad news. She stood up in a hesitant movement. Her strength was very small.

"Louisa," said Richard, "I've brought her home. You'll need to see to her. She isn't happy with me." He walked forward, and both women could see his jaw was held so tightly that the bones of it were showing against skin. The chickens come home to roost, thought Alice. Now I've hurt Louisa, too.

"Is she ill?" asked Jerusalem.

"No. My horse—" He stopped, unable to go on.

"Pharaoh? Not Pharaoh?" said Jerusalem.

"Dead."

Alice began to weep. She sat back down, face in her hands.

"She's weeping for more than Pharaoh," Jerusalem said. "Oh, Richard, I'm that sorry. I'll go see to your sister." She touched her hand to his shoulder but walked out of the arbor, back to the kitchen to give the baby to her mother. Interesting, she thought, that he should ride all this way to tell me, only it is not me he comes to tell. Now why has he brought Louisa home? Into her mind came the vision of her daughter the last time she'd been in London whenever the Duke of Monmouth was near, and she suddenly knew.

"Annie," she said to Susannah's granddaughter, sitting dark and glowering on a stool because she must have disobeyed Susannah, "guess who's come to see us."

In the arbor, Richard knelt before Alice. "Don't weep," he said. His throat was tight. He'd cried like a boy at the sight of Pharaoh. He took a hand from her face, began to kiss it, unable to help himself.

"You mustn't touch me," Alice said.

He walked away.

SUPPER WAS QUIET, strained. Louisa refused to eat with them. A tiny moth came in to play with the flame at one of the candles, and Jerusalem kept waving it away, looking from Richard to Alice and back again. Alice looked weary and drank more wine than Jerusalem had seen her do since arriving at Tamworth. Richard played with the food on his plate, gave short answers to any questions Jerusalem asked.

"How did he die?"

"He just stopped breathing."

"Have you your letter to Turenne?"

"Yes."

"You've resigned, then?"

"Yes."

"Was anything said of it?"

"Yes."

"For example?"

"I don't wish to speak of it."

"Nan Daniell wants a word about Walter. Will you take the time to speak with her?"

"Walter's gone."

"Gone? Where?"

"We don't know. Effriam thinks he's run away."

"But why would he run away?"

"I don't know, Mother."

Jerusalem threw her napkin on the table. "Why don't you both go out and look at the stars? Alice, take your shawl." She walked over to her flute, began to play it.

Out on the terrace, Alice and Richard were silent. Stars were bright, spattering the sky. I can't breathe, thought Alice. It was because of him.

"I'm leaving the army, Alice. I'm going to France."

"I think that's likely a good thing, Richard."

"What if I loved you, too?" he said.

She couldn't answer. Dreams, as far as she could see, did not come true. She felt desperate, weak. "If you touch me, Richard, I'm lost. Please don't."

In answer, he put his hand up to cup the back of her neck, entangling his fingers in her hair, and like the moth at the candle, she stepped into his arms, and his mouth was on hers, not in friendship, but in deliberation and desire and something else, and she was lost, everything she'd felt and seen and grieved and loved welling up in her. She could not have enough of him, his mouth, his taste, his tongue, his body against hers. She ran her hands along the sleek bones of his face, the strong muscles of his neck. She would die for him. She was his to do with whatever he pleased. She was fire and light and love from head to foot. When he lifted his mouth from hers, she had to bunch his coat in her hands and hang on to him not to fall. He put her head against his heart, and she could hear it pounding. I will go anywhere with you, she was thinking, and then lovelier verses floated into her mind, tamping down some of her heat, painting it with something sacred, which was part of her love, also, Wither thou goest, I will go. Jerusalem read the Bible to the household at night, the verses echoing in Alice's mind when she closed her eyes to sleep.

"I could lie with you right now, here, with your mother in the other chamber," she whispered.

"And in the morning?"

"I would rise and tell Balmoral."

He stepped back, and the distance between them loomed huge. "Why?"

"I owe him truth. And there's more truth to be told. I asked Monmouth to flirt with your sister. Whatever's happened, I'm a piece of it."

He stepped even farther back from her. "What a meddling fool you are, Alice."

"Yes."

The sound of the flute ceased.

"Children," called Jerusalem, "time to come inside."

ALICE STOOD AT the window staring at stars long after Poll was faintly snoring. What if he loved her, too, he'd said. She hadn't a shred of pride to separate her from him. Pride. What a meddling fool you are, Alice. Though your sins be as scarlet, they shall be white as snow; though they be red like crimson, they shall be as wool, Richard's mother read. She adored him; she was besotted. Except that she'd hurt his sister. Except that she owed Balmoral her honor. Oh, Barbara, you said it was so sweet. Here was why Caro betrayed—she could so easily betray Balmoral. Richard had only to walk through that door, and she would lie down wherever he wished and open herself to him, meet him kiss for kiss, touch for touch, wild, wanton, feverish, not think of consequences, a slave to this desire she felt for him. There was such longing in her heart, such sadness. What was there to do? Step back from Balmoral? At this late stage? How could she? How could she not? Clever Alice, no longer clever. Would you be a soldier's wife, follow the drum for him? Yes and yes again. Would you live as nobody, hidden away on a farm? No and no again. Would Balmoral ruin Richard if she should marry him? Yes, it was likely. Would Richard forgive her the mischief with Louisa? Who knew? She could scarcely forgive herself. The kitten mewed, leaped down from her bed, came to threaten and fight the tail of her nightgown. The headache was here, growing on each side of her head. "Stop it, Dulcinea." Alice lay down on the floor, pressing her forehead to the cool of the floor, as the kitten leaped and tried to kill her dark and riotous curls.

AT MIDNIGHT, THE little owl flew once over the stable and then back to the wood. Richard led the saddled horse out of the stall.

"Did you mean to leave without saying good-bye?" His mother stood in the door of the stable, a lantern in her hand.

Richard walked his saddled horse toward his mother and out into night that promised morning.

His mother touched the nose of the horse he'd chosen. "There's a yearling of Pharaoh's that Winston Ashford has. I could buy him back. You didn't tell me how he died."

"I don't know. Effriam came to find me, and when I got to the stables, he was down, gone." He put his arm around her, looked into the pale oval of her face. "I'm not coming back, Mother."

"To France?" Tomorrow was Easter. She bit her lips to stop the words, Stay for Easter.

"Yes. I leave trouble behind me. His Grace the Duke of Balmoral is unhappy over a failure of mine, angry that I've resigned. He called me a fool, and—" He stopped. He wouldn't mention Renée's tears, her begging him not to leave. I've ruined you, she had cried, and of course, her unhappiness meant King Charles could not be a happy man at the moment. He wouldn't mention mortgaging Tamworth for every pence, of buying into Prince Rupert's Hudson Bay Company. It was enough he had brought Louisa home, her fighting him every step of the way.

"Do you love her?"

"Who?"

"The French one."

"Yes, I love her."

"And this one?"

"Her too."

"You've food?" It was one of the ways she had known he was leaving, the cook coming to her late and telling how he'd packed food for the young baron, a stable boy telling her he'd asked for a horse to be saddled, Annie saying he'd put a miniature portrait of his father in his saddlebag.

"Yes."

"Let me get some coins from the strongbox."

"I just want to be on the road, away from here. I have no letter for Alice. I sat up half the night trying to write one, but there was nothing I could think to say." He spoke jerkily, holding emotion in check. "Will you say good-bye for me, tell her that I—tell her that she will always have my deepest regard, tell her I forgive everything? Make sure you say that word—everything. It's important. Will you bless me?"

He knelt before her in the dark, the horse, her reins dangling, waiting for him a few feet away. Jerusalem put her hand on Richard's head, closed her eyes, feeling all the things she would not say to this man whose body encased the boy she had loved, the boy who looked back at her often even now when she met his eyes, but who had transferred his heart's allegiance elsewhere, as was fitting, even though she did not entirely like it. So his father had done once upon a time. In her mind, she hugged the boy to her, seeing all his eagerness for life, all his sweet innocence, enclosed forever in a man's body and a man's needs and a man's ambitions. She spoke prayers for him, putting him in God's care. Nothing was ours to keep forever. So it had been. So it would always be.

After he'd ridden away, she walked along the side of the house to the kitchen. Cook was up, and to her gladness, so was the baby. She took her from a sleepy, weeping Nan, who wept because Walter was gone and had sent her no good-bye.

"Oh, ma'am, you mustn't bother yourself with us," Nan said.

"But I want to." This child-mother had no idea how precious it was to have a baby in the household again. She sat in a rocking chair near the window and began to play cat's cradle with the child's hands. "Annie," she cooed. "My sweet little girl." All the little heartbreaks, thought Jerusalem. Louisa, upstairs, cried and raged hers. Alice and Richard tried the opiate of duty, Nan simple tears.

"Bah," said a voice from the corner. It was Tamworth's other Annie, up because Richard had left. Doubtless she'd witnessed the farewell, lurking somewhere as was her way. "I don't like her having my name."

"What shall we call her, then?"

"Stupid."

Later, Poll came to tell her that Alice was ill with the headache again. Jerusalem went into her stillroom, mixed St. John's wort with safflower while Poll held the baby for her. Cook brought some warmed wine, and Jerusalem mixed the herbs into it, thinking all the while about love and its many circles.

IN THE MORNING, Alice glared at Poll. "I don't believe you."

"It's true. He left late in the night, Nan Daniell says. Good riddance, I say, what with your eyes glowing like candles whenever you see him. I want to call you 'Your Grace,' not Mrs. Nobody."

"Get out." Alice threw a pillow. "Out!" She didn't weep. Some things went too deep for weeping. She didn't go to Easter service that day. There was no Jerusalem and no Louisa at supper that night, just Alice. She sat in the opened windows of one of the house's bays, looking out into the twilight. He did not leave a letter. Better that way. He did what he had to do, and so would she. It would have been so sweet to have a letter, but she would have been a fool over it, treasuring it. Jerusalem found her in the arbor that night, sitting on a twig bench in the dark, and held up the lantern. "Poll is fretted about where you are."

"Let her fret."

"Richard left this morning for France. He asked me to say goodbye for him and give you his deepest regard. He said he forgave you everything. I'm sorry it has taken me all day to tell you."

Alice twisted fingers together in her lap, glad for the dark, her thoughts flying out everywhere, dropping back to the arbor only when she heard Jerusalem say, "It seems your lord was displeased with Richard's leaving for France."

Displeased? How dare Balmoral be displeased? That would not do. She would see that Richard got every glory he deserved. Yes, she could do that, couldn't she?

"You've not answered the letters from your father, from His Grace. They'll be showing up on my doorstep demanding to know what I've done with you. Only a few weeks until your wedding."

"Am I well enough to marry just yet?"

"Are you?"

"I had the fever today."

"Did you?"

They were silent, listening to a chorus of frogs croaking their night's serenade. Jerusalem spoke. "June is as good a month for a wedding as May."

June, thought Alice, and her chest seemed to expand.

"We could write a letter asking for a more time, explain you're not quite well."

"Poll ought to go back with it, to pack and put my things in order in London."

A month here. She could rest and lie in the sun on the hillock and play with her kitten and grieve Barbara. She could think about this day's death and resurrection, wondering if any of her old self would resurrect, if any of it were worth saving. She'd think of Richard and let him go. She'd never imagined he might be hers anyway. It was a trick of circumstance that he'd come to her. Oh, she could breathe again. A month and she could face the fate she'd done her best to create. "There's one more thing."

Jerusalem waited.

"I asked the Duke of Monmouth to flirt with Louisa. My father liked her, and I didn't want a stepmama. And so I asked him to flirt, thinking she'd be sidetracked. It's my fault she's hurt now."

After a time, Jerusalem said, sternness like iron notes in her voice, "A portion may be yours, not the whole, but a portion."

"I need to tell her. I have to tell her. Will you send her to me? I don't feel strong enough to walk to the house. And if you don't want me to stay, I understand."

"We'll let Louisa decide that, shall we?"

Alice listened to Jerusalem's shoes on the gravel of the path, to frogs calling plaintively for love, here I am, here I am, to night rustles around her. Purge me with hyssop and I shall be clean. Wash me and I shall be whiter than snow. Might that ever happen? Might her soul ever be free of its burdens? She could smell the lavender from Jerusalem's gardens.

She'd never felt sadder in her life.

Or more alive.

RIGGS KNOCKED ON the door of Balmoral's closet. "It's Sir Thomas," he called, raising his eyebrows to Sir Thomas. His Grace was in a mood, not receiving visitors, he'd tried to tell him, but the man would have his way. To Riggs's surprise, Balmoral opened the door.

"I've a letter to you from Alice." Sir Thomas spoke quickly, feeling suddenly as if the door to the cage of a lion had been opened and he stood beside the lion.

Balmoral moved so Sir Thomas could enter, slammed the door

behind him, took the letter, ripped past the seal, read it, then crumpled it with his hand to throw it down. "I've a good mind to go to Tamworth and wring everyone's necks."

Sir Thomas picked up the letter and read what Alice wrote.

"Is she trying to fob me off?" Balmoral demanded.

"It says here she's not quite well. She's on her way to London, it says—"

"I don't like put-offs."

"Well then, Your Grace, we won't have one. The moment she sets foot in London, we'll have the marriage. She can mend just as well as your wife as she can a spinster."

"Get out."

"Your Grace, I'll leave for Tamworth this moment and fetch her myself!"

"Out!" Balmoral called for his servant. "Riggs, show Sir Thomas Verney the way out."

"I'll call again tomorrow—" Sir Thomas began, but the door slammed in his face. He stood where he was, the expression on his face aghast.

"It's a mood," Riggs began, but there was no explaining. "More like a fit. It will pass."

"I hope to God it does." Sir Thomas took himself down the stairs in a huff, but under bravado was fear. Had Alice's put-off ruined things? He'd strangle her with his bare hands! In fact, after he called on His Grace tomorrow, he was riding to Tamworth to meet Alice somewhere on the road, kill her, and bring her body back for Balmoral to do with as he wished.

Riggs straightened this and that in the bedchamber, listening for sounds from the closet, but all was silent. Struggling with his demon, thought Riggs, unhappy over young Saylor's leaving. He had had plans for young Saylor, but best-laid plans . . . If he weren't afraid it would kill him before his wedding, Riggs would have walked in and poured the first glass himself.

Balmoral sat in his chair, the cabinet straight ahead of him, what he wanted, what he craved, what every part of his body cried out for, just on the other side. He'd promised himself. He had promised

Alice. But the confounded hair on his confounded head was crawling with need. That man Ange claimed was Miguel was gibbering like an idiot in the Tower. Swearing under torture he was the servant, not the master. The king was furious that Henri Ange was gone—he'd had to make up some cock-and-bull story about escape, spreading bribes from one end of the Tower to the other. Buckingham was mild as toast. No opinions. And no support. He'd wanted to hold Ange's letters accusing Buckingham, keep them as extra coins in this game of chance, but now it looked as if he'd need to present them right away to force Buckingham in to save him. . . . He needed only a month. Could he last a month? When Ange brought the evidence of the secret treaty with Madame, Balmoral would be in the coachman's seat again, and Buckingham's betrayals could be put to real use.

Only a month, she wrote. But he couldn't manage another month, not if every night was to be like this. And it was. He would have one drink. Except he wouldn't stop at one, would he? Would it kill him this time? So that she never became a duchess? He wanted that for her. Where was she, anyway? He could do this if she came and walked with him, talked to him. She got sick, left him alone, on his own. He opened the cabinet, set the beautiful crystal decanter before him. Lovely rich pool of red, calming his heart, calming his mind just at the sight of it, taking him down glorious paths of possibility. He'd find Ange and kill him slowly. He'd obtain the casket and know the king's mind. He'd use Buckingham, then ruin him.

He held up the decanter, swirling the liquid, the best sherry in Portugal, sweeter than nectar. A part of him sorrowed as he poured it out into a wineglass. When he drank it down, it seemed to him it burned a new way, a purifying way, and before the explosion within him stopped all, verses came to mind, from a long-ago time when his God had lived outside the fermented grape, sacred verses, hallowed verses, holy verses—create in me a clean heart, O God.

CHAPTER 46

How her head hurt. With each roll of the carriage wheel, the pain had grown greater. Bits and pieces of Louisa's furious accusations kept dancing in amid the pain. How dare you, Alice. He did not flirt with me because you asked it. He loves me. And Jerusalem's cool rejoinder: what nonsense, Louisa. Without truth and duty to anchor it down, the greatest love will fly out the door.

Alice lay in a bed, the breeze from the opened window cooling what felt like a fever in her. Outside, she could hear talk from the innkeeper and his stable boys as they took harness and reins off the horses of the carriage in which she traveled. Poll was somewhere fetching soup, something to drink. And she, well, she was in bed, feeling on the verge of illness again, hating that she'd had to leave Tamworth on bad terms. Love, truth, duty. She could bring Balmoral only two of the three.

The innkeeper called a greeting, and something in the answer made her sit upright. Could that be her father? In spite of her headache, she moved to the window. There in the yard stood Sir Thomas, with him Perryman. Alice stepped back before he should see her. Had her father come to fetch her? As if she were some straying sheep that must be herded back? She lifted her chin in spite of a pang that vibrated down her spine. She needed no fetching. She had been thrown out of Tamworth, thank you very much, and was on her way home now to perform her duty. If he thought she was going to listen to one word of reprimand, he was sadly mistaken. She had swallowed Louisa's bitter words because she deserved them. She wouldn't swallow his.

She climbed into the bed, listening to steps on the stairway. They sounded imperious, impatient, and sure enough, her door was flung open and Sir Thomas stood framed in the doorway.

"At your leisure, are you? Taking your time returning?"

"I have the headache. Go away, Father."

"You'll have more than a headache when I am finished with you." He stepped into the chamber. "Alice . . ." He ran a hand over his face. "It's done," he said, "finished. I'm done, too."

"Balmoral has called off the marriage? Not likely."

"He's dead, Alice."

She leaped out of the bed to attack him, to slap him once and for all, for teasing her, for testing her, for pushing her as always he did. "Why must you say things like that? Look at me! I'm returning. I'm doing my duty, as forever I've done! Whether I wish it or not!" She shouldn't be shouting. It made the ache consume her, made nausea rush up and close her throat.

"Poppet, he died three days ago."

To the surprise of them both, she fainted.

WHEN SHE OPENED her eyes again, she was in bed and he was sitting at her bedside. She pulled the wet rag from her head, struggled to sit up.

"I came to beat you, Alice, from wherever I found you all the way back to London." In spite of his words, all his bombast, all his vigor, had deserted him. "He died three days ago, and all London is mourning. He's the last of the old ones, the last of the foundation stones that we rebuilt this kingdom upon. We're like children who've lost a father."

Bad, willful children, thought Alice.

"He's lying in state in Whitehall, will do so for at least a week. There's to be a ceremonial march of the body, with full escort, through London on its way to his estate outside Newmarket."

"But who has made these arrangements?"

"His Grace the second Duke of Balmoral."

Alice caught her breath. Colefax. "Has he dared to have the will read without my presence?"

"No, but only because I found him and reminded him that he'd betrayed you once already and that I wouldn't stand for a second time. I told him I'd call him out in a duel and do my best to kill him."

"I'm duchess in all but name. They mustn't read the will without me, they mustn't have the funeral service." She clutched at straws, the shock of the news that Balmoral was dead not yet real to her.

"So I've told them. I've sent a message to His Majesty and to Buckingham." He grimaced on that name. "Went crawling like a whipped dog to Buckingham, I did. He patted my head and said he was certain the new duke would do all that was proper." Sir Thomas went to the window, standing with his back to her, staring out at the inn yard below.

Staring at broken dreams, thought Alice, ambitions crushed one more time. I'm not to be a duchess. It's over. I cannot believe it. I let Richard go for nothing.

"So I came to fetch you," he continued, his back to her, "to bring you back to London to take your place as his affianced, the wife he would have had, had you not—" He broke off.

"It will be fine, Father." She spoke as if she were the parent and he the child, "You'll see. We'll rise first thing in the morning and reach London by afternoon." Where I will be the almost duchess, honored for a day or more, then forgotten. Everything changes and nothing does. She shuddered and put her hands to her eyes. How could it be that she was not to be duchess now? Why hadn't he waited for her? She'd refused Richard for him, kept her honor for him. Damn him. There should be tears for her duke. Where were they?

The smell and hurry of London exhausted her: barking dogs, muddy streets, cries of street vendors, sedan chairs jostling carriages for place. Poll found the black gowns made for Princesse Henriette's death. Draped in one, her mother's diamonds at her neck and ears, her father at her side, Alice went to Whitehall to see the lay of the land. They went immediately to the body, lying in state in the banqueting hall, Balmoral's guard, the Coldstream, standing at attention inside and outside, the hall crowded with courtiers, clumped into whispering, gossiping groups. But the gossip, the whispers, stopped at the sight of Alice, who walked regally toward the coffin lying on its satin-draped dais.

The wax effigy atop was dressed in the duke's purple cloak trimmed in fur; it wore a long and curling periwig. It frowned. Alice clutched her father's arm, her eyes on the profile—the effigy's face would have been made, from custom, as Balmoral's death mask. So. He had gone into death with a grimace on his face, this warrior, this hero, this last bastion of the old days, who had played her savior, who had been willing to give her titles and honor. Tears—here they are, she thought—made their slow way down her face. I would have liked to see you once more before you died, she thought, and reached out to touch the velvet of the cloak.

"Mistress Verney."

Here was Colefax, in black, properly somber, but a triumphant light in his eyes. Well, why not? He was the new Duke of Balmoral. She swept into a curtsy, suddenly dizzy in the movement. The walls of the hall whirled around her. She fainted. When she came to, she had been carried to a small chamber adjoining the hall, and her father leaned over her.

"Poppet, you're worse—"

She put a finger to his lips to hush him, as Colefax leaned in over her father's shoulder. "Let me have a moment alone, please, Father."

Reluctantly, he stepped back. Brows drawn, he warned Colefax, "I'll be just there," pointing toward a corner.

Colefax knelt beside her, his expression anxious. "Are you still ill, then?"

"I don't know."

"I can scarcely believe this, Alice, any of it. Have you need of anything?" He took her hand, and in her weakness, she allowed it. "Please let me know."

Would he be so gracious when he learned that she would be given one of Balmoral's estates? "You haven't given me your condolences, Cole."

"My deepest condolences, Alice."

"I loved him." Weren't friendship and regard some pieces of love?

His face twisted. "Alice, don't play the martyr with me, of all people—"

But you of all people will be the most amusing to play the martyr with, she thought, some of her old spirit reviving. "I wish to go to his house, to pay a call upon his servants to see how they do."

"If you feel you must. My wife is seeing to the house."

"I don't need your permission, Cole. I am still his affianced."

"Yes, your little faint reminded one and all of that. Well done, Alice." He was no longer holding her hand.

"You imagine I did it for effect?"

He shrugged, stood, looking down at her. "You'll need to call me 'Your Grace' now, Alice. Or will it choke you to do so?"

"It will choke me."

At the house, she asked for Riggs, waited in a small salon, her eyes flicking over paintings, vases, silver candlesticks. She didn't really see them. She saw instead times past, fragments of a song in her head: Old time is still a-flying, and this same flower that smiles today, tomorrow will be dying.

Caro, the new Duchess of Balmoral, entered the chamber. Sir Thomas rose hurriedly from the chair in which he sat. "Your Grace."

"W-will you excuse u-us a m-moment, Sir Thomas?"

When they were alone, Caro stared at Alice until Alice blushed and dropped into a curtsy, feeling her dizziness again. "Your Grace," Alice said, and found that she wasn't angry that Caro was the duchess.

"D-did your t-tongue curl on t-that?"

Alice straightened. "No, Your Grace."

"Oh, d-don't call me t-that! W-what is it you n-need?"

"I came simply to see about His Grace's personal servant, Will Riggs. May I sit down? I feel very weak. If it doesn't please you to allow me to see Riggs, perhaps you might tell him for me that Mistress Verney called to see how he did? I haven't come to plunder the house, Your Grace."

"D-do you h-hate me so that y-you cannot say m-my name?"

"It's you who hates now, Caro."

"Y-you h-hated first. I simply r-return the favor."

So I did, thought Alice. She stood, even though her legs did not feel strong enough to bear her. In her throat were the words Caro, forgive me, I was wrong, but she couldn't say them. Outside the house, she could feel how ill she was, how much her pride, once again, was costing her.

"Father," she whispered, before falling.

WHEN SHE WOKE, she was in a litter being carried home. Will Riggs was walking to one side of her. She said his name.

"Oh, ma'am," he said. "I'm that sorry he's died."

"Are you well, Riggs? Have you what you need?"

"Well enough. The new duke has his own manservant. It's to be expected. But I'm assured of a place in the household."

"Come to me if you should need anything. Come to me if you and he should not suit."

"Here's your house now, ma'am." Riggs bowed his head and was lost to sight in Perryman picking her up, her father calling out orders, the settling of her once more in bed, where, once done, Sir Thomas stood solid, anxious, beleaguered at its foot. "If you die—"

"Send to Tamworth for Lady Saylor's fever powders. They cured me once. They'll do so again." She had a part to play in the next days, until the coffin was on its way. And she would play it if it killed her.

"The queen sent word to ask how you do. She says she holds a position for you."

As maid of honor? To romp once more with Kit and Luce and whatever mindless four and tens they'd added to the mix? No. Her time as a maid of honor was over.

"Call upon her to thank her, Father, but I cannot be maid of honor again. Tell her as soon as I am well, I will make my obedience to her."

He sat on the bed. "You are everything to me. Don't die, Alice."

Did he think he could command death? Poor fool. Ah, her head ached, and her body. She wasn't afraid to die. She hadn't been afraid when she walked into the river. If death desired her, he could have her. But until he took her, she had things to do. "Ask John Sidney to call, please, Father."

"Sidney? Why?"

She had to sleep, had to close her eyes to the flame that was flickering somewhere deep and low inside her. The coming month was her birth month. Gather ye rosebuds while ye may. A girl needed to wash her face with May's hawthorn dew to make herself beautiful for her beloved. The court would dance around the Maypole, and she was the best dancer. And then there was Richard. That was something to live for, wasn't it?

"IT'S JOHN SIDNEY, Mistress Verney," Poll announced.

Alice sat in her bed, a Portuguese shawl about her shoulders. She considered Sidney as he approached. His face was pinched, far too thin. He was as thin these days as she was. Mourning Barbara. Someone that fine, that rare, needed a long time getting over.

"How kind of you to call on me. I feared you might not."

"You were her dearest friend, and at the end you showed it. She would have wished me to see to you."

"I have a favor to ask of you. Will you write Captain Saylor of the duke's death?"

She had surprised him. "Yes. Of course."

"I did not give you your due. She loved you so. I ought to have loved you, too. It would be my happiest wish if you might—someday—forgive me." She saw in his face that he couldn't do that, but the dreaded words, forgive me, were out, and her heart felt easier for it. Perhaps now she'd be able to say them other places, to other people. Sidney bowed stiffly to her and left the chamber.

"Who else is waiting?"

"Some of the maids of honor," answered Poll.

"Go and fetch them."

But it was her father who appeared. "That's enough for this day. You need to rest, Alice."

"I go tomorrow to the banqueting hall. I don't care if you have to carry me on a litter, Father. Carry me in even if I'm raving, and make certain I wear Mother's diamonds."

"You'll thwart Colefax to the end, will you?"

"Yes."

He kissed her forehead. "I always wished you were more like your mother."

"But I'm not."

"No."

Neither of them minded anymore.

THE NEWS OF the death reached Richard in Paris before John's letter did. The English duke had been too well-known. Richard walked into the cathedral of Notre Dame, sat in a pew, all around him the vast dark cavern of the nave, hundreds of candles glimmering for souls, stone statues waiting for supplicants' prayers, arches above him soaring to their privet's point, priests and nuns in dark robes gliding over the cold stone floors. Walter was on his mind. And Henri Ange. Richard roamed the streets of Paris half expecting to see him. He composed the letter to Alice in his mind, but later, when he went to write it, he ended penning only three words—folding parchment and dripping hot wax, red as heart's blood, to seal it. There was news, too, of Renée. Her climb continued, and the French crowed; she was their invaluable link to the king of England, a replacement for Princesse Henriette. They saw Richard's retreat as a practical thing. King Louis's minister Colbert had called upon Richard personally, thanking him in the name of the king, assuring him his sacrifice would be rewarded, telling him that the position of colonel in the French army was his. My honor does not require rewarding, Richard had replied. Colbert had smiled the cold smile he was known for. To refuse would insult my king. Never let it be said that I am impolite, Richard had answered.

THE CEREMONY FOR Balmoral was spectacular. Everyone who was anyone in the kingdom was there, as well as the people of London, who crowded outside the cathedral in silent respect. Alice had to be carried in on a litter, and her bearers were Lord Mulgrave, the Duke of Monmouth, Prince Rupert, and her father. The sight was impressive and set off a wave of whispers from one courtier to another. Boys whose voices rivaled angels sang hymns. The Archbishop of Canterbury preached a sermon. Various other bishops read prayers. Afterward, as many courtiers came to speak to her as they did the new duke. She would have laughed aloud if it hadn't hurt so much to laugh. But the fever powders from Tamworth had arrived, and one was inside her now, making its miracles, and while she would not accompany Balmoral to his final destination, she had done what she could, grieving over him publicly as if he were her beloved husband and her lord. Now she went home to rest. To wait for word from Richard. There must be word, or she would die.

But when it came, it enraged her. She ripped past the heart-red seal, her eagerness making her hands shake as much as her illness. "Wait for me," she read, incredulous at his brevity. That was all? He did not write love or devotion? Did not ask for her hand in marriage? She crushed the letter into a wad and threw it away, and her kitten flew off the bed to pounce on it.

THE FIRST DAY of May arrived. The court danced around a Maypole erected in the privy garden until lanterns had to be summoned to light the darkness, and then they danced some more. But Alice took fever powders and refused visitors, which was so unlike her that the rumor grew that she was truly ill unto dying, and it was said to be because of her devotion to Balmoral; what a pity she'd not been the duchess. It made Colefax clench his teeth, which were already shut tight at the reading of the will. Alice stayed in her chamber or had herself carried into her father's garden to sit in the sun. She took Jerusalem's powders and dreamed feverish dreams and wondered what next to do.

The days passed slowly. She was in her bedchamber with Poll and Fletcher, who talked himself past the servants and brought a violin and gossip. Courtiers were taking bets that Renée had finally yielded. The bet was not upon that, but rather upon what position the event might have been consummated. York had not walked forward to receive Communion at Easter. The court buzzed that the heir to the throne had turned Catholic. The actress Nellie Gwynn was again with child. The newly married Knollys and his bride quarreled. All the time Fletcher talked, he watched Alice's face.

"It's said you're dying from devotion to the duke. The queen is most distraught."

"Then I'll call upon her someday soon and quarrel with Kit and Luce and show I am my old self."

"Are you?"

"No."

"John Sidney looks wretched."

"Yes. He mourns with every breath he takes."

"And you?"

"I'll never forgive myself, Fletcher."

"Never is a long time."

"Don't be flip."

"Oh, I'm a believer in the adage 'The less one lives, the less one sins.' Why don't you come to court?"

"As almost widow of the duke? As the oldest maid of honor?"

"As an eligible young woman any man with sense would snatch up in a moment. I'm told Mulgrave calls every day to see how you do. Does the wind blow in that direction?"

"The wind doesn't blow at all. I'm going to match him with Louisa Saylor."

"Why?"

"It amuses me."

"To fling away suitors? That will make three."

"I did not fling away Colefax, and Balmoral's death can hardly count as my doing."

"Is it true His Grace left you an estate and all the furnishings in his Whitehall apartments? They say the new duke was overcome with a nosebleed when he heard it."

"If he had the nosebleed, it's because he's climbed too high. You're making my head hurt. Play some music."

"Do you remember how to dance?"

"Play something, and let us see."

The music soon had her feet tapping, and then she was up, turning and tiptoeing at first carefully, then losing herself in the thing she loved. She pulled Poll out into the middle of her bedchamber and danced around her. She saw Perryman in the doorway and beckoned him forward as a partner. When he moved, Richard stood behind him.

She stopped where she was.

Richard stepped into the bedchamber. "You're so thin. They told me you were dying." He wasn't caressing. There was no smile on his face. He looked tired and strained, not the lover at all.

"Is that why you deigned to visit? Because you thought I was dying?"

Fletcher and Poll and Perryman were silent. Were they witnessing a lovers' meeting or a final rupture?

"Damn it, I am absent without permission from General Turenne! Are you well or not?"

"Not! Your note made me so!"

Suddenly he smiled.

She refused to be dazzled. "It would serve you right if I were married three times over! I could be, you know. What if I am dying?"

"I'd ape John and taste every drop I might and sleep at your feet until the final closing of your eyes and then carry your memory in my heart until the day I died." He had moved forward as he spoke, had a hand on her arm. "What's this in your sleeve?"

"A letter. A short one."

"Will you quarrel on my deathbed?"

"Yes!"

Richard stared down at her. Fletcher put his hand to his heart. The intensity betwen the two was palpable; he half expected lightning to strike and thunder to sound.

"The only person you will ever marry is me. I love you." Richard stepped closer, reached his other hand to cup the back of her head.

Alice shivered. "Yes, I will quarrel on your deathbed to talk you from it because if you were to die first, I could not bear it."

"Sweetheart." Richard put his mouth on hers, and they held each other in an embrace so passionate, so white-hot with love, with longing, that later Fletcher would swear he smelled smoke and heard a distant rumble. Richard kissed Alice's eyes, her nose, her lips, again and again, hard, not the way one ought to kiss an invalid. Alice kissed back with all the furious joy struggling in her.

"Yes, I wait," she whispered to him. "Yes," she said as she bit his full mouth. Yes, yes, yes. Home. I am home at last, she thought. He was her beloved.

"My heart left my body when I heard you were still ill."

"I mend."

"You'd best, because I must return at once to France to avoid disgrace. There's to be a war, Alice—"

"What's all this now?" Sir Thomas stood in the doorway, surveying the scene with eyes that were not warm. "Unhand my daughter at once, sir!"

Richard kept his eyes upon Alice, his smile as wide as the chamber around them, his eyes scalding in their promises.

"Our bed," he said to her, "will be green."

AND LATER, WHEN he recited the verses of Solomon on their wedding night, she understood. When love and truth and duty united, possibility had no end. A bundle of myrrh is my well-beloved unto me; he shall lie all night betwixt my breasts. My beloved is unto me as a cluster of camphire in the vineyards of Engedi. Behold, thou art fair, my beloved.

Also by Karleen Koen

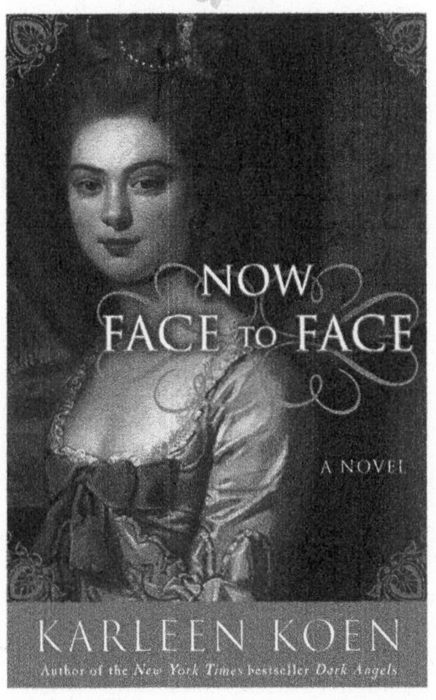

The beloved heroine from Koen's bestselling *Through a Glass Darkly* returns in a passionate, unforgettable, romantic tapestry. A widow at age twenty, emotionally and financially ruined by the death of her husband in scandalous circumstances, Barbara Devane leaves colonial Virginia for London to confront her enemies and to pursue a deeply satisfying yet dangerous clandestine love.

Now Face to Face
978-0-307-40608-8
$15.95 paper (Canada: $21.00)